ear. From the frilly Victorian embedded clauses of Henry James to the whimsical characterizations of Tom Robbins, Helprin swerves effortlessly through the ages of English literature to create a world at once completely artificial and utterly believable." —*Star Tribune* (Minneapolis)

"Humorous in its parodies and hilarious in its slapstick schticks and verbal tom-foolery, *Freddy and Fredericka* is delightfully rich. Helprin's most recent work, *The Pacific and Other Stories*, centered on characters of integrity who find happiness in living honorably, and it's no coincidence that the title characters of his new novel evolve in a similar way. With a Midas touch, Helprin unapologetically brings out the best in his characters and renews one's faith in mere mortals." —*The Miami Herald*

"(A) hilarious, picaresque adventure." —*Bookpage*

"A boy's adventure tale for adults, a romance novel for people who can read a complex sentence. . . . If you can envision a *People* profile of Prince Charles written by J. K. Rowling (if she could write half as well as Helprin), then you have a sense of the novel's style. . . . There's no other writer like him." —*Elle*

"Helprin generates a delectable tension between his impeccable style and unbridled imagination. . . . His first novel in over a decade, following the sumptuous *The Pacific and Other Stories*, is a satirical, picaresque romp. . . . This irresistibly mischievous fable draws freely on Don Quixote, Mark Twain, Monty Python . . . yet is in the end pure Helprin in its narrative agility and celebration of nature's glory and human kindness, courage, and love." —*Booklist* (starred review)

"On the face of it, Helprin (*Memoir from Antproof Case*, etc.) is just about the least likely to produce a slaphappy comedy, yet that's exactly what he's done here. . . . What a lively romp Helprin makes of the whole affair, packing it full of vaudevillian wordplay and rapturous flights of fanciful prose. . . . A comic call for greatness in a mediocre age." —*Kirkus Reviews*

"Wickedly witty." —*Library Journal*

"Helprin does farce as easily as he does philosophy, and the result is a book that may emerge as the summer's great comic escape." —*Boston Phoenix*

"*Freddy and Fredericka* is as searing in its denunciation of contemporary life as anything in recent fiction, possessing a greater satirical breadth than anything written by Evelyn Waugh, and as relentlessly probing as Don DeLillo at his most acutely paranoid. It's also a richly sympathetic work . . . and, concurrent with its fierce satirical bite, deeply and truly heartening. . . . Helprin's capacity to make his readers laugh is equal to his skill at making them see what a mess human beings have made of contemporary existence. . . . [It] is a work of great seriousness, hilarity and simple aesthetic enjoyment." —*The Globe and Mail* (Toronto)

ABOUT THE AUTHOR

Mark Helprin was educated at Harvard, Princeton, and Oxford, and served in the Israeli army, Israeli Air Force, and British Merchant Navy. He is the author of *A Dove of the East and Other Stories*, *Refiner's Fire*, *Ellis Island and Other Stories*, *Winter's Tale*, *A Soldier of the Great War*, *Memoir from Antproof Case*, and *The Pacific and Other Stories*.

FREDDY

and

FREDERICKA

MARK HELPRIN

PENGUIN BOOKS

PENGUIN BOOKS

Published by the Penguin Group
Penguin Group (USA) Inc., 375 Hudson Street, New York, New York 10014, U.S.A.
Penguin Group (Canada), 90 Eglinton Avenue East, Suite 700, Toronto,
Ontario, Canada M4P 2Y3 (a division of Pearson Penguin Canada Inc.)
Penguin Books Ltd, 80 Strand, London WC2R 0RL, England
Penguin Ireland, 25 St Stephen's Green, Dublin 2, Ireland (a division of Penguin Books Ltd)
Penguin Group (Australia), 250 Camberwell Road, Camberwell,
Victoria 3124, Australia (a division of Pearson Australia Group Pty Ltd)
Penguin Books India Pvt Ltd, 11 Community Centre, Panchsheel Park, New Delhi – 110 017, India
Penguin Group (NZ), cnr Airborne and Rosedale Roads, Albany, Auckland
1310, New Zealand (a division of Pearson New Zealand Ltd)
Penguin Books (South Africa) (Pty) Ltd, 24 Sturdee Avenue,
Rosebank, Johannesburg 2196, South Africa

Penguin Books Ltd, Registered Offices:
80 Strand, London WC2R 0RL, England

First published in the United States of America by The Penguin Press,
a member of Penguin Group (USA) Inc. 2005
Published in Penguin Books 2006

1   3   5   7   9   10   8   6   4   2

THE LIBRARY OF CONGRESS HAS CATALOGED THE HARDCOVER EDITION AS FOLLOWS:
Helprin, Mark.
Freddy and Fredericka / Mark Helprin
p. cm.
ISBN 1-59420-054-8 (hc.)
ISBN 0 14 30.3725 0 (pbk.)
1. Great Britain—Kings and rulers—Succession—Fiction.
2. Great Britain—Colonies—America—Fiction.   3. Imperialism—Fiction.
4. Colonies—Fiction.   I. Title.
PS3558.E4775F74 2005
813'.54—dc22   2004065312

Printed in the United States of America
Designed by Marysarah Quinn

For E.L.H., too late

Misconstruction is the emblem of a lost age.

CONTENTS

FREDDY

and

FREDERICKA

As penance for departure from the royal ideal and instruction therein, Frederick and Fredericka, the Prince and Princess of Wales, are forced to travel through America penniless and incognito, with the object of reacquiring the deviant former colonies for the British Crown.

PROLOGUE

THOUGH IT IS HARD to be a king, it is harder yet to become one. This is especially true if among those who are to be your subjects and in international opinion it is generally accepted that you are not quite in your right mind, and are some sort of bloody idiot who repeatedly does stunning, inexplicable things that embarrass your wife, your family, and the nation—but not you, because you believe, and state, that you are impeccably sane, and you cannot understand what all the fuss is about.

You refuse embarrassment because you hold that kings and those who would be kings must struggle to find and define their duty and their special place in the world, and are meant to live on the edge. Why do people expect kings to be unlike anyone else, and then punish them for it? Why is a king, who by accident of birth must submit to the will and expectation of scores of millions, or even (as in the case of the British, world-apparent monarchy) thousands of millions, savagely held to account as he forges a tormented youth into what must appear on Coronation Day to be a royal being of evident perfection?

Like a Roman gladiator alternately reviled by or beloved of the crowd, prior to his ascension to the throne the future king lives a life of overwrought luxury, dreadful isolation, and constant challenge. He desires above all to be an ordinary man, if only because a king is kept from the world as ordinary men are not, and the world is an inestimably better and richer prize than any throne. And yet he will fight savagely to achieve his destiny, not because it is attractive to him but because his sense of honour will not let him desert the field. How strange.

But that is theory, and this is the story not only of the royal state but of two people, Freddy and Fredericka, who had to come to terms both with it and with each other. After so many articles in the press and years of frothy gossip, you may think you know them, but you don't.

My account of what befell them is as unvarnished and pure as a tree on an ocean promontory that has been stripped of its leaves in storm, or a sheep that has been shorn to the pink. It is brutally, literally, and mortifyingly true. This is not because I hold no brief for these two dear friends but because I was asked—commanded—to present their story without argument, polemic, defence, or excuse. For the most part it is a story that I know only as it was told to me. How do I know then, and how can I assure others, that it is accurate?

I know because I was present at the many hypnosis sessions at Sandringham, during which I was absolutely sure that the king was not pretending, for as brilliant and versatile as he may be, he does not have other than in the hypnotic state the ability to read, memorise, and recite backward the Karachi Yellow Pages at high speed, all the while simulating with intense bodily jerkings the paroxysmal death struggle of a salt-water game fish. I know because I used every means to verify all that was related to me, and I know because I have it on the word of someone who has suffered mightily for the sake of such things as keeping his word. But I know most of all because it was told to me, bereft of embellishment, as a duty of the heart and in memory of one who is gone.

I do admit to having taken some liberties of narration. How else could I convey the scope both of their adventures and their transformation? But you cannot trust me, you must trust only the story. I myself am but a cipher to their great account, and what follows is not mine but theirs. And, when you enter, you will be not with me, but with them most certainly. Imagine, therefore, that within these paper portals is an ancient monarchy brought to a parlous state, and a warlike and restless prince lost in a time that for its lack of passion, modesty, and truth was inappropriate to him and broke his heart again and again, but could never break it all the way.

GEOFFREY, LORD PIGGLESWADE
Gower Lodge, Mortlake

I.

THE

GARDEN

of EDEN

The Man Who Would Be King, Who Would Rather Not

The wind was luffing over the tablelands of Skye as a storm built up at sea, but its slow passage promised hours more of sunshine and that the lakes would stay blue. Toward the end of a morning that for September was quite warm, a boy of Kilmuir was cutting across the open land on his way to Staffin. The way was long, with neither road nor path, but the more empty the places in which he travelled and the more space to separate him from all else, the more, in his eyes, he achieved.

At the northern tip of the Isle of Skye are mountains resting in a skirl of cloud risen from the firth. Here, storms are seen from far off and cannot surprise. They mount in black even as the sun shines upon the oceans of purple heather over which they will sweep. Sometimes, if the west wind is slow, the storms stay still and their bright thunderbolts flash like neon lights against unmoving walls of dark cloud.

One such storm had risen at sea and was at the back of the boy from Kilmuir. Like the farmer who fills the bin of his combine with a golden stream of grain, he had a sense of adding to his riches, not with every second that passed but with every step he took that carried him away from the settled world. He was fourteen and did not tire: his strength only grew as he crossed the flatland and climbed to the plateaux. Though the storm behind him billowed higher and higher, he was confident that were he not to slacken but rather to build strength upon strength and speed upon speed, he could outrun it. What a triumph not to have taken the road but to have crossed the landscape with no engine save his own heart.

With rhythmic ease, he ascended a wide apron of broken rock to what seemed the highest and most deserted plain in all of Scotland. For a moment, with his senses attuned to wind and sky, everything was perfect. But then perfection broke, when he saw, as if in a magazine advertisement come to life, a green Land Rover parked on a rise and facing west. Unlike most military Land Rovers, it gleamed. It had impressed into the grass a track that would take a year to heal. If twenty or thirty like it were set loose upon even so wide a place as this, they would crisscross it with thread-like cuts, collapse burrows, and crush nests.

Abandoning a line of travel that he had bent only to skirt lakes, he turned toward the offending object. Surely whoever had broken the spell of these Highlands was inauthentic, someone who did not and could not belong, who was soft and pale and would shrink before this young Scot who would shame him into going back to London or New York. Thus a victory of the wild over the settled, farms over industry, the pure over the polluted, the gold over the dross, the wheat the chaff, and so on, although it was true that he himself wanted quite badly to go to London.

As he closed on the Land Rover he saw through its windows someone who was standing on the other side and very colourfully dressed. Were it a girl, confrontation might be inappropriate, especially were she pretty. She would probably be a London girl, beautiful and elegant, with expensive clothing and a Florentine scarf draped over her shoulders like the petals of a crocus, though he had neither seen such a thing nor heard the words for it. He understood, however, that the appearance of a girl like this might be possible and that something was out of the ordinary, for he saw painted on the passenger door behind the driver's position one of the involved little crests that grace many things, from postboxes to bottles of cologne, over two familiar letters: *PR*. This signified Queen Philippa. He didn't know why she might be called Philippa R. Had he known that the royal family's last name (taken upon the abandonment of their German dynastic name during the Great War) was Finney, according to his lights her initials would have been *PF*.

From the shine of the car and the painted crest he thought that it might belong to a travel company of the type that takes people to places where they think they cannot walk but where, when they do, they walk all day through torrents of clouds and sky. Swinging around the back of the spotless vehicle, he saw who had brought it there. It was neither a girl from New York nor a girl at all, nor even an Englishman, but a massive, white-haired, kilted Highlander, with a face that had been shaped by many battles. On his wrist was a falcon the size of an eagle, which, to register the intrusion, lifted its still-folded wings and cupped the air.

Unwilling to be dumbstruck, the boy of Kilmuir held his ground, saying in the pure accent of Skye, "I thought you were a girl."

"Whom are you addressing?" the falconer asked, imperturbed.

"You. I thought you were a girl."

"Did you."

The boy nodded.

"Why?" asked Bannerman, the falconer, narrowing his eyes, but in a kindly way he had for adolescents.

"Why?" came the echo, as if the boy were just as curious, and had put the question to himself as if he had not known the answer.

"Why did you think I was a girl? Do I look like a girl? Have you never seen a girl?"

"It's a touring company car," the boy said, as if that explained anything.

"No it isn't," Bannerman replied, turning away to stare into the immense sunlit space and at the storm that hovered over the sea and isles to the west.

The boy followed beside him. "It isn't?"

"No."

"What is it, then, a Royal Mail car?"

"Does it look like a Royal Mail car?"

"What's the thing on the door, that they've got on marmalade jars?"

"The thing on the door is the queen's coat of arms."

"Queen Philippa?"

"Aye."

"What's it doing on your car?"

"It isn't my car."

"Whose car is it?"

"Whose car," the falconer asked, pregnantly, "do you think it is?"

"Queen Philippa's?" the boy replied.

"That's it."

"I don't believe you." But he did believe him, because, among other things, there was more inlaid wood and fine leather inside this military vehicle than in a Rolls-Royce. Nonetheless, he kept up his line. "What would the queen's car be doing here?"

"I drove it here."

"What for?"

"Will you please stop asking questions?"

"What do you mean, 'stop asking questions'?"

"You ask question after question."

"Why?" asked the boy.

"I don't know. How should I know? You should get on your way. If it rains, as it will, I will nay let you in the car."

"I don't care if you let me in or not. The rain doesn't bother me."

"All right," Bannerman said, noting that the boy's threadbare waxed jacket and bedraggled boots would keep no water out, "just give me some distance, if you will."

When the boy was hurt, he was stubborn. "Nah, I won't," he said, voice breaking but still nonchalant.

"To hell with you, then."

"To hell with *you*," came the echo.

"Aren't you going to go?" Bannerman asked. "After you tell someone to go to hell, you walk away." When the boy didn't move, he asked, "Don't you?"

"Not me. And why'd you make those tracks with the queen's car? This isn't England, you know, where the grass grows easily; it's Scotland, where it takes a year."

"I know it's Scotland. I'm here for a reason that's worth some tracks in the heather."

"What reason?"

"If I tell you will you promise to go?"

"I'm not gonna. I'll hang about. What are you doing with the queen's car, anyway? It's her bird, too. It's got the marmalade thing on its leathers."

"Aye, it's got the marmalade thing on its jesses, and it is the queen's."

"What is it, a chicken?" the boy asked, as part of his war against the falconer.

"A chicken!"

The falcon, who seemed to understand English, flexed his talons.

"This is no chicken," Bannerman said with unshaken pride. "This is Her Majesty's falcon Craig-Vyvyan, the son of Finlaec, the son of Gueldres, the son of Habicht, the son of Duff, the son of Grimnock the greatest falcon of them all. He's a tiercel; that is, a male, a boy. Ordinarily, you don't call tiercels falcons: they're not big enough. But Craig-Vyvyan here, male or not, is the biggest falcon in England. Scotland, too. Britain. Maybe the world."

The boy was stunned, and stood perfectly still, his mouth ajar as if in dementia.

"I thought you'd be impressed," said Bannerman.

"I don't care about falcons," the boy said, "not at all. Couldn't care less about falcons."

"I see," said Bannerman, doubting him.

"What did you say his name was, again?"

"Craig-Vyvyan, the son of Finlaec, the son of Gueldres, the son of Habicht, the son of Duff, the son of Grimnock the greatest falcon of them all."

"That's *my* name."

"Grimnock the greatest falcon of them all?"

"No, Craig-Vyvyan. That's me, Craig-Vyvyan. I've got the same name."

"With a hyphen?" Bannerman asked.

"What's a hyphen?"

Bannerman made a hyphen in the air with his right index finger.

"Aye, a hyphen."

"And the Vyvyan spelled with two *Y*'s?"

"Yes."

"What's your last name?"

"Cockaleekie."

"Cockaleekie. Did you ever think of changing it?"

"Why would I do that?"

"Just a thought. But your first name is Craig-Vyvyan?"

"I told ya."

"How'd you get it?"

"My grandma's brother was Craig, and Vyvyan was my father's friend, who was with him in Normandy in Lord Lovat's Number Four Commando, and died in my father's arms. My father cannot say the name without tears coming to his eyes, so he calls me by the first part, and when he calls me by my whole name, well, he cries."

"Your father must be my age, then."

"He is. My ma is his second wife."

"Well, Craig-Vyvyan, stay a while."

"I don't want to."

"Now you don't want to."

"I don't like having the same name as the bird. It's kinda spooky. I think I'll just be gone. I'm on my way to see my uncle in Staffin. He's my mother's brother, and he's just had an operation on the bones of his foot. I'll go see him now. Good-bye."

"Wait," said the queen's falconer. "You mustn't go. You're part of history now, even if you don't know it."

"And how is that?"

"I shouldn't tell you just yet, although to keep you here I will, if I must, and if you promise not to talk to the newspapers."

"Newspapers?" Craig-Vyvyan asked, picturing himself talking to a newspaper held at arm's length. "Why would I talk to newspapers?"

"Everyone does."

"They talk to newspapers?"

"That's why so much about the royal family finds its way into print."

Imagining people all over Britain declaiming to their newspapers, Craig-Vyvyan said, "I never even read newspapers."

Here was a natural creature who seemed largely untouched by what the world had become. He still looked like a child; his hair was sandy, sun-bleached, probably cut by his mother; and he himself was sunburnt, with a peeling nose.

"Can you read?"

"A little. I was schooled in the croft, but my ma took ill two years ago, and we moved to Kilmuir. I work now, outside."

"Do you have a television?"

"No."

"A radio?"

"No."

"You've heard of the queen."

"Yes, and of the king. My father was a soldier of the king."

"Aye, her uncle, and a great king he was."

"Not her husband?"

"No, the queen's husband is a duke."

"A duke. That doesn't make sense."

"Yes it does. And have you heard of the Prince of Wales?"

"I've heard of the Prince of Peace and I've heard of Jonah and the Whale, but I've never heard of the Prince of Whales."

"Wales the place, not the creature. Do you mean to say that you haven't heard of Frederick, the Prince of Wales?"

"I do."

"And Princess Fredericka?"

"Are they English?"

"Yes, they are English."

"This is Scotland."

"I grant you that, but you are among the few people in the English-speaking world who don't know of Prince Frederick and Princess Fredericka. A thousand million people watched them wed, and every day they are found on the covers of hundreds of magazines all around the world."

"Oh," said Craig-Vyvyan, who read neither newspapers nor magazines, whose father tended sheep, and whose mother spun wool.

"I see the wheels turning," Bannerman observed, assuming that the boy was beginning to understand fame.

"How many is a thousand million?" Craig-Vyvyan asked.

"Twenty times the population of the United Kingdom."

"What did they do with the leftovers?"

"Craig-Vyvyan," Bannerman asked, which caused the bird to cock its head, "when did you last eat?"

"Dinner yesterday."

"You've gone twenty-four hours, and you've been walking in the wind. What did you have for dinner yesterday?"

"An oatcake, a bit of lamb, and a baked potato."

"Just one potato?"

"And a cup of milk."

"That's hardly enough for a boy your age," Bannerman said to Craig-Vyvyan, as he opened the tail-board, knowing now that he would not have to beg or cajole him to stay. "Here, take some chocolate to hold you until we eat. Have you ever heard of King Richard's dog?"

"I didn't know that kings bothered with dogs."

"Kings love their dogs. Philippa feeds her dogs filet mignon, which Freddy pinches for his barbecues. And they're not palace-trained, so footmen have to follow them around with soda siphons and rags. Why do you think royalty like dogs? It's because dogs don't grovel and beg like people. A long time ago, the Earl of Kent had a dog. He was a tall, white dog with long limbs, short hair, floppy ears, and a face like Charles de Gaulle. Unlike most dogs, who are instinctive loyalists, he was an opportunist. He calculated all the time, like a cat, and the earl kept him not because he liked him but because he was afraid the dog would think too little of him were he to abandon it.

"When Kent's prospects were in decline, the dog, who knew before anyone, stood up, marched out, and left the castle without looking back. He walked all over England quite deliberately until he found the future

Richard the Second. The dog stayed even after this new master had become king, but with the same contemptuous detachment he had shown for Kent. One day, before anyone else understood what was about to happen, he walked out on Richard and went straight to Bolingbroke, who shortly afterward became Henry the Fourth. I wouldn't have liked him, but that dog really knew what he was doing."

"How did he know?"

"Only God knows, and Freddy, who thinks he knows."

"Freddy? The Prince of Wales?"

"The tabloids and those close to him call him Freddy."

"How does he know about the dog?"

"He has a theory. He believes that plants and animals were denied the gift of speech because they can see past, present, and future as one and the same thing, and that were they to tell human beings (particularly princes) what they see, it would be too difficult to bear. He talks to plants, the Prince of Wales, like his ancestor George the Third, because he thinks they are wiser than Einstein or the Archbishop of Canterbury. They're certainly wiser than the Archbishop of Canterbury."

"Who are Ein . . . who?"

"Don't worry about them. Consider, rather, that not all dogs can tell kings, just some. Only one dog in the history of England was like the walking horseradish that went from Kent to Richard to Bolingbroke. You don't just trot off to the RSPCA and pick out a dog that can tell kings. But," said Bannerman, holding his index finger in the air, "the talent exists. The trick is to find it if you can, to find the rare person who can tell about animals that they can tell about kings, and then," the falconer said, quite heatedly, drawing Craig-Vyvyan with him, "when you know which animal can do it, to breed the talent, to preserve it from one generation to the next, down the line, so kings and their heirs would always be able to know who was worthy of and destined for the throne."

"Who is the person who can tell about animals that they can tell about kings?"

"Ah," said Bannerman, "it's a rare gift, which has only come once, five hundred years ago, when the son of an Oxford organ maker was chosen by the Yorkists to impersonate the king who would have been Edward the Sixth.

"His name was Lambert Simnel, and, along with the Germans and Irish who backed him, he was defeated at Stoke in a fierce battle with Henry the Seventh, who proved both merciful and wise. Lambert Simnel was a boy like you. He had no corrupt desires and did not know the world, so the king spared his life, and for several years Lambert was made to turn the spit in the royal kitchen."

"Is this true?"

"It's history, Craig-Vyvyan."

"Is history true?"

"More or less. Lambert would have turned the spit until the day he died—in which case I would not be here and we would not be talking now—had not a bakery maid who had once been Chantal of Cleves peered through a crack in the wall by the ovens as Lambert was engaged in conversation with the birds who had come to peck the floor of the courtyard of its stray grains. They would hop onto his finger or his arm, depending on their size, to converse with him."

"Like Freddy."

"Like Freddy, except that plants and animals don't talk back to Freddy, but to Lambert they did. The king called Lambert before him and asked if this were so. Lambert said it was. 'What do they say?' the king asked. 'They say what is the future, and what is the past.' 'Do they say who will be king?' 'They do.'

"As you can imagine, the king was quite taken with this, and worried. He asked if Lambert could teach him to understand what the birds said. Lambert replied that although he could not teach how to converse with the birds, not knowing how he himself could do it, he might teach the birds how to give a sign. But, were he to do this, Henry the Seventh's falcons would have to cease killing other birds.

"As the trade seemed much to his advantage, the king was willing. He made Lambert Simnel the keeper of his falcons, who had no use now except as the subjects of Lambert's tutorial. The falcons agreed to refrain from attacking all creatures that flew, and Lambert trained a line of them to fly only from the arms of those kings who were fit to be kings."

"What did the falcons get from this?" Craig-Vyvyan asked.

"Nothing but someone to talk to for the first time in ten million years."

"And this falcon, with my name, is descended from them?"

"He is, and you must keep it to yourself. They have their secrets, kings, that go back thousands of years, and we don't know the half of it. I'm the queen's falconer, and I know only one or two secrets, but they live with them as if on a battlefield of ghosts. Since the beginning there have been secrets, and since the beginning there have been kings. The kings know the secrets, which is why they are kings."

"What about him?" asked Craig-Vyvyan, pointing to his namesake.

"He knows who has the heart of a king or queen, and will fly only for a true monarch. When Edward the Eighth became king, Gueldres would not fly for him. He never had flown for him, not even when poor Edward came back from France after the Great War, having seen with his own eyes what few kings ever see.

"I was a boy then. My father had been keeper of the falcons for George the Fifth. Though Gueldres had not flown for Edward when he was the Prince of Wales, we were sure he would fly for him when he became king, given how his heart had been broken in the war. But Gueldres, the bearer of the line, refused, and Edward was forced to abdicate. They made up all that nonsense about Mrs Simpson to hide the secret. Had it not been for Gueldres, history would have known her, had it known her at all, merely as one of Edward's mistresses. Then came George the Sixth, who had to abdicate after the war because of his asthma, and the nation was in a terrible pickle with refusals, scandals, and all that sort of thing, until the unknown brother, Harry, George the Fifth's very strange son, became king for all of a month and died. Thanks be to God that his daughter Philippa has been so unlike him."

"What was wrong with him?"

"Oh," said Bannerman, "let's see. You don't receive foreign dignitaries while sitting on the throne in diving goggles and flippers. If you pride yourself upon speaking fake Chinese, you nonetheless avoid doing so with the Chinese ambassador. You do not—or at least you try not to—address the nation in Pig Latin. You see how delicate is the fate of kings? As delicate as ours or more so."

"But what about Craig-Vyvyan?" Craig-Vyvyan asked again.

"He flies for Philippa. For her he soars and dives at great risk to himself, as you might expect for this lady who is a natural queen, born to be queen, the very emblem of a queen."

"Then why are you here? The bird won't fly for you. Why have you brought him to a place so wonderful for flying?"

"You've got it," said Bannerman. "I am here because this is a wonderful place for flying. Today, we want to fly this bird, we want it badly. And if he needed encouragement or temptation, he would get it here, wouldn't he? Look ahead. There you see a horizon so wide that the curvature of the earth is almost visible, and yet what lies before it isn't merely a disk of flat water but a great stage with an apron of islands, of channels and the blue sea, of a rising storm that multiplies the expanse of this theatre in volumes of blackening depth. And here the sun is still shining, so that were Craig-Vyvyan to fly he would float and swoop through air both light and buoyant."

"But he won't fly for you, so why did you bother?"

"Because this time, God willing, he will fly for the Prince of Wales."

"Him again? Why would he fly for him?"

"He's the heir to the throne."

"Wouldn't the heir to the throne be the queen's son?" Craig-Vyvyan asked with mocking superiority.

"He is the queen's son."

"That's a coincidence."

"No, Craig-Vyvyan, it isn't a coincidence that the Prince of Wales is the queen's son. If he weren't the queen's son, he wouldn't be the Prince of Wales."

"Who would he be?"

"He would be anyone."

"Then why isn't he?"

"Who?"

"The Prince of Wales."

"He is."

"He is what?"

"He's the queen's son."

"That," said Craig-Vyvyan, "is the coincidence."

"All right," Bannerman conceded, "it is a coincidence. It's one of the most amazing coincidences in the world, that the Prince of Wales is the queen's son. Will wonders never cease?"

"No, they won't," said Craig-Vyvyan, "not as long as there's an Earth."

"Today, the prince is coming here, on foot, just as you did, alone."

"From where?"

"From a landing somewhere on the west coast of Skye, where *Britannia* put him."

"That could be fifty miles."

"That's no problem. Look there." Bannerman pointed over the escarpment, to the west-south-west. In the distance a figure, which though hardly visible was neat and trim, moved at military pace along a barely perceptible trail on the high shoulder of a blue lake. "That will be he. You can tell by the walk. The SAS have a certain way of moving across country. Forget that I said that. You're not supposed to know."

As they watched the prince making for them with prodigious speed, the boy asked if this would be the first time Craig-Vyvyan would test him.

"I'm afraid not," Bannerman told him. "The first, as required, was when the prince was seven years of age. Some, like Philippa, get confirmation the first time. For them, life has fewer worries than for those who undergo the test in childhood, adolescence, young adulthood, middle age, and immediately before the coronation. It's a sensitive subject for Frederick, but, as a boy, he failed the test. Craig-Vyvyan peed on him and made him cry. Then he failed as an adolescent, and he failed as a young man. Now, as he enters middle age, he will be tested once again. If he fails, he will have only one chance more, after he becomes king and before he is crowned. If he fails then, he will have to abdicate. May God grant that today he has the heart of a king, so that in his middle age he can know the beginnings of contentment, which is why I've asked you to stay. Your name being the same as Craig-Vyvyan's must have significance in such a place as this, so far from so much. The prince will decide, of course, whether or not to ask that you remain, but I cannot imagine that he will not at least invite you to lunch."

"I hope he does," said Craig-Vyvyan. He thought for a while, and then said, "I never ate with the Prince of Wales or even a constable, and I wouldn't know what to say, but I'm hungry enough to risk it. What do you call him?"

"Unless he bids you do otherwise, address him as Your Royal Highness, and then, sir."

"I don't think I like that."

"If you want to eat, get used to it. We all do."

They heard quick footsteps as the prince rose above the escarpment. First came the slightly thinning head of hair, then Wedgwood-blue eyes rather too close together, big ears, and a face that radiated in equal measure both extraordinary confidence and deep sadness. He had an alert and expressive visage, a strong body, and a strapping frame. In the uniform of a Scots' regiment, with knapsack and assault rifle on his back and a tartan-banded cap folded beneath his left epaulette, here was the Prince of Wales, standing in the sun and wind.

·   ·   ·

HE UNSLUNG RIFLE and pack and leant them against the Land Rover. After he dropped the weight his shoulders rose, and he stretched modestly for someone who had walked so many burdened miles.

Even if Craig-Vyvyan the boy had not heard of the Prince of Wales twenty minutes before, he was frozen at the sight, and looked like a mental escapee who had wandered for days across the heath.

"How do you do?" asked the prince, hopeful of receiving an answer though not necessarily expecting that he would, as Craig-Vyvyan could neither move nor speak. "A citizen of the area?" the prince asked his mother's falconer, raising his eyebrows.

"Yes, Your Royal Highness, a boy, of Kilmuir, I believe, on his way to see his uncle in Staffin."

"Bones of his foot," Craig-Vyvyan managed to rasp.

"I beg your pardon?" asked the prince.

"Bones of his foot," Craig-Vyvyan rasped again, before his jaw fell, and stayed.

"Whose foot?"

"Bones of his foot," came the sound, barely audible, once again.

"Is that your name?" the prince asked. Without speech, Craig-Vyvyan moved his head from side to side. The prince looked inquiringly toward Bannerman.

"Sir, I think you might wish him to stay."

"This is always done privately, Bannerman. You know that."

"I know, sir, but, just the same, I think you may want him to hang about."

"You do?"

"I gotta have something to eat, that's why!" Craig-Vyvyan shouted, fearful that, stoked to flame, his expectation of a royal lunch would be dashed. The worst kind of hunger is hunger that was not expecting to be hungry.

"I invited him to lunch, sir. We've more than enough food."

"Certainly," the prince said. "Do come to lunch, but could you just walk over that hill and stay until we call you?"

With a quick shake of the head, Craig-Vyvyan indicated that he would not, which amazed the prince, who was further amazed when the boy said, as if letting the prince in on the secret, "I want to see if the bird flies."

"You told him?" the prince asked.

"I did, sir."

"Everything?"

"Yes, sir."

"Who the hell is he?"

"His name is Cockaleekie, sir. He had never heard of you, until I told him just now."

"Why did you do that? Not only does he now know what virtually no one save my family and a few discreet—and previously discreet—falconers have known, not only that, but you have taken one of the few people in the British Isles to whom I might have spoken as if I were just a man, and corrupted him with knowledge of who I am. Think of what he might have told us had he the power of speech that you destroyed."

"I've got the power of speech," Craig-Vyvyan blurted out, resentful of being spoken of as if he were a block of stone.

"Good," said the prince, offering his hand to put Craig-Vyvyan at ease. "You can call me Freddy. Just call me Freddy. Try it."

"Freddy," croaked the now pacific Craig-Vyvyan, as if it were the first word man had ever spoken, and he pronounced it *Friddy*.

"No, not 'Friddy.' Freddy. Bannerman?"

"Sir?"

"Please explain."

"You'll want him to stay, sir, I am guessing, because of his name."

"Cockaleekie?" the prince asked. Then, turning to Craig-Vyvyan, he said, "Have you ever thought of changing it?"

"No, why would I?"

"That's his last name," Bannerman said.

"I assumed that. Bannerman, are you well?"

"Aye. You'll want to know his Christian name, sir."

Turning to the boy, the prince asked, "What's your Christian name?"

"Craig-Vyvyan, sir."

"Truly?"

"It is."

"With a hyphen?"

"With a hyphen, which I didn't know what it was until today."

"A good omen, sir, isn't it?" Bannerman asked, as rhetorically as he dared. "He just wandered in here with his name. I thought of King Richard's dog."

"It can't hurt, can it?" the prince asked, as rhetorically as he pleased. "Craig-Vyvyan?"

"Sir?" snapped Craig-Vyvyan, now fully alive to his part.

"I've just walked thirty-five miles, all night and all morning."

"Why the rifle?" Craig-Vyvyan interrupted. "I've never seen one like that."

"It's an HK," the prince told him, "standard for this regiment, and protection from the IRA. They rhyme."

"But you don't look like you've walked thirty-five miles. You look fresh. Look at me, and I've walked just eight. Is it because you're royal?"

"No, it's because I carried a change of uniform and I stopped to bathe in a lake."

"The lake must have been cold."

"It was, and it made me hungry. Let me tell you what's for lunch. Bannerman, tell him what's for lunch."

"I'm quite looking forward to it myself," Bannerman said. "Have been. Very hungry, I assure you. We have a broth of venison, a salad of wild greens and cherry tomatoes with Stilton-walnut dressing, grilled quail, baguettes just flown up from Paris, splits of Lafite '64, Badoit, chocolate mousse, ginger biscuits, Champagne, and tea."

Craig-Vyvyan was as unmoved as if he hadn't heard, so Bannerman repeated what he had said, but, still, it was as if Craig-Vyvyan had not heard. "How does that sound?" Bannerman asked, leaping into the air so that he could cinch up his kilt.

"Is it food?"

"It's food, and I'm sure you'll like it," said the Prince of Wales. "It was prepared on *Britannia* and helicoptered in: the greens and the quail are local."

"Freddy," Craig-Vyvyan asked, "do you have any fried dough?"

Freddy said that he had not.

"Fried Mars bars?"

The response was the same.

"Lard pasties?"

And so it went, a recitation of the most vicious buffet known to man. Bannerman closed his eyes and banged his hands together. "Two steel blocks," he said, "as smooth as ice. That's what I think of when I'm going to be sick, two perfectly smooth steel blocks, smashing together, over and over again."

"That's odd," said Freddy, "so do I. Let's get on with it."

"Indeed, sir. Craig-Vyvyan, we've got warmers and coolers, and china kept hot. But if after lunch you aren't happy, I'll give you all three of the bars of Swiss chocolate that are left. I'll give them to you anyway."

Then a silence. Everything for the test had been made ready beforehand. Bannerman had tended to Craig-Vyvyan the falcon, set up a perch, found the best line for the falcon-step the prince would take. He had even brought a Bible. It was good that the boy had stumbled upon them. The prince had forgotten for a moment what was to take place, and was moved— not only by the boy's poverty and raggedness but by his innocence and strength—enough to decide to reward him whatever the outcome that day. He had a joyful feeling and was contented as well, for the world seemed with him, and as the wind rose slightly and sang past the sharp whistle-like places in the car, he said, "I'm glad of this. How is the falcon?"

"He's good, sir. Many a time today he's cupped his wings."

"Perhaps he's ready."

They walked to the perch, where Bannerman left the bird. No one said anything, and the wind rose strongly, which was a good sign, for all Craig-Vyvyan had to do was spread his wings and it would lift him. Bannerman tugged at the boy to follow. The prince had become oblivious of them and all else, and concentrated upon the restless falcon sidling to and fro on the perch, against a background of wind-thrashed purple cloud that stood over the sea like a castle wall.

THREE TIMES ALREADY he had done this, and three times he had failed. First it had been at Balmoral, then Caernarvon, and then in England at Blenheim Palace, with the grounds emptied of all onlookers except Bannerman, the queen, and Freddy's father, Prince Paul, Duke of Belfast. As a child, Freddy had been used to failure on the first try—not hitting a tennis ball the first time it came over the net, sinking when tossed into the pool during Paul's primitive swimming instruction, failing to deal correctly with invisible cricket balls, sword tips, and badminton birdies. It was therefore not surprising that Craig-Vyvyan had not flown, although it was humiliating when the bird chose to pee on him. Young Freddy was glad to get over that test, and the ten years until the next seemed to shelter him like an infinity. Besides, at seven he imagined that at seventeen he would have the powers of a giant of the earth.

At seventeen, however, he was famously unsure of himself and awkward, and though he had more hope that the bird would fly, he suspected that it would not, and that it would be offended by his tentativeness—as it was. When on the high battlements of Caernarvon he made the forward step, it had refused to leave his wrist. Still, three more chances remained, and any misery he might have had in his seventeenth year was dashed away by the spectacular torrents of his sexual apprenticeship to Lady Phoebe Boylingehotte, who, three years his senior, had a mesmerising, inexplicable, ineffable gift. Though she was green-eyed, blond, firm, well defined, and boiling hot, it was her face—the shape of her lips, the brightness of her eyes, the curve of her smile, the indecipherable combination of it all—that spoke volumes of sex. Her powers of seduction were rivalled only by her powers of delivery. Not one woman in a hundred million had such talent. Whence it came, no one knew. Nor did they know what it was, how it worked, or where it was going, but Freddy had decided that he needed it for the rest of his life. What a pity that she was married.

Though he had failed at seventeen, by the time he was in his late twenties he was absolutely certain Craig-Vyvyan would respond to his strength and fly from his arm. When he was a soldier, his lot for years had been one test after another, each beyond the capacities of most men, some extraordinarily so, and all predominantly fierce. It is remarkable what a man can do in such a frame of mind, and not only did he do such things then but he carried them forward. For example, after lunch with Bannerman and the boy Craig-Vyvyan, the Prince of Wales knew that he would pick up his rifle, shoulder his pack, and walk across Scotland to Balmoral, travelling in the high and empty places by day and through more settled country by night. Having been born to his station, he demanded from himself unceasing proof that he was worthy in his own right. But, still, the bird had been unimpressed by the prince as soldier, and had once again refused to fly. Perhaps he would rise on the fourth try, when the Prince of Wales had not only strength but, by now, the beginnings of wisdom.

That which is required of a king, other than being born to it, is strength, courage, wisdom, and forbearance, all of which Freddy had in some degree, some in great abundance, and some on its way. Now he wanted the falcon to fly not for him but to save England from a crisis of abdication.

So it was hardly of himself that he was thinking as he took Craig-Vyvyan from the perch, quieting him with soft, confident words, but of Britain, and of his obligation to both the past and the future. "England needs a king, Craig-Vyvyan, by the right of succession, the practice of self-abnegation, the harrowing of the body, cultivation of the intellect, and clarification of the soul. Grant me confirmation that I will be worthy in the name of God and for the sake of my country."

But as he removed the falcon's hood and released him from his bonds, he had the sense that something was missing, although he did not know what. He felt within him quite an evenly balanced war of his own virtues and vices—his right and proper sobriety, his disastrous marriage; his high achievement, his terrible temper; his exemplary asceticism, his expectation of the best of everything; his devotion to family, his magnificent adultery with Lady Boylingehotte; his integrity in his duties, and the sin that he had married a woman he did not love.

He knew his good qualities and shortcomings. Surely the falcon would not expect him to be perfect. In her modesty and reassuring grace, his mother was almost that. Though he had been only a small child before her inheritance of the throne, he had always thought that her success in royal matters was at least partly due to circumstance. As a girl, she was content to be the daughter of a king, and nothing more if need be, all her life. Happy with her station, satisfied with her lot, she received the kingly sword having been already blessed with tranquillity. Freddy, however, was a man, with the need to forge his way, conquer, and surprise. Her greatness was feminine, and was within her from the start. His, were it to be, had to be made by his own deeds and strength, and yet none of his deeds and no part of his strength could be directed to winning the crown, as that would be a war against his own blood. All he could do was wait and endure, and this was not natural for a young man of any station.

He had very many good qualities, had worked hard, and been devoted, if not to Fredericka then at least to the kingly ideal, which a thousand or more years of history had made difficult to understand, much less to match. Were he to be judged as he stood upon this cliff looking over the sea, he wanted to be judged as having the heart of a king. Something was missing, however: a quality, a virtue, the thing that would hammer on the falcon Craig-Vyvyan's doors at dawn and tell him, as it had with Philippa, that here was an arm from which God had given a tell-tale falcon full permission to lift away on the wind.

Though indeed something was missing, Freddy did not fail to notice a single detail, not the sunlight streaming down, the westward-flowing sea of purple heather, or the storm lit by jagged shavings of white and yellow lightning. This was a great place in which even to fail, its nature offering consolation sufficient unto the day of the final test.

And this, rather than the certainty of result, made him confident. The wind had risen and was rising still. All the falcon need do was arch his wings and let it open them, keep them straight and let it take him. Lifted and blown back, he would then tilt forward to move into the air below the escarpment. What bird would keep himself from such oceans of air? How could he? He must be aching to go.

In wind now raging, and having risen to the occasion, Freddy elevated his arm, turned to the falcon Craig-Vyvyan, and took the falconer's forward step, expecting to see wings gloriously unfold.

But they did not. Instead, the talons gripped tighter to hold Craig-Vyvyan in place despite his forward momentum, and he turned his head away from the wind and to the Prince of Wales, as if to say, I was willing to fly, I was wishing to fly, and I was wanting to fly, but you have failed me once again.

Craig-Vyvyan the boy did not know what to make of this. Bannerman sighed. And Freddy bent his head in disappointment. He had only one more chance, and now, for the first time since all this had started, he truly doubted the result.

"I'VE FAILED," he said, looking up, "again. Given the state of things, if I fail the next time I may take the monarchy with me. It's one thing if it ends, and even if it ends with me, but it's another if I myself end it," he continued, now pacing. "Other people, ordinary people—watchmakers, hairdressers, and taxi drivers—don't have to stake everything on the whims of a bird, do they?" He shot Craig-Vyvyan the bird an angry look, and seemed to be addressing him even as he spoke out at the heath. "They eat birds, that's what they do. They go to the bloody supermarket and buy dead birds wrapped up in plastic, they take the bloody bus home carrying the bloody birds, and they throw them into a microwave oven." He moved toward Craig-Vyvyan the bird.

"Now," he said to the bird, who stared back with one eye as big as a marble, "we are going to have some birds. We are going to eat them. They're just fuzzy little quails, the kind you've never had, because Lambert Simnel made your great-great-to-the-fifth-power-grandfather promise not to eat them. But who is to say we cannot eat bigger birds? Birds as big as a chicken, for example. A capon. A turkey. It can be done, and one does not have to be a king to do it. Have I made myself clear?"

"Your Royal Highness," Bannerman said quietly, "they'll die in service rather than give in. They're not politicians."

"I know," said Freddy. "And I'm grateful for it."

Bannerman went about getting the lunch. Swinging open the doors of the Land Rover, he revealed an extraordinary field kitchen in highly polished brass and chrome, at which he began to work, adroitly lighting the ovens, warming the china, dressing the salad, and plunging the Champagne into a silver ice bucket. He set up a folding table and camp chairs, and pulled precut firewood from a bin. This he piled on the ground and lit with a blowtorch the size of a nightstick. It blazed up easily in the wind. Bannerman knew that the same wind would blow away most of the fire's warmth, but he made it to sear the quail just before they were eaten, and for the sweet smell of the hardwood and its clinging lichen as they burned. He used a lull in the cooking to feed the falcon a few bits of raw steak. Sometimes arching his wings, the bird Craig-Vyvyan seemed to be flying vicariously upon the distant storm. As the prince watched Bannerman give him water, he said, "He wants to fly, doesn't he?"

"He does," Bannerman replied, "and he will."

"Then come," said Freddy, "and for God's sake, let us sit upon the ground, and tell sad stories of the death of kings." He often quoted Shakespeare inappropriately. Looking for recognition, he found none, and sat down on a camp chair, motioning for his two companions to do the same. "Shakespeare," he said to Craig-Vyvyan.

"No, sir, Craig-Vyvyan."

"*Richard the Second,*" Freddy added.

"No, it's me," said Craig-Vyvyan.

"Have you not heard of Shakespeare?"

"Shakespeare who?"

"Ah, yes," said the prince. "Shakespeare was a playwright, the greatest Englishman."

"I've heard of Jackie Collins: he writes books about racing cars, I think. Have you read them?"

"My loss."

"Soup," said Bannerman, putting down untouchable china bowls of almost boiling soup in front of each diner, including himself.

"Do you always eat this fine, Freddy?" Craig-Vyvyan asked as he began to work up a sweat with the soup, which was most pleasant in the cold wind.

"On occasion, it gets more complicated," Freddy told him. "State dinners can require an interpreter to explain what everything is, and they can take hours. I have eaten more than my share of the kind of things that Dumas describes: you know, 'first take the tongues of a hundred hummingbirds. . . .' And, then, Fredericka is very dainty about what I eat. Fredericka is my wife. The last time we ate in a restaurant—always *her* favourites—I had medallions of veal, four of them, to be precise, each the diameter of a shilling and the thickness of a pound note." They finished the soup and were on to the salad and bread. The bread was hot, the butter was sweet, and Freddy continued. "These *médaillons,*" he said contemptuously, "came on a plate with a combination of sauces the colour of buildings in Santa Monica, California: vapid, pastel, berry-tinted. I put them on my fork and ate all four in a single bite. And then came the salad. The vegetables were Lilliputian. I can't think of anything more overly precious than a whole cucumber the size of a pea, or an asparagus as thin as a hair.

"But then again I suffer all kinds of tortures. In Africa, I must out of politeness eat grubs and worms; in Southeast Asia, rotten fish; in Kazakhstan, the eye of a sheep. And then there's my father. He's the opposite of Fredericka, and will question your manliness if you don't eat the four-pound wildebeest cutlet with which he bombs your plate. 'Not a problem,' he says, 'I killed it myself. If you wash it down with a gallon of ale, you won't choke, and you'd better not. No Heinrich Himmler manoeuvre here; we beat those Nazi bastards and we don't have to do their bloody manoeuvres. Only nine hundred grams of fat. Eat the bullet, too. It's got vitamins.'

"He's never been an ounce overweight, and has no compassion for those who would grow plump on his twenty thousand calories a day. And, on occasion, my mother cooks. Had she cooked for Napoleon we never would have had to fight at Waterloo. You see, she has a deep hatred of cellular structure, which in her cuisine must be broken down at all costs. Not even Fredericka, however, whose motto is *miniature and raw,* refrains from eating it, whatever it may be. And who knows what it is? It's all the same colour. You can't really tell whether it's meat, fish, or vegetables. Why boil lettuce for an hour before it goes into a salad? Does spinach really need peppermint? And toast should not be black. She is England's greatest monarch since Victoria and its worst cook since Nigel Dalrymple."

Although he was used to holding forth, Freddy knew when to hold back and let others hold forth proudly before him. "What do you eat, Craig-Vyvyan?" he asked as if he didn't already know. "What are your favourites?"

"Fried Mars bars, pasties, haggis, sheep's brains, sheep's feet, sheep's tail, sheep's innards," said Craig-Vyvyan, with an angelic look, "eggs, beer, toffee, and lard."

"Spoken like a true Scotsman," Bannerman declared.

To avoid ill-mannered mockery of his guest, Freddy went on earnestly about his own eating habits. "In the next five days," he said to Craig-Vyvyan, "I'm going to walk the one hundred and seventy-five miles overland from Skye to Balmoral, with all the twists and turns. I'll do thirty-five miles a day, carrying sixty pounds in weight. I will sleep in a sack, bathe in lakes, and keep off the beaten track. I'll get water from streams, and berries from the bush. Other than that, I carry dried venison, salmon, and quail; dense Russian corn bread; lime juice, salt; a large tube of tomato paste; two pounds of pasta; five bars of chocolate; dried fruit; and a Dalvey flask of Laphroaig. I have yet to touch it, and will not until tomorrow at lunch. That, Craig-Vyvyan, is my favourite cuisine, what you carry on your back and what you take from the land when you walk. Thank God this is open country and I'm free to do that. The newspapers think I'm on *Britannia,* and will write that neurotic little Freddy never comes out on deck, and spends all the time in his cabin reading Schopenhauer and *Popular Mechanics.* To hell with them," he said, raising a glass of Lafite.

Bannerman and Craig-Vyvyan did the same, Bannerman because he shared the sentiment, and Craig-Vyvyan because he was delighted to be a friend of the Prince of Wales. He did like Freddy, and would have liked him, had he not been the heir to England's throne, perhaps even more, as would most.

"I shall probably never be king," Freddy said, partly because of the wine.

"Yes you will!" Craig-Vyvyan cried, entirely because of the wine, with one eye on Freddy and one eye on the quail in their final sizzle over the smoky fire. "You're the Prince of Wales, or whatever it is."

"I am. It's commonly accepted. It goes without challenge. Nonetheless, as I see it, it is a fact in brilliance that my head is too small for my mother's crown. Do you know of this crown that on some sad and happy day is supposed to be mine?"

"You don't have a whole bunch of them, like a bunch of hats dangling from hooks?"

"We do, in fact, but I speak of one in particular. It weighs three pounds. Mounted on it are four rubies; eleven emeralds; sixteen sapphires; two hundred and seventy-three pearls; two thousand, seven hundred, and eighty-three diamonds, including the second part of the Star of Africa; and the Black Prince's spinel, worn by Henry the Fifth at Agincourt. Quite a hat," he said, between claret and quail, "a hat for which I am not fit, because I am too fat."

"You're not fat," Bannerman said, becoming familiar because he too had been free with the claret. "It's only your father that calls you fat, and it's an injustice. You're in magnificent shape, man, and have been for twenty years. No one in England believes you're fat except your father and you."

"I am fat."

"Be gone!" cried Craig-Vyvyan. "You're lean."

"No," Freddy said, as if wine were truth, "I am obese."

"He's crazy, isn't he?" Craig-Vyvyan asked Bannerman.

Freddy nodded gently, and Bannerman said, "In this."

"Why does he think he's fat?"

"Since he was a wee lamb," Bannerman began, but was interrupted by his prince, who said, "Oh don't start, Bannerman, about the wee lamb."

"It was then that I told you, sir, the story of Wee Wee Ba Ba Sheep."

"A hundred million times."

"You begged for it, and you loved each telling."

"I did."

"I was there when your father would turn to you, a stripling as skinny as a thread, and tell you that you looked like a sumo wrestler. We laughed at first, thinking it was a joke. Bless the duke, but it was not a joke, and he kept at it. He and the queen would have terrible rows about it. He was and is the head of the household, but she is the queen of England, and she squarely contradicted him each time he suggested that you were fat."

"I know that."

"Though I address you, I'm telling him. The prince had a thousand ways of drilling into you that you were fat, and she had a thousand ways of drilling it out. He would call you a hog, she would call you a cat. He would call you a boar, she would call you a deer. He would call you an elephant, she would call you an ibex. He would call you a hippopotamus, she would call you an anaconda. He would call you a whale, she would call you an eel. It was very confusing to you."

"Yes," said Freddy. "Once, he called me a Javanese Opunga, and she called me a Bulgarian Mantis. I didn't know what the hell was going on."

"But I did. Although I couldn't say it, as it was not my place, I knew that it's easier to drill things in than to take them out."

"It's like a screw!" Craig-Vyvyan shouted in his cups, almost falling into the fire. "If you pull off its head, you never get it out!"

"Or a barbed splinter," said Bannerman, "born and bred to flee from a needle or tweezers like a fax from hounds."

"Did you say 'fax'?" Freddy asked.

"Yes, Your Royal Highness. I'm trying to be contemporary."

"Carry on, then."

"You were always a good boy, good boys listen to their fathers, and your father did this to you. You were an anxious child, born after the war and soaking-in all that the grown-ups carried with them of it. You were so serious and grave. And you started each day with a Bible story. You are not fat, sir. No one who fences, runs, swims, rides, rows, and fights, not to mention the polo playing, the three-hundred-mile walks, the two thousand sit-ups, the Aikido, the bayonet. . . . You're obsessed, aren't you? You're six feet tall, twelve stone, and as muscular as an Olympic gymnast. And yet you think you're fat."

"I would be fat if I didn't do all that."

"But you do, don't you."

"I won't be able to keep it up forever."

"Aye, not even for ten more years. Something happens to the body at fifty that at twenty you can't imagine, at thirty you don't suspect, and of which at forty you have just a hint, but cross that bridge when you come to it. You'll be a different man then. You'll forgive yourself. The chase will be over and you'll have learnt to love the world for what it is and to see yourself for what you are. It happens to everyone, even to kings."

"But, Bannerman, I will not be a king. Craig-Vyvyan on the perch has told me so four times. Though I always have thought that I have the heart and stomach of a king, and a king of England, too, he says I don't."

"You've got one more try." The sweet was almost gone and the water was boiling over the fire in an old battered military kettle that Bannerman had brought because he knew the prince was fond of it. "Who knows what will happen between now and then?"

· · ·

TEN MINUTES of silence later, as they drank their tea before the storm would begin with stray shots of rain in huge droplets that could hit as unexpectedly as the darts of Amazon Indians, Craig-Vyvyan asked the question of his life.

"What about me?" he said suddenly. "Maybe you'll be king and maybe you won't, but what about me? I'm from the people who wave as you pass, who beat the brush with sticks to flush the birds you shoot with silver guns. You have palaces: we have roofs that leak. What about me?"

The Prince of Wales was silent in consideration. Ofttimes he was begged, but this was not begging. The lightning that approached may have sealed it, he did not know, but, remembering Henry VII and Lambert Simnel, he was determined to be generous in proportion. Henry had spared Lambert's life even after Lambert had taken up arms against him. Craig-Vyvyan had done nothing, and his name was an omen from which the prince did not wish to be separated.

"Craig-Vyvyan, you're right, and today you might have brought us luck had we been more generous from the start."

At this, Craig-Vyvyan perked up, hoping that he would get not only the bars of chocolate but perhaps something like a five-pound note. After all, the prince's mother was on each one, and they must have been extremely easy for him to obtain from the many free samples with which the royal family was provided.

"If I become king, much will be open to me. Of late the queen has been reserving some of the vacancies in non-hereditary peerages for my use later on, and today I promise my first."

Craig-Vyvyan did not immediately understand the extraordinary thing that was happening to him. As he began to comprehend, he said, "Uh-oh."

"In December," the prince continued, "the Earl of Strathcoyne, who during the nineteen twenties was known for wearing party hats that were often mistaken for dunce caps, surfaced through the window of a Bahamian glass-bottomed boat, severing his carotid artery in the presence of a number of large sharks. His entitlements that have reverted to the Crown are several thousand acres, a house in Belgravia, and two hundred thousand pounds a year."

Bannerman was breathless for a moment and Craig-Vyvyan thought he would never breathe again.

"Craig-Vyvyan Cockaleekie, if you are with me on Lochnagar when I next and finally try to fly the tiercel falcon Craig-Vyvyan, and if he takes wing, I will make you Earl of Strathcoyne—or something or other: you know there are always pitfalls. This I swear on the honour of my family."

"Thank you, Freddy, but what about him?" Craig-Vyvyan added, at first boldly but then trailing off somewhat nervously in fear of compromising his luck.

"Bannerman?"

"Yes."

"Don't worry about Bannerman. He's already an earl, a Knight of the Thistle, and a good many other things. I suppose the Garter is next."

"He's an earl," Craig-Vyvyan wondered, "and he carries firewood, tosses salad, and serves the likes of me with dishes and puddings?"

"I served you," said Bannerman, "first in your capacity as a guest of the Prince of Wales, and then as my guest. Believe me, for my sovereign and my future sovereign no task is too menial for me to perform. It is an honour to serve the queen in any capacity, and the honour is mine as well with the prince, who. . . ."

"Bannerman, please," the prince interrupted. "In the face of such a storm, what does royalty mean? It means nothing. Let's get going."

As Bannerman began to pack up the Land Rover, rain and wind crossed the moor like an army. "Two hundred thousand pounds a year?" Craig-Vyvyan shouted over the wind not only to Bannerman but to the wind itself and perhaps even the whole world. "I've never seen more than ten pounds at once. Is it true? Will he forget?"

"It's true, and he won't forget. What will you do with the money, Craig-Vyvyan?" Bannerman asked. The prince, attending to his pack after having extracted his rain gear, was out of earshot.

"I'll buy every single thing at the tobacconist's," Craig-Vyvyan proclaimed, "and keep the chocolate and penknives for myself and give my father all the tobacco."

"That wouldn't be good for him."

"Why not?"

"Tobacco is bad for the health."

"It is?"

"Yes, definitely."

"Then I'll buy all the tobacco and throw it into the sea."

"And then what will you do?"

"I don't know."

"I recommend," said the prince in a voice that, to carry over the storm, he would have used in hailing someone across a river, "that you get educated. Arrange for tutors. Set up a household at Oxford or Cambridge. Study and read. Transform yourself."

"Why?"

"So that you can be worthy of expectations. So that you can have children who, with no titles, will be great in their own right. So that you may balance the gift, and return fair service. For a gift that does not find balance and a service that is not returned are worth less than a curse."

"How do you know that?"

"Because my family has been in the business for a thousand years. Now, give Bannerman your particulars so he can stay in touch with you. I look forward to when next we meet."

Having finished the loading, Bannerman was standing by the driver's door of the Land Rover in what was now a driving rain. "Craig-Vyvyan, do you want to come along? I'm going through Staffin."

Craig-Vyvyan looked at Bannerman and then at the prince, who stood with hooded rifle and pack, a lonely figure in a landscape gone wild and dark. "Aren't you coming in the car, Freddy?" he asked.

"I'll be walking," the prince replied.

"In this storm? Even the bird's in the car."

"Yes," said the Prince of Wales, starting on his way, "give him my regards."

. . . AND THE WOMAN
WHO PREFERRED THAT HE WOULD

MOOCOCK, the country house of the Prince and Princess of Wales, was set upon a hill overlooking the Weald of Boffin, at the centre of an empty three-mile stretch between the villages of Brooms Hoo and Pestwick-on-Canal. Until Fredericka succeeded in allowing it into two dozen glossy magazines, it had been a secret. And then, although Freddy had been able to keep the photographers from his library, the green room, the tack room, the gym, and the baths, he had had to give up everything else. Thus, half the world had seen the pools, indoor and out; the reception rooms; the bedrooms; and, always the favourite, the kitchen. As a result, the security force had to be doubled, ugly electronics mounted upon the otherwise classical roof, and seismic devices embedded in the weald, like potatoes.

Freddy and Fredericka's first theme argument, when Moocock was still unknown to the public, was occasioned by her insistence upon changing the name of the house and allowing it in magazines, and his determination not to do either. One weekend, having driven out unobserved, they had dismissed the servants and ordered the police to remain at the perimeter. Blissfully alone, they gravitated to the pool. For two days they stayed in an August sun that made them glow like roses. At night, though the lights were on in the water, which spoke back to a diamond-lit sky like a sapphire in a band of green, not an insect was in sight, and the sharply cut waves, like once-molten glass, went unblemished by gnats. The temperatures of water and air were perfect, and a slight wind warmed with its heat exactly as much as it cooled by evaporation.

Hanging on to one another while Freddy held fast with one hand at the tip of the diving board, they were breathless from intimate coupling beneath the surface in the glare of underwater lights. It had been like swimming through Champagne, quite a bit of which they had consumed before tumbling in. In fact, a used magnum rolled around the bottom of the pool like a mine. And of all the appeals to their senses that evening, the most memorable was the scent of flowers carried ceaselessly on the summer wind.

"Freddy, why is it called Moocock?" Fredericka asked in a voice that despite its aristocratic lineage sometimes veered toward the dialect of a refined Cockney shopgirl, which in her youth she had picked up first from her favourite nanny and then during her brief and disastrous career in the theatre. Freddy thought that these touches were like bright red poppies scattered across fields of gold. The queen did not, viewing them not as surprising colour but as constant irritation.

"The chap who built it called it Moocock," Freddy answered.

"What kind of name is that?"

"English."

"It doesn't sound English."

"Yes it does. *Moo,* and *cock.*"

"But what could that mean?"

"Cow penis."

"What's a cow penis?"

"I don't know. What do you think it might be?"

"The penis of a cow?"

"Yes."

"But, Freddy, cows don't have penises, do they?"

"They don't."

"Then why would he have called his estate that?"

"Because he didn't want anyone to find it, and a cow penis is nonexistent."

"If I had a name like that, I'd change it."

"So would I, although I haven't changed my name from Freddy Finney, have I?"

"You might have changed it had it been Freddy Cow Penis."

"I don't think so. In fact, I might change it *to* Freddy Cow Penis."

"Whether you do or not, let's change the name of the house to something other than Moocock."

"I've been at Moocock for fifteen years and never had a problem. Moocock is a splendid name."

"But won't it be funny when the television visits us and they say, 'Here are the Prince and Princess of Wales at Moocock'?"

"No, because neither the television nor anyone else will ever know of this place."

"But it's so beautiful. It should be in magazines."

"Never in magazines, Fredericka, never. It's got to be a secret. But if you really want to change the name, perhaps we can."

"That's a start."

"You see, when I first bought it, I had intended to call it something else, something magnificent and noble, something that, ever since I was a boy, I had wanted to call an estate in the country."

"Nothing like Moocock, I hope."

"Nothing whatsoever. Rather, it's the name of what is supposed to be the mythical white rhino of Bechuanaland, which actually is real, although no one ever believes me. I've always been fascinated by it, and I see no reason why we can't use it instead of Moocock."

"What is it?"

"Mohoohoo."

"Mohoohoo? Not really."

"Yes, so elegant," said Freddy. "I had wanted to name it Ostrichhurst, but then I found out that this is the name of one of my father's secret retreats, in St Mary's Hoo. Mohoohoo is better anyway, more sophisticated."

"Why not something like . . . Cliveden, or Hampton Court?"

"Those names are taken."

Now rather tense, they were no longer touching, and had forgotten the smell of the roses. "I can't live in a place called Mohoohoo," Fredericka declared. "It's ridiculous."

"Then we'll keep it Moocock."

"Imagine that in *Vogue,*" she said. "I'd be so embarrassed."

"You survive embarrassment in regard to your father's house, which, in case you have forgotten, is called Feta."

"What's wrong with that?"

"It's a cheese."

"It's a delicious cheese, Freddy. And Moocock is such a beautiful, magnificent house, why call it Moocock or Mohoohoo? What about something more conventional?"

"Such as?"

"Edam, or Gorgonzola."

For a moment, Freddy was speechless. "Those are cheeses," he said.

"So?"

"You can't name an estate after a cheese."

"Of course you can," she said, as if she were speaking to a child. "Why not? What about Sapsago Hall, or Mozzarella? I know: 'The Princess of Wales at home at her country estate, Camembert.'"

To Freddy's astonishment, this dispute would drag on for a number of years. Although he loved Moocock in every way, she hated the name and was determined to follow her family's tradition and call it after a cheese. It is said that marriage is a long war between ancient families trapped in close proximity by lust. That's not the half of it. The next morning, Freddy stood fully clothed and forlornly looking at the dead Champagne bottle at the bottom of the pool. He was about to dive in after it—soldiers are used to swimming in their clothes—when Fredericka appeared. Dressed only in a short silk robe, she was as beguiling as ever she had been. He felt that Eden, or, perhaps Edam, might yet be restored, for the wind still carried the scent of flowers, the sun was hot, the sound of a nearby fountain was hypnotic, and there they were, the two of them, a study in the statuesque. Horses had never been bred better. Bread had never been buttered better. Batter had never been better beaten.

"Were you in my bathroom last night?" she asked, breaking the spell and seething for a fight.

"I was," he said, innocently.

"When I was sleeping?"

"Yes, just making sure everything was safe."

"Safe?"

"Secure."

"Was it you who turned around the paper roll in the WC?"

"It was."

"Why did you do that?"

"Someone put it in the wrong way. It was coming from behind and off the roll like a scoop rather than from off the top and hanging down like a beef tongue."

"Who says?"

"Says Frederick, the Prince of Wales."

"That's wrong. It should come from the bottom."

"Certainly not. If it comes from the bottom, when you rip it off you can't control it and it might not tear evenly."

"Who cares if it tears evenly?"

"Fredericka, there is a right way to do things, and a wrong way. At Moocock, and everywhere else I live, it must come off the top of the roll."

"I'm sorry," she said. "Yours can come off the top of the roll. Mine comes off the bottom."

"I won't be able to sleep, and you know it."

"Then at night I'll remove the roll from the holder and lock it in my suitcase so you can sleep like a badger."

"Good idea," he said, "a good compromise."

"If you'll do the same."

"Why would I have to, when mine is inserted properly?"

"So I can sleep."

"All right."

This was, more or less, what their lives together had become. But such things as they disputed are not important, and can easily be overridden by mutual passions and compulsions, deep spiritual sympathy, and intellectual compatibility. As Freddy was by inheritance and constant physical training a spectacular physical specimen, and Fredericka was by inheritance and constant physical training an even more spectacular physical specimen, he assumed that she, parallelling him, would be content to spend the rest of their days absorbed in the challenge of sport, the contemplation of history, the mystery of fate, and the beauty of nature. All his life he had been either engaged in explosive and exhaustive physical pursuits or lost in thought. Everything in between—sociality, ceremony, conviviality, petty cares, and display—he thought witless.

Naturally, he understood how such things might be of interest or attraction to people who had to work their way up the ladder. But to him and to his family they seemed pointless. Having no place higher to go, why would he waste time flapping his wings? Though he had to cut ribbons and banter with tense Melanesians, on his own time he had Shakespeare, Liddell Hart, Newton, Mozart, and history. He loved history. The history just of his family was a field unto itself. He never had enough time left in the day to read. How could Fredericka, born to a high family and destined to be the queen of England, be unlike him?

Once, in London, when they had not been married long, the first cold evening of autumn came suddenly from the death of a lingering summer. Autumnal winds lifted in their wake the bat-like leaves that roar through darkened parks, and the lights of the city glittered from countless placid windows. Poised to strike, rested and intense, in excellent health and perfectly dressed, Freddy and Fredericka stood in a long gallery of Buckingham Palace, looking out at the night.

He could not decide what to do, but there were many possibilities: a private tour of the Tate, or, better yet, just wandering alone through the National Gallery; a visit to the prime minister or Stephen Hawking; a helicopter flight over London, which would flicker like a galaxy clouded with smoke and stars; a walk through Hyde Park as the wind swept it empty; an opera or a play; or perhaps just sitting by the fire, with a book. And that was hardly exhaustive, for here was the greatest, most civilised city in the world, and within and without his palace of six hundred rooms the heir to the throne had many options.

Then came ten piercing words that shattered his peace of mind like a dagger clattering upon a marble floor: "Freddy," she asked, "you know what I've got? I've got disco fever!"

"What?"

"Let's go to a disco. We'll just pick one and walk in. The excitement will be awesome, and it will make all the papers."

Freddy stepped toward the wall. Staring at the elaborate silk wallpaper as if he were deeply hurt, he ran his eyes along the patterns as he spoke. "First of all, Fredericka, please don't say 'awesome.' Secondly, we don't want to be in the papers other than on controlled, appropriate, and dignified occasions. Generally, it is good to avoid the papers." She hadn't moved from the centre of the red runner, and was resplendent in gown and tiara. Her savagely blue eyes outshone the great weight of jewellery on her, and her golden hair outshone the tiara.

"Discos," Freddy went on, "are for people whose empty heads require a filling of drugs, achingly bad music, and hideous lights. I never have been to them, I never will go to them, and I hope that if you have been to them you will from now on leave them behind."

"But they're fun."

"We've discussed this."

"We have?"

"Before we married, I told you, and you agreed, that though there are many things we can do that most people cannot even dream of doing, there are many more things we cannot do that most people could not dream of doing without."

"Like going to a disco?"

"And walking through Chelsea in daylight, having tea in a hotel, sitting in a park while reading the paper, holding regular employment, being unnoticed, not bearing the weight of a thousand years of tradition, et cetera. It is indeed awful in the modern sense of the word, and it is why, if I had a choice, I would not be king."

"You're just saying that," Fredericka told him nervously.

"I am saying it, but I'm not just saying it. I mean it. I've considered it all my life. Given the choice, I would not be king."

A look of misery and panic crept over her. "It's that bloody bird. What has he done to you? He's made you this way. Why don't you just have him killed?"

"He comes from a royal line many hundreds of years old. My patience with him is the patience that I myself am granted by others, and to break such a line would be a sin such as I would never commit."

"But he'll stop you from being king."

"And if he does?"

"What will we do then? We'll have to live in Paris, like your great-uncle, or in a little village somewhere, and no one will care about us."

"Fredericka, no one cares about us now."

"Oh, no, Freddy, the whole world cares about us."

"Not a bit. We're merely an amusement, a distraction. As the whole world does not really know us, cannot be close to us, and has no real need of us, nor does it love us, it merely uses us to fulfil certain of its needs. Anyone in our position would do. A thousand million people saw our wedding, to be sure, but you cannot count on a single one of them any more than they can count on you."

"That's nonsense. I feel adoration now more than ever in my life."

"Adoration is for God, saints, and babies, Fredericka. It has only one direction. Even if you contrive somehow to return it, accepting it is a sin."

"A sin?" She was astounded.

"Adoration will betray and ruin you, take the life from you, and leave you a charred shell."

"All I want to do, Freddy, for God's sake, is go to a disco."

"You've touched upon things that have taken the deaths of kings and princes to be learnt. I never expected you to come into this immediately or to learn all you must in an instant. It will take time to clarify, but then you'll understand."

"Understand what?"

Freddy sat down on the floor and leant against the wall. Still hopeful that they would go out into London, Fredericka sank like a flower and knelt in the centre of the red runner. Soon she lay down on her side and was as relaxed as he, her right hand cradling her head, her elbow on the floor.

"You'll understand in time that all the things that we have—the palaces, properties, and farms, the paintings, uniforms, fame, and jewels—are a burden, a trial, and a test. Most people are lucky in that they spend their lives working constructively for such things, though they may never get them. Our bad luck is that we need not work and we have them. When you do get them, the process of destruction begins. It is inevitable. These things rot and corrode not only the souls of men but the spirit of dynasties, and it has been that way since the beginning of time."

"Why?" Fredericka asked, not because she wanted to know, but because she knew he loved it when anyone asked him why.

"Because they are things, and when things are the end of the road they must be vested with a significance they cannot support. The enterprise, which is often a life, is then bankrupt. There is only one solution."

"And what is that?"

"To do without them."

"You don't do without them, no one in your family does without them."

"Ah," said Freddy, "that's where you're wrong. It's one of our secrets, and it goes back quite far. We find these things repulsive. All this stuff is the enemy, foisted upon us by our inherited position. The world dreams of it and imagines that we are enjoying it, for the world wants what we have. Our job is to pretend that we want it, too."

"You don't?"

"We detest it."

"I must say, you fooled me. You have the best of everything and you're very critical of everything else. You made me throw out my boots."

"White patent-leather boots are for chorus girls, prostitutes, and circus ladies, not princesses of Wales."

"You're always sending things back, saying they're not good enough."

"One gets addicted to that kind of behaviour. And nothing I've said means that I think smoked salmon and caviar are inferior to cheese puffs, or that a Mini Morris is superior to an Aston-Martin. Given a choice, I'll choose the best, naturally, based purely on objective criteria. You can feel it in the wood, see it in the cut, smell it in the leather, hear it in the way the car door closes, and, of course, you can taste it. What would you rather have, a cooked pig's foot . . . or a burgundied cutlet of venison? That choice, which, when you get down to its elements, is physics, has nothing to do with what I'm saying."

"Freddy, can't we just go to the disco and talk about this tomorrow? Life is slipping away."

"No. Life is right here. We don't have to go anywhere. Kafka never left Prague."

"There are a lot of discos in Prague. I've been to them. I may have danced with Kafka."

"Probably not: he was a bit of a bug."

"And so are you. All I want is to go out into the air."

"We'll walk in the garden."

"Where you'll talk, and tell me how your family, which has more things than anyone in the world, doesn't like things at all. That makes me nervous. I want lights, people, and busy streets."

"Very well. I'll tell you not in the garden but here, and if at the end you still want to go out, we'll go out."

"How long will it take?" Fredericka asked, gathering herself more happily.

"Not long."

"And can we go anywhere I'd like?"

"Yes. Where shall I begin?" Freddy asked, in a hall in which two dozen kings, staring silently over the years at sons and daughters, rivals, ancestors, fathers, mothers, old friends, and descendants and heirs they had never known, were imprisoned in their portraits, without words and largely forgotten in their lively particulars.

"Begin with yourself."

"That's the fashion, but I'd rather go back to Richard the Second, though he is hardly the beginning. He was, however, the first sumptuary king. In times when most people lived on earthen floors, ate gruel, and broke the spell of darkness only briefly with smoky tallow, his court was brilliant with light, he flew falcons, and he had ten thousand retainers. It took three hundred kitchen servants just to cook the food, and three hundred others, all in silk, just to keep house."

"What's so terrible about that?" Fredericka asked. "This palace has six hundred rooms, and grooms, postillions, pages of honour, pages of the back stairs, pages of the presence, yeomen of the plate, under-butlers, yeomen of the glass and china, footmen, polishers, sweepers, gardeners, mechanics, soldiers, and God knows what else. You know better than I. No one can keep track of them."

"I know," Freddy said, "and you forgot the bargemaster, the swan warden, the armourer, the deputy clerk of the closet, the hereditary carver, the apothecaries, the astronomer, the extra and temporary equerries, the heralds and pursuivants, the extra women of the bedchamber, and diddle diddle diddle all the way home. It's a disease that's been festering for a millennium, and we are supposed to be enthralled by it. The public pretends to want to take it away from us, and we pretend to fear. If a Labour government had the courage, and did, it would be like cutting Prometheus from the rock."

"Who?"

"Think of it. When Edward the Seventh, as Prince of Wales, was roughing it on the Nile, he went in six blue-and-gold steamers and six barges, and took four thousand bottles of red wine, three thousand of Champagne, four French chefs, four riding horses, and a laundry. If you build a whole house around your picnic, it's no longer a picnic, and that's what these people did with everything.

"But then there was my great-great-great-great-grandmother, Drina—that is, Victoria. After the death of Albert, she understood that her choice was between futility and simplicity, and she chose the latter, rejecting the burden of nonsense out of hand. She came on her visits in a carriage pulled by one horse, and in a bonnet such as a shopgirl might wear. She saw right through it."

"The bonnet?"

"No, the things that still excite you. And why shouldn't they? You're new to them and they to you. We have a different view. George the Fifth, the first Finney, preferred to live modestly in York Cottage, and for good reason. George the Third, the most misunderstood of my ancestors and a great and good man (although the Americans refuse to look into the question), was much the same. They called him Farmer George, and he took as much real life as he was allowed. His routine and dress were by preference like those of a dairyman. He was modest. He refused to be captured by things. We try to follow his example."

"It doesn't look like it from a distance, does it?" Fredericka asked archly, for Fredericka.

"Granted, not a bit, but of that which surrounds us, in masses of things and masses of ceremony, a vast proportion belongs to the state. Much that is left belongs to the monarchy as an institution and is no more ours than we can claim history. It does not belong to us; we belong to it. Of what remains, which year by year becomes less and less, much is in a 'museum state,' and untouchable. We are curators who cannot use what merely weighs upon us. And then, and only then, have we our personal possessions, and if you sift them from the mass of all else they are surprisingly little, at least from my perspective.

"Despite appearances, we have learned not to need, not to want, not to succumb to fame, flattery, and the material. It is our only chance of survival. And no good Prince of Wales in the modern day would want to be king. I would rather be a normal man, for then I could have a life with"—he hesitated—"texture. What is brittle fame compared to the peace of anonymity? What is adoration compared to love?"

"But you won't abdicate."

"Of course not. It's my duty to go on, to maintain the line. I can't possibly fail in that. It's as if you and I were throwing a ball back and forth to establish a record, and had been doing so for a millennium. You cannot drop a ball that has remained airborne through good effort for most of a thousand years. You cannot stop an unlikely heart that has been beating for so long. I would rather die than betray continuity, for its own sake if for nothing else. And Britain needs a king, just as it needs motormen and cooks and a prime minister. Just as it needs soldiers who will die for it if they must. It's my job, or it will be, but you should know that I've never wanted it. I was only born to it, as if with a deformity, to which I hope I can respond with grace."

Fredericka had been running her finger over the carpet, tracing a pattern in the way children do when they have learnt something overwhelming and are moved, but cannot say so. Freddy expected her to look up, with tears, and that in this moment she might have begun the long and arduous process of becoming a queen. She was so beautiful. To embrace her now, with high emotion flowing from her physical majesty, was all he wanted in the world. Her finger stopped moving, and she turned her eyes to him.

"Freddy?"

"Yes?" he answered.

"What's raw egg? I read a recipe in *She* that called for a cup of raw egg. What is that?"

After a long silence, Freddy asked, "Which part of the formulation escapes you? Egg? Raw? The link between the two?"

"The two what?"

"Fredericka?"

"Yes, Freddy?"

"Would you like to go dancing?"

"Oh, yes, Freddy!"

"Come, then. We will."

THOUGH FREDERICKA did not seem . . . rapier-minded, Freddy had from time to time been unsettled by her mysterious ability to come up with instantaneous answers to the most arcane questions. For example, once, she was doing her nails (checking them, actually: she had legions of nail-doers) while Freddy was flipping through the television channels. Thinking to irritate her, he settled on a university courses programme in which a professor of mathematics, who looked like an insect with a lot of hair, asked one of his students to write on the board the Cauchy Integral. "That's easy," said Fredericka, without looking up, "$\int_c f(z) \, dz = 2\pi i \, \Sigma$." The student wrote exactly that.

Stunned, Freddy asked, "Have you seen this programme before?"

"I don't think so, Freddy. It's a live broadcast and I don't have a time machine."

"Then how did you know?"

"Know what?"

"That integral."

"I don't know. It just seemed obvious."

Perhaps she was protected by angels. Probably they had been with her all her life, and were the agents that had delivered her to the Prince of Wales. The logic of angels is not always apparent. At first, he loved her—as one can love paintings, views, or houses—purely in response to her ravishing beauty, which was such as to suggest that she might have elicited the protection of angels because she had once been one of them, before falling away by accident, plummeting to earth, and bumping her head. Had she been injured in any other way she might have done well enough on her own, but an angel who strikes her head must be attended at every moment, and this is what the other angels did.

Because he had eyes, Freddy knew she was exquisite, but he underestimated the rest of her continually and to his detriment. He was fairly sure that she would quickly alienate the press and, through it, the public, and for this reason be forced to see her position in a light closer to that which illumined his own, which would bring her closer to him as she deepened in spirit and intellect. That, with Lady Boylingehotte on the side, would have been perfect. The thing about Lady Boylingehotte—Phoebe—that he could not do without was that she was crazed with lust for him, as Fredericka and the rest of the world were not. Too many more years of this and he would be dead, so he envisioned that when he was in his late fifties and Lady Boylingehotte had reached sixty, they would cut their throbbing engines and coast quietly through the rest of their lives as friends or acquaintances, and that, after he had given her a plumper title and some lands out of gratitude for their many decades of molten couplings, she would not write a book. He thought that even at sixty she might be quite fetching, what with modern creams, injections, surgery, diet, and spas. Fredericka, because of her unique and splendorous constitution—Freddy had once described it as more impressive than the Constitution of the United States—probably would not have to revert to such things until her middle seventies, and then who knew what would happen, or to what measures she might resort, she who thought that the best remedy for asthma was roast beef, osteoporosis was an island in Greece, and stuttering could be cured, as she delicately put it, "by fucking." (Freddy had made sure that he and not she had become the patron of the League of Scottish Stutterers.)

Despite her lack of medical knowledge, Fredericka did not, however, alienate either press or public. Say what she would, it would pass through the invisible trumpets of angels. In fact, this was getting to be a problem not only for Freddy but for all the Finneys, who, with the possible exception of the queen, were not protected by angels.

One autumn afternoon almost a year before Craig-Vyvyan met Craig-Vyvyan on Skye, the Prince of Wales was in his offices at St James's Palace at work on a study of the philosophy of history. Unlike most academics or public intellectuals, who in his view were just glorified peasants, he had no need to write, and did so only because of his genuine interest, which, in shining through, afforded him great advantage. Nonetheless, those whom he threatened professionally linked their pitchforks and viciously attacked him, but he relished it because it was a fight with consequences.

The sun was weak and the traffic of London sounded like surf or wind. How he loved it when an electric lamp shone in a room just on the edge of darkness, for then the light was mobile, its condition like a sunrise or sunset, the relative strengths of room light and lamplight changing in infinite gradation, at first the lamplight unneeded and then the only thing left, having become a sun. It was four o'clock, just at the point of balance after which the war of the lights would intensify.

He was dressed in high riding boots, khakis, a military sweater, and brown velour tie. That morning as London awoke to tabloid layouts of Fredericka resplendent in blue, in images that stopped pedestrians and held them in place, he had run, ridden, and swum. He was as fit as, indeed fitter than, the soldiers half his age who stood outside his open windows to protect him from terrorists. Surrounded by books, dark wood, and richly coloured works of art, he was in his princely element, and had forgotten that his head was wrapped in a bandage and his arm was resting in a sling. At polo just two hours before, Sir Battiscombe Finwit had backhanded his mallet far too high and struck the Prince of Wales in the temple, knocking him from his horse. "At least," Freddy had told Sir Battiscombe, "you generously granted the gash on my head the companionship of the sprain in my arm." He carried these wounds with some pride, but because he thought it unmanly to look in mirrors and hardly ever did so, he did not know that they profoundly affected his appearance.

When she was young, his mother had been beautiful in her way, and had chosen his father, as Freddy would eventually choose Fredericka, by sight. Though these two had collided as Venus and Mars, they had produced an asteroid. Freddy was strapping, strong, and lean. Due to his many years of tortured thought and iron physical discipline, his face showed almost as much martial character as his father's, and he was exceedingly graceful, in the royal way, in movement and expression, even if half of it was attributable to the simple trick of standing with one's hands behind one's back, the left hand loosely clasping the index and middle fingers of the right, accompanied by a barely perceptible three-degree lean forward. His presence overall was striking, and yet, an asteroid is an asteroid.

Though much obscured by character and resolution, the shape of his face was very like a potato. His eyes were miraculously close together—he could not use binoculars, because they did not fold in enough—and his ears, as immense as Pacific atolls, were, in shape, potato-like echoes of his face. Though sincere and endearing, his smile emphasised the spiny ridge of his nose. His was without doubt a most wonderful face, thoroughly endowed with kindness and character, but, nonetheless, on the day he was born God blessed the cartoonists.

One can always compensate, and he did, with the best haircut in London and clothing that fit with divine perfection. But with the bandage covering up his hair except for a sheaf-like tuft that spilled over the top, and the sling breaking the noble fall of his raiments, he presented quite a picture. One of his guards, using a nickname for him derived from his title, said quietly to another who had just joined him at the street entrance, "Have you seen Moby-Dick?"

"Have I seen him? I was just in there for two hours while he was writing his bloody article on Gibbon. He read parts of it to me and asked what I thought. 'Your Royal Highness, I don't know much about Gibbon.' 'Yes, but what do you think of the writing?' 'I think it's beautiful, sir, very noble.' Jesus Christ."

"But have you seen him?"

"Of course I've seen him."

"He looks like he just got off the barricades of the French Revolution."

"You mean because of that thing on his head?"

"Yes."

"He does, doesn't he. But I think he looks more like that bloke Alfred E. Newman."

"Is that the new Serjeant-Major of the Greys?"

"No, the American."

"Who's that?" A passer-by halted and put up his hands. "No, no. Keep going," said the soldier, waving his HK.

"He's in the magazine."

"What magazine?"

"I'll bring some in and leave them in the ammunition locker."

"Has it got naked girls?"

The other soldier paused, and a smile crept across his face. "So to speak," he said.

Up in the office the prince's revery was cut short by the ringing of his private telephone. Probably Fredericka, he thought, wanting to know if she can waste another ten thousand pounds on a dress. Just as peasants are always yelling and screaming, Fredericka is always buying clothes.

"Hello?" he said, pulling himself away from a fifteen-clause sentence on the theological implications of Empire.

"Freddy?"

"Yes?"

"It's Fredericka."

"I know."

"What are you doing?"

"I'm working."

"On what?"

"Gibbon."

"The monkey? What do you mean, 'working on him'? Are you giving him a massage?"

"No, I'm not giving him a massage, and it's the other Gibbon."

"The designer? He's so out."

"The historian."

"Oh, I didn't know there was one. We should have him to tea. Listen, Freddy, I know that you don't like to do things on short notice, but a courier just brought over an urgent request from the Royal Historical Society. They'd like us to do an event."

"When?"

"This evening."

"This evening!" He looked at the clock. "It's four-thirty."

"It would be at seven. Do you have something to change into?"

"Say no."

"I couldn't. I've already accepted."

"You've what?"

"I said yes."

"Why didn't you ask me? How do you know what my plans are?"

"I looked at your schedule."

"Where?" He didn't believe her.

"On your computer."

"You don't know how to operate it."

"I just turned on the switch and started the honky disk drive, and then it showed a picture of what looked like a pork cutlet and asked me a lot of questions."

"No. You don't know the password."

"I guessed it."

"Really?" he asked, convinced that she hadn't. "What is it?"

"Hippopotamus Boy."

"How did you do that?"

"It just came to me. You had nothing for tonight, so I said yes."

"What is it?" Freddy asked, resigned.

"It's a symposium on Samuel Pepys" (which she pronounced not *Peeps,* but *Peppies*) "and they've asked me to give the main speech."

"You? Not me?"

"Uh-huh, but they wanted you to be there, of course. All the press will be there, especially on account of the chairman of the RHS dying this morning. That's why such short notice."

"Lord Pipstoke is dead?"

"Totally. Heart attack. It's his memorial, so I couldn't say no."

"But surely you're mistaken. They want *me* to give the address."

"No, me. It says so right here." She began to read.

"I understand," he interrupted. "Very well, I shall see you at the RHS at seven."

"Not at the RHS, at the Natural History Museum, on the Mammal Balcony."

"On the Mammal Balcony at the NHM?" Freddy asked. "You know that will bring up complications."

"Yes, but it has a wonderful blue floor that goes with my eyes. I said we would do it only if they moved it there, and they agreed. Go in through the main entrance, then push on through dinosaurs, reptiles, and fish."

"What about dinner?"

"I've made reservations afterward at La Bonne Hottentote."

"I don't like eating little pieces of African snakes in mauve-coloured sauce," Freddy said.

"They're very healthy. Snakes are rich in anti-oxidants, and their venom reduces polyponimides and other forms of industrial pollution that cause wrinkles and cancer. And tonight they have fringe theatre."

"Oh God," said Freddy. She was winning every battle.

"Freddy, I do have a problem."

"Dearest?"

"I've been doing a lot of public speaking, although just a few lines each time, and the press loves it."

"I know."

"I'm quite confident that I can do this well, but I don't know a thing about Samuel Pepys [*Peppies*]. I've never heard of him."

"I see," said Freddy, eyes shifting rapidly. It was too good to be true.

"You must know about him, being a historian and all. Could you fill me in, so I don't have to look in the encyclopaedia? They're so heavy. I'm sure just five minutes will be enough."

. . .

AFTER BRIEFING Fredericka on Pepys not for five minutes but fifteen, Freddy rang off and rather rapidly slipped into a kind of euphoria. Only Napoleon could actually work when euphoric. Freddy, like everyone else, was distracted from his labours by the feelings of pure joy that took hold of him and would not let go. For an hour or so he tried to work on Gibbon, but was distracted by his own chortling.

Staring as if into the distance, he thought painlessly for the first time of Fredericka's glorious press coverage—the whole world had fallen in love with her: she could do no wrong—and contrasted it with his own. In the public mind, one of her smiles or one of her strapless gowns was worth a decade of his study and reflection. In fact, he was mocked by the press for being too private, too serious, too studious, and too grave, while she never failed to carry everyone after her as if on a rising wave. Half the planet was mesmerised by her breasts alone. He, of course, did not have breasts as such, not female breasts anyway, and even if he had, he would not have contrived with couturiers to have them carried in front of him half naked as if riding on a tray.

Little did it or they matter any more. The honeymoon was about to end, and if it would do so on the Mammal Balcony, so be it. She probably had chosen the Mammal Balcony not only because the carpet matched her eyes but to embarrass him. Freddy, who had many ideas that he was able to realise solely because he was the Prince of Wales, had long objected to the fact that most books are about mammals. Not an ideological complaint by any means, his object was to protest uniformity. So, in his late twenties, he had proposed to a publisher that he become the general editor of a series of books not about mammals, and because his offer had arrived on stationery with purple plumes, this had come to pass. In every bookstore in the United Kingdom one could see displayed the *Not About Mammals* series, edited by HRH The Prince of Wales. The first sentence of his general introduction read: "Though the volume that follows is by a mammal, it is not about a mammal, and a jolly good thing, too."

Now he was about to claim his due, on, of all places, the Mammal Balcony. Inexplicably, this, too, elated him. In fact, he was so euphoric as he dressed that, like Napoleon invading Russia, he lost track of what he was doing. Not wanting to take his arm out of the sling, he threw on what he thought was a tartan robe, but which actually was a car shawl that said

Schweppes in bright orange letters now hanging across his back. He whipped off the velour tie and quickly tied on the bow tie of one of his regiments. As he had taken it from the cupboard, another bow tie had come down with it in a tangle. This he threw behind his back to disregard, but rather than flying onto the shelf it hit the wall, bounced forward, and landed on top of his head, its weight borne by the bandage and unperceived. It was a fat, Churchillian, polka-dotted butterfly, and it now rested in the tuft of his hair potted and sheaved upward by the head wrap. Its two polka-dotted leads trailed behind him like pigtails; but, of course, he didn't know this.

He thought that now, to hit the nail on the head, he would play a little of her game, bending a little her way as she went down. Wherever she went she was followed by fashion critics, all of whom dismissed his mode of dress as hopelessly staid, military, and boring. But not this time. This time he would liven things up by adding to what he believed to be his otherwise unremarkable costume two armbands of animal bones given to him on his last tour of Africa. This little touch would be his subtle bend in the direction of her bare bosom.

When he went out to his car, neither the guards nor the driver said anything. They assumed he was off to a fancy dress party, where he would once again be the recipient of the "Extremely Strange and Dowdy" prize. "To the Natural History Museum," he told his corporal.

"Yes, sir."

Halfway there, Freddy wondered if perhaps he should do without the bones. "Do you think these are too much?" he asked the driver, rattling them.

"Not in view of the overall context, Your Royal Highness," the driver responded.

Freddy thought he was referring to the Natural History Museum. "Exactly!" he said, confidence soaring.

As he walked through the museum halls he thought he must have looked sharp indeed, because people were even more shocked by his presence than usual, and stopped short. "Splendid," he said to himself under his breath. "This is my moment."

Quite so. His entrance upon the Mammal Balcony had the all-consuming character of a Fredericka entrance. The assemblage was startled. The last time such a thing had happened was at a remote village in Brazil, where he had been mistaken for the Pope. The strobes went crazy, like a shower of shooting stars, just as they did whenever Fredericka turned her head or smiled. How did they know in advance what was going to happen? Was it just the bone necklaces? Perhaps it was his aura.

"Freddy?" Fredericka asked, obviously rattled. "What are you wearing?"

Unaware of the bow tie on his head, the effect of the bandage and sling, his coiffure, and the *Schweppes* banner, Freddy said, "You're not the only one who can dazzle."

"Freddy, that sounds so unlike you."

Flapping his arms like someone imitating a chicken, so the bones would clink, he said loudly enough for everyone to hear, "Sometimes I shake my bones, too. I can shake my fat fanny. And I will shake my fat fanny!" This was a line from American music, that he had picked up completely unawares from his recent correspondence with the president of the United States, former senator and governor August Self. Freddy was an accomplished bassoonist, a brilliant theorist, and such a superb singer that had he not been, as he liked to say, "an accident of birth," he might have been famous upon the stage. But of jazz, rock and roll, the blues, anything North American, he knew absolutely nothing.

"Freddy, I've never seen you like this. Are you all right?"

"Don't worry about me," he replied, supremely confident.

"Are you sure you don't want to go home and change?" she asked conspiratorially.

"Why?" he asked, looking himself over as far as he could. "It's glorious." Then they were seated.

She was wearing a gold lamé gown, a sunshine-coloured, snake-like thing of chain mail that stopped dead at her sternum. The guests of the RHS were given a choice between this and the attire of the prince, and even though they were mostly male, they could not choose between sex and astonishment. To those seated on the dais the audience looked like spectators at a tennis match, with eyes that went tightly back and forth as if tracking the movements of a metronome, though, absent a ball, they were unsynchronised.

After the customary pap, some words of mourning, and a short introduction by Freddy—"I cannot wait to hear the princess's remarks on Pepys, of whom she has been a serious student all her life"—Fredericka stood to a lengthy ovation, and Freddy leant back, one hand clasped behind his head, ready to savour the results of his tutorial.

She had it down, and would not depart from the line he had supplied. In fact, he would be astounded at how faithfully she reproduced it. And she was by now a perfectly polished speaker of brief orations, who knew how to exploit to the fullest the public perception that she was new to the game.

"No one is more appreciative than am I," she began, "of the efforts made by Sir Samuel Peppies, who sacrificed himself for his native Australia, for its women, for its men, and for the twin causes of Acute Reticular Self Esteem Syndrome—ARSES—education, Aboriginal art, and Gandhian self-violence and masturbation. One might have expected Sir Samuel as a person to have been deeply concerned with ARSES, but it is all the more remarkable that he, a disciple of Gandhi, rejected the path of self-violence and chose selflessly to inflict violence upon others in his famous armed raid upon the Australian Parliament. And it is only the more remarkable to us, the privileged and safe, that he was concerned to spread the message among his own people, the Aborigines of Northern Australia, where ARSES do not even exist.

"Not even one documented case! And yet, Sir Samuel carried his message undaunted to each woman and man across the face of Australia. Plagued since birth by an aversion to land travel, Sir Samuel devised an ingenious method of bringing to each Aboriginal woman and man the essential message. In the blimp *Compassion* he floated over the Outback and—like some great princess dazzling the people—would frequently surprise Aboriginal women and men by appearing over their campfires.

"What tragedy that *Compassion* was directly in the path of the piece of flaming Jovian moon that hit the Earth last summer and destroyed the town of Alice Springs. Never again will Sir Samuel be able to work compassionately, as I have, for ARSES education. Never again will he work compassionately, as I have, for Aboriginal art. Never again, to paraphrase the words of Joseph Biden (who?), have so many owed so little to so few.

"May God bless you, Sir Samuel, and each compassionate person who would live the life of a Peppie. God save the Queen."

The prince had been listening as if from an opium dream. Her earnestness of delivery, her passion, her eloquence of expression, her heartfeltness, and her complete faith to his briefing, made it that much more pleasurable for him. He waited for the deluge to engulf her, and it did, but it was a deluge of applause. Never had he seen more thunderous a reception for anyone or any words, and as the thunder echoed through the museum the mammals shook on their posts.

Not only did retired officer types (the kind who had spent decades

guiding little survey ships through ice fields in Antarctica or operating he-
liographs on purple mountaintops in Nyasaland) jump to their feet and call
out, "Bravo! Bravo!" but they turned to each other as they stood, and embraced. From the pit of his shock, Freddy could only wonder what had
happened to England.

To make matters worse, the carpet did match Fredericka's eyes perfectly, and the press photographs would be spectacular, though not of
Freddy. He discovered the bow on top of his head only as he was eating a
piece of poached snake and listening to a nude woman scream obscenities
about Claude Monet and Golda Meir, who, in her view, were linked in a
monstrous conspiracy. The next morning, the leader in *The Times* read:
"Princess of Wales Delivers Heartfelt Speech As Prince Looks On in
Bizarre Attire: Palace Refuses Comment." *The Guardian:* "Fredericka Attempts to Speak to Oppressed While from Sidelines Freddy Mocks Poor."
And the tabloids: "Freddy Mad with Jealousy, Fredericka Brilliant,"
"Freddy's Bananas and Fredericka's a Peach," and "Prince Really Quite
Insane." By evening the television commentators had joined in questioning his sanity, though no one said a word about her speech except to praise
it, and to note that she was the most compassionate royal ever to have
graced the monarchy.

"DEAR FREDDY," wrote the Duke of Belfast from what he refused to call
by anything but its old name, Basutoland.

> Returning from a well spent morning watching rhinos, your mother
> and I found yesterday's papers brought to us by courier. It used to be that
> when we were far from home we had the news only on the wireless. Now
> it is entirely different, and it is not only advantageous but sometimes, un-
> fortunately, unpleasant, as today has proved.
>
> You are the heir to the throne, our son, and a married man entering
> middle age. Your behaviour is a disgrace, and so, might I add, is Freder-
> icka's: she shows entirely too much bosom. The Princess of Wales is not an
> aspiring starlet at Cannes. We find the subject so embarrassing that we are
> not able to discuss it with her, but you must.
>
> Quite frankly, it appears that she is trying to overshadow the queen. We
> do not know why. Perhaps she simply enjoys it. Perhaps it is a result of

problems with you. There is no use speculating, but the effects are grave and rapidly worsening. If our surmise is correct, and you donned the beatnik costume to compete with her for the attentions of the press, you know not how dangerous a road you have chosen. First of all, it is, *sans phrase*, beneath your dignity. In the contest for turning heads, she must always win, but, remember, *Schönheit vergeht, Tugend besteht;* beauty fades, virtue stays.

Even the tabloids in Capetown were full of stories about the two of you, hinting of a rift. Several items concerned Lady Boylingehotte. I have always warned you about what for you are the two great dangers: Phoebe Boylingehotte and rocky road ice cream. If you are still polishing your torpedo below her decks you had better stop immediately. And you must never touch rocky road ice cream, as you cannot eat a spoonful without going on to a gallon. Meat, Freddy, eat more meat.

Your mother is extremely distressed. Not about your weight—you know that she loves you even though you're a butterball—but because she senses that Fredericka wants to upstage not merely her but the monarchy, and not merely to upstage the monarchy but to destroy it. She says she has not felt such a sense of peril since the war or, as a child, during the crisis of abdication. All this may be premature, but I think not, as I trust her instincts. As you know, they are extraordinary.

Listen to me, Freddy. I have come by this, as it were, *per vias rectas*. You must straighten things out, and you must do so quickly. If when we return nothing has changed for the better, or, God help us, the situation has worsened, we will have to take some drastic steps of which you have no idea, as you have never been told of all the options available to the sovereign. They are not in your history books, having been carefully kept out. Of all people living, only your mother and Mr Neil know the remedies, and I dare say she has kept some even from me. If things are as bad as your mother feels, she will be forced to turn to Mr Neil, something that in all her reign she has never done. Though you have now been informed of his existence, you must not mention it to anyone. Save a threat to king or country, you were not supposed to know until your coronation.

You are doubtless familiar with the charming story of how, after being crowned, the young Queen Victoria rushed home to bathe her dog. All clever disinformation. She rushed home to . . . well, I'm getting ahead of myself. Perhaps all this, *orando laborando*, will disappear. You must have a talk with Fredericka. Although she may sometime have to learn of Mr Neil, do not tell her now, but let her know that she will not enjoy the consequences if as a result of her present course she unleashes a power that the queen of England during almost half a century on the throne has not wished to employ. Take Fredericka to Moocock, and make sure she understands.

And Freddy, remember that *embonpoint* does not suit a prince. In this world you must be lean and strong. I have always been ready for combat, and my body has always been as hard as steel (metaphorically, of course). Try to turn your attention away from delicious foods—here in Basutoland I have been surviving solely on warm water and raw rhinoceros chops—according to the theory that the worst pig eats the best acorn. Freddy, eat the worst acorn, and be the best pig.

> Very best,
> Da

Freddy let the letter drift from his hands to the surface of his desk, a wood of splendid and daily polish. Having shed the sling and head bandage, he looked his old self, and having beaten his fencing master several hours earlier, he was tired and content. He picked up the phone and ordered a helicopter to Kensington. As his father had made it plain that this business needed attention, he would fly Fredericka to Moocock. He rang her up.

"What's that noise?" he asked.

"It's a hair dryer. Demeter and Dimitri are doing my hair. Freddy, I bought some dresses today. They were too beautiful for anyone else to have."

"Good."

"You don't object?"

"No," he said, distractedly. "How much were they?"

"Each was thirty-four thousand pounds and a bit over. I bought three and a handbag."

"The helicopter will touch down on the lawn at three-thirty. We're going to Moocock, alone. We need to talk."

"Why can't we talk here?"

"Things will be more relaxed at Moocock."

"Moocock is always so boring, Freddy."

"That may be, but this is important."

"Ow! Dimitri!" came over the phone. "Not the hot pack, the cold pack!"

"Fredericka?"

"Yes, Freddy?"

"It will be just the two of us. No guests." He thought for a moment. "No hairdressers. No coaches."

"Oh, all right. I'll even bring a book. Lord Louey sent me a book on compassion that I have to read because he wants me to be the author. I'll be ready."

Upon hanging up the phone, she turned to Demeter and Dimitri. "Can you imagine, Demeter and Dimitri, I'm going to have to spend a weekend in the country, with insects and weeds."

"Oooooo!" they said, horrified.

"And I'm going to have to read a whole book."

"Oooooo!"

"And I'm going to have to be alone."

"Oooooo!"

"With Freddy."

In his offices at St James's, Freddy walked to and fro, brows knit, with what one of the guards who glanced in the window took to be a monastic prayer bumble-beeing from his lips. It wasn't a prayer. He was saying, "Who the hell is Mr Neil? Who the hell is Mr Neil?"

FREDERICKA HAD COME to dislike Moocock, and it was difficult to get her there, but the surest way to do it was by air. Not only did flying cut the travel time by three-quarters, but she loved the vibrations of the helicopter engines as they swept through her, and even likened them to therapy. Then, again, she likened everything to therapy.

"Very interesting," said Freddy. "I suppose that's the secret of organs in cathedrals. When the liturgy is magnified and echoed so powerfully that one's diaphragm vibrates in sympathy, as if the impetus were from within, it takes the soul out of the body and frees it of extraneous and distractive impulses that block it from weightlessness and ascension."

"How would you know?" Fredericka asked. "Men don't have diaphragms."

At least he liked to fly helicopters and she liked to fly in them, or, rather, to sit in them as the engines strained. She was not actually interested in flight, but vibrations. As a princess she had precious few opportunities to lean against a warm washing machine, and so resorted to military helicopters. By the time they entered the one that had touched down on a Kensington Palace lawn, it was dusk.

"Let me give you a hint about the press," Fredericka said, as she climbed to take her seat next to Freddy.

"I've been dealing with the press since I was two. What hint have you for me?"

"Things have changed, Freddy. The world has changed."

"I haven't."

"That's the problem."

"No, it's the world's problem, Fredericka. It's not that the world has betrayed me, it's that, by almost any measure of quality or dignity, the world has betrayed itself."

"Whatever the world has done, you have no sense of dealing with the press."

"I think what I say to them is rather eloquent, thank you," he said as he started the pre-flight check.

"Who cares about what you say?" she asked, buckling her seatbelt. He went on, in silence, with a long list of pre-flight items. "Words don't matter any more," she told him. "Didn't you know? It's just pictures. You can say anything you want. No one understands or cares. It's not what you say, it's how you look. And you just don't have a feel for it."

"Why? I'm usually pretty well turned out." He moved the throttles and gently grasped the controls, feeling every detail of the huge craft's movement in his feet and fingers.

"That's not what I mean," she said as they lifted off. "For example, you like photographers to take your picture when you're flying this thing, because the ear muffins hide your ears."

"Photographers use special architectural lenses to make my ears seem big. They do the same for Michael Heseltine's eyebrows."

"Freddy, Demeter and Dimitri do his eyebrows for Question Time. They say they're fabulous and they're real."

"Demeter and Dimitri think everything is fabulous, even rabies."

"What you don't know, Freddy, is that the press actually likes taking photos of you in this machine, because the ear muffins don't hide your ears, they emphasise them. Everyone knows you have big ears, so when you wear ear muffins, people assume that the ear muffins are as thin as silk and your ears fill them completely. That's what I mean. You didn't know that. You have no flair for picture publicity."

"And what if I don't?"

"You'll be left behind."

"Nonsense."

They rose into the air above dusk-coloured London gleaming below them from Battersea to Hampstead in white, green, and buff. Unlike most great cities, which at this time of evening begin to sparkle like astronomical prints, London hid its masses of lights amid cliffs of stone and brick, in sheltered squares and curtained windows, and behind fonts of royal foliage that during daylight and blue sky projected upward in autumnal colour like the plumes of fireworks.

This was Freddy's London, soft and gentle in its colours and as perfectly balanced as a good sword, not at hilt and blade but at the juncture of the drive of life and history's tranquil comment upon it. As Prince of Wales or king he could fly over the city and see it with dream-like mastery. But though he might float above it he could not live in it, and unlike anyone else, he could never be lost in it. His mother had described this to him as swimming so buoyantly upon the sea as to be unable to get wet. "In that sense," she had said, "you and I, my father, and your heir, will have given up our lives for the sake of our duty. People don't know, and they'll never know, that no collection of things and no human deference can ever make up for not being able to ride home, tired and alone, on the train to Camden Town, and disappear into a block of flats unwatched, in glorious and absolute privacy."

Absorbed in the demands of piloting the helicopter, meditating upon the beauty of London, and thinking about his unusual fate, he had lost track of Fredericka. He turned to glance at her, and then, watching once again the sky ahead and the strobe lights of aircraft moving through the air over London like fireflies, he said, "Damn it, do you have to do that? We're over a miracle of civilisation!"

"I want beautiful nails!" she snapped, and resentfully went back to buffing them.

"It's time to observe."

"Do I have to?"

"Yes."

"Oh, Freddy, you know I hate it."

"It's a family tradition."

"Christ."

Fredericka opened a compartment and withdrew a set of image-stabilised, low-light binoculars. With practised skill, she scoured the streets below, calling out: "Red Jaguar . . . brown Mercedes . . . yellow lorry . . .

Citroën, can't see the colour . . ." to which Freddy's response was to call out points and keep a running tally.

"Army truck!" she screamed.

"Ten points!" Freddy cried.

"I see an American car, I don't know what kind."

"You have to know the type or it doesn't count."

"I think," she said, straining her neck to follow as they left it behind, "it's an Old Mobile or a Cat Alack. They have such strange names for their motors."

"Which is it?"

"I don't know. It's a UFO."

"That's all right. Keep at it."

Even before they began to trace the illuminated ribbon of the M11 they had racked up 160 points, which put Freddy in such an excellent frame of mind that when they landed at RAF Moleturd on the weald near Moocock, he agreed to address a contingent of French air force cadets, who wanted not to hear him but to gawk at Fredericka. They were assembled in a brilliantly lit hangar, looking, with their moustaches and sideburns, like a group of small, physically fit bartenders. Even as the Prince of Wales spoke, they did not move their eyes from the princess. For his part, Freddy casually improvised in what the Foreign Office wincingly called "Freddy French." His accent was perfect, which made everything that followed seem exceedingly strange, for someone had once told him that the French language exists virtually without rules or restrictions.

> Bon soir mes petites grenouilles aériennes, le bon Prince des Baleines vous adresse. Moi vous conclerez, et vous me semblez toujours trop poufaites. Au clou du poisson, la dégasse faible exprime offensement le Maroc. Contre rapetassage restent les hommes d'état et les cuillers. Pour moi et pour vous, brugnons ensemble, il faut seulement éclabousser. Vivent la France, le droit, et le roi. (Nous, nous ne tuons pas nos rois, merci beaucoup.)

Little speeches like this had puzzled the French for years. Had they known what he was trying to say, or even had he known, or had they had a written text for their linguists to try to decode, a crisis would undoubtedly have ensued. But no one had the vaguest idea of what was coming out, and the cadets had the look of puzzled rapture seen occasionally in the paintings of Hieronymus Bosch, having been glued with Gallic urgency upon the sight of Fredericka while Freddy turned the tables on them and ravished their language.

AT MOOCOCK, an informal dinner awaited and a lively fire burned in cool air fresh with the scent of flowers. "It's very romantic," Fredericka said.

"I've never understood what it is," Freddy replied, "that moves women to think that a bunch of burning paraffin sticks and some flowers have anything to do with that awful word, *romantic.*"

"Then what would you call it?"

"Elegant and appropriate."

"Ah," she said. "Look at this. It's so . . . appropriate."

At the shake of a bell, Sawyers served the dinner: consommé, petit pain and pâté de mer, green salad, poached salmon, New Guinea potatoes, a rare white Haut-Brion, a chocolate-ginger torte, and Champagne. They were absolutely alone at Moocock, with only fourteen servants, and could talk privately.

"Fredericka?"

"Yes, Freddy?"

"Pretty good, a hundred and sixty points, in semi-darkness."

"We've done better," she said, uninterested.

"Only two UFOs. That's marvellous. Usually we have six or seven."

"That's because I've learned all about BMWs. Did you mention tonight's game to that officer?"

"Yes. I always do. He's very keen on the UFOs."

"I don't think you should. The press, Freddy, the press."

"Major Fattiston is completely reliable. Good family, shot throughout my father's regiments and my own like sprinkles of gold. He assured me that as long as he remained in the RAF he would keep our observations entirely under his hat. His word is his bond."

"As long as he remained in the RAF?"

"For goodness' sake, he's a career man, a professional. What would he do outside the RAF?"

"Be an airline pilot," Fredericka said.

"Oh."

"Don't say I didn't warn you. The press is an octopus. It sucks up everything, catches everything that falls, seizes everything that floats."

"Fredericka, I didn't know you could speak that way."

"I believe that's from a song by Elton John."

"Who?"

"Never mind. The press, Freddy, is too powerful, too omniscient."

"You've done very well with it."

"Yes, I know."

"You could be more retiring."

"Really?"

"Absolutely. In fact, both my mother and father are rather upset about the inordinate amount of press attention you get."

"It's their game, after all," she said, "isn't it?"

"A game they don't like to play, whereas you seem to enjoy it."

"Perhaps they might enjoy it, too."

"They hate it, don't you see? And, being new to it, you don't. All they ask is that you pull back a bit, and become a little more private."

"Will you be private with me, then?"

"Yes," he said, unconvincingly.

"I don't believe it, and I don't want to be private all by myself."

"We can be private, Fredericka. That means that we don't have to go to restaurants every night, or to so many parties."

"But I like parties. You can be private and go to parties. I used to go to parties alone."

"I hate them, as you know, and I very much want to be private with you, except that you seem to think that privacy excludes reading. Every time I pick up a book or a journal, you sigh in pain."

"What am I supposed to do while you're reading?" she asked, woundedly.

"You could do the same."

"Sit for two hours and read about exchange rates in Namibia? No, thank you."

"You read *She,* especially when you're on the cover."

"I like to *do* things."

"As you get older, you will naturally become more contemplative."

"Does that include water-skiing?"

"Not really."

"Freddy, I want to live my life."

"You must learn to live the life of the mind."

"And talk to plants?"

"Do you know why I talk to plants, Fredericka?"

"Why?" she asked.

"They listen."

"Rot."

"Indeed not, but let me state something bluntly. Someday, I am to be king of England. People find that endlessly intriguing, even if I do not. If I chose to, like some princes of Wales, I, too, could draw the spotlight from the sovereign. I could be like Edward the Seventh, who with horses and hounds chased a deer into the precincts of Paddington Station, killed it, and galloped off with his retinue into Hyde Park. But I'm not. I could become a dissolute, epicene, hermaphroditic, deracinated, drugged-out user of catamites. But I don't. I could become ferociously political, and by proxy run three quarters of the Tory Party. But I don't. Even in my youth, I knew. Do not upstage the monarch. Do not upstage the third-oldest surviving institution in the world. Do not upstage the queen of England. And," he said, raising his finger, "with a bosom, no less."

"What?"

"Your bosom."

"Why do you say that, Freddy? Why do you talk that way?"

"Because," said Freddy, with the urgency of a huntsman who has got his fox in a barrel, "it is a fact in brilliance that you upstage the queen, the duke, me, my brother, my sister, the monarchy itself, indeed, the whole bloody country, with—what?—a bosom?"

"*A* bosom?"

"Yes, *a* bosom."

"But Freddy, why do you say that? You know I've got two."

This shut Freddy up like a stun grenade. "Two what?" he finally said.

"Two bosoms."

"No you don't, you've got one bosom. One, only one."

"No I don't, I've got two," she said proudly, holding a hand up to cup one breast, and then another. "One here, and one here. Sit down, Freddy. Sit down there."

Freddy complied.

"Okay," Fredericka said, as if talking to an agitated hospital patient, "look at me."

"Yes?"

"Now, Freddy," she said, pointing to her head, "how many heads do I have?"

"That's ridiculous!" Freddy protested.

"How many heads do I have, Freddy?"

"You have one head, Fredericka."

"Good. Now"—she lifted up her blouse, exposing her navel—"how many *boutons de la ferme* do I have?"

"What are *boutons de la ferme*?"

"That's what the French call farm buttons."

"What are farm buttons?"

She pointed at her navel.

"Since when is that a farm button?"

"It's always been a farm button. The question is, how many do I have?"

"One," said Freddy, derailed.

"And how many hands?"

"Two."

"Nose?"

"One."

This went on for a while until Fredericka paused dramatically, smiling because Freddy, like a circus horse, had counted flawlessly in ones and twos. "Now," she asked, "tell me. How many bosoms do I have?"

"One," said Freddy.

"You're hopeless," she said. "I have two. You used to be quite fond of them."

"You have one, and I am quite fond of it."

"Freddy, look," she said tentatively, "just look. Two. Not one. Two. Two bosoms."

"Sorry, Fredericka, but the fact is, and I know it for sure, and would stake my life on it, that you have only one."

"The hell I do!"

"Yes. You've got one bosom, two teats (spelled t-e-a-t and pronounced *tit*), and two breasts. And that's a fact."

"Oh! So now I've got five!"

"Five what?"

"Five bosoms."

"No, you've got only one."

She narrowed her eyes and dropped her head in a position of exasperation. "Make up your bloody mind. Have I got one, two, or five? The papers are right, and I didn't even know it. You go around in bizarre costumes and talk about UFOs. Everyone knows you're mad. Who the hell are you to tell me I've got one bosom? Have you got the opposite of crossed eyes? Or can't you count? No one ever told me I had one bosom, and no one ever told me I had five—no one, that is, but you, and you can't even make up your mind. Is it five, or is it one? Or is that too difficult a challenge to take up?"

"Hardly," said Freddy, in warrior mode. "It's an easy challenge. And here, Fredericka, is a challenge for you." He stood, strode across the room, took *The Shorter Oxford English Dictionary* from a shelf by the fireplace, returned, and slammed its blue-jacketed bulk on the dining room table so hard that not only did all the plates and utensils jump four inches in the air, but a fine mist of sawdust fell to the carpet beneath.

"Goddamned mealy-mouthed worms!" he shouted, upon seeing this. She hadn't seen it, didn't know what he was talking about, and was quite nervous because there were swords in the room.

"That," he said, pointing at the still slightly vibrating dictionary, through air still ringing with the clatter-sound of silver and crystal, "is a dictionary. You might try, for once in your life, consulting it. To do that, I know, you must open it. And it is, God forbid, a book. But! It's not the kind of book you read from cover to cover. No! You can just dip into it, like *She.* Try it! Try it for the word *bosom.* You might actually learn something: that is, how to speak in reference to the history of the speech of the world, rather than in reference to what you merely feel. It's called exactitude. It's called objectivity. It's called classicism. And it has nothing to do, nothing, nothing whatsoever, with compassion."

She glared at him. He glared at her. The fire crackled joyfully, as fires do during combat. And in the midst of the war of two worlds came a polite, indeed, an obsequious knock at the door: Sawyers' knock, instantly recognisable.

They stood back to compose themselves. No matter that he had probably heard every word. "Yes?" they said, aristocratically and in unison.

He entered. "It was very quiet. I thought Your Royal Highnesses had left." This was intended to assure them that their privacy was intact. Relief was visible in both their faces.

Sawyers cleared his throat. "I'm very sorry to say, sir, that the bosom has escaped."

"The what?" Freddy asked.

"The dog, sir."

"The dog, again?" Freddy asked with more exasperation than heat.

"I'm afraid so, sir. There's nothing he can't bite through, even the heaviest chain link."

"Did you go after him with cheese? You scream 'Cheese!' and when he gets near, you lie on the ground and put the cheese on your face, leaving your arms free, so that, when he approaches, you—gently—clip a lead onto his collar."

"We have the cheese, sir."

"Well?"

Sawyers had a pained expression on his face. "Sir, the only person other than yourself who is qualified to do this—he is a pit bull, you know—is Douglas, his keeper."

"Then get Douglas."

"He's in Basutoland, sir, with the queen. She asked if he might go along to help with the gift animals. You know what a terrible ordeal they had last time on the plane with the rhinoceros after it contracted diarrhoea."

"Do I have to do this again?" Freddy asked.

"If Your Royal Highness doesn't," Sawyers said, with perfect logic, "the dog will remain loose and may kill someone."

"Very well," Freddy told him. "I'll change while you bring the cheese around."

"Thank you, sir."

Freddy stormed upstairs, with Fredericka following. "Obviously, he was listening," she said.

"It doesn't matter."

"How will you find my doggy?"

"He always goes toward one village or the other." Freddy pulled on his boots. This was unpleasant after a full dinner. "It's your blasted dog," he said. "I hate it."

"You're the only one it won't bite. You have a royal way with dogs, like your mother."

"You mean, 'as does your mother,'" Freddy growled.

"Yes, that's what I mean," Fredericka averred, innocently.

"I don't like having a pit bull lick Gorgonzola off my face, if you don't mind. I also don't like pit bulls. He should have been destroyed."

"I couldn't."

"Just because his master died of AIDS?"

"He didn't die of AIDS, he died of malnutrition."

"Your nutrition counsellor died of malnutrition?"

"So?" Fredericka asked indignantly.

"He was some piece of work."

"What are you driving at?"

"Perhaps you would expect," said Freddy, "that someone who dispenses advice about nutrition would be able to eat well enough to keep himself alive."

"It was an accident."

"Fredericka, one does not die of malnutrition by accident."

"Oh Freddy, he was always so melancholy. It's difficult for Chinese people in London."

"But you didn't have to name the dog after him."

"Who should I have named the dog after, François Mitterrand? He wasn't François Mitterrand's dog, was he? If the master dies, you name the dog after the master. It makes perfect sense."

"Well, fuck him."

"No, Pha-Kew."

"Yes, I know."

Another polite knock. "What!" Freddy screamed.

"Sir," Sawyers announced upon entering, "Melody is waiting by the front door with the Gorgonzola. She can't hold out much longer. Besides, Pha-Kew may be halfway to Glasgow by now."

"Sawyers," said Freddy, bitterly, "I always find him, and he always gets the cheese."

"Thank you, Melody," Freddy said to the gagging servant as he took a kilo of semi-spoiled Gorgonzola and walked into the night. He doubted that Pha-Kew would be on the grounds, so as he walked across the lawns and through familiar hedges and fields he was silent. As his eyes grew accustomed to the darkness he felt calmer. The silky lawns in the cloud-blinkered moonlight seemed purple and soft. It was cool, but not cold enough to kill scent, and a hundred different aromas—of plants, soil, water, and Gorgonzola—came at him on the wind, like regiments passing on parade. Along the canal he seemed to glide on the towpath, the black water on his left half the time shimmering in moonlight and half the time as infinitely dark as death. Leaves floated on the surface, as curled and dry as potato crisps. Every now and then, he called the dog's name, and every now and then, he called out, "Cheese!"

When he reached the village, he thought he might simply take a tour in hope of finding the dog purely by luck. Having been misunderstood on several previous occasions as he passed through Pestwick-on-Canal or Brooms Hoo shouting the dog's name, he was wary of active measures, so he hiked-up his collar, bent his head, and tried to be unobtrusive. At least this time he would not be chasing after Fredericka's late blue-eyed Savoyard Gabinetto, Taxi. In one distressing incident, Freddy had walked through Brooms Hoo for an hour, screaming: "Taxi! Taxi! Taxi!" This, naturally, brought out the otherwise dormant Brooms Hoo fleet of taxis, both of which sped to oblige.

"I don't need a taxi," he had told them.

"Oh," they said, and pulled away.

"Taxi! Taxi! Taxi!" he shouted an instant later.

They rushed up again. "Changed your mind, Your Majesty?"

"No," said Freddy, looking at them scornfully, "not at all."

"Oh."

"Tell me," Freddy went on, "have you seen Taxi?"

"Well, governor, we're taxis," one of the taxi drivers said.

"Yes," said Freddy, laughing, "but have you seen Taxi?"

"No, sir."

At that moment, Freddy saw Taxi disappear behind a dustbin, and he shouted, "Taxi! Come here! Taxi! Come!"

The taxi drivers cleared their throats, and said, "Here we are, Your Lordship."

"No, not you, him," Freddy said, pointing at the dustbin.

"Would you like us to take you somewhere, Your Majesty?" they asked, hopelessly.

"No," said Freddy, who then bounded toward the dustbin and, as he rattled it violently to dislodge the dog (who had already left), yelled, "Taxi, Taxi! Damn you! Taxi! You never come when I call!"

The taxi drivers, terrified by now, approached Freddy and asked, most meekly, "Aren't our taxis good enough for you sir? We can wash them?"

"Look," said Freddy, turning to them with great irritation, "I'm not looking for a taxi, I'm looking for *Taxi*."

"Oh," they said. This went on for at least another hour, but they never gave up.

Now, in Pestwick-on-Canal, two old men were standing in front of the Post Office, trying to think of something to say, when they saw him coming. "Oh, look. It's him," one said. "Not this again."

The other replied, "You know what I say, I say, royalty or not, give him as good as he gets."

"Excuse me," Freddy told them, "I wonder if you've seen my dog, Pha-Kew."

"No, I haven't seen your dog, and fuck you," was the answer.

"No, no, no," Freddy said. "You don't understand—Pha-Kew!"

"But yes, yes, yes, we do understand. Fuck you!"

"The name of my dog," Freddy said, laughing, and then pausing, "is . . . Pha-Kew."

"If you don't want to tell us the name of your dog," the other man said, "then fuck you, too."

"But I do want to tell you the name of my dog. I've been telling you the name of my dog."

"Oh, really? What is it?"

"Pha-Kew."

"Fuck you too, and you can go to hell, you royal bastard!"

Just then, a wedding reception surged out of the White Louse, spilling onto the pavement in good suits and fine dresses. Freddy and the two men turned to see. It was lovely. The women's voices carried through the night like bells. Anyone beholding the scene would be drawn to it, as were, indeed, the two men and the Prince of Wales. But for Freddy it was more than just an attractive bevy of women, it was deliverance, for Pha-Kew poked his head from behind a bush just beyond the wedding party.

Freddy was off, running toward the bush and screaming at the top of his voice, "Pha-Kew! Pha-Kew! Pha-Kew!"

One of the old men turned to the other, and said, "Just pray that the old lady hangs on."

Meanwhile, the men in the wedding party stepped forward to protect their women. Freddy was very big, and he ran like a commando. Though they were scared, they were prepared to do their duty. But he ran right past them, screaming, "Pha-Kew! Pha-Kew!" and stopped at the bush, into which Pha-Kew had receded, like a moray eel, before anyone had seen him. "Pha-Kew! Pha-Kew!" he said to the bush. "Don't do this to me, Pha-Kew. Not again."

"Is that the Prince of Wales?" one of the women asked, "or have I had too much to drink?"

"It can't be."

"But it is. It is."

"Oh, look," the bridegroom said, "look what he's doing."

Freddy had lain upon the ground and put the cheese on his face. "Cheese!" he said. "Cheese! Cheese!"

And then, out of the corner of his eye, he saw Pha-Kew darting onto the towpath beyond the Post Office. Pha-Kew disappeared in a white blur, which befit a 125-pound horseradish travelling in the moonlight, and Freddy realised that the dog would be halfway home in a trice. Still, he was so worked up that he rose, yelled "Cheese!" and began to run after the elusive Pha-Kew, calling his name many times.

As he passed the wedding party he felt strangely uncomfortable, and stopped. "What's that?" he asked a small blond woman who was pointing something at him. When she failed to respond, he asked, again, "What is that?"

"It's a video camera, Your Royal Highness," was the reply. She kept on shooting.

"Oh," said Freddy. "I see. Oh. Oh my."

The last scene on the tape was of Freddy running off into the darkness, shouting, "Off with his bloody head!"

The Lord Cecil Psnake and the Lord Alfie Didgeridoo

The Lord Cecil Psnake's Moncay House had been a royal palace. That was why he bought it. Ten acres in the middle of London, a Palladian villa of forty rooms, a mews, gardens as if from paradise, and a sports complex with two pools, tennis, squash, and half a million pounds' worth of chrome-plated muscle machines that Lord Psnake was no more likely to touch than he was to take out the rubbish or clean the bathrooms. And Moncay House was not even his home. Most of the time he lived either in Switzerland or on Cap d'Antibes, and when in London he stayed in a twenty-thousand-square-foot triplex penthouse perched over his offices in the Media Royal Building, headquarters for the holding company that owned half of Britain's newspapers and private television channels.

The others were the property of the Lord Alfie Didgeridoo, an Australian who drove himself in an ordinary ten-year-old car with stuffed dice dangling from the windscreen mirror, who dressed in rumpled off-the-rack suits, lived in a small terrace house appropriate to a young professional and his family, ate unrecognised in workingmen's pubs, and who, partly because he had neither yachts nor Swiss nor African estates nor Moncay Houses nor retinues nor aeroplanes nor entourages, not to mention mistresses, former wives, and business interests outside those he understood, was worth five thousand million pounds.

Didgeridoo's papers and television stations ran neck and neck with Psnake's, but Didgeridoo could watch the race from atop an electrifying mountain of cash. Psnake, less single-minded, had motives more complex than building such a mountain. This, Didgeridoo knew, and thus he was apprehensive when he received from Psnake an invitation to dine at two in the morning at Moncay House. "Why such a time?" Didgeridoo had asked, having made the call himself, of Psnake's aide-de-camp. The answer was because Lord Psnake had wanted to make absolutely sure that their meeting would go unremarked.

"How do you do?" asked Psnake of Didgeridoo, at the door of Moncay House, as the wind blew through, and the moon was anchored over Hyde Park like a barrage-balloon.

"Quite well," replied Didgeridoo. "A bit tired."

"I apologise for the late hour, but I have something of immense importance to discuss with you, and no one must know. Please come in."

Lord Psnake, a counter-eponymous hippopotamus, slowly led the way. His little feet and little legs smoothly moved his immense bulk, as if on wheels, into a cavernous reception room only one corner of which was lit, and that hardly at all. No whippet himself, but svelte by comparison, Didgeridoo followed, wondering on account of Psnake's seeming ability to glide if underneath his purple satin dressing gown were more than just two legs and feet. Didgeridoo imagined there a mechanism comparable to the action of a piano—something busy, bony, complex, and spindly. Psnake's thin hair was matted as if he lived on the street, a sign not of bad hairdressing or inadequate hygiene, for he undoubtedly had the best of both, but of ill health.

Didgeridoo felt that he was in some sort of wilderness den, and yet this room in Moncay House was splendid even when shrouded in darkness. Out from the corner fled a ballroom-sized floor of ancient reddish-brown planks that seemed to glow of their own accord. The air was perfect in its temperature and refreshed by banks of rooted flowers beneath the windows, while Ming vases holding cut flowers stood watch like sentinels of white light subdued in nets of Pacific blue.

The lighted corner was rich with browns and gold, and a hypnotic Persian carpet soaked up the light of the single lamp in a muted Technicolor so vivid it seemed to move. In Moncay House the shadows were sharp, the chairs leather, the trays upon which refreshments waited actually of gold. "Eat if you like," said Psnake. "I'm past eating. It's edema that has given me all this horrible gravity. I eat, but I don't enjoy it."

"Thank you, but I've already had dinner."

"It's there," Psnake said, sitting down and breathing hard, "if you want it."

The lateness of the hour and the goldenness of the light made for trust, which led Didgeridoo immediately to suspect a trap. Psnake, after all, who before his elevation to the peerage had been Cecil Birdwood, was his constant rival. The circulation of one set of papers varied inversely with that of the other, as did the viewership of their television channels. What could he be up to?

"As you know," Psnake began, "we've never met. We've been in the same room from time to time, and perhaps in the early days we were introduced, but I don't recall it."

"Nor do I."

"Knowing of our rivalry, people have assiduously kept us apart, which I have always thought to be silly."

"So have I."

"After all, if we're rivals it's only because we seek the same prize. I've observed among those who work under me that disdain is only as intense as similarity. Why shouldn't the two of us admit it? I don't suppose a foreigner could tell the difference between our papers, could he?"

"Can you?" asked Didgeridoo.

"Never could," he said, "and who wants to? Tell me, how are things coming along?"

"In business?"

"What else?"

"They're excellent, as usual. And I know that you, too, are doing quite well."

"Yes," said Psnake, "but our hill of cash is as flat as the lawns at Hampton Court, whereas yours is the height of the Matterhorn."

"Do you want me to buy you out?" Didgeridoo asked, in shock. The thought had never occurred to him. If such an arrangement were to go forward, 80 percent of Britain's newspapers and private electronic media would rest in one hand, a Didgeridoo hand.

"Did I say that?"

"Not yet."

"Nor will I." Psnake leaned forward as best he could, and in the light his lips looked neither red nor pink but alarmingly vermillion. "I don't want you to buy me out, and I wouldn't want to buy you out even if I could."

"Then what do you want?"

"I want"—breathing hard, he looked like an old lion about to make the last kill of his life—"to give you something."

"To give me something?" Now Didgeridoo had all his defences up.

"Yes. Don't worry about Trojan horses. Everything will be entirely transparent, as I will explain."

"Please," Didgeridoo replied, realising that Psnake obviously had not many years left, if even a single one, and was about to make something like a deathbed confession. Didgeridoo had always been able to sense opportunity. For him it was like smelling the scent, blown out to sea, of orchards and grasses. He could be tossing on the waves far from sight of land and suddenly he would be aware of the whereabouts of a great garden. Others would have no sense of it and smell nothing, but he would be in the Garden of Eden. "Please," he said, "do go right ahead. I'm interested in what you might say."

Cecil Birdwood, Lord Psnake, leaned back in his leather seat and looked up into the darkness before he began to speak, as if to infill with ancient desire.

"WHERE SHALL I BEGIN?" he asked not Didgeridoo and not even himself, but the unseen presence that drives accomplishment and is the goad of genius. "It's always hard to begin, because every story begins at the beginning of the world.

"Leaving out a bit, then . . . on the twenty-first of February, nineteen seventeen, I was a boy of seven in a Midlands town that, although the twentieth century had begun, was fixed in the nineteenth. If you looked about, you might have thought that it was eighteen seventy-five. Those years, which I had never seen, left their calling card in the things we had, which were battered and familiar; in what we believed, which was reassuring and unchanging, or so it seemed to me; and in what we said, how we felt, and how we treated one another. I imagine it was much the same for you."

"It was," said Didgeridoo, remembering Australia.

"Toast made on the rack in a wood-oven," said Lord Psnake, "coal heat, no piped water, marmalade and tea our most extravagant luxuries, steam trains and steam whistles, and great politeness, especially to women. Things moved slowly and we hadn't much, but when things moved slowly they were lovely, and because we had so little, what we had seemed like a great deal."

"Yes, I remember."

"My father, who had married my mother in nineteen ten, was a pressman. In 'fifteen, he was called from his steel cylinders and inks into the artillery. He became a shell handler, which was appropriate, I suppose, for a man who had lifted steel all his life. When they took him, when I was five, he could, without assistance, lift and mount above his head (one end at a time) a five-hundred-pound roller. In those days, after he had run a mile down the beach with me on his shoulders, he breathed as lightly as if he had been stirring tea and reading a newspaper.

"But when they sent him back to us, on the twenty-first of February, nineteen hundred and seventeen, he had neither his feet, nor a right hand, nor a lower left jaw. For twenty years, until he died, we fed him mush through a tube, and he was sick every day. It's a mystery what was wrong with his innards, but from the time he returned until his last I often could not sleep, because of his screaming.

"He had been a man of dignity and unerring grace, which, for a poor man, he had in surprising abundance. 'What I did,' he used to tell me, 'I did for king and country, and I do not regret it.' And then I would say, because I loved him, and because I was young, 'But if you did it for king and country, why doesn't the king visit you, to thank you, and help you along?'

"He would just pull me to him, and kiss me with the side of his face, which was all he could manage because of the way he was, and say in speech that sounded like the speech of someone drowning, 'You're a good boy, and all I want in this world is for you to be happy and safe.'

"Of course, the king never visited or sent a card, even when my father died. And look what my father had done for him, suffering without complaint.

"What was the king doing while my father took twenty years to complete the process that had begun with the explosion not even of a shell but of a fuse? What was he doing that he could not visit, or even send a note? I saw that he was on holiday a lot, enjoying himself. And he went from palace to palace, and raced his yacht. Being young, I envied him, and could hardly blame him, as I would have done these things myself. But I did blame him for not knowing about my father.

"How could he have known? There were so many men like my father, and only one king. But, as I saw it, there was only one of my father, and so many kings that they had to have numbers after their names. Still, I understood why it was not practical, and because I did I wondered why things were arranged in such a way, how they had come to the point where they were so hurtful.

"My mother thought of kings as gods. In this country in those days the common people sometimes found it difficult to breathe in their presence. Why was this, and who were they, and how did they get to be that way? My curiosity was driven by the presence of my father. I was not moved by hatred, but by love. So I read history, and I found out how these kings got to be kings, and who they were originally.

"When I discovered that they had become kings mainly by killing whoever stood in their way, or, if that did not suffice, by trickery, plots, and manoeuvre, I realised that not only are the kings of today ordinary people floating upon the habitual deference of other ordinary people, but the bloodlines to which they refer as the only justification of their state are as black as pitch.

"Despite this, and although I believe that all men stand equally before God, I believe as well that England needs a king. But which king? Or which queen? The throne is an institution and a prize. It has always been in play, it always will be in play, and it is in play now. The most riveting moments of our history have been those moments when it is contested. And, I ask you, why should history cease to be interesting?"

"You mean to say," said Didgeridoo, rapt and amazed, "you mean to say that you, Psnake, are contesting the throne of Great Britain?"

"I am."

"Not really!"

"I have worked all my life with that hope ever present within me. It has kept me alive and driven me forward. I haven't always done well, but am now in a position to begin."

"To begin what?"

"One of two things."

"You can't be serious," said Didgeridoo, agitated not so much by the prospect of what he heard as by his intuition that the opportunity he sensed for himself was real enough, but dangerous.

"Look here," said Psnake, "the queen is immutable other than physiologically. She will remain on the throne for as long as she pleases or until she dies. She is a brilliant and faithful woman and a great queen. I would no sooner try to unseat her, or want to, than I would wish to blow off my own leg. The weakness in royal lines, as in everything else, is at the joint, during the transition.

"In the Second World War, in which I fought for king and country with luck greater than my father's, I learned in stupendous battles that the place to strike an enemy formation of any size is at the seam. Military echelons are arrayed so as to protect their centres rather than to interlock and overlap, and the more mobile forces are, the less they tend to blend with those adjacent. The seams, Didgeridoo, the joint: that is where I shall strike, at the younglings, who are spoilt and confused by the long and just reign of their great mother. They have not been tested, and for me that is all the advantage in the world."

"What are you going to do?" asked Didgeridoo, "have them murdered like the princes in the Tower?"

"These are modern times. One murders differently. I will murder them with headlines, and my dagger will be speech. My poison will be the half-hidden mockery in a sentence read by millions, forgotten, and then re-called unknowingly by the reading of a sentence laden with half-hidden contempt. Their bodies shall be untouched. I will assassinate only the public persona, which, though it cannot be touched and has no weight, which though it merely floats through the imagination and has only the ethereal blood of words, exists nonetheless. When we kill the public persona of a man, Didgeridoo, his physical body, though it may not die, reels and re-treats. He goes to ground as if wounded. He breathes hard. He thinks only of rest. He surrenders and is grateful to live out his days in obscurity."

"But, my good Psnake, you can't possibly hope to be king, can you?"

"Of course not. My deepest hope is to live another two years. And even were I twenty I would have no desire to be king. Why would I?"

"Why then are you contesting the throne?"

"I want the new king, whoever he might be, or the new queen, to be different. I contest the throne to change the king, even though the king be the same. I care not about which body seats its arse on the fancy chair, I care about which soul. The soul is what I will contest. The soul is what I will change. The soul is what I will . . . shake up."

"But why?"

"Because I loved my father. He was a good man. He gave his life for king and country, and the king did not even notice. In this the king was wrong, for he should have noticed. He should have laboured all day to do so. He should have given the shirt from his back to those who, in his name, suffered and died in Flanders and France. For the sake of God, it was in his name. If I were king I would never cease to honour and serve the widows and young children of the men who fought for England in my name. I would pray for the rest of my life, and give up everything I had, for the sake of those who died in my name.

"That would be royal conduct, royal rectitude, and royal honour. Though kings who would comport themselves so have been few and far between, they have existed. These royal children must be pushed hard in that direction, to save the idea of monarchy, to give it substance, to restore its honour, to make it worthy of my father."

"My God, Psnake," said Didgeridoo, "this is real stuff, isn't it."

"In every age, there's always someone who moves the real stuff, and, at this moment, I'm it."

"But it's madness, Psnake. You cannot expect a modern sovereign, especially one from this bunch, to be a saint."

"On the contrary, the age calls for it. The royals and the people both have drawn precisely the wrong conclusions. They imagine that in modern times the king must be loose in his ways, lack morals, and drift as if there were no God and no task in life. But they are wrong. In modern times, with sin and death magnified and the king's armies so immense and battles so bloody that not hundreds but millions of men die in his name, the king must be medieval. He must be pious and devout. He must be holy, bookish, and restrained. He must be naturally full of sorrow. If he is any other way, the monarchy will fall."

"You want the king to be an ascetic? With no money and no palaces? You want a bicycle monarch as in Holland and Denmark?"

"No, I want the monarchy to be filled with glory and state treasures, but I want a king whose way of life makes the bicycle monarch look like a sumptuary."

"How will you get that?"

"First," said Psnake, "I have an ally, a fifth column in place at the heart of the matter, ready to move."

"Who?"

Psnake paused with delight, and said, "Freddy."

Then began a curious recitation of Freddy's name, almost an incantation, as Didgeridoo, in disbelief, questioned it, and Psnake, understanding the astonishment, patiently and insistently confirmed it.

"Freddy?"

"Freddy."

"Freddy?!"

"Freddy."

"Freddy?!"

"Freddy."

"You mean, Freddy?!"

"Yes."

"Oh!" said Didgeridoo.

"I have been watching him," said Psnake, "since he was born. And, let me tell you, had he been born a year later he would have been truly a child of the twentieth century, and thus, for my purposes, hopeless. But his mother felicitously gave birth just before the midpoint, when the tendrils of the previous century were still strong enough not merely to make an impression upon him, but to claim him. That, in my view, is the source of all the troubles. Though he may not fully understand it, he is one of the last of his age.

"His difficulties stem from the fact that his nature and ideals are a hundred years or more behind the times. Not only do they clash with the loose and sybaritic mores of today, they clash with some of his own characteristics. He is, after all, a relatively young man. He does not know that he is of the last century, except in his heart.

"I saw it in him even during his infancy, when I beheld him for the first time, in a newsreel. Soon after I had bought my first daily, I went to a motion picture house near the Strand to get ideas for using images in the paper. Images had begun to gallop at us like the cavalry of an invincible army, and I wanted to play the odds correctly. I was young. I had survived the war. I thought, why not be comfortable even as everything I cherish slowly dissolves, with its great champions, like Churchill and Lloyd George, senescent or dead.

"And then a little baby appeared on the screen, and I sat bolt upright, corrected in my lack of resolve, ashamed that I might weaken. He was an infant who could not even walk, and yet in his face I saw a quality of seriousness and reflection that his father could not match in a million years and that even his mother did not have. Here was someone to be reckoned with once he was free to make his own imprint. Here was someone of truly independent mind, who understood as if by instinct that there is a purpose for every one and every thing, and especially for him. He seemed totally possessed of destiny.

"I watched as he grew. He was isolated from the first, left to his own devices, bullied at school, ignored at home, misunderstood. And yet he came out of it with gravitas and good humour. Had he been able to raise a family and practise a profession, to learn the normal lessons and suffer the normal slights, I am sure he could have made history on his own. But the lessons and slights were royal, he has had neither his own family nor a real profession, and he must spend his life waiting for something that may never come.

"Didgeridoo," Lord Psnake said, looking into the eyes of his guest, "his temperament—by accident of history or birth, by nature, circumstance, coincidence, or plan—is exactly what the monarchy and England need in this most dissolute hour. The problem is that all advice and influence runs contrary to it. They want him to be modern, when, indeed, he must be medieval."

"I have to say," said Didgeridoo, "that I must be mad, because I see just what you mean and I agree with you. Tell me, then, how you mean to make this prince more medieval."

"He must be pious."

"Yes, he must."

"He must be grave."

"Oh yes."

"He must be ascetic, and spiritual."

"Of course."

"And he must have a quest."

"Well, yes, I suppose so, but that doesn't answer my question. How are you going to do it? You can't just say, 'Now, Freddy, go fetch the Silver Chalice,' can you?"

"That's right."

"Then how will you do it?"

"I'm going to shake them up, make them fight back, force them to bring in Mr Neil."

"Mr who?"

"Mr Neil."

"Who's that?"

"If you don't know who Mr Neil is, Didgeridoo, you don't know a thing."

"Oh," said Didgeridoo, ashamed that he did not know, "Mr Neil! I thought you had said, 'Mr *Eel*.'"

Lord Psnake shook his head to indicate that he had not, in fact, said "Mr Eel."

"How're you going to do this?" asked Didgeridoo, meekly, and wondering in a chamber fairly close to the front of his mind who, exactly, was Mr Neil, or Mr Eel, or whoever he was.

Lord Psnake raised his left index finger, pointed upward and slightly to his left, closed his left eye, and nodded his head knowingly. "Do you know," he inquired, "why you sit on a mountain of cash and I sit on the flat?"

"The great number of your former wives?"

"That's part of it."

"The yachts, cars, and houses?"

"Another part."

"Your Indonesian chicken farm schemes?"

"Definitely a contributing factor."

"So I do know."

"But you don't know why."

"Why what?" asked Didgeridoo.

"Except for the wives—I married for love even if they did not—it was all to intertwine my fortunes as much as I could with those of the royal family, so that when it was time to budge them I wouldn't have to do it with a guided projectile from four thousand miles away."

"All for that?"

"All for that. For almost thirty years, I have been at the edge of their circle. The chicken farms in Indonesia? Freddy invested a great deal of his money in Indonesian egg farms that had not a single chicken. I positioned myself to be his main chicken supplier, and was there when he needed me. Yes, I took a loss, but it was worth it. Although he is unaware of my purposes, I have known Freddy since he was a boy. He likes me, I think. We speak of things that have consequence. I have measured his wit, liveliness, and intelligence. He is what I thought he would be, though it will take something like an earthquake to bring out the true king in him."

"But how, Psnake, how?"

"Ah. I have my own mountain."

"Of cash?"

"Of what use is cash? Of enough stuff on Freddy, and, of late, Fredericka, to drive him from the throne ten times over."

"You do?"

"I do."

"But if you want him to be king, why drive him from the throne?"

"I want a king who will by his own devices meet all challenges and beat me back, or I want no king at all."

"Are you going to release what you have?"

"Indeed."

"What does this have to do with me, except that, when you do release it, you'll kill us. What will we run on our front pages, two-headed alpacas? We've already done that, and so have you."

"You think," said Lord Psnake, "that I'm about to steal your mountain of cash."

"I do."

"What would I do with it? Would I keep it in my coffin as a cushion? Would I reside upon it, as on a bed of crisp lettuce, for eternity? Would I use it to fluff the silks of my catafalque? Why in heaven's name would I need it? Don't worry, Didgeridoo, I'm not going to make you fake any more two-headed alpacas. I'm going to share with you what I have, split right down the middle."

Didgeridoo was excited but not exactly overwhelmed, and he said, "I see, and I think I see why."

"Certainly you see why. If only Psnake papers carry these stories, people will think I've got it in for Freddy."

"And of course you don't!"

"Not really, given the splendid outcome that may result. If just the Psnake papers run them, they will be dismissed, but if for every Psnake bombshell there is a Didgeridoo bombshell, no one will be able to say anything, and, believe me, I have the stuff."

"How much?"

"If you tease it out, enough to last for years. It's amazing what you can do with things like that. People don't care about history or astronomy, they care about what Sheila told Teddy."

"Oh splendid Psnake! You're just going to give it to us?"

"I'm going to give it to you," Psnake replied with a quiver of delight, "and then you and I will give it to them."

THE NEXT MORNING at ten o'clock Didgeridoo brought his son and heir, Jerry, and Lord Faintingchair, editor-in-chief of *The Noon Behemoth*, Britain's largest newspaper, to a meeting with Psnake at Moncay House. In keeping with Psnake's desire for secrecy, the Didgeridoos and Faintingchair were disguised as charwomen. In flower-print dresses, scarves binding their hair, heavy lipstick, and stockings, they carried mops and buckets. It was not unusual for *Noon Behemoth* investigative reporters to don disguises, and the delegation was untroubled by its attire.

That *The Noon Behemoth* was the country's (and, if you discount Japan and China, the world's) most popular newspaper did not upset Psnake as it might have, given that the second and third biggest papers, his own, bracketed it every day and together claimed one and a half times its readership. These were, as everyone knows, *The Morning Psnake* and *The London Afternoon Omelette*. The three organs combined had a circulation of eight million and sold as reliably as the tide. Elaborate marketing studies and surveys done several times a year indicated consistently that if the regular page-two (in the *Psnake*), page-three (in the *Omelette*), and page-six (in the *Behemoth*) photographs of voluptuous nude women were to have been discontinued, combined circulation would fall from eight million to 2,420. When first instituted, they had been a scandal. Then the scandal had become the norm. Knowing how these things worked, the press lords had inscribed above the doorway of their association the motto *Whatever it takes.*

Psnake's publisher and protégé, Watson Axelrod (who was used to hearing, after stating his name, "It's what goes between the wheels"), received the Didgeridoos and Faintingchair. When everyone had sat down, stirred his tea, eaten a biscuit, looked into the fire, and observed that the rain was pounding on the gravel paths in the garden, flying back up into the air a foot or two as it bounced, and slanting now and then against the windows so that, wind driven, it washed them clean, Axelrod began. Psnake said nothing, and listened carefully. Axelrod was casually but extremely well tailored. He wore the thin, entirely round, tortoise-shell eyeglass frames popular in Britain until the 1960s, and spoke like an Oxford don, which, once, he was.

"Gentlemen," he said, hesitating as he looked at their lipstick and head-scarves, "very kind of you to come. We are exceedingly grateful. As you know, we would like to share with you a series of news stories, for purposes that the Lord Psnake has outlined to the Lord Didgeridoo. The question of scheduling, order, and timing will have to be studied after first release and initial reactions, but, notwithstanding that, let me acquaint you with the substance of our material."

"Yes, do," said Jerry Didgeridoo.

Axelrod opened a portfolio, exposing a typed, coded, and colour-keyed list of eighty or ninety entries. "I'll acquaint you with some of the more volatile of these," he said, "which the others serve as dunnage, spacing the hits and allowing oxygen to rush the fire.

"For instance, the rather infamous dinner at the Royal Historical Society, at which the Prince of Wales appeared in. . . ."

"That's not news," protested Lord Faintingchair. "The *Behemoth*'s chewed that one until there's not a bit of gristle left."

"We understand," said Axelrod, "but we have three hundred colour photographs of Freddy and Fredericka at the occasion, not a single one of which anyone has seen." He produced a portfolio. "They're all like this," he said, holding up a picture of Freddy with closed eyes and a contented smile, happily staring into inner space, the bow atop his head emphasised by the angle of the shot. "You see, it's all a matter of juxtaposition. You take anything he says, anything—'Good morning,' 'Delighted to be here,' 'England's youth are its future,' 'Yes, I did fall from my horse'—and run it with this picture, and it will be like a V-2 in Grosvenor Square.

"Looking through at random . . . yes . . . for example, from Major Fattiston, retired, formerly RAF Moleturd and now chief aviation correspondent of the Psnake Group, we have a long and detailed account, backed up by tape recordings, of the Prince of Wales' claim to have seen UFOs on the streets of London—repeatedly and as a matter of routine."

"Is that true?" asked Didgeridoo.

"Quite so. He keeps a running tally, and claims to have seen almost a thousand over a period of twelve years, in broad daylight and in places like Chelsea and Lincoln's Inn Fields. Taken directly from the tape, we have the following statement, in what is clearly the prince's own voice. 'Fattiston, you'll never guess what. I saw a UFO in Marylebone, right in front of Wigmore Hall. We had no idea what it was, but an African woman jumped out and disappeared into the night. It was very big, and it moved off toward Portman Square. We were going the other way and couldn't track it. You don't get many UFOs up here, do you, but they're all over London. I see them from my windows every day, and feel like crying out in frustration. They do distract one from one's work.' Note this," Axelrod said: "'It was Mummy who introduced me to them, you know, but I wouldn't repeat that if I were you. It might be misinterpreted.'"

"You have the tapes?" Faintingchair inquired.

Axelrod nodded.

"Extraordinary, extraordinary. Go on."

"It seems that since time immemorial the Prince of Wales has been carrying on an absolutely stupendous, totally uninhibited, wall-banging, roller-coaster-screaming, positively thermonuclear sexual affair with Lady Phoebe Boylingehotte, and although we have far more than we can use, it's a doomsday weapon if we're ever backed into a corner."

"Then what good is it?"

"We can freely use parts of it: tape recordings of telephone conversations, for example."

"How did you get these? It's against the law."

"We took them off the air. The royals are as promiscuous with cellular telephones as they are with money, hot water, and mistresses. Listen." He produced a tape recorder and played a static-laden phone transmission. It was Freddy, who said some things that were very embarrassing, and some that were only mildly embarrassing.

"What's that? What's that?" asked Faintingchair. "Play it back."

"I wish," said Freddy, recognisably but clouded with static, "that I could be your tarpon."

"Your what?" Faintingchair interrupted.

"Your tarpon," Axelrod said, resting his chin on clasped hands like a country vicar.

"What's that, a tarpon?"

"A muscular and silvery game fish that lives in the Atlantic Ocean off America. He had just come back from Florida and was. . . ."

"No no no!" Faintingchair shouted. "Can't you see!"

"See what?"

"See that this is worth a hundred million pounds."

"Because he wants to be her tarpon?"

"I didn't hear it that way," Faintingchair said.

"You didn't?"

"No, and I print things as I hear them. Give this one to us."

"You may have it if you wish, though I must say that I can't see that it has any sensational value at all."

"Live and learn," Didgeridoo declared in a way that was trusting and proud, although he had no idea what Faintingchair had in mind. "He knows all about fish."

"Go on," begged Jerry Didgeridoo, now more interested in this than in his racing cars.

"We have," Axelrod continued, pressing a button to close the curtains and darken the room, "a marvellous series of photographs taken by a former royal servant who shall remain nameless."

"And rich," added Psnake.

"And quite rich. She/he took them. . . ."

"Wait a minute," interrupted Jerry Didgeridoo. "You said he'd remain nameless."

"Yes. She/he will."

"Well, if his name is Sheehy," Didgeridoo the younger said triumphantly, "he's not nameless, is he?"

"Her/his name is not Sheehy."

"Who's Herhiz, an Iranian?"

"What are you talking about?"

"You said his name is Sheehy."

"No, I didn't. I said *she* slash *he*."

"She attack him?"

Axelrod had had students like this. Usually they had come in caravans of Rolls-Royces and urinated out the windows of their rooms for a week or two before they understood enough English to find the WC. He knew what to do. "She did attack him, Herhiz, that is. He's dead, and she went back to Cork. You won't let on, will you?"

"No."

"Good. Anyway, as I was saying, Ms Sheehy has provided us with splendid photographs. She has now opened a portrait studio in Cork, where she is working her way up rapidly in the world of infant portraits." He flashed a colour transparency upon a glass-beaded screen.

"Oh God, look at that," exclaimed Didgeridoo the elder.

There was Freddy, covered in viscera and gore, pulling the innards from a huge stag and smiling like the Cheshire Cat.

"This was taken in Scotland a few years ago," Axelrod stated. "We thought that, without mentioning that he was doing the job of a gillie who had been injured in the hunt, we would run it on one of our front pages, or all of them, above Freddy's statement to the crowd at the reopening of the Children's Zoo: 'All my life, I've loved animals and children.'"

"It's a gold mine," said Faintingchair.

"What about these?" Axelrod continued. "We have no idea what he was doing, but with the right captions we don't really have to, do we?"

The first in this series of pictures showed Freddy dressed in a deer costume, antlers and all. Then came Freddy lowering his head as if to charge. Then a speeding Freddy, legs off the ground. Then a dramatic collision with the side of the stable at Moocock. Then Freddy lying on the ground, apparently having lost consciousness.

"All those people in the back, laughing," said Didgeridoo the elder, "make it quite obvious that he's entertaining them."

"My lord," Axelrod said, "we will of course edit them out, and supply a caption such as 'The Prince of Wales Atones for His Crime in Scotland,' or 'Freddy in Attempt to Reduce Demolition Budget During Moocock Renovations,' or some such thing."

"Have you got anything on the Princess Royal?" Faintingchair asked.

"Not really. She's having another affair with a bull-fighter."

"Which one?"

"Number ten. There's no more juice in it, not even a drop. How many times can you run the banner 'Sydney Takes a Bull by the Horn, Again'?"

"Every time we've done that," said Jerry Didgeridoo, "we've sold an-other million papers."

"If this programme is properly exploited," Axelrod told him, "you'll double, treble, and quintuple your circulation on good days, and move as a matter of course a million more papers than you do now. Permit me," he continued, opening the curtains, "to show you a videotape taken by a member of a wedding party at Pestwick-on-Canal, a village near Moocock."

At the end of the showing, the assembled conspirators were silent, and only after five minutes was the silence broken. "What could he possibly have had in mind?" Psnake asked, quite out of character.

"Is that," asked Lord Didgeridoo, "what they call Tourette's Syndrome?"

"No, my lord," Axelrod answered, "it is what is called Royal Tourette's Syndrome."

"Are we really to go ahead with this?" asked Faintingchair. "It is the monarchy, and these things are like atomic bombs."

"Buck up," said Psnake. "The Americans dropped them on the Japa-nese, didn't they?"

No one answered.

"Didn't they?"

"Yes," spoke Jerry.

"Then what's the problem? I see no problem. I've been planning this all my adult life. I'm sure it will go smoothly. Why wouldn't it? It's history, after all, and history always works itself out."

"Indeed, my lord," said Axelrod, "history always works itself out."

CRISIS OF THE ROYALS:
THE PRIME MINISTER
V MR APEHAND,
LEADER OF HM LOYAL OPPOSITION

IT WAS FITTING that the House of Commons was packed, because London itself was packed, its theatres, restaurants, and hotels swarming like beehives in July. A dozen plays pulled-in English speakers and admirers of the language from the Continent and much woollier places all around the globe. Mongolians, Africans, and Javanese milled with the inhabitants of the former Axis powers, Texans in Stetsons, and Gulf Arabs in burnouses. They were everywhere, all the time. They were in chophouses and oyster bars; buying ski simulators, jewellery, and toupees at Harrods and ropes of pearls in the Burlington Arcade; riding about in buses looking exhausted; filling the lobbies of hotels while they read newspapers in eye-crossing alphabets; trying to take taxis from Trafalgar Square to Nelson's Column; standing in the minor glare of theatrical marquees as lonely snowflakes came like scouts from the region of cold night, all in the days before Christmas.

Parliamentarians were eager to work through the dark evenings. How lovely it was to go from a division to a late dinner party in a house that sparkled and beckoned at the edge of a square emptied by December wind, and find there, among open fires and in candlelight, women gliding about like Milton's angels. When in winter the natural world was inhospitable, by comparison the works of man shone like gold.

Winter beat MPs from their constituencies to London like grouse flushed before a gale or Teutons forced down to Venice by the action of the summer sun. It would have been even more excellent than it was, as Psnake could have affirmed, had a Churchill or Lloyd George been either in government or opposition, for then the House would have had irresistible allure. But without a crisis or crisis-in-the-making, without a threat to the life of the nation, and in any but a golden age, no leader could be great, and great men seemed out of their element on the green benches of the Commons, having no more place amid the saccharine boo-hoo-hoo-ing and bureaucratic chuckering than Moses in a tea room or Joan of Arc in an aerobic dance class.

It was a sad time for great men. Their day was over, and their customary positions were occupied by arrogant snot-nosed hacks who dreamed of being gods, by waddling adenoidal Morlocks full of studied indignation, and by the always-so-reasonable middle, who spent their political lives offended by action, embracing indecision, and wooing extinction. The prime minister, Nigel Pimcot, was elected to his safe seat every year by the Conservative marble chewers of Beeton–St Bartholomew. His Labour counterpart, the beetle-browed V. I. Apehand, came from a constituency in the North Midlands that nobody quite knew the name of because there was too much smoke to see the signs. He coughed a lot. Hillary Lamb, his Liberal nemesis, was in perfect health, ate no fat, and could not understand how anyone could be so phenomenally low as to attend to self-interest.

Parliament seldom packed itself to hear these three or their variously semi-human substitutes. Not since Lady Hilda beat the potatoes out of the Bolivians in the Easter Island War had the House of Commons been a hot ticket. She had said of that war, "It is for Britain today a glorious victory. It would have been, for Britain in twelve ten, a glorious victory. But for Britain at any other, reasonably vigorous time, it would have been just a bloody blip, and you know it."

Lady Hilda was the queen's favourite, the favourite of Prince Paul, and Freddy's favourite, too. Had she been younger, he would have married her, or he would have tried. When Lady Hilda was twenty-five, she was the most beautiful woman in England. She was upright, strong, and willing to cut to the quick, which was once the hallmark of the English woman before the whole island, according to Freddy, went soft, as its timbers rotted into what its intellectuals thought was the marsh of history. According to Freddy, only the moderns saw history as a bog. He thought it was quite the opposite—full of sharp lines, hard surfaces, and sparkling lights, like Lady Hilda.

When she had been the queen's first minister, she and Freddy had often met at ribbon cuttings and receptions, and had appraised one another with a regretful non-Disraelian regard that telegraphed their sorrow over the two decades that stood between them. He imagined her as young, she imagined herself as younger, and in this was a tenderness that neither could express. Neither publicly admitted to anything but official thought of the other. She was, after all, the prime minister, and he the heir to the throne. Still, when he married Fredericka, her note had said, "Congratulations, but if only you could have married me," and his, in answer, "For which God may forgive us but I cannot forgive Him." And then not a word passed between them, ever, until no word could.

Fredericka had read Lady Hilda's note and become enraged. It was one of the early artifacts of the war between them, which was what now packed the House as if it awaited not Pimcot, Apehand, and Lamb, but Disraeli, Churchill, and Pitt. No one was concerned, really, about the numbing particulars of government, even in a petty age when men feared above all the rapaciousness and terror of their own food. No one cared a whit if the cost-of-living allowance were to increase at a rate .003674 percent faster for civil servants than for council employees with less than five years' seniority. The people sent gladiators to Westminster to argue about details that would otherwise bore them to death. Although they did not care, the predilections they had inherited for caring and for fighting were still partially intact, and they went through the motions in the same way that the comatose, when pricked with a pin, sometimes jerk a limb.

Now, however, along with a season of very good plays, the MPs had something to look forward to—a royal fire, fed with newspapers, that blazed over London like the flames of old. They felt alive again. Here was something, though not entirely serious, that they could fight over not like beetles but like bulldogs. Here was something, the fitness of royalty, the question of succession, the implications for representative government, that arose from a stilled sea like a great whale breaking mirror-smooth water into cascades of insolent foam. At Question Time the MPs were backed up through the halls and into the courtyards. They knew they would enjoy even the normal business that would come before everything about Freddy and Fredericka, because now even normal business would have a captivating edge. The speaker, a woman of hefty fortitude and original character, rose to invite questions for the prime minister. Pimcot walked to the dispatch box, put down a looseleaf notebook, responded to the first question with an announcement about his scheduled meetings, and then steeled himself for a battle in which he would defend his king.

"Number two, Mr Lovelace," the speaker called.

Up sprang Lovelace of Spofford-Treacle, as nervous and eager as a greyhound. The prime minister turned to his right to receive the question from this friendly member of his own party, who could set down the lines without challenge, guiding the debate to come. Thank God for that. Lovelace was relatively new and could not fail to seek such an opportunity for his party and himself. In fact, even before Lovelace opened his mouth, Pimcot was trying to match him up with something for his reward.

"The prime minister must be aware," Lovelace began, "of the tremendous importance of hogs in the economy of these islands. Even the Romans had hogs, and were very fond of them, actually, as pets, guard animals, and assistants. Every hog is covered with a great number of bristles, and these are the hog's hairs."

With tremendous but well practised irritation, the speaker rose to say, "Will the gentleman please put his statement in the form of a question."

"Is the prime minister aware," Lovelace asked, "of the tremendous importance of hogs in the economy of these islands? Is he aware that the Romans had hogs, and were very fond of them, actually, as pets, guard animals, and assistants? Does he realise that every hog is covered with a great number of bristles, and that these are the hog's hairs? Does he possess the knowledge that hog bristles are highly valued in Japan as well as in other luxury markets around the world? Does he understand that the Japanese company, Kumato-Kuragai, has opened a brush factory in my constituency, in the village of Spotwich-Piggy? Does he consider that twenty-eight jobs have been created in the last month for a population of one hundred and sixty-seven souls? Is this not, proportionately, a record eight times better than that of the Labour government the last time 'round? And isn't it true that this government encourages opportunity and job formation as none other before? And will the prime minister visit Spotwich-Piggy to inspect the Kumato-Kuragai factory?"

Much more smoothly than silk, for silk seemed smooth only to medieval people used to itchy fabric, Pimcot picked up the baton of speech and carried it with him as he floated. "I *do* value pigs," he said, "this government values pigs, and very few civilised people in the world today are unaware of the value of the bristles on hogs or that these exist in great number. I hope that my travels take me soon to the vicinity of Spotwich-Piggy, in which case I will be eager to tour the Kumato-Kuragai factory. How many Japanese factories did the last Labour government bring to Spotwich-Piggy? How many to this country? I'll tell you. None. They have not created wealth and jobs themselves, because they are too busy worrying about how much money other people have, and too busy trying to take it away from them. That is the difference between us and the party opposite. That is the difference."

A great lowing and mooing arose from the Labour benches, met with a kind of high-pitched yodelling from the Conservative benches. But it stopped dead when a small voice from the Conservative side pierced the air like a javelin of weakness. This was the voice of Rupert Bertie Bethune, the oldest member of Parliament, a man of the previous century who not only listened through but spoke through an ear-trumpet, so that on those few occasions when he did speak it was uncanny: a strange centenarian feebly declaiming through a clogged tube. "Aren't we at war with them?" he asked. "We don't want their bloody factories! We should drop bombs on their factories!"

"May I respectfully remind the Right Honourable Gentleman from Snettisham that the war with Japan has been over for half a century," the prime minister said. In Westminster, you could hear a kilt pin drop.

"It has?" asked Rupert Bertie Bethune, in the sweetest voice imaginable.

"Yes."

"Oh," he said. "Then I take it we've won. No one told *me*. I didn't hear any bells. Why don't you go out and ring the bells?"

"Today," the prime minister told him to his evident delight, "all the bells will ring at exactly twelve noon."

"Mr Apehand," the speaker said, and up rose V. I. Apehand, a Welshman with alarming eyebrows, sack belly, and a nose shaped like a loaf of bread. Many years older than Pimcot, he approached him always with a frontal attack, certain that, though this never worked, he would somehow pick up, on the other side of nought, all the votes he lost, because, as he was fond of saying, "Politics is redistribution, and no one ever thinks he has enough."

Pimcot closed one eye as Apehand began.

"Is the prime minister aware of Mrs Fanny Albingle-Epworth, a pensioner in Leeds, who was, at her tragic and unnecessary death, eighty-seven years of age? Is the prime minister cognizant of the fact that Mrs Albingle-Epworth, a war widow who had been receiving the heat allowance year after year, was denied it by his government, and that she died ten days after she was cruelly cut off during the recent cold snap? Is this government so indecent as to allow war widows to freeze to death? To me, it's like Mussolini putting babies on hillsides to die. What do you have to say for yourself . . . and for your wretched government?"

How could Pimcot possibly explain away such cruelty? The Conservative backbenchers who had pushed for cutting the heat subsidy were feeling rather queasy, sure that not even Pimcot could save them. They thought, Well, if he can—and we cannot imagine how he might—that is why he is the queen's first minister.

Pimcot let a long time pass, as if he had no response or had not heard. He seemed utterly calm and even amused, which upped the stakes. From long experience, Apehand knew that all was not well.

"I am aware," the prime minister recited gravely, "of the death," he continued, pausing rhythmically, "of Mrs Fanny Albingle-Epworth, of Leeds. I am aware that, ten days before she died, Mrs Albingle-Epworth was denied her heating allowance by my government. For which," he said dramatically, "I take full responsibility, and express no regret. Am I regretful? No, I am not. If Mrs Albingle-Epworth were to rise from the dead and walk before us now, and approach this bench with the words 'Please, please, may I have my heating allowance?' I would say, 'No, no, and no again!'"

The House roared in almost hysterical disapproval. Every Tory was terrified. Had Pimcot gone mad? "Killer! Killer!" screamed Labour, and not just one or two, but a hundred or more.

He took the opportunity to work them up yet again, aiming for a state of froth. "'No, no, and no again, Mrs Albingle-Epworth! No heating allowance for you! Not a chance!!'"

The House was half insane. Apehand rose, and after five minutes, when the jeering had subsided, he cautiously sought to drive in the stake that he thought Pimcot had placed pointing at his own heart. But he was still worried. "And why, Prime Minister, why, I ask, why in the name of God, would you deny to this poor woman a few lumps of coal?" The pathos was as thick as apple-butter.

Pimcot waited until not a single member was not on the edge of his seat and holding his breath. "I would deny her those few lumps of coal," he replied to Apehand, as gravely as he possibly could, "because," he paused for what seemed like forever, "she didn't need them. She didn't need them, because she gave up her flat in October, moved to Jamaica to live with her son and daughter-in-law, and died there, on a ninety-eight-degree day, of heat prostration. That's why."

The Conservatives now rose as one and cheered as if indeed Japan had just surrendered, which Rupert Bertie Bethune believed to be the case. "And that is why we are on this side of the House, and you are on that side," Pimcot said, bearing down. *"We do our homework."*

Next up was Hillary Lamb, terrified by the display of Pimcot's resilience but determined as a matter of faith to take the shot he had prepared. Lamb was a ladies' man, and this everyone knew. Evidently his Roman haircut, military background, and genuine astonishment that anyone could disagree with his obviously sensible views were, to women, in Apehand's phrase, "like fresh vegetables for an Eskimo." His party had discovered that 88 percent of its adherents were professional women who wore scarves and brooches and bathed with perfumed soaps. When this was made public, Pimcot had opined that not one member of Apehand's party used perfumed soap, and that only a few used soap at all. Apehand, engaging the totality of his wit, had shot back that he did use soap.

Now Lamb stood with the troubled, earnest expression for which he was famous, and spoke in his cashmere voice.

"The prime minister is aware, is he not, of the recent case of environmental atrocity at the Royal Naval Station, John O'Groats? One of my constituents, a Mr Coningsby Isaac, had been employed by the Royal Mollusc Society to care for molluscs in the marges of John O'Groats. He was obliged, therefore, to expose himself to the highly dangerous high-frequency emissions from the radomes at RNS John O'Groats, which the Royal Mollusc Society suspects are responsible for the very low rate of reproduction among the local mollusc community.

"Molluscs at John O'Groats are stunted and puny, and virtually never achieve orgasm. Why? Because of the Royal Navy's ludicrous assertion that it must guard the seaward approaches to Britain."

The speaker rose. Always when addressing Lamb she had a special tingle in her voice, but now she was irritated as well. "Would the gentleman please put his statement in the form of a question."

"Certainly, Madam Speaker. Is the prime minister aware that Mr Coningsby Isaac, after more than forty mollusc expeditions to John O'Groats, has suffered the same fate as his charges?"

The House perked up.

"Mr Isaac, having been irradiated like a mollusc, is no longer capable of satisfying his wife. Or, for that matter, anyone else. Has the prime minister read, in *The Noon Behemoth* of yesterday, Mr Isaac's courageous, exact, and detailed account of his many unsuccessful attempts at sexual relations? Is the prime minister not impressed by the man's courage in publishing so exhaustive an account, replete with photographs, to illustrate not only the plight of British molluscs but his own? And can the prime minister tell this House, and the British people, what he is going to do about it?"

"I have always thought," the prime minister replied, "that men after whom women lust uncontrollably are fools. It is unthinking to consider them exemplars of manhood when in fact they have given up their manhood, willing as they are to keep it so unbalanced. A man is many things. He is the sober protector of his family, the earner of wages, the fighter of wars, the father of his children. In his life he discovers that the greatest part of being a man is standing fast in the teeth of those forces that whittle away at his existence and eventually will destroy him, so that he may do his duty to his God, his family, and his country. This you cannot do offhandedly, for in the end it takes everything you have. But a man whose life is filled mainly with the prospect and attraction of adoring women has, perforce, abandoned those things that most make him a man. Women of substance know this. The last great duty of a man is to stand alone. He cannot do that if he is courted by ten thousand women. He becomes a gigolo, a powder puff, a kind of perfumed cushion, who, with his bevy of admirers in the seraglio gossips about nipples and tarts."

The House was stunned. Lamb said, "Why, may I ask, is the prime minister addressing such a topic?"

But Pimcot had made his statement only as a Parthian shot, and had no desire to debate what was clearly obvious. "We are, are we not," he asked, "addressing the matter of Mr Coningsby Isaac's impotence?"

Lamb nodded.

"I have read the account in *The Noon Behemoth,*" Pimcot stated. "Who has not? After inquiring of the minister of defence, I am relieved to inform the House, although Mr Isaac may not share in my relief, that RNS John O'Groats reports that though the radomes at the installation are still standing, the equipment that had been inside them was removed in nineteen seventy-six, and there have not been radar emissions at or from RNS John O'Groats for years. Do you get my drift?"

Not only Tories, but Labour and even the Liberals smiled. Even Lamb. Pimcot gave the already spinning wheel a little pat. "Will you then please convey to Mr Isaac my wishes for a speedy recovery, if such a thing is possible. And I do hope that in future more molluscs have orgasms. Meanwhile, I will be able to sleep at night with the knowledge that my government has not robbed them of this enjoyment."

Who would dare challenge Pimcot now? After such an exhibition he seemed invulnerable. Every sensible member of the House, knowing that Pimcot would defend the monarchy unto death, feared to ask about the scandalous behaviour of the Prince of Wales. This was a huge piece of meat, a whole ox, that could cook either way. The House was silent for fear that Pimcot had saved his most devastating ambush for the very question that had brought them all out. Pimcot, who had absolutely nothing left in his quiver and not a single bolt for Freddy, showed as much confidence as he could, hoping to bluff his way.

The House was silent, but then, to Pimcot's distress, the speaker recognised the one Labour backbencher who caused the Tories more pain than any other. At the mention of his name they closed their eyes and cringed, for although only four and a half feet tall, with the visage of a troll and the speech of a broken irrigation pump, he was all hide and no nerves, and he was from the safest seat in England, Mold-on-Gruth, a dark and melancholy depression filled with rubbish dumps, coal pits, and chemical factories. "Mr Mallet Scuffs," she said, and, though it was hard to tell, he stood bolt upright.

On this occasion he was wearing a rust-coloured jacket that matched what was left of his rust-coloured hair and beard. On the left (naturally) lapel of this jacket was a button that read *Please piss off.* Like all arresting characters, he did not let fear push him too early into speech. Instead, he surveyed the House as it surveyed him, slightly altering his expression, letting the silence deepen. And then he did what virtually no one had ever done during Prime Minister's Question Time. He actually asked a question.

"What . . . about . . . *him?*" he said, in words that boomed and echoed through the House chamber like summer thunder.

"What about who?" replied the prime minister, although he knew.

"You know who. The Prince of Wales," said Mallet Scuffs, with the undiluted singularity that had attended his rise.

"The Prince of Wales?" inquired the prime minister, hoping to get through the next few seconds, as if he had never heard of him.

"Yes, Prime Minister. *I'm* asking the question of *you.*"

"But what about the Prince of Wales?" the prime minister asked. Already, the House was tittering like an aviary.

"We're not French, we don't have to be coy," said Mallet Scuffs, finally content to make a statement. "I do read *The Morning Psnake*. I read the *Behemoth*. I read the *Omelette*. And I cannot imagine, Prime Minister, that you don't."

"And the question?"

"What about him? He's bloody mental, isn't he? I mean, he's quite 'round the twist, ain't he? And someday he's supposed to be king. I say, throw them out when they're ripe. People in my constituency are starving and born with sixteen fingers. Did you ever eat weasel shish-kebob? Freddy doesn't walk by the side of the motorways to gather dandelions for his salad, but the people who sent me here do. Why are we supporting him? He doesn't deserve it. The Tories won't give milk to children who go to school hungry and come home to baked cat."

Happy that Mallet Scuffs had larded up his attack, Pimcot knew he had a chance at division. "The last time the Right Honourable Gentleman raised the accusation about the policies of this government forcing his constituents to resort to inedible foods—in that case, as I remember, it was ants, earwigs, and glowworms—the National Health looked very seriously into the matter, and their inspectors. . . ."

"Division! Division!" cried out some who had got the scent of blood, and Mallet Scuffs himself, successfully diverted, cried out, "Weevils, too! Weevils and grubs!"

"Their inspectors. . . ."

"Weevils, too, weevils and grubs! Weevils, too, weevils and grubs!" chanted a Marxist anti-missile faction.

"Their inspectors," insisted Pimcot, "found that it had long been a custom in Mold-on-Gruth to barbecue unusual edibles." The inspectors had determined no such thing. Pimcot had made it up out of whole cloth for the sake of outraging the House into a division.

But just as Pimcot had by brilliance and skill risen to the leadership of his party, so had Apehand and Lamb risen to the leadership of theirs, and they prepared to cross his T. First, Apehand stood to put the debate on course, speaking in the magical voice of Wales. "I believe that the question, Prime Minister, was not about weevils and grubs but about the Prince of Wales. Would the prime minister be so kind as to answer the question?"

When Pimcot was cornered, he assumed the expression and mannerisms of a hurt and resentful child. This habitually cost him as much as his vaunted ability effortlessly to exploit victory habitually brought him advantage. Nonetheless, he persevered. "England needs a king," he said, "as much as it needs its weather. The sovereign is the point around which everything in this country has revolved for so long that without the sovereign everything would fly apart. To cripple the sovereign would be an act of efficient self-destruction. No wonder you want it. I have always taken hostility to the queen and her family as the manifestation of just such a tendency. Indeed, though it is difficult to say of Englishmen, I have always taken it, and am not the only one to do so, as hatred of country. As the royal power has decreased, its symbolism has increased, and it stands now for Britain as never before. Is it not a fortunate circumstance that, given our own direction of our own affairs, we may enjoy it without anxiety? And why bother now to strike at the sovereign, when the balance of our power and his position has reached perfection?" He sat down.

Up popped Apehand on his side of the Sceptre. "No one is talking about abolishing the monarchy, Prime Minister, so you need not display your put-upon look. What my colleague holds up for the consideration of the House is the behaviour of the heir to the throne, certainly a legitimate concern, especially if, as the prime minister says, the throne is inextricable from the sinews of state. When I see a nut, Prime Minister, I am not afraid, I am not afraid to say, there, there is yon nut. And I do see a nut, Prime Minister, and I do say, there, there is yon nut. And what do you say?"

"It is really very unfair," Pimcot insisted, "to make a judgement of the Prince of Wales based on what one reads in newspapers that every day owe their circulation to photographs of nude women in ludicrous and provocative poses. Yesterday the *Omelette* had a picture of a nude gymnast in an aerial split above a trampoline made to look like a buttered scone. And what about the 'Naked Ms Napoleon'? Based on such nonsense would you seriously question the foremost representatives of an institution exceeded in longevity only by the Papacy and the Chrysanthemum Throne?"

Slowly and languorously, Lamb rose, and was recognised by the speaker. So what if his party held only seven seats. He always looked marvellous.

"Thank you, Madam Speaker." He had a great, impatient air, a magnificent flustration, and a velvet voice. He was not thinking of what he said, but, rather, feeling it. And knowing that an unprecedented number of women would now have their eyes bonded to his image, he would speak somewhat rashly. In fact, many members of the House would believe that, after Pimcot's earlier attack upon his character, he had been waiting for his chance. The riposte, however, would strike not Pimcot but Freddy, who could not be present to defend himself. Lamb's constituents were confused about the monarchy, not Apehand's, who wanted to abolish it, so Apehand was delighted for Lamb to do the work and leave him high and dry.

Lamb looked about the House with the tortured look that some thought made him a modern Mark Antony and others attributed to a digestive complaint. "Madam Speaker, does the prime minister not realise that all the accusations are true? Does he not realise that they are founded upon evidence—photographs, videotape, voice recordings and transcripts—that is incontrovertible? Does he not realise that simple, blind support of things royal will not in the end preserve the monarchy? That, Madam Speaker, is the real danger." He sat, hoping Pimcot would take the bait.

Pimcot rose and did. "The Right Honourable Gentleman simply repeats the foreign affairs and defence positions of his party in another guise. 'We want a strong Britain, but the way to strength is to be courageous enough to do without weapons and armies. We can catch more birds with honey, so let's cooperate with our rivals, enemies, and detractors. In fact, we'll show them. We'll show them that we're strong enough to capitulate to them!' It's always the same. In this case he advises that the best way to defend the monarchy is to refrain from its defence. Is it his view that not only is the strongest army the army with no soldiers—or perhaps half a dozen, as in Andorra—and no weapons, but that the queen is best served by a chief minister who abstains from her defence? And as the Right Honourable Gentleman has stated that the tawdry newspaper allegations are based on incontrovertible evidence, does he believe then also that infant survivors of the *Titanic* have recently been cast up upon Beachy Head, that the prime minister of Norway is a space alien, that the Pope is repeatedly struck by meteorites, and that the American singer Barbra Streisand is actually the panicked reincarnation of Frederick the Great? If the honourable member has incontrovertible evidence, I invite him to show it."

Lamb stood. "Madam Speaker, may I?" he asked. She indicated that he might, and he did. He lifted some sheets of paper. "This," he said, "is a transcript taken from the recording of the Princess of Wales speaking to Mr Thor Früsengladje, Her Royal Highness's former hairdresser. It is the voice of the princess. I can attest to this. I know women's voices. Allow me to read."

"Madam Speaker, this is highly irregular," Pimcot said. The Tories were so anxious that, amazingly, each and every one of them was awake.

"May I remind the prime minister that it was by his own invitation? Does he now urgently request a ruling against himself? Really. Go ahead, Mr Lamb."

"I will simply read from the transcript.

"'Thor: Let me suggest to Your Royal Highness an icy-blond highlight for the back sweep. It's called Fantastic Alaskan Vanilla Frost.'

"'Princess: I liked the Icy Jamaican Platinum Orange better, and *She* loved it.'

"'Thor: They don't make that any more, I fear.'

"'Princess: Oh dear.'

"'Thor: Madam seems dejected.'

"'Princess: It's just terrible.'

"'Thor: Tell me. I won't tell a soul.'"

"Except his bloody tape recorder, that's all!" screamed a Tory, who in the Magdalen College production of *Pinocchio* played the whale.

"It is," said Lamb, "no matter what its origins, the truth." He then returned to the transcript.

"'Princess: I think Freddy's crazy. He's been acting so strangely of late. I'm frightened.'

"'Thor: What did he do?'

"'Princess: I don't know if I should tell.'

"'Thor: It will never leave this room.'" (General laughter in the House.)

"'Princess: He's crazy. He assaulted me with an encyclopaedia. I'm lucky to be alive. He threw it at me and called me a mealy-mouthed worm. It was blue. I don't know what it was, but he's always reading it.'

"'Thor: Oh my God.'

"'Princess: Even so, that's a kind of normal thing to do, isn't it? I mean, people do throw things at each other. But what was so crazy was why he did it.'

"'Thor: Why did he do it?'

"'Princess: He called me a cyclops. What's a cyclops? Is it bicycle shoes?'

"'Thor: He called you a what?'

"'Princess: A cyclops. He just started screaming at me, and saying, "You're a cyclops! You're a cyclops! You've only got one bosom!" Just like that. That's why I'm going to lower the cut on my dresses even more. I've got to show him that he's wrong.'

" 'Thor: But doesn't he know?'

" 'Princess: Of course he knows. He knows bloody well, but he's crazy. He was just screaming and screaming. It frightens me so. Then he said I have *five* bosoms. Really. I mean, obviously I don't have only one, and obviously I don't have five. Where would I put them? What would I do with them? How can he think such a thing? I tried to convince him, I even held my two bosoms up for him to count. And what did he do? He started to call me things. He called me a mealy-mouthed worm, a cyclops, a tart, and a strumpet. And then he threw that big blue book at me. He said it was a book about bosoms. That's what he reads. He reads books about bosoms, bosom books. I'm frightened and I'm angry. You know, it runs in his family.' "

Lamb sat down, assuming the pose of Rodin's *Thinker* to show that he was thinking. In the House as it was constituted, this was a magical gesture, as if he had snapped his fingers and become invisible, rendering him immune to counterattack. It was also a signal to Apehand, who shook his head to and fro in exaggerated pity.

Pimcot jumped up. "The charges as delivered, Madam Speaker, even if true, serve only to vindicate the Prince of Wales, for, indeed, as everyone knows, the Princess of Wales, and every other woman on earth, has only one bosom, as has each man." He sat, thinking this would be indisputable.

But on the Labour side, mouths hung open in disbelief. Then there was sniggering, which quickly turned to derisive laughter. Apehand assumed his post. "Now we know," he said, anticipating a cheer from his own benches, "what is wrong with the Tory Party!" The Labour benches rose as one to cheer. "Does the prime minister, or does he not, stand by his remark that men have bosoms?"

Pimcot rose in amazement. "Of course I do," he said to a storm of mockery from the Labour side. "And I would like to edify further the member for Rhode-on-Tyne. A man, like a woman, has only *one* bosom." Astounded by the hilarity that ensued, Pimcot screamed, "Look it up! Look it up!"

"Where? In the Prince of Wales' bosom book?" Apehand asked, completely overpowering the Conservatives, who were too shocked to protest. "Would the prime minister next be throwing such a book at me, as the crazed, overprivileged, spoilt, ungrateful, and unnecessary Prince of Wales throws blue bosom books at his wife?"

Pimcot was now enraged, so he took the kind of trapeze-artist's leap that had made him famous. He had kept his eye on the Labour benches during their mockery, searching out Swindon Michael Worry, a university member and Marxist lexicographer so thin he might have been mistaken for fishing line. Swindon Michael Worry looked embarrassed. Even if Labour was his party, words were his life. Which would he choose if put on the griddle? Pimcot remembered his own Oxford days, when, for principle and truth, most of the people he had known would have died (and the rest would have died for an invitation to the right dinner party). He hoped that some of this great quality, that had held the planes aloft until victory in the Battle of Britain, still ran in the veins of those such as Swindon Michael Worry, who could not rise in the House without including in his remarks the words *principle* and *fairness.* "Would the member for Rhode-on-Tyne put the question to Mr Swindon Michael Worry, the renowned authority on all things lexicographical?"

At first a chill ran through Apehand's round body, but then, when he saw Bracken Hornwood, Pimcot's Chancellor of the Exchequer, overcome by a sudden grimace of pain at the prime minister's gamble—speaking without words the question, How can you gamble the monarchy on a Marxist?—he turned with an easy look about him, full of hope, to seek out Swindon Michael Worry. The House was so silent you could hear the throbbing engines of tugs far up the Thames, the little beeps of horns that carried on the wind from Marylebone, and the cry of Dutch seagulls shocked that the winds had borne them from Leyden to London.

Swindon Michael Worry rose, in agony. Many of the MPs understood this agony, and not a single hardly breathing one of them would have been unwilling to give him an hour or more to come to terms with himself. It was the kind of decision some men could not make in a lifetime, and he had less than a minute. The Conservatives hoped that he would simply tell the truth, but their own memory and their hearts told them that he might not. Most of the Labour members assumed that he would say that, obviously, a woman has two bosoms, a man hasn't even one, and that would be that. The Lambs, as they were called, were tortured. Some of them had eyes more dewy than usual.

"Actually," said Swindon Michael Worry, "words are continually evolving, and they mean what we want them to mean. After all, we invented them." Pimcot felt the fall of a kind of inner guillotine. "And in the modern usage, which is the controlling usage, I think it is rather clear, is it not, that men have no bosoms and women have two." And then he sat down to the kind of cheers that once had come for the victories in North Africa and the crossing of the Rhine.

"The world turned upside down," said Pimcot bitterly as he and his ministers departed from the front benches. As they came into the quiet of the halls into which they customarily strode as the first wave out, they heard a boisterous chant from the House chamber.

It rose, and then, when the chanters had got it right, it thundered. For the first time in years, Pimcot felt that his government was in danger. "What are they saying?" he asked. All stopped to listen. Through the baffle of the halls, stronger and stronger, came the swelling chant: "Cyclops! Cyclops! Cyclops! Cyclops!"

To TRANSFORM impending crisis into crisis itself, that night Canal Didgeridoo ran the wedding-party tape both in its original version and in a computer-enhanced edition in which focus was sharpened, light amplified, and close-ups provided of Freddy's face. A man running full speed at the camera while shouting obscenities might be something of note. Certainly it would command attention, but it would be put in context by the action of his body. With context deleted in a skilfully executed close-up of the royal person hustling along, his face became an emblem of madness. The odd expression, concussive breathing, fixed and horizon-skewering eyes, and the flesh of the cheekbones and jowls vibrating inexplicably up and down, were absolutely arresting. Accompanied by the bellowing of an apparent obscenity and aired seventeen times in one evening, it was the beginning of a constitutional crisis.

The queen was not amused, and neither was her consort. They were, as always, unflappable—given their perspective and protections, they never needed to flap—but they did want to see Freddy right away. In fact, Freddy, who was merely annoyed, grew anxious after opening the note that the duke had sent to his office via a page of the back stairs. Freddy had known his father to use idiomatic expressions quite often. To be colourful in language is a soldier's prerogative. But this was the first time in Freddy's experience that his father had made use not only of colourful Anglicisms but of a strange Americanism. The note had read: "Freddy, get your bloody fat arse over here, pronto."

"Pronto?" Freddy had actually said out loud.

When he saw his parents the next day, Queen Philippa smiled her gracious smile, as she could not help but do when her children came into her presence. Prince Paul scowled the vacant scowl of the county aristocrat, something he had adopted merely as a class tribute. He was sitting with legs crossed (a dangerous sign), his left hand grasping and hanging from his right shoulder (also a dangerous sign), and his right hand resting limply on a marble side table, fingers drumming (a very dangerous sign). It was just before Christmas, the cold had slipped down England's spine after shattering off its hooks above the polar sea, and a fire was burning in the fireplace. This was all the more lovely because of a mass of yellow roses in the background, and snow falling flake by flake past the long Palladian windows.

"Good God, Freddy, what have you been eating?"

"Me?" Freddy answered, not like a prince but like a park squirrel pointing its little grey fingers at its little white chest.

"I see no other pachyderms in the room."

"He's not a pachyderm, dear," said the queen, "he's a pinworm."

"Pinworm like hell. He's a cetacean."

"No, dear, he isn't a cetacean, he's a crustacean."

"Whatever he is, he's peeled the wrappers off a thousand too many Violet Crumbles."

"I don't even like those," Freddy protested.

"That doesn't mean you wouldn't eat them, does it? You eat anything that moves."

Freddy looked at his father with puzzlement. "They don't move—they're not game, they're manufactured sweets—and I haven't had one in twenty years."

"Would you stake your existence on that?"

"When I say I haven't had one in twenty years, it means approximately twenty years."

"Yes, and when I say you've gained weight it means you're a bloody hippopotamus."

"He's not a hippopotamus," said Philippa, crisply, "he's a hummingbird."

"I'm in excellent shape for someone of middle age, as you very well know. I could go right back into service without adjustment."

"No, Freddy, the last time we used fuel bladders was in the Normandy Invasion."

"Really," said Freddy, "you'd think I was fat. Because I exercise all the time I have to eat a lot, but that doesn't make me fat."

"You look fat."

"I have a different body type than you have."

"That's right, you're fat. You've got a fat body type."

"No, I'm not fat. My body type is somewhat like Mummy's. What's wrong with that?"

"I'll tell you what's wrong with that. Mummy is a woman. . . ."

"Yes," the queen said.

"And you are—that is, you are supposed to be—a man. Sydney looks like Mummy. Sydney is a girl. That's good, because Mummy is a girl. You, on the other hand, are a boy. You are supposed to look not like Mummy but like me, who are a boy."

"Who are a boy?"

"Who am a boy?"

"Who am a boy?"

"You and me, that's who."

"But I'm different than you. If I were the same, I would be your clone."

"Freddy," said Paul, who understood this as the proper pronunciation of *clown,* "you're not my clone, you're Fredericka's clone."

"Fredericka's clone? I am?"

"Yes."

"Not physically."

"Yes, physically."

"Do you think so?" Freddy asked, feeling his hips and looking at his sleeves.

"Precisely, Freddy, exactly. Big shoes, red nose, plucked eyebrows, the works."

Freddy stared at his father, not knowing how to respond. The queen leant toward her husband and whispered in his ear. Whatever she said, it contained the word *circus.*

These things happened, and with Paul they happened every day. Once, for example, Freddy had absent-mindedly rounded a corner in the private secretaries' corridor as his father absent-mindedly rounded it at high speed in the opposite direction. Colliding like two jousting knights, they knocked one another to the floor. The duke then lunged ferociously at his son, grabbed him by the lapels, and shouted, "Who the hell are you? Why are you here? And where the hell are you going?"

"I'm your son," Freddy had said, "I live here, and I'm going to breakfast."

Now, Paul said, "Sit down, and take off your cloak."

Freddy, who was not wearing a cloak, felt a shudder of fear. Could it be that his father, like Wolf Larsen, the captain of *Sea Wolf,* was blind, and had been fooling everyone all along? Not likely, as his father played polo, shot well, and read books about horses, dogs, and ducks, all without assistance. But one could never be sure, so Freddy walked up to him, as if the duke could not see, and waved a hand in front of his face.

Using only the muscles of his neck, Paul drew back his head in irritation and disbelief. Then he waved his hand before Freddy's face, and said, "What! Monkey see, monkey do?"

"No," said Freddy, relieved that his father was not blind, "it's the new way of saying hello."

"Sit down, and shut up!"

Freddy sat down, and began to drum his fingers.

"Don't do that," commanded the queen, "it reminds me of Mussolini." She sighed. "What are we to do?"

"I'll tell you," her husband answered. "You, young man, will have your things brought from Moocock, St James's, and Kensington, and stay here until it blows over."

"Until what blows over?"

"Until *what* blows over?"

"What?"

"Do you think all you've done of late has gone unnoticed?"

"I don't see that what I do in private is anyone's business," said Freddy. "After all, I don't go around sticking video cameras in other people's faces. I suppose if I did, it would be a scandal: 'Prince of Wales Invades Privacy of British Subject.'"

"What exactly were you doing in that film?" the queen asked.

"Nothing."

"Nothing?" Paul repeated. "Were you not shouting obscenities at an innocent wedding party and a shrub? Were you not lying on the ground and rubbing cheese on your face, all the while screaming, 'Fuck you'?"

"I can explain. Do you know Fredericka's horrid little dog?"

"That horrid little dog," said the queen.

"His name," Freddy began, and then he held up his index finger to signal them to wait, took a pen from his jacket, and wrote on a card the dog's name, passing it to Paul.

"Ah, I see," said the duke. "Pha-Kew." He passed the card to the queen.

"Pha-Kew," she said. "Who named him that?"

"Fredericka," Freddy answered. "She named him after one of her nutritionists, who died of malnutrition."

"Not surprising," Paul said. "Nutritionists don't know anything about nutrition. They're prejudiced against meat. Five pounds of meat a day is what I say. But what of all this other stuff? What were you doing in deer antlers?"

"Viscount Baring's fourth birthday party. The children loved it."

"Are you in Fanny Baring's knickers?" Paul asked.

"Of course not."

"Why did you let them videograph it?"

"It would have been impossible not to: it was a birthday party. The *Omelette* air-brushed out everyone but me. I can't fathom any of this. Fredericka goes to a children's hospital, poses for photographs with some poor child for less than a minute, drops him like a hot rivet, and all over the world she's lauded as the new Albert Schweitzer. I put on a deer costume and suffocate for an hour so a bunch of four-year-olds can ride on my back, bite me, kick me, and spit on me, and then I knock myself out against a brick wall to make them laugh, and who am I? The Marquis de Sade."

"Did you throw an encyclopaedia at Fredericka?"

Freddy laughed. "Yes, the *Britannica*. It took eight minutes."

"Why was it stated in the House?"

"I slammed *The Shorter Oxford English Dictionary* down on the table because I was enraged that she thought she had two bosoms. I was trying to get across to her the point you asked me to make, but I couldn't because she doesn't really understand English."

"Has she at least made less display of her bosom?" the queen inquired.

"Oh God no," Paul answered. "I just saw her on the television. She had everything hoisted up in front of her as if she were carrying a plate of uncooked grouse. Does she imagine this to be aristocratic?"

"I think yes," said Freddy. "She doesn't understand how much better we are than aristocrats. I haven't been able to explain that to her, because, you see, she herself is just an aristocrat."

Philippa addressed her son. "Freddy, as a woman, I must ask this question. Are you doing anything that might alienate her affections? Sometimes one's woundedness can be manifest in outrageous behaviour."

"I'm not wounded," Freddy answered.

"I want to know if Fredericka has been wounded by anything you've done."

"No."

"Think, Freddy."

"No. I haven't done anything."

"What about Phoebe Boylingehotte?" Paul asked.

Freddy put his hand over his mouth so the queen could not read his lips, and said, silently, "Does she know?"

"Of course I know," said the queen. "In time I know bloody everything."

"Oh."

"From this moment forward," the queen declared, "speaking not as your mother but as your sovereign," and Freddy always knew the difference, "you will not see that woman. Is that clear?"

"Yes, ma'am."

"Ever," the queen said, holding her right index finger bolt upright and moving it as if quickly signing a document.

"Ever," said Freddy.

"Good."

"Ever?"

"Get it right!" Paul insisted.

"I understand." Freddy thought of Lady Boylingehotte's intense desire and total lack of self-consciousness, which would never be duplicated, even by Fredericka, who, though voluptuous, was not Boylingehotte.

"What are you thinking about?" Paul asked.

"Mozart," said Freddy.

"Well, get off that and consider this. You have been giving every anti-royalist in the world succour and sustenance, and I don't care how it happened or how blameless you may be, it's got to stop. Get Fredericka here. Stay on these grounds for as long as it takes, and keep low."

"But she likes to go out."

"That may be," said Philippa, "but I'm fond of the throne."

"She'll go mad. You know, it isn't as if she can amuse herself by doing quadratic equations. I don't think she's ever read a book."

"We'll see," said the queen. "It may be too late, anyway. Apehand has this in his sweaty palms, and you cannot predict what he'll do with it. We need quiet above all. No more disturbances, or for the first time in my reign I shall have to call upon Mr Neil. Bring Fredericka to the palace. The both of you must drop out of sight."

"Who is Mr Neil?" Freddy asked of his father. "You mentioned him in your letter. I can't place him. Is he a privy councillor? Who is he?"

"Freddy," the queen said, "you shall know in time."

"But who is he?"

The duke stood. "Get about it, Freddy, and while you're here we'll do some physical training and drop a stone or two of fat from your whale-like corpus."

"It's not fair. I haven't got an ounce of fat on me."

"Nonsense. You're a hippo."

"He's not a hippo, he's a hare."

"No he's not, he's a rhino."

"He's not a rhino, he's a rattlesnake."

As this continued—both the queen and Paul knew a great deal about animals—Freddy walked off into the long halls that were to be his prison.

AFTER A LONG CONFINEMENT in which Fredericka read and reread every extant issue of *She,* and Freddy ran so many circuits of the grounds that had his course been a straight line he would have reached Madrid, the Prince and Princess of Wales very nearly dropped from the news. Psnake and Didgeridoo were aware that, though they had not shot their last bolt, without something fresh their campaign would fail and might possibly backfire. But because the two principals had been cooped for weeks within the palace, completely out of touch, there was nothing fresh. Once in a while, like Mao Tse-tung, they appeared in the distance to let the world know they were still alive, but in the main the royal public relations gnomes promoted a period of tranquillity during which Freddy was said to be translating Latin epigrams, and Fredericka carrying out botanical experiments on arugula.

Despite huge headlines speculating upon their reasons for withdrawal—"Is Fredericka With Heir?"—they held their own. When *The Noon Behemoth* implied that Freddy had contracted leprosy, that Fredericka refused to nurse him, and that both had converted to Hinduism, public sympathy began to flow toward the royals and away from the obviously mendacious *Behemoth* and other like and gigantic organs. The queen was happy. She thought the battle might turn. After all, this was the throne of England, which had prevailed throughout history, starting earliest, rising most high, and lasting through. Freddy was no blowsy, dissolute, intoxicated, Eurotrash flea.

To the contrary, he was eloquent; perspicacious; a fit officer in the SAS reserve, who knew five modern languages, Latin, and Ancient Greek, and was the author of well received historical studies and essays on historiography. Apart from Lady Boylingehotte, whom he had now dropped, he did not womanise, he drank little, had no experience with drugs, and had exactly the grave, devoted, sacrificial temperament appropriate to a monarch.

But Fredericka, though statuesque and golden, was narcissistic in the extreme, astoundingly superficial, and totally uncaring. That is to say that although she was known throughout the world for emoting about endangered pandas, the wives of African political prisoners, people with various diseases, and whales, she actually cared very little about anything. This they had discovered by her behaviour and in conversation.

How much could she have cared about anything but Fredericka and not known where the North Sea was? No, Manitoba was not the African chief who killed and ate Rudolf Hess, and electricity did not come from rabbits rubbing together. Vladimir Lenin, she had told the Soviet ambassador, had done some of the greatest guitar riffs she had ever heard. All Fredericka cared about, really, was being adored.

And she was the darling of the world. Although she could seem less intelligent than garden mulch, this was not because she was dumb, it was because she had a way of gliding through things, and spent no more energy than was required to drift along in silken orbits, adored by masses of people who were in many ways just like her and not at all like Freddy. The queen understood such popular appeal but was not yet ready to believe that the practice of looking up to exceptionalism and virtue had been supplanted in power by the idea of worshipping the lesser, the least, the mediocre, the vacant, and the corrupt.

FREDDY WAS AN EARLY RISER, monastic by temperament, and quite happy with their new routine. Fredericka was not. With no ribbon cuttings, trips, state dinners, or even the slightest public contact, she did begin to go slightly mad, especially after many hours of listening to Freddy practising hearty Japanese phrases that ended with many exclamation points. So she made him play a lot of tennis and she did a lot of stretching. In fact, during Freddy's four-hour Aikido–Japanese Language study period each day, seven days a week, she stretched.

"How can you stretch for four hours a day?" Freddy had asked her.

"How can you study Japanese and Aikido for four hours a day?"

"I'm honing my body and mind."

"That's nice, I'm stretching mine. Where is it written that honing is better than stretching?"

"In the book of the world."

"Show me this book."

"You are in the process of being shown the book. You aren't even on page one."

"No, I've seen a great deal of the book, and I have yet to see where it is written that honing is more godly than stretching."

"Perhaps if you had honed more and stretched less, you would have seen it."

Despite a continuing undercurrent of domestic friction, things were on the mend. By May the newspapers were out of stories, having repeated themselves so many times that the public was shagey-eyed. Psnake and Didgeridoo had always known that the royals were clever. The press lords had their plans, but no matter. Freddy and Fredericka did nothing to supply fresh grist for the mill.

In early May, Fredericka insisted upon more tennis than ever, having read in *She* that this was the best way to utilise anti-oxidants. Freddy was only too willing to oblige, and each day at the end of Japanese and stretching they played for two hours. They had a good tennis court, hidden away. Except for the roar of traffic, somewhat muted by the massive wall that enclosed the palace grounds, they might as well have been in Arden.

Freddy had inherited and learned his noted thrift (he preferred to sleep on the floor, wrapped in an aged army blanket; he happily ate rations straight from the tin; and his favourite jacket was twenty-nine years old and looked it) from both his father and his mother, but especially from his father. Paul was so thrifty that he saved used matchsticks, cut off the heads, and sent them as gifts to children with hamsters. Once, his gift to the eight-year-old grandson of Field Marshal Montgomery had been switched inadvertently with his present to the president of the United States. The puzzled little boy had received a large humidor of the finest cigars, and the president a box of used kitchen matches, with a note that read: "From HRH Prince Paul, Duke of Belfast, for the little fat one with a broken tooth, affectionately known as Hermann Göring. Have fun, because when you grow up you may become a statesman, and all fun will cease."

Like his father, Freddy didn't like to part with things, even tennis balls. "I like playing with dead balls," he said one hot day at about the midway point of tennis with Fredericka. "You have to move faster and hit harder."

"I don't," she said, "not at all, especially when they come over the net and just flop down."

"You've got to run them."

"Which is why you have that waffle-print on your cheek."

"It will go away."

"Freddy, we need new balls. We can afford them."

"We'll get some tomorrow."

"We need them now. We're playing tennis now."

"We don't have any, and it would take too long to send for them."

"I don't understand. You just received a huge package of Dunlops from Lord Mewshaw."

"We can't use those."

"Why not?"

"They're imprinted with photographs of Psnake and Didgeridoo. If one were to go over the wall, all these months of confinement would be for naught."

"Then we won't hit them over the wall."

"I don't hit them over the wall, Fredericka, you do."

"We'll switch sides, and I'll play with my back to the wall. Really, Freddy, I'm tired of playing with tennis balls from the forties. I simply will not ever touch them again, full stop."

"Most of them are from the sixties," Freddy informed her. He paused, hoping that this might satisfy her, but it didn't, because they were more than thirty years old and some of them didn't even have any fuzz left.

As Freddy left to get the Psnake and Didgeridoo balls, he worried. Not to worry. If Fredericka had her back to the wall, what could happen? In the tennis pavilion he drank some water, seized the box of imprinted balls, and started back, energised for another match. Fredericka was a good tennis player, with long arms, long legs, and distracting blue eyes. Her shorts were short and her shots were hard. Sometimes they went wild, but he loved the intense way she bore down on an incoming round.

They switched sides, and before play Freddy ostentatiously calculated the ballistics. With Fredericka's back to the wall and the wall's height and distance from her, he claimed, no matter with what force she connected, a ball she hit could not leave the palace grounds. Even were she to slam it supernaturally, which sometimes she could, the ball would not have anything flat enough or hard enough from which to ricochet. "Hit it as violently as you please," he said, lobbing a Psnake-imprinted ball her way. She did. In fact, she had been hitting decades-old dead balls with such extra panache that she failed to make the adjustment and smashed this first shot so hard that, striking Freddy flat in the centre of his forehead, it knocked him both down and out.

"Freddy! Freddy!" Fredericka cried out as she jumped the net (which she could do from a standstill). "Oh Freddy! Freddy! What have I done?" He was still out, so she ran to the pavilion and seized what she took to be a red pitcher of cold water, which actually was a clear pitcher of the juice of American tomatoes. Though he had revived and was lying with his eyes open, wondering what had happened, she emptied half a gallon of tomato juice onto his face. He sputtered, choked, and rose. The first thing he did, in disgust, was to take off his soaked shirt and toss it away.

"What happened?" he asked.

"You were hit on the head with a ball and knocked out."

"A dead ball from the sixties?"

"No, the Psnake ball."

"The Psnake ball, the Psnake ball," said Freddy, still woozy from the blow. He tried to think things out. "Where is it?"

"It bounced from your head and went sailing back over the wall, just as you said it couldn't. So much for ballistics."

"We have to get it."

"How? The gates are locked from the inside as well." They were, so that they could not be opened for terrorists.

"I know where the key is," Freddy said.

They hurried to the wall, where Freddy retrieved a key from behind a loose stone.

"Freddy," Fredericka cautioned, "you can't go out there. You'll be seen."

"Not a problem. There's no traffic. They're tarring the road. I can get the ball and pop right back in."

"This isn't a good idea."

"What, to step beyond the wall of the palace? Don't be ridiculous." He turned the key in the massive lock and smoothly retracted the bolt. The door opened on oiled hinges. Freddy leaned out and pulled himself back in. "I've made a reconnaissance," he reported. "There isn't a bit of traffic. The road is covered in fresh tar and the workmen are gone. A derelict is lying in the high grass, eating a box of fried chicken. He may not even see me, and if he does, so what?"

"I don't like it."

"Nothing to fear. I'll be back in a minute." As he stepped out, he remembered that he had to give the key to Fredericka so she could let him back in. Pivoting to accomplish this, he inadvertently slammed the heavy iron door shut on his foot and his shorts. The pain propelled him outward. "No!" he cried, to the sound of shredding fabric. Losing his balance, he realised that he was naked and about to fall into a bed of fresh tar.

By lifting his head and pushing his arms out before him, his front was tarred only from instep to neck. But while struggling to his feet, he fell back into the tar in a sitting position. When finally he managed to stand, he stood completely naked except for a pair of blackened tennis shoes and a partial appliqué of glistening pitch. He stumped angrily to the door. As he reached it he heard the derelict squealing. "Look! He's got a black arse! Look! Look at it!"

Turning to him with an obscene gesture, Freddy screamed, "Rot in hell!" Fredericka, whose feelings had been wounded when Freddy had so abruptly slammed the door, thought this was directed to her, which made her cross. When the key came flying over the wall, she picked it up, tossed it into a bank of pachysandra, and stalked off to an appointment with one of her hairdressers.

"Fredericka? Fredericka?" Freddy called. "Fredericka? Fredericka!" When, after a minute, she didn't answer, he began to bang on the door.

"*You* rot in hell, that's what I say!" the derelict squealed. "Now you know what it feels like to be on the outside with people like me. Going around naked. *You* rot in hell!"

After five minutes during which the still somewhat bleary Freddy, who thought he might be dreaming, stood at the door in the hope that Fredericka might open it, the road workers began to filter back to the head of the street. They put on their fluorescent vests and started to move cones and fire up their roller. Freddy knew that he was in a bad situation, but what could he have done? He was naked, tarred, and the wall was too high and too smooth to climb.

Suddenly, like Fredericka, he needed clothes above all things, and the only source of clothes was hatefully staring at him as it ate its chicken.

Regretful that he had been curt with one of his mother's subjects, Freddy approached him, and said, "Oh, hello there."

"What's in your hair, tomato juice?"

"Yes," Freddy answered. "It is."

"Why did you put tomato juice in your hair?"

"It was an accident."

"It can be," squealed the derelict, mysteriously. "You're the Prince of Wales, you are."

"I am."

"Well, now you're out here with me, only I've got the chicken!" He squealed like a hyena. "I've got the chicken! I've got the chicken! Chicken! Chicken! Chicken!"

Freddy sensed that perhaps this was not going to be easy. "Yes, you have. You have the chicken. I don't want the chicken."

"And you're not going to get it!" the derelict screamed. "And not the box either! And not my pillow!" He held up a filthy down pillow.

"You can have those," Freddy said as if he were a bank manager talking to a man draped in bandoliers of dynamite. "I don't want those, but I'll tell you what. If you give me your clothes, I'll give you a hundred pounds and ten roast chickens."

"I like my chicken fried."

"Very well, ten fried chickens."

"And what would I wear?"

"I'll send you to Hobby and Richard for ten suits. Hobby and Richard will come to you. They'll measure you."

"It's a trick."

"It isn't. As you can see, I need clothes."

"What about me? So do I."

"A thousand pounds, ten fried chickens, and ten suits."

"Me mum always said don't go 'round naked. It was a rule in my family."

"Ten thousand pounds, a hundred fried chickens, and twenty suits."

"I'll get back to you."

"I don't have time for that!"

"And you don't have any clothes, either, do you?"

"A hundred thousand pounds, a thousand fried chickens, and fifty suits."

"Not good enough."

"What do you want?"

The derelict grew focussed. "I want ten million," he said, vessels throbbing across his forehead.

"Ten million pounds?" Freddy asked, aghast.

The derelict shook his head to indicate that he did not want ten million pounds.

"Ten million what?"

The derelict smiled broadly and almost toothlessly.

"Ten million fried chickens?"

"With waistcoats," the derelict said.

"What do you mean, *ten million fried chickens with waistcoats*?"

"I want each one," he said, "to have a waistcoat. Before I eat them, I'll take off the waistcoats, and put them in a Turkish closet."

"You're insane," said Freddy.

"Oh," said the derelict, "am I? I may be, but everybody knows about you for sure."

"How can I possibly come up with ten million fried chickens?"

"You're the Prince of Wales," the derelict said, as if this answered the question.

"That's every chicken in England, with waistcoats."

"They don't have to be fancy waistcoats. They can be basic black. Buttons, toggles, I don't care. Chickens look good in waistcoats."

"Fried."

"Golden and crispy."

"What about ten million pounds and a million fried chickens?" Freddy asked, feeling completely out of control when, just a few minutes before, he had been the prince inside the palace grounds, the envy of the world.

"What's money to me?" the derelict asked.

"All right!" Freddy shouted. The construction workers were getting closer. "I agree."

"Good," said the derelict. "Payment in advance."

"Madness," Freddy said.

"Is it? The last time, the other Prince of Wales—I forgot his name—sank my boat. That's why I have to be this way."

"I can't just create ten million fried chickens, with waistcoats."

"I understand that. I'll make allowances. I'll take half."

"I can't do that, either."

"Ah! Just to show you who's dealing in good faith here, I'll take ten percent."

"A million fried chickens?"

"One percent, in advance, on the barrel head."

"A hundred thousand fried chickens?"

"I'm being entirely reasonable, am I not? One percent?"

"I can't give you even one fried chicken in advance."

"How about a drumstick?"

"Nor that."

"You aristocrats are all alike. All you do is talk."

Freddy lunged for the derelict's pillow, with the intent of taking it from him by force to make a loincloth. They fought and tumbled, contesting the pillow until in one particularly savage exchange of pushes and pulls the pillowcase broke in half and a mass of yellow-white down was laid bare to the sun . . . and wind. "Oh no!" Freddy cried out as a sudden puff of air lifted the feathers and they flew toward him. Instinctively, he covered his face, but they would not have stuck to his face. And then he turned, re-membering that, dorsally, only his posterior had tar. "Now you've got them on your arse, too!" the derelict said in triumph. "Look at you, you look like a giant white chicken! I've never seen anything like you. No one has, no one in the world!"

"Bugger off," said Freddy, fully aware of what he looked like. "And give me that box of chicken."

"Do you want a drumstick or a thigh?"

"I want the box, to hide my face, damn you."

After using his thumbs to punch holes in the box, Freddy put it over his head and set out the long way around to the palace mews. From having looked at the schedule that morning, he knew that a German television crew was going to be filming the Changing of the Guard, and of course tourists were always at the main gate, with cameras. Loping along, he began to feel better. Most probably everyone was, indeed, looking at him, but they didn't know who he was. The farther he travelled the more hope-ful he became that he would emerge from this unfortunate episode un-scathed, but then he saw a police car coming down the road, and when it reached him it jammed on its brakes.

The window went down, and as the police car paced him in reverse Freddy heard the call. "This is P-Seventeen, Grosvenor Place and Duke of Wellington. We have a large, male, possibly RC Three—it's very hard to tell—running south on Grosvenor Place. Please send gas, nets, and crowd control goo. He is without doubt very fit and very crazy."

Freddy turned back and ran so fast that the wind lifted his feathers until they were parallel to the ground. The police couldn't follow him on the tar, and didn't, but this route channelled him to the main gate just as the guard had begun to change. He had thought for a moment that he might be ignored, but the German television crew swivelled its cameras and began to eat up the scene. Tourists as well ignored the magnificent ceremony in favour of the tarred and feathered nude runner with the fried-chicken box on his head.

When Freddy got to the first gate the police converged upon him, having come around the palace. He turned to go back, but was hemmed in. Why, he wondered, were people shrieking and shouting? They seemed to be afraid of him. A palace guard in a bearskin helmet pointed his automatic rifle at Freddy as if at a terrorist. Presumably he was doing this to protect, among others, Freddy. What is that sound, Freddy wondered like a man surrendering to sleep, that lovely, peaceful, summer sound? It was like crickets. But why crickets? Then he realised that it was the sound of camera shutters.

"Slowly, nut thing. Slowly. Remove the box from your head," the soldier commanded.

"May I speak to you privately?" Freddy asked.

"No, you may not." The soldier's adrenaline was flowing as if in combat. "Take the bloody box off," he said, bracing himself alarmingly as he tensed around his rifle.

Then an idiot tourist said, "Is there a bomb in the box?" despite the fact that, obviously, Freddy's head was in the box, and people began to scream, "He's got a bomb! He's got a bomb!"

"Take the box off!" the soldier ordered in the particular voice that comes before pulling a trigger.

"Serjeant," Freddy implored, as he looked at the world through sad, greasy holes, "the only thing in the box is my head. Why don't you just arrest me, but leave the box on. Please remove me from public view."

"I'm going to count to five, and then I'll fire."

"I'm going to count to four," Freddy said, "and then you're fired."

"Just a moment, Serjeant," one of the police said. "You don't have to do that."

"Do what, count to five and fire, or let him in?"

"Neither."

"He does have to let me in," Freddy said. "I live here."

"You shut up," the policeman said. And then, to the guard, "The net's here. After we fire it at him at forty miles per hour, the box will come right off."

"Enough," said Freddy, who already had a waffle-print on his cheek. "I'll remove the box. Oh God," he sighed. Then, in the obverse of Napoleon crowning himself, he raised his two hands, gripped the chicken box, and lifted it from his brow.

Shutters clicked into a frenzy until they sounded like surf. The Germans with the television camera stepped back as if pushed by a wave, but they kept on recording. Finally, the guard, now near tears, inquired of the Prince of Wales, "I didn't know it was you. What are you doing? Sir, what's going on?"

Freddy spoke gently. "I was practising," he said.

"For what?" the guard asked, not impertinently, but from pathos.

"I don't know," Freddy said. "I think I hit my head. You see, Fredericka refuses to play with my balls."

THE SPECIAL SOLVENTS used to remove the pitch were very painful and turned Freddy blazing pink. His father would not see him, which was not a problem, because Freddy himself would not see anyone, not even Fredericka, who was so contrite that she went without having her hair done for an entire day. And though he faintly wished that his mother would come to his sickbed, as of old, she did not. Days passed, and except for occasional communications with his doctors he spoke only to Sawyers, who brought him caviar and chopped truffles, his comfort foods.

"Sawyers," Freddy asked eventually, "where are the papers?"

"I brought you the *Journal of the Royal Services Institution,* and several monographs about computational warfare."

"But where are the papers?"

"You might not want to see them, sir."

Freddy winced as if jabbed by a knife. Then he stiffened. "Right. Carry on."

Never in the history of journalism had newspapers sold in such volume all over the world. People who had long since ceased to read suddenly began to buy ten different newspapers a day. And repetition seemed not to blunt their appetites. Front pages were filled with three genres of photograph: Freddy standing, tarred and feathered, with the box on his head; without the box; and walking dejectedly into the palace, feathers at the rear.

For the first genre the school of headlines included: "At It Again," "Guess Who's Coming to Dinner?" "Peekaboo!" "It *Is* Who You Think," "2000 Years of Inbreeding," "What Hath God Wrought?" "Rule, Britannia," and "Let's Play Chicken," among hundreds of others in every language, such as the magnificent French headline, *"Poulet Royal!"* The second, of Freddy's face exposed, was slightly more subtle: "Practising for What?" "Mater Said There'd Be Days Like This," and "Kidnapped by Aliens." The third group's headlines tended to the overtly political: "Just Go!" "Can Pimcot Survive?" "Walking Toward the Palace but Away from the Throne," and "Sun Sets on British Empire, Chicken Style."

Freddy did not need to see these. He knew. And he had no idea how to turn things around. He doubted very much that Mr Neil, whoever he might be, could restore to him the dignity that he had squandered. But for the time being Mr Neil was his only hope.

Five days after what Freddy had come to call "the incident," his father appeared. Freddy could hardly look up. "They found the tennis ball, too," Paul said, "with Psnake on it. His papers now suggest that the House of Finney be abolished and Fredericka take the throne. Your mother is not very happy. She hasn't been as upset since the war."

"What about the Commons?" Freddy asked.

"Pimcot's government may fall on a vote of confidence scheduled for tomorrow. In that case the Greenham Common ladies will run the government while Apehand spends most of his time in Bermuda in the company of women who have wasp-thin waists but are otherwise so buxom that the laws of physics would have to be abridged for them to get their heads wet."

"What did Pimcot say?"

"When?"

"At the audience."

"He could hardly speak. Mummy did most of the talking."

"Pimcot unable to speak?"

"He suspects he's finished. That's enough to shut up even him."

"I understand."

"No, you don't. He wanted you committed to a mental institution. He said it was the only way to save his government and the monarchy as well. That's the order he put them in, too, the bugger."

Freddy looked at his father anxiously.

"Your mother told him that mental institutions don't take people as overweight as you, and that in any case we wouldn't have it."

"Mummy said I was overweight?"

"To save you, Freddy. She still suffers the illusion that you are not. Pimcot was suitably put off. But we did have to make up some rubbish to tell the press."

"What rubbish? You do realise that whatever you told them will follow me long past my death."

"Of course I realise it. It's part of the price we pay. We said that you were in the care of several physicians who, consulting with Fredericka, would see you back to health."

"Consulting with Fredericka! Do you know how much Fredericka knows about medicine? When Baron Florizel Beeston was stricken with appendicitis and had to be rushed from Henley Regatta in a water ambulance, she said, 'Oh! It's so horrible! To think of them opening up the brain to find the little appendicitis and then killing it before it gets a heart attack!'"

"I know, Freddy, but people think she can heal the sick and bring back the dead. We said that you would be confined indefinitely to Balmoral, and that you were to follow a regime of nature foods and Banlucopyroxidine Metasalicylate Tri-Arf-Popsiculine."

"What was that?"

"Pimcot made it up."

"Am I to stay at Balmoral for the rest of my life? I suppose I wouldn't mind too much if I could go outside. Can I?"

"You're not going to Balmoral. We are awaiting Mr Neil."

"Who, exactly, is Mr Neil?"

"You know. You're being coy, aren't you?"

"No."

"In that case, I can't tell you. Only those who can by themselves discover who he is, know who he is. I think it should come clear when you meet him. We hope that he will appear. Your mother has never been in such straits. She must choose between her duties as queen—her obligation not only to millions upon millions but to history, her forbears, and her oath—and her son. She loves you very much, Freddy. I don't think that any force can overcome the bond between mother and child if the mother's love has been allowed to develop. Nor do I think it should. But, then, as queen she has a duty to God and country. Never have I seen her suffer so, and this, I believe, will bring Mr Neil."

"Can't she just summon him? Whoever he is, she is the queen of England."

"Oh, no, Freddy, she cannot. Not even the queen can summon Mr Neil, but only hope that he will come."

Parley at Windsor

Though it was announced that Freddy would go to Balmoral, upon instruction from his mother he went to Windsor to await the puzzling Mr Neil. Neither Philippa nor Paul would speak of Mr Neil, and when Freddy did they lifted an index finger—left or right, it did not matter—to their closed lips to signify that they would say nothing.

Freddy ransacked to no avail every biographical reference he could find. "Is he a marriage counsellor?" he asked one evening at dinner. "He isn't registered as such. Nor is he listed anywhere as attached either to the royal house, the government, the universities, or elsewhere. I found many a *Neil,* but none appropriate."

"How would you know?" Paul asked.

"Perhaps I was rash, but I ruled out hydrologists, economists, barristers, solicitors, surveyors, ships' captains. . . . It is a common name."

"Precisely."

"I looked in your address files."

"Did you ask my permission?"

"I'm your son. I take certain liberties."

"You may be my son, but that doesn't give you the right to look in my address files. What next, using my toothbrush? Borrowing my cufflinks? Sitting in my chair if you could fit? Mr Neil isn't in any address files, mine or anyone else's."

"To calm you, Freddy," said Philippa, smiling nasally, "I'll tell you a fact about Mr Neil, a person to whom we will trust the fate of the monarchy, and to whom the fate of the monarchy has been entrusted before. But only if you promise to leave off about him until he comes—if he does."

"One fact?"

"His profession. To restore your confidence in our judgement."

Freddy said, "I agree. What does he do?"

The queen looked at Freddy. Fredericka, who had pushed her dessert aside, was listening raptly. "Mr Neil," the queen said, "at the moment, at least, is employed as a mould maker in a rubber sex toy factory in Naples." Then she and her consort chortled royally and went back to their chocolate mousse.

After some time, Freddy said, "That isn't true, of course."

"Yes it is," said the queen. "It is true. It is literally and precisely true."

"But it is your way of telling us," Freddy insisted, slightly losing his mental footing and beginning to slide, "telling us something in an indirect way, or metaphorically, is it not?"

"Metaphorically my arse," said Paul, resplendent in a linen summer jacket that glowed against the ancient dark panelling. "He does that work, and don't underestimate him."

"Don't underestimate him," Freddy repeated. "Certainly not. Why would I be tempted to think any the less of a man to whom, evidently, I am to entrust the course of my life, just because he works in a rubber sex toy factory in Naples? That wouldn't make sense, would it?"

"Freddy," warned his father.

"No, really. Why bother with, say, the rector of a university, a former prime minister or Speaker of the House, a panel of Nobel laureates, a bishop, or a distinguished philosopher or historian, when you can get him. He doesn't! Does he?"

"Yes he does," said the queen.

"We've been waiting here a week for what reason, exactly? Why not send the ambassador in Rome to get him?"

"No more questions, Freddy. You promised," his father reminded him.

"It's not actually a question," Freddy declared, holding up both his hands in a gesture that said, Bear with me as I continue, and do not interrupt me. "Not a question. Here we are, the royal family of England, waiting like supplicants for someone whom the queen cannot summon." He interrupted himself. "You can summon the prime minister, the Archbishop of Canterbury. . . . You can summon just about anyone in the world except the Pope, who, perhaps coincidentally, also lives on the Italian Peninsula."

"What is your point, Freddy?" the queen asked dryly.

"That you cannot, you cannot summon Mr Neil, who works in a . . . what? I don't know, do I? I haven't a clue, have I?"

"No," the queen said. "Just wait."

"I will," Freddy assured her, relaxing his entire body into aristocratic submission, which somehow did not seem aristocratic. And then they adjourned for the after-dinner walk. Freddy and Fredericka went off into the park, alone together in the fading light.

"You know, Freddy," she began, "when we married, I knew that the cumulative effect of centuries of being king or queen would be detectable in a hereditary sense, perhaps even pronounced. But I thought that the privilege, rank, and amenities you enjoy would enable you to carry on, to muffle it, so to speak."

"What are you driving at?"

"Forgive me, Freddy, but I really think something is wrong with your family. It's not just you. It comes from them, doesn't it?"

"It wasn't that way—we were doing fine—until I met you."

"Coincidence and excuse."

"Perhaps it is," Freddy admitted.

"Do you think," Fredericka asked, "that they think we're sexually incompatible, and that they themselves may have had such a problem at some time, and this Mr Neil solved it for them, with . . . ?"

"Don't say it."

"Well, do you?"

"They're not idiots."

"Then who is he?"

"Perhaps he served with my father and was his confidant during the war."

"Do you think he's a long-lost relative? A brilliant member of the family but with a huge hump?"

"Every Finney, Fredericka, is meticulously recorded and accounted for, even the fifth cousins who married Gypsies and run tawdry grocery stores in the former East Germany."

"What about illegitimacy? What if King Harry had an illegitimate son, your mother's brother, who's, let's say, a diving instructor or something?"

"No, he works in a factory, remember?"

"I didn't say he had to be a diving instructor."

"Were he my grandfather's son, they would have taken better care of him, his name would not be Neil, and he wouldn't have been allowed to work in a rubber sex toy factory in Naples or anywhere else."

"Perhaps he's out of control, as you're supposed to be."

"Then why would they consult him?"

Freddy and Fredericka went to bed that night while it was still light, though the light was faint. Surprisingly, they slept deeply. When finally the sky grew ink-black, the trees were visible only as their swaying branches blotted out the stars that crossed in blazing showers, as sometimes they do. The language of the stars, seldom read and heeded less, told beautifully and in silence of all the victories that had ever been won and all the defeats ever suffered. In uncountable lines of light across the widest sphere, the stars spoke of everything notable even down to a leaf blowing rhythmically in the wind.

THE NEXT MORNING was as hard and bright as the evening of shooting stars had been soft and dark. Windsor Park sits in the midst of England like a jewel. The castle walls stretch on so much like a headland by the sea that it was almost strange not to see white birds sliding on the wind and squawking past vertiginous nests in the battlements.

No matter. At seven-thirty exactly came the noise and excitement of horses streaming from the gate. On two of the noblest horses in England, matched in their deep brown by the dark leather of their tack and the boots of their riders, were the Prince of Wales and the Duke of Belfast, perfectly attired and as used to riding fast as bank clerks are to cashing checks.

When they reached an isolated field, they swept by a stand of polo mallets and picked up what they needed. Freddy, on Napoleon, wheeled around and smashed the ball. This began a breathless ballet the likes of which can be equalled only by wolves in moonlit snow oversailing one another as if they can fly, and turning on the super quick. But these were not wolves moving as deftly as the shine of a needle that flies through soft wool, they were great animals heavy enough to make the ground shake.

In polo skirmishes and long and furious rides through mist, sunlight, and rain, Freddy's father, a man of remarkable strength and courage who would all his life stand beside his wife as she held sway, spoke to his son as he could not speak in words. Perhaps because he knew the world had been created before words, and because he wanted what he had to say to outlast them, he spoke in the grace of movement that he knew his son would remember indelibly. When they flew across the field at great speed, the father was speaking to the son. When he hit the ball dead centre and it left his mallet like a shot, it was the same. And all throughout, the message was, Here are the movements to follow—now explosive, now smooth, now perfect, now ragged, now abrupt, now surprising, now full of grace— and when I have left the field and these actions are not mine, they will be yours.

Because Paul was aware of what had been said and did not want to be embarrassed in the lull thereafter, he broke off. "Very good; see you at lunch," he said, and galloped away, leaving Freddy alone on Napoleon amid the trees where he had retreated to leave his mallet.

He walked the horse and listened to the beating of his own heart as it returned to rest. The world for Freddy was full of noted places, of views down corridors and of castles in the field, of particularly beautiful cornices that no one knew except the future king, who loved to see them from a certain angle against deep or brilliant skies. This put him at odds with the architects, because, for him, architecture was neither theory nor experi- ment, but beauties with which he was a familiar and upon which he was dependent. He had lived all his life amid the great architectural mass of royal Britain. What the theorists had in books and in neck-craning field trips had been his at every moment, dusk and dawn, in privacy, in loneli- ness, at all hours and in every kind of light, in snow, fog, and pouring rain, when the grey walls in their massive acreage looked like the sea made vertical.

And then came, literally, while Freddy was thinking about architecture, a bolt from the blue, lightning striking from a cloudless morning sky, near enough to bend the limbs of the trees and make the well trained horse sidle and shiver. As Freddy reined in the horse, too busy to survey the sur- roundings, he thought it might have been a bomb. He galloped out of the copse of trees, ready to race back to the castle in a hail of fire, but there were no volleys, rattles, or bursts.

"Did you hear that?" Freddy asked an old man standing in the middle of a freshly raked patch of bare soil as brown as coffee beans.

"No, but you did."

Though certainly used to seeing the royal family, the Windsor groundskeepers did not speak with such impertinence. Not only had he not addressed Freddy as "Your Royal Highness," he hadn't said "sir," and he seemed provocatively unimpressed.

Eighty or older, he was straight, strong, and in good health. Too old to have been a gardener, he was dressed in a ratty purple velvet jacket, a shirt

with Edwardian collar, striped black trousers, and tennis shoes. He was a
Bohemian according to Freddy's definition of such people, which was that
their hair seemed to be in pain. Perhaps he was a relative of someone on
the staff, who understood neither the rules of the palace nor that he was
speaking to Freddy. But that was unlikely, if only because of his air of authority. The hair, in pain or not, was wild and white, the face ancient and
powerful, the posture as straight as if he were wearing a brace.

But then Freddy, who remained mounted, felt some relief, having de-
duced that this was simply a retired groundskeeper who had returned, as
former employees sometimes did, to exercise at former tasks. Freddy had
not recognised him, because he would have taken his pension long ago. His
clothes were alarming merely because he had been free for decades. He was
presumptuous and belligerent because he was saying that these had been his
grounds to care for before Freddy had even come into the world, and he
wanted Freddy to know it. And the strongest proof of this lay in the fact
that he had himself tilled the exquisitely brown patch in which he stood.
He had to have, because he stood in the middle, and in the soft and impres-
sionable loam not a footprint was to be seen. Freddy confidently acquainted
him with his excellent deductions.

"Oh really?" was the answer. "Where's my rake?"

"Behind your back," Freddy said pompously. It had to have been behind his back: the tilled area was large enough so that not even an Olympic
javelin thrower could have propelled a rake out of sight.

The pensioner turned around to show that he was rakeless.

"How did you do that?" Freddy asked.

"Do what?"

"Get to the middle of tilled ground while leaving no footprints."

By this time, the old man was halfway to Freddy, having left a line of
footprints deep in the soil. "There," he said. "I did leave footprints. Always
have. Are you calling me a smynk?"

Freddy had never heard the word. "The footprints are only in one direction, out from the centre," he insisted.

"If you are calling me a smynk, young man, you'll have hell to pay."

No one spoke to the Prince of Wales that way except his father, and
certainly not retired gardeners. Perhaps he was senile. "I am the Prince of
Wales," Freddy said, to put the man back in his traces.

"You," the old man said, "are a pipsqueak, a shit bug, and a glothwind.
You have rubbed me the wrong way already. You," he continued, "are an

arrogant, snot-eating snail, and you had better pray that I am in a better humour when I meet you, Flip, and the others in St George's Chapel, on the instant, as fast as you can move your blooming royal arses."

Needless to say, Freddy was stunned. Never in his life had he heard such talk. In school and in the various branches of the military in which he had served he had been treated with unusual severity, but never, never, had his mother—for God's sake, the queen—been brought into it. No one had dared.

Aghast and amazed, Freddy knew who it was. "You are Mr . . ." he started to say, but, before he could finish, Mr Neil touched the horse, and as if stabbed with a hat pin the animal rocketed forward completely out of control.

"Do as I say, shit bug!" Freddy heard from behind him.

Usually Freddy could control Napoleon or any other horse. He had ridden all his life, was extremely strong, and totally unafraid. But he could not control this horse, and it did not stop its flight until it was home safe, overturning a dozen buckets and stools and nearly decapitating the Prince of Wales as it entered its stall.

LIMPING AT HIGH SPEED into the family quarters after banging his leg against a post as he ran from the stable, Freddy discovered his mother and father in conversation with Pimcot and Apehand. They were somewhat startled when he rushed in, gimpy, flushed to purple, sweating hard, and with laboured breath, shouting, "He's here! He's coming! Into the chapel, into the chapel, all of us! He stabbed Napoleon with a hat pin, and Napoleon almost killed me, damn him!"

The queen knew from their expressions that her prime minister and the leader of her loyal opposition now believed that every rumour about Freddy was true. She could see them calculating the political repercussions attendant to a flagrantly mad prince.

Before she could intervene, Pimcot and Apehand stood, and Pimcot said, "It's nice to see Your Royal Highness. How are you, sir?"

But Freddy was so shaken that he ignored them, saying, "I've never had any problem with Napoleon, even when he was parted from Josephine. What do you expect, however, if he's stuck with a hat pin?"

"Who stuck who with a hat pin?" Apehand asked.

"Interesting that you should ask," Freddy answered. "A mould maker in a rubber sex toy factory in Naples, that's who, a nonagenarian in a purple velvet jacket and Edwardian collar, a perfectly vile creature, that's who."

"It is he," the queen pronounced. "What did he say?"

"He said to get your royal arses to St George's Chapel as fast as you could. Can you believe the impertinence, the gall?"

But as Freddy was complaining, the queen was already rushing out the door. He had never seen her run. Neither Pimcot nor Apehand had ever seen her run. Her husband had never seen her run. No one had ever seen her run. She had never run. Now she was running, and she loved it. "Get Fredericka, too!" she shrieked like someone being tickled. "I love this! It feels so good! I'm going to do it every day!"

The guards on duty watched the queen run through the inner court and shriek with apparent joy, followed by Paul, a limping Prince of Wales, the prime minister, a heavily panting Apehand, and Fredericka, in a sun dress, clutching her hat.

"What do you think this might be?" asked one Royal Marine of another.

"Obviously, what Freddy has is catching."

"It's too bad we don't have a video camera. Psnake would pay a million quid."

"Well look at *him*," said the other guard, pointing at a fusilier on the roof, who was carefully filming the scene. "His ship's just come in."

The chapel door was locked, but the queen produced a key from out of her handbag as if she had known that she someday would need it in a pinch. When they were all in, clumped near the entrance, she closed the door and locked it from the inside.

"How will Mr Neil get in?" Freddy asked in the tones of a Roman conspirator. They felt strange in the vast chapel, which was colder than the outside, perfectly silent, and dark but for the light filtering in agelessly through coloured glass.

"He's already in," the queen told him, although no one could see him.

"But how can that be? The door was locked."

They walked forward, and as their eyes adjusted they saw—in rose, blue, and yellow light that flowed as if through reefloads of translucent water and gaily coloured fish; beneath heavy, straight, and parti-coloured flags; between multiple banks of yellow-lacquered choir stalls; upon the grave of

Henry VIII and Charles I; and amid the blue and white tiles set in the floor of the airy and towering vault—a man. He stood as if floating in blue light, his white hair almost glowing, his purple jacket as shiny and mysterious as the skin of an aubergine, which knows not whether it is purple, blue, or black. His eyebrows stood out, at a hundred feet, better than the most clubulous aristocratic colonel's. As he breathed, light seemed to ebb and flow around him like water against a rocky coast. The room was charged with a presence, and it had no relation to the queen. Nor was it due to any of her family or the prime minister, and certainly it was not on Apehand's account. This candle was lit by Mr Neil, whoever he was, and burned with an exciting brightness that Freddy hoped might make things right.

Even were it not good news that he would glean from whatever was to happen here, at least Freddy might be freed from waiting powerlessly in royal suspended animation. The prospect of resolution was for him like coming out of an airless tunnel onto high cliffs above a bright June sea. His sense and courage seemed to flood back as if from nowhere, making him ashamed of all the foolish things he had done. Just a moment before, he had burst into the family quarters like a lunatic, speaking words that might be misconstrued, sounding too eager and very likely insane.

The first impulse that overtook him was to counter the power of Mr Neil. His parents, Pimcot, Apehand, and even Fredericka might fall under the spell of this person, this Rasputin, but he, Freddy, would not. Freddy, who supposedly was insane, would be the rock of sanity, the sceptic, the Holmesian barrister. Whoever Mr Neil was, he was undoubtedly a fraud of the type that takes advantage of beleaguered and declining aristocracy. People like that were exceedingly dangerous.

Freddy watched as his mother, Philippa, by the grace of God, of the United Kingdom of Great Britain and Northern Ireland and of Her Other Realms and Territories Queen, Head of the Commonwealth, and Defender of the Faith, approached the man who stood upon the grave of her ancestors Henry VIII and Charles I. He did not bow, and he certainly did not address her properly. "Hello, Flip," he said, "haven't seen you since you were a tot."

"Hello, Flip?" Freddy said to himself, with no sound, his eyes darting and wandering, his brows knit into a puggle.

"I've seen your picture in the newspapers, but that's not the same. You were a pretty girl with a sweet face, and now you're a handsome woman with a sweet face."

Freddy waited for the upbraiding that was sure to come on the heels of such ripe familiarity, but rather than that he witnessed the unthinkable. His mother looked down demurely, closed her eyes like a bashful schoolgirl, and curtsied.

She what? She curtsied, deeply. To whom? To an insolent mould maker in a Neapolitan rubber sex toy factory? And then he put his arm around her shoulders and led her, as if she were star-struck, to a place in the front stall that was not even hers, and in which she, the queen of England, obediently took a seat.

Mr Neil merely pointed at the other seats in the same row where he wanted everyone present to sit, and they went there like zombies. Freddy didn't like this at all, and remained standing.

"Sit there," Mr Neil said offhandedly, pointing at the last unoccupied place.

"Thank you, I'll stand," Freddy announced, his anger apparent.

Mr Neil froze, like a perfectly still stalk of *Aurorians bucra,* or an ancient bubble trapped in stone.

"Freddy, sit where he tells you," his father ordered.

"Freddy!" the queen seconded.

Mr Neil slowly lifted his left foot from ground that was the grave of two kings, until he was standing like an old stork.

Freddy was undeterred. "I am the Prince of Wales," he declared. "Who are you?"

"I am Mr Neil. Who are you?"

"I just told you."

"Who?"

"You."

"You are me?"

"No," said Freddy. "I am not you. You are you, and I am I, and I am the Prince of Wales."

"I know that song!" Mr Neil exclaimed. "I used to sing it in the navy." And then, bursting with energy as if he were in a music hall before five thousand people, he sang.

Oh, I am not you, pass me the stew,
In the navy they serve it in pails,
You are you, and I am I,
And I am the Prince of Wales!

Oh, I am not you, the ship's built with glue,
You'd best never lean on the rails,
For you are you, and I am I,
And I am the Prince of Wales!

"Will you shut up," Freddy said.

"Yes, I will. Do you know why? Because you are the Prince of Wales. You are the Prince of Wales! You! You are! You are the Prince! Of Wales!" Mr Neil proclaimed. "Well. My oh my. The Prince of Wales himself."

Freddy was immobile. He might not force Mr Neil into anything, but then again neither could Mr Neil force him.

"I am standing on the grave of two great kings, my boy," Mr Neil said. (Freddy could not place his accent, which was, perhaps, a fusion of Welsh and Cornish.) "Hank and Chuck. Compared to them, you are nothing but a bad pup. Whereas you have yet to accomplish anything, they were kings who made of kingliness something more when they finished with it than what it was when they began."

"And what of it?"

"Undoubtedly you know that one of Chuck's vertebrae was made into a salt cellar, and that a finger bone of Hank the Eighth is now the handle of a cheese knife."

"I thought it was a dessert knife," Freddy said, happy to catch Mr Neil.

"Cheese," said Mr Neil, "which is often a dessert. But you see, Prince Goat Vomit, even if you are lucky—that is, lucky to be alive after provoking me, lucky to live until you can be king, lucky to become king, and lucky to be great—even if you are lucky enough and good enough to pass the tests and to last on, you are still nothing more than goat vomit whose more stolid substance should be flattered to serve as a salt cellar or a cheese knife."

"And what about you?" Freddy asked, contemptuously. "I picture you eventually as a bowl brush, or perhaps the ivory button on a sex toy."

"They don't have ivory buttons."

"Yes, and you should know, shouldn't you. We're all mortal and have the same end. I have no illusions to the contrary. Even if I did, it wouldn't excuse you from proper conduct in my regard, or, for that matter, in anyone's regard."

No one said anything, not even Mr Neil, but the queen and Prince Paul looked at Freddy in a way that confidently contradicted him.

"Excuse me?" he asked of his parents. "He's not mortal? He won't die?"

They kept their expressions fixed exactly where they had been.

"Oh no," said Freddy. "What rubbish. You mean to say that you think this old loon is immortal? What can he have done to you? This is the twentieth century, is it not?"

"It is, Freddy," said the queen. "Now, will you please sit down?"

"I will sit down," Freddy said, "but I will not take this sitting down," and he sat down.

"Your Majesty," Apehand asked, "is he a privy councillor?"

As the queen nodded, Mr Neil said, "Ha!"

"What do you mean, 'Ha!'?" Pimcot inquired, coolly. "I know the list, and despite what Her Majesty has indicated, you, sir, are not on the list."

"I, sir," said Mr Neil, "am a councillor of the Witan, which gives me rank superior to that of a mere privy councillor."

"The Witan?" asked Apehand.

"Mr Apehand," the queen said, "Mr Neil is indeed a member of the Witan, and what he says is correct."

"But the Witan," Apehand held, restating anyway what everyone knew, "existed in the time of King Alfred."

Mr Neil approached the leader of Her Majesty's Opposition, and, in the most savage and unpleasant way, said, "You filthy peasant. I hate peasants. They smell, they stink, they know nothing, and all they have is appetite, like beasts."

Needless to say, as a Labour politician all his life and a member in good standing of the Socialist International, Apehand took offence.

"You are a peasant elevated by accident of history from the dark earth into the high halls of Westminster, like a termite in the rafters. It is wrong that you participate in governance with knights, lords, and kings. One of the great sins of all times is that your power is greater than that of those who once possessed you. Dare you argue with me, stinking peasant?"

"At last," said Apehand, "an honest Tory."

"That's hardly fair, Doyle," Pimcot protested.

"Doyle?" Freddy asked. "I never knew his name was Doyle. Doyle Apehand?"

"It isn't," said Apehand. "It's Vladimir Ilich, but Tories can't pronounce it."

"Look at you," Mr Neil said. "Clearly, you are inferior. Your body is inferior. Short. Obese. Dark. Bandy legs. Ill health. Fleshy lips. Tufted eyebrows that are thick, gross, and black. You move so slowly that, in a quest, you would surely fail and die."

Pimcot broke in. "And what about you, you spindly, bilious, malicious old bastard? Surely, you, too, would die in a quest, and how dare you insult my honourable friend, who represents the strength of Britain and its soul as much as I do, and, at times, when the people declare it, more so. The prince is right, Your Majesty," he said, addressing Her Majesty. "Must we listen to this . . . this gentleman?"

"Oh!" said Mr Neil, "three against one! The prime minister, the leader of the Opposition, and the Prince of Wales. What am I to do?"

"Yes," Freddy said, feeling that the moment was about to be his, "what are you to do?"

"As this is a democracy, of which all of you seem enamoured, why not put it to a vote, and if necessary I will break a tie?"

Certain that Fredericka would vote as he would, even were his parents momentarily enchanted, Freddy accepted. Apehand and Pimcot winced. As experienced politicians, before agreeing to a vote they reflexively would have polled, cajoled, and twisted arms.

Mr Neil framed the resolution: "A nay vote will deny me my rightful opportunity to speak—after all, I was invited, I graciously accepted, and I came a long way. An aye vote will express the confidence of this assembly in my powers and prerogatives. So?"

"I vote nay," Apehand said, starting the process after conspicuously failing to insist upon a careful definition of what Mr Neil called his powers and prerogatives.

"Nay as well," added Pimcot.

"Absolutely nay," said Freddy, looking confidently at Fredericka.

"Aye," said the queen.

"Aye," said Paul.

And, "Aye," said Fredericka.

"How could you, Fredericka?" Freddy demanded.

"He's so nice, Freddy. It doesn't matter what he says, he's nice."

"He's nice? He's a nasty son of a bitch."

"No he's not. You can tell from the story of the rabbits."

"The story of the rabbits?" Freddy asked. "What rabbits?"

"Freddy," the queen said, as if to a small child with conceptual difficulties, "we have been sitting here for two hours listening to the tale of Pacatooth the Rabbit."

"We have?"

"Yes."

"Pacatooth?"

"Pacatooth."

"Have we?" Freddy asked the politicians. They nodded in the affirmative.

"I will now break the tie," Mr Neil said, "by voting aye. Let us proceed."

"I don't understand," Freddy said. "How can you presume to direct the assembled leaders of Great Britain, you, who work in a sex toy factory?"

"He does?" Pimcot asked. "I thought it was a joke."

"I do," volunteered Mr Neil. "Fascinating work. You see, I'm an old man whose powers are declining, and in place of them I want to know absolutely everything. I worked in a nuclear weapons factory, making warhead triggers. I was a baker. I am about to learn tree surgery."

"You should study the history of democracy," Apehand said.

"That, I have seen with my own eyes. It started here, you know. I've never liked it. I much prefer the idea of royalty menaced by threat."

They had no idea what he was talking about, but Pimcot took him seriously. "What do you mean, 'It started here'? It started in Greece."

"Not quite," said Mr Neil. "The Greeks had noble ideas but couldn't put them into practice. We have from them mainly democracy's name. The fact of democracy started on this exact spot."

"What spot?" Freddy asked.

"Right here," Mr Neil said, softer now, as if moved by his account—whatever it was—of the origins of the democracy he refused. "Here, with the Round Table." He pointed to the floor.

"You mean, here at Windsor," Freddy, ever the historian, corrected. "The Round Table was in the Round Tower, not here."

"No," Mr Neil said. "Because the Round Tower is round, people got it into their heads that the Round Table was there, but it wasn't. It was here."

"How do you know?" Paul asked, crisply, though not as a challenge.

"This is Winlesora," Mr Neil answered, almost dreamily. "I know it well. Arthur chose it not because it was near the river, or because of the hill, but because it smelled so good. He rode here in late spring, in the company of Sir Gavin de Mildrep and Sir Gondred and Sir Gawain—he liked to do things like that, taking out three G knights at once—and when they were on the hill they smelled a marvellous perfume, from what plant they did not know, but it grew near the river and was fed by its waters, and every spring it made Winlesora heaven.

"The Round Table was right here; it was too windy up at the tower, too cold in winter. Arthur sat there," he said, pointing to an empty space above the floor. "You, sir," he said to Apehand, "are sitting where Sir Launcelot sat. That is why, perhaps, I was so severe with you. My heart was pained. I offer my profoundest apology."

"What does this have to do with democracy?" Pimcot pressed.

"Because the table was round, everyone got the idea that he was the equal of the others, including even the king. That's what started it. Arthur had endless troubles thereafter."

"Why did he choose a round table, then?" Pimcot asked.

"He didn't. It was an accident. He said to his carpenter, 'Build me a table so big that I can sit around it with all my knights.' The carpenter was a literalist, and when he heard the word *around,* democracy was born."

"I need a drink," Freddy said.

"Drinks for all," Mr Neil proclaimed, and out from the shadows three extremely grubby, long-haired boys dressed in black and brown rags appeared with wine-glasses of chilled mead, six in all, and nothing for Mr Neil.

As they drank the wonderfully sweet and cold mead, Mr Neil went on. "He was stuck with it, but because he saw that it was God's will, he made the best of his trials. He was a king unlike any other. He was *the* king, *rex quondam, rexque futurus,* and when he died, Britain lost its shield, if only temporarily, for he still watches over it. He even grew to love democracy, and to practise it, didn't he, Philippa?"

"Yes," the queen affirmed.

"How do you know this, Mater?" Freddy asked, feeling as if things had moved far beyond his control.

"I knew him, Freddy," the queen said, "and so did you, thank God."

"You knew him?" Freddy asked. "I knew him?" He pointed to himself.

"Don't you remember when he showed you the pistol he used at Omdurman?"

"Mother," Freddy said, compassionately (Fredericka perked up), but as if the queen were insane, "that wasn't Arthur, that was Churchill."

The queen smiled gently.

"Oh God," said Freddy. "You believe that Churchill was Arthur?"

"Once every thousand years or so, Arthur returns," Mr Neil said, matter-of-factly, "but only when Britain is in mortal danger. I'm so sad now—no, I'm heartbroken—that he will not return for a millennium.

You, Frederick, had the misfortune of being born at the end of his glory, but at least you had the privilege of knowing him, of being touched by his life. He was liveliness itself, greatness itself, and when he was in the world, the world was magnificent. But, when he died, the moths came out to eat the fabric of time."

"Splendid," said Freddy. "Very entertaining, fascinating—almost plausible. By the way, who were the boys who brought the mead?" He asked this of Mr Neil and his parents both, not knowing who would answer.

Mr Neil did. "That would be Swinebert, Borlock, and Chuffy the bastard of Sir Gavin de Mildrep. They assist me."

"They assist you," Freddy repeated dryly.

"Yes."

"In the sex toy factory?"

"Naturally not, they're too young. In my idyll they have little to do, and have spent most of their time in social intercourse with the street urchins of Naples. Unfortunately, I caught Chuffy the bastard of Sir Gavin de Mildrep smuggling cigarettes, so I made him run up and down Vesuvius twelve times."

"Mr Neil," Freddy inquired somewhat insanely himself, and certain that his mother was in the grip of a madman, "did *you* know Arthur?"

"Arthur Goldberg?" Mr Neil asked.

"No, the king."

"The king?"

"Yes, the king. King Arthur."

"It all depends on what you mean by *know*, what you mean by *did*, and what you mean by *you*."

"What about the punctuation?" Freddy shot back mockingly.

"That, too. You can end a sentence with a barst, a frid, a sylapse, a dipont, or a teetingle, and unless you know what you've ended it with— which you cannot from mere speech—you cannot know what it means."

"Did you know the first kings of England? I end that sentence," Freddy said, throwing all to chance, "with a frid."

"You don't even know who the first kings of England were, so how can you ask such a question and end it with a frid?"

"I do indeed know who they were."

"Oh no you don't," said Mr Neil, swinging his right leg to and fro like a pendulum, which seemed childlike and incongruous. "You think you do, but you don't."

"Pray tell, Mr Neil," the queen asked, "if it is not who we think, who was the first king of England?"

"Gershwin, the Baby King, in the Age of Blue."

"Do you mean George Gershwin?" Pimcot inquired, now happily stunned by his mead. "How could that be?"

"I don't think his name was George. I don't think he had a first name. It was thousands of years before Arthur."

"Thousands of years before Arthur," the queen echoed, delighted to hear this, as it deepened her pedigree.

"Thousands," said Mr Neil. "Arthur was a newcomer, like all of you. But of the hundred kings or more before him, there had to be a first, and that was poor little Gershwin."

"The Baby King," Freddy interrupted, "but not George Gershwin."

"The Georges came later, twit. Gershwin, just Gershwin. What is the matter with you people? Learn something, will you? Little Gershwin was just fourteen months of age when in the autumn (there were no calendars then) two hundred boatloads of Pontic and Fippian Norsemen beached at what is now Scarborough. Ten thousand warriors burned their way across England, filling the sky with heat and ash. The nobles and headmen of the time could not even conceive of an army that size. The biggest army in England was the forty-five-man force of Sir Bakwin De Muth."

"How could Sir Bakwin De Muth have been a knight?" Freddy asked contentiously, "with no king to knight him?"

"I'm translating," said Mr Neil. "His actual title was *Lachpoof,* and his name was *Bachquaquinnik Dess Moofoomooach.* I'm just updating the terms, much like expressing prices in current or inflation-adjusted sterling. Anyway, you can imagine the state of Bronks if Lachpoof Bachquaquinnik Dess Moofoomooach's was the largest military force."

"Excuse me?" Freddy asked. "The state of what?"

"Of Bronks, or, as they would have said then, *The* Bronks."

"What was that?"

"That was the first name of England as a whole."

"The Bronks?"

"Yes."

"You mean like that awful place in New York, where I dedicated what I believe was called a Methadrone clinic?" the queen asked.

"How would I know?" Mr Neil asked. "I've never been there."

"What language did they speak?" Pimcot asked.

"Bronksian Snep and Bronksian Chia," was Mr Neil's answer. "Often Snep and Chia were indistinguishable, as in *Thumswak inchka entlama bisko frigadooka,* which was exactly the same in both dialects, and which meant, in today's parlance, 'Ghastly bad luck that you're so small and like not to bathe in the sea.'"

"Let's keep this to ourselves, shall we?" Paul suggested. "Can you imagine what the Americans would do with it?" They all agreed.

"Gershwin," continued Mr Neil, "lived with his parents on the Cornish cliffs. They were birds'-egg gatherers, and though the Norsemen had been burning their way across England for a month, they had not heard. One day, out of the blue . . . I should explain. Everything was much bluer then, and not only the sky and the sea. Most things that now are grey and brown were shades of blue and silver-blue. When the waves broke, they turned not white but lavender. Out of the blue, then, came the Norsemen. Gershwin's mother hid Gershwin in the hay and ran toward the cliffs to warn the father, who was on his way back with an armful of eggs. Terrifying and leather-clad, the Norsemen, having come joyously to the sea, the end of their conquest, slew them more casually than if they had been animals.

"Knowing somehow of his parents' deaths, Gershwin cried. The Norsemen heard him, came into the barn, and pulled him from the hay by one of his little legs. They took him out and laughed at him as he cried, holding him upside down, and swung him in a circle like a hammer. The one who did it, a giant in black leather and stud armour, thought it amusing, and so did the rest. As he swung the baby, now silent perforce, the Norsemen parted ranks so that he could move closer to the edge of the cliff. And when he was close enough, he twirled and twirled, and near the slain father and mother they laughed as he hurled Gershwin over the edge of the cliff high above the sea. The conquest of England was complete, they thought.

"But that was not so, for at that very moment, as the child hung in the air over the water far below, after England had been crossed and recrossed by savage armies that bled it deep and held it down, and no man would have dreamt that the conquest was not permanent, at that very moment, God turned His long-absent gaze to this island. And seeing a baby about to fall into the waves, He commanded everything that was blue to rise. The waves tried to come up to the dizzying height of the cliffs to catch him, and blue haze and mists over distant strands rushed to his defence, but it was the blue sky that saved him, cupping him in a sapphire-coloured cradle that held him gravityless above the sea, and infilling his soul with kingliness.

"The silver-blue rocks begged to help, and from them came, at that instant, the kingly sword. It was the first sword known to man that was of bright steel and strong enough to break all others. It lay across the cradle of sky as the baby was comforted by visiting clouds. England had a king. He was, Madam, your first royal ancestor, and though the stories of his boyhood, youth, and reign are as great as one might expect, suffice it to say now that he found the very Norsemen who had slain his parents, and the very Norseman who had thrown him from the cliffs, and put them under his sword. Though they were in their old age, he was neither merciful nor slow, for at that time he was in the midst of reconquering England, which, with armies clad in blue, he did.

"He was Gershwin, the Baby King, the first king of England, crowned by God, in the Age of Blue."

Freddy looked about. Fredericka was dabbing at her eyes. The queen breathed deeply in satisfaction. Paul seemed reflective and grateful. Pimcot, as usual, was hard to read. The only hope was Apehand, who had been called a stinking peasant, and who could not have been kindly disposed to Mr Neil. Freddy was not happy, however, to appeal to Apehand, who, after all, wanted to abolish him; who once, on the hustings in his constituency, had referred to Freddy as "that mindless royal pipsqueak who thinks he's Pope Innocent the Tenth"; and who in private habitually referred to the royal family as the Romanovs-in-waiting.

"Mr Neil," said Freddy, the voice of reason and restraint. "How do you know all this about Gershwin the Baby King? No one has ever heard of it."

"Ask Chuffy."

"Chuffy's gone, it seems. I'm asking you."

"No one living may have heard of it, that's true."

"Yes, well, then, how *do* you know? Is it written in some great source that until now has been hidden from historians?"

"No," said Mr Neil, blinking like an owl.

"Then how do you know?"

"Believe me, I know."

"How?"

"I just know."

"It's a legend, perhaps. Did you make it up?"

"I did not make it up. It is no legend. It is the literal truth."

"Mr Neil," Freddy asked, thinking that perhaps the tide had begun to turn, "were you there? Did you see all this, thousands of years ago?"

"Look," said Apehand, in a way that made Freddy think he was coming to help, "I just want to know what this is all about. What's going on?"

"You, peasant," cried Mr Neil, "with nose- and ear-hair like little straw brooms; you, porcine, flatulent, and pale; you, from a bog house with no candle; you shut up! What would you know about kings?"

"That's just the point," Apehand told him. "We're surrounded here by kings, royals, and nobility, living and dead. Even though you're obviously from some asylum, even you have that air. Pimcot is a distant cousin to the queen. I'm the only one here who's not in on this, I'm the only sane one, and, I say, what the hell's going on? I came here for a meeting to discuss him," he said, pointing at the heir to the throne. "It's all very nice and all about Baby Gershwin. Lovely. But let's get down to business."

Once again, Freddy was checked by the flow of things.

"You are correct, Mr Apehand," the queen averred.

"Thank you, Your Majesty."

"The subject," she continued, "is Freddy . . . and Fredericka."

"Me?" Fredericka blurted out. "What did I do?"

"This all began after Freddy married you."

"It did not. What about when he ran through Chelsea wrapped in toilet paper?"

"I was trapped in a boudoir and had to escape without my clothes."

"It had nothing to do with me," Fredericka stated in triumph. "And, if you recall," she told Freddy, "before our marriage you called Konrad Adenauer 'a Blackpool drag queen before the age of cosmetic surgery,' and then you had the nerve to stay in his hotels."

"Those were the indiscretions of youth," Paul said. "Now you are man and wife. Mr Neil, are you aware of the situation in which the Prince and Princess of Wales find themselves?"

"I've got the gist of it from the Italian papers. Have you ever read an Italian newspaper? I imagine it's like being on drugs."

"What shall we do?"

"Just like that?" Freddy asked. "You'll put my fate in the hands of a lunatic, without even a minute's discussion?"

"He knows what to do, Freddy. You must listen to him."

"When they don't listen to me," Mr Neil said, "they go the way of Chuck the Second and George the Fourth." He shook his head. "And worse: Elfredge, the idle king killed and stuffed by Hollanders; Vastain, the sumptuary king mistaken for a hog and butchered in his own palace yard; King Bullfinch, enamoured of. . . ."

"King Bullfinch?" Freddy asked. "Who was King Bullfinch? That's not a pre-Arthurian name, or are you translating?"

"Not translating," said Mr Neil. "King Bullfinch is a future king."

"A future king?"

"*Rex futurus.*"

"Who will not follow your advice."

"Correct."

"How do you know?" Freddy asked.

"Frederick," Mr Neil said, closing his eyes and then opening them, again and again, "you have much to learn about time, something of which you know almost nothing. You probably believe in the primitive concepts that allow frightened men to hallucinate a passage through time's dangerous swirl. Your weakness compels you to imagine that it is a river, that it flows always forward and always straight. But it isn't, and it doesn't."

"Really." Freddy was stony.

"Really."

"What is it then, Mr Neil?"

"It's a storm, the most magnificent storm man has ever seen, a vast explosion of wind and waves—tresses, tori, whirlpools, crowns, spindles, pillars, falls, flumes, and foam. And yet, it is as still as a planet of absolutely clear ice. When you have reconciled these contradictory states, you will understand not only time but many other things as well. And, if you are lucky, what happened to the Thane of Rumpelstiltskin will not happen to you."

"The Thane of Rumpelstiltskin?" Freddy asked, his voice dripping with contempt, his mouth curled like that of a pirate in the cinema. "Couldn't you make up a better name than that?"

"I suppose so, but that was his name."

"And where was he from, this Thane of Rumpelstiltskin?"

"I believe he was from Dorking."

Freddy stared at the cool planes of stained glass that stood vertically to the light. Where they were blue, they were as blue as a cold and sunlit sea. Where they were red, they were as red as a tropical fruit. Where they were yellow and gold, they were like the harvest ground in a medieval minia-ture. All this was his, and always had been. To keep his tranquil life, he might have to suffer some sort of penance, but it would be worthwhile. Given what he had done, what could be asked of him? Were Mr Neil rea-sonable, as he might prove to be, the punishment for looking foolish on occasion when Fredericka had trapped him into it would have to be of a minor sort—turning in his Aston-Martin, a ten-percent reduction in his revenues from the Duchy, more charity work?

"What do you recommend, Mr Neil, as my penance?" Freddy asked al-most impatiently.

"You think it will be a tap on the wrist," said Mr Neil. "I know what you think."

"I have no idea."

"You think that, as formerly a knight who was unchaste was disallowed the use of his riding animal . . ."

"You mean horse?"

Mr Neil ignored him. ". . . you will be disallowed use of a road engine, and that will be all."

"They're called motor cars."

"Do not presume to instruct me in a language that you know only in its gutted, burnt-out, non-musical, desiccated remains. You idiot, you don't even know what you have done."

"What have I done?"

"You have betrayed your God, your country, your family, and your dignity."

"I beg your pardon. How have I done that?"

"In being an ass. You are supposed to be a king, not an ass. Kings may not go through Chelsea wrapped in toilet paper. They may not run about Buckingham Palace in tar and feathers. They may not appear day by day in ungainly compromised situations, with horns atop their heads, in foolish costumes, speaking nonsense, falling over, laughing at hospital patients."

"I can explain all that," Freddy said.

"It doesn't matter," Mr Neil told him. "Your explanations are irrelevant and demeaning. A king is not a hapless idiot. He does not allow such things to occur. He does not allow himself to be the subject of misinter-pretation or the butt of jokes."

"Shall I have killed Psnake and Didgeridoo?"

"It would have been the honourable thing."

"And all over for me. I would have been confined for the rest of my life to the royal cell at Froghampton."

"It would have been over for you, perhaps, but better for the kings who followed. What is important is not you but what you represent."

"I have told him that, Mr Neil," the queen said firmly, "but on no account shall he kill either Psnake or Didgeridoo. I forbid it."

"Of course, Your Majesty. He must do more than simply kill two old scribes."

The queen nodded gravely. Freddy was alarmed.

"He must conquer! Like a real king, a king *ex nihilo,* someone who, though not born to royalty, puts his hands into the hurricane of time and shapes the rushing winds into a crown."

"Mr Neil," Freddy said earnestly, "I was born for that. All my life I have yearned for a moment such as my grand-uncle had in North Africa during the war. He stood on a verandah overlooking a beach where thousands of troops were bathing in the surf. Recognising him, they ran forward like the tide, until he was surrounded, as they would soon surround the Afrika Korps. He did not know what to say. Nor did they, but they were fighting in his name, as of old. Because life and death contended through their days, they lived so intensely that in this desert they were as royal as he. In the silence, a lone voice began 'God Save the King,' which was then taken up by thousands, many of whom were soon to die. He understood at that moment, as the sun bore down and the waves crashed against the strand, the sacrificial glory of kingship, and so did they. That is the kind of moment I seek, and the kind of king I wish to be.

"I was born for such a thing, Mr Neil, but this fortunate time is hardly kind to kings. George the Second was the last British king to lead an army into battle, a quarter of a millennium ago. I wish I had been born into another age, but I will know only this one, misconstructed as it is in so many ways. My test is to hold myself back and learn the strange and dishonourable contentment that now we call success.

"For the monarchy is like an old mountain range, once sharp, high, and glittering with snow, and now worn smooth, now comfortable and quiet. Such evolution may be right and proper, but it does not match my temperament, and it is my temperament in these times that often leads me to be taken for a madman or a fool. Times that are bright and dangerous have come before, and they will come again, but I am destined to be king throughout a long and placid afternoon."

"No, you are not destined to be king," said Paul, "no longer. The succession is on hold: you will have to earn it."

"I've never heard of such a thing," said Freddy. "It's impossible."

"Sorry," said Mr Neil, "it's possible. Shall we break for lunch?"

"Just a moment," Freddy commanded, rather tensely. "I don't want to break for lunch. I've just been informed that the order of succession is on hold." His voice was rising. "To hell with lunch."

"You, young man!" Mr Neil shouted, gaining, it seemed, several octaves in depth and a foot in height. His eyes narrowed in anger. "You will eat lunch, and you will be gracious, and you will shut up. Shut up. Is that clear? Discipline. If you cannot summon the discipline to do such a small thing, then how will you conquer lands?"

"All right," said Freddy, roping himself in like a man who, as he is burnt, is silent. "I shall say not a word during lunch, and will retain my composure. After you, Mr Neil."

A lunch had been laid out in the narthex of the chapel. How it got there no one knew except perhaps Mr Neil, but neither Swinebert, Borlock, nor Chuffy the bastard of Sir Gavin de Mildrep was in evidence. In fact, no one was in evidence. A first-class table was set with fine china, silver, and crystal. Venison broth, Freddy's favourite if made by Mrs MacGregor at Balmoral, as he assumed this was (it tended to follow him around England), steamed as alluringly as tea from a sunny orange cup, a sprig of cress floating almost unwilted upon its hot surface. On a plate near each individual tureen of soup were several thick slices of bread of a heavy, golden, continental type, its origins unclear. Then a perfect salad, a vin ordinaire as good as the finest claret, mineral water from Sweden, and the entrées—two Scottish smoked salmons with capers, dill, and three kinds of sauce; seared tenderloins of wild boar on wild rice; and an Italian pasta that Apehand regarded as if it were the Holy Grail. A dessert table held a large white teapot suspended above blue flame, many gold-rimmed cups of chocolate mousse, a plate of half a dozen cheeses, various fruits, lime biscuits, chocolate-covered cherries from Belgium, and some freshly baked rolls, as if whoever was responsible knew that Freddy would not eat sweets without plain bread.

He would eat silently and go through the entire meal before he learned of the changes in succession, because he was a soldier and could submit to discipline.

"What are you doing, Freddy?" Mr Neil asked incredulously.

"I'm sitting down at table, Mr Neil, for lunch, as you bade me."

"Not you," Mr Neil said. "Not you, or her," indicating Fredericka. "As the rest of us eat, the both of you will stand over there in that patch of light."

"Then why is the table set for seven?" Fredericka asked crossly, as Freddy led her to a patch of light shining upon the cold floor.

"Fredericka, pay it no mind," Freddy told her. "Stand with me and show what you are made of."

"But I'm hungry."

"Fredericka."

"Are we supposed to stand here like servants and watch them eat?"

"Get used to it," barked Mr Neil.

The queen found this rather funny, and laughed as she spooned up her soup. And Paul said, seemingly to everyone, "It's about time, you fat thing."

"You see," began Mr Neil, as those who were to eat eagerly awaited their lunch, "I know more about you than you think."

"Who?" asked Apehand.

"Freddy, and everyone else, too, but now I'm addressing Freddy."

"Then why don't you look at him?" Pimcot asked.

"I don't have to look at him: I can see him through the collarbone of time. There. There he is," Mr Neil said, pointing at the tablecloth beneath a vase of yellow roses. "Freddy, you need not assume from my question that I disapprove of what you did, but why did you jump in mud puddles at construction sites?"

"You did what?" asked the queen.

"On one occasion, Maman"—he addressed her in French only when under great stress or delirious with fever—"I did swim in the foetid sink that forms when a large building begins to take shape and the rains are heavier than normal."

"Why on earth did you do that?"

"Another officer and I were on a twenty-mile run in a pouring November rain. It was quite cold and we were soaked through to the skin, and yet our rushing blood and the heat of exertion made us perfectly warm, so we decided to take a swim. I like to swim in my clothes. And I like to swim in natural waters."

"In a construction pit?"

"The mud was welcoming, as in Africa."

"Bloody good that Psnake doesn't have pictures," Paul declared. "'Prince of Wales Cavorts in London Mud Puddle.'"

"But he does," Pimcot announced. "He has those pictures, and any others he might need."

"That's what I've been saying," said Mr Neil. "It's gone too far, and we've got to bring it back. That's why you called me."

"How?" asked Pimcot.

"When this kind of thing happens, the king or heir is banished from the kingdom and sent to conquer savage lands. That's why England has an empire. Historians have it all wrong, because it's a secret, as it must be, or the people would lose confidence. The Voyages of Discovery, the Conquests, all that remarkable stuff, were driven by royal decay."

"They were?" asked Pimcot.

"Yes. The greatest and most courageous navigators, merchants, and generals, the spearheads into the darkness of the unknown, were all well disguised marginicidal kings."

"What is the meaning of *marginicidal*?" Pimcot asked.

"Dehiscent by the disjunction of the united margins of the carpels," Fredericka said, stunning everyone in the room.

"That's right," said Mr Neil. "How did you know that, Princess?"

"I read it in one of Freddy's botany books, a long time ago, when we were driving up to Baldershot and he threw my copy of *She* out the window."

"That book is a thousand pages long," said Freddy.

"I thought it was very interesting," she said. "Plants are cute."

"Be that as it may," Mr Neil continued, "your grand-uncle who abdicated, Freddy, was a marginicidal king who was sent to conquer, and failed."

Freddy did not answer. He was not allowed to.

"King Tatwin the Seventh, for example, was dispatched to the summit of Cairngorm to smite the Dragon of Penrith, who had fled when fire was brought to England by the sweet young girl who was the grand-daughter of what's his name. What's his name? You know, he was very unpleasant and he never paid back the money he owed you. Terrible cook, always burnt everything. Ah! Prometheus, that's it."

"King who?" Paul asked.

"Tatwin the Seventh."

"I've never heard of him, have you, dear?" the queen asked Paul.

"No. Are you sure of such a person?" Paul asked Mr Neil in turn.

Standing still on his square of floor, from which the sun had almost entirely disappeared, Freddy had a look of vibrant disgust.

"Yes," said Mr Neil, seemingly unsure and perhaps a touch senescent. "Was it Tatwin the Sixth? Let's see. Tatwin the First was, well, you know. Ah, Tatwin the Second, yes, and the Third," he mumbled. They couldn't really hear what he was saying. It sounded like the noise that emanates from a beehive after an early August rainstorm.

"Right," he said, getting back his energy in the way that a machine with a loose electrical wire will fade and then forge ahead. "Tatwin the Seventh was the bad one. Unspeakable. It was he who was sent, naked, as is the custom, to Cairngorm."

Freddy silently repeated the word *naked*.

"And he," Mr Neil continued in a hysterical sing-song, "and he . . . he . . . he was the one who was supposed to smite the Dragon of Penrith."

"What happened?" Apehand asked. "Did he smite the dragon?"

"No," said Mr Neil, wagging his finger, "the dragon smote him. And then ate him. Hence, no Tatwin the Eighth."

Freddy was mumbling to himself. "Shut up, Freddy," his father said almost reflexively.

"Why have we never heard of the Tatwins?" the queen asked.

"Oh," said Mr Neil, hands fluttering like pigeons trying to fly from a closed coop, "in history are many gaps in time, bloodlines, chronologies, ladders, steps, and trees. Oxbows, as it were. They get fistulated. Besides, the Tatwins weren't worth the candle. History lacks nothing in their omission."

Freddy whispered to Fredericka, "I'm rather worried."

"I should say," Fredericka whispered back, "but you needn't be. Whatever you have to do, I'll send you things to make it easier, and I'll be waiting when you get back."

"Disasters happen to kings, and then they must put them to rights," Mr Neil stated, sounding perfectly reasonable. "What do you think happened to Hank the Second when his pet monkey tore up all his private papers and notes? Sent to conquer Africa, that's what. And what do you think happened to the monkey?"

"Where shall Freddy be sent?" asked the queen, as if inquiring after a diplomatic posting for a wayward viscount. She was so calm. It made Freddy livid.

"He must be sent," was the answer, "to find a New Caernarvon in the most savage, strange, and unconquerable region of the earth. There he will either subject it to his rule or fail in his quest. It cannot be an easy place like the Land Beyond the Sea of Snow. No. It cannot be empty, like the summit of Cairngorm. It must be inhabited by fierce, clever, and industrious creatures—monsters. It must be a vast place where power arcs from point to point like the whiplash of sparks. It must be as smoky as hell, as bright with fire and sparkling with dangerous things as the land even the Norsemen dared not mention. In fact, it is that land, the most unconquerable, savage land on earth. Aaah Hooo!"

"Bless you," said Pimcot.

"That was not a sneeze. It was the horror of such a place coursing through my body and jumping from my lips."

"You have found such a place, Mr Neil?" the queen asked.

"The very place."

"Pray tell, is it in Africa?"

"No, no, not Africa."

"The Amazon?"

"Too much litostis in the Amazon, Your Majesty."

"What is litostis, Mr Neil?"

"Solidified thegram of tekla, much like West Egyptian gruth."

"I see. Is it in Asia?"

"Asia is a very civilised place. I summer there."

"The poles?" asked the queen.

"No, Madam, their cuisine is too deadly."

"I mean the earthly poles."

"Theirs too."

"Icebergs," the queen said, with urgency rather than irritation.

"Not there."

"Then, where?"

"I have looked long in my scrolls for such a place," said Mr Neil. "Three marginicidal kings have perished there. It is beyond the dissilient cliffs of pure water that cleave the great ocean and fall through infinite tunnels of mist. It is where the vast stinking body of the expired Dragon of Penrith was laid to rest, only to vapourise and disappear immediately upon contact with the white-hot ground. Oh, devils! Oh, God forsaken! Oh, darkness, stench, and flame!"

"Oh, get out with it," said Freddy, breaking discipline and taking what he wanted from the dessert table. "If I'm going to go there, I should know where it is, shouldn't I? What is it called?"

"It is called, Your Royal Highness," Mr Neil said quietly, using the noble form of address for Freddy for the first time, *"New Jersey."*

"I've flown over that," the queen said. "I didn't know there were people in it. It looked like it was on fire."

"New Jersey?" Freddy asked. "Am I supposed to conquer New Jersey? I told you, Mother, that he was mad."

"New Jersey is but a tile in a land so vast that, as far as anyone knows, it has no name," Mr Neil said in a mad whisper.

"Yes it does, you idiot," Freddy told him. "It's called the United States of America."

"It is this, then, that you must conquer."

Certain that Mr Neil was indeed an escaped inmate of a perhaps no-longer-extant asylum, Freddy relaxed and sat down with his tea and chocolate mousse. Fredericka followed, relieved, because she could see that he felt the game was his. And he did think so, because obviously neither his mother nor his father, nor the prime minister, nor the leader of the Opposition would require him to go nude into New Jersey and conquer (whatever that might mean) the United States.

"Is he an actor?" Freddy asked his father, who was known for staging elaborate practical jokes. "He appears to be asleep." Mr Neil had once again run short of power. Jaws aslack, mouth open, and eyes closed, he slept as he sat, most pitifully.

"Don't joke at a time like this, Freddy," his father whispered.

"What do you mean, 'at a time like this'?" Freddy responded, very loudly, startling Mr Neil back into consciousness.

"You must leave in three days," Mr Neil said, as if to himself, "when the dark side of Venus will be at fourteen-degrees semi-perpendicularity to the plane of the Jovian orbital conjunction with Mars. That is when tree frogs make their most secret sex sounds, and, in Devon, the moon rises mauve and pink. It is the day when chalk cliffs crumble, and bellboys electrocute their fish."

Freddy laughed nervously.

"The government will provide the requisite transportation, and any other services needed," volunteered Pimcot.

"I suppose it will have to be a covert insertion," said Paul.

"Thank you, Prime Minister," said the queen.

"What!" exclaimed Freddy.

"It will be necessary during the prince's absence," said Paul, drawing upon his wartime experience, "to craft a scenario of deniability, and, I imagine, to convene a working group at the highest level to plan for the reaccession of the Colonies should he succeed."

"This is why we brought you here," the queen told Pimcot and Apehand, "in your capacity as privy councillors."

"Your Majesty's Loyal Opposition is in full and harmonious agreement," Apehand said, smiling. "We ask only that, if the Colonies are reacquired, a strenuous effort is made to achieve a coordination of collective bargaining rules in the mother country and among the colonials."

"All in good time, Mr Apehand," the queen assured him. "We assume that, when they are informed, Mr Lamb's Liberals will press for coordination of environmental rules. But we're not going to inform them."

"And why not, Your Majesty?" Pimcot asked.

"Because, Prime Minister, they cannot keep their mouths shut."

Everyone was in agreement, and the air was charged as when a great ship is just about to get under way.

"Oh come now!" Freddy shouted, in disbelief.

"Quiet, Freddy," his father countered. "You've been a very bad prince. Now you must go to New Jersey."

"Naked?" Freddy asked.

"You will have," said Mr Neil, *"hracneets."*

"And what, Mr Neil, are *hracneets?*"

"Modesty panels of golden rabbits' fur. They attach to the body with thin straps of green snakeskin."

"It sounds like the bathing suits we saw at Cap d'Antibes," Fredericka said. "I wish I could have one. Three little rabbits' fur panels, and some lines of sexy green snakeskin."

"You *will* have one, Princess," Mr Neil said, eyes crossed.

"Oh! Lovely," she said, and then blinked. "Why?"

II.

PARADISE LOST

ANGELS

THE LUMINOUS JUMP clock in a black C-130 droning its way across the Atlantic off the air routes had been set to Eastern Daylight Time. Thus, as icebergs scrolled underneath in the salmon-coloured light of the sub-Arctic sunset, the Prince and Princess of Wales could readily see that it was eight o'clock in New Jersey, where at this time of year so close to the summer solstice the sun would set in another hour or so, blood-red from the noxious gases through which its weakening rays struggled to pass.

Wrapped in military blankets because their *hracneets* were insufficiently warm over ocean so close to Greenland, they sat on uncomfortable web seats, silently staring at their parachutes. Except for leather flight caps, aviator goggles, and *hracneets,* they would be naked when tossed from the aircraft into New Jersey. Neither shoes, nor clothing, nor a wallet, nor a watch would go with them, nor a pen knife, a cellular telephone, a toothbrush, nor even any feminine appliances.

"What if I need feminine appliances?" Fredericka had asked of Mr Neil.

"What are they?"

"You know."

"No, I don't know, which is why I asked."

"You're ten thousand years old and you haven't found out yet what feminine appliances are?"

"I have great gaps in my erudition, Princess. Perhaps you can enlighten me."

"All right," she whispered, blushing marvellously pink across the spacious top of her chest, "what if, what if it's that certain time?"

"Springtime in Paris?" Mr Neil asked.

"No."

"The mating season?"

"No."

"Chestnuts roasting on an open fire?"

Fredericka looked at Mr Neil as though next she would kill him. She was at her most beautiful when her expression was fierce.

"I don't know what you mean," Mr Neil said, "and whatever you mean, no, no, no. Naked, naked, naked—except for *hracneets.*"

"Who's going to do my hair?" Fredericka asked, not quite comprehending what was in store.

"The air," said Mr Neil, neither cruelly nor kindly.

"Thir?" echoed Fredericka, mistakenly. "Wonderful. He's Icelandic. I don't know what I'd do without my Nordic hairdressers. My highlights are now in Spicy Lapp Tundra Permafrost Gold, with a touch of Stockholm Silver Sprat Delicious."

Observing the expressions of pity in those around her, she finally understood that things were about to change.

In the aeroplane, Freddy, who was used to dropping from black C-130s and thought his seat rather comfortable, tried once again to comfort his wife. "Buck up," he said. "If we don't die on the way in. . . ."

"Die? We have parachutes. You told me that because they're on static lines I don't have to pull the umbilical cord. You said it was a 'nothing jump.'"

"Well, yes," Freddy said with military candour, "but the drop zone is undefined and we'll be parachuting at night. One can drown, or be electrocuted on high-tension lines, or land in the path of a train or vehicle, be impaled on saplings or spikes, mangled in the trees, or hit the side of a cliff and suffer chute collapse. You can even have your limbs severed by man-made objects, or be blown out to sea. Then there's quicksand, exsanguination, head trauma, internal bleeding upon too violent a landing, wild animals, hostile tribes, snakes, poisonous plants, pirana, infectious worms. . . ."

"Don't be an idiot, Freddy. We're going to *New Jersey.* I read about it before they took us to Northolt. Across the river Hudson from New York, New Jersey, the Garden State, is a bucolic flat land where vegetables are grown. And, besides, once we get there, we're going straight into Manhattan to the Carlyle. I'll need a bath, bed, and clothes, not to mention something to eat. As we won't be able to go to a hotel until we can wire for money, do you know someone in New York who will shelter us?"

"Don't worry, I've made provision."

"You have?"

"I can pack a parachute as well as anyone," he said, leaning toward her. For some reason, he wanted very much to kiss her, as if he never had, as if nothing had ever gone wrong between them. And though he didn't, he did hesitate, in a kind of fume of desire, before he went on. "Last night, I arose at four, went into the parachute loft, and taped ten five-hundred-pound notes to each of our chutes. Keep the parachute after we land. With ten thousand pounds, at least we'll be able to buy clothes, food, a car, and whatever else we'll need to get where we're going, wherever that may be."

"Are you sure you've packed the parachutes properly?"

"I always pack my own."

"And mine?"

"I let the monkey do it."

"Really, did the jump master, or whatever he is, check it?"

"Serjeant Munchkin-Tito?"

"Who?"

"Serjeant Munchkin-Tito. Rex." The jump master to whom Freddy referred was a rough-looking sort, with sharp features and very black hair. His father was Croatian and his mother from Didcot.

"Serjeant Rex Munchkin-Tito?" she asked. "You can't even say it. Is he English?"

"He's as English as I am."

"Yes, but you're German."

"Let's not get into that again."

"Whatever happened to names like Smith, Abernathy, and Churchill?"

"It was like ships passing in the night," Freddy said. "Now people who live in Ruthenia, Bangladesh, and Japan have names like Smith and Jones, and England is packed with Al-Waziris and Chongs."

Darkness had fallen, and they sat close for warmth. There is something very soothing and dreamlike about flying over icebergs floating in dim seas. The sight of them drifting like imagined alps in an endless grey ocean is theological in nature. So white, clean, and fanciful, they seem to have no mass. And each has the virginal quality of an artifact fresh from the hand of God. No one had ever seen these particular vast dollops of ancient snow parading in the frigid sea like an invasion fleet or the dead souls of polar bears proceeding to a silent Valhalla after a long and alingual life.

"Serjeant," Freddy asked.

"Sir!" the serjeant replied, saluting like a vibrating railway semaphore.

"Ask the pilot to go low over the icebergs."

"Is that what you wish, sir, or, on account of the princess and all, would you prefer some happy median?"

"As low as possible, and bring me about fifty feet of line and a vehicle chock."

"Right off."

"What are you going to do, Freddy?" Fredericka asked. "I sense that this is the kind of thing of which your father would not approve."

"He's not here."

"Nor would Mr Neil."

"Mr Neil," said Freddy, "is a lunatic who thinks he's ten thousand years old. I don't have to follow his instructions and neither do you."

"If you don't have to follow his instructions, what are you doing in a rabbits'-fur-and-green-snakeskin bikini, about to parachute into New Jersey?"

"That has nothing to do with him."

"Of course not."

"Not at all. The government and my parents have forced us. They follow the lunatic's instructions, and we follow theirs. That makes it bearable. You've never been in the army so you wouldn't know, but it's always easier to follow an insane order from someone who hasn't originated it. It spares your dignity if you know that the person relaying the order shares your perplexity and disdain."

"In regard to orders," she asked, "where are we supposed to go? What are we supposed to do?"

"You were there," Freddy reminded her. "We are to find the live ash circle and conquer the United States."

"But what is the live ash circle?"

"I don't know, and I don't know if we're supposed to find it and then conquer the United States, or conquer the United States and then find it. That's half the fun of a quest, isn't it, not knowing what you're looking for? The other half is not knowing where it is."

"Whatever it is, we'll never find it."

"Of course we'll find it," Freddy said, perfectly confident.

"How can you possibly think so?"

"Because for a thousand years my bloodline has been victorious and supreme. I don't mean to be immodest, but, for a Finney, this kind of stuff is old hat. As Queen Elizabeth my grandmother many times removed once said, 'I thank God I am endowed with such qualities that if I were turned out of the realm in my petticoat, I were able to live in any place in Christendom.' I have never yet heard of a king who did not succeed in a quest. It's what kings do."

"But what about your grand-uncle? And all the others that Mr Neil named, who did fail?"

"I was just making an allusion."

"To what?"

"To William the Second, who, upon putting to sea in a storm, said, 'I have never yet heard of a king who was drowned.' My unfortunate grand-uncle and the others were not destined to be kings. They did not know how to carry on the royal line through unprecedented danger, as I do."

"How do you know that?"

"It's in the blood."

"You're cracked," said Fredericka. "Your whole family's cracked."

"We may be cracked, but we have ruled Britain and much of the world for a millennium. Don't discount this. I'm royal. I have good vibes."

"You have what?"

"Good vibes, the American equivalent of royal blood. An American of great hereditary merit is said to have them."

"How do you know?"

"I've committed a number of Americanisms to memory. You, too, should learn them."

"Where did you find them?"

"In 'The American Language As It Is Really Spoken.'"

"Who wrote it?"

"It's a manuscript that is yet to be published."

"Who wrote it?"

"My father."

Fredericka drew back. "What does he know?"

"He's been there a number of times."

"So have you."

"Yes, but when he goes, he speaks to academics. I go to turkey farms and furniture factories."

"Freddy, I don't think your father really knows how to speak American English."

"But he does, and it's all been checked by some professor in a red-brick, who's also an MP, I think."

"Not Swindon Michael Worry," Fredericka said.

"I don't think so. No, no, it's all on the up-and-up. Guess how they say 'How do you do?'"

"I don't know."

"'Vus machs die, meshuganeh?' And if you want to say 'Fine, thank you,' you say either 'Like a bird from a crisp corn pie,' or 'Straight up, bro.'"

"Are you sure?"

"Certainly. I now know lots of these phrases. We'll blend right in. For instance, do you know how to say, 'I'm famished'?"

"How?"

"You say, 'Amaw make me a date wit da colonel.'"

"It does sound American."

"Absolutely. Do you know what they call bobbies?"

"What?"

"Pigs, if you want to be formal, but, idiomatically, porkos, piggies, or badge hogs. They'll never ever suspect that we're English."

"But Freddy, they will. They'll recognise us. We've been on the cover of nearly every American magazine, and the embassy reports that we're continually on their televisions."

"Mr Neil swore they wouldn't."

"I know, but do you believe him?"

"Yes. Context is all, and, besides, in a short time we won't look like ourselves, you especially. God knows what we'll be wearing, who will cut our hair, or what happens to the face during a quest. In battle, one's features change. It's remarkable but true."

"We're going down now, sir," the serjeant said. "Here are the line and chock."

Freddy seized a fire bucket and dumped out the sand. After attaching the line to its handle, he threaded the chock so it slid down the line, tilting the bucket like a drag scoop and giving it twenty pounds of weight. "Otherwise," Freddy said, when he had it rigged, "the wind would keep it too high."

The serjeant understood what was about to happen, and as Freddy buckled Fredericka's seatbelt, the serjeant strapped on a safety harness affixed to a bulkhead. Freddy then donned another on the opposite side. The plane lost altitude and the serjeant opened the ramp. The sound of servomotors and wind was no less new to Fredericka's ears than it was to the untouched sea. Though the atmosphere in the cabin had been fresh enough, the Arctic air that now flooded in was inexpressibly pure, voluminous, and sweet. Why the air above icebergs would be so sweet Freddy did not know. "The air is lovely," Freddy shouted above the wind, and Fredericka nodded.

The ocean now was so close that they could see bubbles, froth, and the gauze of fragile wind lines that crazed its surface during the passage of the plane. The first iceberg they flew over at low altitude was so close that their hearts leapt. Almost as near as the snow ramp at the exit of a ski lift, it was only about four feet below them. They felt eddies of cold air drawn into the cabin from the untouched surface of the ice, and then the warmer air over the water as it followed on.

Freddy looped the line around a winch and let the bucket slip off the ramp until it trailed the plane at 30 degrees of declination. The weight of the chock was greater than the force of the lift against the bucket's curved aerofoil. When the bucket was thirty or forty feet from the plane, Freddy stopped. "Hold on," he said, leaning back with the rope end that came off the winch. Seconds passed, then a minute, and then the rope vibrated, shuddered, and was kicked taut. The bucket was dragging along a flat-topped iceberg over which they glided, planing up a rooster tail of glistening detritus. "I've got it," Freddy said as he started the winch.

As the bucket drew closer to the plane, Fredericka bent forward to look. Freddy had snagged a gallon of the kind of crushed ice one finds underneath extremely large prawns in extraordinarily expensive restaurants. It looked perfectly edible. When it was in and the ramp was closed and the wind shut out, Freddy offered Fredericka the first taste. She received it gently. It was something few people had ever experienced, and she said, "Freddy, is this where iceberg lettuce comes from?"

"No, Fredericka. Lettuce doesn't grow here. This is ice from the Sea of Snow—the first evidence of the quest. When they calve from glaciers, icebergs up-end. The freshness you taste now may be snow that fell twelve thousand years ago, and has slept in immobility until this moment—twelve thousand years ago, when the world was infinite and an utter mystery to those who lived in it, in short, direct lives pressed hard into every facet and sensation of nature. It may have been that when this water fell as snowflakes, it was snowing in England, too, where not a single wall had been erected, nor a single tent pitched, nor a single garment stitched. And, yet, people may have listened to the hiss of the snow landing in that dark night, hoping the sky would clear and bring to them a round and opalescent moon."

SOMETIME AFTER TEN, the C-130 crossed the Hudson near West Point and banked southward at fourteen thousand feet. They would gradually descend for a landing at McGuire Air Force Base, where the unmarked cargo plane was to take on a load of classified electronic equipment. There had been no flight plan, and there would be no record. At any point between the New York–New Jersey state line and the landing, Freddy and Fredericka were to quit the aeroplane. Freddy had thought that Mr Neil would have had a set of coordinates picked out, but Mr Neil had not been to New Jersey, and where to jump was up to Freddy himself.

On the way across he had studied the map. "Our best option," he had told Fredericka, "is to jump into these meadows opposite New York."

"Bayonne Meadows," she said. "That sounds lovely. Being so close to New York City, they must be like Hampstead Heath."

"Yes. We'll go to a boutique and buy some clothes. I imagine a boutique in Bayonne Meadows will be upscale enough to take sterling."

Fredericka liked the site. Being just across the river Hudson from Manhattan, it was probably very trendy. So they arranged with the serjeant that they jump over the heath itself. Their worry was that they might parachute into a chamber music festival or a Shakespeare performance, but the chances were that they would land softly in a windswept field, unseen except perhaps by dons making astronomical observations.

"We've just crossed the New Jersey frontier," an officer shouted from the front of the plane. "Look at the gorgeously lit bridge ahead, which I believe is named after the rebellious George Washington."

"Oh, Freddy, I'm so nervous," Fredericka said. "I just want to get it over with. I can't move."

Freddy knew that the first jump was like facing execution. "Don't worry," he said. "The moment the chute opens, your fear will vanish and in its place will be elation."

"It feels like dying. Why do I want to rush it?"

"Fort Lee!" cried out the serjeant, on his way back to open the ramp, with the excitement and urgency always present before a jump. As the ramp was lowered they had to shout ever higher above the sound of wind and servomotors. "Static line check!"

"Check static lines," Freddy repeated, confirming not once, not twice, but three times that all was in order with the lines.

"Check chutes and harness," was the next command. They did, and the serjeant, as if before battle, followed on.

"Ten thousand five hundred feet, check harnesses again." They did. "Static line final check." They did.

"Chutes, lines, and harnesses in order," Freddy barked.

"Chutes, lines, and harnesses in order," Munchkin-Tito repeated.

"Confirmed," Freddy shouted.

"Ten thousand feet. Thirty seconds."

Freddy and Fredericka moved toward the edge of the ramp. Below them the lights of Hoboken and Bergen shone to the right, and farther right and to the north the George Washington Bridge sparkled with a bluish-white light more entrancing than any diamond necklace Fredericka had ever worn. "Oh God," she said, for the lights seemed so far below, and the intervening emptiness impossibly vast.

"You will be jumping on my command. Altitude ten thousand feet. Plenty of time to manoeuvre to the centre of the heath. Are you ready?"

"Go," said Freddy.

"Ten, nine, eight, seven, six, five, four, three, two, one."

Expecting to die, Fredericka followed Freddy from the ramp. As she fell, time seemed to stop, her heart seemed not to beat, and she did not breathe. Never had she fallen so far—several hundred feet until the chute deployed—and as she fell she forgot entirely about her hair. For years, whenever she had been conscious, she had thought about her hair. But not here, for here she fell through the black air with her soul momentarily in the hands of God. Then she felt the tug of the lines. "Freddy!" she called.

"I'm right here," he said, "circling you. Do you see my red light? I see yours."

"Yes, yes, I do." Though they were not supposed to, they had little red diodes in the front and back of their harnesses—a gesture from the serjeant, who had reservations about sending a novice parachutist into the dark above an untested drop zone.

"Good," said Freddy. "Now. Pull the left toggle. That's right, that's right. Enough, let go. Very good. Just relax. We're going to make some broad circles, and we'll touch down right in the centre of that black mass, away from roads and structures."

"This is marvellous!" she exclaimed. "Why haven't we done this before?"

"I've always considered it part of my work rather than entertainment. It never seemed like something to do for pleasure. Usually, you know, I'm weighted down with equipment. And, besides, I've never been able to get you even to go off the high diving board."

"I love this!"

"Right toggle," he said. "Some more. Good."

"And I love you," she said, her heart buoyant. She really did love him, although each time she said it and he could not reply, she loved him perhaps a little less.

They toggled again and wheeled through the darkness until they faced Manhattan below and to the east. Were he not able to tell her that he loved her—he wanted to, but could not state what was not true—at least he could show her this. England was civil, splendid, ancient, and deep. Nothing was finer than its perfectly bright colours softly combined against a field of misty blue sky, and nothing could ever be more eloquent or beautiful. But now, as if floating among the stars, they looked out upon a world burning in white. Uncountable lights were crushed together in gleaming walls or strung in chains across silvered bays lit as if by the dust of the moon. In depth, it was infinite, disappearing into all points of the compass, though gracing the quadrant of the Atlantic with a few sparkles only, of ships at sea mounted as if on a pewter shield. Each and every one of the uncountable lights blinked and sparkled. Summer air gave them their restlessness as their rays were bent in its rising, but hundreds of thousands had a life of their own, flashing on and off, changing colour, flaring, fading, burning, appearing through smoke, blocked by cloud, peeking out again. And many more hundreds of thousands were actually moving in traffic, gliding softly upon rivers and bays, or sailing in smooth trajectories along the high decks of bridges. From altitude, the clutter of moving lights looked, in its abrupt starts and stops, like illuminated diamonds shaken back and forth in a box. And in the sky itself hundreds of busy planes levitated above the city like gnats in an August clearing. Blinking and floating, they gave the darkness its immense depth.

South of the black heath were cities of flame set upon the horizon like castles under siege. Each had scores of brilliant towers topped by flares or bulging plumes of smoke that on their undersides mirrored the yellow and orange flames but at their cloud-like tops were pure ebony. On the plain that they enclosed, in a tangle of light, were roads, factories, and yards from which flashes emanated as if from ranks of artillery. Welders' torches, arcs, acetylene, and pantographs scraping their cables made a continuous dance of sparks and fire.

"Freddy?" Fredericka asked. "I've never seen anything like this. How was it done?"

"Heaven and hell collided," he said.

"Perhaps the heath isn't as trendy as we thought. It seems a bit industrial."

"This area is certainly industrial," Freddy answered. "Left toggle. Left. Hold. But the heath itself is black, perhaps playing fields for the workers. You see there? Off that way a bit? I think it's a bonfire. Probably an association picnic. We'll try to land close to it. First, as they probably have had a cricket or football match, it would be near a field. Second, in reasonable proximity to the sports park are undoubtedly expresso bars and boutiques. Probably they're open late, as in the Via Veneto. Right toggle."

They took ten minutes to descend, and as they dropped lower and lower they saw, heard, and smelled evidence of untrendiness. "You would think," said Freddy, "that if this were like Hampstead Heath, it would not smell so sulfurous."

"What about fashionable restaurants with highly spiced cuisine?" Fredericka asked. "Remember the one in Paddington Mews?"

"Yes," Freddy answered, forgetting for a moment that he was parasailing. "Two days later I was in a receiving line, and when I breathed into the face of a beautiful Swedish princess, she closed her eyes and reeled."

"What princess?" Fredericka asked, also forgetting that she was dangling from a parachute.

"Imogen of Fätso Bruggen."

"What's so special about her?" There was a blade in Fredericka's voice.

"She was one of the most beautiful women I have ever seen, and yet she was as big as a sequoia."

"What's a sequoia?"

"Right toggle."

"What's a sequoia?"

"Right toggle!"

"Freddy, what is a sequoia?"

"A tree."

Fredericka toggled right, which put them back on track. "You've got to respond quickly," Freddy told her. "As you can see, there are many obstructions below. We don't want to land dangerously. Had I known that the

Bayonne Meadows were surrounded by industry we could have parasailed right over the river and landed in Central Park."

"Why didn't we anyway? You can see it from the Carlyle."

"Don't you know, Fredericka, that Central Park is dangerous?"

They were low enough now to see and hear distinctly what rose to meet them. Huge arterial highways and thick bundles of railway track wove the landscape into thousands of patches, some of which seemed empty, others overwhelmed by ships in inland slips, yards for trucks and trains, factories, pipelines, transformer stations, stadia, and residential streets.

"Look there," said Freddy. "Houses all across the hillside. It *is* like Hampstead."

"Yes," said Fredericka. "I saw it on the map. It's called . . . Ho-Ho-Kus."

"No," said Freddy. "You're mistaken. I believe it is called . . . Ho-Bo-Kus."

"I don't care what it's called, as long as I can buy a decent dress and some shoes, and get something to eat besides iceberg. I feel like *médaillons* of boar with a citron-lingonberry relish."

"I'm sick of boar," said Freddy. "I want some wasabi ptarmigan."

"Freddy?"

"Yes?"

"What's that?"

Freddy looked around, and just as he saw what was approaching he heard its roar. Not an eighth of a mile from them a commercial jet had begun to bank and descend. Freddy looked over his shoulder to ascertain the position of the airport. Then he looked at the plane. Long a pilot, he understood the problem.

"If we don't drop faster, we'll intersect. Pull both toggles hard!"

"What's 'intersect'?"

"Pull!"

They pulled their toggles and plummeted. As they fell, the jet closed in on them, headlights blazing, engines screaming. Fredericka was terrified as much by the high-speed fall as by the plane bearing down on her. For a long moment it seemed as if they would be hit, but they fell below the plane's nose, and its belly passed a few feet from the tops of their collapsed chutes, jerking them into the turbulence.

"Release! Release!" Freddy screamed as soon as they had come into the clear.

At first Fredericka held the toggles clenched in her fists, but then she opened her hands. "Too fast! Too fast!" Freddy called out. "Right toggle, left toggle. Right toggle, left toggle." He wanted to manoeuvre into aerial switchbacks to keep them over a thermal that would slow their descent, but she was confused by his instructions. Trying to stay close to her erratic path, Freddy, too, lost control, and they were both dropping too fast for the little altitude they had. As he was attempting to guide her, they collided head-on, smashing face to face, body to body, as in the dalliance of eagles but with none of the grace.

When their mouths struck as if in a Dantean travesty of a kiss, each lost the two upper front teeth, and when an instant later their heads banged together yet again they were quickly dazed and incapacitated. Their blood was spattered by the wind against their goggles and into their hair as they fell in a rubble like broken kites, unable to scream or think. And then, in a breathtaking, solar-plexus-paralysing thud, the universe was transformed from a realm of ethereal lights to one of foetid black water in which they could neither breathe, see, nor move, and into which they sank tangled in the white parachutes that like the wings of angels had wrapped about them in their fall.

THOUGH FREDDY had parachuted into water many times, in most cases he had been able to see it as he approached in the day or by moonlight, and could release himself from his harness fifteen feet above the surface, dropping into the sea and swimming out from under the potentially fatal shroud as it settled upon the waves like snow. Even when for one reason or another he hadn't been able to release in advance, he had had a knife with which to cut himself free. And he had been trained to do this, first in a swimming pool and then in the sea with divers by his side.

Now, it was dark, the impact had been unexpected, without release, and after injury, and he had no knife. For him it was rather difficult, but Fredericka was certain to be overwhelmed. When he broke the surface and held up the parachute enough to get a breath of air, he heard nothing, which meant that she was trapped underwater. He had to hurry to save his own life so that he could save hers. He called out to her reflexively, but his cry was muffled in the black and malodorous water.

He pulled his emergency pins to untie from the billowing nylon and tangled lines, but still he was trapped. The cloth that in air was light, compliant, and diaphanous took on immense weight in water, like a sea anchor. He tried to dive down and swim under but couldn't because he was too enmeshed. Normally he might have had several goes at it, but to save Fredericka he would have to be quicker.

In savage, painful, animalistic motions, he gripped the fabric in his now gapped teeth and tore at it like a mad dog. Eventually he bit his way out and swam across his dead parachute toward the other lotus-like bloom, which he feared was Fredericka's grave in the waters.

"Fredericka! Fredericka!" he screamed as he swam to her languid parachute. She didn't answer. He dived down and sought her from underneath. He could see virtually nothing. Nor could he feel her body. There he stayed, embracing the filthy mud, pulling the lines with his hands, swallowing the poisonous water until he had no more breath and had to surface.

Again he was trapped. This time he was so out of breath that he thought he would never get free. Again, though with less energy, he tore at the parachute with his teeth. It went slowly, but he made a hole big enough to get his head through, and then, after breathing, he enlarged the opening and swam out of the confines that he was sure had taken his wife.

Treading water, heart pounding, he began to weep. Perhaps she had lost and never regained consciousness. Otherwise, it would have been too terrible a way to die. The water stank of mud and chemicals, and was covered with an oil slick. Oh, how horrible, he thought, and his fault entirely to have allowed it. If he had simply refused instead of letting himself be backed into what was really not even a corner, she might yet be alive. Had it not been for his weakness and indecision, they might have had a simple life together, and though he had no idea why, he was sure that in a simple life he would have learned to love her.

For the next half hour he grimly sought her body, diving down to no avail, swallowing more and more water, bathing his bleeding wounds in the sewer-tainted swamp. Finally, unable to find her, he swam to the bank in misery and defeat. He was too tired even to climb out, and simply lay on the mud, his face resting upon a pile of muskrat scat.

And then he heard a voice, and the voice said, "What are you doing there? It's so boring, watching you swim around in that disgusting water. Can we go now?"

"Fredericka!" he shouted. "Fredericka!" He flopped toward her and threw his arms around her mud-coated shoulders.

"Get away, Freddy. Your face is covered with muskrat shit."

He drew back.

"Wipe it off in the water."

"How do you know it's from a muskrat?" he asked.

She tightened in disgust. "I saw it. I saw it doing it," she said.

"That's all well and good, but how did you know it was a muskrat?"

"I've read a book about muskrats."

"You have?"

"Yes."

"When?"

"On our honeymoon, when you left to help Phoebe Boylingehotte move, I read a book about muskrats. Your father gave it to me because, at the time, he pitied me. It was the last time he pitied me. Now he hates me. He thinks I'm an idiot, and I suppose I am. I was so happy that he gave me the book, because I thought that after I'd read it we could have long conversations about muskrats, but he's not a bit interested in muskrats. It's just a pose. And what's more, he hadn't even read *The Complete Book of British Muskrats*."

"I read it," said Freddy. "It was remarkably well balanced. Most books about muskrats have a bias."

"Yes, I loved it," Fredericka said plaintively.

"But the British muskrat is different from the American," Freddy said. "Are you sure that what you saw was a muskrat?"

"No, I'm not sure, but the resemblance was uncanny," Fredericka answered, "and whatever it was it was doing its business right where you rested your face. Which brings up the question, now that we are injured, bleeding, and exhausted, how do we get to a five-star hotel?"

"The money!" screamed Freddy. In an instant he was back in the water, where for the next half hour he worked as hard as ever he had worked in his life. This was the first ten thousand pounds he had actually earned, and he came back to her with it as if it were the Silver Chalice, which it wasn't.

Dragging the Opheliated parachute through the brine had further exhausted him, but the money in it was not the only reason to do so. They could not walk about Manhattan, or hope to register at a hotel, in mud-coated *hracneets*. But with Fredericka's internationally famous touch for clothing, they would convert the many yards of parachute nylon into something acceptable, if not even chic, for street wear. Fredericka thought upon the fact that the world's fashion magazines might eventually be full of parachute dresses: it was not unreasonable. In Devon, once, she had pinned a few sprigs of goldenrod to a crème-and-lavender Ben Metumtam cocktail dress, and the fad had swept the globe, netting her more than twenty thousand letters of thanks from allergists alone.

But they had nothing with which to cut, and were unwilling to risk enlargement of the now prominent gaps in their upper front teeth. "Not to worry," Fredericka said, after seeing how difficult it was to rip through the reinforcing grids of heavily woven nylon, "we'll bunch them up the way Chaco did two years ago in Paris."

"I confess to having missed it."

"It was extremely hot. Chaco said that all the balloony, gauzy white fabric sent a message of sex. *You can come to bed with me even while I'm standing up. Deep in the clouds of Zanzibar lies the dark delta of Venus,* or something like that."

"That's what Chaco said, is it?"

"Yes."

"Somehow, I think that Chaco might not be interested in that himself."

"Oh no," said Fredericka, "Chaco is unambiguously bi. He's also ambidextrous."

The end result of Fredericka's swamp couture, however, probably would have pleased Chaco a great deal. They kept their leather flight caps to keep the mud and filth off their hair, and so seemed to have completely bald, moose-coloured, pointy heads. Freddy's two upper front teeth were gone, as were Fredericka's. Instinctually, they repeatedly ran over the empty spaces with their tongues, which had a pronounced effect on their expressions—it did something especially peculiar to the eyes—and made them appear perhaps less intelligent than they were. Their heads stuck out from the centres of their parachutes, which hung fashionably caftan-style from their arms, but to walk they had to bunch up the material they could not cut away, and it circled waist, thighs, and knees in ever larger rings, as if they were walking in a tower of white doughnuts. This, Fredericka had accomplished with the great deal of line available, and it was fairly trim.

"Shall we keep the goggles?" she asked.

"Let's hang on to everything we've got."

"I don't want to wear them on my head."

"You're the *couturière*."

"Ah, I know. We'll bunch them up in this fabric here that trails, and carry them in a ball in front of our stomachs. It's the Mali look from three years ago."

"Chaco again?"

"No, Berenice Edouard Bluvair."

"You do realise, Fredericka, that your breast *hracneets* are visible every time you move your arms."

"That's marvellous," she said, "and fashionable. It's called a cadenced peek-aboo. It drives men crazy. Far more hypnotic than flat-out bare bosoms."

"Tonight," Freddy promised, "you will have your five-star hotel," but he was not absolutely sure. Though his royal confidence, when conflated with his oft-felt black despair, was always victorious, this was an unusual place, where the rules might be incomprehensible.

"Follow me," he said. They set out into a landscape of mud, reeds, and the hulks of mechanical things. This detritus—what remained of cars, televisions, refrigerators, boats, metallic construction debris, and sharp rusty things of indeterminate origin—mysteriously littered the swamp. How did it get there? It did not float. After a few minutes' consideration, Freddy surmised that it must have been dumped from barges at high tide.

Their royal cuts and abrasions were soon joined by scores of razor-like wounds inflicted by the reeds, and their feet were punctured many times by reed stems and other sharp things embedded in the mud. They walked toward the houses on the hill, which Freddy judged to be at least a mile and a half away. In the other directions lay only roads, rail lines, and frenetic industry. The houses looked more inviting, though in the moonlight even they had a sinister air, their windows being almost Halloween-coloured and dim, and their dark unrelieved shapes on the palisade as forbidding as the most derelict castle.

"Though we may not find help in one of those houses," Freddy said, having given up hope of boutiques or expresso bars, "we should be able to find a taxi. Taxis come to me even when I don't want them."

"Would it take sterling?" Fredericka asked.

"I should think so. After all, it's New York."

"New York is across the river. This is Ho-Ho-Kus."

"No, Fredericka, it is Ho-Bo-Kus."

Their progress was slow, but after a time they had come far enough so that they were able to glimpse, off to their left and toward the motorways, the bonfire they had seen while floating down.

"Do you still think it's an association picnic?" Fredericka asked.

"Perhaps not, but there must be people there, and if they came in, there's undoubtedly a road out. The walking will be easier even if they don't help us, and why wouldn't they?"

. . .

LYING AMIDST the khaki-coloured reeds quite comfortably on their doughnut rings of parachute cloth fifty feet from the fire, they made a reconnaissance. A breeze had come up, the stars were phosphorescent, the blaze in front of them was as gold as the refinery flares miles away on the horizon, and all around, in chains of light and garlands of red, were necklaces of unending traffic.

"It's dry here," Fredericka whispered, "and it doesn't smell so bad."

"The wind," Freddy said.

"But what is that coconut smell?" Fredericka asked, lifting her nose in the air like one of the royal beagles. In her leather aviator's cap, she did not seem quite human. She was, however, alive to everything around her.

"Merely a noxious gas from a refinery or chemical works."

They peered at the scene before them. "Who are those people?" she asked.

"I don't know."

"What are they doing?"

"They're cooking."

"Why are they all dressed in black?"

"Leather," Freddy whispered. "Motorcyclists require it in view of falls or slides upon the macadam. You see the motorcycles beyond the fire? The silver rods are high handlebars: for a style of motoring that, on a long trip, counterintuitively relaxes the arms and back. That's where the music comes from."

"From the motorcycles?"

"They've got big amplifiers and speakers. It isn't allowed in England because it would disturb the peace, but here there is no peace to disturb. Everyone in this country makes as much noise as possible. It's that way in all barbarous places. Remember the Maoris?"

"I do, but, Freddy, aren't those swastikas? This isn't Germany."

"Neo-Nazis," Freddy said.

"They have swords."

One of them had drawn a bayonet and was brandishing it in a drunken altercation with another, who followed suit and drew his own. In slow motion timed to the music pulsing through the flames of the bonfire, they struck at one another.

"Two twenty-two-stone drunks with bayonets," Freddy said, "and not the slightest idea how to fence."

"We'll go around them," Fredericka proposed.

"Why?"

"What do you mean, why?"

"Why should we?"

"Because they're thirty drunken Neo-Nazis with bayonets, in the middle of a swamp in New Jersey, that's why."

"They're just savages, Fredericka. They may be mechanically inclined, but they are savages. We've never faced such people except with friendliness and confidence. I was not born to skulk in fear, and, besides, Mamie Eisenhower was always very nice to me. She used to make excellent hot cocoa laced with something that made me feel extremely relaxed—for a child. She would carry a bottle of it in her purse and drink it herself."

"They aren't Mamie Eisenhower, and there are thirty of them."

"Thirty," he said, wistfully. "Britain has subdued whole regions of the earth with, in some instances, just a few thousand or even a few hundred men. The essence of being British is not to flinch from such encounters."

"The essence of being British," Fredericka asserted, "is compassion for one's fellow man."

As Freddy rose up in his full doughnutted grandeur and began a procession through the reeds, she followed.

The motorcycles were parked in a semicircle blocking the road, and the motorcyclists gathered around the bonfire were standing, sitting, squatting, dancing, prone, or out like a light. Their chiefs with their consorts sat on several car-seat benches and a couch without cushions. They ceaselessly lifted silver-coloured containers of beer to their lips, draining them in a few swallows. The litter of beer vessels through which they lurched and danced was a foot high. They did what those who sit on disembodied automobile seats in a swamp and drink beer by a bonfire do. That is, they smoked cigarettes and cocked their heads back as if reading messages in the sky. And for some reason they walked backward and sideways, with a staccato step, as much as they walked straight ahead. This led to occasional collisions and collapses, and seemed to be a sign of the last stages of drunkenness before a long sleep.

As Freddy and Fredericka approached, they were able to count some on the ground who had been unseen. All told, there were thirty-eight, including what appeared to be nine women, with twenty-six motorcycles in waiting. Some wore Wehrmacht helmets, SS insignia, and swastikas, others simple bandannas. The men's extraordinarily thick forearms suggested that they trained with weights or were removal workers. On the backs of their jackets was a painting of human bones, a dancing cat, and a kitchen blender beneath the words *Paramus Devil Cats*.

From force of habit, when Freddy walked into their midst he showed a gracious smile. Fredericka, at his side, had the air of someone trained not to flinch at flashbulbs. Freddy knew what Fredericka looked like in her tori of parachute cloth and brown leather cap, and she knew what he looked like, but each gave himself the benefit of the doubt. Never having seen anything like these visitors, and fairly speechless ordinarily, the Paramus Devil Cats were silent as if mesmerised.

"How do you do?" asked Freddy. "Frederick and Fredericka Finney." The prince and princess smiled. "And you?" he asked the stunned Devil Cats. "You are, I take it, Paramus," which he pronounced *Para-moose,* "Neo-Nazis?"

Some of the Devils looked away as if to clear their vision, but when they looked back Freddy and Fredericka were still there.

"Hey, man," said one of them. It didn't mean hello, and was not a greeting. No one knew what it meant, not even the one who said it.

"How do you do?" Freddy repeated. Fredericka displayed her charming look, a tortured smile that said many things, none of which was true in any respect. No one came forward or said anything, so Freddy, clutching the ball of cloth over his stomach, occasionally thrusting his finger into the gap in his upper teeth, and now and then wiping the dirt and oil around on his besmottered face, took the initiative. "Say," he said, "do the taxis here take sterling?"

"What the hell are you?" asked one of the Devils, apparently their chief.

"I'm the Prince of Wales, and this is my wife, the Princess of Wales."

None of the Devils evinced any reaction whatsoever, until finally one turned to the others and said, "They're not human, are they?"

"You see," Freddy said, "we thought this was something like Hampstead Heath. We thought it would be surrounded by bookshops, clothiers, antiquaries, and expresso bars. We even thought that this was an association picnic, or the outing of one of the big investment banks." He looked at the Devils. "Perhaps the very back office."

"*You* thought," Fredericka said.

"Very well, I was wrong, but at least I thought something. You thought nothing."

"Isn't it better," Fredericka asked, "to think nothing than to think something that is completely idiotic?"

"It wasn't completely idiotic, it was entirely reasonable, but when you are about to jump from an aeroplane into an abyss it is in fact not better to think nothing than to think something that is completely idiotic."

"Hey, man," one of the Devils said, as if he were on a timer.

"You shut up, I'm not finished," Fredericka commanded. "You see, Freddy, you're always getting us into trouble like this because you feel that you have to have an answer for every question."

"If you're going to jump, Fredericka, you have to choose a landing zone."

"What I am saying, Freddy, is that you don't."

"You mean, just throw yourself from the plane at random?"

"One mustn't do *that,*" she said. "If you did that, you might almost drown in a swamp and then have to muck your way through a mile of reeds and an army of Neo-Nazis."

"We're not Neo-Nazis," said the chief.

"You're not?"

"No. What makes you think so?"

"The way you dress," said Freddy.

"Hey, man, we're having a party. You wanna start something?"

"Freddy, just shut up," Fredericka commanded.

"I will not," said Freddy. Then, turning to the Devils, he said, "Resolved, you are Neo-Nazis."

"Bull . . . shit!" said a Devil.

"Then why," Freddy pressed, "is each and every one of you sporting one or more swastikas, SS insignia, Afrika Korps badges, Wehrmacht helmets, and/or Nuremberg daggers?"

"We don't like Nazis, man. We hate Nazis. My father was in World War Two," the chief said.

"On which side?"

"America's side."

"Then why do you dress this way?"

"I don't know," the chief replied, a blank look on his face.

"You don't know?"

"No." He didn't.

"Is it drugs?" asked Freddy.

"Yeah, it's drugs. What is it?"

"The way you are."

"Yeah. It's drugs, drugs and alcohol."

"Who are you?" Freddy asked. "Why do you behave this way? What do you want?"

"What do *we* want?" the chief asked. "Hey, we want to party. We want to ride our hogs. We want to kill some Pagans or Angels. We want to kill someone famous. Stuff like that. That's how you get on television."

"Have you killed anyone famous?" Freddy asked.

"There isn't anyone famous in New Jersey. If you get famous, you move *out* of New Jersey."

"*We're* here."

"Freddy!" Fredericka protested.

"I'm making a point. You, are you the leader?"

"Yeah."

"What's your name?" the prince asked.

"Peanut."

"Is that a surname or a Christian name?"

"It's my first name, man. Otherwise, I'd be *Mr* Peanut." The Devils laughed. "Nobody in his right mind would call the head rider Mr Peanut."

"They would in the antebellum South if you hadn't reached your majority and you were addressed by a slave or white trash, wouldn't they, *Mr* Peanut?"

"The dude's crazy," said one of the Devils.

"Freddy," Fredericka said, trying to pull him away.

"Fredericka, please! Would you prefer that I address you as 'Peanut' or 'Mr Peanut'?"

"Me?" asked Fredericka.

"Him," said Freddy.

"Don't call me Mr Peanut."

"Then I shall call you Peanut, and you shall call me Freddy."

"Yeah."

"Peanut, you say that the *Para-moose* Devil Cats would like to kill someone famous."

"Yeah?"

"And that you can't find anyone famous in New Jersey."

"Freddy," Fredericka asked, "are you mad?"

"Please, Fredericka."

"It's supposed to be a secret."

"No it isn't. Mr Neil said we could operate as we wished. How else could one possibly expect to conquer single-handedly a country of more than two hundred and eighty million people? Just because they've given us noms de guerre doesn't mean we have to use them. And, as you know, we haven't even had a chance to open the capsules."

"We could make up a name. I could be Lady Clydesbee, and you could be Lord Danforth."

"We've already told them who we are."

"We didn't hear," Peanut said. "We're drunk, and we're, like, focussed on what you look like."

Freddy stood to his full height in his doughnut suit and moose-coloured cap. "Do you imagine that we are more ludicrous than you?"

"Yeah," said the Devils, but they were drowned out by a jet flying over-head. When it had passed, Freddy resumed. "Let's get back to the point. You said. . . ."

"I know what I said," said Peanut. "No one's famous in New Jersey ex-cept Thomas Edison, Molly Pitcher, and that bitch Joyce Kilmer, and that's only because they're rest stops."

"If you killed someone like, let us say, Joyce Kilmer, would that be satisfactory?"

"Yeah. It would be big stuff if we killed a chick who was a rest stop."

"Joyce Kilmer was a man."

"No shit."

"Then," said Freddy, "what about us? We're famous. I'm the Prince of Wales. She's the Princess of Wales. Here we are, in New Jersey, *voilà*."

Fredericka sat on the ground and put her face in her hands.

Seeing that they had never heard of him or any other prince of Wales, Freddy sought to clarify. "The Prince of Wales is the heir to the British throne."

"What does that mean?"

"It means," Freddy explained, "that the queen is my mother, and that when she leaves the throne I will be the king of England."

"So fuckin' what?" asked Peanut. "This is New Jersey. Who fuckin' cares?"

Fredericka looked up, her hands still held as they were when they cradled her face. "You don't care?"

"Why should I?"

"I'll tell you this," said Freddy, to Fredericka's considerable frustration. "If you kill us, you'll be on television for weeks, and years later you'll be in the crime and biographical retrospectives."

"No shit!"

"Think Charles Manson. This is my proposal. I saw you with the bayonets. Why don't you pit your best man against me. That would have to be you, Peanut, wouldn't it? And if you kill me, you'll be famous and you can have her," Freddy said, pointing to Fredericka.

"He can *not* have me," Fredericka said indignantly. "I'll be the judge of who will have me."

Freddy turned to her and said, "Be quiet, you're spoiling it."

The Devils, more than Peanut, who would have to do the fighting, liked the proposition. "But what do I get?" Freddy asked.

"You get killed," Peanut said, a little nervously.

"But what if I don't get killed? What if neither of us gets killed, or I kill you?"

"I don't understand."

"If I win, what do I get?"

"What do you want?"

Freddy pointed toward the biggest motorcycle, which was standing alone and had the most music coming out of it.

"You want my hog?" Peanut asked.

"Put the keys to the other hogs in a bag on the handlebars of yours. Yours, engine running, will sit two hundred feet down the road, with her on the back seat." Fredericka gave a hrrumph. "All the Devils shall stay here, and we will fight twenty-five feet from the hog. If you win, you win. If I win, we're off and I'll drop the other keys at the end of the road."

"Don't you trust us?" Peanut asked.

"As a rule, I don't trust people who wear swastikas, no," Freddy said.

"Okay," said Peanut, too drunk to think.

The prospect of a duel charmed the Devils into near sobriety. They rushed hither and yon, and no longer did they walk in staccato steps sideways or backward as they collected their keys and moved Peanut's motorcycle. Peanut himself managed quickly to become undrunk. Perhaps it was because his twenty-two stone could soak up alcohol like a sink, and he had had only thirty bottles of beer.

Walking up the road, Fredericka asked, "Have you ever fenced with someone who weighs as much as a grand piano?"

"If anything, it's to my advantage. Clarence is very slight but it's hard for me to best him."

"That's with foil or épée. What about sabre?"

"Darnley is also slight."

"And short."

"Yes, but he's the best in England, Fredericka."

"Do you use your strength against him?"

"In a way."

"What if you couldn't?"

"I don't think I'll have difficulties," Freddy said. "Peanut is neither fit nor agile."

"The bayonet is shorter than the sabre, Freddy."

"These are long bayonets."

"But they are shorter. Have you fought with one?"

"This is not the time, Fredericka, to sap my confidence."

"Can you back out? Why don't we just run away on the hog?"

"I've given my word."

"Freddy, what if you're killed and left in this swamp, and I'm gang-raped and become the chattel of Mr Peanut?"

"It's too late to fear," was the answer. He started the motorcycle.

Fredericka sat herself on the back seat. "It's such an ugly machine," she said. "Am I to wear a helmet?"

"No, we shan't wear Nazi regalia."

Freddy turned to walk toward Peanut, who approached with a bayonet in each hand. One blade was about two and a half feet in length, the other less than a foot. When Peanut drew close, Freddy said, "I hope the long one's for me."

"It isn't," said Peanut.

"That's not cricket," said Freddy, picking up the small one after Peanut had thrown it to the ground.

"We made an oral contract," Peanut told him. "You specified bayonets, I accepted, and you raised no objections. You didn't narrow the terms."

"Are you a solicitor," Freddy asked, trying to fix the rickety handle of the short bayonet, "a lawyer?"

"I am," Peanut said. "I am, in fact, a fuckin' litigator, if you must know."

"I would imagine," Freddy told him, trying to delay, "that for duelling with bayonets and wearing Nazi accoutrements you might be disbarred."

"What I do in private is my own business, guy."

"In England, it wouldn't be."

"This is New Jersey. It's like *Born Free.*"

"Whatever that means, it isn't quite fair that your bayonet is a sword and mine is a paring knife."

"We made a contract," said Peanut, lifting his bayonet above his head and bringing it down with tremendous force where Freddy would have been standing had Freddy not jumped to the side. Though the ground bounced with the impact, Freddy jabbed Peanut's side with the short bayonet. It went through Peanut's leather but was stopped before it touched flesh.

"You've got body armour," Freddy announced. The answer was a bayonet stroke that would have sliced through oak. Freddy blocked it with his own paltry blade, which flew into the swamp as Freddy fell backward, hands stinging. Peanut raised the long bayonet above his head as he had before.

Were Freddy to roll too soon, Peanut would change the path of his stroke and catch him as he went. Were he to roll too late, he would be hit. Still, he was unafraid. The narrow band beyond which action was in vain appeared to him almost as if it were a glowing graphic superimposed on the warm night air. Associated with what he knew would be his correct timing and subsequent survival was a burst of joy that welled up within, a gift from on high that guided him to exactly the moment he sought. As the blade was forced down, he saw it blur in the air. He delayed his roll, and felt motion building within. And then, seemingly too late, he did roll, the blade missed, and the ground vibrated once again.

In a moment he was up on his feet, dodging the bayonet as it came whistling past in a horizontal sweep. He did not have to say words of encouragement to keep himself in the fight, for he wanted to be nowhere else, even if he had no idea what to do next. As far as he was able or willing to think ahead, he would dodge without end, confident that his energy would not flag before that of his adversary. In fact, though it was not a thought, he sensed in the part of the mind that can deal with such things during a combat that this alone kept him alive. He seemed to float, his reflexes on fire.

Peanut's blade went up, but in the clear space it left came a long bayonet thrown by Fredericka, handle first, flying as if of its own volition into Freddy's grip. In a split second born of a lifetime of swordsmanship Freddy parried well. Now it was cricket. Freddy was so much a better fencer than Peanut that he relaxed and stayed in place, parrying each attack with ease. He had never been able to do this with his fencing master, who was far too good, but the perfect defence had always been his ambition, in that he would suffer no harm and do no harm. Thus, he stood for the next five minutes, rooted on one spot, while Peanut moved mountains of weight in thunderstorms of grunts, breathing and sweating like a water buffalo, before he finally collapsed.

"I won't kill him," Freddy told the surly Devils, "but you see that I could. We're off now, like birds from a crisp corn pie and faster than a falling raccoon." He and Fredericka mounted the idling motorcycle and drove away. Moments later they heard the sound of many motorcycle engines. "They had spare keys," Freddy said, increasing their speed on the sandy track.

"Can you drive this?" Fredericka shouted over the wind as they whipped through the reeds at fifty miles per hour.

"I've just learnt."

Coming out onto the road, they flew off the curb, and when they hit the pavement the radio came on. The beat of the music thundered louder than their engine and made their growing speed seem natural and safe. Going too fast to know where they were going, they enjoyed it despite the absurdity and danger, both of which they assumed were characteristics of the country itself. By driving at first on the left side of the road, which proved disconcerting to oncoming traffic, they lost the Devils. Freddy was a jet pilot and sometimes drove very fast, but now he drove particularly fast because of the strange music. Trained to the highest standards by Britain's finest musicians, conductors, and theorists, he had been lifted to the celestial sphere by Bach, Mozart, and Beethoven, and he knew his Handel, Verdi, and Brahms. That is all true, but nothing in his experience had prepared him to be rocketed ahead by the blues, in a new world and a new life. He knew instantaneously that deep in the heart of American civilisation was its music, and that deep in the heart of its music was the miracle of the open road.

Entering the New Jersey Turnpike at 140 miles per hour, they could afford neither to take a ticket nor to choose their direction. Physics sent them south, and they found themselves hurtling into the summer night, flanked on all sides by machines gliding with them in the direction opposite or at cross purposes. Even the air was crowded with activity. Planes flew above in bug-like, slow circles, flashing multi-coloured, rising with a roar, or descending floodlit onto vast prairies of concrete spotted with soft violet lights.

With their parachute silks trailing behind them like courageous brush-strokes, the air and oxygen forcing into their lungs, and the roar everywhere, they passed at unthinkable velocity through an unthinkable landscape of light. Here were mantis-structured refineries where amber lamps blinked in unknown code beneath sheaths and coronas of flame. Here were bridges that leapt bays, distant lighted towers, flags spotlighted against the sky, thick traffic that flew in air, ships pulled up to land, and nothing still, fixed, or set.

"I believe," Freddy shouted above the wind and the insane mumble of the engines, "that we are on our way, more or less, to Philadelphia."

"Isn't this dangerous?" Fredericka shouted in turn.

"I suppose so," was the answer. "I'm inexperienced and we are going a hundred and forty miles per hour."

"Why don't you slow down?"

"We're being chased by Devils."

"We lost them," Fredericka averred, "when we went the wrong way on that single-direction ramp and crashed through the hedge."

"I didn't do it deliberately. The wheels have a gyroscopic effect. The machine wants to go in a straight line, and I'm loath to lean into a turn: it's so heavy I don't know if it will come back up again."

"Freddy, just slow down."

They dropped to 120, which seemed more civilised. "We must buy dollars," Freddy declaimed into the wind, which carried it back to Fredericka, "we must find a hotel, we must sleep, we must wash, we must get new clothes and a car, and we must see a dentist."

"After the hairdresser," Fredericka insisted.

"I advise that you have your hair cut short. We'll run out of money soon enough, which means that you'll have to wash it yourself. Even now we can't really afford a hundred pounds a day for hair, can we."

"If I have it cut it will be a lot more."

"Why? I pay six pounds. What do you pay?"

"I don't have my hair cut in an army barracks, thank you," Fredericka said. "It's a bit more complicated."

"How much more complicated could it be? How much have we been paying?"

"Thir charges five hundred and fifty pounds for a full cut, which includes everything else, so you come out radius, ready to dedicate an orphanage."

"Do you mean, *radiant?*"

"Everyone looks at you."

"Where does he get off charging that kind of money? It's madness."

"No, it's because he cuts my hair that he can do that. Everyone wants him now."

"I'm aware of the effect," Freddy said. "The trick is to let them charge other people more because they do business with us, but to demand that they do it for us for nothing. You tell them at the beginning that it has to be that way. It's a kind of tax."

"And what if they won't?"

"They're finished, and they know it."

"But Thir is already known for cutting my hair."

"You could destroy him by putting egg and ink on it and showing up at the Royal Albert Hall. I've done that kind of thing."

"I know."

"It works. Why am I so hungry? We need a good *relais de la campagne.*"

"Freddy, what kind of car can we buy for less than ten thousand pounds?"

"I suppose it will have to be previously owned."

"That's disgusting. Who knows what people do on the seats?"

"A plastic Yugoslavian mini, probably."

"You mean the kind you can lift? I'd rather use the train."

"In America, Fredericka, they don't really have trains for people. The trains here are used mainly to transport pigs, television sets, and fruit."

Far south of Rahway, where the road cut through trees and fields rather than the busy floor of hell, two New Jersey state troopers sat in their cruiser hidden behind an abutment. They had decided to rest for a few minutes before they darted out to give another ticket, and were enjoying the night air and the sounds of tree frogs and crickets when Freddy and Fredericka sped by.

"What was that?" one asked.

"I don't know. It clocked at a hundred and twenty-eight point three."

"But what was it?" the driver said as they pulled out onto the road.

"It looked like a two-humped camel draped in cheesecloth. It was like two guys with big fat white bodies and little tiny brown pinheads."

"Was it a motorcycle?"

"Whatever it was, it had only one headlight. You'd better turn on the siren."

A few minutes later, when Freddy saw the flashing lights in the mirror on the windscreen, he shouted to Fredericka that he thought their speedometer was defective. This was because what he took to be either an ambulance or a fire engine seemed to be gaining on them from very far away. As it grew in the mirror, he calculated that either it would have to be going 150 miles an hour or he and Fredericka would actually be travelling at sixty rather than 120.

"It seems that we're going quite fast," Fredericka said.

"That's just the wind. The speedometer must be broken. What I'll do, taking a leaf from the theory of relativity, is to keep them in my mirror at a constant size, or make them shrink. Then we'll know we're going ninety or ninety-five."

By increasing his speed to keep the police car the same size in his mirror, he led the troopers to increase their speed to 165, beyond which they could not go faster. They breathed tensely and dared not call for a roadblock. A hundred people might be killed. Shooting past other cars on the road, they hoped for the best.

Freddy could no longer hear Fredericka, or himself for that matter, and though the speedometer hovered near 165, he did not credit it. In his judgement, the sensation of great velocity came from speeding through open air. Drivers he passed, cruising at sixty-five, could hardly comprehend another sort of vehicle whistling past them a hundred miles per hour faster.

As Freddy and Fredericka raced down the passing lane somewhere south of Hightstown, a huge lorry ahead suddenly veered left. They had to move right so quickly that they were forced into a roller-coaster-like manoeuvre that made Fredericka pound on Freddy's back and scream for him to slow down. As he, too, had been startled, he did, and they both exhaled in relief upon decelerating to eighty, which seemed so slow that it was as if they could jump on and off. "I'll let that bloody ambulance pass us," Freddy announced, but when it came up behind them it began to demand over its loudspeaker that they pull to the side of the road.

"It isn't an ambulance, Freddy."

"We can't pull over," Freddy said. "We have no accessible documents."

Pulling up on the left, the troopers motioned for them to stop. When they saw what they had been chasing, their hair stood on end.

"There's only one thing I can do," Freddy told Fredericka, after he had given the troopers a royal wave and a gracious smile. "We must find a forest."

"What if they shoot us? They do that in America, you know."

"They won't if you smile and wave."

Until they reached the next exit, Freddy and Fredericka waved and smiled at the troopers, rolled their eyes, and scratched their heads. The troopers couldn't even speak. At the first exit, Freddy veered right just before the smash barrier and accelerated up the ramp, while the police car had to come to a stop, back up, and resume. By this time the motorcycle had run through the tollgate, triggering alarms that summoned additional police.

"All we need now," Freddy said as they raced down a country road, "are trees that we can pass through and they cannot. There."

Ahead was a pool of undeveloped blackness where the road passed through a pine forest. They left the pavement, thudded across a ditch, and moved between the trees, with Freddy taking many branches in the face. But no car could follow, and he was strong enough to push on, sometimes taking roads to increase his lead, but going mostly overland. They travelled through the night until, far from where they had started, the motorcycle ran out of petrol, and they abandoned it in bushes at the edge of a field. Walking on in what remained of the moonlight, they got to a quiet glade that was narrow and well protected, and there they lay on the pine needles and soon were able to sleep. Various insects crawled into their garments, and mosquitoes bit them, but the air was fragrant and warm and the floor was soft. They had reclined on their backs because of the parachute balls on their stomachs. After Freddy had fallen asleep, Fredericka had looked at the last of the moon through the trees and said, "How lovely it is here. I must be mad."

The next morning, Freddy was awakened by a golden bug flying in circles above his nose. It sounded like a cheap alarm clock ringing in another room, which reminded him of his public school days, and then it stung him. Despite the throbbing pain, he didn't care. In fact, he hardly

noticed. This was now the way things were going to be, and he was determined to make the best of it. *"Quelle jour magnifique!"* he said when he
turned his eyes to a deep blue sky framed by virgin evergreen boughs
swaying in a cool wind. A front had pushed down from the Commonwealth to bless the royals' first incognito North American daylight, and,
like an obsequious ambassador, it had followed them from a rare and spec-
tacularly clear summer evening in New York to perfect Danish summer
weather in a copse of Lakehurst Pines not far from Philadelphia.

"Freddy, I'm hungry," Fredericka told him when she awakened. "Don't
you know any tricks about making omelettes in the wilderness?"

"Nothing about omelettes as long as we have no eggs, but we could
bathe in a stream and breakfast on crickets, grubs, and raw frog. We might
find some berries and edible roots, and we could chew balls of resin."

After a moment of paralysis, Fredericka said, "Let's push on to the Four
Seasons in Philadelphia."

"Yes, let's. And after that we can go to Washington. Why not a coup?"

"A coup?" she asked. "How do I look?"

Her leather flight cap was so stuffed with her thick golden hair that it
seemed as if her skull had swollen or she was from a different galaxy. Her
nose and cheeks were bright red from windburn and abrasion, she was
missing her two upper front teeth, and scores of little evergreen sprigs had
tangled in her peculiar clothing, which, like Fredericka herself, was filthy
dirty and covered with smudges, mud, and tar.

"Apart from the impression you create of being the sister of the
Michelin rubber boy," Freddy said, "you look splendid." He wanted to
keep up her morale.

"Do I really?" She began to glow through the smudges.

"You look outdoorsy, but feminine; rugged, but sexy."

"I don't look strange?" she asked, placing a finger in the vacant space
where two huge Chiclet teeth had been.

"No, not at all. The unfortunate accident involving the teeth—which
shall be fixed—makes you rather fetching, actually. How do *I* look?" He
smiled broadly, the gap in his teeth as black as an architect's clothes.

"You look, you look . . . very masculine I would say. Tough. More than
that. Warlike."

"Really?"

"Definitely."

"Which war?"

"The one you just wrote about."

"Eighteen twelve?"

"No, the other one, where everyone killed each other."

"That doesn't really narrow it down."

"The one that lasted forty years."

"Forty years," Freddy said, wondering. "Do you mean the Thirty Years' War?"

"Yes. I thought the costumes in that war were very sexy."

"Indeed, why should we be the slaves of fashion?" Freddy asked. "For centuries the pantaloon has been strongly associated with hardened soldiers and men with very long pikes. Why should I be reticent about my mode of dress, especially when it is we, after all, who are the arbiters of fashion."

"You're right," she said, "but isn't it *artichokes* of fashion?"

"That's the feminine. I am an arbiter. You are an artichoke."

"What's the other one you told me?"

"Which one?"

"You know."

"Obtuse?"

"Yes."

"A man is obtuse," he said, "but a woman . . . is a Watusi."

"I must confess that I think I used it to great effect, even if you won't like it."

"What do you mean?" Freddy asked, shooing away another golden bug.

"I shouldn't tell you this, but before we left I taped an interview with Brian Kidney of the BBC."

"Why? You weren't supposed to. When?"

"We were shopping in the same store, and he's always been so nice to me. That afternoon, I let him come 'round for an interview. Don't worry. It's good. It even makes things seem normal, as if we were still there. They'll show it next month."

"You shouldn't have done it."

"No, I was really very good. I wore a ravishing *framboise*-and-*crème*-coloured Dimitri Rashpagin. And I made the distinction just as you told me to. Brian Kidney asked my view of the queen's personality, and I was very high-blown. I said that in every respect you can understand her if you understand that she is actually a Watusi. He said, 'Do you mean, literally, that she is a Watusi?' And I said, 'Of course. Look it up. Freddy is the one who opened my eyes to this.' And he said, 'Freddy says that his mother is a Watusi?' And I told him that that's what you had told me on a number of occasions. Didn't you?"

"Yes," said Freddy. "I did."

"You seem distressed," Fredericka said. "You mustn't be. This is a new situation."

"You're right," said Freddy. "The first thing we must do is find a bank, buy dollars, and get to the Four Seasons. There we shall wash, shave, eat, brush, rinse, sleep, and get new clothes. The next day, *chez le dentiste.* Then, properly dressed, coiffed, accessorized, rested, and repaired, we shall make our way to Washington."

"The embassy?"

"We can't go to the embassy, but my good friend Edmund St John du Plafond—Plaffy—is now a first secretary there. Do you remember when I flew over quietly to play polo in Virginia?"

"Yes."

"He let me use his digs. The embassy may have been alerted, but even if he's in on it, he'll help. I was always generous with him. I'm sure he'll set us up with whatever we need, and then we can look to the conquest."

"Wouldn't that be cheating?"

"Not at all. It would be cheating if we used a credit card, obtained a loan, commandeered the embassy, or announced ourselves to the press— assuming that the press would believe us. This isn't cheating any more than was taping the hundred-pound notes into the parachute."

"Which was cheating."

"Shall I just bury them, then?"

"No."

"I thought not. How can the two of us alone conquer this immense country unless we're flexible?"

After wandering around the forest for a while they broke out into a subdivision shining in the now strong sun. Beyond dozens of one-and-a-half-storey houses scattered about the fields like giant pencil sharpeners was the silver-blue skyline of Philadelphia, as glossy and cool as a glacier. They were much cheered by this, and despite their discomfort and no shoes, they walked a good pace.

"Shoes," said Fredericka, looking at her bloody feet. "My palace for a flip-flop."

"You shall have better," Freddy proclaimed. "Press on. Where there is a housing estate there is a shopping centre, and where there is a shopping centre there is commerce, and where there is commerce one can exchange currencies."

After half an hour of walking, now on sidewalks, during which many a mother grabbed her baby, they came to a strip mall. Proud of his predictive ability, Freddy read the roll: "You see," he said in the same tone his father used when describing an animal he had just killed—*The Vladimir Ibex must be shot between cheek and ear*—"Vinton's Tropical Fish; Mattress World; Napoli Pizza; Tapeworm Video; Mr G's Lavender Tux; Samos Travel; Schoenbaum, Pakistan, and Graziella, Attorneys-at-Law; Mary Ann's Paints; Sub-Total Aquatic Fitness; and . . . the Bank of Cherry Hill."

They strode up to the Bank of Cherry Hill like conquerors. "Where's the door?" Fredericka asked, as only a machine and a car lane faced the street.

"It is a detached structure," Freddy said. "The door must be on the other side."

They walked around the bank like pilgrims at the Kaaba. On each of the building's sides was an automatic teller machine that whenever they passed was supposed to say, "Welcome to the Bank of Cherry Hill," but said, rather, ". . . ank of Cher . . . ank of Cher . . . ank of Cher. . . ."

"What does 'ank of Cher' mean?" Fredericka asked.

"Where are the people?" Freddy added. "Where is the door? Where is the room?"

They walked on, cutting across the back of a decaying shopping centre, where weeds, broken glass, and sheet-metal refuse littered the asphalt. They had seen from afar the signs, windows, and door of the Utz Bank of New Jersey. Utz, Freddy informed Fredericka, was an ancient German banking house with longstanding connection to the Hanseatic League and the Fuggers.

"The who?" Fredericka asked.

"The Fuggers. I'm sure that the Utzs are actually Fuggers. Perhaps in America they didn't want to call themselves Fuggers."

"I should think not," said Fredericka.

"In Germany it's *Steinweg,* but, in America, *Steinway.* Should we need some leverage in this transaction, we have it, because in my economics tutorial I wrote a monograph on Hartmut Utz. When he extended his operations to Silesia, he changed his name to Fugger. All the Fuggers, therefore, are Utzs, so, conversely, the Utzs must be Fuggers. This may prove useful in charming them."

"All I want is to be clean, to have a clean bed, to bandage my feet, to eat, to wash. . . ." Fredericka said, limping up the few steps of the bank.

"Don't worry," said Freddy. "We've made it."

HAVING FORGOTTEN ENTIRELY their strange appearance, they entered the bank as if nothing were amiss, and all movement ceased. Tellers, officers, and customers became as still as suddenly discovered deer who believe that lack of motion creates invisibility, as sometimes it does.

Near the door was a silver punch bowl half full of M&Ms. When they saw it, Fredericka shrieked, "Look, Freddy! Sweets!"

"Yes," Freddy answered, just as excited as she. "I know those! They have chocolate inside. The president eats them," he screamed, shovelling them into his mouth as Fredericka did the same for herself. "They're called W&Ws!"

"Ummh! Ahhh!" Fredericka said, scooping handful after handful from the bowl and eating with tremendous speed.

Barely audible through the crunches and crackling, Freddy went on, but the only phrase that survived was, "He keeps them in a bowl on his golf cart." The rest, along with his wife's comments as well, was subsumed in moans of near-sexual pleasure. Though the audience—tellers with money in hand, customers holding cheques and deposit slips, bank officers leaning forward in their chairs—was still immobile, when Freddy picked up the almost empty bowl and, like some sort of very odd Norse celebrant, raised it to his lips, they pulled their heads back, pigeon-style, unbelieving.

Meanwhile, Fredericka had started to drink tea from foam cups. In between drinks she ripped open packets of cream and sugar and emptied them directly into her mouth. Freddy followed suit. When nothing was left on the table but empty wrappers and the silver punch bowl drained of W&Ws, they trotted in a sugar high up to the counter. They had their pick of tellers, as all the customers were leaving the bank. "Hello," Freddy said to a woman fleeing ahead of her tilted shopping bags. "Delighted to be here, how do you do?" he asked, as if he were opening a highway or consecrating a cathedral. The four tellers behind the counter watched with painful perplexity as the two creatures who had just eaten several pounds of W&Ws struggled with the white balls of cloth tied to their stomachs.

As they had hurtled through the trees, the strings had been caught on the branches and pulled tight beyond redemption. "Drat!" said Freddy, "we'll have to do a Caesarian." He stepped toward an officer. "May I impose upon you for some scissors or a sharp knife?"

The woman was so stunned that, though she could not conceive of witnessing the operation Freddy had mentioned, she gave him papershears from her desk drawer anyway. "Thank you so much," Freddy said, and then, as the woman fainted, stabbed the ball and cut into it violently. Presently he removed a pair of parachutist goggles, which he put on his head, and a fistful of hundred-pound notes. Then he went to work on Fredericka. Another pair of goggles emerged, which she put on her head, and more notes, which she gave to him.

With pronounced relief, they stepped up to a teller and greeted her with wide smiles. Where teeth remained, they were chocolatised. "How do you do?" Freddy asked.

"How do you do?" the teller echoed sceptically. She had very black hair, red lipstick, glasses that were shaped like a butterfly, and she looked like Jack Palance.

"We would like to buy some dollars," Freddy declared, "with ten thousand pounds sterling."

"You would like to what?"

"Buy dollars."

"You would like to 'buy' dollars?"

"Yes."

"You can't 'buy' dollars, sir. Dollars are money. You can't buy money."

"Of course you can."

"No, you can't. Sir, this is a bank, not a store."

"No, no, look. I have here," said Freddy, holding up the money, "ten thousand British pounds."

"British what?"

"British pounds."

"Whatever those are, sir, I can't sell you money."

"I want to exchange them. What is your rate?"

"Do you have an account with us?"

"No."

"Do you bank in Cherry Hill?"

"No, I don't bank in Cherry Hill."

"Where do you bank?"

"Coutts," he said, naming the banker to the royal family.

"Where?" she asked.

"Coutts."

"Are you trying to say something?"

"Coutts!" he shouted. "Coutts! Coutts! Coutts!"

She drew back, convinced that he was mocking her with birdcalls. "Sir, you don't have to do that. I simply asked what bank you used. Why don't you speak to Mr Guthwin?"

There was Mr Guthwin, hand extended to usher Freddy and Fredericka politely to the chairs facing his officer's desk. "Are you related to Gershwin, the Baby King from the Age of Blue?" Freddy asked.

Mr Guthwin, who was very timid, replied in a barely audible mumble, looking down as if in shame, "No, no, no, I'm not, no."

They sat. Freddy and Fredericka were used to dealing not with tellers but with bank chairmen. And only rarely did they go to a bank. Usually the bank sent a delegation to them. Their statements came bound in leather. Their questions were answered immediately, their requests filled instantly, their expectations met invariably.

Entwining his hands, Mr Guthwin rested them on the edge of the desk and put his head down to them so that his nose sat on the saddle of his index fingers. He closed his eyes, breathed-in a deep breath, looked up, and said, "What can I do for you?"

"A standard transaction," Freddy stated confidently. "Something quite ordinary." He held up the banknotes. "What is your rate on sterling? I have ten thousand pounds and would like to buy dollars."

"The Utz Bank doesn't do foreign exchange," Mr Guthwin said. "We're not equipped for it. I'm sure that in Philadelphia you'll have no trouble. Just across the river." He pointed.

"Mr Guthwin, you don't have to be equipped for this transaction," Freddy lectured. "You need not be holding yen or roubles or kumquats. You have in inventory exactly what we need: U.S. dollars. Now, if we have to pay a premium because foreign exchange is not common in Cherry Hill, we will. That's because we need a taxi, we need food," his voice began to rise in passion, "we need shoes, we need clothes, we need to cut ourselves out of these suits, and we need a goddamned bloody dentist!"

Mr Guthwin looked at them. He looked at the trail of blood that marked where they had walked. He looked at Fredericka's huge long nose that was like a horseradish but which in conjunction with her immense cheeks, high cheekbones, and broad aristocratic face had fired the imagination of the world. Now, however, it stood out in red and it was, without her masses of silver-blond hair to balance it, not quite of the world. Who were these people? Were they people? He didn't know. They were very large, they were tremendous. And they seemed so angry and desperate. He didn't want to say no. "We may be able to arrange it," he told them. "I'll have to call Mr Utz, our president, at the main office."

"Don't they do foreign exchange at the main office?" Freddy asked.

"No," said Mr Guthwin, picking up the phone. As he dialled, Freddy and Fredericka felt hope return. "Mr Utz please. Serge Guthwin at branch seven." He looked up and smiled, as if to say, *Here comes Mr Utz, and all this will be taken care of.*

"Mr Utz, this is Serge Guthwin. Fine, sir. Thank you. Yes, we have two foreign gentlemen here. . . ."

"Gentlemen?" Fredericka asked. "Gentlemen!" She ripped off her aviator's cap and out fell masses of paralysingly beautiful tresses that spilled like a waterfall and shone in the light. "I'm a lady," she said severely.

"I'm sorry," Mr Guthwin said. "Excuse me. Mr Utz, a gentleman and a lady." Her nose was now in context, and assumed the hypnotic anteater quality that some men found irresistible. "They would like to buy dollars with pounds sterling. Yes. Cash, one-hundred-pound notes. I have no idea, how can I tell?" He listened for a while, covered the mouthpiece of the telephone, and said, "Mr Utz says he's sorry, but, because we don't ordinarily deal with it, we have no way of knowing if the sterling is genuine."

"Of course it's genuine," Freddy said. "There's a picture of my mother on every note."

"He says, Mr Utz, that it is genuine, and that there is a picture of his mother on each note."

"And tell him," Freddy said, pulling his ace, "that he's a Fugger. Go ahead, tell him."

"Mr Utz, he says to tell you that you're a Fugger."

They heard, from the phone, a tiny voice that said, "A what?"

"A Fugger."

"Tell him," Freddy said, "that all Utzs are Fuggers, and that I know this because I'm a historian."

"He says, sir, that all Utzs are Fuggers, and that he knows this because he's a historian."

"And tell him that, although he may not have known it, I am certain of it, and that I will be happy to go into it in detail if he would like to come here to interview me." Freddy removed his own leather cap, with some relief.

Mr Guthwin relayed this message to Mr Utz. As he was doing so, Fredericka said, "Freddy, with your cap off and in that white balloon dress, you look like a duck in drag."

"Mr Utz says," said Mr Guthwin, pressing the phone against the same place one presses the butt of a rifle, "'Fuck you.'"

"No, no," Freddy said, "with a G." This was relayed.

"Mr Utz says, 'Fuck you, with a G.'"

"Please," Freddy asked, "let me speak to him."

"He would like to speak to you, Mr Utz." Mr Guthwin handed the phone to Freddy, whispering, "He's mad as hell."

"Mr Utz," Freddy said in his most regal voice. "I'm so sorry, sir, that there appears to have been a misunderstanding. Who am I? Actually, I'm the Prince of Wales, and the princess and I will forever be in your debt if you will simply authorise Gershwin the Baby King to . . ."

"Freddy, he doesn't know."

". . . complete this rather simple, hello? Hello? He's rung off."

"He's like that," Mr Guthwin said. "I'm afraid we just can't help you."

Freddy's visage suddenly went dark. He gathered himself up in his chair, pointed his right index finger at Mr Guthwin like a gun, and said, "Look, we've been in your country for less than a day, and we're starving, bloody, and cut. We've been attacked by Devils, chased by ambulances, stung by golden bugs, and insulted by Fuggers. I'm tired, angry, covered with muskrat shit, and all I've eaten in days has been the top of an iceberg, a pound of W&Ws, and fifteen packets of fake cream." Freddy now hovered over Mr Guthwin, the blood vessels in his temples signalling real danger.

"This is good money!" he shouted. "My mother guarantees it. I'm even on it. See me in the background, near the gate, in the baby carriage? I demand that you accept this as legal tender and give us dollars. I insist."

During this oration, Mr Guthwin had pressed the silent-alarm button on the undersurface of his desk. The police would be on their way, and now he had to delay. He was unaware that the woman with the butterfly glasses had previously pressed her own button, and that the police were already sealing off the perimeter.

"Let's see," he said. "I think it isn't impossible to do such a thing. It shouldn't be, should it?"

"Why not," Freddy asked, falling back in his chair, "seeing that I myself am on each note?"

"We'll need documentation. You have identification, of course, Social Security numbers?"

"Of course not," Freddy said. "We're aliens."

The Cherry Hill Police burst through the front doors of the bank. It might have been in the commando style had not the door hit one in the face and knocked him down, and had not the lead man charged in so fast that he tripped and slid on his belly along the waxed marble floor for ten feet, his pistol clattering in front of him and out of reach. When they had righted themselves, they pointed their guns at everybody, as one of them, a greying walrus of a man in a suit, approached Freddy and Fredericka. "Are these the ones?" he asked.

Mr Guthwin nodded. The uniformed police approached and tried to frisk the Finneys but found it impossible to get through all the folds of parachute cloth. Royal personages are notoriously ticklish, and the frisking was the occasion for bursts of high-pitched laughter. Satisfied that if Freddy and Fredericka did in fact have weapons they would not be able to get to them, the police holstered their pistols, although two officers outfitted with backward SWAT caps and AR-15s, and seemingly no more than twelve years old, remained on guard.

The uniformed police called-in some codes and the walrus sat down on the edge of Mr Guthwin's desk. "I'm Detective Mancuso of Cherry Hill PD. Who are you?"

"Serge Guthwin, president of this branch."

Detective Mancuso turned to Freddy and Fredericka. "Who are you?"

Freddy and Fredericka were silent. Their eyes darted. They looked caught.

"Who are you?" Mancuso repeated.

"They said they're aliens," Guthwin told him.

"I didn't ask you," Mancuso said. Then he turned to Freddy and Fredericka and spoke to them in a cautious, patronising fashion, as if they were insane. "Are you aliens? Did you tell him that you're aliens?"

A look of absolute dread crossed Freddy's face, because he realised that before he answered any official questions he would have to open the capsule.

"Well?"

Freddy was silent.

"Do you know where you are?"

"Cherry Hill."

"Good. Do you know who we are?"

"Pigs," said Freddy.

In a somewhat less friendly tone, Mancuso asked, "What's your name?"

Freddy almost answered but caught himself and was silent.

"Are you aliens?" Mancuso asked again.

"We don't know yet, pigs," Freddy said, thoughtfully. "May we use the WC?"

"What's that?"

"The *water closet,*" Freddy answered, as if talking to an idiot.

"What's the water closet?"

"The *toilette.* I can't tell you my name, and I can't tell you if we're aliens, until I use the *toilette.*"

"How 'bout you, ma'am?" the detective asked Fredericka. "Is that your position?"

"I haven't the slightest idea who I am," Fredericka said, "and neither does he. Since we fell to earth we haven't had time to look."

"You're aliens, then?"

"We don't know."

"But if you go to the *toilette,* you will know? Is the *toilette* some sort of communicator?"

"Yes, Constable, in a way."

"You're not getting up out of that chair, alien shitbird, until you identify yourself."

Fredericka shuddered in angry exasperation. "Unfortunately," said Freddy, in a burst of heat and irritation directed, puzzlingly, not at Mancuso but elsewhere, "we ourselves will not know who we are until we read the information on tiny scrolls in capsules that we carry in our rectums."

"Excuse me?" Mancuso asked.

"I don't want to repeat that," Freddy said.

"Are you drug mules?"

"We are not drug mules. We are not mules of any type."

"What are you, then? What do you do?" Turning to Fredericka, he asked, "What does he do?"

"What do you mean, 'What does he *do*?'" Fredericka asked contemptuously.

"I mean, 'What does he do?'"

"He's a prince," said Fredericka.

"I didn't ask you, Ms, what you think of him. I asked you what he does. How does he make a living?"

"I told you; he's a prince."

"I don't understand."

"I knew you wouldn't," Fredericka said, almost wickedly. "That's why I was able to tell you."

"Then why can't you tell me your names?"

"As I have said," Freddy told him, "we will, if we are given the opportunity."

Mancuso turned to Guthwin. "Does the bathroom have a window?"

"Of course not, we're a bank."

"Were they in there at any time?"

"No."

"Okay. Vogelman, check out the bathroom. And you," he said to Freddy, "if somehow you come out of there with a gun, it'll be the last thing you ever do."

"You mean," asked Freddy, "no more orphanage dedications, no more visits to labour training centres for hoodlums, no more accursed motorway spur openings?"

"You're not suicidal, are you?"

"Hardly."

"I want you to sing every second that you're in there. You, too," he said to Fredericka. "We don't want any suicides."

"Do you think," Freddy asked as he rose, "that I'm going to kill myself because a bank in Cherry Hill, New Jersey, can't change pounds sterling?"

"Sing," Mancuso commanded.

Freddy had a magnificent singing voice. From someone so shy, it was totally unexpected, a masterful bass and baritone that could shake cathedrals. Had he not been born a prince he might have trained for the opera. The moment he closed the door to the loo, he began a startlingly powerful rendition of *"Don Giovanni, a cenar teco m'invitasti."* It was, in its mass and gravity, absolutely chilling. Mancuso had assumed that Freddy would sing something like "Home on the Range," or "Take Me Out to the Ball Game," but this, this glimpse into the darkest recesses of sorrow, delivered with the power of a ship's whistle, paralysed everyone in the bank.

"Jesus," Mancuso said, reverentially and in awe. Even Fredericka was amazed.

The water ran, and eventually Freddy came out, smiling a huge, gap-toothed smile, and holding a little red capsule as if it were the Holy Grail.

"Freddy," Fredericka said. "I didn't know you could do that."

"It's not so difficult, and you'll feel a lot better when it's out."

"I mean the singing."

"Oh. I sing when I'm on the way to Moocock, hunting UFOs, as I float above the rooftops alone."

Satisfied with this answer, Fredericka left to retrieve her capsule. Her song was a lovely rendition, as if by an English choir girl, which once she had been, of "Up on the Roof."

"You float above the rooftops," Mancuso said to Freddy.

"At times."

"When you're hunting UFOs."

"Yes," Freddy answered, in a pleasant tone.

"Do you do that a lot?"

"Yes, Mummy invented the game."

"The Mummy invented the game?"

"I'm on more familiar terms," Freddy said condescendingly. "I just say 'Mummy.'"

"I know," said Mancuso. "When I talk to the Bride of Frankenstein, I just say 'Bride.'"

"Do you?" asked Freddy, convinced that Mancuso was insane.

"You and she," Mancuso said, meaning Fredericka, "hunt UFOs on the way to Moocock. That's what you do."

"That's what we do, yes."

"Not at Moocock."

"Never."

"Why not?"

"Because UFOs could never get to Moocock. Moocock is like a fortress."

"What is Moocock?"

"It's a secret."

"Like your name?"

Fredericka came back from the WC, clutching her tiny red capsule.

"We can't tell you about Moocock," Freddy continued, "but now we can tell you our names."

"Okay," said Mancuso, "what are your names?"

Freddy and Fredericka both opened their capsules and took out tiny little scrolls that they unfurled to about ten inches in length. The print was so small that they had to hold it right next to their eyes, like jewellers. "My name . . ." said Freddy, reading. "Just a minute, I'll find it. I'm surprised it's not at the beginning. My name . . . is . . . Christ!"

"Your name is Christ?"

"No. My name is . . . Lachpoof Bachquaquinnik Dess Moofoo-mooach, which is my imperial and Druidic name . . . hold on a moment . . . but the name on my Louisiana driver's license is . . . here it is . . . Desi Moffat. My name is Desi Moffat. That's a strange name, but not bad, really. I can live with that."

"Who's she?" Mancuso asked, as if in a dream.

"She's my wife."

"What's her name?"

"I don't know. She hasn't opened her capsule yet."

"I have too, Freddy."

"Oh, sorry," said Freddy. "What's your name, then?"

"My name," she said, reading down the little scroll so near her eye, "is . . . just a moment . . . is . . . *Mrs* Lachpoof Bachquaquinnik Dess Moo-foomooach, or," she said, actually reading, "'tell them *Mrs Desi Moffat,* which shall be the prince's name. Your Christian name is Popeel.' Popeel?" she asked. "That's a name? What kind of a name is that?"

"Is that your name?" Mancuso asked.

"Yes."

"Have you ever heard that name before?" he asked Freddy.

"No."

"And neither have I," volunteered Fredericka.

"And she's your wife?" Mancuso continued.

"Yes."

"You didn't know her name until now, and I take it you didn't know your own name until just now, is that correct?"

"Obviously," Freddy said.

"How can you explain that?"

"I have no idea."

"Desi?"

Freddy did not respond, but looked around as if Mancuso were speaking to someone else.

"Desi!" Mancuso shouted.

"Are you addressing me?"

"What do you do? I've got to know. I don't know why I've got to know, but I do."

"For a living?"

Mancuso nodded. Freddy held the scroll up to his eye again. "I'm a dentist, it appears, in Ahlahbahmah," by which he meant *Alabama*.

"You . . . are a dentist?" Mr Guthwin asked, looking at Freddy's teeth.

"Shut up," Mancuso ordered. "If you're a dentist in Ahlahbahmah, why do you say you have a Louisiana driver's license?"

"Perhaps in Ahlahbahmah I live close to the frontier. How would I know?"

"What frontier?"

"The Louisiana frontier."

"Between Louisiana and Ahlahbahmah, you will find Mississippi."

"Surely I'm not expected to know things like that. Can you name the *départements* of France, or the provinces of Romania? Really, Constable, don't be absurd."

"But you're *from* Ahlahbahmah."

"Yes, but I didn't go around tracing its borders. I was always more interested in history and aesthetics, and teeth, of course."

"I think you people are insane," Mancuso said.

"We're perfectly sane," Freddy declared, "and we are who we say we are. You may check in Ahlahbahmah, where an unimpeachable record has undoubtedly come into being. All we want to do is exchange some money."

"What are you doing in New Jersey?"

They both referred to their scrolls. "Tourism," they said simultaneously.

"Where's your car?"

"Which one?"

"The one you came in."

"We walked."

"You walked from Alabama? You don't have a car?"

"There are many footpaths, Constable. And I have many cars. The smallest," Freddy said, thinking of the miniatures in the dollhouse at Windsor, "is this big." He held his thumb and forefinger three inches apart. "It's real, and it really goes. The largest is cavernous. And I have carriages, too, and railway wagons, and many other modes of conveyance, including a yacht as big as an ocean liner. Though all technically Mummy's," which Mancuso heard as *mummies,* "they are as good as mine. These things I find sometimes comforting and sometimes a curse. When you inquire about them so blindly it shows me that you and I exist in different worlds."

"Yes, it does, and you're under arrest."

"It's over," Fredericka cried. "So soon after it began. We didn't last a day."

"Damn!" said Freddy.

Mancuso turned to his men. "Cuff them and read them their rights." He said to his prisoners, "I'm arresting you for making false statements in a banking transaction, attempted extortion, disturbing the peace, and public endangerment." As Freddy and Fredericka were handcuffed and their rights were read to them in a sort of low Gregorian chant, Mancuso turned to Mr Guthwin. "I was a cop in Philly for twenty-five years," he said. "I've never seen anything close."

"I know," Guthwin told him sympathetically. "They thought I was George Gershwin."

A CROWD HAD FORMED in front of the bank. Freddy and Fredericka were used to walking between police lines and seeing the ropes and barricades groan with the weight of masses of their admirers, though not quite this way. "I am the Prince of Wales, heir to the throne of Great Britain," he said, at wit's end, "and I demand that you remove these manacles."

The response was derisive laughter, as if he and Fredericka were being brought through London in a cart on their way to the headsman. Many ancestral memories welled up. Stress, odd diet, and lack of sleep all took their toll. But things rolled on, and they were put into a police car at the end of the barricaded corridor, heads pushed down so that they would not be able to bump them deliberately and sue the city of Cherry Hill.

As the door closed after Freddy, his trail of parachute cloth was caught up in it. Pulling hard, he undid the lock, leaving the door slightly ajar.

"Fredericka," he whispered. "The door is open. We may have an opportunity to flee."

"I see," she whispered back. "I'm ready."

Two patrolmen got in the car and, without belting themselves or looking at their prisoners, drove. After all, Freddy and Fredericka, handcuffed, were locked in the holding compartment. The glass was kickproof, the doors dead-bolted.

"I haven't had a doughnut in what, an hour?" one patrolman said to another.

"Stop at the White Hen."

A few minutes later, they did. Turning to the prisoners, they asked, "Would you guys like something to eat?"

"That's sweet of you," Fredericka said. "I'd love some Bovril and a crumpet."

"How about a doughnut?" one of them asked. "That's what we eat on Earth."

"Thank you."

"What about you?" they asked Freddy.

Freddy asked for haggis. They promised him a doughnut and disappeared into the White Hen. As soon as they did, the Prince and Princess of Wales escaped into Cherry Hill.

"Do they see, Freddy?"

"I don't think so. Just run."

Running at full speed, they turned a few corners and soon were lost in a forlorn district of threadbare stores. But the streets were vital and packed with people. "Everyone here seems African," Freddy said. After eight or ten more blocks, stopping for breath, they heard sirens in the distance. "Look," said Freddy, pointing down a side street, "*Reggae Style*—the Commonwealth."

A woman who unlocked the door said, "Ella don't sell no ganja to no more professors since last year."

"Do you take sterling?" Freddy asked.

"I tol' you," she said, "I'm tru." Her Jamaican speech with its pickled English and Celtic under-rhythms was a delight to Freddy's and Fredericka's ears.

"Not for ganja," Fredericka said, "for clothing."

"Oh! Of course I would, darlin'," Ella said. "I goin' to London next week to visit my sister."

"And do you have a hacksaw?" Freddy asked, holding up his hands.

Ella closed her shop and quickly made an arrangement with Freddy that would see Freddy and Fredericka completely reattired, their manacles removed, and their hunger sated. To help, she summoned her nephew, Desmond.

"Desmond what?" Freddy asked as soon as Desmond arrived, looking just like Jimmy Cliff.

"What?"

"What is your last name?"

"Moffat."

"That's *my* name," Freddy said, amazed.

"You in luck, mon," said Desmond. "Here." He held up a handcuff key on a key chain anchored by a miniature plastic car in the shape of a hot dog in a roll.

"Marvellous," said Freddy. "Why do you carry that?"

"I got tousands of them, mon. I drive the Weeny Car. I give them away."

"Keys for manacles?"

"Oh, that. Every brother who drive on the road have to have it."

"Why?" Freddy asked as he and Fredericka freed themselves.

"Because, mon, if you don't look at the police when they pass, they tink you hidin' someting. If you smile at them, they tink you mock them about. If you look at them an' not smile, they sure it's a challenge. The only time they don't stop you is if you driving a company truck."

"What is the Weeny Car?"

"You ain't seen the Weeny Car?" Desmond asked, holding up the key chain. "It look just like this. A whole lot of fibreglass, pink-an'-bread-coloured. On the East Coast, a mustard stripe, an' on de West, ketchup."

"How many does it seat?"

"Four. It can't get past fifty even if the wind is at the back. Great soun' system."

"Will you take us to Washington?"

"I can't, I can't drive in Delaware no more."

"For a thousand pounds? We could go through Pennsylvania."

"I not insured in Pennsylvania."

"Who would know if we just drove through?" Freddy asked.

Desmond held up the key chain. "Everyone. I can take you to the Delaware Memorial Bridge, an' you don't have to pay." He lowered his voice and said, "You been in this country long, mon?"

"Not even a day," Freddy answered, "and I'm ready for the insane asylum."

"I know," said Desmond. "Tings happen here you can't explain to a normal person. Sometimes, we switch Weeny Cars, an' all the West Coast drivers move to the East, an' all the East Coast drivers move to the West. The only sane time is on the great migration. I like it out there. It's quiet."

"Tell me," said Freddy, "when that occurs, does the East Coast get a ketchup stripe and the West a mustard?"

"No," Desmond said. Fredericka had a look of daft wonder.

"How is that avoided?" Freddy asked. "You don't trade vehicles, do you?"

"We meet in Salina, Kansas, all hundred of us, at a old drive-in theatre. There, we switch the mustard an' ketchup stripes. They plastic, and they snap on an' off. It take a few hours in the middle of the night, an' by dawn we back on the road again."

"Isn't it astounding?" Freddy asked Fredericka. "All our lives, we have been unaware of that."

"Freddy, we need a dentist. Let's go while it's light."

Freddy agreed. Ella asked, "What you want to eat? Desmond will get it while I fit you wit' the clothes."

"I would like," Freddy said to Desmond, "some smoked salmon, caviar, capers, and truffles *en potage* to begin, with a glass of Laphroaig. Then some roast lamb, *haricots verts,* and a mixed salad with goat cheese and walnut oil dressing, with a good claret and some Ramlosa. For dessert, something like a *bûche de noël,* but *en travine,* with expresso and a glass of '28 Pol Roger, super-chilled, thank you. Fredericka, what would you like?"

"I don't want to be demanding," Fredericka said, "I'll have the same."

Desmond blinked. "Okay, barbecue chicken! I have a big iron shovel outside I foun' in the dump, an' I put Ella's oven rack over it. Chicken do not fall tru like hot dogs."

"That sounds lovely," Fredericka told him. "Do you have Red Stripe?"

"Plenty," Desmond said, and left to make the fire.

As Desmond cooked, Ella buzzed about in service of their wardrobe. First she cut them out of their parachutes, exclaiming, "Nice underwear, mon!" when she spied their *hracneets.* Freddy and Fredericka had always been aware, being who they were, of the power and magic of vestments and drapings. They were not surprised at their transformation as Freddy donned cheap denim and calico patched with red velvet velour and zebra trim at the hips, a banana-yellow shirt, ox-blood high-heel spats, a lime-green chiffon cravat, and a huge hat, big enough for six heads, with a tiny crescent brim. Fredericka was willing to be less conservative. Her body shone in spirals of gold lamé, and she let Ella put a two-foot-high dollar-green turban on her head.

"Don't you have something perhaps a little less . . . forward?" asked Freddy, who, dressed as he was, had already begun to speak differently, walk in a kind of dance, and snap his fingers while he half-closed his eyes and held his lower lip between what was left of his teeth.

"Why?" Ella asked. "It's the best stuff. Flow."

"Flow," said Freddy.

"Someting is missing," Ella told him.

"My teeth."

"Someting else."

"What?"

"I don't know," Ella said, knowing exactly. "Desmond!" Desmond appeared. "Desmond, when you get done wit' the chicken, go to the store an' get these people *Tan Automatique,* four tubes. It has to on them real heavy."

Of the three Jamaicans riding south from Cherry Hill in the late afternoon in the Weeny Car as its prodigious sound system filled the air with rock and roll, one was authentic and two were forgeries the colour of Krugerrands. Now deeply gilded, Freddy and Fredericka had been fed at last, with chicken, plantain, Red Stripe, and mango. As the Weeny Car hit fifty and stayed there, the wind blew their flowing clothes back from them until they looked like hood ornaments.

Freddy turned to Fredericka and removed his white-framed sunglasses. "We not doin' too bad, Ricka," he said in a passable Jamaican accent (except perhaps to a Jamaican). "We got nine tousand pouns left, we full a' chicken, mon; we got new clothes; we runnin' hard to Washington, DC; an' it ain't even four o'clock in the aftanoon."

"Yes, Freddy," Fredericka said, all the while waving at children who, as they passed, whipped around in their seats to stare at a car shaped like a frankfurter, "but are you sure it's wise to have become black?"

"It not wise," Desmond said, "an' you not black, you gold."

"Whatever," Freddy said. "All in all, I think it was the correct decision."

"Why?" Fredericka asked.

"Because the police, Fredericka, are looking for us, and we are white. Now that we are sort of black, we have no problem."

Desmond looked heavenward.

"Freddy," Fredericka asked, "don't you think that the police might be looking for some black people, too?"

"My point is that we are no longer the white puffballs who resisted arrest in Cherry Hill. They might stop us, but then they would let us go."

"I don't think they would let us go, Freddy. I think they would hold us until they figured us out, and that might take forever."

"Nonsense. Habeas corpus."

"They would send us to an insane asylum, Freddy."

"An insane asylum? Are you mad?"

"Freddy, we're peculiar."

"Peculiar? Why are we peculiar? We need only behave with dignity to carry ourselves effortlessly through any situation. The day is not even over," he said, holding up his hands as if worshipping the sky, "and here we are, running along at all good speed, with quintessential American music cutting a path for us on an endless American road. I wish only that Mr Neil had allowed us enough preparation time to learn how to hot-wire an automobile."

"We're not criminals, Freddy."

"I know, but automobiles are the river of life in this country. When you get one, even this one, you're back in the game, but as soon as you lose one, you're in trouble. Haven't you noticed that? In America, the car is the second chance. They lift you from your troubles and set you into the heartbeat of the country."

"And what is the heartbeat of the country?" Fredericka asked sceptically.

"Being nowhere, on the way to somewhere, with music, on the open road," Freddy told her. "All the rest is the baggage of Europe, sometimes well developed and extended, sometimes not. But this motion, this ongoingness, this rolling, these hypnotic wheels, this particular glory, is exclusively American—their transcendence."

"Freddy, shut up!"

"But it's true. The pulse of the road . . . I've been to America many times, but never felt it until now, when we're poor, on the run, and sort of black. By the way. . . ." He trailed off.

"Yes?"

"You look," he said, blushing even through his *Tan Automatique,* "you look, in that colour. . . ."

"Yes, Freddy?"

"Very, I would say, very, well, very beautiful, Fredericka, and, and . . . numbing."

"Thank you, Freddy. Even without the teeth?"

"Even without the teeth."

They rolled south toward Delaware, which was beyond Desmond's range, and he dropped them at an entry ramp of the Delaware Memorial Bridge, to hitch-hike. Then he drove off in the Weeny Car toward his duty station of the evening, the amber-lit and diamond-blue arteries of New York.

Fredericka wondered if perhaps they should have gone with him.

"We couldn't have," Freddy informed her. "On a quest, you cannot re-trace your steps."

"Who said?"

"It's common knowledge. We must go forward, always. Don't worry, I used to hitch-hike at school. When a car comes by, you do like this."

Freddy threw out his arm, thumb extended, with such verve and au-thority that a nursery truck approaching the ramp braked to a stop. "Are you going across the bridge?" the driver asked. "There's room in the back. I'm just going over to the other side. I can leave you at the Delaware Pike."

"Thank you," Freddy replied graciously as he and Fredericka began to climb into the back. As the truck engaged its gears and began the run over the bridge, they seated themselves high amidst a mountain of freshly cut evergreen branches that made as fragrant a bower as any they had ever encountered, and they had encountered quite a few. To elevate their souls, rajahs had made flowery tents for them, and had not succeeded half as well.

Gypsies

THE WIND SWEPT OVER them as the truck crossed on the bridge's northern span, which rises like an aircraft above the broad expanse of the Delaware. Freddy stood amid the branches and looked out upon cities, near and distant, that were like ancient walled towns with glinting spires. The spider-work of chemical plants sat upon the shore, a forest of white grid-lines through which the breeze whistled as it came off the estuary. Eight lanes of traffic flowed across the bridges, and, in the channel below, massive ships rumbled up and down: monstrous rust-and-steel constructions of a hundred thousand momentous tons moving at twenty knots. Not two or three, but a dozen gliding as smoothly as swans. The sound of their engines, and the vibrations without sound, drummed in Fredericka's chest.

"It never stops moving, does it?" Freddy asked rhetorically, meaning the whole country.

Fredericka nodded, quite taken with their rise through summer-blue air.

"And this is just the smallest piece, the littlest part, of the perpetual ignition. Over three hundred and sixty degrees, engines are throbbing, ships and lorries moving, birds gliding, wind flowing. The emblem of the Americans, who have no idea where they're going, is that they never stop."

The entrance to the short and unimposing Delaware Turnpike was busy and dangerous, and hitch-hiking where the traffic divides was like making oneself a ten-pin. But not knowing where else to go, they stood in a triangle marked on the roadway and tried to get a ride. For five or ten minutes, cars and trucks rushed by. At one point a car was in the right lane and its driver wanted to go not toward Baltimore but to Dover. This meant transecting the triangle, cutting off two streams of traffic, and flattening the Prince and Princess of Wales. Nothing would deter the driver, even had his grandmothers in their rocking chairs been dead—or about to be— in his path. He veered against all chance, forcing Freddy and Fredericka to leap back to save their lives.

"Here comes a Bobby," Fredericka warned, of an officer headed toward them on a motorised tricycle.

"A pig," said Freddy. "When in Rome. . . ."

As the policeman arrived, lights flashing, Freddy smiled semi-toothlessly and cheerfully said, "Hello, pig!"

Embarrassed by his tricycle, the patrolman was ill-tempered to begin with. For a while, he tried to classify them. Finally, he asked, "Mexican or Chinese?"

"We've eaten, thank you," Fredericka answered.

"That's good, because you're under arrest for hitch-hiking, trespassing on an interstate, and public endangerment. I'm going to circle around and come back," he said, twisting his body to look behind him, "and stop over there with my flashers on. When I give the signal, cross and jump that rail. There's a sidewalk on the other side. We'll wait there for a car to take you in. If you try to get away, I'll come after you with my gun drawn. Is that clear?"

"I suppose it is," said Freddy, disturbed that though he had been in America for not even a single day, he had now been arrested twice.

"You be there," the patrolman said as he remounted and rolled forward, and as he left he shot them a piercing, hateful look.

"My bloody foot, pig!" Freddy shouted.

"Why did you do that?" Fredericka asked. "What good does it do? We've been arrested again."

"Not if we can get a ride in the next minute," Freddy said, hitch-hiking with psychiatric intensity.

"If he sees you doing that, it'll be worse. He might shoot us."

"For hitch-hiking?"

"He thinks we're Mexicans."

Just as the patrolman reached them after doubling back on the other side of the rail, a boat-like white Cadillac squealed to a stop in the triangle. Its passenger door was flung open and a swarthy fat man commanded them to get in. As soon as they did, he pressed the accelerator to the floor and the three of them were pushed back against the red-leather bench seat. With the acceleration, the door slammed shut, and Freddy and Fredericka felt the fluids in their bodies migrating to the rear. This was not unpleasant, and because of its high horsepower the engine seemed only to whisper.

"I think we should warn you," Freddy told the driver.

"I know. I saw him. That's why I stopped."

"He'll be after us."

"We'll get to the state line before he does."

"What if he radios ahead?"

"I just want the pike for my initial burst. Then I'll get off onto the back roads."

"Thank you," Freddy said, but it was stilted. He was so used to people giving him things, doing things for him, and praising him that he could not express gratitude. It was the same thank-you that he would have managed when receiving a hideous ivory carving from the monarch of a Southeast Asian principality.

"I didn't do it for you, I did it for me. I know that cop and I don't like him. He saw me, he knows my car, so now this is between him and me. You don't have to be grateful: you're just a prawn."

During the initial run on the turnpike they were going too fast for the passengers to study the driver or vice versa, but after the initial rocketry, on nearly empty roads between waist-high corn in neatly laid out fields, they looked to see with whom they were riding.

He was a Gypsy, with a fat dark face and shiny hair and moustaches that were as black as Palasimnos and as soft as mink. He had at least two rings on each finger and one on each thumb. They were the gold anchors for shell beds of diamonds and pearls that impressed even the Princess of Wales. So many gold necklaces weighed him down it was surprising that he could breathe, and yet he was as buoyant as a natural politician or an empty bottle—a huge, scheming baby with sparkling, voracious eyes. And he dressed more flamboyantly than even his passengers, in purple, paisley, and a rakish white hat.

They studied him and he studied them. Their hats alone were a wonder, and all the garish colour against the Chinese-red leather looked like an explosion in a paint factory or an accident involving lobster Cantonese.

"Soul brothers," he said. "I always pick up soul brothers. The pigs really dump on them."

"Yes, the pigs most certainly do," Freddy answered, without the slightest effort to conceal either his accent, which was captivating and regal, or his bearing, which was much the same. "It appears," Freddy went on, "that the pigs and the soul brothers are locked in obsessive conflict."

Still looking at the road, the Gypsy cocked his right ear the better to judge every puzzling inconsistency.

"As best I can tell," Freddy said as if he were holding forth to a delighted expert he had summoned to one of his magnificent libraries for tea and conversation, "the object of the pigs is to provoke the soul brothers until they reveal what the pigs believe is their true criminal nature. Thus, in the eyes of the pigs, provocation is merely an investigative technique to overcome barricades of falsity. And the object of the soul brothers is to protect their dignity by gratuitous and provocative defiance, as if that would do so. This must lead to one confrontation after another."

"Right on," said the Gypsy. "Are you some sort of radiologist?"

"No."

"Come on, you've got a talk show."

"What is a *talk show*?"

"Where they talk on the radio."

"Is that a question?"

"Is what a question?"

"You said, 'Where they talk on the radio?' I don't know where they talk on the radio, except on the radio."

"Do you?"

"Do I what?"

"Do you talk on the radio?"

"On occasion."

"I thought so."

"Not as a profession," Freddy volunteered.

"You're a guest."

"Yes, I'm a guest."

"What shows?"

Freddy put his finger in the spaces of his missing teeth, and explored.

"What shows?" the Gypsy asked again.

"Really, I don't remember."

"Imus?"

"I beg your pardon?"

"Imus?"

"You can do whatever you wish."

The Gypsy looked at his passengers obliquely, then quickly back at the road. "You haven't been on Imus?"

"Whatever that means, and I don't know what it means, I imagine the answer is no."

"Then what do you do?"

"I'm a dentist," Freddy answered.

"I see," said the Gypsy. "Yeah."

Fredericka was sitting between the two men, and as Freddy conversed with the Gypsy, Freddy's eyes rolled over her like hands on silk. When the driver said no more and just drove, listening intently to every sound from his right, Freddy found himself looking at his wife in a kind of daze.

"You know," he said, "you have an enormous proboscis. I never noticed before how immense it is. It's like a country—a small country, mind you, one of those long islands in the South Atlantic, with shorelines of thousand-foot cliffs on which millions of white seabirds perch. It's like a runway, a long gallery, a projecting boom, or an architectural ornament in a beautiful palace."

"Thank you," said Fredericka, staring ahead with intense concentration as she tried to deduce from Freddy's comments the meaning of the word *proboscis*. The Gypsy was also at work.

"It extends at a perfect angle, especially from the side. It's just so beautiful. When we were white puffballs I couldn't really see it, and before that, when we were just white, I failed to pay it enough heed. Now that we're black or gold, or whatever we are, it's strongly contrasted. It's as if I hadn't ever seen it. I would like to kiss it . . . and . . . I would like to. . . ."

Freddy had no more words. Fredericka, though she still did not know what a proboscis was, reddened with pulse and pleasure. "Please, Freddy," she begged. "We're hardly alone."

The Gypsy stared ever more intently at the road, listening with a hair-trigger ear.

"What *is* a proboscis?" Fredericka asked.

"Elephants have them," Freddy said.

"They do?"

"Famously."

"And what do they do," she asked hesitantly, "with their proboscises?"

"Proboscides."

"Yes, their proboscides."

"They roll logs with them, pick things up, spray themselves with water, eat peanuts, that sort of thing."

"You mean their. . . ."

Before she could finish, he leaned over and kissed her first on the nose and then hard on the lips. Inexplicably, she felt a surge of pleasure throughout her entire body. "A little trick I learnt when I was in Africa with . . ." he said, before she smashed his face and chest with both her fists.

"I don't want to hear that woman's name ever again, and don't do any elephant sex tricks on me!" she said, enraged.

"But Fredericka, it was just affection. You always say you want affection."

"You don't know what affection is, you idiot," she said, seething down. "And I don't want affection while sitting next to another man, a commoner no less."

"He's just the driver," Freddy protested.

"No I'm not," the Gypsy said. "I own this car. This is a Cadillac El Dorado with red-leather seats. You're just hitch-hikers. You don't even have a car."

"I assure you," Fredericka said, now a lioness defending the lion she had a moment before mauled, "that he has a great many more cars than you have."

"I don't think so," said the Gypsy.

"Well, I do," Fredericka told him.

"Yeah? How many cars does he have?"

"Let's see," said Freddy. "Do I count my immediate family?"

"Meaning what?"

"My mother and father."

"Sure. You can throw in all your cousins, too."

"All my cousins?"

"First cousins."

"Over a hundred automobiles, more or less," Freddy said, "of every conceivable type: Rolls, Duesenberg, Aston-Martin, Bugatti, et cetera."

The Gypsy smiled. "That's all?"

"And how many do you have?" Freddy asked, assuming that he was riding in most of the inventory.

"Me? Depending on the time of day, anywhere from five-to-seven thousand."

"Automobiles?"

"Yeah."

"How is that?"

"I'm in the wholesale car business. I supply South America with used American cars. Every day we load a ship. Sometimes, on holidays when the stream backs up, or in a storm, we have ten-to-fifteen thousand cars in the yards, and if a car is in the yard, I own it. It's a big business, with a lot of cash flow."

"Where do you get all the cars?" Freddy asked.

"Everywhere. I've got more than a thousand people working for me, and not a single one on the books. Lots'a soul brothers."

"I've always wondered what the mechanism was for placing all those older American vehicles in poorer countries around the world," Freddy said.

"Now you know."

Vindicated and relieved, the Gypsy pulled onto an entrance ramp of the Maryland Turnpike, where the afternoon traffic was light. The three of them stared straight ahead into the glare. Freddy was embarrassed both because Fredericka had hit him and because the Gypsy had many more cars than even the royal family. Fredericka was embarrassed that he had been so forward in such an inappropriate venue, and because her gambit to defend him had failed. And though the Gypsy wasn't embarrassed, he did wonder about his passengers. They were American types that he hadn't encountered before. Everyone was silent until the Susquehanna, but after they had driven over it, marvelling at a Georgian mansion that overlooked it and at the ongoing breadth of the river as it forged inland, they all had the urge to talk. Perhaps it was because, having crossed the Susquehanna, they were now in the gravitational field of Washington.

"Did you see that house?" the Gypsy said. "I could buy that house."

"So could I," Freddy said. Fredericka kicked him.

"No you couldn't. That house would be in the millions," the Gypsy told him. "You couldn't even dream of that. And I'll bet it's filled with art."

"Already I miss the presence of great paintings," Freddy stated before Fredericka kicked him again. "I do."

"You have to put certain things out of your mind," she insisted.

"That's all very well for you to say, but one gets used to a specific standard, and then when it vanishes the world seems impoverished. It seems especially impoverished when buildings have flat roofs and undivided windows wider than they are high, and when I can see as if with X-ray vision that behind a wall of tawdry-board is a bunch of glass wool insulation and a lot of plastic. The heart, Fredericka, can sense itself beating off stone, and the solidity of stone is one of the heart's great comforts. But when the heart hears the flimsy echo of claptrap, it is much aggrieved."

"He talks like that?" the Gypsy asked.

"No, Freddy, it isn't walls that speak to the heart," Fredericka stated, ignoring the Gypsy. "You have, as you frequently tell me, embraced a lie."

"I take it you were happy when you lived in that wretched little flat in Brompton Road, and drove that wretched little automobile?"

"I was."

"But you jumped like a trout at the chance to marry me, didn't you."

"What does that have to do with it?"

"I come with palaces."

"That's not why I married you," said Fredericka, and anyone in the world who might have been listening would have known that it was true—anyone, that is, but Freddy.

"How do you know?"

"You spoke about the heart?"

"Then why do you make perpetual trouble?"

"Because," Fredericka said, almost knocking her green turban against Freddy's giant ballooning hat, "the queen treats me like a dog. No, she's kind to dogs. It's so unfair. She's the queen. What can I do? To whom can I appeal? She's older, she's your mother, and she's the queen, but she is wrong, and she is cold, and I am right."

"What do you want of her?"

"I want her to treat me with benevolence and respect. I will someday bear your children. How can she not embrace me like a daughter? Something's wrong. It doesn't make sense. It's unfair to me, to the children not yet born, to the way things should be. Freddy, it's so gratuitous. That's why I make trouble."

"Fredericka, you tried to rush the royal way, but the royal way cannot be rushed. Currents run subtly beneath the surface, and rather than wait until you were able to apprehend them, you roiled the waters so that apprehending them is now impossible. The duke and the queen have a very high standard. They need not be patient. They need not compromise. They need not extend themselves to anyone."

"Where are you dudes from?" the Gypsy asked.

"Why?"

"I can't make you out. What's your name?"

Freddy extended his hand across Fredericka and the Gypsy shook it. "Desi Moffat, and this is my wife, Popeel."

"What are you? Are you soul brothers?"

Freddy pulled out a little piece of paper that he unfolded many times. Reading it so close to his eye that he seemed to be using a loupe, he said, "Yo."

"But you're gold."

"Our grandmother was Jewish," Fredericka told him.

"You're entertainers. You gotta be entertainers."

"We told you," Fredericka said, "we're dentists."

"You too?"

"I really don't know. It didn't say. Perhaps I'm a dental hygienist."

"What didn't say?"

"The instructions."

"What instructions?"

"We work from instructions," Fredericka said, "according to a sort of plan that just happened and that we don't quite understand, so we follow the instructions and we sleep in the woods, on the ground."

"Don't you have any money?"

"We have sterling," Freddy said, "but no one knows what it is."

"I do, and I'll give you one point four nine five."

"You will? Now?"

"When I get to my desk, but you can do better than that, a lot better, if you listen to my proposition."

For perhaps the first time in his life, Freddy needed to hustle. "What proposition?"

They hurtled along. Something about the road south of the Susquehanna accelerates cars toward Baltimore in an almost supernatural sense. Perhaps the wide Susquehanna rolling toward the sea and seen only briefly gets the blood up and puts the accelerator down. Perhaps the jewel-like qualities of American cities accelerate travellers on the road like a celestial slingshot. Certainly the Gypsy, despite what, in his idiom (and Shakespeare's), he was about to "lay on them," and even Freddy and Fredericka, who did not know what was ahead, wanted to see a glass city sparkling and bronzed in the dusk. Lights there would flash amber-coloured by the million, and the sun would track across the mirrored towers in clockwork motion, deeper and deeper in colour as distant traffic rolled upon high viaducts tracing a path around the orrery. On hot summer evenings as the streets released their heat, the cities seemed to burn in muted chestnut-coloured phosphorus.

"How much sterling have you got?" the Gypsy asked.

"Nine thousand pounds," Freddy told him, thinking he would be impressed.

"Too small."

"Thirteen thousand dollars is too small?" Fredericka asked. After all, that was the price of a sun dress.

"Thirteen thousand, four hundred, and fifty-five," the Gypsy said. "But for small, uneven lots, you can't get the rate I quoted you. That was the rate on a million-dollar contract. If I did the trade, and I'm not saying I would, I'd give you one point three six, which would be twelve thousand, two hundred, and forty dollars."

"You calculate rapidly," Freddy said.

"I'm a businessman."

"How could you have assumed that we were carrying a million-pound lot of sterling?"

"I didn't. In fact, I figured that you had less than a thousand. I quoted you the best rate because the lot was unspecified. That's what you do. Look, I sell seven thousand cars a day. Do you know how much money is involved in that?"

"Millions, I imagine."

"Ten, fifteen million a day. You know how heavy I am into foreign exchange? We're not always paid in dollars. I have my own trading desk."

"Are you an arm of General Motors?" Freddy asked.

"I'm nobody's arm. The IRS doesn't even know I exist."

"Is that so?" Freddy asked, beginning to doubt his veracity. "Who are you, that the Inland Revenue knows you not?"

"You had no idea," the Gypsy said, "but you're sitting next to a king."

"What kind of king?" Fredericka asked.

"An A-one, top-of-the-line, hot-shot king. I'm the only king you'll ever meet, the only king in America with real royal blood in his veins. And you're sitting next to me, riding in my car."

"You're the king of the wholesale car market, if that is, indeed, true," Freddy ventured.

"I may be. I am. But I'm also the king of the Gypsies."

"What's your name?"

"Kitten the Tenth."

"Kitten the Tenth?"

"In Romany the word *kitten*, pronounced *kitten*, has a meaning different than it does in English. It means—and it's impossible to translate directly—a small, agile, young, flexible, playful cat."

"Are you the king of all the Gypsies in the world?" Fredericka asked.

"We don't have a world king."

"Are you the king of all the Gypsies in the Western Hemisphere?"

"No, we don't have hemisphere kings, either."

"North America, then?"

The Gypsy shook his head from side to side.

"America?" Freddy asked, as the kingdom was whittled down.

"No, too many Rom in America for one king."

"East of the Mississippi?" Fredericka inquired charmingly. They were now rooting for him. He was silent. "Where, then?" she asked.

"I'm the king," he said, drawing an air map quickly with his right index finger (Freddy could read air maps), "of all the Gypsies in New Jersey. Well, northern New Jersey east of the Saddle River, north of Hoboken, and south of Englewood."

Freddy considered this. "Some kings don't have large kingdoms," he said, "but they're great kings nonetheless. A king's fame and reputation depend not on the size of his country but on his virtues, and it has always been that way. For example, the kings of England have had for centuries a special respect for the kings of Portugal. Now, it is true that this is related to Portugal's geographical position vis-à-vis Britain's former great rival, Spain, and that Portugal had a great overseas empire. But, still, Portugal is, well, Portugal. Kingliness comes from . . . inside. We have a special place in our hearts for kings in exile, and though kings in exile have not a single subject, the place in our hearts is always open. It is the duty of one king to defend the nobility of another no matter what the indicia of the other's power."

"Really?" asked Kitten the Tenth.

"Absolutely," said Freddy, exploring with his tongue the now familiar gap in his teeth.

"You know," declared Kitten, "I like you. I don't know if you're soul brothers or not, but it doesn't matter. All the races of man—Gypsy, soul brother, anchorman—are the same. There's no difference between them."

"Then how do we know there are different races?" Freddy asked.

"Stereotypes."

"But how do we know which person fits in which stereotype?"

"It's random."

"It's random?"

"You never know what you are until someone abuses you. That's what happened with the Indians."

"You mean that the Indians, who didn't know who they were, and the Europeans, who also didn't know who they were, were indistinguishable until the Europeans began to mistreat the Indians?"

"No," said Kitten. "The Indians killed the Europeans to get their horses. *They* mistreated *them*."

"Who mistreated whom?"

"It doesn't matter. They're all the same. You're walking a real thin line here."

"Tell me something," said Freddy.

"What?" asked Kitten, feeling the road to Baltimore vanish into the black hole of his exhaust pipes. With all the horses under the hood, it was almost like flying.

"Are you really a Gypsy?"

"Part Gypsy, part Italian, actually."

"What part Italian?"

"In percent?"

"Yes."

"I don't know, maybe a hundred."

"Then you're not Kitten the Tenth?"

"I can't prove it, but I am. I'm also part Romanian. This is America, right? I mean, who are you, exactly? You can say anything you want, but you'll never convince anyone in the world that you've got a clear bloodline. Look at you two. A census taker could spend the rest of his life figuring out what box to check."

"Moofoomooach," Freddy said inexplicably, like a frog on a lily pad.

"What shall we call you," Fredericka asked, "rather than Kitten the Tenth?"

"Sal."

"Sal what?" Freddy asked serenely.

"Sal Foppiano."

Freddy withdrew, but Fredericka briefly put both hands on Sal's right shoulder. "I shall call you Kitten the Tenth."

"Seven thousand cars," Freddy said, devastatingly.

"All right," Kitten admitted, "seven hundred."

Freddy sneered.

"Seventy."

"Please," Freddy said.

"Seven to ten—I swear on my mother's grave—over a week's time, sometimes two weeks, or three. In the winter, maybe four."

"And how do you get these cars?" Freddy asked.

"You tell me."

"You steal them."

"You're right."

"And that's your proposition. You want us to steal cars for you."

"No."

"Freddy, you said you wanted to learn to hot-wire."

"I'll teach you to hot-wire, just for the hell of it," Kitten told them. "If you want, we'll have dinner in South Baltimore and I'll show you in the parking lot of the Crab House. Then you can pick a car and be on your way. It's up to you. But maybe you'll want to stay. Maybe you'll want to take my deal, which, believe me, is a lot better than thirteen thousand dollars."

"How much better?" Freddy asked.

"A hundred thousand, guaranteed. If you have a little patience, another hundred and fifty. You can't beat this deal, and I'll buy dinner."

He took a powerful right as the road forked, heading in the dusk toward the tunnel that dipped under Baltimore's liver-grey harbor. Right and ahead the city rose up just as it was supposed to have, with the sun gleaming on it and a vast number of lights now sparkling and shining in the dance of dying heat.

"THIS LOOKS FAMILIAR," Freddy said as they glided through the twilight in South Baltimore. "I think I dedicated a bridge here once."

"You probably did," said Kitten, "one of those bridges that goes underneath the water."

"Aren't those called tunnels?" Fredericka asked.

"Perhaps it was a ship," Freddy added.

"Which is your favourite kind of ship to dedicate?" Kitten mocked.

"Ballistic missile submarines."

"You do a lot of those?"

"Some."

"What did you say your name was, again?"

"Desi Moofoomooach."

"Moffat," Fredericka said. "Desi Moffat."

"Let's not be confusing," said Freddy. "Our names are Lachpoof Bachquaquinnik Dess Moofoomooach, and Mrs Lachpoof Bachquaquin-nik Dess Moofoomooach. But you can call us Desi and Popeel Moffat."

The Cadillac moved like an arrow down leafy blocks of row houses with sugar-cube doorsteps until it reached the Crab House, where half a dozen people greeted Kitten as he came in, but only stole quick glances at his guests. The three royals sat at a round, deeply varnished table that pulsed with the bass beat of a jukebox. Various neon and electric bar signs flickered almost in time, crawling along motionless paths like hallucinogenic worms. Waitresses moved about as quietly as sharks at the bottom of municipal aquariums, though they looked less like sharks than like décolleté pigeons. Kitten ordered three pitchers of beer and three crab roasts.

"What is a crab roast?" Freddy asked the waitress.

"You take three kinds of crabs," she said, "Alaska King, Chesapeake, and Stone; shell them; marinate them in spices, extra-virgin olive oil, and sherry; and then sear them on a superheated grill. They cook right through and stay hot. We give you a whole pound, and I tell you, honey, it's a dish fit for a king."

"Then we'll have to take it," said Freddy.

A little later they heard three pounds of marinated crab hit a white-hot grill, and when the crab arrived, it was truly magnificent. They ate, gratefully. "Not even a day, Fredericka," Freddy said quietly, "not even a full twenty-four hours, and here we are, in a cooled banquet hall, dressed in the clothes of nobles, with music, and the richest fruits of the sea. You see how, after falling from the heavens, we have been able to agitate fortune in our favour?"

Kitten listened in true puzzlement as, after several pints, Freddy was oblivious of being overheard.

"I think," Freddy continued, "that not only is the reacquisition feasible, but desirable. I like the way of life here, the road, the music, the crab. I would like to be this people's sovereign. They speak English in their way, they're mad, and they're vital."

"I don't know, Freddy," Fredericka whispered, though within the range of Kitten's cocked ears, which moved like radar dishes. "Can you imagine them at the Garden Party, dressed in leather, chains, turbans, and street clothes born in the circus, speaking in their atrocious accents, with pierced body parts, tattoos, and rooster hair?"

"We wouldn't invite the intellectuals."

"But even the real people here are like that."

"Though it's true that they have a certain wildness, like Indians or Celts, it's part of what gives energy to their empire. When Phoebe Boylingehotte dresses as a Cel. . . ." Knowing that he had erred, Freddy nonetheless could not stop the memory, and it made him take a long deep breath.

"Is that what she does?" Fredericka asked, like a munition about to explode. "Dresses as a Celt?"

Caught, Freddy instinctively told the truth. "Body paint, feathers, and furry things like *hracneets.*"

"Damn you, Freddy!" Fredericka shouted, half-rising in her seat, stilling the conversation in the room. "With her and not with me? Why not with me!" She was deeply hurt, but, also, a bit excited.

Freddy said, "I don't do it, she does it." He looked sheepish. Behind him, in a pocket of darkness, a beer sign blinked in purple light. "I thought you'd be embarrassed, but if you'd like we can do it, too."

Fredericka seized her glass and threw a pint of beer into Freddy's face. "Never again," she said, like a dog growling through a tight muzzle. "Never again. From now on, it's just business, and you can go fuck yourself."

Everyone in the restaurant began to applaud, though from experience they assumed that this was anything but a lasting declaration. For his part, Freddy began to streak. His face looked like a gold coin that had spent time on a hot grill. Catching a glimpse of himself in a distant mirror, he saw that he looked like a cross between a tiger, an angelfish, and a baked apple.

"Who are you dudes, really?" Kitten asked.

"That's not important. What's your proposition?" Fredericka said, nursing her wounds.

"How do I know you're not cops?" Kitten asked, and then quickly answered himself by laughing.

"We would like to hear the proposition," Freddy said. "We need a lot of money."

"For what?"

"I can't really explain, but we have a great mission, something very difficult, possibly impossible. We have no idea whatsoever how to accomplish it, but it may come to us on the road, and it shall almost certainly involve a major fiscal commitment."

"I know," said Kitten.

"On the road things occur that don't occur to people who sit still. If we keep moving, the way may be illumined. Have you ever been on a quest?"

"No, but I've eaten one," said Kitten, thinking that a quest was a chocolate-covered pastry like a Ring-Ding or a Ding Dong. He hadn't the vaguest idea of what Freddy was talking about. "It's a big country. You ever been to Arizona?"

"I dedicated a bridge there, or was that in Hawaii?"

"Of course."

"The bigger the better. The more you move, the more likely you'll find the divine rhythm. You have to throw yourself into the storm of the world even before it takes you, or it won't. It's like riding a wave."

"Yeah," said Kitten. "You lost me."

"A man never rises to greater heights than when he does not know where he is going."

"I know," said Kitten. "Like, you take the high road and I'll take the low road, and I'll get to Scotland before you."

"Afore ye," Freddy corrected.

"Whatever. But why do you need money, apart from the fact that everyone needs money?"

"Money," Freddy said, "is the store of power and effort. Properly understood, it can be a bolt of lightning. It is the compression and compressor of time, the frozen accumulation of motion, the battery of many engines too numerous to name, and the theory and history of effort. On a quest, one must accumulate it so that when the opportunity comes to cast or block lightning bolts one can draw upon its fluid power in reserve."

Kitten pondered this. "Will two hundred and fifty Gs do it?"

"One has to start somewhere," Freddy said. "What's the proposition?"

"You've heard of Swastika 34 Egg."

"Yes, I believe I have," said Freddy. "It's an ingredient in German shampoo."

Kitten thought this was funny.

"It isn't?" Freddy asked.

"Obviously," Kitten said, "you don't read *Time* magazine."

"We don't, so tell us."

"Okay. One of my clients is an accountant in Chevy Chase. His life is like an air crash in slow motion. Anything that he can do to destroy his family, not to speak of himself, he does. He overeats, he takes drugs, he drinks, he gambles, he whores, he steals from his clients. You know the type. He's got a big house, he goes to fancy restaurants, dresses like Antonio Fantangami, drives a Ferrari, and keeps up all appearances. Something's gotta break, right? He owes his bookie half a million dollars and is a million in debt to the banks over and above his mortgage. He covers himself by embezzling, and keeps all the plates in the air by shifting money around from client to client in a scheme so complicated it would take the math department at Cal Tech to figure it out. Even he can't figure it out, but he knows he can't last too much longer or go too much deeper. The string has got to run out, because he can't stop gambling, and each week he spends on drugs twice what he makes in a month. So he wants to make a clean breast of it."

"Turn himself in to Scotland Yard?"

"Yeah, turn himself in to Scotland Yard. You really get me. What good would it do to turn himself in? He'd go to jail. How could he pay his bookie? No. He's desperate. So he comes to me. Why me? I got him a liver-and-onion-coloured BMW 750-IL. It was hard to get the right car. We went all the way to Atlanta. He knows I have connections, and that I can do things he can't. 'Let's go into business together,' he says. 'One time, then it's over.'

"But it'll never be over for him, even if he thinks it will, because he's a born suicide. Still, that doesn't mean I can't help him. Who knows, maybe he'll give all the money back, pay off his debts, become a vegetarian, and take up a hobby like building harpsichords. It can happen. Meanwhile, he cuts me in, and I cut you in."

"To what?" Freddy asked, warily. He had no intention of committing a major crime, although he would consider the possibility and judge the nature of the act before entirely ruling it out.

"He goes to a lot of parties, right? He knows a lot of very rich people. Some of them have great art in their houses, but only a very select group of burglars can do art. Why? You have to have a special fence. As it happens, the accountant knows such a fence, and has been stealing his money for years.

"So he knows that he can get rid of certain works. The fence says to him, 'If you knew what I would pay for a Swastika 34 Egg, if only you knew.'"

"What *is* a Swastika 34 Egg?" Freddy asked.

"Art."

"I'm sorry, but I don't really understand what you're saying."

"The artist, one of the most expensive artists in the world."

"Really? I've never heard of Swastika 34 Egg." Freddy knew almost as much about art as Kenneth Clark, but was uninterested in the avant-garde.

"She died last year," said Kitten. "That's why she's so hot."

"Who was she?"

"She was on the cover of *Time* magazine, nude, but they put letters in the strategic places. She's the greatest American artist after Frank Sumatra."

"I think I've heard of him," said Freddy. "He's some sort of entertainer."

"No, he's an artist. He's half Italian and half Indonesian. He puts dirt in rooms, screams a word for ten hours, chops off his foot, and eats government documents."

"That's very interesting, but what about Homer, Eakins, Sargent, Whistler, Henri?" Freddy asked.

"I've never heard of them," Kitten said. "They didn't jump out of a sixth-storey window into a three-storey pile of horse manure, did they? Frank Sumatra did. They didn't wear a brassière made of miniature colour televisions tuned to the Golf Channel, did they? Swastika 34 Egg did. She's really hot. She completed only thirty-four works and then killed herself, as she promised, for number thirty-five. She had the art world holding its breath for years as first one thing and then another was finished. Last year, they exhaled. Of the thirty-five, fifteen were things like jumping out of windows, committing suicide, or sweeping the ocean with a broom. There are only twenty Swastika 34 Eggs that can be bought and sold. Of those, ten are held in a vault by a public corporation—this scheme was one of the fifteen other works—and you can buy stock and futures in them. The value, as of the last time I looked, was a hundred and thirty-four million dollars. The prices fluctuate, but you have to figure that any of the ten in

the outside world is worth about ten million. The fence can get five. My
client the accountant can get three from the fence. He keeps two, and I get
one, of which I give two hundred and fifty Gs to you."

Both Freddy and Fredericka were stunned. As sabre-toothed tigers
were to the children of cavemen, art thieves were to them, which was perfectly understandable given that Freddy was the eventual owner of the
world's greatest private collection of paintings. His face showed through
his tigrine stripes that he would have none of it, but Kitten thought he was
merely sceptical.

"Don't worry," said Kitten, spreading his arms in a winged gesture. "It's
a sure thing."

Freddy began to get up.

"Wait," Kitten commanded. "You don't have to do anything now but
listen."

Freddy sat down and Kitten continued. "All right, the accountant goes
to lots of fancy, big-time parties. One night in Kalorama—he's stoned, he
hardly knows where he is—he finds himself at the home of Arthur and
Marina Clovis."

Freddy looked up from his plate of crab. "Don't know them," he said.

"You've never heard of Arthur and Marina Clovis?"

"No."

"Office parks."

"Office parks?" Freddy asked.

"Don't you know what an office park is? You must be from another
planet. Trust me, they're billionaires. And they have huge parties. So, last
winter, in a snowstorm, the accountant finds himself, without knowing
how he got there, in their living room, with two hundred people watching
an actress do a striptease in a fur coat, like Anita Ekberg in *La Dolce Vita,*
but you wouldn't know about that, either."

"I know about that," Freddy said. "I taught myself to use a projector so
I could sneak into the screening room at three o'clock in the morning and
run it for my own edification."

"What screening room?"

"A screening room in the ghetto," said Fredericka. "They have them,
you know."

Kitten took a bite of crab. "Whatever. My friend turns from Anita Ekberg because he's not interested in that for the moment, because he's hungry, starving, but the college students and actors who work for the catering

service are busy watching Anita Ekberg, and their trays have gone empty. So Larry—that's not his name, but let's call him Larry—glides around the house in search of something to eat. He's as kissy as a skunk and doesn't know at all where he's going. And then, according to him, the Red Sea opens, and he has what he calls 'the three great visions.'

"He walks down a little hall, into an elegant study—a gas fire, dark walnut panelling, a big globe. You know, the way a decorator would make a place not for someone to study in but to feel important in. If you want to study, you go to the library and sit with a hundred people who smell bad. Doing that is to concentration what a hot oven is to baking bread. I used to study refrigeration mechanics in Central Park. When a place is not yours, it holds no distractions."

"What did he see?" Fredericka asked with the curiosity of a child.

"In one corner, lit by a little spotlight, one of the world's ten free-agent Swastika 34 Eggs, just what his fence was dreaming about. He waltzed toward it and turned a bewildered circle or two before he got there, but it was a Swastika 34 Egg, one of the top three.

"He didn't even have time to regret that it was in a house that dripped with alarms and servants, and that therefore he'd never be able to steal it. Why no regret? Because he went back out the door—he says he felt as if he were on an invisible conveyor belt—down the hall, and into the kitchen. Ah, he says, food. The kitchen is tremendous, filled with Ecuadorans, Ethiopians, and Vietnamese working at black granite countertops under diffused fluorescent light that leaves no shadows. In a kind of cathedral of black stone, frosted glass, stainless steel, and polished birch, they roast beef, make hors d'oeuvres—those are snacks . . ."

"I know," said Freddy.

". . . and open Champagne. Larry by this time has forgotten all about the Swastika 34 Egg. All he wants to do is grab a roast beef, hold it in his hands like a concertina, and eat it like an ear of corn. The Champagne is irresistible because he's extremely thirsty. His mouth is so dry he's afraid he won't be able to open it so he can drink, but he knows he wants at least a magnum, and that he'll get it."

"Oh dear," said Fredericka.

"And the cakes, caviar, and grilled shrimp don't escape his notice, either. But for some reason he holds back, and sits down on a duck press. The duck press is in a little alcove, in shadow, and no one in the kitchen notices him. It's as if he's invisible. Who knows, maybe he is?"

Kitten took a long drink of beer. "Half an hour passes, maybe an hour, and he doesn't move. Now they really can't see him, because they've actually seen him a number of times and yet been unaware that he was there, so they've accommodated him out, so to speak, and he's just a part of the landscape. An Ethiopian puts on his coat and leaves by the kitchen door, two feet from invisible Larry. Then the two Vietnamese go. Who's left? The Ecuadorans, not a single one over five feet tall. They have to stand on stools to work at the counters and get to the cabinets. One of them works full time for the Clovises and lives in. The other two are day workers, or night workers as the case may be. The live-in takes off her apron, kisses the man, and goes off toward her quarters. Larry remains invisible.

"He watches her walk right past him and down the hall. But she stops, turns around, and goes back. Larry turns and sees that the man and woman who remained are in a corner near the cookbook shelves, kissing. The man's hands are doing a customs inspection of her inner thighs. Uh-oh, thinks Larry, because even in the state that he's in he remembers that the live-in kissed the man goodnight.

"Live-in walks back to the granite island in the centre of the kitchen. No one sees anyone else, but Larry sees everything. Live-in gets up on a stool and reaches toward the centre of the counter, where two daffodils are sitting in a crystal vase, as fresh as daisies. For a moment Larry and live-in are held by the bright yellow and green beneath the very white light. It's beautiful. Even in the cold of winter, daffodils come from the Clovis greenhouse, which, at the edge of a cobblestone courtyard, sits in an ultra-violet haze like a beached flying saucer.

"Live-in seizes the flowers and, remembering where they came from, perhaps because she herself had picked them, glances toward the greenhouse. What does she see in the corner? A brown mass, like a bear, moving slightly, cutting off the clean lines of the greenhouse etched by the ultraviolet light. She shades her eyes to see better, squints, and grimaces. For a moment, time freezes.

"But then comes an explosion of Inca curses such as the District of Columbia has never heard. Have you ever been in the seriously overcrowded kitchen of a Chinese restaurant when a fight starts? It's worse even than that. Thank God they're all so small. It's like the Battle of Verdun, with Teddy Bears. Larry, of course, is just sitting there. Live-in goes through a ten-minute tantrum and then turns and marches to a closet, whams open the door, pulls a coat off a hanger—breaking the hanger in two—slams the door, puts on the coat like a four-year-old in a huff, and storms out.

"From habit, she stops by the keypad near the door and arms the alarm. Then she steps out and the door shuts behind her. The alarm is blinking and beeping, its way of saying that it's about to arm, when someone moves in another room that isn't programmed for exit delay, and half a dozen sirens go off. Live-in turns about on the path and runs back. As soon as she enters she punches in the disarm code, a couple of feet from Larry. He's an accountant. The four digits appear in his brain like that big building they have in Hollywood that says *20th Century Fox*—I always wanted to go there—and they glow in front of his eyes.

"Then she goes to a phone at a little built-in desk, dials an eight hundred number, states the Clovises' account number—six digits permanently engraved in Larry's brain—and speaks the passwords. Then she storms out, and the man runs after her. The woman takes two coats from the closet and follows, leaving Larry all alone in the kitchen. He's perfectly free to write down the codes and passwords, but he doesn't have to any more than he would have to write down his own name.

"This is only the second of the visions, but he doesn't know, so he grabs a magnum of Champagne and drains it. Why not? Feeling really happy, he orbits back into the living room, where most people have gone home."

"You mean *whence*," Freddy said.

"No, I mean *where*."

"You mean that their homes are in the living room?"

"No, their homes are on the streets, in lots."

"No, their *houses* are *off* the street, *on* lots."

"Fine. *Whence*. Okay?"

"Just go on," Fredericka said.

Kitten went on. "You know when a beer bash or something is almost over and it gets very quiet and sad? People who have been screaming for six hours suddenly talk as if they're on their deathbeds. Larry fit right in, because no one knew him and he didn't say anything. He just sat on a couch and stared at a fish tank. Or maybe, according to you, Moofoo-mooach, or whatever your name is, he sat *in* a couch, and stared *whence* a fish tank. Behind him, Marina Clovis, lubricated with drink though degreased by time, was having an earnest conversation with a friend. What do rich people talk about?" Kitten asked, anticipating that the soul brothers could not possibly know.

Receiving no answer, he asked again. "What do rich people talk about?"

"History," said Freddy.

"Nope."

"Clothes," said Fredericka, with great authority.

"Uh-uh."

"No?"

"No. Rich people talk most about, in ascending order, furniture, vacations, breast implants, watches, smoked fish, adultery, and servants."

"That's new to me," said Freddy.

"What would you know? Do you know why they talk so much about servants? Because they live with them. They're surrounded by them, and naturally there's a lot of tension. The servants have to go through their whole lives and bring up their own children on less money than sits on the mistress's dressing table in the form of little sparkling rocks. Let's say the Clovises pay live-in three hundred dollars a week and the value of her room and board is another three hundred. That's six hundred. After deductions from the paycheck, live-in's got the equivalent of five hundred a week and change, let's say five-fifty. That means that if at home she neither ate nor drank, nor fed her children, nor dressed, nor spoke on the telephone, nor had any medical expenses, went anywhere, or did anything, she could in ten years accumulate as much money as the Clovises paid for one of their BMWs parked near the greenhouse. They have three BMWs, a Rolls, and a four-wheel-drive thing with cup holders. I don't steal those: people who want one won't buy one hot. They're for dentists and college professors."

"So what?" Freddy asked.

"One Rolls, one fuckin' piece a' metal, and it's more money than live-in, her husband, and her parents—who are still in Ecuador because they can't afford to come here—see in their whole lives. It's a big attention-getter. These people see their children die sometimes, in front of their eyes, because they can't pay to save them, and then they see all that money immobile in the houses of the rich, unused, unthought of, forgotten in a quiet corner."

"Are you some sort of revolutionary?" Fredericka asked.

"Of course not, I'm a car thief. If there was a revolution, no one could afford cars, or, for that matter, anything else."

"Then why are you telling us this?"

"To explain why rich people talk about servants."

"They don't," said Freddy.

"They do," said Kitten, "because they know, underneath, even if they don't know that they know, that these people with whom they live in the same house and to whom they entrust their alarm codes, their cooking, and their children, would in many cases slit their throats. Hey, look, it's better than Ecuador, but these people are not idiots. They look, they see, they adjust, they wonder, and they say, 'Why not me?' Wouldn't you? That's why a rich man's house is never at peace. A rich man's house is a nervous outpost in a long and never-ending war."

"Actually," said Freddy, "the tension of which you speak is an all-pervasive poison that restricts the natural breathing of the upper classes. I should be glad of its absence and to be unoppressed by its weight."

"Yeah," said Kitten. "So Mrs is talking to her friend. All Larry can see when he tries to turn his head is lighted Plexiglas, goldfish, and big hair. Ecuadorans, according to the lady of the house, are great. She calls them 'my little Inca dinca doos.' They're cheap. Terrific. If they can't feed their children protein, it's okay, because Marina Clovis can buy a Frank Sumatra or a Swastika 34 Egg. They're not surly. They don't mind being four foot ten and washing Señor Clovis' underwear. You should get a few: it's cheaper than lunch at the Palm.

"And as Larry sits there, his eyes floating in their sockets and every word sucked into his brain like Libyan cell phone transmissions drawn into Fort Meade, she summarizes the Inca dinca doos' schedules and habits. Monday is their day off, and, at two, Marcia, the live-in, leaves for Fairfax, where her sister lives with a family of Pakistani opticians. That's great, Marina Clovis says, because except for the first Monday of each month, when she and Arthur go to the board meeting of their foundation from four to seven in the evening, the house always has someone in it. 'It's only unattended three hours a month, and, of course, it's alarmed to death.'

"Larry's eyes were like the windows of a grand-slam slot machine. We know where the Swastika 34 Egg is. We know that it's genuine. We have a fence for it and a price. We know when the house is unattended. We know the alarm code. And we know the password."

"Why don't you just steal it?" Freddy asked.

"Are you kidding? Larry's an accountant. Accountants don't steal *physical* things. And I can't, because in DC I'm galactically hot. We need soul brothers."

"Us?"

"Why not?"

"I'm sorry," Freddy said, recoiling. "My upbringing and inclination do not lend themselves to the theft of paintings."

"It's not a painting," Kitten said derisively. "You think modern artists can paint? It's grocery string smeared with zebra blood, attached with blue thumbtacks to the ceiling and the floor so that it stretches at a forty-five-degree angle. It's called *Piece Twenty-three of Thirty-four Egg at Forty-five Degrees.* Yo, grocery string smeared with zebra blood. We need soul brothers to carry it away."

"Why?" Freddy asked.

"Come on," Kitten said. "You know."

"I don't believe we do."

"Lawyers don't steal physical things, either."

"What does it have to do with lawyers?"

"There are two kinds of people in the District of Columbia: lawyers and soul brothers. Anyone else sticks out like a camel in a funeral procession. If you're going to get out of there unobserved, you have to be one or the other, and we can't get a lawyer who's honest enough to commit so straightforward a crime. That's why we need soul brothers. That's why we need you. You were born to it."

Two golden shadows moved quickly down Rhode Island Avenue, accelerating purposefully near rubbled lots or burnt-out houses where addicts in stupors were splayed in the heat and humidity. After crossing several sets of railway tracks, they came to more populated areas where they occasioned comments such as, "Hey, Stokely Carmichael joined the circus," and, "Catch this, Odetta and her brother."

"Freddy, I'm nervous. Do you think these people know we're royalty?"

"No, they think we have dietary deficiencies."

"Can't we take the Tube?"

"The American tube doesn't accept sterling in large notes."

"Couldn't we go back to Kitten?"

"We're not thieves, Fredericka, and even were we, the only way to contact Kitten is through Raphael at the squid shop in Benning Road. I don't know where that is, it's probably closed on a Sunday night, and, given a choice and the fact that it's probably closer, wouldn't you prefer the British Embassy to Raphael's Squid Shop?" That sealed their course, and they pushed on until Logan Circle, from which it was easy to make their way to Embassy Row. At the gate of the British Embassy they were met by an American policeman.

"Would you ring up Edmund St John du Plafond, the first secretary?" Freddy asked, with the happy air of someone who has survived a dangerous wreck.

"Embassy's closed."

"I know the embassy's closed. Still, I would like to speak to the first secretary, Mr du Plafond."

"You can come back tomorrow."

"Of course I can, but I would like to speak to him tonight."

"But you can't."

"Why not?"

"I told you; it's closed."

"Officer," said Freddy, "he's a friend of ours. Please ring him up, won't you?"

"All right, I can ask. Who are you?"

"Say 'The Master of Moocock.' He'll understand."

The policeman stepped away and seized a phone. "Lunatics at the gate," he said. "What should I do?" He listened, and then turned to Freddy and Fredericka. "Are you British subjects?"

"No," they had to say.

"They're not." He listened to instructions, and said, "Go to your own embassy."

"This is our embassy," Freddy said. "It really is ours. We're not over-awed. To us, it's like a garden hut at Hounslow. Let me have the phone." He snatched it. "Hello, I'm so sorry for this irregularity. I'm looking for Plaffy. We thought we might try here before we went to his home. I'm not asking where his home is, I know where it is. Oh, I see. I see. Very well. Thank you."

Freddy took Fredericka's arm and pulled her back down Massachusetts Avenue. "They softened when I referred to him by his sobriquet—very few people know it—but he's in Tokyo."

"Oh no," said Fredericka. "Where are we going to sleep?"

"On the ground, as we did last night."

"Not again."

"Sometimes I sleep on the ground for weeks at a time."

"I don't."

"Then what do you suggest?"

"We can stay with a friend of mine who lives in a gorgeous house in Georgetown. It's not far from here."

"You have a friend in Washington?"

"I do."

"Is that where you were when I was with the president at Camp David and you threw a fit?"

"Yes."

"Who is she?"

"He," said Fredericka.

In the leafy darkness near the Turkish Embassy, Freddy stopped still. "He?" He felt his stomach floating about, just as it had before his first parachute jump.

"Yes, he."

"But I was gone for the entire weekend."

"And so was I."

"Oh, Fredericka," Freddy said, almost in tears, his mind absolutely swimming. "Oh, Fredericka, did you stay . . . did you . . . ?"

"Do you know how many times," Fredericka asked without any sympathy whatsoever for his jealousy, "while we were propagating, as you call it, or in your sleep, you have screamed the name Phoebe?"

As if to plead guilty and take his punishment all in one breath, a beaten Freddy asked, "Who is he?"

"Jus d'Orange."

"That little French military attaché with the manners of a headwaiter? That brilliantined little slug in a pillbox hat? Him?"

"*Oui,*" said Fredericka.

Now that they were walking, Fredericka had a difficult time keeping up with Freddy's pace. "He was at Spithead last time. If I had known, I would have killed him."

"He's very kind," said Fredericka, "and gentle. . . ."

Freddy wanted to die, but, before he did, he wanted to kill. "We'll go to Georgetown," he declared, to the bewilderment of some passers-by.

"I'll put the squeeze on Jus d'Orange and throw his filthy body into the Potomac."

"No, Freddy, you can't."

"And why not?"

"Because then I'd have to kill Lady Boylingehotte a thousand times over, would I not? You have many faults, but you are eminently fair when put to the test. Tell me that you won't touch Jus d'Orange."

"What if you got pregnant by him?" Freddy asked angrily. "The next king of England would be a bloody grapefruit."

"It was more than a year ago, Freddy. Put it out of your mind."

Deeply hurt, Freddy passed through Dupont Circle as Fredericka, many steps behind, followed the sound, like that of an idling outboard motor, of his grumbling. She was relieved when instead of turning south-west toward Georgetown he pointed them down Connecticut Avenue. Just after a store filled with wonderful things to eat, he halted in front of a movie theatre. On one of several publicity posters a magnificent-looking woman was pictured, mainly in the nude, in a most seductive pose. Her body was taut and long, with every bit of definition precisely where it belonged, and other areas enticingly lax. But it was her face and its expression that did the seducing, her eyes mainly, and her mouth, and the slight numbness of her cheeks that, even in a poster, proved that she was intoxicated with desire. It was hell for Freddy, because the movie was French, and its title in English was *Anyone but My Husband*. It was as if knives were cutting into his interior all on their own, and he almost cried. Though Fredericka was happy to have vengeance, and could have kicked his Jamaica-clad rear quarters like a football, she did love him. She didn't know why, but she did.

A passing bus left them in a night-cloud of bittersweet diesel exhaust, the scent of which, Freddy had told her one night long ago in Scotland, reminded him of Rome. "It's like Rome, isn't it?" she asked, as the street-lights shone through the trees, dappling the sidewalk according to the intervention of swaying branches.

"It is," he answered. "When I was young, they let me stay in the English Cemetery for a few hours to honour our dead. I was alone. I sat by a wall and breathed the air, which was sweet despite the exhausts of buses and Vespas. For that short time, I was like everyone else. I pretended that I could walk out of there and no one would know I was a prince, that I would not have to ride in a motorcade, that I could see the city as if I were invisible. I've always wanted to be anonymous."

"Now that you've got your wish," she said, "what are we to do?"

"Connecticut Avenue," he told her, with the voice of someone who was just coming out of a dark place and in great danger of falling back, "leads to the White House."

"The *coup d'état?*"

"No, a hot bath."

"But we're not supposed to tell anyone, Freddy."

"We weren't supposed to tell Plaffy, either, or Jus d'Orange. We just need a little respite, and then we'll be pulled back into the quest."

"What would Mr Neil say?"

"I really don't care what Mr Neil would say. I think that tonight we should sleep in Blair House. I would like to have a hot bath, with salts. I would like to start off tomorrow on a new foot. I don't exactly have to say who I am. That's the point. The president has a name for me that only he and Evita would know, a name that will both get us in and keep us from betraying, technically, what Mr Neil expects from us."

"But only technically," said Fredericka. "What name?"

"At Camp David, in the bowling alley, I heard him refer to me by this name. I had gone toward the tenpins to try to get my bowling ball free of the machinery, and because I was far away they thought I wouldn't be able to pick up their conversation, but the acoustics gave me a leg up. I don't know exactly what it means, but I believe it's a word that in the American idiom signifies a close and faithful friend. And if he's forgotten that, there are a number of intelligence passwords and replies, known only to heads of state and heirs, that I can use to bring him to the gate."

"Freddy, I don't know. . . ."

"Don't worry, I have it down to a science. Princes, presidents, kings, we're all part of the same fraternity. I promise you, Fredericka, that we shall, as they say here, blow right into the White House."

EVEN BEFORE the two gap-toothed and golden Rastafarians reached the north-west gate of the White House, a radio call went out and a man in a vest too bulky for a hot night appeared as if from nowhere to stand in the shadows, from which he could rake the path to the West Wing with shot-gun fire if someone were to make a mad dash. Inside the White House, amber lights on several consoles began to flash, and the approach was logged.

The Rastas pushed through scores of dangerous exhibitionists moving at high speed on Rollerblades over what had once been Pennsylvania Avenue and was now a playground for narcissists who wanted mainly to be seen by President Self or the television cameras with their celebrity correspondents working on the front lawn (they did not, of course, cut it), which was just, because President Self himself, the chief narcissist of the Western World, wanted mainly to be seen by the other narcissists and the television cameras. Freddy assured Fredericka that within half an hour, as soon as they could tear themselves away from the president's greetings, they would be across the way in Blair House reading the British papers and eating sushi.

But just as they approached the sidewalk by the White House fence, a purple-clad behemoth in lobster-scale helmet and pads came rushing at them out of control. He was headed for Fredericka in such a way as to make collision unavoidable, so Freddy did the chivalrous thing and stepped between them to take the blow. The concussion was tremendous, at least for Freddy, who was thrown to the ground like the head of a gavel rapping on a slab of walnut. The skater was gone in an instant.

"Freddy? Freddy?" Fredericka pulled him to his feet. "Are you all right?"

"I'm all right. What was that?"

"One of those idiots knocked you down."

Freddy bled from a cut under his right eye. "He must have hit me with an edge of his armour."

"Shouldn't we recover before we see the president?"

"All the more reason to go now."

They walked ahead until they came to the guardhouse, where they greeted a uniformed Secret Service officer. "Good evening, sir," he replied.

"I usually arrive in an automobile and get out under that lantern," Freddy said. "Do you recognise me?"

"No, sir."

"We would like to see the president, please."

"The president is not available. If you would like to see the president, he often appears at public functions. Should you have need of an appointment, write to the White House, Washington, DC."

"No no no," said Freddy, laughing politely, "I'd like to see him now." He lowered his voice and sounded urgent but assured. "Call upstairs to the

family quarters and tell the president or Evita that *the nudnik* is here."
Freddy pulled back, as if this would do it. When the guard appeared not to
react, Freddy thought to clarify. "That's my secret name. That's what they
call me, in there."

"You'd better move on," said the guard. "There's a procedure that we
have to follow, and at this point you'd best go."

"You don't believe us. I thought you might not. I also thought that the
president himself might not remember his name for me. That's forgivable,"
he said, holding up his hands magnanimously, "and not a problem. Just
tell him that . . . *the yellow crow of Baghdad* . . . is in . . . *the cross-hairs of the
tenth stooge.*"

"I will," said the guard. "Wait here." He went inside.

"Freddy, what if the passwords have changed?" Fredericka asked.

"You're right," said Freddy. "I'll have to go deeper. Officer? Officer?" he
said, shouting very loudly and pounding on the bulletproof glass. With the
shouting came, invariably, a high level of gesticulation. "I'm *Chuckles*! I'm
here to see the *Dalai Lama,* and we're going to play . . . *cross-dressing.* Tell the
president that I'm going to plunge my *knife* into his *breast.* He'll understand,
and if he doesn't, he can ask the Director of Central Intelligence."

"Freddy, he's not going to call the president."

Freddy looked into the gatehouse, where several officers were unfurling
a net. Others were briskly walking down the driveway. "Funny," said
Freddy, "another net. I think perhaps we should go."

They burst through the narcissists, knocking quite a few off their
skates, which seemed just and was certainly enjoyable, and then went west
toward Georgetown, a place that Freddy mistakenly thought was named
for his favourite king. "I'm hungry," said Fredericka as she ran.

"I am, too," her husband added. "Do you think trendy little restaurants
in Georgetown take sterling?"

"They might," she answered, "but we'll never know."

"Why not?"

"Because they won't let us in."

TOO EMBARRASSED to sleep on the street, though it might have been safer,
they walked along the canal and found a wide doorway with a broad granite step. There they stretched out, too tired not to. "Do you think it's safe
here?" Fredericka asked.

"No," said Freddy.

"We could go to Jus d'Orange."

"That Franco-citric bastard? I'd sooner kill him."

"Then what do we do?"

"Suffer until the banks open. Tomorrow we'll change our nine thousand pounds. With more than twelve thousand dollars, we'll go to a hotel for two nights, where we can rest and have a bath. That and some decent food will set us back only a thousand dollars, leaving eleven. Then we'll have our teeth fixed at a public dispensary. . . ."

"Public dispensary?"

"We can't afford to have it done privately."

"What if they don't match?"

"Why wouldn't they?"

"That would be awful. Colour-matching is a subtle art."

"Don't worry. Say that's another thousand at most. We'll have ten left. If we spend a thousand on passable casual clothes and shoes. . . ."

"A thousand dollars for the two of us? A thousand dollars won't even buy a brassière!"

"Those days are over. It will buy, as it will have to, some khakis, cotton shirts, and strong shoes for both of us, as well as belts, underwear for you, socks, toilet kits, and backpacks. We'll need sweaters and jackets for cold nights or when we go into the mountains. With the nine thousand left we can buy a secondhand car—something rugged with four-wheel drive—and still have enough left over for a few weeks on the road."

"Where are we going?"

"I don't know, but I can feel the mountains rising to the west, and, beyond them, in the thousands of miles stretching onward to the sea, a promise that we will succeed."

"Where do you get such confidence?" she asked.

"It wells up in me like a spring. Even when the spring seems drained and I'm prostrate with shame, I need only rest, and it reappears like a mad river rushing down from the Himalaya."

"I never had that," Fredericka told him, her voice slurred with fatigue, "but, then again, I haven't needed it. What would we have done had we not had the ten thousand pounds?"

"For one thing, we wouldn't be in these clothes, would we? And we'd still be white."

Soon they fell asleep. It was not too bad a place to be. Often the canal was drained of water, mud-bottomed, and foul, but some event far away, where rivers ran over sharp rocks and had risen to foam, filled it with clean water as black as obsidian and saturated with oxygen. The long, dark run of the canal was covered in thick overhanging boughs heavy with summer leaves, not a one of which had yet died, and lights shone through, as they do on summer nights, making luxurious shadows, frosted patterns, and optical illusions. The step upon which the prince and princess slept was cool, and because their headgear was so huge and puffy they did not need pillows.

They had been in America for a day. Here, colours were neither soft nor light and sound was not muted as in England. Now in their dreams they were carried over dark plains where lights were at war, and the daylight of these dreams was as clear and bright as the modern paintings Freddy did not like. In this country everything had an edge, and where there was no edge, where time and tradition had worn against the blade of the new, rebellious angels floated invisibly alongside, honing without sound and sharpening with glee. As they slept, the prince and princess shuddered and moaned: you would have thought purely from the soundtrack not that they were sleeping but that they were in a battle. In their dreams they saw devils, angels, blinding colours, cities that arose in ambered towers, obelisks sheathed in flame, wheels, knives, engines, and all things and everything floating freely and cut loose from the past.

THIEVES

WHEN MORNING CAME in a half froggy light, some leaves that had fallen, their still-green stems cut by a force unknown, floated upon the canal like lily pads. Stiff from sleeping upon stone, the prince and princess slowly awoke. "What's this?" asked Freddy, propelling himself instantly into a seated position and inspecting the many ribbons into which his clothes had been cut. "I've been julienned."

"What do you mean? Oh! I have, too, like a potato. Why would anyone want to do such a thing?"

Freddy patted himself down. "They've taken the money. We have no money, not even a farthing."

After making their way across the District of Columbia to the squid shop in Benning Road, they had to wait because it had not opened. Watchless, they did not even know how long they had remained in the doorway in expectation of Raphael as the afternoon sun turned their forsaken quadrant of Washington into the Rub al-Khali.

"Did you notice all those people whom normally we look down upon," Freddy asked, "looking down upon us? People clutching briefcases and newspapers in a clearly barbaric way and scurrying to their upper-middle-class jobs in monumental buildings and glass boxes, asserting with every step their status in life?"

"I did."

"They viewed us with revulsion, pity, and amusement. I've never treated people that way."

"Not ordinary people, they were too far below you, but you did treat the nobility as these people treat us. Did you see their women? They were all wearing business suits and running shoes. It's like a tribe in the Amazon."

"We're all God's creatures," Freddy proclaimed. "We all moulder in the grave. What foolishness to believe that we can lord it over others because of some meaningless variations that we ourselves have made up."

"Look who's talking," Fredericka said.

"Get the hell outa here," Raphael ordered, moving between them to unblock his decaying wooden door.

"Are you Raphael?" they asked, following him inside.

"We're not open yet."

"Kitten sent us—Sal. Would you ring him up?"

"I'm busy," Raphael said, as he began to cut apart the first squid of the day.

"But we have no other avenue," Freddy told him.

"Lots'a avenues out there," Raphael informed them, gesturing with his knife. "This is a squid shop, not AT&T."

Taking Fredericka tenderly by the shoulder, Freddy pointed at an exhaust fan so encrusted with congealed grease that it looked like an illustration in a cardiology textbook. "I've never seen anything like that," he said. "Think of the vast amount of cold blue ocean entrapped and distilled on that frame and fan. This five pounds of the most ethereal oil of the squid is the raffinate of ten thousand cubic miles of ice-blue seas. Here is the conqueror of Moby-Dick, the biggest living thing in the world, a nightmare of the ancients, clinging to a fan and covered with the dust of Benning Road. God, it's just like *Ozymandias.*"

"You know that cat?" Raphael asked.

"Shelley?" Freddy answered.

"No, Ozzy."

"Yes . . . Ozzy. Of course."

"Why didn't you say so? I've been cool with Ozzy since we were five years old—like, before there were birds. Any friend of Ozzy's is a friend of mine."

As Raphael washed his hands so he could use the telephone, Freddy turned to Fredericka and said, "I must be destined for the throne."

KITTEN BEGAN to go over the plan even before the car door was closed. Though it may have been foolish to drive up and down the streets of Kalorama in a stolen Cadillac so conspicuous that it might as well have been *Titanic,* he did, passing the Clovis mansion forty times. "Wait a minute," he said. "It just grabbed me. You're white people."

"Yes, we are white people."

"How did you do that?"

"We were born that way," Fredericka said.

"You weren't white yesterday."

"We washed our faces in the canal after we were robbed," Fredericka said.

"And that made you white?"

"It washed off the gold."

"It washed off the gold," Kitten said to himself, trying to understand. "Was it water from a special place?"

"It was just water, Kitten. You see, Desmond told Desmond that the gold would last far longer than it did."

"Desmond told Desmond," Kitten echoed. "You two are so strange. . . ."

Fredericka smiled, the gap in her front teeth just as charming as it had been when she was gold.

"I thought those blue eyes were contacts," Kitten said. "You, too," meaning Freddy.

"No, these are our eyes."

"We got our eyes by washing in the river Oxus and the river Styx," Freddy added, as a witticism.

"In Maryland, right?" Kitten asked.

"Kitten," Freddy said with the decisiveness of a soldier who knows that apprehension looms ever greater in the absence of action, "all we need do is go into a house and bring out an *objet d'art*. If we ride around all day talking about it, it will never happen."

"This is a big hit," Kitten said, unbelieving that two novices were unafraid while he, a professional, was, as he put it, real jumpy.

"I have no anxiety," Freddy said. "Do you, Popeel?"

"Not at all," Fredericka answered.

"You've never done anything like this before?" Kitten asked.

"Never."

"How can you be so calm?" He rapped his steering wheel, which beeped the horn.

"I was brought up," Freddy informed him, "not to suffer anxiety about decisive initiative of all types."

"Okay," Kitten said, stopping the car. "It's two blocks down. After the hit, meet me where I showed you on Connecticut Avenue. Be confident. Act like you own the place."

"We will," Freddy promised, and as Kitten accelerated away in his half-a-block-long automobile the Prince and Princess of Wales in their shreds walked gracefully down a deserted street, hearts filling with the joy that flows from the sight of beauteous things. Here were noble trees, carefully shaped hedges, old brick and iron in the shapes they had known and loved since birth. Here were pediments, architraves, and plinths. Just the properties and proportions of windows, eaves, French doors, and roof lines were enough to energise and refresh them.

"It's a pity the Clovis family doesn't live in a Georgian house," Freddy said. "I'd enjoy myself much more looting a Robert Adam or a Christopher Wren than a refrigerator turned on its side with trapezoidal windows and dirt on the roof. But what can we do? The great forms speak directly to the heart, but in this age so many people have been robbed of their hearts that they no longer understand what is spoken."

"I don't know about you," Fredericka said with immutable determination, "but I'm looking forward to a trip to the Clovis kitchen."

"Why not? In for a pound, in for a penny. If we're going to steal a ten-million-dollar 'art' work, we might as well take a chicken leg. I had no inkling how delightful it is to come by one's food, day by day, with neither money nor assurance. I suppose it's like hunting or illicit sex."

She looked at him with an injured expression. Many of her expressions were injured. He had never before realised this. "Just the two of us, Fredericka, in the Clovis kitchen," he said by way of apology. "Just the two of us. We're in it together. The pleasure will be ours alone. For the rest of our lives."

This meant a great deal to her, and when they opened the gate and went up to the Clovis kitchen door, she was happy. Neither of them felt any apprehension about the burglary, perhaps because they had been brought up knowing that they were entitled in the literal sense and also to things in far greater profusion than they had ever been able to take. "I'll kick in the door," Freddy said, looking about, "you get to the keypad and disarm the alarm, and I'll close the door expeditiously. It should take about five seconds. Are you ready?"

She nodded. Then Freddy aimed a martial kick at the lock plate, and the door exploded inward. "I've got it," Fredericka said, arriving at the keypad. Freddy gently closed the door. Even the door frame was undamaged, for the wood had been supple enough to bend so that the deadbolt had simply popped out of the strike. They were in.

"Wait," said Freddy, holding up his index finger, lifting his eyes, and listening. "There's no sound. Perhaps the system wasn't armed, but, then again, it may be silent. Enter the code and be prepared to cancel it."

Fredericka entered *4020 Off.* Marina Clovis was a tractor heiress, and in her family's glory days the 4020 was a popular tractor. Nothing happened except a chirp. Freddy told Fredericka to hit *4020 Away,* which she did, and the system came up armed. "Forty twenty Off," he said. She complied, eliciting a series of chirps.

"That's strange," Fredericka said. "It wasn't on. Do you think someone's home?"

"Let's find out," Freddy said. "Hello? Hello?" He marched through the house, calling out, "Hello! Hello! We've come to check the flexes and points, and the door was wide open. Is anyone home? Hello! Local authority here to check flexes and points. Is anyone there?"

No one was. "They forgot to turn on the alarm," Freddy said. "That means they may realise it and come back."

"I doubt it," Fredericka offered. "Just after they'd left, perhaps, but if relatively soon they hadn't remembered what they'd done, they would have become unconcerned. That's why houses explode when the cookers have been pumping gas into them since boiling over at breakfast."

"You're probably right. Shall we eat first?"

WHEN THE CLOVISES came up the walk, having left their board meeting after remembering that neither of them had turned on the alarm, two people in shredded clothes and outlandish headgear were seated at the kitchen island partaking of cold filet mignon with Acapulco lime chutney, French bread, *salade aux tomates,* and lots and lots of Champagne. Freddy and Fredericka had been thirsty all day, and fortunately the refrigerator contained a row of Dom Pérignon magnums, from which they had conscripted and nearly drained two. Perhaps because of this, they took the return of the masters of the house more lightly than they might have. "Look," said Fredericka, "here come the Cleavises."

"The Clovises."

"Whoever they are. What shall we do?"

"We're servants."

"You may be," she said, "but I'm no servant to any Cleavises or anyone else. I'm the goddamned princess of you know what."

"I went out on enough moonlighted catering jobs with the palace staff to know exactly how to be servile and obsequious. You do it your way, and I'll do it mine."

"As always," she answered, the Champagne having brought out some hostility, as in a grave rubbing.

The door opened and the Clovises entered. Although they were startled to see two very large, oddly attired strangers drinking their Champagne and eating their filet mignon, Freddy and Fredericka's absolute ease made the Clovises think that they had overlooked some sort of new organisation accomplished by the servants.

"Didn't you used to work for Ladislas and Fifi Brown-Vanilla? Did Velda arrange for you to be here?" Marina Clovis asked, half deferentially and half as a challenge.

"Indeed," said Freddy. "It was Velda, Velda, Velda, a better man than I, the regimental Inca, with a finger in the pie. Though I've belted her and flayed her, by the living god that made her, she always gave that good old Inca try."

"Are you . . . Arthur? Is he? Are you part of the Inca community?"

"Can't you tell?" Freddy asked, with the manner of his father dressing down a page. It was the Champagne. "I am Tuhalpac Amaru, Velda's cousin. But she," meaning Fredericka, "is Woffe Ababa, an Ethiopian."

"Arthur, they've got blue eyes and they're tall," Marina Clovis said under her breath.

"I heard that. I'm Anglo-Inca, and she's Ethiopian of Icelandic extraction."

"Why are you drinking our Champagne?" Arthur Clovis finally weighed in, belligerently, his last belligerence of the evening.

"Why do you bloody think we're drinking your Champagne? We're bloody thirsty, that's why," Freddy said, jumping up to his great height, with a foot added by his Jamaican hat. He towered over the Clovises and was much bigger in every way. "Considering," Freddy went on, "that every social-climbing bastard ever born comes to nick *our* Champagne, which flows like a river and bankrupts us out of house and home, what are two lousy magna?"

"Oh, I didn't know," Arthur said pusillanimously.

"Do you think it's fair?" Freddy asked.

"What's fair?"

"That everyone," Freddy said, waving his right arm back and forth drunkenly, like a madman directing traffic, "drinks our Champagne and never says thank you—as if it comes from trees."

"As if it grows on a vine," Fredericka added, smugly.

"Of course it's not fair," Marina Clovis agreed, like the psychology major she once had been, and the coward she was.

Freddy took a long drink. He was under a great deal of strain, but he did notice Arthur Clovis moving toward the keypad, sideways, like a prodigiously slow crab. "Oh oh ah," said Freddy. "I see that, Arthur. I know everything there is to know about panic buttons. My family had them when they were velvet ropes." Arthur stopped moving, and smiled. "Where are some more of these wonderful Argentine steak knives?" Freddy asked rhetorically.

"How does he know that?" Marina whispered to her husband. "It's not written on them that they're Argentine, and they cost a hundred and fifty dollars apiece."

"Here," Freddy said, opening a drawer and taking one up. "We have them, too. They're perfectly balanced and tempered. Arthur, attention!" He raised his arm and threw the knife into the wall next to the keypad. It went in up to its little nickel hilt. "Wallboard," said Freddy. "Wallboard . . . is for poor people."

"I didn't know you could do that, Freddy. I mean, I didn't know you could do that . . . *Moofoomooach*."

"Yes, *Mrs Moofoomooach*. I practise in the Orangery, in the corner opposite the harpsichord."

"Who *are* you?" Arthur Clovis asked, screwing up his face in irritation and amazement.

"I'll tell you who I am," Freddy said crisply but over-emotionally. "I am a person whose various kitchens have walls of stone."

"That's who you are?"

"And I can throw knives as if I'd been brought up in the circus."

"Yes, but you're not above the law," Marina said defiantly.

"I am above the law, quite above the law, in many respects. If, for example, I were to kill you and I were sent to gaol, I would be allowed to take my clothes with me, and I have enough cummerbunds to string together so that I could lower myself to the ground even if my cell were at the top of your Empire State Building."

The Clovises were breathing hard, terrified of his inexplicableness.

"So sit down and shut up, and speak only when spoken to."

"Freddy, that's not nice. It's their house."

"They're prisoners of war."

"Don't be absurd."

"I'm not absurd, they're absurd. Look at the house they live in."

"We really don't have that much money," Marina Clovis stated reflexively.

"I can see that," Freddy said, but they thought it was sarcasm.

"Really, we don't. We gave most of our wealth to the foundation."

"With what intent?" asked Freddy, who knew all about foundations.

"To help animals."

"That's nice," Fredericka commented.

"Help them do what?" Freddy asked.

"Live more productive lives."

"Give more milk? Fatten up?"

"Oh no, of course not."

"What's this, then?" asked Freddy, pointing to what was left of his filet mignon.

"That's meat," Marina Clovis answered, "but it's for guests. We don't eat meat, and we endowed the Clovis Foundation for Research in Animal Psychiatry."

Freddy thought about this for a moment. "Of what use would a psychiatrist be to an animal? Animals cannot speak."

"Children can't speak, either," said Marina Clovis, triumphantly, "and they have psychiatrists."

"What do you mean, 'children can't speak'?"

"Well, not like adults."

"At the Clovis Foundation," Freddy asked in a scathing tone undermined by the huge gap in his teeth, "do a bunch of Freudians analyse chickens who are neurotic because they're fryers and they want to be broilers?"

"Chickens have just as much right to medical care as you do," Marina Clovis told him.

"What about sea anemones?"

"Why not?"

"Because sea anemones cannot have psychiatric problems."

"How would you know, not being a sea anemone?"

"How would you, not being a sea anemone, know they did?"

"Better safe than sorry," Marina said. "We are the world leader in cat biofeedback."

"Do you mean fur balls?"

"I mean, however you may mock me, serious study into the. . . ."

"You don't study into something, you make a study of it."

"Oh! A pedantic burglar. How lucky we are. That aside, we are on the cutting edge." She swallowed in fear of what she had said. "We developed Clovis B, which cures feline baldness."

Freddy stared at her in as much disbelief as she had for him. "That's important," he said. "Think of all the poor bald cats to whom you have given hope. You should know that I have developed Freddy A, which shuts up fat super-spoiled matrons with intelligence quotients of less than fifty."

Marina, who in her anxiety had heard imprecisely, and thought Freddy had been referring to her age, said, "Forty-six! In fact."

"I don't think so, milady. I'd say about twenty-three."

"Thank you," said Marina, softening unbelievably.

"Please," said Arthur Clovis, "take anything you want. I swear, we won't tell the police. You can lock us in the closet. We won't get out for days."

"How will you eat?" asked Fredericka.

"We'll bring cookies and sandwiches."

"We're only going to take one thing," Freddy announced, "and then, in a year or so, you'll receive five times its market value either of today or then, whichever is higher. We are not thieves, we are borrowers."

"You're borrowers."

"Yes, and we don't care if you tell the police or not. We walk upon this earth with virtual invincibility. We are not who we are, you don't know us, and we don't give a fig."

"Arthur, they're completely psychotic. They're going to kill us," Marina whispered, but Freddy heard.

"We're not going to kill you, but we would like to kill your decorator. Look at this place. It's all of fashion. It all comes from cheap magazines. Have you ever looked at such magazines from the past? It makes you dizzy with revulsion. Everything seems like a conspiracy that failed, and of course it did, as the conspirators' prime value is simply to move *en masse* from one craze to another. I wonder where in the world there is a hole big enough to swallow all the granite countertops that in a few years will be marching out of kitchens like an army of the dead. Other than with the addition of modern appliances, the kitchens in my houses have hardly changed since eighteen forty."

"Oh, stop it, Freddy. You're insufferable when you get this way. Leave these poor pathetic people alone. You mustn't torment them just because they're of low station. It must be the Champagne. You rail against the low aristocracy every time you have a drink."

The Clovises knitted their brows like cavemen. They really had no idea what was going on. All kinds of permutations raced through their minds, but in the end they suspected that they were hallucinating. "Are you Jamaicans?" Arthur asked.

"Speak when spoken to!" Fredericka commanded. "And it's 'Your Royal Highness.'"

"No," said Freddy, "not here."

"You will address me," Fredericka ordered Arthur Clovis, correcting herself, "as Popeel."

The Champagne made Freddy and Fredericka forget the presence of their captives, whose eyes were fastened upon the royal couple as if with glue. "You, Moofoomooach," Fredericka said, "are simply too aggressive."

"You're the one who screamed at the peasants."

"You started it. I think it's because you model yourself after George the Third."

"What's wrong with that? He was a great and gracious king, the most learned king, a good man, in the wrong time, who happened to have been ill."

"Granted, but modelling oneself after someone who is ill is asking for trouble, isn't it? And all you do is get into trouble."

"Name one instance."

"Freddy, I could name a thousand instances."

"Moofoomooach," he corrected.

"Moofoomooach," she continued.

"No you can't."

"Yes I can."

"Name one, then. Go ahead."

"When you thought the Australian High Commissioner had bought a residence next to the lands of Moocock, and threw boomerangs at him and sang 'Tie Me Kangaroo Down,' but it wasn't the Australian High Commissioner, it was the Papal Legate."

"How was I to know?"

"For one, he was African. The Australian High Commissioner would not be African."

"Why not? We're African."

"No we're not."

"Yes we are."

"No, we're not. Arthur?" Fredericka asked, "are we African?"

"I don't know what to say," said Arthur, fearfully.

"Say the truth, chucklewit."

"No, you're not."

"We *were* this morning," Fredericka said to her husband.

"That's right," he answered. "I remember now that, like Achilles, we made our ablutions in the canal."

"Please don't hurt us," Marina begged, holding her hands like an angel at prayer.

"Why would we hurt you?" Freddy asked. "All you are are *nouveaux riches* who strut about like guinea hens, spending the unimpressive amounts of money you have in the most ostentatious way and without restraint, wasting your lives in senseless competition with other *nouveaux riches* who must have this and must have that, never realising that no matter what you do to appear higher than others, no one is ever thinking about you, they're thinking about their own lot. No one is impressed by you, they are impressed only by themselves. What you imagine to be their impression is them begrudging you a meaningless point in a meaningless game. Position means nothing unless it's an accident of birth, an unwanted obligation. Then it can be a test, and only then. But if you seek it, you cannot be noble."

"I don't know what you're talking about," Arthur told them. "I don't know who you are, what you are, or why you're in my house."

"We're here to appropriate your Swastika 34 Egg," Freddy said, like a messenger asking someone to sign a receipt, "but, as I have stated, and given that we are subjecting you to duress, we'll make it worth your while. Would you like a Gainsborough? A Rubens? I suppose I could even spare a Caravaggio or a small Raphael, if he's finished cooking the squid," Freddy said, as a joke for Fredericka. "How could you possibly be so stupid as to consider a piece of grocery string and two thumbtacks a work of art?"

"Why would you steal it if you think it of no value?"

"Frankly, we couldn't care less. The king of the Gypsies wants it."

"If, because of the schizophrenic delusion that you are directed by the king of the Gypsies, you do this," Marina told them, "you'll be running from the police for the rest of your lives."

"Of late we've been running from the police quite regularly," Fredericka said. "I've been thinking about that, and I know how to deal with it."

"How?" asked Freddy.

"We shouldn't run *away* from the police when they chase us, we should run *toward* them."

"Why?"

"Remember when Stephen Hawking came to dinner and told us all about Einstein and Lawrence of Arabia?"

"No, Popeel, it was Einstein and *Lorentz*."

"Ah!" she said, "I thought it was Lawrence of Arabia. Anyway, if the police are chasing us at sixty miles per hour, and we are fleeing at sixty miles per hour, as Einstein said, we will be frozen in time. The chase could last forever, or they would only have to increase their speed a tiny fraction and they could catch us—or, if we decreased our speed by a tiny fraction, or if we both decreased but we decreased more, or if we both increased but they increased more."

"Yes?"

"That's why, the next time we're chased, we should run *toward* them. Let's say we're going at the speed of light, and they're going at the speed of light. If we run toward them, when we pass them we'll be moving apart at twice the speed of light. What better way to get away from someone?"

"I'm willing to give that a try," said Freddy. "It does have a wavering charm." He addressed the Clovises. "Don't you realise that in supporting the destructive currents of modernism you are destroying the world? The only thing that makes art of a bloody piece of grocery string hanging from a bloody fucking tack is the power of coercion. There is such a thing as art, grounded in a universal language derived from all human experience and the absolutes of nature, and when you destroy the limitations and definitions of art by the inclusion—via sterile decree—of absolutely everything, you destroy civilisation. Or didn't you know that?"

"Are you saying," Marina Clovis asked meekly, "that Arthur and I are destroying civilisation?"

"Yes," Freddy said, "I am."

. . .

THE ROYALS FOUND KITTEN, stepped into his car, and disappeared in traffic. Kitten looked grim.

"What's the matter?" Freddy asked. "We've got it."

"I can't pay you," Kitten said. "I was just on the cell phone with Larry's wife. The FBI arrested him this morning for conspiracy to import prohibited lizards. The deal is off."

"Bloody hell!" said Freddy. "We did that for nothing?"

"Don't worry, you have a distinguished career ahead of you. You were just in the big game, and you sailed through."

Freddy grumbled.

"At least get us new teeth," Fredericka begged.

"I'm the king of the Gypsies, not the Tooth Fairy," Kitten said. "What do Gypsies know about teeth?"

"You're neither a Gypsy nor a king, and you've left us in a most difficult position," Freddy told him.

"If there's anything I can't stand," Kitten said, "it's someone who thinks I owe him a living. This was a business proposition that failed. I don't owe you anything. That's the law." He stopped the car at K Street to let them out. "But, here," he said, handing Freddy a twenty-dollar bill, "get yourself some sashimi. You don't have to chew it."

As they emerged from his car into a sea of young lawyers, both male and female, in dreary suits and rushing to and fro, Kitten said plaintively, "You're taking the string?"

"We stole it," Freddy stated, "so it's ours. That's the law."

Kitten drove off, they threw the string into a dustbin, and the impoverished couple walked aimlessly toward Pennsylvania Avenue. "What are we going to do, Freddy?"

"Tonight we'll sleep in the park, and tomorrow we'll get new teeth, new clothes, a bath, and perhaps some exercise."

"How?"

"Somehow. Look," he said, holding up the twenty-dollar bill, "we're on the right track: we've got twenty bob." But as he finished his sentence a bicycle messenger dressed in metallic green the colour of a fly's eye flew past them, snatched the bill from Freddy's hand, and was gone before they knew what happened. "We're even again. The only direction is up."

They slept in the aura of a great white temple that looked east over the reflecting pools. Here Lincoln sat, day and night, through the years, in tranquil marble and heroic size, his expression that of a man whose understanding of things ran deeper than his powers to alter them. It was this expression that stripped its onlookers of all pretensions and allowed them to hear in their hearts the song of the Union dead.

At first Freddy and Fredericka did not even see Lincoln. They found a place near one of the monument's walls, where they lay down on soft earth amidst fragrant bushes and slept for six or seven hours. No one saw them or even came near, and they were safe, being so indigent that not even the robbers of people who sleep in the bushes would have bothered with them. This was an unusual circumstance for two people who had lived in great houses and palaces always under guard, but as one feels less safe when one is guarded than when one has no reason to be guarded, they slept peacefully and well. In England, when Freddy was by himself on the heath, he was identifiable. And even were he not, his kit and rifle were a far richer prize than what he had now, which was nothing. When they went to sleep, the fragrant air that gently swept across them was a perfect temperature, and the ground and walls were warm. It felt like the Garden of Eden.

But in the middle of the night a Potomac miasma, sticky, cool, and perhaps the very agency that addled the minds of politicians, settled over them like the spinnings of a silkworm. Awakened and miserable, neither spoke as the minutes passed, until Freddy asked, "Are you awake?"

"Yes, are you?"

"I just spoke."

"I'm cold."

"I am, too, and thirsty."

"And I'm hungry, Freddy, but we have no money."

"Perhaps we can break into a tea wagon and find a stale pastry, or what they call a hot *dog*," which Freddy always pronounced with the stress on the second word.

"Oh, Freddy, I'd love a dog. It would be just what we needed."

"To eat?"

"No, just to love." She turned away and said, to the night, "Or a baby." He didn't hear.

"How would we feed a dog? We can't even feed ourselves."

"Perhaps we could hunt."

"In Washington?"

"They must have game preserves."

"I thought you were against hunting."

"I am, but I'm hungry."

"Let's walk about."

"Isn't it dangerous?"

"Why? We're the criminals."

They went around the steps of the memorial and looked at the statue of Lincoln. Then they walked inside. "You know, I've been here before, with the president-before-this-one, but it was in daylight, we faced outward, and I had to give a speech. I didn't really see. Look at his face. Of all the kings of England, none was half as noble. Nor Nelson, nor Wellington, nor Marlborough, nor Churchill.

"In the middle of this crazed, materialistic, common country, where the lowest of the low is turned up by the strong currents of progress and rides upon the glittering surface of national life more buoyantly than an aristocrat; in the midst of all this that I thought so unimpressive—Gypsies, Cadillacs, houses with flat roofs—we have been outdone by the visage of a peasant, a soul speaking through marble, in a history not our own."

"Who is that?" Fredericka asked.

"Lincoln."

"He's the one who shot Kennedy?"

"No, no, Fredericka. He himself was assassinated, a century before Kennedy. He freed the slaves."

"Is he a big deal, then?"

"Look at him, Fredericka. He suffered and died for an undeniable principle. They had a great war here, and lost their sons. He lost his, too, though not in the fighting. It shows in his face: love that is ever awaiting."

"Oh, I know about that," she said.

"You do?"

"I do."

"I see," said Freddy, looking down at his feet. He always regretted that he hadn't come to love her. She had a good heart, she was beautiful, her eyes were blue. She was willing to walk in the mountains, sail into a gale, and propel her long frame alongside him in running or in the waves. The problem was that she appeared to have no sense of what was noble or sacrificial. Were that so, and he was not absolutely sure that it was, how could he live with her forever? Strong, facile, powerful, and at his peak, he wanted a woman who, though she might grace the cover of a magazine, was also able to lose herself between the covers of a book and feel the tide of serious things. This was his dream, and had been all his life. Occasionally Fredericka did show flashes of wit and understanding, but these flashes were for Freddy like the lightning storm over Tunisia that once he had seen from a mountaintop in Sicily: silent, dim, and achingly remote. And though physically she was nearly perfect, she was ill-educated. Just as he was determining to ignore that, for, after all, she was his wife, she asked, "Did they have World War One to free the slaves, or World War Two, or both?"

"The War Between the States," Freddy answered.

"There are so many states, more than a hundred. How did they keep track of which ones won and which ones lost? It must have been confusing."

"They were organised into two opposing camps."

"That was a good idea, but how did they decide who would be on which side?"

"It was the South versus the North, the slave-holding states versus the free states."

"They're very creative, aren't they, those Americans. They're so organised. I wish my wardrobe was half as organised as their country. Freddy, how are we going to eat? How will we get clothes? How will we replace our teeth?"

"We'll have to work."

"But who would hire people like us? We're so dirty and strange."

"YOU GET ROOM and board for a week, a voucher at the thrift shop, haircuts, referral to a dental clinic, and delousing," a Salvation Army major told them. "In return, you will behave in a civil fashion, neither smoke nor drink nor fight, attend chapel twice a week, and work in the job we send you to so that you can begin to pay your own way. If all goes well, you'll gradually move up to full payment for services, and, eventually, God willing, you can move on."

"I've always contributed to the Salvation Army," Freddy said. "My entire family has. We were right to have done so."

"Thank you," said the major, a kind of Irishman. "We appreciate that."

After they were deloused—though they had had not a single louse on them—they were shown to a shower room where, because they were mar-

ried, they would be allowed to be together. Green operating-room clothing and plastic slippers awaited them when they finished. They had
stripped off and thrown away their clothes, and stood now without anything of their own, not a single thing, not even an earring or a ring. And
yet they felt confident and strong, perhaps because, though they could
easily have fallen further—at this point they hardly knew difficulty or
degradation—they thought they had reached the bottom. They had nothing and so could not have had less. They stood with no accoutrements,
props, or illusions. To reach this state is worth an earldom or two, in light
of what it does for you, and after the addition of such a thing to the
princely qualities that had been Freddy's since birth, it was not surprising
that for the first time in his life he actually felt like a king.

They stepped into a shower stall of enamelled tin and pulled a plastic
shower curtain across the gap. Above them was a fluorescent light, and a
new bar of white soap rested in a cheap plastic holder. When Freddy
turned the taps a strong stream of hot water issued from above like a waterfall in the mountains. Produced in an industrial boiler, it would last as long
as they wanted.

In fluorescent light, Fredericka's body was like an Elgin Marble. Un-
adorned and perfect, she was now her essential self. When she took her
turn in the stream of water and pulled her wet hair back, and the stream
beat against her breasts like the overture of a Wagnerian opera, Freddy was
not unmoved. For all her faults, this was she. Her bones, her flesh, her
teeth (that remained), the musculature that allowed her to stand nobly
straight, this was Fredericka, with not a thread of fashion and no place in
any order but that of nature. This was Fredericka, the wife whom he had
never loved, and she was royal not in the royal way but in the way of things
that exceed and confound hierarchy and privilege. She was something that
could have lived in and mastered the sea. She was the centre, and vital,
as lithe as a porpoise, with blue eyes like sapphires, and the shoulders of
Aphrodite.

THEIR ROOM for the time it would take to save them was three or four
storeys above the street, just beyond the crowns of trees that protected
them from the heat as a jetty holds back the waves. Even the trees that were
rooted beneath the sidewalks shimmered in daylight, were reservoirs of
cool shadow, rustled at night with every breeze, and early in the morning

were luminous green hives for birds. Just over them was the top of a stone building across the street. Its roof was flat and undistinguished, but undulating in the air above it were the mirage-like images of whited sepulchres—domes, pediments, friezes, roof lines like the Parthenon's—real buildings as bleached as bone, floating in the blue as if on the ocean on a summer day.

Two twin beds, a white laminate desktop between them, two graceless metal chairs with vinyl cushions, a lamp, a sink, a mirror, and a parchment-coloured window shade that moved to and fro in the wind, were all they had other than their operating-room pyjamas and a small pile of clothing they had purchased with their coupon in the thrift shop. For most of the first afternoon of their salvation, Fredericka lay on her bed, listening in the heat to the wind as it argued with the shade, to traffic flowing down the street, and to the sound of Freddy sewing industriously on the bed across from her.

Sewing is quiet, but not silent. If you listen closely you can hear the cloth as it is pulled and flopped over and even as it is bunched. You can hear a strange sound, a cross between breathing, talking, and distant singing, as the tailor attends to his task. You can hear the thread as it is pulled, and sometimes, if the world is still, the needle as it pierces.

"I didn't know you could sew," she said. "I've never even threaded a needle."

"It's a military virtue."

"But it's feminine and tranquil."

"Feminine or not, when your clothes are torn in the field you have to repair them, and you must also be able to sew up a wound. Then there's sailing, where you must sew, so I've had three reasons to be a tailor, and at the moment I must say it seems a lovely occupation. Do you hear the birds? There are not that many lines of work in which you can listen all day, intently, to songbirds."

"I've been listening."

"I'm almost done. They said they'd come at three to get us for the dentist. Very kind of them, really, and impressive that they understand that people like us don't have watches."

"You mean royalty, or paupers?"

"Take your pick. We didn't need to wear watches—though goodness knows I have quite a few—because we had our staffs. I must say I hated it when rather than just being able to wander I was driven, escorted, and timed. All those poor secretaries and pages thought we wanted to blast through the traffic lights and have doors held open for us, when we had, in fact, an insatiable desire for the ordinary frictions of the world. They aren't imaginative enough to understand," Freddy said, finishing the button on a dusty-rose polo shirt for Fredericka, "that potatoes have much more staying power than caviar."

"If you put them in a cool dark place," said Fredericka.

"I mean that our diet in all things should not be as rich as everyone imagines."

"I thought one of your favourites was caviar *on* a baked potato."

"I'm speaking metaphorically," Freddy said.

"I know," was the answer. He turned sharply to look at her. She *had* known.

My God, he thought, had she known all the time?

THEY HAD DONE VERY WELL in the thrift shop, as Washington has many highly placed lawyers, lobbyists, and officials. In fact, because they were judicious and had an eye for clothes, they had done splendidly well. Fredericka now had, in addition to her dusty-rose polo shirt, one in navy and one in white. She also had a beautifully cut pair of khakis, some olive-coloured shorts, a Fair Isle jumper, and a yellow shell-parka. It was a sailing wardrobe and very versatile, down to the gum-soled Top-Siders.

Freddy too had piqué polo shirts, though in navy only, and he had acquired a grey lamb's-wool sweater, khaki trousers and shorts, a yellow parka like Fredericka's, and the same kind of shoes. They each had a tan rucksack with leather straps and bottom, and Freddy had a bridle-leather belt with a surcingle buckle.

When they were dressed and had carefully arranged their gear, Freddy said, "You look beautiful, as always. All we need now are teeth."

She did look beautiful. In fact, shaven and clean, they looked like the people they once had been—as long as they did not open their mouths. It was not surprising that they seemed like what in America are called preppies, in that they were the Mecca toward which all preppies pointed. If they had been able to keep their mouths closed they could easily and without challenge have swept into any yacht club or polo ground in the world.

But their destination that afternoon was the *pro bono* dental clinic of Dr Jay Popcorn.

Dr Popcorn made them recline on chairs on either side of him. Poor people are used to having a dentist between them, swivelling from one to the other like a mechanic working on two Vauxhalls at once. Dr Popcorn was a celebrity dentist with curly grey hair, horn-rimmed glasses, and an aquiline nose. Usually he gushed over his patients, though not at the clinic, where they didn't pay. But this was different.

"You have," he told both of them, "magnificent, magnificent teeth. I would have to think that either you're from a mineral-rich-aquifer area like Texas, or you've had monthly dental care all your lives. Are you from Texas?"

"Ahlahbahmah," said Freddy.

"Alabama, Alabama. Hmn. Were your parents dentists?"

"No."

"Neither of your families?"

"No."

"What did they do?" he asked, curious about the background of patients who seemed unlikely for a *pro bono* clinic, and whose traumas were identical.

"My father was in the army, and my mother does a lot of gardening," said Freddy.

"I see, a military brat. And you, Mrs Moffat?"

"My parents are farmers," she said, after hesitating a bit. It was true, in a way.

"And what, may I ask, do you do?" Dr Popcorn asked.

"We're dentists," Fredericka blurted out. After all, that was what it said in the capsules.

Knowing that this could lead to trouble, Freddy clarified Fredericka's answer. "Not for people, though," he said, holding up his right index finger.

"Not for people? For what then?" A long silence followed.

"Crocodiles," Freddy finally said. He seemed to think about it in awe.

"Crocodiles?"

"It's mainly periodontics."

"Is that true?" Dr Popcorn's hands fell to his sides.

"There are tens of thousands of crocodiles in the South, where we come from. They have a lot of problems with their teeth, and they have a lot of teeth—a lot of teeth."

"But there are no crocodiles in America."

"There aren't?" Freddy asked.

"No, just alligators."

"Oh," said Freddy. And then, turning to Fredericka, "You mean all that time, all those years, we've been working on alligators, and we thought they were crocodiles?"

"What's the difference?" Fredericka asked.

"I have no idea," Freddy answered.

"Whatever they are, they make nice belts and bags," Fredericka continued. "Did you know that Bunny, the middle daughter of the Duchess of Trent, has a speedboat with crocodile upholstery? Or alligator, I don't know."

"How do you get them to the point where you can safely work on them?" Dr Popcorn asked. "I can't even do that with a lot of my own patients."

"I guess you shoot them," Freddy said nonchalantly.

"To anaesthetise them."

"To kill them."

"You do periodontics on dead alligators?"

"Alligators or crocodiles, whichever they are."

"What for?"

Freddy was hard-pressed to think of an answer. "We're animal lovers," he said.

"But you shoot them."

"We have to. They're terribly vicious. They can swallow a Corgi in the blink of an eye."

"How do you know?" Fredericka asked.

"I saw it."

"Where?"

"At the Crystal Palace."

"What was an alligator doing at the Crystal Palace?"

"It was there for the handbag show, Fredericka. Will you stop asking questions?"

"*I* was at the handbag show, Freddy. I didn't see any alligators, not live ones."

"This was before it opened. We were on a private tour."

"Why wasn't I invited?"

"Perhaps you were, but no one could find you, because you were having breakfast with Jus d'Orange."

"I hadn't yet been introduced to Jus d'Orange. I wasn't invited, because your mother doesn't like it when the photographers gather around me. And I know your mother was there, because how else would the alligator have swallowed a Corgi?"

"You've jumped to conclusions, as always."

"That may be, but you know as well as I that she can't stand it when the people pay attention to me and not her."

"She has every right."

"I walk behind her, as I'm supposed to. Talk to the photographers."

"Popeel!" said Freddy, angrily.

"Yes, 'Desi'?" Fredericka answered, with acid dripping from both words.

"Shall we?"

"Shall we what?"

"Shall we shut up so we can get on with our dental work? We're not bloody crocodiles. Let this man do his job."

Fredericka thumped the dental chair, crossed her arms petulantly, stared up at the ceiling, and opened her mouth.

THEY WERE USED TO services performed expeditiously and the undivided attention of professionals—from horse trainers to bankers to yoga or sabre masters—devoted solely to them. Where a normal person might wait a week for a procedure or its results, they might not wait at all. So when their teeth were ready early the next day, before they were to start work, they affected no surprise, and did not suspect that the teeth were not bespoke but had instead come off the rack. And that Dr Popcorn installed them in under an hour did not, for the prince and princess, seem remiss.

When he finished, he said, "Well, at least the colours match perfectly."

"Do they?" Freddy asked politely, having failed to appreciate both the slapdash nature of the *pro bono* clinic, where standards were always relaxed, and the fact that, because of the business about crocodiles, Dr Popcorn had come to feel that they did not really respect him.

"Perfectly. Please realise that I have never seen the teeth these have replaced, and, not having anything to go on, I had to make a guess. I think it came out all right." He shook his fist and knitted his brows. "Strong," he said. Freddy and Fredericka both quieted their breathing and followed him with their eyes. "Don't be alarmed. Anything new in the mouth takes some getting used to."

"Do you have a mirror?" Freddy asked.

"We used to," Dr Popcorn replied, "but a patient smashed it."

Freddy and Fredericka rose simultaneously, bibs on, and rushed to their room. Once inside, they leaned against the door as if Satan were in the hall. Freddy threw the deadbolt. Both were pressed against the door, eyes half closed. They had not dared look at one another. "You first," she urged.

"I will, in a minute."

"What are you afraid of?"

"Nothing. Well, perhaps the mirror. If Dr Popcorn has been too enthusiastic, if he has violated the rules of proportion. . . ."

Freddy was interrupted by a scream. He turned to see Fredericka falling onto her bed, left hand against her forehead, palm out, in the nineteenth-century signal of feminine distress. Her right arm, hand and fingers extended, pointed away from her at a forty-degree angle, as if at a sinking lifeboat. She had landed on her back, head on the pillow, perfectly. Freddy ran to her.

His eyes widened. There before him was still one of the world's most beautiful women, but changed. Her new front teeth were perfectly matched in colour to those that existed already, but they were twice the size they had been. They curved like a beaver's teeth, slightly but certainly, and protruded over her lower lip. Freddy was distressed, because though it was endearing, striking, and even sexy, it wasn't quite human. Even Freddy, who could hardly afford to cast stones, had the uncontrollable urge to ask her how many trees she had felled that morning.

As she recovered, he approached the mirror, eyes half closed in a deliberate fog, face all screwed up. Then he opened his eyes wide. "Jesus," he said. He ran his finger over his new teeth in wonderment.

"What are we going to do?" Fredericka asked meekly from the prone position.

"We can never go back to England."

"Why not?" she asked indignantly. "Half the girls in my school had teeth like these. That's why riding clothes are cut the way they are."

"One thing is for sure," he opined. "It will make it either much more difficult to conquer this country, or a lot easier."

"Make up your mind."

"It's impossible to know, but if we fail and cannot return to England we can go to the wilderness of Canada. We own it, you know. Mummy is on the stamps."

"Will you stop that? Everywhere we go, 'We own it. Mummy is on the stamps. Mummy's on the coins.' Really! Who cares? It's such a stupid thing to say, because you don't own it. You don't own Canada, you don't own Jamaica, do you."

"Perhaps not technically."

"Perhaps not at all. God, Freddy, if you become king and I'm queen, all the pictures will have to be retouched."

"Don't be foolish. We'll get new teeth long before then."

"How? We don't have any money."

"We'll go to a public dispensary again."

"They won't give us new teeth just because these are too big. Cosmetic dentistry isn't covered by the National Health."

"Perhaps in Beverly Hills," he speculated.

"By the time we get there, given that we'll have to walk, we won't need new teeth."

"Why not?"

"Because, Freddy, Beverly Hills is three thousand miles from here, and America is full of hunters."

"We're not finished, Fredericka. We'll carry on. Come, if we hurry, we can catch the bus to work. It's our obligation to the Salvation Army. We agreed, and they've been feeding us. I've grown rather fond of corn dogs. Buck up. We're healthy, well fed, suitably attired, and now our teeth are weapons."

"I don't want to work. What if someone photographs me?"

"No one does that any more. We're free."

"No, Freddy. We're beavers."

"And what do beavers like to do?"

"Have sex?"

"No, they like to work." Freddy hesitated. "You knew that, didn't you." She smiled mischievously. "Let's go," she said.

. . .

AFTER A SHORT RIDE in slow traffic, a grey bus discharged its load of street people and royalty at a social services centre where they were to be taught how to work. In a room that was so ugly it crushed the soul, Freddy and Fredericka waited with their fellow trainees for the appearance of what they had been told would be their team leader. This team would win no prizes for alacrity or health. Save the prince and princess, everyone was deeply depressed, half asleep, internally ill, and off on drugs. The air in the room, even with all the windows open and a breeze blowing through, was heavily nicotined just by being drawn weakly into the lungs of these people and feebly expelled. Their blood pressures were so high that sitting next to them was like training with the bomb squad. Even though they were on average a decade younger than Freddy, they seemed on average two decades older. What struck Freddy with nagging force was that so many of them possessed the traces of aristocratic features. Here were once beautiful—beautiful in their bones and in their blood, beautiful as children, beautiful as girls—Appalachian women of almost pure Scottish lines, and men who had undoubtedly descended from the noble Masai. These were the sons of chieftains, clan leaders, and even Pygmy headmen. These were the daughters of the daughters of the daughters of thanes and earls. They were the natural aristocracy of the British Isles and Africa. And yet they were weak and ill before their time, their faces hollow, their eyes laden with the long story of defeat.

Where had they been and what had happened to rob them of the spark of life? Freddy was disquieted by the remnants of their once noble bearing. He felt like a man who, having built a new house, comes upon the smouldering ruins of one that has just burned. Fredericka was deep in the throes of compassion and could not fully contain them. "Freddy, don't you feel compassion for these poor people?" she asked in a whisper.

"No."

"Why on earth not?"

"We've been through this, haven't we? What good does it do these people what you feel? And what good does it do you?"

"It helps them."

"No, it doesn't. Helping them helps them, maybe, if they can be helped, and if they are helped in the right way. Having compassion for them doesn't do a bloody thing except perhaps for you. It's like an orgasm, isn't it. You have it and then you want to go to sleep."

"That's fine," she whispered, "but as they said in Hermione's ashram, if you don't have compassion you won't be compelled to help."

"I don't see why not. I don't have a bit of compassion, not a smidgen, and all I do is patronise hospitals and orphanages."

"You do that because if you didn't they'd take you to the guillotine, that's what."

"What better reason? And that's why I do it so well. Would you prefer that the lower classes had no leverage, and that we cater to them purely out of the goodness of our hearts?"

"Yes, it would be nicer that way."

"Until one of us with perhaps no goodness in his heart at all simply decided to end the game. Don't you know, Fredericka, that being the object of pity ultimately makes one angry?"

This dialogue was interrupted by the appearance of the team leader, who swept in with an entourage and spoke to the limp collection of ne'er-do-wells in the strangest idiom Freddy had ever heard. It was as if a mad doctor had made a creature who was one part hysteric, one part Karl Marx, and one part Mother Goose. He never stopped shouting.

"Use your brains, break your chains! Don't work for another, work for your brother! To hell with money, it ain't honey! Aim high, or you won't fly! To hell with elections, we want protections! Capitalists suck, and to hell with their suction, we want to own the means of production!" he screamed, just for a warm-up. Between the rhymes he blistered the walls with oratory that, though it had a spectacular lilt, a seductive cadence, and tremendous emotional power, made no sense whatsoever.

Freddy raised his hand. "What does all this have to do with getting us on our feet?"

"Be-cause! I have got to moti-*vate* you! *Challenge* you! *Raise* your self-esteem, that has been broken *down*! I want you to *know*, that you can *take*, pow-wah! Pow-wah! Pow-wah!"

"How misleading," said Freddy, addressing his peers. "All you need do is refrain from smoking, drinking, and the use of drugs. Eat only wholesome, low-fat foods, with the emphasis on vegetables, grains, and fish. Seek work. Work hard. Show up on time. Do more than is expected. Think of ways to make the job efficient. Don't complain. Shave, bathe, and wear clean clothes. Be cheerful. Don't gamble. Live within your means. Save. And then, when you have all this in balance, study things of substance. Read to satisfy your curiosity. Don't father children out of wedlock or bear them as a single mother. Exercise. You will find that you will be promoted—perhaps not knighted, but promoted. If that doesn't happen, look quietly for a better position. Find a husband or a wife whom you love and who has the same good habits. Invest. Assume a mortgage if you must. Teach your children the virtues. And then, having become the means of production, you will own your share of the means of production, and if you do these things, all of which are entirely within your power, you will own your lives."

They looked at him as if he were an armadillo that had just spoken to them in Chinese. Not having assimilated a single phrase, they all got up and went out to the bus. "You don't have to be a king to do these things," he told them, despairing at their passivity. "Most people live like that. Most people, every day. It's a matter of will. If you can get up in the morning, if you can put one foot in front of the other, you can do it. And either you will, or you won't."

The bus driver turned on the radio and fiddled with the dial. He wasn't being rude to Freddy, but, for him, Freddy and what he said simply did not exist. Without further ado, Freddy was completely drowned out by someone singing, "Honey pie, sugar pop, you know that I love you so. . . . Can't help myself. . . ."

FREDERICKA WAS AFRAID that she might never see Freddy again and that she would be drawn ever further into the incomprehensible bowels of this odd country, to end her days as an old woman in an almshouse somewhere on the prairie; but she left him nonetheless, and as he travelled on to his own assignment she went into a vast office building to take up hers. How shocked she was to discover that for eight hours that day she would clean toilets. Her heart seemed to shrivel and die, and she contemplated suicide—not fake, attention-getting suicide but the real thing—as she walked down a brilliantly lit hallway, where all was silver and fluorescent and the world only a dream, with her vision blurred by tears.

She was ignored by everyone she passed. Even men went by without a glance, like bats or manta rays, in badly tailored suits that glistened in the light because they were made of petrochemicals that saluted the fluorescence with their own slithery gleam. That these men did not even glance at Fredericka, with her sapphire-blue eyes, buoyant blond tresses, and statuesque body (an immense amount of exquisite leg showed from her flattering olive-coloured shorts), was because she guided a trolley that held buckets, mops, squeeze bottles, and toilet paper stacked as high as the Eiffel Tower. Riding on the side like passengers hanging on to a cable car were two yellow plastic sandwich boards that would announce in English and Spanish for time immemorial (such things are never thrown away, and they do not rot) that the floor was wet.

The prospect of cleaning toilets before ending her days in an American almshouse was not as hurtful as that she had been overlooked. The way people held themselves, walked, and spoke, as in the dances of ants or bees, seemed to Fredericka to have the object not merely of excluding but of killing the people who, like her, were at the bottom. It was the single cruellest thing she had ever experienced, not because it was particularly intense—it wasn't—but because she understood intuitively the untold number of times it had been and would be repeated. Thousands of millions gone and thousands of millions yet to be born had and would suffer through it. She had heard orators in England permanently impassioned by their memory of such a thing, not as it had applied to them but as it had applied to their parents and would to their children. This was the source of unquenchable anger and pity, and she had learnt it in the short time it had taken her to push her cleaning cart down a crowded hall to the first lavatory. When she arrived, for the first time in her life her head was bowed not as an insincere demonstration of humility but from heaviness and something like shame.

She knocked on the lavatory door. It was a men's room, and she had been told to do the men's rooms first. When she had set up her barriers and entered, she waited as the stragglers left. They were completely unembarrassed, for her status had trumped her sex. Then she had the lavatory all to herself. Fourteen urinals, five sinks, seven toilet stalls, several mirrors, and an ocean of white tile faced her, having been neglected for a week. The floor was littered with paper towels and newspapers. Urine and excrement had leapt beyond their confinements and had had days to cure and dry. Cigarette butts, spittle, and hair had mixed with the dirt tracked in and compressed by foot. She had never faced anything like this, she was alone, and she wanted to run away. But she had no place to go, so she looked at the room in cold fluorescent light as if it were an enemy, and her eyes narrowed. She remembered what Freddy had told her about battle. To survive, he had said, find the rhythm of the battle, and never let it go. This she began to do.

With a mop and heavy galvanised bucket, she attacked the first filthy toilet stall. To clean it took a great deal of strength and movement, but as she made headway it was just as Freddy had said. A certain music arose, a beat, a rhythm. She heard it in her breathing and in the blood as it pounded through her, and this she channelled into how she moved. The harder she worked and the more steadily, the more things gleamed. When she would burst from a stall and slam the door, headed for the next, she was like a gladiator coming into the arena. It was actually beautiful, in its way, when the porcelain sparkled and the chrome was a flawless mirror of quicksilver in which she saw her face now rosy red with hard work.

A report like a gunshot signalled that the last stall was done, and then she took up arms against the urinals. Her teeth were clenched and she breathed hard, for it was a struggle to wrest one's dignity from the act of cleaning a urinal, but this is exactly what she did. To her own surprise, she was singing softly to herself a furious song that she had never heard before and that now possessed her. Somehow, though bound and low, she was freer and higher than she had ever been.

A man walked in, having ignored her yellow plastic sandwich boards, the tape stretched between them, and the sign hanging from it. He had ignored how the floors shone and that they were wet. He had ignored her work. And now he ignored her. Perhaps she would have accepted this an hour before, but that hour had passed.

"It's closed," she said quietly. "Didn't you see the sign? I'm working on it."

His answer was to smirk and turn slightly away as he approached the urinal. Then he took his place and began to relieve himself.

This Fredericka found so demeaning, such an attack upon her dignity, her person, and her honour, that something snapped. She cocked the mop behind her right shoulder like a samurai sword and took two swordsman's steps toward her blissfully unaware antagonist. Then she brought the mop-head down like an executioner's axe, separating him from the urinal—in the shock of his life—like a faggot split from a round of oak by a twenty-five-pound maul. The force of the strike threw him against a toilet stall, where he rapidly collapsed. Before he knew it, the sharp end of Fredericka's mop was pressed against his windpipe, and a huge, fit, crazed woman, her magnificent Norse-blond hair shining in the light like metallic fire, her noble nose like the prow of a galley, had been smart enough to choke up on the shaft so that even had he dared he could not have pushed it aside.

And then, as much with her sea-blue eyes as with her savage, growling voice, she ordered him, a mouse-tinted person who did not know how to fight, to leave her lavatory. "Get out," she said, "or I'll presently cleave you from your tiny apparatus." Still holding his apparatus in his hand, he did.

Then she cleaned up the uncleanliness he had left, and fell back into the work by which, as surely as if with sparks flying, she was forging a new self.

AFTER A MEAL of compressed turkey with colloidal gravy, ultra-soft succotash, instant mashed potatoes, weak iced tea, and papaya Jell-O, they took an armful of junk food to a bench overlooking an expressway. It was seven o'clock, the sun was still high, they were freshly showered, and their muscles burned as if after a full day of skiing or fox hunting. They had loved the dinner and taken seconds and thirds, thanking the ancient serving ladies with a sincerity that bespoke their hunger. Now they were exhausted, and looked forward to an hour or so of sun, during which they would watch for license plates. America was a paradise for license-plate hunts, with fifty states, the District of Columbia, the Canadian provinces, Guam, the Virgin Islands, Puerto Rico, Mexico, and various European countries in the running. Freddy knew that with its Congressional staffs, lobbyists, diplomats, and tourists, Washington was the best place in the world for his favourite game after polo, so he had expressed the wish to play it while they could. In North Dakota, the thrill was not the same. He had been there once, to hunt buffalo, and his take had been one buffalo, three Minnesotas, two Manitobas, a Saskatchewan, a Colorado, and a dozen South Dakotas. You could do better, he said, in Nigeria. But in Washington, Fredericka wrote down the plates that she saw or Freddy called out, and within ten minutes they had Alaska, Wyoming, Prince Edward Island, and Curaçao, not to mention so many multiples of so many other states and countries that Freddy was almost in tears. "Did you have a good day?" he asked. "North Carolina, California, Maine."

"Yes. I almost castrated a middle manager. Maryland, Arizona, Peru."

"Peru! Why did you do that?" Freddy asked, exultant over Peru.

"I was cleaning lavatories—Massachusetts—and he came in when he shouldn't have. Iowa, Ontario."

"Isn't that—Montana—a rather Draconian punishment? I don't mean
to take his side against yours, but if I were castrated every time I went into
the wrong room or parked where I shouldn't have, you would long ago
have divorced me even had I been a kind of centipede. You haven't let
American feminists brainwash you, have you?"

"You don't understand. Texas, Oregon, New Hampshire."

"Ahlahbahmah. That's where we're from. Jolly good."

"He just came in, as if I didn't exist. I asked him to leave. I asked him
nicely. And then he smiled and began to relieve himself. You should have
seen his expression. What would you have done in my place?"

Freddy took his eyes from the road and looked with interest and respect
at his wife. "Sometimes," he said, "it is right only to be unreasonable."

She felt wonderful. Marriage is, among other things, having someone
deeply and unreasonably on your side, and Freddy had often been infuriat-
ingly impartial. They ignored the traffic, and stared at one another.

"You cleaned toilets?"

"I don't mind. It's my job. I've never seen lavatories cleaner than the
ones I cleaned. It made me happier than water-skiing off Skiros or being
on the cover of *She*. They wanted to hire me full time, with medical,
401(k)—isn't that a vitamin?—and two weeks' vacation per annum. I told
them I couldn't, but that I was honoured. They begged me to think it over,
and said that you could work there, too. They like hard-working immi-
grant couples better than anyone else."

"I'm fond of my job loading trucks," Freddy told her. "The other
workers, however, are not fond of me. They say I work too fast and too
hard, like someone who's going on to something else. Indeed, I loaded a
lorry with five hundred Die Hard automobile batteries. That was ten tonnes,
or twice as much as my nearest competitor. The temperature in the trailer
was one hundred and forty degrees Fahrenheit. Work like that makes me
feel worthy of my ancient forbears who were not kings, and for some reason it is they whom I wish always to impress in my imagination. It is they
who I pray are watching as I cross the heath, cut wood, or fish for trout on
the gravel bar of a deafening stream. Why do you suppose that is?"

"I don't know."

"Perhaps it's because, in being separate from and above everyone, my
family have fallen. We live the dream of the common man, but haven't the
courage to tell him that what he has is far better than what he wants. It is
his imagination that is faulty, not our execution of our role."

"Freddy, how much money do you have?"

"Thousands of millions, if you count land, paintings, real estate. . . ."

"In your pocket."

"Forty dollars. My wage was six dollars fifty, but after taxes and deductions I've come out with considerably less than what I earned. What do you have?"

"The same."

"If we clear eighty dollars a day between us, that's four hundred a week. Let's say we paid a hundred and fifty a week for a room, and a hundred and fifty for food. That would leave a hundred per week for supplementary medical care, insurance, clothing, travel, furniture and decoration, entertainment, books, utilities, subscriptions, and savings."

"Freddy, how can two people live for a week for the price of an entrée at Citron, Foie, et Feu?"

"Citron, Foie, et Feu is an expensive restaurant."

"How much did it cost to have the window fixed on the Rolls?"

"The one that caught my head?"

"Yes. That was the grey one, wasn't it?"

"It also happened in the green one. Both times it was two hundred and seventy-five quid, which is more than the two of us earn in a week. What of it?"

"It's not fair."

"But, Fredericka, poor people never have to fix the windows of Rolls-Royces: they don't have them. Things are not symmetrical, and never have been. That doesn't render them unfair. As long as the competition is free and open. . . . What is the name of that fellow who makes all those arrogant and pretentious computer programmes that are physically ugly, offer only a Hobson's choice, and are so riddled with frivolous junk that they break down all the time?"

"Oh yes," she said. "I know. The one who looks like he works in a butcher's shop. He seems very nice, actually. What's his name? He lives in a town on the West Coast—Sea Eel? Sea View? Tree Eel?"

"Whatever his name is, he's now the richest man in the world, richer than we are, and he was born in his parents' garage."

"Why would he be born there?" Fredericka asked. "Why wouldn't they at least have had him in the bedroom?"

"I don't know," said Freddy, "but, think of it, a baby born in a garage became the richest man in the world—practically before it grew up. That's

America. The rich can become poor and the poor can become rich. Now and then they trade places, and anyone can go anywhere."

"Isn't that Socialism?"

"No, it's Capitalism, and it's why we, having dropped from the sky with nothing, have a chance of acquiring anything. There is no limit. We might even bring in Mexico as well. Why not? We already have Canada."

"Who cares?"

"I do."

"But why?"

"It's my job, and I want to do my job as well as I possibly can. You see, it's like cleaning toilets."

"Ah," she said. "I understand."

BECAUSE THEY WERE such good workers that each had earned promotion and a higher wage, and because they had told the Salvation Army that they would leave Washington at the end of July, they were allowed to stay for longer than usual. Every evening they wolfed down the cafeteria dinner and went out to the bench near the expressway, junk food in hand. After a while, they had five Guams, a hundred Idahos, two Perus, two Czechoslovakias, a Yemen, and thousands and thousands of Marylands, Virginias, and Districts of Columbia. In fact, they stopped counting Districts of Columbia after ten thousand.

On weekends they would go on daylong rambles through Washington, happily and easily covering twenty or thirty miles, taking in the sights anonymously. This was one of the greatest pleasures of their lives, especially after Dr Popcorn had agreed to grind down their teeth for only $200 and they found themselves casually but elegantly clothed, in magnificent physical shape, smiles debeavered, well rested, and finally comfortable. After the rambles they would read in the Library of Congress or go to the National Gallery to refresh their souls with the most open, beautiful, and promising scenes man had ever witnessed or imagined. All through the capital they found fountains; shaded grottoes in which to sit; cool marble halls where, with educated commoners, they took refuge from the heat; and river prospects along which they walked relaxedly.

On a trip to the periodicals room at the Library of Congress, they discovered that the world thought they were still in their ordinary habitat. "Look," Freddy said, leafing through the glossies. "Here we are in the

Aegean, and here we are at Balmoral. With old photographs you can lull the world. We could be dead and no one would know—like an American politician or Mao Tse-tung. I wonder whose idea it could have been to grant us a year of press holiday in exchange for regular pictures and stories?"

"I haven't been on the cover of *She* for three months," Fredericka said not even wistfully. "It's hard to believe."

"But you're inside, and half-naked, too."

"I am?"

"Look."

"Oh, that was last summer. Don't you remember? There you are, on the terrace at Sorrento, reading that book about Leonard O."

"Who?"

"Leonard O. The Italian."

"Oh yes, him."

"I was trying to tan absolutely all over. You didn't even notice."

"Yes I did, and so did the photographers. How long were you able to stay upside down?"

"Only a minute or so each time. The blood ran to my head."

It was strange that the public thought they were carrying on normally, because, finally, they were. They ate ice cream once a week, and had their hair cut. Freddy asked his barber to cut his hair like the Prince of Wales', and the barber told him that he couldn't, because "Your hair isn't like that. It doesn't go that way. And what do you want to look like him for? He's an asshole." Fredericka was told, on the other hand, that she did bear a passing resemblance to the Princess of Wales, but, rather than imitate, she should go her own way, as she was much prettier.

"Am I?" she asked.

"Oh yes. Fredericka's horsey, and has a huge nose. They hide it in pictures. You're beautiful, and although you have a strong nose, it's not even half the size of hers."

So Fredericka got a new hairstyle, a French braid that nonetheless made her look very Scandinavian, very young, and very gorgeous. This delighted Freddy, who was pleased not only with her appearance but with her. Now she had far less appetite for nonsensical and petty things. At one point, it had seemed as if, while sitting on a bench in the trees near a fountain, she was thinking. But he had no proof.

He, too, had changed. For the first time in his life he thought a great deal about money. They had paid the Salvation Army for room and board, and after the outflow to Dr Popcorn, fifteen dollars for each of their week-end excursions, and minor purchases of toiletries, sunglasses, a folding knife, and a water bottle, they were left with $1,600, which seemed to them like a fortune. They had no intention of spending it unless they had to, and resolved that wherever they might land they would work to support themselves, drawing from savings only during travel.

Freddy was vexed by how much it cost to go anywhere. Flying was out of the question unless they were to proceed directly to the West Coast, but what then? The train was out of the question as well, and the bus cheap but punishing, and, in a sense, too fast. They needed to see the country, and, for the country to open to them, they needed friction.

When they decided not to pay for transport, the prospect of working at each extended stop left them with what suddenly seemed like superfluous wealth. Freddy thought Fredericka would want to buy clothes or go to an expensive restaurant. He himself wanted to buy books, and they both had a yearning for staple foods—smoked Scottish salmon, caviar, huge prawns, seared quail, truffles, dry Champagne. But a change from the simplicity of their routines would only have bankrupted them and broken their lovely, trance-like equilibrium. Now they were incognito in letter and spirit, and dared not jeopardise it. Perhaps the best thing would be simply to save. This appealed to Freddy and, eventually, to Fredericka as well, who had never saved money or known anyone who had to, and had thought it a religious practice.

"Are we Buddhists now?" she asked.

TRAMPS

FREDDY HAD SEEN goods trains rumbling across bridges over the Potomac. "Americans leap upon them and travel west," he told Fredericka. "What's his name, the comedian who married his mother, or his daughter—or was it his sister?—Woody something, sings songs about it. They have so many goods trains because they have so many goods."

His heart had fastened upon the idea of leaping onto a train to ride into the mountains. It was as if he knew already the nature and character of the railway sidings, the colour of the walnut trees, and the feel of heat from the rock that covered the stony ridges over tunnels that pierced the hills, that then spread out to the open plains. And it was as if he knew what he was going to encounter there, and that it was good—or at least Hemingwayesque.

They went to a train yard, where Freddy taught Fredericka to vault into a goods wagon, to climb the ladder at the corner, and to run along the catwalks, leaping over gaps and couplings. Fredericka was unaccustomed to this, but as the athletic descendant of fifty generations of stag hunters, she learned quickly. So trained, they retrieved their packs from the Salvation Army and went to lunch at a restaurant on Capitol Hill. They ate unsparingly, convinced that they would have to rely for a long time on the stores they carried, from which they assumed they would have to draw lightly. The restaurant was expensive, but they had earned this money and were confident that they could earn more.

After brushing their teeth in the fountain grotto near the Capitol, they made their way to a sunken rail siding near the Potomac. A train came through at about three. The light above the engine was yellow like the sun, and formations of wavy air rose behind it like a waterfall recoiling backward. The thundering goods wagons, which Freddy had learned at his job to call freight cars, or boxcars, were almost all empty, each an essay in colours—pumpkin-orange, green, yellow on black, maroon, teal, and blue—and in names of far places like Santa Fe and the Pacific, and of some that were close, such as Norfolk, Richmond, and the Chesapeake.

Four engines and fifty cars had passed, and the train was still coming without an end in sight when Freddy asked, like a coxswain on the Isis, "Are you ready?" He knew Fredericka appreciated the query, as she had rowed, and he frequently said it to her. She had a knot in her stomach, never having jumped onto a moving freight train—which is as much like one that is still as a picture of a lightning bolt is like the lightning bolt itself—but she lowered her head and concentrated upon the thing to be conquered, in a demure but absolutely determined way that caused Freddy to delay their spring, because he couldn't take his eyes off her. She seemed so vulnerable and yet so strong and admirable. He felt something deep within him at the sight of her and her expression at this moment, although he did not know what it was.

"Now," Freddy commanded. They ran for an open door in a clean steel-red car that said *Union Pacific*. Freddy placed his palms on the wooden floor and pushed himself up so vigorously that he almost rolled out the opening on the other side. Fredericka was still running. She hadn't the arm strength to vault in as Freddy had, so he held the doorpost with his right hand and reached toward her with his left.

"Wrist to wrist," he ordered. Even as she ran along the stones, she smoothly extended her left arm toward his. He grasped her wrist in his hand, closing about it completely. She grasped his, getting a grip, though not circling it. And then, in synchrony with the rhythm of her steps and her breathing, Freddy bent down, she leapt, and he stood and stepped back, pulling her in.

"That was wonderful," she said.

Leaning against their packs, they sat on the clean oak floor of the goods wagon, the blood rushing through them after their sprints and vaults, and they were taken up in the booming of steel on steel as the bridge that spanned the Potomac rumbled below them. The water was a colour somewhere between saddle-brown, café au lait, and gunmetal blue. The sky was what Royal Delft was made of, and all the monuments that they were leaving were as white as the whitest ruins of antiquity.

· · · ·

THEY ROLLED PAST the Pentagon and clusters of cheaply built little sky-scrapers until, soon after they had recovered their pulse, they began to see forest and field dovetailing with airports and shopping malls. And then even the rapidly balding outskirts were left behind as the train wound through real woods, over fields blond with sun-bleached grass, and past springs, cabins, and hills. The sound of the train moving through the Virginia countryside was like a song.

"Keep an eye out for the live ash circle," Freddy told Fredericka.

"You look on that side, and I'll look on this one," she said. "What is it?"

"I don't know, but it must be a circle, it must either be made of ash or be ashen in colour, and perhaps it moves or undulates in some way, as if it were alive."

Fredericka looked intently for five minutes, with the expression of someone in the Underground waiting for a train to take her to an appointment for which she was already late. "Why didn't Mr Neil tell us what it was?"

"Because he's a lunatic, and when a lunatic sends you out to look for something, he doesn't always tell you what it is."

At four o'clock, with the sun still hot and high, the train swung left to the south-west and picked up speed. Now they were rushing through glades of rhododendron and forsythia, then forests of pine, and half the time they broke out onto fields the size of prairies that nonetheless were fenced for horses or cows or farmed for hay and grain. Rivers ran between the green foothills, and to the west the Blue Ridge rose abruptly in a very long line that never faltered no matter how many hours passed, its pale blue like that of the mist on the Thames on a clear morning in June.

The land was beautiful, and other than when the smell of diesel smoke came in through the open doors, one could not escape the fragrant air of newly mown hay and of flowers growing in the shade of the woods. Now completely disconnected from their former life and alone in a broad and colourful landscape, Freddy and Fredericka sat together shoulder to shoulder. To his surprise, he embraced her. It was not merely that her statuesque form, which he held close, was speaking to him sexually, as almost always it did, but that he thought she was beautiful, though not because she was but rather because of something else. Despite his many doubts about her, and the way she irritated him so often and sometimes drove him mad, despite their troubles and their history, to be with her now, on a freight train, riding free *en plein air,* was just what he wanted, and he wanted nothing more. She looked up at him, doubting herself, doubting him, having always been rejected, and then she looked down sadly. Her expression was as hopeless as that of a prisoner, a refugee, or a child in a cruel orphanage.

This moved him deeply. "Fredericka," he said. And then he touched her face, and kissed her.

THEY WERE AWAKENED by silence. Outside, a congress of gnats was riding on the remnants of the afternoon's heated air. The train had been stopped at a siding for an hour or two. They heard birds, and an unfamiliar, whirring noise. To the right was a white wall that completely filled the door of the goods wagon. They looked out and saw that across a ditch and a fence was an enormous building a hundred feet high and perhaps a quarter of a mile long on the side they could see. Written on the wall that faced them, in immense blue letters, was *Gemeischen Pipsfindert Haubrecht Gesellschaft Virginia Abflangen Ochsteif.*

"I thought we won the war," Fredericka said.

"We did. Just because there's a big building in front of us on which is written *Gemeischen Pipsfindert Haubrecht Gesellschaft Virginia Abflangen Ochsteif* doesn't mean we didn't win the war. After we finished with it, there was nothing left of Berlin."

"There is now."

Freddy leaned slightly outward and looked up the track. Twenty or thirty wagons away, a uniformed guard was being pulled toward them by a dog on a lead. "Let's get to the factory side," Freddy said. With packs in hand they jumped from the train. On the other side, the guard dog began to bark. Leaping the ditch and pushing through honeysuckle and brambles, they found themselves up against a waist-high wire fence. Fredericka asked if they had to go over it. "No," the more experienced Freddy answered. "It's held up by these splintered posts. That means that the wood in contact with the ground has been there long enough to rot. A fence like this is like our last government: it stands merely out of habit. Look." He walked to a post, grasped the top in both hands, and put his weight forward. It broke at the ground and the fence leaned over, compressing the brambles on its other side, which they then crossed with ease.

Now they were on the grounds of the factory, where people were coming out and getting into their cars. A little traffic jam formed as these people headed home for dinner. "What shall we do?" Fredericka asked.

Freddy led her to the main entrance, where a line of people was waiting to enter. There they stood as if they knew why. A woman who had come up behind them asked, "Y'all here for a job?" and then they did know why.

"Indeed," Freddy told her. "We always wanted to work at *Gemeischen Pipsfindert Haubrecht Gesellschaft Virginia Abflangen Ochsteif.*"

"You'll probably get the job," she said, "if you can say that. No one else can."

"Freddy," Fredericka whispered, "we don't want to work here, do we? We've just started out, and it was so lovely a train."

"I want to see what's inside."

The lobby was ultra-modern and full of potted trees. The royals looked impressive and self-possessed, and the instant the interviewer stepped into the cubicle in which they had been seated he wanted to hire them, but he had to follow procedure. A friendly man with a hippotine face, he shook hands with them, bade them sit down, and said, "I'll get to your applications in a moment, but first tell me why you want to work at *Gemeischen Pipsfindert Haubrecht Gesellschaft Virginia Abflangen Ochsteif,* or, as we say, GPHGVAO," which he pronounced *Gippy Hog Vow.*

"As you will see on my application," Freddy said gravely, not having even seen an application, "I'm an electrical engineer. My wife, too, is an electrical engineer."

"I thought we were dentists," Fredericka protested.

"No, Popeel, we're electrical engineers."

"Oh," she said, as if she didn't really know what an electrical engineer was, which she didn't.

"If your wife is an electrical engineer," the interviewer asked, "why did she think she was a dentist? And why did she think you were a dentist?"

"We used to be dentists," Fredericka said.

"The positions we advertised have nothing to do with either dentistry or electrical engineering."

"We'll change professions," said Fredericka. "We've done it before. We're very flexible."

Freddy took up the challenge as well. "We're extremely interested in what you do here—in boosting productivity, rationalising systems and sub-systems, strengthening morale, and increasing the synergistic networking potentiality of employee clusters and nodes of action. It's an exciting time."

"It is, but these are entry-level jobs for which you seem vastly over-qualified."

"Ah," said Freddy, like his father about to throw a logical dart at something Freddy had said without thinking. "That's just the point. Love of an operation starts at the bottom, with the fundamentals. You know, face in the dirt, eating stones, chewing rocks. We need a comprehensive view. What about a summary tour?"

"I suppose if you've got half an hour I can give you a tour. I don't know if I can hire you, though."

"We're very grateful," Freddy said.

"There is electrical equipment that you'll find fascinating, and if the second shift is in, perhaps you can glance at their teeth."

"Good idea," Freddy told him, "although, without bite-wings, I can't speak with authority. No one can."

"What makes you so interested in fulfilment?" the interviewer asked as they walked down a corridor.

"The very name," Freddy answered, "is perfectly expressive. Every man, *and every woman,* wants fulfilment. Don't you, Popeel?"

Fredericka blushed, and said, "Oh, Freddy."

"Oh, who?"

"I mean, 'Oh, Moofoomooach.' No, I mean, 'Oh, Desi.'"

"What are your names?" the executive asked, having stopped before a huge set of double doors.

"Popeel and Desi Moofoomooach," Fredericka said, holding out her hand to be kissed.

"Popeel and Desi *Moffat,*" Freddy corrected.

"That's right," said Fredericka.

"Which is it, Moffat or Moofoomooach?"

"Moffat is the short form of Moofoomooach," Freddy offered.

"And what kind of name is Moofoomooach?"

"I don't know," said Freddy, "but there are lots of Moofoomooachs where I come from. The telephone registers are stuffed with them. I went to university with a bunch of Moofoomooachs, didn't you?"

"Yes," he said. "Come to think of it, they were a bunch of Moofoomooachs."

When the doors opened, Freddy and Fredericka found themselves looking down a corridor a quarter of a mile in extent and a hundred feet high beneath a ceiling covered in dim golden lights. The place was almost dark, but saved by golden lamps as if on some malicious winter afternoon the dying sun had peeked beneath a lid of black cloud and briefly gilded the world.

Now and then a little cart with a flashing light upon its roof would appear, darting into the corridor from one of the many aisles that branched out from it, and then darting away into one of the others, like a fish penetrating the refuges and crevices of a reef. In each row, platforms that moved on tracks could swiftly take an operator a hundred feet up and five hundred feet along the line, or in any combination on the fifty-thousand-square-foot grid. Each platform had a fork-lift system that could reach into the many levels of shelves and retrieve pallets or cartons.

"What's in the boxes?" Freddy asked.

"Books, of course. We have fifty million books in this building, and it's possible to get a box of ten or twenty of any one of them in less than twenty seconds."

Freddy was sceptical. That was a great many more books than were in the British Museum. How could so many be in this building in the middle of the Virginia countryside, surrounded by horse and cattle farms, rotting fences, red earth, and honeysuckle?

"In this one building, Mr Moofoomooach, there are five times as many books as in the Library of Congress, but we have only sixty thousand titles. In some sections, we have more than a million copies of a single title."

"The Bible," Freddy said. "The Oxford Shakespeare."

"No. We don't have that many of those, but we do have a million two hundred thousand copies of Melinda Harridan's *Makeup and Self-Esteem*."

"I read that!" Fredericka said, her enthusiastic declaration rising in the vastness like a tiny spacecraft shot beyond the solar system. "It was wonderful."

"We're drawn down now, but recently we had eight million copies of Wesley Joshua's *Nantucket Orgasm*. The next one should be coming soon—he does about three a year; books, that is—and the trucks will be pulling in night and day. Then we've got the first lady's book about the president's pet snail."

"I remember him," Freddy said. "But I don't remember his name."

"Sidney. He passed away quietly."

"No he didn't," Freddy said. "I was there. I met him. That was no accident. Dixie Self, the president's daughter, wanted to take him on a campaign trip, but Evita would hear of no such thing so she flushed him down the loo. It was murder."

The *Gippy Hog Vow* executive continued, not sure of what Freddy had meant. "The other part of the facility is for grouping returns. There we keep books on shelves individually. As they come in we pack them in cartons of ten, but sometimes we have to wait for the right number. So, if we cover a hundred and twenty thousand titles for what we are currently shipping and what we shipped within the return limit period, we might have, in theory, up to a million and eighty thousand individual copies waiting to be boxed. But the actuaries looked at our records and told us we need never have more than the space required to shelve a few hundred thousand individual volumes. That's not exclusively because of probability, but because of the groupings. If you get a hundred thousand returns of one book, the maximum number of loose copies is nine, but the average number will be five. You see?"

"Yes," said Freddy. "Take me to the Melinda Harridan section, if you will, and then to the Shakespeare section."

"This way."

As they walked they looked up at the many rows of shelves disappearing toward the golden ceiling. Each little box of ten books had the author's name stenciled upon it. It was like being in an Italian cemetery, in the narrow marble alleys with the little garage doors behind which bones were stacked, like books, in hope of eternity.

"Here's the Harridan aisle." A hundred thousand brown boxes with *Harridan* stenciled on them were stacked to the ceiling. They stretched to the ends of the aisle in both directions, their mass overwhelming. "That's thirty million dollars, retail," the executive said, "for a penny's worth of bad advice. A lot of money. You'd think that with between a hundred and fifty and two hundred fifty million dollars' worth of inventory in this building at any one time we'd have remarkable security. We don't. We have a ten-redundancy fire system and a watchman. Masses of books are very hard to steal. By the time anyone broke in and started to move even a few hundred dollars' worth, the entire Virginia State Police would be here."

"That's right," Freddy said. "Nobody steals books except kleptomaniacs and university students. In most places you can leave a book on the street and come back for it the next day."

"I've found exactly that," the executive said, warming to Freddy and his beautiful wife. "I'm somewhat embarrassed to say that I'll have to look up the Shakespeare section." He consulted a computer terminal at the junction of the Harridan aisle and the *grande allée,* and led them on a march that lasted five minutes. At the end of one of the last rows, almost in a corner, was the Shakespeare. Not a single carton was stacked any higher than Freddy could reach. It extended fifty feet or so, and the rest was silence.

THEY ALMOST KILLED THEMSELVES getting back on the train, which when they left the *Gippy Hog Vow* was moving down the track in a slow acceleration that would begin an ocean-craft-like run across the continent. As it picked up speed headed for the mountains in the blue of evening, they breathed hard and their faces were flushed. Their legs were covered with stinging scratches and clean crimson lines, but the pain was as pleasant as a mild sunburn. Fredericka had never seen Freddy's face look as it did when he stood in the door of the boxcar watching the countryside flow past the train, and the mountains loom ever more excitingly larger. "What's happened?" she asked.

Freddy's eyes moved in answer to her question, but it was only a partial answer. Then he filled it out. "For a thousand years," he said, "the history of my family has had a single keel. It has been a single work, with a constant aim. For a thousand years, we have lived within a context of expectations that, though often broken, has just as often been restored. And do you know what?"

The train shuddered darkly underneath them. "What?" she asked.

"It's over. It's shattered. Let's say it was a river. Now we have come to the falls."

"Is that good?"

"No."

"Is it bad?"

"No."

"Then what is it?"

"It's only what it is. It means that even if we find whatever we're supposed to find, and go back, and I become king and you queen, this is where our story will be, this the place by which we will be remembered. And this is not home. Take it in. You'll see many beautiful things and many things that are great, but they will leave but a short trace, like the evanescent lines of momentary particles about which physicists talk incomprehensibly, like life itself. Nothing concerning us will any more be properly memorialised except in the eyes of God, which is the way it is and has always been for most people. What you see is what you will get, and then it will be gone, like music that you cannot perfectly remember—which is why you must take it in your heart in full."

"But I do, Freddy. I always have. It's all I can do." She smiled in what appeared to him, to his shock, to be wisdom greater than his own. And then they were taken up by a number of things that filled the world of a summer evening—the sun lacing the tops of the Blue Ridge with a piping of molten gold, rhododendron blooming deep in the woods, the perfume of night air streaming from copses already sheltered in complete darkness, the beautiful rhythm of the rails, and the feeling that in the endless country ahead were things that in their great and lively action could redeem them.

Sleeping in a moving freight car was hardly as pleasurable as riding in it during the day. The floor vibrated like a gravel sorter and the rumbling that otherwise was exciting became a torture. Once they were asleep, however, to stay asleep they had to sleep deeply, and thus when they awakened they were well rested. They awoke after first light, when the land had already begun to warm, in the dryer, less insistent heat of altitude. All around for as far as they could see was a mountainous wilderness. They didn't know the distance they had covered or in which direction the train had run during the night, but neither did they care, for they looked at things as a bird might, wanting to go this way or that because of a clear alley in the clouds, or because the glint of rock on a distant peak made a bull's-eye in the light of day, or because the wind turned a meadow on a hillside into an alluring sea of waving grass.

They had a large amount of food left but had used up most of their water, and they wanted to bathe. This made them partial to finding a lake or river, which, in turn, decided their course. Not a single work of man was visible other than what belonged to the railroad. The rest was an endless view of rock, sky, and trees that made a continuous conquest of mountains that ran in corrugated rows, with clearings on the highest slopes and in the widest valleys. Because the train was headed south-southwest, they were able to see in the flawless morning light every leaf to the west and north.

Now and then they would go into tunnels. And because they were high on a ridge, and going down, the train moved slowly. "I don't want to go south," said Freddy. "I feel that we should go west. Look there, in the distance," he said. "You see that line that looks like a thread? It's probably a rail line, or at least a road, and it points in the right direction."

"Which direction?"

"North-west, which would take us to the Great Lakes. Their waters are cool and fresh. Have you ever seen them?"

"I've flown over them, I think."

"Right in the middle of the continent there's an open horizon on a sea of sweet water."

"That's where we should go," Fredericka said. "I'd love to take a long swim in a freshwater ocean. Can you drink it?"

"In the northlands, where the water is pure, I believe so, but it's too cold there to swim."

As they were absolutely free to go anywhere they pleased, they determined upon the Great Lakes, and as their timing was all their own they simply jumped off the train at the first grassy bank they saw. It was steep, and they rolled. Had a rock been hidden in the meadow they could have been killed, but though gravity took them and bounced them bruisingly down the hill, knocking the wind out of their lungs, they felt well guided and safe. And when finally they came to a stop, they laughed in relief. The train progressing into the distance made a sound like the ocean, and they lay where they were.

Fredericka rested in the meadow, her arms outstretched, her hair somewhat dishevelled, and Freddy saw her as if for the first time. Overcome by the fall of her braid, the curl of her fingers, the depth of her eyes, the sweetness and beauty of her face, he took her in his arms, lifted her toward him, and gently cradled her head in his left hand. Now she nearly floated up to him, because for the first time she was getting what she deserved, and for the first time he was looking at her with love for all she was, even her imperfections, which no longer put him off but drew him in. As the thunder of the freight train echoed in the valleys, softened, and finally disappeared, they were left with the sound of the wind moving through the pines like water cascading through the teeth of a weir, as if the tops of the trees were willow branches dangling in a stream, and the sky were water trailing through them.

THEY DID NOT REACH the base of the mountain until midday, which was surprising to Fredericka, who asked how long it would take to get to the other railway. Freddy replied that this was, by line of sight, about thirty miles distant. Taking into account rest and obstructions, they could travel at about two miles per hour, but these were mountains of insistent corrugation, and therefore the distance would be double that of flat land. "Thirty or forty hours," he said. "But allowing for sleep, darkness, and troubles, it might take two or three days. In war it could be done in a day."

"How long would it take in a car?"

"At seventy miles per hour, with Swiss bridges and viaducts, about half an hour."

"Is this what you do," Fredericka asked, "when you go off into Scotland, or when you walked from Innsbruck to Venice?"

"To Trento. Yes."

"Why?"

"I enjoy it," he said, as they pushed toward the sound of a river, moving through evergreen branches that brushed them like ostrich plumes.

"What's that?" Fredericka asked.

"From the cry, I believe it's a red-tailed hawk, although it's hard to be sure."

As they moved through the fragrant evergreens, Fredericka said, "Freddy, this is so lovely; it really is like Eden."

"You know," Freddy stated academically, "although he was unaware, Adam loved Eve. He came to know it only after they were thrown out and they had wandered."

"Oh," she said.

Then they came to the river.

IT WAS WIDE for a river that ran so high in the mountains, and it ran fast for so late in summer. Fresh water that is channelled between walls of rock and pine runs with a certain rhythm even when it is not rushing, but when the flow is rapid, mists are released in arcs of counterpoint, the surface oscillates in a steady beat, and the water breaking against rocks and leaping over them is the melody. A good river is nature's life work in song. It winds and cuts through the land, connecting the high places with the low, mountaintops with estuaries, light blue sky with deep blue sea. And always above it is the action of water purifying air, of air giving life to water, and of light lost in rainbows that float above the fast dip of the stream.

They looked at this stream, breathed-in the air above it, and let its sound command their senses. Never had they seen a more beautiful or perfect thing. They leant down on a flat rock and put their faces in, drinking from the heaving flow.

"Now we have to cross the river," Freddy said. "It's waist-deep, a hundred yards wide, and running fast. You won't be swept off the ends of the earth if you're knocked over, you'll only be carried downstream. When that happens, avoid the rocks. Keep watch for them, and hit them with both feet if hit them you must. As you flow downstream, continue to work your way straight across. The mistake people make is to swim either upstream or down at angles other than the perpendicular. You must cross as if you're in perfectly still water. That way you can confound even a great river simply by following your aim. It's vector analysis. I'll go first with my pack, make my way back along the bank twice the distance the current will have swept me downriver, and recross to join you, landing probably right here. Then I'll take your pack, and help you cross."

"That sounds reasonable."

"Each time you go in a river like this," he said, "you're supposed to shed your sins and be forgiven your trespasses."

"What trespasses?" she asked.

"For me, more than I can enumerate. As you get older, they accumulate and you acquire the ability to recognise them."

"Freddy, someday you'll be the head of the Church of England. You will appoint bishops and archbishops, you'll take vows. . . . I always thought it would be just a formality, that you didn't like what they do in the Church."

"I don't any more. It's too goddamned smarmy."

"But you do believe in God," she said.

"I do, and so will the bishops I appoint."

"You do, even in these modern times?"

"Look about," he told her. She swept her eyes from the river to the sky, and looked up and down the river course and at the curve of the pines that lined its banks like a great wreath.

"The evidence is here," she said, having understood. "In this river. In this forest. In these trees."

"Toute la nature crie qu'il existe," Freddy said, and Fredericka, having been finished in finishing school, understood exactly the meaning of the words, even if she did not know who had said them first. "All nature cries out that He exists."

FREDDY THREW HIMSELF in without hesitation. He had crossed many a river in Scotland, the Alps, and elsewhere, and knew that when water ran full you had to give it full attention. Once in, there was indeed nothing else but the crest of the waves and the onrush of looming rocks. Sometimes he swam furiously, and sometimes he let himself go, turning to kick off a boulder against which he was thrown, pivoting about after contact, holding still for a moment, and then resuming the downstream slide. Until the next hazard, he would move straight across. In this kind of procession, punctuated by danger and its relief, he made his way to the other side, where he came to rest in a sunny pool that rocked violently at its outer edge and then was made still by walls of granite at the bank. He pulled himself up, shedding water, and placed the waterlogged pack on a dry ledge. Then, he climbed the wall until he was in the forest. He ran the half mile or so back to where he had started, waved to Fredericka, and continued upstream for another half mile. In the water once again and now accustomed to it, he moved with greater assurance. His emergence from the river at the place where he started struck Fredericka as superb.

Without comment, because he saw that she was apprehensive, he shouldered Fredericka's pack and said, "Into the river." Once she was in, she would have neither time nor space for fear. The water seized them in its delphinine curves and silver flow, and for five minutes they used every sinew and every nerve to keep alive. Freddy lent her his strength and experience, shouting now and then what to do, which she accomplished well. In the peculiar moment when the current twirled them around after they hit their first boulder feetfirst and were accelerated once again into the stream, they were united in fear. It all went so quickly that before they knew it they were in the slowly rotating pool.

Twirling in the sunlit caldera, they held together and could not take their eyes from one another. With the water-darkened pack straps pressing against his muscular shoulders, Freddy no longer had the face of a ridiculous man. Sunburnt and unshaven, his eyes clear alight, he had the nobility he had longed for and that his grandfather had had in that great moment in the desert when the troops had come up from the beach and sung "God Save the King" entirely unbidden. All the foolishness that had been impressed upon him by the conscious and unconscious wishes of scores of millions, and the distorting burden of being so close to and put upon by a role in history, were gone. He was just a man, and she loved him.

He held her, she held him, and they floated. Who was this now so close to him, with her broad back, her nose that jutted out and was too big but ravishingly beautiful nonetheless? In her expression and in her eyes he saw a woman he had never known. He didn't understand why he was shaking but he knew he wasn't cold. Her hair was wet, and in the French braid it looked as if it had been made to drip with the water of rapids. Perhaps he had slighted her. Perhaps he had underestimated her. Perhaps he had not been patient enough in seeing her come along. But now she had come along, and in pure water and bright sun, with speech made impossible by the thundering of the river, they embraced and rocked slowly back and forth not like the Prince and Princess of Wales, but like an anonymous couple locked in embrace on a dance floor long after the music has stopped. And, like that couple, had their lives ended there, their lives would have ended in perfection.

III.

MANIFEST
DESTINY

Anglo-Saxon Times
in Chicago

THE MAN WHO LIVED on the floor above—which is to say the ground floor, because they lived in the basement—had a scratchy voice that went well with the four hundred and fifty pounds that were the rest of him. Throughout the winter, even when the temperature fell to fifteen below, he wore a Hawaiian shirt. His most prepossessing trait, however, was not the way he dressed but the way he sang, and he never was without song except when he slept, except that he sometimes sang in his sleep. And why not? He sang when he ate. He sang, *bien entendu,* in the shower. He sang when the fire engines roared by, as often they did, because the fire station was next door, and he sang when they didn't.

And he sang only one kind of song, those about the city of his birth, the city he had never left, that he loved, and that was, for him, the world. "My kind of town," he would scrape out from the chalk, "Chicago is . . . my kind of town," and this he would repeat over and over because it was the only part he knew. Then he might switch to, "Chicago, Chicago, that wonderful town, that wonderful town, Chicago, Chicago, I'll show you around. Bet your bottom dollar you lose the blues in Chicago, Chicago, the town that Billy Sunday could not shut *down,*" and that was it, repeated ad infinitum, because he did not know the verse about State Street that great street.

Freddy's favourite was, as it was rendered upstairs: "*In* Chicago, *in* Nebraska, go go Pogo. *In* Milwaukee, *in* Alaska, go go Pogo. Virginia to Virginia, with everything that's in ya, you can even get as far as New Mexico. Oh! *In* Chicago, *in* Nebraska . . . , " and so on. When the royal couple sat at dinner, their faces half hidden in the kind of headgear that is called a Chicago hat and is worn only in Chicago, the Gulag, and adult homes, they would look up at the vibrating ceiling and a swaying bulb at the end of a frayed cord—Freddy had wrapped the bulb in a slowly oxidizing cone of saffron-coloured foolscap—and let the rhythm envelop them like a Tibetan chant.

It was not only the rhythm of his gravelly, unconscionable bass, but that of the house shuddering both as he danced and at the behest of the navy blue wind that came off the lake and froze solid anything unheated by flame or glow. If you looked north, before your eyeballs iced over you could follow a line that stretched in the dusk across the solid white top of Lake Michigan, the rock-cold Canadian ground, and the Arctic ice, a line that, without tarrying in a single firelit domain, stretched all the way to the pole itself. With the possible exception of the Navy Pier and the jetty, no bulwark against the absolute existed for Chicago. The city's parlours, offices, and institutions, its banks, kindergartens, and intimate restaurants, its libraries, bedrooms, and all the rest, were the first wall against which broke the snowy wave of polar winter that knew nothing but the black of starlit space and an ocean of tundra covered in a death shroud of white.

Buildings of stone and glass—gold and grey, black and silver, sometimes amber—were the first breastwork hit by the wind. Freddy said it was as if the Palace of Westminster had been constructed atop the last wet rock at the tip of Land's End, so that as legislation was crafted inside, the sea could thrash against the windows. "What a place to put a city," he declared, "right on the front line of absolute zero. No wonder a cow burnt it down."

"A cow?" Fredericka inquired.

"Yes, a cow owned by a Mrs O'Leary."

"How do you know?"

"Because I know," he said, almost sweetly, without upbraiding her for her ignorance, even though he knew that she would think he had just made it up, and that in a minute or two she would say something like, "That's funny, because it was Mr O'Nero's cow that burnt down Rome."

"That's funny," she said, after a pause, "because it was Mr O'Nero's cow that burnt down Rome."

He patted her hand. "No," he said, "it really was Mrs O'Leary's cow. He kicked over a lantern."

"He?"

"Yes."

"How could a cow be a he?"

"I call cows *he*. I always have. Really, whom does it hurt?"

They were not unhappy. Quite to the contrary, they had learned to love pork shoulder and dollar-a-pound canned mackerel that Fredericka whipped into interesting pâtés with Cheez Whiz or soy protein substitute, whichever was on sale. They made wonderful soups of potatoes, leeks, and chicken parts other than breasts, legs, thighs, and wings. Their meals steamed up the room and thickened the air with an aroma even stronger than what came from their ever-burning kerosene fire and its dancing ring of Druidic-blue flame. With day-old bread and some sort of green vegetable, this was, to people who expended three or four thousand calories a day, far better than the most refined cuisine of a youth spent almost entirely without hunger.

After dinner they would clean up, brush their teeth, and boil water to humidify the otherwise painfully dry space and add heat to the air. Then they would take their two glass mugs and fill them with boiling water for tea, wrap themselves in ragged but clean army blankets upon which was written *US Cavalry—Ft Sheridan,* and sit before the kerosene fire, a steady source of warmth and light that became the centre of their world. After hot soup, doing the dishes in scalding water, and tea, they might actually feel warm. Just beyond the occasionally quivering wall that they faced was the unforgiving darkness into which, if one were to penetrate, one could snake one's way to Siberia. Down a slope of dirty snow was a river of some sort that was even more filthy than the Cleveland river that Freddy had ignited in an effort to douse a burning brand that another vagrant had used in an effort to maim him after Freddy was unable to identify, much less recite, the Pledge of Allegiance. "Allegiance to what?" he had asked.

If the river (or possibly canal) in Chicago was a tad less flammable than the one in Cleveland, it was filthier with that which was floating upon or gelled within it: tyres, shopping carts, animal body parts, plastic containers, mats of algae, condoms, oil slicks, and offal. It didn't freeze, but it did thicken enough to support dirty snow. And beyond it and a rubble-strewn rail line, on rubble-strewn rocks against which rested a million tons of lake ice stacked by wind and waves, was the void.

Their walls were painted the same ungainly green as the inside of armoured personnel carriers and tanks, and the stove, which according to its embossed metal tag had been installed on 2 July 1915, had probably not been cleaned since. The seal in the toilet tank was rotted, so the water ran all the time, which was the only thing that prevented it from freezing. The cupboard in the kitchen area was warped and didn't close, and termites had made the floor underneath the ancient impetigoed linoleum as foamy as kapok. Freddy had lifted a splotched corner and seen, in a hollowed-out area, a she-rat nursing her litter. She had looked at him as if to say, *I beg your pardon,* which caused him to replace the flap apologetically.

On one wall was a picture of Jesus, in blues, whites, and silvers as in the Orthodox rite. On another wall was an automotive air filter company catalogue with a nude for each month. And over the bed someone had long before tacked the famous picture of Mao Tse-tung swimming, in which all you could see was his head floating on the Yangtze. With neither the kerosene fire nor the cooker burning, when the wind was blowing, which was all the time, the refrigerator was a lot warmer than the room. The constant cold brought Freddy and Fredericka physically closer together than they had ever been.

The highlight of each week was bathing in the kitchen vessel on Tuesdays and Fridays. They didn't know, and didn't want to know, exactly what it had been, but it was a three-by-three-by-three stainless steel sink with rolled edges, a huge drain that emptied it in a minute, and a bronze plaque that said *Armour & Co.* Before their bath they would boil water in two huge cauldrons on the stove. Then they would fill the Armour vat with all the hot water the hot-water heater could produce, while standing naked at the kitchen sink and sponging themselves with dish rags, Japanese style, so as to be immaculately clean upon entering. When the water filling the vat started to go cold—which they knew by the temperature of their wash rags—they stopped it, rinsed themselves, and like two nude, shivering elves, poured in the cauldrons of boiling water. Then, almost dry because the wind passing through the apartment would have evaporated the moisture that had clung to them, chilling them to the bone, they climbed in.

Half from the water heater and half from the cauldrons, the water was as hot as they could bear, and turned them quickly pink and red. This was what they dreamt of at work, on the street, and even in their room as they huddled by the kerosene fire. Except for this, their moments of warmth were never moments of heat. They needed heat, if only once in a while, to bring them back to life.

It was as hot as hell for fifteen minutes, after which they would get out rather than cool in the water. During this time they were by necessity pressed together, completely entangled, locked, set, penetrated, and mixed. They sat in the hot water that came as high on them as it did on Chairman Mao, and that lapped clearly over their shoulders and three quarters up their necks, fully floating their embrace. Though they spoke a great deal these days, in the bath they seldom spoke but only breathed, often with eyes closed and sometimes simply staring at one another as if in pleasant shock.

There was no place in Buckingham Palace quite as fine as this, or in St James's, or anywhere else, for although tubs were to be had and the water hotter and more plentiful, a lack of contrast made them far less welcoming and their luxury was dulled by its assurance no less than by its abundance. Here they existed simply in one another's embrace, with no worry of anything beyond their hot confines, not even the wind whistling—sometimes screaming—through the boards. At the end of the fifteenth minute measured by a heavy white Westclock on a table nearby, they pulled the plug.

As soon as they were dry they dropped their thin towels, hit the light switch, and flew into their creaking bed. Even had they had night clothes they would not have worn them, for they warmed one another far better when flesh was pressed to flesh. Entangled as in the vat, but now stretched out in blankets, their limbs braided like rope, they would sometimes awaken having fused so completely together that sleep had failed to pull them apart.

They were obsessed with one another as if they had just fallen in love. At work there was plenty of time for their minds to wander, and, to their surprise, when their minds did wander they wandered not so much to their royal pasts or to imagination of the future, or to appraisals of the world and all that was in it, but to one another. He dreamt of her and she of him. She became his world, and he hers. He found in her, in her body, in her laugh, in the way she moved, in what she said, more than he ever had thought he could find. And she found in him the same.

They had a forbidding lake and supernatural winds. They had night, cold, and the exhaustion of work. And they had the stainless steel vat and their warm bed. One evening, as they stared into the kerosene fire, he said, "We're like poor people, who have nothing but each other, and are happy. What is it called when two people have such a passion only for one another?"

WEEK AFTER WEEK, month after month, they arose before dawn and rode the buses with the sickly and exhausted people who travel to menial jobs

in the earliest hours, but their habits, their background, and the short du-
ration of their tenure enabled them to do what these others did, without
destruction. They ate only what they required, and despite being pushed
toward pork shoulder, most of the time they ate well, preferring vegetables, whole grains, and fish above all else. Of course they did not smoke,
they drank as much alcohol in a month as some of their co-workers did in
a day, they watched no television, and they went to bed extremely early
and were able to regenerate for the next day's hard labour, in which they
did so well that it seemed—although it was not—inexplicable.

Each day, Freddy walked to a freight yard from which he rode, in a converted mail car with a woodstove, to stretches of track in Indiana where he
would swing a hammer and carry rails for six hours, with a break out of
the cold for lunch of half an hour. Machines had been doing this kind of
work for decades, but some stretches of rarely used, torn-up line were too
irregular for mechanised equipment, unworthy of replacement, and yet
not ripe for abandonment. So out of Chicago the rail gangs came, winter
and summer, to straighten track, replace bad ties, and redrive spikes that
had worked themselves loose in frost and sun. Such stretches, as dishevelled
and broken as pensioners with bad teeth, went on for miles. What was
done would have to be redone in a year or two, so there was always work.

The men who did it had to wield a twenty-pound hammer all day in
sub-zero temperatures. They were mostly blacks from the South Side, but
quite a few were whites from the coalfields of Appalachia, or Poles,
Czechs, and Irish from the wards, and immigrants—Bosnians, Mexicans,
and Russians who proudly didn't mind the cold. The head of the hammer
had to strike the top of the spike at just the right angle to drive it effi-
ciently and not glance off to hit the rail or splinter a tie. As the spikes stood
at differing heights, the men had to make continual adjustments in their
stance to carry through. They pivoted, stretched, extended, arched, leant,
and aimed. It exercised every sinew in their bodies, and to do it down a
hundred yards of broken track was like fighting your way through a
Roman legion.

After three weeks Freddy hit his stride and came to feel an incompara-
ble exhilaration in nailing a stretch of line, especially as the snow flew and
darkness lifted or fell. The train followed, rumbling as it crept after them,
smoke issuing from its exhaust pipes and the chimney of the woodstove.
There he stood, the heavy hammer flying perfectly timed over his head,
hurtling through light snow to explode against a spike and drive it as deep

into the wood as it would go. The sound of his strikes and those of the others combined to make a strange and beautiful music that rolled onto the snow-covered fields. An incessant counterpoint of bell-like notes wove about an elemental beat that each man took into his heart and to which he unconsciously timed his strokes, so that the upshot throughout the day was that thirty men in thirty places were all doing the same piece of work.

Were it not for half an hour in the heated railcar, scalding hot bean soup, and scalding hot coffee (tea for Freddy), they could not have done it. Once, early in February, they went inside at eleven-thirty, leaving fifteen-below-zero and a twenty-mile-an-hour wind. There was so much smoke in the car their eyes ran, and for a moment before they melted and dropped, the tears became little white pearls of ice on their cheeks. On days like that no one talked much, but on this day a huge, bullet-headed, black ex-con suddenly grew curious about Freddy.

"Hey Moofoomooach," he said, eschewing all subtlety, "you got a woman?"

"Without question," Freddy answered crisply.

"Is she white or black?"

"As white as a polar bear," Freddy told him, which occasioned a some-what lewd chorus of approval, "but as far as I'm concerned, she could be as black as ebony."

"You saying you like brown sugar?"

"I'm saying I like Popeel."

"Popeye?"

"Popeel."

"Who Popeel?"

"Popeel . . . is my wife."

"And where Popeel at?"

"Chicago," Freddy answered.

"Where she at in Chicago?"

"She washes dishes at a cafeteria."

"You married, Moofoomooach? You sound like you was married yesterday."

"We've been married," Freddy said, "in some senses for quite a few years, but, in another sense, for just a few months. It was America, I think, that did it."

"America? Then why didn't America do it for me?"

The others laughed.

"I don't know," Freddy answered earnestly. "We were riding in a freight car and something happened. Maybe it had been happening already—I can't say for sure—but the heat, the crossing of the Potomac, the mountains. . . . We jumped from the train into a meadow that sloped down a hillside." Freddy put his spoon in his soup. "We may have hit our heads."

"Where was this meadow at?"

"It was in West Virginia, I think, or perhaps Kentucky, I really don't know."

"But it's been cool ever since?"

"Yes, it's been marvellously cool."

Not a man stirred. The only sound was the crackling of the fire. The ex-con, a man bigger than a bull, it seemed, extended a boxer's fist to Freddy, and they grasped hands. Then they finished eating and went out into the cold to swing their heavy hammers in the wind. Later, as the train trundled back to Chicago in the dark, rolling past a landscape of grey steel and refinery flares in Gary, Indiana, in the precincts of hell, Freddy burned with rose-coloured heat.

FOR EIGHT HOURS A DAY Fredericka washed dishes at a huge sink beneath a clock. Like Gaul, this sink was divided into three parts. The first received dishes and slop from a continuously moving conveyor belt. Though people were supposed to throw napkins and other trash into a bin at the receiving point, often they didn't. But one of the laws of nature is that, as in politics, slop rises to the top, so Fredericka would quickly skim the floating things from the surface with a wire wok ladle, and, once in a while, lift a mesh basket from the drain and dump its contents in a garbage can. In the first sink, Inferno, the water was always hot and always running. This did a great deal of her work for her, especially in light traffic when she could let things soak.

From Inferno the plates, cups, and silverware were lifted by the princess into Purgatory, where she scrubbed and soaped them before passing them through a continuously running water curtain into Paradise. In Purgatory, too, the water was always hot and always running, entering in the curtain wall used for the rinse.

Then, in Paradise, the clean and rinsed tableware and cutlery soaked in extremely hot, faultlessly clear water, which did not run except through the overflow as it was displaced by the growing masses of china. When it could no longer subsume all that was put into it, and white rims poked above the waves, like Mao's head, Fredericka would drain the sink and stack the dishes before returning them to their racks. The beauty of the system was that though the things that came to it were filthy, they left perfectly clean—by the thousands, the tens of thousands, and, eventually, the hundreds of thousands.

None of Fredericka's friends had ever done this kind of work, and would not have been able to appreciate its pains or rewards, thinking themselves above it, though sure to remember to express sympathy for the oppressed people who did it, which was yet another way of raising themselves in their own estimation and that of the world. But now, after six months on the job, Fredericka knew its rewards, of which there were several.

She depended on no one. No allowances were drawn, no interest returned, no capital gained, no principal depleted. She made her living, albeit modestly, by the strength of her own hand. Every week she took home in her pay packet two hundred dollars. It is true that this was the price of an entrée at Le Chat Rôti, that she had left on the table bad bottles of wine costing five times as much and thought nothing of it, and that, not long before, a hundred times her current recompense for a week's hard labour would have escaped unnoticed had it vanished from her accounts or her purse.

Now that she worked so intensely for forty hours to amass two hundred dollars, a dollar seemed like a lot, and two hundred of them were something of which she was very proud, week after week. Coupled with Freddy's three hundred, it allowed them to pay the rent, eat, save, and enjoy themselves in ways that were surprisingly elegant. This was no summer job: she would starve without it. And although she knew she would not be condemned to it forever, nothing would lift her from it but her own determination, of which she was confident if only because she believed that she could last in the job indefinitely.

Indefinitely. They had spoken of this many times. What if they simply were to stay this way, with perhaps an adjustment for declining strength; i.e., Freddy eventually becoming a baggage handler or a mechanic once he could no longer abide the severities he now loved, say in his middle fifties? She told him that she could go on at the sink, supervising the salvation of dishes in a three-step apotheosis, for another forty or forty-five years. They knew they wouldn't—it was not their destiny—but they considered that they might.

Fredericka found a satisfaction in what she did unlike any she had ever enjoyed before. The rhythm and certainty of the dishes coming off the line, getting clean, and taking their places once again in newly formed ranks gave her the pride of a serjeant-major forming up his platoons in good order. Some battles are never won except in continually fighting them. People eat, so the world needs clean dishes so it can keep on running, and she was a soldier of the line, a non-com, classless, independent. She measured her work in integral units, organised it by the clock, and watched the meals pass, like the seasons, quietly.

In the repetitive motion she discovered a tranquillity that she loved. She was tied down to the work as if by gravity, but the motions of her hands and arms, her tight and frequent glimpses, the counting and planning, the lifting and scrubbing, again and again, was like the beating of a heart, and now, she thought, at last, I have a heart other than my own, and I am aware of it every day.

She spoke to Freddy of these things philosophically, as he had so often spoken to her. He didn't know quite what to make of it. For example, as they were settling in during the bleak period after Christmas, when the cold seemed to be accelerating toward absolute zero, she had been asked to find someone to help her on Martin Luther King Day, when traffic was heavy because of school holidays and the parade. Freddy had the day off, so he joined her. Slowly but certainly as they worked they were pulled into the trance of steam, plates tumbling into the sea, and hands revolving around the clock.

"Freddy," Fredericka said after hours of silence and a perfect work flow in which they could have passed the plates even had they been blind, "I've been thinking."

"Yes?"

"Should one live, or should one die? That's the question."

"In some senses, I suppose, it is."

"Is it better in your opinion to suffer outrageously, or to stand up to all one's troubles and just end it? I mean, what if dying were like sleep, and just by going to sleep you could end all the thousands of pains and heartaches you otherwise would feel? It seems attractive. Maybe dying is like sleep, and maybe you dream."

She thought on, and her face lit up. "Ah, but there's the catch, because who knows what dreams you may have when finally you've checked out? You have to wonder. Maybe that's why people are willing to grow old and get fat and ugly, and suffer awful people, and snobs, and disappointment in love, and a rotten inefficient judicial system . . ."

Freddy looked at her in wonder.

". . . and stupid bureaucrats, and all that and such, when all you have to do is stab yourself with a fish knife. Why would anyone go through all these things and work and sweat day after day except that they were frightened that in death, from which no one has ever returned, it might actually be worse! Better a bird in hand than hell knows what in the bush. We're just afraid, I guess, and whenever you think that it's time to end it, your fear turns your resolution to mush. Oh, be quiet now. Here comes Louella, and she's in a bad temper because they made her work on Martin Luther King Day."

Freddy was stupefied, because she didn't stop there. In the weeks and months that followed, she slept-walked through many a choice passage, all as if by magic, not only from *Hamlet* but from everything from *Timon of Athens, Lear,* and *The Tempest,* to *Richard III, The Merry Wives of Windsor, Troilus and Cressida,* and *Titus Andronicus.* Freddy's eyes bulged when suddenly, on the El, she began an idiosyncratic paraphrasing of *Henry V:* "It's just us that will be happy by doing this, while all the toffs in England lie around in their beds." Freddy had a good knowledge of Shakespeare, but because he was weak on *Cymbeline* and had never read *The Rape of Lucrece* or *Love's Labour's Won,* he feared that he might be missing a great deal when she spoke.

She didn't do it like someone with a Ouija board, or like a medium or a mystic. She chirped it out in her normal voice like a salesgirl at Marks and Spencer. Whence did it come? Was it the conscience of their race, that had hitherto been sleeping in her well known breast and only now, by stress and strain of seas colliding, erupted from her with the power and surprise of a volcano and the innocence of a schoolgirl? He never told her what she was doing, because he didn't want to shock it to a stop. And for the rest of their lives together she would speak this way now and then, especially when she was moved or tired, and he never ceased to be amazed, for he knew that she had not studied Shakespeare for even a minute in the finishing school to which she had been committed, for in that place Shakespeare had been deemed far beyond the reach of all the girls who, nonetheless,

had come up like flowers in the spring rain from the very loam in which
the man himself had risen and was buried.

ALTHOUGH when they had arrived in Chicago they went every day to
swim in the lake, October got them walking. They would use Michigan
Avenue like the barrel of a cannon to launch themselves northward into
various city neighbourhoods, suburbs, and towns that took their elegance
from the lake as if with a pump. They hardly ever went inland, preferring
to stay by the fresh and curious sea strangely devoid of ships.

Then Freddy's demanding work and the winter put an end to these
walks. Although to stay fit Fredericka did ballet exercises for an hour each
day, Freddy had more than his share of exertion on the railroad. On weekends they followed the pattern they had established in Washington of
going to a modest restaurant after a day in museums and libraries. Though
Chicago's museums and libraries were neither as varied nor as rich as those
of the capital, they were more than enough.

Fredericka now took notice of Freddy's vast knowledge of history,
science, and art. "How do you know all these things?" she asked as they
were walking through a museum, having just entered a room of pre-
impressionist landscape painters.

"I read. The more you read, the more the world opens up to you in a
place like this, and the happier you are and more comforted you feel. It's
up to you. No one is educated who cannot educate himself."

"Could I educate myself, then?"

"Certainly you can."

"How would I start?"

"In the library."

"It has millions of books," she protested. "I wouldn't know where to
begin."

"Start in the reference collection. I did."

"Reading encyclopaedias?"

"Read what you find interesting, and then follow your interests. You'll
find that in doing so you always generate enough to illuminate the next
step. On Saturday, while I'm checking our press—after all, it doesn't take
two—you stay in the reference room and I'll join you when I've got a
good selection."

"That's fair," she said. "You get to read *She*, and I read the *Dutch Encyclopaedia*."

"I've already read that," said Freddy. "Besides, I find no pleasure in reading *She*."

Saturday, in the library. Outside it was insanely cold and the wind made buses sway like metronomes. Inside, the lamps glowed and chairs made wood squeals and scuff sounds as only library chairs can. Freddy took a few hours to collect their press on a library cart, and when he wheeled it to Fredericka's side, she hardly noticed. Semi-enclosed within a rampart of books, she was reading intensely, oblivious of everything except the volumes she had gathered around her.

Freddy tilted his head and read the titles on the bindings, whispering them as he read. He had assumed that her selection would be heavy on fashion, makeup, and "celebrities," but he was wrong. With her left hand resting possessively on *Who's Who in Zimbabwe,* she was deep in *Sources and Methods of Hiccup Diagnosis.* She had also chosen the *Directory of Polish Hydraulic Fluid Wholesalers;* the *Encyclopaedia of Angels;* the *Catalogue of Chuvash Books in German Libraries; Aboriginal Science Fiction; The Register of Non-Existent Churches; A Bibliography of Indonesian Military Poetry; Orators Who Possessed Horses; Lloyds' Survey of Failed Board Games; A Dictionary of the Efik Language; The Picture Book of Albanian Idioms*—a list in her handwriting lay next to the latter, beginning with the entry, "*I ka duart të prera,* 'to have one's hands cut off,'*"—The Language of the French & Indian War, Vol. I, Obscene Expressions; Glossary of Dead Architects* (Freddy couldn't wait to read the latest entries); and, finally, though not least, *Nicknames of Popular Fish.*

"You see," he told her, "it's fascinating."

"Yes, I love it. Now go away."

"I have our press."

"I couldn't care less about our press." She held up *Who's Who in Zimbabwe.* "There's a whole world out there, Freddy, that has nothing to do with us."

"You didn't know that? I've been telling you so for years. Nonetheless, reading about oneself is addictive. You'll be amazed at what they think we're doing." He spread out half a dozen glossy magazines and another half dozen newspapers. "It must have taken some time to ramp up, because when we looked in Washington they really hadn't got going, but now it's Bob's uncle."

"That's us in Turkey, two years ago, on the yacht of Sir Archibald Spoo," she said of a brilliant *She* cover photograph in which she and Freddy were backlit by the glowing azure of the Aegean. "How can they do that?"

"How do you know where it is?" Freddy asked. The only background was blue water.

"Because I'm in my safari-cloth bathing costume. I wore it only on that trip, on account of your mother's complaint that when it's wet you can practically see through it and it sets revealingly around the nipples. Right there," she said, pointing, "and there."

"Right. That's why *She* ran it, and that's how you know and no one else does. Everything's cropped out. Even Sir Archibald Spoo wouldn't be able to tell just from the picture. No one would. There are dozens of articles about us, all completely fraudulent, with pictures, quotes from non-existent people, precise times, reports of what we ate and accounts of our minor spats."

"That's a popular fish."

"Sprat."

"We could be dead and no one would know," Fredericka said.

"Exactly. Are you aware that we went skiing in January and stayed at the chalet of Blavica Chelinsky in Gloom-Bierbat?"

"Who the hell is she? And we've never been to Gloom-Bierbat. It's too dark there and they're always drinking and hitting each other with bottles."

"She's a Bulgarian countess who's like an older sister to you."

"I've never heard of her."

"Here she is." Freddy held up a picture of Fredericka with her arm around a deeply tanned matronly woman loaded down with so much gold jewellery that she looked like a fat Sammy Davis Jr.

"She smokes," said Fredericka in disgust, "and she's got a tattoo."

"She looks to me," Freddy said, "like someone Psnake got from a hotel pool in Beirut. The rest is computerized manipulation."

In quiet astonishment, Fredericka read the text out loud: "'Blavica has for many months now been Fredericka's closest confidante, and is credited with substantially repairing her relations with the prince. Fredericka wept as she told Blavica of the strains of public life, and Blavica sang six Bulgarian folk songs that the princess claims have won Freddy's heart anew. The one Fredericka sings to him the most is entitled "Brajfila Konyaffa," or "The Little Grey Goat." Its first verse goes as follows:

Papoola konyaffa, Brajfila trazhits,
Blagomir setaslava da sborniki pazhoy,
Brajfila konyaffa armanda sofaht,
Obonya fulina ingrappia coleh,
Brajfila konyaffa, prazhymsky klashitz.

or,

My little kind goat once ate fish oil and trash,
I sold him to the butcher for handfuls of cash,
Now I regret deeply all that I've done,
As I sit drinking grappa and stare at the sun.
My little grey goat is my teacher and cousin.'"

Fredericka was stunned. "What cheek!" she commented.

"It's not Bulgarian," Freddy added. "It's not anything. But, you see, we're not anything either. We were always, to some extent, a fictional construct. Now we are entirely a fictional construct. That's what happens when you live in the press, and it is why, sort of, Bedouin are enraged when you take their photographs."

"Isn't Bedouin the king of France, and why would he not like to be photographed? I'll tell you," Fredericka said proudly, "because he's not! He's a college in Maine."

"Let's not even try to answer that one."

"Freddy, why don't we just stay here?"

"In Chicago?"

She nodded.

"I admit, it is my kind of town, and it was lovely in those weeks when we swam in the lake, bobbing up and down in the wind and the sun, with an immense and vibrant city just beyond the beach."

"Everyone went by on their roller skates and no one bothered us except those old men who wanted to sell us worms," Fredericka said.

"They didn't bother me," Freddy asserted. "That is, after all, how I got my job. But what would we do if we stayed?"

"We could improve our lot. We could find more prestigious employment, make more money, and buy a semi-detached house in a Polish or Irish neighbourhood."

"It would have to be Polish."

"Then we could be Polish, or Ukrainian. No one would know. I look Scandinavian. We'd have a little car and go to dinner theatre once a month. We could buy some simple furniture and a little sailboat. We'd have one another. What else would we need?"

"I don't know," said Freddy, "but because it won't be warm enough anyway to strike out for the West until May, perhaps we can see about better jobs. I like what I'm doing, but it's trying to body and soul. Let's get the classifieds and peruse them in our hovel."

"If we buy the Sunday paper," said Fredericka, keeper of the household, "you do realise that we shan't have enough money for octopus sandwiches."

"Don't be ridiculous," Freddy told her. "We're going to dip into principal and get double octopus sandwiches to celebrate our new jobs."

"What new jobs?"

"Anyone can get a job, Fredericka. There are millions of them."

AFTER DOUBLE OCTOPUS SANDWICHES and several decanters of hot sake, they decided not to get new jobs but to start a business. When Freddy had begun his biscuit business at home it seemed that everyone in the world had wanted to be in on it, and it was very easy to hire staff and get things rolling. True, various stuffed shirts had stopped him from implementing some of his best ideas, such as the meat and fowl colas—"Straight-up Chicken Soda," "Pheasant Cooler," and "Liver and Lime"—but the Chocolate Cherry Biscuits, the Royal Scotch Caramel Cookies, and the Princess of Wales' Staffordshire Double Lemon Bristols were a huge hit.

While reading the want-ads, Freddy had come up with a brilliant idea. They had considered answering the call for Federal Express drivers, because, among other things, Fredericka would look smashing in the uniform, especially the summer shorts. But why work for Federal Express rather than compete with it? Freddy was easily able to get an appointment with a venture capital specialist at Grabben DeKessef. His phone manner and eloquence put them right through. So on a bleak Tuesday they found themselves on the eighty-ninth floor of one of the glass towers that Freddy so hated, face to face with a man whose temples were silvered and whose self-assurance was imperious.

Freddy got right to it. "We need several million pounds to start a business that I'm sure will grow like wild licorice."

"You want to grow wild licorice?"

"No no. We're sure the business will grow with great fecundity."

"How much money do you want?"

"A few million dollars, let's say four or five. I've started a successful business before."

"What was that?"

"I baked cookies, and everyone loved them. I didn't actually bake them myself."

"A factory baked them."

"Certainly not. They were baked in a castle, by footmen and pages."

The banker stared at them intently. "Now you want a different kind of challenge."

"Exactly. You are familiar," Freddy asked, "with the great success of Federal Express?"

"Yes."

"Which is, essentially, based on three principles: competition with a hitherto frightfully inefficient monopoly; the idea of a hub-based delivery system; and crisp, fast, guaranteed service. A splendid success," Freddy said, pausing dramatically, "*except locally.* It would be too expensive. So, what I've come up with is fast, same-day, hub-based, guaranteed delivery for localities. We'll start in Chicago and eventually cover every major city in this country and in the world."

"But who would spend nine dollars to deliver a letter locally?"

"It wouldn't cost nine dollars. It would cost just a dollar, and it would be based on the courier principle. In Victorian times, the post was delivered several times daily. We could return to that. Our couriers would bring packets to a central hub and deliver in reverse. They would have routes to walk, or, in some cases, drive, four times daily. The first trip would be solely to pick up, the second and third to pick up and deliver, and the fourth solely to deliver. Each customer would have three pickups and three deliveries daily. At a dollar per envelope—I've made estimates—a courier could easily produce five hundred dollars a day.

"Whereas Federal Express is a long-distance service and its colours are red, white, and blue, we would stress the local and medieval quality of what we offer—you know, making a great city as intimate as a village—and our colours would be brown, tan, and black. The couriers of our service, which we would call *Feudal* Express, would be dressed like medieval varlets and serfs, in linsey-woolsey jerkins and hose, codpieces, and leafed hoods. They would carry their loads in muslin sacks, and always plod about with staffs."

The Grabben DeKessef specialist was paralysed in place.

"The couriers would be very poor people with bad teeth—illiterates and fools, cloddish peasants, semi-criminals, torturers, dungeon-keepers, et cetera—and their supervisors would be burghers. The executives would ascend in rank from squires and knights through a peerage of various marquises, viscounts, and dukes, and, of course, I would be king."

"You would be king."

"Popeel would be my queen. That unusual business structure in itself would be revolutionary, or perhaps anti-revolutionary."

The specialist smiled. "Don't you think," he asked, "that you should look into the feasibility of actually running a medievally based business?"

"Oh, I know all about that. My family has been doing that in England for a thousand years."

"What about America?"

"It broke away."

"I mean, shouldn't you see how a medievally based business runs in America?"

"How can we? None such exists."

"Ah, but it does. And you're in luck."

It was a modest space about the size and shape of the Circus Maximus, with a high roof built over it and galleries for spotlights tucked into the corners just underneath the black ceiling. At one end of the oval arena was a platform about five feet above the sand. Here were two gilded thrones upholstered in cloth of royal blue dotted with golden fleurs-de-lys. On either side of the thrones, rigged on Roman tripods, were Sears Roebuck kettle barbecues below signs that said S.P.Q.R. Blue flame from many cans of Sterno rose from within them.

Upon the thrones sat King Bonticue, also known as Frank Bonticue, and Queen Devore, also known as Gina Bonticue. They were dressed in togas and wore crowns that Freddy understood were appropriate to a viscount. Queen Devore had difficulty squeezing herself into her throne chair, and could not get up without one varlet pulling her out of it by the hands as two others pushed against her behind. King Bonticue was twice her size but his throne had no sides. She wore eight to ten pounds of makeup, he at least three. Both were tattooed, and both wore earrings. On his wrist lived a huge Japanese digital watch with a square orange face, and she chewed gum as if she were being paid to generate electricity with her jaw.

In this kingdom ten miles north-west of Chicago, Freddy was a serf who carried Styrofoam lances for the Jolly Green Knight, who rode his charger half-naked, with a laurel of asparagus and other vegetables upon his head. When he made his appearance on horseback he circled the arena near the perimeter, and as he looked into the faces of a thousand people arrayed upon benches at continuous plank tables, he lifted his sword and shouted, "Ho ho ho!"

To which, almost as one, as if in a secret ritual that was not at all secret, the entire crowd responded, "Ho ho ho!"

Then the Jolly Green Knight shouted, "In the Valley of the Jolly . . ." and paused.

Always, the pause had exactly three beats, before the crowd responded, with massive force that shook the walls, "Green Giant!" To his dying day, Freddy would never understand how each batch of a thousand people knew, at performance after performance, to hold the pause for the requisite number of beats and then answer as if they were as practised as the Vienna Boys' Choir. Then again, they wouldn't have the vaguest idea about Andy Pandy, would they? But they never missed a beat or failed to shout, "Green Giant!" although the knight was in no way identified as such. What stupefying force could decree such synchrony?

"Why do they call him the Green Giant?" Freddy had asked one of the knights who was sitting in the sun drinking a beer and eating chocolate-covered doughnuts, "and am I not his valet?" Freddy pronounced *valet* in the American way, because he was, after all, speaking to an American in America.

"Not *valet, valley*. He plants corn in the valley," was the thoughtful response.

"What corn? What valley?"

"You know," said the knight, " 'the Valley of the Jolly, ho ho ho, Green Giant.' "

"Where is that?" Freddy asked.

"In California."

"I see," said Freddy. "Is someone supposed to kill this giant?"

"Yeah," answered the knight, unwilling to resist the line of questioning.

"Who?" asked Freddy, hoping to hear that a prince from a foreign land would, in the course of his quest, kill the giant and find the live ash circle.

"The American Tourister Gorilla."

Freddy cocked his head and looked up. After a moment, he asked, "Who?"

"The gorilla that jumps on the suitcase. You know how they get him to do that?"

"No," said Freddy, looking dangerously toward the sun.

"They fill it with Baby Ruths."

"The suitcase."

"Yeah. He goes apeshit trying to get them out."

"The babies?" Freddy had no idea what the knight, Sir Rocky Spreckles, was talking about.

"Yeah."

"Now, let's summarise this," Freddy said. "The Green Giant will be killed by the gorilla that jumps on his suitcase because he goes apeshit trying to get the babies out of it. Is that right?"

"Right on."

"Does this have anything to do with the live ash circle?" Freddy asked.

"The live ass circle?" Sir Rocky repeated, and belched. He had had only eight beers, but it was morning.

"Ash."

Sir Rocky thought, weighing the question, bouncing his head back and forth a little. "Yeah," he said, "it does."

"It does? You've heard of the live ash circle?"

"Yeah, I've heard of it."

"But you thought it was *ass*."

"Sometimes it is ass."

"It is?"

"What is it?"

"What is what?"

"Whatever it is. Which is it?"

Sir Rocky motioned Freddy to bend in close to hear a whisper. "It's in Kankakee," he said conspiratorially, "Kankakee."

The knights didn't like any serf, but they particularly hated Freddy because they thought he put on airs. He was always telling them how to ride, hold a sword, or carry a lance. "Hey, what the fuck do you know?" Sir Randy Shifflet had asked. "You're a fuckin' serf, so shut up."

Because of his rodeo background, Sir Randy got to be king three times a day. Sir Mildred of Iraq would shoot a poison arrow at King Bonticue, and in the king's death soliloquy he would command his knights to fight for succession. He always died in the arms of Sir Randy after Sir Randy had "knocked" all the other knights off their mounts and swung onto the throne platform on a velvet bell rope. That was his job, to become king thrice a day. Freddy hated him, especially because the combat was obviously fraudulent. They carried Styrofoam lances, and their hollow aluminium swords were no more dangerous than deck chairs.

Freddy had picked up one of these swords once and had begun to exercise with it, when a fellow serf said, "Put it down! If Sir Buster sees you, you're a dead man!"

"Why?"

"We're not allowed to use a knight's sword. Are you crazy?"

"Why not?"

"We're serfs."

"We're not really serfs," Freddy protested.

"Yes we are."

"Yes we are?"

"Yes. They're our betters. They can ride, and use swords. They'll beat the hell out of us if we try to be like them."

"I can ride and use a sword," Freddy stated, "far better than they can."

"Well, you can't let them know, because they'll really do it."

After a moment's thought, Freddy seized the other serf by his jerkin. "Do what?"

"They're knights. She's a serving wench. You know."

"I know what?"

"They get to take every new serving wench to their trailers. It's the right of the lord of the manor. Sir Randy wants Popeel."

"Popeel is my wife."

"That doesn't matter. They're knights. That's the way it is."

"I've never heard of such a thing! Actually, I suppose I have. But why haven't we been told?"

"That's because, in the system, Popeel goes to Sir Buster, but Sir Randy wants her and they've been arguing about it."

"What does Popeel get to say about this?" Freddy asked indignantly. "She's not a slave."

The other serf looked at Freddy as if Freddy were an idiot. "She's a serving wench, and her husband is a serf. She doesn't have anything to say about it."

"Forget about me for a moment," said Freddy. "What about the law?"

"What law?"

"The law."

"As far as I know," the serf told him, "no one has paid any attention to the law for at least twenty years. Bonticue steals all the money from the show and drives around in a stolen car. Gina's a fence. Randy's been selling drugs since before they were invented."

"Thank you for the briefing," said Freddy, graciously departing.

"Popeel," he said to Fredericka, who, sweating gloriously, was carrying a tray of twenty roasted chicken halves, "I must speak to you at once." There was an immense traffic of serving wenches going in and out of the kitchen, and they could hear.

"Desi," she answered, "we're filling the microwaves up top in preparation for the second show. Might we speak later?"

"No, now," he said, manoeuvring her and the tray of chickens into a corner, where he told her what he had heard.

"That pig," she said. "He invited me to his trailer for an apéritif—although I think he may have used a different word."

"What did you say?"

"I said I would talk to you, and he said he was certain you would say yes. I thought he meant that you would come, too."

"I'm just a serf. Stay away from him, Fredericka. He's of immense size and thinks he owns this place."

"Not even King Bonticue owns the 'Times,'" Fredericka said, using company jargon. "The wenches say it's owned by investors in Florida. What are you going to do?"

"I don't know. Obviously, I can't let this happen, but, needless to say, the idea of a peasant rebellion makes me ill."

"WELCOME!" King Bonticue screamed at the top of his voice, head raised and bathed in purple and blue theatrical lighting, "to Anglo-Saxon Times!" He stressed the last word as much as he could, and the crowd went wild, all thousand men, women, and children, as if he had actually said something.

Pressed against the wall of the arena in darkness except for the occasions when a gold or rose spotlight briefly illuminated him as it swept wildly across spectators and performers alike, Freddy wondered why the king put the emphasis where he did. It had to be significant. The king pronounced it in his deep Chicago accent—if something flat can be called deep—as *Timsse*, with a closing of the lips that made it almost, if not quite, *Timessah*, or *Timessuh*. Freddy had noted also the existence in Chicago of *bearsse, bullsse,* and *puhleesse*.

"I am King Bonticue! And this is Queen Devore!" the king thundered into a hand-held microphone. "After the show, please stop by the store! There you will find, for your shopping pleasure—what else?—Anglo-Saxon treasure! Swords and shields, flags and flagons, plastic castles, rubber dragons! Perfumes and soaps, foods of all nations, Anglo-Saxon clothes for those of all stations. We take Visa and American Express; if I ask you to shop, you've got to say yes. For I am your king, and I talk no jive, this is not now, it's *eight ninety-five!*"

The crowd always went wild when so commanded by the king, for they had been trained since birth to respond to advertisement. For Freddy it was very unpleasant, especially because it signalled the onrush of his least favourite part. "And, *now,*" the king said, cockeyed of emphasis as usual, "in *honour,* of the serving wenches of *Swabia,* who will serve you chickens when the music begins, let us enjoy a ritual entertainment made famous by my great-, great-, great-, great-grandfather, King Jerry of the Angles and Jutes. Let the musicians play . . . the . . . *Mexican . . . Hat Dance!*"

All the lights came up blindingly. As offstage the knights screamed obscenities and made foul gestures, Freddy and a bunch of other serfs ran into a circle at the centre of the arena, put on huge sombreros, and did the Mexican Hat Dance. The crowd seemed not to question the authenticity or appropriateness of this, or anything else, ever, and the king and queen drank from enormous flagons of malt liquor.

As Freddy danced and the knights, hidden from the audience in the passage from which they would burst forth on their chargers, continued to mock the serfs—in parallel dances, by dropping their pants, and in many vulgar pantomimes—Fredericka was working her hardest. She moved along the narrow lines between rows, dishing out half chickens and petite loaves of bread. Following her were beer wenches who filled and refilled the plastic cups. The object of this exercise was to allow the men to look down the dresses of the serving wenches, which they did nearly without exception in tell-tale silence and sudden immobility, as if their wives wouldn't notice. Fredericka paid no attention, and focussed on the heavy trays of food that lightened mercifully as she served out her half-chickens. After two or three trips she would be sweating as if in a sauna, which put the men in a trance. She felt like an enchantress as one by one their mouths dropped open and they went numb as she passed, even though she smelled like chicken "roasted the Anglo-Saxon way." In fact, when they got home after the shows, Freddy found her new perfume the most potent aphrodisiac imaginable. "Why?" she had asked him. "You used to hate it when I picked up the slightest smell of food, and would make me bathe, and now all you want to do is lick me. What will happen if we serve fajitas?"

When the hat dance was finished, the spotlight turned on the king, who emptied the last of his half gallon of malt liquor and rose unsteadily to tell a tragic story. As he warbled drunkenly, the crowd was rapt. The audience felt privileged to hear this lay straight from a king, and he would have been believed no matter what. He could have said anything.

"This is a sad story of Anglo-Saxon *timsse*," he began, "of tragedy and threnody, royalty and rhapsody, of a chicken separated from its egg, and a castle moaning and groaning in the wind. Do you want me to tell it?"

"Yes!" the crowd screamed in one voice.

"Do you want me to tell it like it is?"

"Yes!"

"Do you want me to sock it to you?"

"Yes!"

"Really?"

"Yes! Yes! Yes!"

"That's what I wanted to hear. For a king, you know, I'm very insecure. I need constant approval." At this, Queen Devore staggered to her feet and bashed him on the head with a huge inflatable rolling pin. "Well, not that constant." The crowd was apoplectic.

From the horse passage, Sir Buster shouted, "Get on with it, you cheap pyromaniac bastard with your goddamn stolen Impala!" Sir Buster had thought that, because of the acoustics of the tunnel, no one but the king would hear this, but it was picked up on the microphones and it echoed around the premises.

"Ah!" said the king. "The knights are discontent. And no wonder. They know not who will be king. You see," the lights went low, and the king swayed, "no one knows who my *hair* is, no one knows the true Prince Arnold. He was stolen from Devore and I when he was a baby, one terrible winter night when the Cornish Sea came up on the land and iced over the forests in waves of all this frozen shit. Where did he go?

"Why, the White Eof took him. We knew that he would live, but he was no longer ours, he was hers. She raised him in a cave so well hidden that none of our soldiers could find it, and, for eighteen years, we grieved.

"Then, one day, Cardinal Richelieu was riding in his sedan and one of those sonic brooms scared the crap out of his bearers. They dropped him, and he rolled down an impassable gully—*right into the lair of the White Eof!*

"And who was there? Why, twelve young men clad in skins and hardly able to speak. We brought them to our castle because we knew that one of them—one of them—was our son. But which one? Who the hell knew? So we had to train them all as knights and put them all on probation. And here they are, the knights on parole!"

Trumpets sounded as the serfs, carrying shields and lances, walked abjectly through the exit of the passageway, immediately leaving the circle of light shining upon it and disappearing into the darkened arena to await the explosion of horses and riders.

"Sir Buster!" said the king, and out shot Sir Buster, bumping around on a western saddle, carrying his plastic armour lightly.

"Sir Ray!" Out burst Sir Ray, cloaked in gold and silver Orlon.

"Sir Joey!" And then the rest, ending with Sir Randy, who was so big and who was on such an enormous horse that everyone knew he was the one.

They lined up in the centre of the arena, and as the spotlight was trained on each one individually—Fredericka meanwhile was dumping chicken carcasses and plastic cups into a huge plastic bag that she carried upon her shoulders—the knights proclaimed, "I am Sir Buster, but, really, I am Prince Arnold, and I shall be king," and, "I am Sir Joey, but, really, *I* am Prince Arnold, and *I* shall be king," and so on through the lot, at the end of which Fredericka was handing out towelettes and double chocolate Anglo-Saxon doughnuts.

The king, who had been drinking from a fresh flagon, rose to say, "Woe is me, for I know not who is my true son, and prithee how shall I tell?"

Out from the tunnel rode Sir Mildred of Iraq, in black robes and black burnous. Chased by the lights, he galloped around the perimeter of the arena until he came to the royal platform and loosed a Styrofoam arrow at the king, who, although the arrow missed him by two feet, fell.

"The king is no more, quoth Sir Mildred," said Sir Mildred, "and the kingdom will know war. Let the princes and their host prove themselves in combat, to see who will succeed this crazy royal wombat!"

Thus cued, the knights broke into anarchic chase not of each other but of the serfs. The first part of the contest, worth half a doughnut, was for the knights to run down and slaughter the serfs, who fled like rabbits before they were struck. Then they half fell, half limped away, supposedly dead, rushing to the locker room to change costumes for the last scene, when Sir Randy was crowned and they would prance about as wood fairies.

During the battle, with his fellow serfs falling piteously all around him and screaming in pain that was sometimes real, for the swords were not entirely weightless, something arose in Freddy that had been in him, great and glorious, all his life. In this state, time slowed and everything deepened, whether it was the glint of the blue spotlights on the polished aluminium swords, the flash in the eyes of the "war horses," the trajectory of flying serfs, the golden dust rising in beams of light that slewed madly across the scene, the bellow of the crowd, or just the sense that history was at a turning point, as at Agincourt or Al Alamein. Battle, any kind of battle, cut him from the pull of the ground and gave him grace and resolution.

Up in the galleries, Fredericka stopped, breaking the rhythm of the line and its tasks, and turned toward the chaotic arena below as if she could sense that something was about to happen there.

Freddy had decided that he had to be king, and that he would, from the ground and unarmed, fight a dozen mounted knights to take the place that God had made for him, because, God having made this place, it would be held open for its rightful occupant.

So when Sir Buster began to gallop toward him from out of the light-woven gloom, Freddy slowly opened his arms and readied himself for the impossibly fast strike that, he knew, can only come from a slow unfolding. The mass of Sir Buster and his horse slipped heavily and quickly across the sand, but to Freddy it was slow motion. The sword made an almost instantaneous clockwise circle in preparation for striking down the serf, but to the serf it seemed to roll slowly through the air, like a Pacific wave moving across blue water in the wind, and he turned as it came, caught it on the flat, and yanked Sir Buster from his horse.

Sir Buster was down. Seeing this, the dead King Bonticue stood up, and said, "Hey! Who did that?"

Long before Sir Buster could catch his breath, Freddy was high once again on a horse. His sense of battle carried from him into the animal like an electric current, and the horse, a huge grey, did what warhorses do under kings, and what no horse had done beneath the rodeo knights at Anglo-Saxon Times since its inception. Nostrils flaring, it reared on its hind legs like the Britannic lion, boxing imaginary enemies before it. And as the spotlight operators went for this as one, all beams converged upon Freddy and the rampant grey. Fredericka's tray cluttered to the floor.

"Cut the lights! Cut the lights!" screamed the dead king. "He's just a goddamned serf!"

But the attitude of the horse, and the way Freddy stood masterfully in the stirrups, sword floating in air beside him, magnetised the light, which would not go away no matter how fiercely the dead king commanded. And then, when the horse's forelegs returned to ground, Freddy took out after the remaining knights. The first was Sir Joey, who nervously rode toward him.

Freddy spurred the grey and bore down on Sir Joey with eyes and sword, and having been a swordsman since he was four, in one fabulous bind he launched the impertinent knight's weapon like a rocket, straight up. It seemed to disappear, and then came down, point first, to stick in the ground with a thud.

Freddy wheeled the grey about and, like a sailboat smoothly knifing forward through the crests of waves, caught up with Sir Joey and knocked him from the saddle with the flat of his sword. This, however, was only the beginning of a fluid motion that then extended to the next knight in line, Sir Eric Chuck, who went flying like an Olympic diver. Never had anyone watching seen such horsemanship or swordsmanship, as Freddy pursued his destiny and that of his family. His movements were not his, he merely filled them as they appeared before him. But they did require strength, grace, and daring, and these he supplied, running down another line of knights, his teeth clenched, to topple them like tenpins. Riderless horses now pranced around the arena or stood vacantly pawing the ground. As the lights followed Freddy, the audience cheered for him. They had come to hate the knights. They had come to hate the false king. And they wanted Freddy on the throne. They were moved by Freddy's revolt—which, unlike everything heretofore, seemed real.

Sir Randy, though, had stayed in place, sizing up Freddy and his manoeuvres. This he had learned in rodeo: let everyone else go first, and then you know exactly what has to be done. In no time at all, he was the only one left.

Theatrical to their bones, the spotlight operators highlighted the two combatants and ignored the squealing king, illuminating him briefly now and then because he was too odd to be left entirely in darkness. Sir Randy was immense, and so was his mount. The knight played with his sword, assimilating what he had just seen Freddy do with his. Then he trotted out.

They faced one another from either end of the arena. In a naturally deep voice that carried over the microphones like rolling thunder, Sir Randy asked, "Where did you learn to ride that way, serf?"

In his most elevated Oxbridge manner—not just with voice but with the whole of his body and expression and more than just the sum of its parts—Freddy answered, royally, "Out Utah way."

The crowd erupted and the horses snarled. "I'm going to take you down so hard, serfer girl," Sir Randy said, "that you're going to wish you were Sir Buster's horse."

"No," Freddy proclaimed. "Not you, not you, who would, in your mobile home with flame decals on the side, take Popeel, or any woman, against her will. Not you, not against a real king."

"We'll see," said Sir Randy, lowering his visor and spurring his horse.

Having lost the initiative, Freddy was off second, which he did not like. When they clashed, neither was unseated or separated from his sword, but Sir Randy's great weight had shaken Freddy as the swords had crossed. Freddy had no time, however, to think about this, and turned the grey for another go.

When they clashed again, Sir Randy lifted Freddy's sword from him and launched it almost as high as the ceiling. Fredericka clenched her fists and brought them to the base of her neck. The crowd drew in half the air of the room and held it. As Sir Randy wheeled around and began to reset for the killing run, what was Freddy doing? What was he doing, looking up as if beseeching God, eyes fixed on the seemingly unpromising darkness above?

And then, eliciting from the audience a strong and wonderful cheer, Freddy spurred his grey a little forward and to the side, and, with great concentration, extended his arm and caught the silver sword as if it had been sent to him from on high. With a restrained but triumphant smile, he turned, not to Sir Randy, but to all the kings of England in their graves. Every man, woman, and child stood and shouted. Doughnuts were launched inadvertently through the air, and the roar echoed everywhere.

In flew Sir Randy, still courageous, and Freddy rushed to meet him. This time, Sir Randy's weight would mean nothing, for this time Freddy had in his sword hand—and he knew it—the weight and expectation of a thousand years. When the knight met the king who had been a serf, the knight was thrown from his saddle as if by a catapult. Off he went in a backward arc that ended on the hard sand and took from him all the breath of his fight.

With every light on him, Freddy galloped his horse toward the five-foot-high platform upon which stood the dead king, now muttering into his microphone so that all could hear, "I'm the director, goddamit. I wrote the fuckin' script. I paid good money for the franchise."

"Shut up, Frank," Queen Devore was heard to say. "Can't you see what's coming?"

At the end of his gallop, the grey took a leap and flew onto the throne platform, where he collapsed the furniture and hangings but missed the king and queen, who stared silently up at Freddy.

Freddy extended his sword tip to Frank Bonticue's throat. "Give him the crown, Frank, give him the crown!" Gina advised, and the dead king removed his crown and hung it on the end of the sword.

As Freddy lifted the sword, the crown slid down the shaft. Holding the sword upright, like an escort cavalryman, he left the crown untouched and would not even look at it. Rather, his eyes swept the darkness that was in turn swept with beams of light, and he said in a great voice that hardly needed amplification: "It is my destiny to be king, and I will let no one take that from me. I was born to it and born for it, and I will, in this life, achieve it."

Like everyone else, Fredericka was transfixed. But, unlike everyone else, she was with him as if their blood and bodies were the same.

A Short Interlude
on the Mississippi

ALL AROUND THE WORLD, the surf breaks in a ring upon the ocean perimeter, never having been still since the beginning of time, and rolling out more steadily than all the looms of India, or those of Britain that once filled the Midlands with their incessant chatter. Were there a choir of everyone who has ever lived, its voice would hardly be as complex as that of the surf, which in its trillion-trillion-fold mass encompasses all frequencies, variations, and choreographies of water and foam. Pieces of it are thrown about as spray and glitter that catch the light as in an infinite glass, and it rocks back upon itself, pausing in scattered silences as new waves rise. But despite its unfathomable variety it heeds the laws that gather it into conforming bales as it rolls across the obsidian waters of the north or over hot turtle-green seas. When the first wave broke upon the first startled strand, it began the never-ending song of the world. Water has long memory and cannot be driven from its original instructions. Even in alpine flumes it stays true as they try to leap their channels, or when the tide rushes up the Thames, or in a flash flood in an arroyo, or off the bows of ships in the ocean, yawls on lakes, or barges on the Mississippi.

The bow wave that preceded Freddy and Fredericka like an endlessly unfurling carpet was the forward declaration of a massive barge train nearly two thousand feet in length and a hundred feet wide. The water was depressed, drawn up in a curve, and then sent out ahead, rising in the light, oxygenated, cast athwart to sink back into the cool Mississippi whence it had come. When the air was anything but perfectly clear, the foam was white with a slight touch of grey, and the water from which it rose was greenish-grey or sometimes brown, but always flowing, with a slightly earthen smell.

Their job was to keep their eyes on the river, looking ahead and to the sides to see those things that a pilot far astern might misinterpret or miss entirely. They would warn off unthinking boaters, because the great barge train could neither stop nor turn except by advance calculation. They would report obstructions and new shallows, and tell everyone astern what the river looked like ahead as they rounded a bend and were thrust into new territory like scouts riding in front of a cavalry column, far in advance of the push-boat as it slid across the water to take the turn.

This was not the first work they did in America, but it was the best. The shore was ever-changing, a world of twisted limbs and bleached tree trunks resting askew on sandbars; of fields under the spray of irrigation machinery that rolled slowly on twenty-foot wheels; of rivers joining the Mississippi like new riders swelling a procession of horsemen; of birds that floated on air cast back by boats and barges; of towns that had died long before but refused to sleep or go under because they could not cease watching the river; of bay-like widenings that promised the sea at the end of flow; of bridges that passed overhead, the bottoms of their decks space-black from a hundred years of coal and diesel smoke; of fields that burned in little worm-like lines of gold wool; of the wind that fed the fires as they crawled across the fields, made safe by the mile of water that stopped their sweeps; and of the progress of the banks as the boat threaded through tangled nature, charging onward and full of the promise of life ahead.

They lived in a little hut mounted on the prow of the leading barge. It had only two single beds and a small bath. But on the ten-foot-wide deck that spanned the width of the barge were some canvas chairs and a little table on which sat a heavy book of bound river navigation charts, binoculars, and the radio with which they reported to the pilot house. Off to the side was a barbecue-smoker on which they cooked their dinners and heated water. In return for pay, accommodations, and passage to New Orleans, they had promised always to keep at least one set of eyes on the river. One would fish or cook, and the other would watch ahead. One would read to the other, or sleep, while the other kept his or her eyes on the river. It was all-absorbing and obsessive, which was perfect for Freddy. They were in the wind day and night, riding upon a white bale of fresh water as if in a wonderful dream.

FREDERICKA HAD ALWAYS feared that were she to have been cleaved from her parents, her estate, her name, class, and connections, she would be lost.

Later, sharing in Freddy's wealth, she had been somewhat reassured by the possession not only of her own ancestral resources but of his. Still, the paradox of receiving an extraordinary living while doing nothing creates a fear that is difficult to convey to commoners, a giddy and nauseating feeling like that of sitting unsecured at the top of Nelson's Column in a high wind.

One night when Hampton Court had been opened just for them and they wandered its long corridors in their finery, Freddy had told her, "You don't have power, power has you. Mummy says we suffer the illusion of the axe handle, which thinks it's powerful because it uses the head of the axe to smash into wood, but hands use the axe handle, which has no real power, and arms use the hands, and the body uses the arms, and so on. Power is a long chain, with each link a captive of the others."

Fredericka had rightfully been anxious in her high and delicate position, because it was accidental, and because she had to rely on so many people to do things for her. What if they had simply refused? What if the mechanics had refused to fix her car, the maids to clean her halls, the cooks to prepare her food, the police to protect, the drivers to drive, the hairdressers to dress hair? What if her fortune had vanished and she could no longer write cheques? What if the bank, where all these monies were kept, said, "Sorry, we have no record of your holdings"? However many pounds she had in various incarnations were invisibly recorded on a silicon chip in ones and noughts. What if these things simply did not report, or if the people who kept them in trust denied their existence, or hers? "But I have a receipt," she might say, handing it over to them to prove that she had not just imagined five million pounds on deposit. And then they would tear it up, saying, "What receipt?"

It was the stuff of nightmares that she had had both waking and sleeping, but no longer. Her three jobs in America had forever changed her. No one had known her when she applied for them. The work in each was the kind of thing that her former friends would not know even in dreams. She had been paid in cash that came in little envelopes, and cumulatively the pay was less than she would require to replace her best pair of shoes. She often thought of those shoes sitting on a rack in her windowed American-style "closet," where they would not get dusty, because the air was filtered. Nor would they mould, because it was dehumidified. Nor would they crack, because the dehumidification was moderate. These shoes would take more money to replace than all that had sustained her, body and soul, quite happily, often joyfully, for almost a year.

On a bright May afternoon, standing on the bows as they slid over the Mississippi, Fredericka threw down a bucket on a line to get water for washing. The bucket hit the surface and bounced, and as it trailed it took on water that she could see frothing and ricocheting inside. As if the rope were attached to a marlin, she tightened both hands, planted her feet squarely on deck, and strained to pull it in. The harder the resistance, the harder she pulled, until the bucket leapt from the water and rose into the air. By the strain upon her body, by her refusal to give up, by her own effort, she had drawn water, and now she stood in the sun. The satisfaction of cleaning lavatories, washing dishes, serving chicken in the dark, or working as a barge lookout was greater than any she had known. Now she understood, from having been high and having fallen, that the very frictions and troubles her peers had unceasingly sought to avoid were the touch of life itself, and she did not want to go back.

As she crossed the deck and was about to pour the bucket of water into a cauldron on the grill, Freddy turned momentarily from scanning the river to glance at her. She was in denim shorts and a blue, floral-print, sleeveless blouse that she had bought at what Freddy called "Wal-Nut" someplace in Minnesota during a spring thunderstorm. She had tied back her hair, and now glorious in the sun it lay across her shoulder like golden flax, touching her collarbone, concaving slightly across the sunburned top of her chest, and then coming to rest on the Bristol blue print. Her eyes were of a deeper, more sapphire blue, and the blouse set them off like a gem in a carefully worked sceptre or crown. She had not worn makeup for months, and some imperfections that Freddy had previously been unaccustomed to now seemed to him to be beautiful—some hardly perceptible facial hairs, blond almost to invisibility, that now he could see; a tiny cup-like indentation to the left of her left eye, a childhood scar that in England he had never seen; her rougher hands, still beautiful, in which there was now obvious strength; the way she carried herself, relaxed and at ease, with more real dignity than she had ever had before. She was content to be unheralded and unknown, which gave her a kind of grace that as a princess she had never possessed.

"Keep your eyes on the river," she said to her husband. Then she poured the water. As the wind blew her hair back over her shoulder, she raised her left hand, in a kind of salute, to shield her eyes from the glare of the sun. The riverbanks rushed away, and were left behind in the stream. "Freddy, I don't want to go back."

"To Chicago?" Freddy asked, sighting a northbound barge train. "Just a minute." He took the radio from the table and reported: "Approaching navigation, port side, two thousand yards."

"Roger that," was the reply from the pilot house. "We see it."

"Not to Chicago," Fredericka said.

"England?" Freddy asked, surprised.

She nodded. She did something to her face when she nodded, a drawing in of the lips and a widening of the eyes, that he loved.

"England? You don't want to go back to England?"

"No. I want to stay in America. I feel so alive here."

"Didn't you feel alive in England?"

"No one does."

"Don't be absurd. That's nonsense. Is it because we're poor here? We can be poor in England, too."

"After you're king?"

"Look," he said, "we can really mess things up if we want. We'd find a way."

"But it isn't just that, Freddy. It's that here the class system is so weak and everything is so big."

"What's so big?"

"The whole thing. Look at it," she said, her arms opening and then dropping as she turned back to him. "I love how vast it is. It totally relaxes me."

"What would we do here, Fredericka? I'll soon be too old for this kind of work. I'm taking my last shot. When I was your age I wanted to stay in the army forever, but things change. I've always wanted to be strong, fit, and self-reliant, but as I age I appreciate my privileges."

"Don't you feel vulnerable and guilty?" she asked.

"At times I feel positively unnerved, and sometimes I even dream that my head is rolling away from my body. I hate it when people stare at us the way they do. God only knows what some of them are thinking. But that's not the point. I feel bad when I kill the fish that we grill, but I do kill them, and we eat them—because they're delicious, that is our fate, and we are imperfect. Sometimes, in this palace or that, surrounded by the world's greatest and most wonderful refinements, I wonder what the hell I'm doing there. It wasn't my choice, such an accident of birth, but, as my father says, steady on. Have the grace to accept a fate that is singular, spectacular, and inexplicable."

"But aren't you happy here?" she asked.

"I am."

"Happier than ever before?"

"Yes."

"Then let's stay."

"What would we do? Where would we live? And if people found out about us they'd want to put us in advertisements."

"We could buy an estate in Virginia or on the other side, on the coast of . . . what's that big state that looks like a banana? I could write children's books or make puppets or something, and you could be a historian."

"We don't have the money to do that, and though they gave me a dental degree they neglected to provide a D.Phil. in history."

"Then we could be dentists."

"We'd kill our patients."

"It's just teeth. It's not like open-heart surgery."

"Can you imagine," Freddy asked, "the screams, the bleeding gums, the lawsuits?"

"I think it would be rather fun."

"Do you?"

"Yes, and very dramatic. Studying all night and straining to do it right the next day."

"My idea of freedom is not to be a frantic, desperate, sleep-deprived, fake dentist."

"I've got it!" she said, snapping her fingers and kneeling beside his chair, as she always did when she wanted to convince him of something. She began evenly and sincerely, as if to impress him with the good sense and so-briety of her plan. "We'll study obsessively for a month or two until our savings run out. It's all in books, isn't it? And we can practise on one another."

"Whatever we do, Fredericka, I don't think we should practise den-tistry on one another. On some poor unwitting peasant, perhaps, but . . . no, not a good idea, not in the least."

"Why not? We've got lots of huge teeth. But here's the key."

"What is the key, Fredericka?" Freddy asked dryly.

"The key is, we can set up practice, temporarily, in some out-of-the-way place, some place where no one ever goes, that no one's ever heard of, in a state that's never in the news—a backwater where they don't even have a dentist and wouldn't know the difference between a real one and a fake one. We'll stay there until we know how to do it, and then move to a place where we'd like to live, practise normally, and make a lot of money."

Freddy took his eyes off the river for a moment and looked at her. She was so beautiful. She glowed in the sun like a buttercup. Scanning the river once more, he said, "But Fredericka, I don't want to be a dentist. I'm supposed to be the king of England."

"It's not that different, really, if you think about it."

He could think of no answer to this, and just blinked.

"And what if it doesn't work?" she asked. "What if we can't conquer this country? We've been here almost a year, and look." Again she opened her arms, not, as before, like a cup holding the light of the world. This time, they pointed downward, with the light of the world spilling out.

He glanced at her for as long as he could. "I think you look very fetching in that blouse from Wal-Nut, like a natural-born queen."

"That may be so, but we're hardly in a position to turn down a lucrative dental career."

"We've been here only a short time," he said. "How do you expect two people, thrown naked from an aeroplane, to conquer the richest, most powerful, and most complex country on earth, in just a year?"

"How long will it take?"

"It might take forever and it might happen tomorrow."

Fredericka scowled, looked at her denim shorts and Wal-Nut blouse, and at Freddy in the canvas chair, clad in frayed khaki shorts, scuffed climbing boots, and a garbageman's green T-shirt. "What do you mean, 'it might happen tomorrow'? How could it happen tomorrow? We haven't even tried."

"Naturally we haven't tried. What are we supposed to do, take over the television stations and play 'God Save the Queen' instead of wolf-man movies? They wouldn't even notice. They watch the television not for what they see but as a kind of energy transducer. You can't conquer a country like this deliberately. You have to wait for the wavelength, and, when it clicks, you get on the wavelength, and it's done."

"What wavelength, Freddy?" asked Fredericka, bouncing the plastic bucket on her knee.

"The sex wavelength."

"The what?"

"Like sex," he said, "it isn't a matter of effort. You can't make it happen, you have to let it happen. Effort impeaches itself. We'll just wait for the country to submit to our rule, as I'm sure it will."

Fredericka was astounded. "What gives you your absolutely lunatic self-confidence?"

"I don't know."

"Is it money?"

"You know that I think money is vulgar."

"Was it your upbringing?"

"I don't think so. As you know, my father pretty much convinced me that I was a hippopotamus."

"Is it all that rot about being descended from William the Conqueror? I'm descended from him, too, and I don't have your confidence. Besides, what did *he* ever do?"

"I was born to be king," Freddy told her, and then went on as if he were instructing her on how to put batteries in a radio. "The road has two destinations, death or my reign, and I simply follow the road that has been laid down."

"Then what about my dental plan?"

"I didn't know you had a dental plan."

"The idea that we be dentists. I've always liked to play with the tools when the dentist leaves the room."

"So have I," said Freddy. "Once, one of them caught me using his grinding wheel to cut a chevron into my signet ring. Mummy had to knight him."

"Freddy, dentistry can provide a good living if your destiny is not what you think."

"Did you read that on a matchbook?"

EVENING WAS ILLUMINED in golden light. The sun lay low on the fields, the air was cool, and the shadows deep. Startled by the barge train's engines and the blasts of its horns, pheasants and quail would explode from stunted hedgerows or clumps of dead branches, filling the sky with glitter.

"If we become dentists," Fredericka said, as she had argued throughout the day, "you would know, finally, what it is to live like a normal person."

"But I do know."

"That's just the point. You've been either the Prince of Wales or an impoverished spike driver. You haven't lived a normal life."

"Yes I have."

"Of course you haven't. You do all kinds of things that other people won't or can't do, and you don't even know it."

"Name one," said Freddy.

"For example, you're inside a room and I'm at the door." She rapped on the deck and, to make sure he understood, said, "Knock knock."

"Who will be there?" Freddy asked.

"You see?"

"See what?"

"You said, 'Who will be there?'"

"So?"

"No one says that."

"They don't?"

"No."

"What do they say?"

"They say, 'Who's there?'"

"That's ridiculous," said Freddy. "I've always said, 'Who will be there?'"

"It's incorrect."

"I don't believe you."

"That's because the only doors you knock on are your family's, and they all say, 'Who will be there?' and no one corrects them or you when you do."

"Fredericka," Freddy said as if she were stupid, "one doesn't really care who's outside in the hall. Servants or guards are always traipsing about or just standing there. One cares about who will be in the room *after* you permit them to enter. Thus, *who will be there?* We've always said it."

"Yes, it probably goes back hundreds of years. But it's wrong."

"It's wrong?" Freddy asked himself. "It's wrong? 'Who will be there?' is wrong?" He laughed. "I'm supposed to say, 'Who's there?' That's insane."

"Freddy, you often cannot even make yourself understood, or understand those to whom you speak. It happens all the time—not because anything is wrong with you, really, but because of your peculiar situation."

"I challenge you to produce an example."

"The professor."

To get to the Mississippi, they had hitch-hiked to Davenport, and had at one point been given a ride by a University of Iowa professor in a Volvo station wagon.

"What do you think of the Hawks?" the professor had asked in regard to the university's football team. But to royal ears unused to his Midwestern speech, he had said, "What do you think of the *hogs*?"

As they were on their way to Iowa, the prince and princess were not particularly surprised. "To be truthful," said Freddy diplomatically, "we haven't actually seen them, though they are world famous."

"They are?" the professor asked.

"Certainly."

"Then, you follow them?"

"Follow them? No, we don't follow them."

"How do you know about them?"

"I suppose I read about them in the encyclopaedia, or was made to study them in geography."

"What have they got to do with geography?"

"You know, those little bundles of wheat, and pieces of fruit, and cotton plants, factories, et cetera, that dot maps."

"What would that have to do with the Hawks?"

"They're on the maps, too."

"They'd be amazed to know that," the professor said. "I know some of them. I'll tell them."

"You know some of them?" Freddy asked.

"Yes, and I'll let them know."

"What good will that do?"

"It'll make them happy."

"If they could understand English."

"They understand English. They're all Americans."

"Indeed," said Freddy, "but they're dumb."

"They may not be . . . Einsteins," said the professor, "but they're not dumb. The rules don't allow it. If they're not capable of doing college work, they're not allowed to train."

Freddy laughed. "Train for what?" he asked. "Being sliced up and wrapped in plastic?"

"They're not that bad," the professor said, "though the Indians always whip them."

"The Indians shouldn't do that," Fredericka said. "You'd think that after what the Indians went through they wouldn't whip anyone."

"What do you expect the Indians to do?" he asked.

"To face up to the fact," Freddy said, "that under our direction they thrived, and when we left they were undone."

"You were an Indian?"

"Of course not," Freddy protested. "We were *not* Indians. That's my point."

"I don't understand," the professor said. "I thought you were fans."

"Fans?" Freddy asked incredulously. "What kind of fans?"

"Hawk fans," which sounded to the royals like *hog fans.*

"Good God, man, that's what electricity's for," Freddy stated.

"So," the professor asked, "how's the weather?"

Back on the barge, at evening, Fredericka said, "You see? You haven't had a real life. You don't know a thing. You're a freak."

"I don't know a thing? That's rich coming from someone who thinks that Cervantes is a dip for prawns, and who once told an interviewer that she wanted to be a reader for the deaf. What don't I know?"

"You don't know anything about women, for example. When Madame Zeitgeist invited you to name her perfumes—the most expensive in the world—you came up with what? *Tuna Salad, Liverwurst,* and *Delivery Wagon.*"

"What was wrong with those?" Freddy asked.

"What was wrong was that, because you are the Prince of Wales, before she went belly-up and died a laughingstock, the poor woman had to use them. And you have no tact, Freddy, no tact at all."

"I beg your pardon. I have extraordinary tact. I learnt it when dealing with people who wear bones in their noses. We have to keep them in the Empire, and so we must be tactful with them."

"You mean in New Guinea?"

"I mean in Soho."

"Freddy, someone with tact would not, at a state dinner, insist upon calling the chief of the French Secret Service 'Harry Covert.'"

"If they hadn't served them," Freddy protested, "I wouldn't have called him that, but the opportunity was too great to pass up."

"But a hundred times?"

"No one got it, that's why."

"The English got it right off. The French would never get it. They thought you were mad, pointing your finger and speaking in Pidgin English at their security chief: 'You! Harry Covert! You! Harry Covert!' and so on. Don't you understand? They thought you spent ten minutes calling him a green bean. The poor man didn't know what to say."

"He kept saying, *'Comment?'*"

"That's what they say. It doesn't mean to repeat it."

"Yes it does."

"No, Freddy, it doesn't. They thought you were insane."

Freddy grew silent. As they both listened to the ever present roll of the bow wave, she thought he was hurt, but it is harder to hurt someone who has lived his life as a prince than it is to hurt an ordinary person. He was thinking. He was contemplating. In the heart of her criticism, in the adversity of her comment, might lie a prize. For he had learnt not to oppose too quickly, and that wonderful things in this world are often carefully hidden. For example, a map of the Middle East that Her Britannic Majesty's Stationery Office had sent over for use in a strategical essay he was writing had stood drably and hardly worth notice on an easel next to his writing table. It was the colour of khaki lentil soup and, all in all, quite undistinguished. Then, entirely by chance, he arrived early one morning and for the first time saw the sun on it. In strong light it had taken on a life of its own. It had become the colour of the desert in morning—light yellows that spanned every possibility of yellow from near silver to far beyond gold, almost pale pinks as if from the glow of flowers blooming in the crease of a wadi. It had become a window looking into the desert itself, a portal of which he had been unaware until surprise and accident had brought it to him like an angel that descends a blinding ray.

"Yes," said Freddy, in his sovereignly, magnanimous tone, surprising Fredericka even though she had been at him in one way or another for hours. "We shall be dentists. Let us find a dreary, forgotten, wind-blown prairie town without a dentist, where no one ever comes and nothing could possibly happen. There we will settle, safe in our anonymity, away from the world, in unbreachable oblivion."

"THE ALUMINUM-TONGUED
ORATOR OF THE PLATTE"

ALTHOUGH NEITHER Freddy nor Fredericka had even a passing interest in American politics, they had parachuted into a nation approaching an election. By June, when they were almost ready to start practising dentistry in Siliphant, Nebraska, Senator Dewey Knott had secured the delegates necessary to claim the nomination of the GOP as its standard-bearer (which he unfailingly called the "standard bear") against the incumbent President Self. This would have made most anyone's heart rise, but not Dewey Knott's, for Dewey Knott was forty points behind a president he detested and who mocked him at every opportunity for his famed reticence and indecision. It was Dewey who had famously said, "Indecisiveness is next to Godliness." How so decent a man who was so indecisive could have become his party's presumptive nominee was one of the mysteries of democracy, but he did, and the president and his supporters revelled in it.

"Do we bomb Iraq, or Dewey Knott?" the president would ask the assembled faithful, who ate it up with a spoon. "Do we raise taxes, or Dewey Knott? Do we say the Pledge of Allegiance, or Dewey Knott? To be or Knott to be, that is the question," the president would boom in his Alaskan accent (he had been a beautician in Juneau), a mass of heavily lacquered hair clinging to his head like a hornets' nest on a gatepost, and horse-like teeth bared in perpetual smile. "America, do we, or Dewey Knott?"

Senator Knott's advisers were made of such stuff that the debate raging among them, details of which were leaked every day to sexual partners in the media, turned on whether or not to change the senator's name. It was not merely a binary question, for the faction that favoured the change was split into a camp that wanted to change his first name, a camp that wanted to change his last name, and a camp that wanted to change both. At this stage, a thousand people were working on the campaign, each with a perfect plan for victory. The only one without a plan, or even an inkling of one, was Dewey himself, but he was willing to listen to anyone, and follow each and every recommendation he received, whether or not one contradicted another. In regard to his name, some wanted to keep things familiar, by naming him Huey Knott, but they fell out of favour with him when others pointed out that Huey was too close to *Huey* in Huey Long. "Look," the senator had said, "Huey is not only like Huey, it is Huey."

So he went with this group for a while, until another pointed out that Louis, which is what the Huey rejectionists had proposed, was too much like Louis XIV. "Who the hell was he?" Dewey asked, and when told that he had been the king of France, asked to be briefed. "Not that I want to be king or anything, but I just want to know."

"Louis Quatorze was a brilliant political operative, a genius who united France," an aide stated.

"Yeah, but what about Louis the Fourteenth?"

"He was Louis the Fourteenth, Senator."

"Louis Quatorze and Louis the Fourteenth were the same guy?"

"Yes, sir."

"How'd they do that? Jeez, what are our other options?"

"Well, there's Mooey."

"Mooey? What's that for, the dairy farmers? They already like me. I'm the father," he said, neither for the first time nor the last, "of the cottage cheese subsidy."

"Not for the dairy vote, sir, for the African-American vote."

"The what?"

"The African-American vote."

"What's that?"

The aide blinked. "Well, you know, the votes cast by African Americans."

"What are they?"

"They're those people who are very dark?" another aide said, tentatively, and in the manner of the American generation (of which he was part) that could not make a statement except in the interrogative, not even their names ("Hello? My name is Britney Hitler? I'm, like, very glad to meet you? My grandfather was, like, the Führer? In, like, Germany? Okay?"). When Dewey Knott showed no sign whatsoever of familiarity with African Americans, the aide was stymied.

"Whadaya mean, dark? Who?"

"They make up more than, ten percent of the vote?"

"They do?"

"Yes."

"Whadaya mean they're dark? I don't understand. Are they depressed? Dewey Knott was depressed, then he took Prozac, but that's a secret."

"They're not, depressed? It's just that, they're not white?"

"Oh!" said Dewey Knott. "I know them. Blacks! It's a generational thing. Dewey Knott calls them blacks. That's my generation, that's all. I'm white, I'm not a European American. They don't call us European Americans, do they?"

"No."

"So, you know, why should we call . . . that's not the point. Why would changing my name to Mooey take the black vote from Self?"

"Because that's what Howard Cosell called Muhammad Ali," the older aide answered.

"Why'd he do that? That's what you call a cow."

"Muhammad. Mooey."

"Oh. Do you think he would endorse me?"

"He might."

"Would I have to become a Muslim?"

"I don't think so, but we'll keep it on the table."

"What else have you got?"

Dewey was speaking to the leader of the faction that had come to be called *the rhymers,* who held his tongue in statesmanly fashion, although some of his young assistants were working on Fooey, Stewy, and Glooey, and back to the mail room for them, although, someday in the far future they too would run presidential campaigns.

Unbeknownst to the rhymers, Senator Knott had secret meetings with the plain speakers. They were simple in their approach, having boldly abandoned the pattern based on Dewey. "What about John?" one asked.

"John. John Knott. Sounds good. 'John Knott will lead you into the future. Vote Knott for president.' I like it. I'll think about it."

That aide left with a glow that came of visions of the flag in his office in the John Knott administration. But, among the thousand, many glowed and danced on air with visions of a flag in their futures, including the proponents of Bruce, Larry, Herman, Arthur, and Cecil, all of which Dewey Knott liked and promised to consider.

They were so desperate to get the votes of women that a faction arose that wanted Dewey Knott to change his name to Alice.

"Why would I do that?" he asked, rather disturbed.

"To get the women's vote, sir. You know how much we're behind. Our polling shows that if you changed your name to Alice, Frieda, or Betty, you'd get back between four and five percent of the women's vote. That could put us over the top."

"How about Cleopatra?" another aide asked.

"Cleopatra?"

"Cleopatra Knott."

"Cleopatra Knott. Cleopatra Knott. Gee, I don't know. I'll have to think it over. What would be the effect on the men's vote if I had a girl's name?"

"We haven't studied that aspect of the question."

"I have," said a young aide, who, for speaking out of turn in the presence of Dewey Knott (thus threatening the position of his immediate superiors), was marked for death by the campaign's middle management. "You'd drop by forty-seven points among men."

"It's not worth it," Dewey said.

"Definitely not. I mean, no."

"Don't ever tell me that you want me to change my name to a girl's name again," Dewey Knott said to the lad who led that faction, "but maybe we'll look at it later on."

While Dewey had been campaigning in North Dakota—because even if he lost he wanted to sweep the plains states, and, to the delight of the antelope, ended up spending most of his time there—a bunch of young Turks arose at campaign headquarters in Washington. They wanted to change his last name, and they, too, were deeply factionalised. The "timids" wanted him to become Dewey Scott. He rejected this on the grounds of rhyme. He was learning, as the campaign progressed, to understand these things. A small group of senior advisers came to him with the suggestion that he change his name to Washington.

"Dewey Washington? That doesn't sound right."

"We know it doesn't, Senator, but what we didn't tell you is that while you were in North Dakota we spent a long time thrashing this out and we've come to the conclusion that you should be really bold, take the bull by the horns, and change both your names. In for a dime, in for a dollar."

"Yeah, that's good, but to what?"

"George Washington. Your polls go sky-high with that name. On trust and integrity, you go through the roof."

"You polled?"

"Yes, sir."

"How much did it cost us?"

"A hundred and fifty thousand."

"It better be good."

"It is good, it's very good," a young politechnician said, and then, reading from the text of the study, he continued: "When asked, 'For whom would you vote if your first consideration were integrity, trust, and honesty . . . the president, or George Washington?' ninety-eight percent chose you."

"Chose me, or George Washington?"

"This is assuming that you change your name to George Washington."

"Did you tell them that I was going to do that?"

"Tell who?"

"The people you polled."

"No, we had to maintain absolute secrecy. But what's the problem?"

So many different factions arose that the senator didn't know what to do. While it was easy to reject names like The Flying Nun, Admiral Dewey, and Berkeley Yamamoto, nothing was rejected conclusively. "Everything's on the table," Dewey had said. "That's how you win. You don't rule things out, and you don't rule things in. You keep those balls in the air. That's how I got where I am, and it's how I'll get where I'm going. By the way, where are we going? I hope it's not California. They hate me in California. But they love Dot (Mrs Knott). They love Dot in California, but they don't love me."

"They do love you, Senator, we just haven't found the right way to get you across."

"Idoh know, maybe Harrison is right, maybe I should change my name to La Pasionaria, Idoh know. We should send Dot there. She's really good. They love her. They don't love me. What has Dot got that Dewey Knott has not got? Dot Knott is hot, and Dewey Knott is not. Dot Knott is a hot Knott, but Dewey Knott is a Hottentot. She's hot, she's hot, and I am Knott, not Knott, but not hot, that's what she's got, Dot Knott. What has Dot got, that Dewey Knott. . . ."

This was what his aides termed the Dr Seuss death spiral, when the plane that held Dewey's consciousness went into a dive. Nothing could stop it except extreme shock. They always tried to avoid this, because for Dewey to be slapped in the face by his aides would be unpresidential.

"Mrs Knott's going with you to Nebraska," an aide said, but this didn't do the trick.

"They love Dot in California. California's a big state. Big. Lotta vegetables. Lotta electoral votes. Surfboards. They'd vote for Dot. But they won't vote for me. They really love Dot there. . . ."

"Senator," an aide interrupted, knowing that a press conference was about to begin and the press liked nothing better than for Dewey Knott to talk like Dr Seuss. "Senator, someone said that there was a *Uganda Tribune* story, or something like that, that said the president punched a little girl in a wheelchair."

"Why Dot? Why not Dewey Knott? Why Dot Knott and not Dewey Knott? Can you figure it? California? They love Dot Knott. . . ." There was a pause. "The president what?"

"He punched, a little girl?" the young aide who could speak only in the interrogative said. "Who was in a, wheelchair? Who was, like, trying to give him flowers?"

"Dear God," said Dewey Knott, "did he really?" He was out of the spiral.

"No, Senator," said a non-interrogatively challenged aide. "He didn't."

"Why'd you tell me that?"

By this time, the young fellow who had told him had left for a week's paid leave. "We didn't."

"Someone did. Didn't someone say. . . ."

"No sir."

"Damn, I thought I heard someone say the president punched a little girl in a wheelchair. Are you sure it isn't true? Run it down. Get a kid on the computer. It would make all the difference in the world if he had. That could give us twenty-five points."

"The press conference is starting in five minutes."

Dewey Knott began to walk, followed by dozens of people, toward the press conference. "Where are we going Monday?" he asked decisively.

"This is Monday."

"Where are we going next?"

"Siliphant."

"That's good. Get back home. Siliphant. My hometown. Maybe if I'm president it'll stop shrinking. Maybe it won't die."

WHEN FIRST they had arrived in Siliphant, to take over the practice of a dentist who had died more than a decade previously, Freddy and Fredericka had seen a ratty sign at the entrance to town. It looked like it was printed in apple butter: *Welcome to Siliphant, Nebraska, Birthplace of Dewey Knott.*

"Is that the Dewey Knott who's running for president?" Fredericka had asked whilst still in the Greyhound.

"I assume so," was Freddy's answer.

"Did you ever meet him?"

"No. I met his predecessor as majority leader of the Senate, Senator Knuckles."

"What if he comes back?"

"I don't think he will, Fredericka. He died a number of years ago, and earthly resurrection is unavailable even to senators, although they themselves may be unaware of this."

"He died?" Fredericka asked.

"Had you read newspapers then you would have known that, in inaugurating a water slide, he bunched up at an elbow and drowned in the water for which he served as the plug. No one knew where he was, only that he had failed to come out and that the water, which was running at a tremendous volume, had stopped. By the time they understood what was happening, many tonnes of water had collected, and when finally he gave way the force of the water shot him out of the tube and he flew through the air like a cannonball."

"How can he run for president if he's dead?"

"Knott is running, Knuckles drowned. Knott is peculiar. It's rather a miracle that he's gone as far in politics as he has. As soon as he garners an advantage he throws it away by doing something honourable. In one moment he's a traditional politician, and in the next he may respond to a crucial question with complete and self-devastating honesty. He's the one who once lost the nomination by saying in debate: 'You know, I don't really know anything about that. I was supposed to read the briefing book, but there was a sale on men's trousers and I just didn't have time. Why don't you ask him'—his opponent—'I'll bet he knows.'"

"I see," Fredericka said. "I hope that Knott doesn't come here. After all, he was born here. He would be sure to bring the press with him, including representatives of the British press, and then what would we do?"

"Why would he come here?" Freddy asked. "What do you think he is, a salmon? He'll never come to this Godforsaken place. It would remind the whole nation of everything he wants them to forget. Don't worry. We're safe."

"I don't know, Freddy."

"And really, Fredericka, even if all of Fleet Street were to arrive on our doorstep, it would hardly matter."

"Why not?"

"We'd take out our new teeth and put back some big ones, brush our hair in front of our faces, put on sunglasses, and talk like idiots. Why would they think that two American dentists in Nebraska, idiots with huge teeth, would be us? Even our parents wouldn't recognise us."

Their first weeks in Siliphant were spent reading dental books and peering into one another's mouths. They studied for fourteen hours a day, and cleaned one another's teeth so often that they had nightmares about wearing them down to pointy little stumps. For the first time in her life, Fredericka lost herself in the tumultuous passion of hard study and concentration. Her brain worked as strenuously as a cowboy driving a huge herd of cattle across a wilderness. Never had she felt this particular kind of exhaustion. With illumination from a blue dental spotlight, she raced across the pages, trying to commit to memory in four weeks the expanse of knowledge necessary for completing four years of dental school. They ate as they studied, usually wretched take-out Chinese food drowning in ketchup, which in Siliphant was the only thing available other than huge steaks that looked like the India rubber balls Amazon natives carry in their canoes down to Manaus.

In the dental practice they had bought for less than a song, the lights often burned all night. Fredericka assimilated in a delirium all she needed to know about teeth, and when Freddy tested her he was as pleased as he had been on the hillside in West Virginia. He saw now that her intellect, her capacity for memorisation, the potential depth of her erudition, and her scholarly discipline, were as great as his, or perhaps—and this was terrifying—greater.

Even as they exercised they jammed every bit of dental knowledge they could into their heads. They did calisthenics, they lifted bottles of water from the water cooler, and they ran at night through the few streets of Siliphant, drilling, always drilling: that is, accomplishing feats of memory and mental training; they had not yet turned to their equipment.

Three o'clock in the morning, 101 degrees, windows open, Freddy sitting on Fredericka's feet and ankles, Fredericka dressed in very short shorts and a royal purple tank top, doing sit-ups, bathed in sweat. Although she had shaved her legs, Freddy could feel a minute stubble on what was otherwise dolphin-smooth flesh, and he found this exciting. Nonetheless, he held in abeyance his intoxication with her sapphire eyes and golden visage, her deep breathing, the taut muscles of her abdomen, the beauty of her movement toward him and then away, the circle of her mouth, through which breaths came hard through brilliantly white teeth that he himself had polished. Her whole body glistened, and though he desired her as one can only when it is over a hundred degrees at three o'clock in the morning and the wind from the plains makes the curtains dance like waves, he said, "Fredericka, tell me about the dental pulp."

As she rose and fell, water dripping from her lasciviously, she answered, "A soft, vascular, sensitive organ made up of myxomatous tissues, containing many blood vessels and nerves that enter by way of the apical foramina. It does not possess lymphatics. The periphery of the pulp is bounded by layers of cells arranged like columnar epithelium, each cell sending one or more branched processes through the basic substance of the dentine."

"And what are these?" asked Freddy, entranced by her beauty.

"These," she said confidently, "are the dentine-forming cells, the odontoblasts of Waldeyer. The blood vessels break up into the innumerable capillary loops which lie beneath the layer of odontoblasts. The nerve fibrils break up into numberless non-medullary filaments, which spread out beneath the odontoblasts, and probably send terminal filaments to the extreme periphery of the pulp outside the odontoblasts."

She took a breath. "Freddy, I'm rock-solid on the odontoblasts and anything to do with the pulp. Hit me with the biochemistry of the stellate reticulum, and then I've got to loosen up after all these sit-ups, so let's put on some music."

After she aced the question about the biochemistry of the stellate reticulum and had finished her one thousand sit-ups, they put on the music. In Siliphant, her intellect had exploded like a supernova, and, finally, Freddy had learned to dance.

Freddy was unusual. Why wouldn't he be? He had grown up destined either to be a king or to die a rotten death. There were many ways of living lively, and one of them, he had discovered, was to live with a perpetual sense of combat—combat against his own limitations and heredity, combat against the prevailing wisdom when it was wrong, combat against the drift and degradation of civilisation. He wanted to win, of course, but this was not his object. His object was to fight on. In fighting, and in risk, was purification. This he had learned from his father, his ancestors, his reading of history and literature, and in the doing. It was why he made his great treks across England and Scotland and climbed to the summit of glacier-clad mountains, why he studied and practised physical combat, parachuted, flew helicopter gunships, ran minesweepers off the Hebrides, and, much more dangerously, took on modernists and the avant-garde, in the bitterest combat of all. He was only one, and they were many, so many in fact that they were a country, an alliance of states, a world. Freddy was not afraid to pit himself, as truth required, against the direction of things. He was well known for participating in disputes of which he had less expert knowledge than the many seasoned gladiators who lined up to bang his shield with their swords. But it was a royal shield, and he held it bravely, spinning in the periphery of his vision those scenes, from deep in his blood, of knights in mortal struggle while encased in gleaming metal. The swords flew in slow motion and the horses accomplished their noble and sacrificial manoeuvres. All of it—the colour and compression of time, the cries, the poignant glances, the risen dust and falling halberds—came to Freddy in intense and wracking silence. Such things were with him even while drinking tea in the midst of vacant chatter, which, at home, he did too much.

A person of this nature is not partial to dancing, if only because, in his eyes, things that move—rising dust, falling water, rampant horses—tend to still or slow. He is too contemplative to dance. But Fredericka had come a long way into Freddy's world, and he thought it would be ungenerous not to reciprocate. Just as certain things had unfolded for her, so they did for him, in the dentist's office that now was theirs in Siliphant, Nebraska, in a fire of prairie heat.

They had an old gramophone—a Victrola—that played 78s and took a while to warm up. But when it did and its vacuum tubes glowed strongly, Freddy put on a ballad sung by a woman long gone, a gentle, measured progression in a minor key. When Freddy took Fredericka in his arms and they waltzed slowly across the room, time stopped within the sheltering vault of this music. Their slow turning built around them a chamber in which they found themselves beneath an imagined deep blue dome in which was embedded a cloth of gently shining stars. And that was of little moment compared with the dishevelled, heat-curled fall of Fredericka's hair, her wise and tender expression, and the great trust that had arisen between them. Who was this woman who had become so wise, sagacious, and true?

She was easily as wonderful as the transcendent combats of which he had dreamt from his earliest and most despondent childhood, and she was not a dream.

NOT LONG AFTER the dance with Fredericka that in Freddy's memory would always be bracketed by white curtains moving on the wind and lifted on the air as easily as doves, there was a different kind of dancing in a hotel in Omaha. The dancers were young women in white cowboy hats, tasselled white boots, and sequined bathing suits that sparkled violently in red, white, and blue. They moved in perfect synchrony to a thundering beat and the enticing clash of cymbals. In light so bright and music so overwhelming, they were white hot, an Omaha Niagara, and they were dancing for Dewey Knott. But Dewey Knott himself did not dance, and neither did Dot. Dewey Knott did not dance, however, in a different way than Dot Knott did not dance.

Dot Knott did not dance because she was as shy as a little girl, and when asked to dance, she would explode in cascades of nervous laughter that conveyed very strongly not only amused embarrassment but an all-encompassing fear and panic that wrenched her soul. Everyone knew that to make Dot Knott sweat all you had to do was to ask her onto the floor, and since day one, Dewey Knott's political opponents had sent operatives to his fund-raisers to ask Dot to dance.

But, for Dewey, not dancing was quite different. When he was alone in his office and had just won a primary or another term, he would put on music and dance with such unmitigated fury that it made the paroxysms of voodoo look like Calvin Coolidge at nap time. He would prance across the floor, jump on his desk, put on hats, throw things in the air, writhe like a snake, and howl like an owl. On the rare occasions that Dot stumbled upon this, she would say, in great distress, "Oh, Dewey!" and leave the room. But it didn't discourage Dewey. Risking that C-Span had placed a hidden camera in his Capitol rooms, he would hop and jump the whole long length of marble in the reception area. He may have been crippled in politics by his senseless honesty, a true love of country, and the oratorical skills of a Popsicle, but he could dance the pants off anyone in Washington.

Never, never, never, however, in public. His ability to experience ecstasy in dance was none of anyone's business. Perhaps his hesitation honoured an ancient Nebraskan taboo brought to the grasslands by the wagon trains. Perhaps it was simple modesty. Whatever it was, Dewey Knott would not dance in public.

Dewey had found the strength to go against the conventional wisdom, and had been inspired to eschew public display, in an essay someone had clipped for him from a theological journal, an essay about public dancing and Western morals—the author of which had just learned to dance in the town where Dewey Knott had been pulled from his mother's womb and slapped on his behind so that he would take his first, magnificent, shocking breath of air, upon which followed his last decisive *cri de coeur.*

But he could not make his views known to the public. Had he simply stated the case from his heart, where it lay, he might have rocketed in the polls and cut the president's lead in half. And had C-Span actually had a camera hidden to record his hops, his shaking, his spinning, his leaps into the air and onto his desk, he would have eaten up the forty-point lag and pulled way ahead. But he didn't know this, and even had he known it he wouldn't have taken the risk, and even had he taken the risk he would have delayed so long and prepared so carefully that he would have danced stiffly and self-consciously, killed the whole thing, plummeted in the polls, and lost the election without carrying even Siliphant.

What was the point of fighting when you were forty points behind? The point was in the fight itself. He refused to give up, he was so dogged, because he was an honest man who had chosen a dishonest way of life and, out of a sense of honour, patriotism, and obligation, he had slogged through that life, hating its every falsity, and hating himself when it overtook him. Losing was, therefore, the kind of punishment that purified him and restored the balance of honour that he needed to survive. He was grateful, then, for every form of distress. President Self had no idea of anything except that he had to be powerful and adored. Dewey understood that having power and being adored was, as Dewey himself would have put it, "a bucket of shit." He was in it for the suffering.

That evening in Omaha, in front of a thousand Nebraska Republicans, Dewey Knott, or George Washington, or Cleopatra, or whoever he was, intended to give a defining (which he pronounced *deafening*) speech to rescue his gangrenous campaign. True, he had already given half a dozen other deafening speeches to rescue his gangrenous campaign, and each had only made things worse, but they had been written by his former chief speechwriter, Campbell Mushrom, which meant that each ended in the phrase, "With liberty and justice for all." And each described Senator Knott as a "mild-mannered legislator," who had come to "Gotham by the Potomac," from "a far-off place, to serve the American ideal."

Most of Dewey's advisers loved this approach and thought it made Dewey seem truly extraordinary and heroic, or, as Campbell would say, "like a man of steel." But Dewey looked at the polls, and canned Mushrom, although Russel Haverstraw, who replaced him, wanted to exult in his new position, and hired Campbell back as a luggage carrier for Dot's valises, a very cruel thing not only because he had to be strapped to the top of the car but because the things he carried were very heavy, which endangered his heart and made him sweat a lot, which plastered down his waterfall of immense curly black hair into two page-boy halves as big as tennis rackets, which caused him to look like a wretched medieval varlet, or, from the perspective of the Secret Service helicopter above the motorcade, and because Mushrom was six feet six, a horribly scrawny deer or some sort of extra-terrestrial moose.

The new speech was to be unlike all others. It was written for delivery in Siliphant, where Dewey's heart supposedly was. As everyone in the United States knew, Dewey's heart was on K Street. But, like the contents of reliquaries, politicians are given the benefit of the doubt, for reasons of state and because one of the sustaining fictions of American life is that beneath the shifting scenery that has replaced his soul a politician has bedrock that can be detected by watching him on television as he walks through his hometown with his jacket off.

He was supposed to deliver the speech in Siliphant, but he refused: "Omaha. Nobody knows Siliphant. Omaha's big. Got a bigger auditorium." That's all he would say, and no one could sway him. But Siliphant was his hometown, not Omaha. People associated Omaha with dainty octogenarian trainers of animals, nuclear weapons, and big bloody cuts of beef. Siliphant, by contrast, was Americana. The shots they had of Siliphant, always with at least one corner emblazoned with the passionate colours of the flag, went so well with ersatz Aaron Copland music that the film editors had to put Saran Wrap over their mixing controls lest their tears short-circuit their efforts. It had to be Siliphant. The speechwriting team almost went on strike. After all, they had produced this masterpiece only for a particular setting. "Nope," said Dewey, "Omaha."

The newsmagazines and networks hired professors and political commentators to figure out why, and they came up with all sorts of reasons. By giving the speech in Omaha, Dewey was putting the Russians on notice, just as one of their leaders would be sending the same rudimentary signal were he to give an important speech from the epicentre of their ICBM fields. It was the candidate's way of asserting himself without any possibility of misinterpretation. (The proponents of this interpretation did not concern themselves with the fact that the speech was to introduce Dewey's proposal that Medicare cover cosmetic surgery for exterminators.) Others claimed that he was making a statement about the quality of transience in American history, Americans' lack of roots, the near but decisive distances between kith and kin, hearth and home, and hell and high water.

In fact, Dewey did leave Siliphant, and his heart was there no longer. But he remembered. He remembered his father and his mother, and his childhood and young manhood before he moved into the public eye. He didn't want to use Siliphant to attain the presidency. Siliphant was a town, full (not so full any more) of good people. They could film it, because it was a public place. They could talk about it. Reporters could go there and ask people about how Dewey drank milkshakes or went to the graveyard on Halloween, but he himself would not go there, because, when he did, he was too moved by the past, and it knocked him akilter.

Dewey was chatting with Dot and trying to eat his fourteen-inch-thick steak when suddenly he went white. Though his body locked, his hands grasped the thick linen tablecloth and began to bunch it up in folds, which knocked over a glass or two and moved the plates of some very important contributors.

"Dewey?" Dot asked, in cold terror. "Dewey?"

They didn't know whether he was having a heart attack or required the Heimlich manoeuvre. Whatever it was, the most important thing, more important even than keeping him alive, was that the press had to be kept away. But two hundred television cameras stood nearby on their massive tripods, like the weapons of alien invaders, topped by blinding lights and manned on the dark side by liberals in ponytails, beards, and leather jackets.

"Dewey?" Dot asked again, thinking that she might soon be a widow.

Then he unlocked, gave a violent shudder, and reeled, except that he held the table and went nowhere. It had taken all his discipline to keep from crying out.

"Dot," he said, "my tooth. I must have an abscess or something. I don't know if I can stay conscious. When I bit into that steak, it all came apart.

My right upper molar. The jaw must be shot. Who the hell knows what's in there."

"What about the speech, Senator? Can you give the speech?" whispered Haverstraw, a nasty preppy who wore tweed pyjamas. "Perhaps you oughtn't to. You're to rise in two minutes."

"I can do it," said Dewey. "Bring me a can of Scotch."

"It doesn't come in cans."

"Fill a Coke can, moron. That's what we do in the Senate."

"Are you sure?"

"Been doing it for years. Why do you think the Senate's like it is?"

"I mean, that you want it now?"

"No. Make it two cans."

"Birds?" Haverstraw asked, as a witticism.

"Birds? Whadaya mean, birds? Get me two cans of Scotch. Hurry up. I'm dying."

Haverstraw sprinted to the bar, took two cans of Coke and a bottle of Scotch, stepped behind a curtain, and emptied the cans. Half the Fourth Estate—perhaps, therefore, the Second Estate—upon seeing two trouser legs and a cascade of foaming liquid coming down between them, came to the conclusion that Dewey's chief speechwriter was very ill. Haverstraw got the Scotch to Dewey just as the lights dimmed (President Self had said, cruelly, that dimming had been invented in Dewey's honour), the noise began to abate, and a spotlight anxiously searched the room. As a harsh amplified voice introduced "the Republican nominee, the senior senator from our own great state of Nebraska, the majority leader of the United States Senate, and the next president of the United States," Dewey Knott imbibed two pints of Scotch like an elephant eating a peanut. Dewey wasn't a drinker, and could not hold his liquor, but Dot guided him to the podium, her smile rigid and moon-like, every muscle in her body as tense as the spring of a mousetrap.

She thought that all might go well if Dewey could complete his text before the alcohol was cleared from his pancreas, or wherever it went just before it screwed up your political career. But what she didn't know, and every pickup-driving, backward-baseball-capped, pimply adolescent boy in America knows, is that Scotch from a Coke can is, as in his glory days Campbell Mushrom would have put it, "faster than a speeding bullet and more powerful than a locomotive." By the time Dewey Knott grabbed the lectern to steady himself in the world that was twirling all around him, he felt able to leap tall buildings at a single bound.

As he gripped the helm and tried to calm the rolling seas, his supporters swayed with him out of something more than politeness: it was like a cross between a tennis match and a group of Girl Scouts singing "Kumbaya" at a campfire. The first thing he said was, "That's why they write it down on little bieces" (he said *bieces,* not *pieces*) "of paper, so you can read it no matter what happens. It's like the Constitution. It's on paper, too." He paused while his eyes swam fifty yards. "So you won't forget it. Right?"

"Right!" his audience shouted.

Haverstraw called out, in a whisper, "Senator, just read the speech."

"No!" Dewey Knott shouted, with peculiar emphasis and emotion. But he was not answering Haverstraw, whom he had not heard, he was taking exception to his last statement. "It's not like the Constitution, it's like an insurance policy, that they wrote it down on a paper, and all it is, is a lotta little lines, that go this way and that way, and this way and that way." He pointed quaquaversally with all his fingers. "Who did the writing?" he asked. "Who?"

"Your team, sir," said an aspiring new Mushrom from behind the lights and the ponytails.

"Not my *team,*" Dewey answered, tremendously irritated. "It was the Fo . . . it was the Fo . . . it was the Fo-something. You know, they had those fishhooks, what was their name?"

"The Phoenicians," offered a really attractive brunette in a really low-cut dress, at a table dangerously near the front.

"Yeah," said Dewey, "it was the Phoenicians. Did they invent the telephone?"

As the audience was almost as inebriated as Dewey himself, and the camera operators were stoned, no one except Dewey's staff, Dot, and the rest of the world knew that anything was amiss. Haverstraw said, "Read the goddamned speech!" His career, too, was on the line.

"Okay," Dewey answered, saying, as he unfolded the paper, "I haven't looked at this, this, whatever it is. I know I was supposed to. I was supposed to look at it. I'm always supposed to look at it, but . . . like a bad little bee, I don't. So here goes.

"Oh," he said. "Okay. Here's the line, up here. Ready? *Three score and nine years ago, Dewey Knott was brought forth onto this continent by his parents,*

Askew and Lola. You see," he said, "this illustrates why you should always use the serial comma. If you thought that you shouldn't, you would think that I was brought forth by my parents, and by Askew, and by Lola, who were midwives or something. But if you did, and it was gone here, as it is, you'd know that my parents were Askew and Lola. See? Who wrote this? Did Mushrom write this? Where's the crap about Superman? Or is that coming?"

Way in the back of the room, Mushrom was moved almost to tears. He had been with Senator Knott for a quarter of a century, and in that time not once had the senator mentioned his name in public, and this was going out all over the world, even pre-empting soccer matches in Brazil.

"No one ever called my father Askew. They called him Ask. When he heard Kennedy's inaugural address on the radio—'Ask Knott . . . what you can do for your country'—he thought Kennedy was talking to him in jive. Let's see," Dewey said, turning back to the text. "*Three score and nine years ago, Dewey Knott was brought forth on this continent by his parents, Askew and Lola. Now we are engaged in a great campaign, testing whether this Knott or any Knott so conceived can long endure. . . .* What is this? Did Mushrom write this? This is the goddamned Gettysburg Address."

"No it isn't," Haverstraw said, standing up. "And I wrote it."

"Abraham Lincoln wrote it," Dewey stated flatly.

"He did not."

"Like hell he didn't, you little shit."

"I resent that, Senator. The speech plays off the syncopes and the zeugmas of the Gettysburg Address, yes, and it is referential in homage to the Gettysburg Address, yes, but it isn't the Gettysburg Address."

"Fuck you, it's the Gettysburg Address."

"How could it be?" Haverstraw asked, his initial anger becoming panic as he was unable to sustain his indignation under a concentrated Dewey attack in front of so many television cameras. "Lincoln wrote it on the back of an envelope. Is that an envelope you've got in your hand? Is it? Is it?"

"Yeah, well I happen to know that Lincoln didn't write it on the back of an envelope, in fact. People think he did because someone made a joke about Lincoln writing the Gettysburg *Address* on an *envelope.* Get it? Other people, obviously your ancestors, were so stupid they didn't know it was a joke—they were too busy screwing around with their syncopes and their zeugmas—and they thought he really did write it on an envelope. You're fired."

Dewey Knott then moved his head up and to his left, grasped his jaw with both hands, closed his eyes, and howled like a wolf. Every network news program opened with this for days. The president's arrogant little snots began referring to the presumed Republican nominee as Wolf Man Knott. Teenagers loved what he did, but they didn't vote. Among likely voters, Dewey Knott was preferred in the instapoll by fourteen percent, as opposed to seventy-two percent who preferred the president, and fourteen percent who "didn't know." These people also "didn't know" when asked which was bigger, the sun or the moon, what country they lived in, or whether they were animal, vegetable, or mineral. All this, however, would be immaterial to the nominee, who wanted only to get his tooth fixed.

As he charged offstage, Dot ran for the microphone and, as unruffled as a bomb-squad robot, began to walk through the audience, reading a speech that Mushrom had been writing as things spun out of control. It was a thousand words long, and she was able to memorise it on the instant. After all, she had been the first female dean of the Harvard Business School, at age twenty-three. The problem was that Mushrom had had a bit to drink himself: "My husband knows that America is great, and he loves freedom, and he knows that we face the future. Like a small child from another planet sent to the world to fight for justice and the American way, he knows that his special powers. . . ."

Waiting in the wings, perturbed in his own inimitable fashion—that is, somehow, very deeply but only slightly—was Dewey Knott's chief of staff, John "What the hell am I doing in this business?" Finney. Ancestrally wealthy, naturally brilliant, and actually principled, he was Dewey's chief of staff primarily because he wanted the Senate to run smoothly, reflect its ancient traditions, and survive. In the unlikely event that Dewey Knott were to become president, Finney was willing to go with him as his White House chief of staff, because he knew that Dewey needed him. He would have much preferred to have been secretary of state, and he knew that Dewey would appear to promise this to him while promising nothing, just as he knew that were Dewey to become president, he, Finney, would stay as chief of staff during the whole Knott administration, for God and country.

"John!" Dewey said when they were alone in the greenroom. "I drank two Coke cans of whisky."

"I know. Mrs Knott is out there saving you."

"Call her Dot, John."

"I will, Senator." He would never call her Dot, but always Mrs Knott. Dewey Knott commanded him to call Dot Knott Dot every time Finney called her Mrs Knott, but Finney was formal in his ways.

"You'll call her Mrs Knott, not Dot, I know you. Call her Dot, not Mrs Knott. I had to drink them. There's a fire in my jaw."

"Abscess?"

"My God!"

"We'll get you to a dentist right away. We'll go now. The speech will be explained by its context."

"No one can know," Dewey squeaked, sweating in agony.

"Why not, Senator?"

"They'll think that if I'm president and I get a toothache, I'll get us into a nuclear war. This is more than a toothache, and when I'm president I'll know I'm president, but I'm not president now, so if I needed a bottle of Scotch to deal with this, it's okay."

"Can you hold on until we get back to Washington? We'll have your dentist waiting and ready to go."

"No," Dewey said, tears streaming down his cheeks. "I can't."

"We don't know anyone here we can trust."

"I do. In Siliphant. My dentist when I was a kid. When my brother shot himself through the leg with a twenty-two, he was the one, even though he was a dentist, who treated it, and didn't tell my parents. He's discreet."

"We'll call him."

"He doesn't like that."

"What?"

"Telephone calls. Very old-fashioned. Uses a foot-drill. Let's just go. He lives in his office and he's always there. Hasn't left Siliphant since the twenties."

"What if he's dead?" Finney asked.

"John," Dewey said, as if he were talking to an idiot, "how could that be?"

Instead of going to the airport, Senator Knott's motorcade turned onto the interstate and sped toward Siliphant, press in hot pursuit, Dewey Knott kicking the front seatback of the limousine like someone doing bicycle exercises on a floor mat. The press were afraid and strangely silent, because they had never been in the void into which they were now headed, but only flown over it. Omaha was bad enough, but beyond Omaha, in the black of night, was nothing.

.   .   .

FREDDY AND FREDERICKA stood at the open second-floor window of their frame house and office in Siliphant, breathing-in a strong current of air that, courtesy of the lightning on the plains and the snows of the Rockies, was clean and relatively cool. They watched the stars blaze and the flickering of distant lights in another town on the plain, which seemed as remote and mysterious as a fully lit ship silently ploughing the dark across a long stretch of sea. They could hear not only the wind but the faint rumble of lorries on the interstate five miles away, patiently grinding toward the Atlantic or the Pacific. The air moved in waves and immense billows, carrying the scents of distant grassfires, cattle, and the innumerable tons of sage that blanketed tens of thousands of square miles and perfumed the night.

No one in the world knew where they were. Thus lost, they had the effortless freedom of ghosts, and felt as if they could float on the wind and blow through solid obstacles without touching them. Had there been trees on the plain, oak or ash, and had Freddy and Fredericka been taken on the wind, like dandelion seeds, they suspected that they might have passed through the tangle of branches and the heavy trunks as smoothly as the dead. But they were alive, they felt as bright as light, and they were framed by gauze curtains ebbing and flowing on the incoming wind.

Freddy stood behind Fredericka, his left arm curved around her back, his right grasping her waist. She had turned her head sharply to the right, and they were kissing. Her skin was sweet and fresh from a day in the sun and because it was always like that anyway, and he could see the lights of the distant town vaguely shining in her sky-clear eyes. In kissing her now, perhaps because they had made themselves insane with dentistry, he was especially aware of her teeth, which were like the perfect snow cliffs of Greenland. Now they had numbers that he knew, and now he knew the anatomy of the lips and tongue, but these things, this knowledge, came and left in the trance he was in, perfumed by sage, as he stroked her cheeks and hair. Sometimes it seemed as if they were moving, slowly revolving like astronauts separated from their ships, and sometimes it was as if they lay together, and sometimes it was as if they were just a foot or two over the floor, having kissed their way free of gravity. "No one ever told me this about Nebraska," Fredericka whispered. As light as the curtains and lost even to time, they might have gone on all night, kissing lavishly by the open window, except that, after a while, they realised that someone was calling to them. They stirred and almost acknowledged a person on the pavement, but sank back into their lovely delirium. Then, as in a double take, they snapped out and looked down.

"Don't you hear me?" Finney asked. "Can you hear? I've been trying to attract your attention."

The doorbell was ringing, someone was pounding on the door, and the street was full of limousines and police cars. Rotating red and blue lights made the neighbourhood look like London in the Blitz, though it was so quiet that, despite the idling engines, crickets and tree frogs still filled the air with their beautiful madness.

Freddy and Fredericka looked at Finney, a compact, foreshortened, impressive figure in a suit. A suit in Siliphant? Limousines? Motorcycles? Range-Rover-like vehicles with the heft (instantly recognisable to Freddy and Fredericka) of armour plate? It could mean only one thing.

"They've found us," Freddy said. "How in God's name did they find us? It's over."

Fredericka was straightening her hair, hoping that she would not be photographed for an hour or so, for the blood had run so heavily into her skin that she was covered in scarlet, and her eyes had that opium look that comes from complete loss of self and the world in lovemaking. At least she and Freddy were still dressed.

"Are you the dentist?" Finney asked, sceptically. Though he couldn't see Fredericka very well in the dark, still, he couldn't take his eyes from her.

"Maybe they haven't found us," Freddy said sotto voce to Fredericka.

"Excuse me," Finney shouted in exasperation, "are you the dentist?"

"I regret that the previous dentist is dead," said Freddy in the same tone that he would have used in giving a Latin oration in the Sheldonian Theatre. Perhaps this was due to his elevated vantage point. "I'm Dr Moffat, the inheritor of his practice. As is my wife, though she is a dontist; that is, an endodontist. Have you ever wondered why there are dentists and dontists, such as endodontists, orthodontists, and periodontists?" Freddy was in his pedagogical mode.

"No, in fact I haven't," Finney said, which brought to Freddy's scarlet face a slightly arrogant smile, until Finney went on, "because I know that one is derived from the Latin and the other from the Greek."

"Which, I take it, you have studied," Freddy said, assuming that this was not so.

"For a number of years, yes."

"I did, too."

"Good for you. I hope you've studied dentistry."

"I have," said Freddy. It was true.

"And that you can see a patient. I know it's late, but it's an emergency. It's Dewey Knott, and that's always an emergency."

BEAUTIFUL WOMEN tend to tie things up in knots. Other women are often jealous of them or admire them to the point of female servitude, and men can become in their presence as ungainly as a giraffe in a neck brace. Fredericka was so spectacular-looking in her dental smock that no one, including Freddy, could take his eyes off her. Finney was greatly moved. Dewey, who had been well trained by Dot not to look too hard at what both he and Dot called "dames," couldn't take his eyes off her either, although he tried. "How'd you get so red?" he asked.

"Sunshine," Fredericka answered, like a princess, ringingly.

"We don't allow relatives in the room when we see patients," Freddy told Finney, whose royal name he did not know.

"I'm not his relative, I'm his chief of staff."

"Or chiefs of staff," Freddy added.

"This is the presumptive Republican nominee," Finney said. "The Secret Service wanted to have an agent present, but I convinced them to let me stay instead." He thought he could impress Freddy (little did he know) into abandoning standard practice.

"Sorry," Freddy said. "If we are to treat the patient, presumptive nominee or not. . . ."

"I *am,*" said Dewey. "I'm Knott."

"Are you, or are you not?" Freddy asked.

"I'm Knott."

"So you aren't."

"I am."

"Look here," Freddy told him, more severely than Dewey was accustomed to, "I don't care if you are or you are not."

"I am Knott."

"Fine. Whatever you are, if you want us to treat you, no relatives or chiefs of staff in the room."

Dewey Knott looked at Finney and said, "Finney, get the hell out of here."

"I beg your pardon?" said Freddy, almost dropping the round mirror, with a hole in it, that he was about to strap onto his head. "To fix your tooth, I must be here."

This last construction struck Dewey and Finney as most odd. "We know that," said Dewey, "but he has to go, right?"

"Who?"

"Finney."

"Yes?" Freddy answered, thinking he had been addressed.

"Why is it a question?" Finney asked.

"Why is what a question?" Freddy replied.

"*Yes.*"

"Yes what?"

"Finney, just get out," Dewey commanded.

"Ah, I see," Freddy said. "*He's* Finney." He looked at Finney inquiringly, though Finney knew not of what he was inquiring. A distant relative, perhaps an eighteenth cousin, Finney resembled Freddy somewhat in elegance. Finney then left, thinking he was in a dream and not at all confident in Freddy's perspicaciousness.

"Did you know Doc Ottabay?" Dewey asked when Finney was gone.

"No, he died long before we took over his practice. For years the dental needs of Siliphant have gone unfulfilled."

"Well, fill mine for Chrissake," Dewey commanded, pointing at his affliction.

"Just relax," said Freddy. "We're going to give you a little nitroglycerine to loosen you up."

"Nitroglycerine?" Dewey asked.

"It's not called that," Fredericka said to Freddy, placing the mask over Dewey's mouth. Dewey was rather disturbed.

"What's it called?"

"I don't know," Fredericka answered, "but it does begin with an *N*. Nitrogen? No. Nitrate?"

Dewey tried to say something, but it was muffled by the mask.

"Fredericka, how can we fix his tooth if the mask is over his mouth?"

"Oh, I hadn't thought of that," she said. "I guess it should be over the nose." She moved it. "There, that's better."

"Don't you know how to . . ." said Dewey, and then a strange look came over him. "Don't you. . . ."

"The question is," Freddy said, addressing Fredericka, "how much of this stuff to give him."

"How are we supposed to know?" Fredericka asked. "We haven't gotten to that yet."

Dewey's eyes flashed like the eyes of a wild horse when a thunderstorm is near.

"What does it say on the machine?"

Fredericka looked down. "There are a lot of numbers. What about eight? That might be good."

"Higher," said Freddy. "Once, I bet on eight at Monte Carlo and lost ten thousand pounds. What about fourteen, that was my regatta number."

Dewey tried to rise from the chair, but by this time he had no body. Flying through the empyrean, with no sense of time, he dreamed ecstatically and with anxiety. He dreamed that he had lost the election. Then he dreamed that he and Dot were young again, and that no one had ever heard of them, and that they were in shorts, walking on a sand road that led to the ocean. They could hear the surf in the distance and feel it pounding every time a wave thudded down. It was a hot day, the United States had just defeated Japan, and when he got up in the mornings he wasn't the slightest bit stiff. He was sunburned, he had all his hair, Dot was a beautiful young woman whose ambitions were of the heart, and no one had built much of anything on the coasts except some gun emplacements, so the beaches were windswept and empty, and the sea was primitive and wild. He could have stayed in that dream forever.

"He looks happy," Fredericka said. "I wonder what he's thinking."

"Fredericka, we're in a rather difficult situation."

"Yes."

"After all, we were going to practise on animals first."

"That wouldn't be fair," Fredericka protested.

"Oh, let's not have that argument again," Freddy said.

"It wouldn't. My shampoo isn't tested on animals, so why should we practise on them?"

"Wouldn't you prefer that your shampoo be tested on animals rather than on people, or on you? Besides, I would think that a gorilla might enjoy having his hair washed."

"It wouldn't have worked, Freddy. How would we have gotten a cow into this chair?" she asked indignantly.

"It's adjustable," Freddy said.

"Anyway, this is not a cow or a high plains drifter or a charity patient, this is the Senate majority leader, whatever that is, and perhaps the next president of the United States. The Secret Service is outside, the press is outside, and we forgot to ask him where the pain was."

"It wouldn't have mattered anyway," Freddy said. "We haven't come to fillings, bondings, or root canal. If only he could have arrived a few days from now."

"You said he'd never come here."

"Yes, well, first we have to make sure we don't put him to sleep permanently."

"You mean kill him?"

"It would be a tragic embarrassment. If we don't kill him, perhaps we can relieve his pain. Or, when he wakes up, if he wakes up, we can speak in gobbledygook and refer him to a babbiodontist."

"What's a babbiodontist?"

"I don't know. Is he alive?"

"I think so."

"Let's examine him. We may not know what we're doing, but he's lucky to have two dentists all to himself."

"But, Freddy, we aren't dentists."

"We are now," Freddy said. "I read in the book that they'll open their mouths even when they're gassed. Open," he commanded.

Dewey's mouth popped open like the lid of a rubbish bin. This startled Fredericka, who jumped back and put her hand on the top of her chest just under her neck.

"Courage," Freddy recommended, peering into Dewey's mouth. "My God, it's like a horse's mouth. If we get a file, we can float some of the teeth. I've done that, and we won't even have to put him in cross ties."

"Do the examination, Freddy, as in the book."

"Very well. Stetson's duct, visible. Lips, normal. Mucosa, normal. Pronounced recession from—three through B-one, and, wait. Just a minute. What's this?"

"What's what?" Fredericka asked, peering into what had been called the widest thing in Nebraska other than the river Platte.

"Look on the upper right, between one and B-two. You see that? I thought it was a wire, but he hasn't any braces. It's a spike, lodged in the gum."

"Let me see," said Fredericka. "Oh my goodness it's a nail, it's right next to the tooth, and from the angle I would guess that it's jammed into the periosteum. If it's long enough, it may have pierced the jawbone. How could he have stood it?"

"He's a politician. That's what he does to other people. Clamp."

"I beg your pardon?"

"Clamp."

"Look," Fredericka said, "you're a dentist, but I'm a dontist. A dentist, when addressing a dontist, is more gracious."

"I'm sorry. May I have the clamp, please, Madame Dontist?"

She gave it to him with a bit of a smoulder. He pulled out a spritzer, washed the area, and daubed at it with disinfectant. Then, with the clamp, he gripped the end of the spike and began the extraction. With the application of a little force, he pulled it out. Freddy cleaned the wound, squirted disinfectant in the hole, and put a wad of gauze in Dewey's mouth. "Bite," he said, and Dewey bit like a guard dog. As Fredericka cut the N_2O and fed Dewey pure oxygen, they looked at the spike. It was metallic grey, as thick as paperclip wire, as sharp as a hypodermic needle, and an inch long.

"We've had some luck, Fredericka, but can you convince him otherwise?"

"Of course I can."

They threw away the spike and leaned back against their wooden drawers of instruments, proud of their work upon their first patient. Their relief was temporary, however, for just as they thought they were in the clear, Dewey ripped off the mask, grunted, and went through some sort of spasm that suggested death.

"What's that?" asked Fredericka.

"How am I supposed to know?"

"Is he dead?"

"Obviously not, he's breathing."

"This isn't England, you know," Fredericka told him as they approached (to use one of Self's insults) Sleeping Dewey.

"What does that mean?"

"This is America."

"Do you think that Americans breathe after they're dead?"

"I wouldn't put it past them," Fredericka said.

"Fredericka, don't suddenly go anti-American just because we're in a stressful situation."

"It's not anti-American," she protested, "it's a compliment."

"You said it with a certain contempt."

"I did not. Freddy, he's not getting up, is he?"

"No."

"Is he in a coma?"

"How could anyone tell?"

"Maybe we gave him brain damage, Freddy."

"You don't *give* someone brain damage, just as you don't catch it. You cause brain damage. You inflict brain damage."

"I do?"

"One does."

"Maybe we inflicted brain damage upon Dewey Knott. Did we?"

"How are we supposed to know?"

"Examine his brain."

"You mean take it out?"

"Of course not. We don't know how to do that yet."

"Dentists don't take out people's brains, Fredericka. Not to worry, he's just sleeping." Dewey had been hurled into oblivion by alcohol and nitrous oxide acting upon his exhaustion and anxiety.

"If he's just sleeping, wake him up."

Freddy shook Dewey, shook him again, kicked him, and commanded him to awake. He didn't.

"Freddy, you'd better look at his brain."

"How am I supposed to do that?"

"Through the ears."

Freddy was dumbfounded. Fredericka had become brilliant, but in some areas she lagged. "You can't see someone's brain through the ears, Fredericka," he said patronisingly, and then gave a little royal laugh.

"Oh really? In fact, if you shine a bright light across the columnar reticulum lying outside the cells of Claudius, a space is visible between the outer rods or corti and the adjacent hair-cells. This is called the Space of Nuel, and in conditions of neuromuscular stress or jaw inversion, the septum of reticulation just beyond the Space of Nuel can become translucent or even transparent, affording a direct view of the brain."

"That's remarkable," Freddy said.

"Use the penlight. It has fresh batteries."

"Fresh *cells*, or, as I have explained, a fresh *battery*. What's jaw inversion?"

"It's when the jaw is inside out. It doesn't matter. Examine him."

Peering into Dewey's left ear, Freddy looked like a sailor trying hard to form an image in the eyepiece of a jiggling telescope.

"What do you see? What do you see?"

"Nothing."

"That's unjustifiably snobbish."

"I mean I don't see any . . . wait a moment. Ah, yes. Yes. I see . . . I see something. It's rose-coloured, and it's shaped like an inkwell."

"Is that his brain?"

"I would hope not, but it is in the centre of his head. What else could it be?"

"Does it look all right?"

"How would I know?"

"Are there any cracks in it, or wounds or anything? Does it look damaged?"

"No, except that somehow I think it knows that I'm looking at it."

"At least we didn't break it."

Freddy drew back and switched off the penlight. "He's sleeping, that's all. Let's have faith that he'll awake."

They were in the midst of washing their hands when they heard someone pounding on the door and rattling the doorknob. It was the other Finney, who yelled, "What's going on in there? Let me in."

"We can't," Freddy said, speaking as if to the door.

"Why not?"

"He's in recovery."

"Is he all right?"

"Yes, he's fine," Fredericka said. "He had an extremely dangerous abscess in his peristootium, which made for complications of the nerve bundle in the Bocage of Venus."

"In the what?" Finney asked.

"The Bocage of Venus," Fredericka said, addressing the door.

"Yes," said Freddy, "the Bocage."

"The Bocage?" Finney asked from beyond the door.

She then continued. "We did a most complicated nerve splicing in the peristootium. He can't move or be disturbed until the Islets of Langerhans congeal and fuse with the Dendritical Horns of Laertes."

"He's got to go on *Nightline* in twenty minutes," Finney said. "After the Omaha speech, the only thing that'll save him is a strong performance tonight."

"Sorry," said Fredericka.

"What's the topic?" Freddy asked. Fredericka kicked him and waved her hands around in an erasure motion.

"Defence and foreign relations," Finney said, "about which he knows almost nothing. We were hoping we might catch his charisma in one of its rare appearances, but I guess it's over."

"Will they take answers relayed from his hospital bed?" Freddy asked.

"What hospital bed?"

"Here, in the office of his dentists, where he is recovering from a life-threatening abscess."

"Why can't he just take the phone?" Finney asked.

"He can only garble," Freddy said.

"We know that," Finney declared. "Why can't he just take the phone?"

"I am referring to the fact that he's got all kinds of tubes and fishing equipment hanging from his mouth."

"Fishing equipment?"

"That's what dentists call it as a joke," Fredericka said to the door. "His mouth is in traction and he looks like a sea bass."

"Can you understand him?" Finney asked.

"Only from long experience," they both said simultaneously.

"Me, too," said Finney. He weighed the choices. "Why not? He's going to crash and burn one way or another. He's had no briefing, he really hates these subjects, he's drunk, and he's in pain. What's your number in there?"

Freddy told him.

"Well," Finney said to no one in particular, "maybe people should see that he doesn't know anything about this stuff. The pity is that Self knows even less and cares not at all. Let's do it. Why not?"

ALTHOUGH THE HOST of *Nightline* (a man, not a vast army) was framed against a backdrop of the most exquisite federal blue, he was so elfin in manner and appearance that most people who saw him imagined that he was sitting upon a giant spotted mushroom. Freddy had once spoken to him in an early morning hookup to Balmoral. After the interview, Freddy had still had time to eat breakfast, walk to his favourite trout-fishing eddy, and begin to cast before sunrise.

Freddy was quite used to the oddly calm and desultory period of waiting before going on the air, as technical people came and went on and off the line and things slowly got rolling. During this time, Fredericka expressed her disapproval, for anything to do with the press might inadvertently throw them back into the pre-dental life.

"Don't be silly," he said, turning his head to her as when she had turned her head sharply to him in the kissing that seemed so far distant now even if it had been only an hour before. His hand covered the mouthpiece of the phone. "They can't see us, they don't even know there are two of us, we're totally out of context, and I'm going to put this cotton wool over the mouthpiece." He then taped a rabbit-tail-sized piece of absorbent cotton across the lower end of the phone. His eyes focussed on a world somewhere else as he listened first to the commercials and then to the introduction.

"Good evening. As you may have heard or seen, Dewey Knott was stricken today by a life-threatening abscess that felled him during what was to have been a defining speech he delivered—in the event, somewhat problematically—in Omaha. He was supposed to have been with us tonight, but instead *Nightline* has an exclusive hookup to his hospital bed in Siliphant, Nebraska, his hometown, where his life was saved in an emergency operation by his longtime friend, the noted oral surgeon, Dr Moffat.

"Hello? Is this Dr Moffat?"

"Moffat here," said Freddy.

"Dr Moffat, is Senator Knott in your care this evening?"

"Yes, he is."

"Can he speak? May we speak with him?"

"He can speak through me," Freddy said. "Otherwise he would be unintelligible."

"I should just speak to you as if I were speaking to him, is that right?"

"Exactly."

"Let's try that then. How are you, Senator? Are you sensible?"

"I'm fine," Freddy said.

"We've just spoken with Dr Moffat, but we'll ask you. Are you in any danger?"

"I'm not exactly lying here unconscious, am I?" Freddy said on behalf of Dewey. "I'm in no danger whatsoever, though I was."

"You were?"

"Yes. Dr Moffat tells me that I had a potentially fatal abscess, which he has now cured, although I will be incapacitated for a while, because, to avoid nerve damage, my mouth has been put in traction."

"Senator? Your mouth is in traction?"

"Yes. I'm going to take the brilliant Dr Moffat back to the Senate with me. There are mouths there and in the House of Commons that cry out for traction."

The interviewer thought this was funny, not because it was, but because it was intended to be, and that's the way Washington is. But something about 'Dewey's' statement lingered. "The House of Commons, Senator?"

"Full of the lowest vulgarians," 'Dewey' said. "And I hope Dr Moffat doesn't stop there. The mouths that most deserve traction are those of the press."

"The print media."

"You wish."

The host looked somewhat disturbed. People would process their grandmothers for tomato fertiliser just to be on his programme for five minutes. No one had ever criticised him on air, or even implied a criticism. "Senator. . . ."

Freddy interrupted. "You know," he said, "they take film and pictures of you when you're swimming off a yacht or hunting ducks in Spain, and then they put a fake story up and everyone looks at you as if you're insane."

"Really."

"Absolutely."

"Is that what happened to you earlier this evening during your Omaha speech? Was that the fault of the press?"

"That was my fault," said Freddy. "I really mucked it up. I did. After the sudden onset of the abscess, to anaesthetise myself I drank a bottle of Scotch. When I gave the speech I was as drunk as an Irishman."

"An Irishman?" the host repeated, almost in shock. No American politician would so gratuitously and offensively say such a thing, especially about so large a dissolving voting bloc. "Senator, what do you think Irish Americans will have to say about that last comment?"

"I don't think they'll say anything. I think they're too busy running guns, raising money for the IRA, and blowing up people in boats, that's what I think."

"But, Senator, you yourself are of Irish extraction."

"I am?"

"On both your mother's and father's sides."

"Knott is an Irish name?"

"Senator, for many years now, you've been the grand marshal of the Saint Patrick's Day Parade in New York."

"I did that to take advantage of those poor drunken bastards who will vote for me because I march at their head. That's called the politics of ethnicity, I believe, and it's repellent. What's good for one man is good for another. Anglo-Saxon jurisprudence is founded on the principle of equality of fundamental rights attaching not to a group or a class but to the individual. You cannot have justice if rank and privilege are accorded by class. I have always believed that, despite the accident of my birth."

Although he did not quite comprehend the accidental quality of Dewey Knott's birth, the interviewer said, "Senator, I've never heard you talk this way, in this . . . style."

"Of late, Wickham," Freddy began in his reflective tone, even though the host's name was not Wickham, "I have been rereading the documents of the Founding: *The Federalist Papers,* histories of the Constitutional Convention, the letters of Jefferson and Adams, and, most importantly, the Declaration and the Constitution themselves. I have for the first time seen the deep and luminescent connexion between these and the philosophy and culture of our mother country, how the greatness of the English oak—solid and strong but fixed and constrained in a tight and settled island—was allowed to flower luxuriantly and in miraculous ease in the great spaces of America. We are like two halves of a broken coin. The English: staid, cutting, seasoned, and reserved. The Americans: youthful in energy, intoxicated with principle, full of spontaneity and song, and irredeemably vulgar. How badly we need one another, perhaps."

"Excuse me," the host interrupted, for Freddy was enamoured of the unity of the English-speaking peoples and would have gone on indefinitely. "Is this Dr Moffat?"

"Yes, Moffat here."

"Dr Moffat, you seem to be relaying Senator Knott's answers without pause. How do you do that?"

"I watch his lips move, and mine follow a quarter of a second later. After interpreting for thousands of patients whose mouths I have set in traction but who must continue to run their businesses and communicate with their families, I have perfected instant recapitulation."

"Remarkable. Let me ask the senator, then, a few questions about military and foreign affairs. I'm amazed, as I'm sure all Americans will be, too, at Senator Knott's . . . what can I say? His leap into quality? His depth of statesmanship? His seriousness. His transformation. I sense in just these few words we've heard the presence of a greatness and wisdom long absent from the American political scene. Of course, I could be very wrong, but I think something has happened here, and I think my colleagues in the press will be most eager to look into this as well. But I do have some important questions that—I apologise—are strictly policy-oriented. Senator, I know you've been ill, and may not have had the opportunity to be briefed, but, may I?"

Freddy had a near-photographic memory, read all the government dispatches supplied to his mother, devoured every fact in literally a score of foreign affairs and military journals, and was—despite a military rank that suggested only tactical responsibilities—a genius of grand strategy. He had no qualms about the questions to come. "Senator Knott says," he told the man on the toadstool, "I have no qualms about the type of questioning you propose. I keep up on these things and, out of charity and modesty, only let it appear that I depend upon my aides. Now that I'm going to be president—and I will be president, because I am determined to win the election and I shall see it through—it's time to dispense with my previous reticence and state to the American people that your next president is not a substanceless, back-slapping, sub-intelligent, moronic twit incapable of anything other than vulgar political machination. I live and breathe the relations between states and the finely balanced interdependency of diplomatic and military power. I know the history, the current operational details, and the broad structure of principle and metaphysic upon which strategic and diplomatic calculation rest, and I will happily submit to your questioning, at any level of detail."

"Senator, I can't tell you how amazed I am at this—how shall I say it? I can only repeat—transformation. I don't mean to be insulting, but are you the man they used to call 'the emperor of density'? I think it's safe to say that this is a new Dewey Knott."

"Thank you, Wickham. That's very kind of you."

"We have assembled a panel of experts here, and they're ready to question you. Are you ready?"

"Of course I'm ready," said Freddy.

The panel that had been assembled to question Dewey consisted of three of the most arrogant, offensive, and aggressive think-tank monstrosities in Washington. They had learned to hybridize the blood-red internecine warfare of the federal bureaucracies with the baseless pomposity of academia. The result was a beast as sure of himself as a professor who comes to believe that, because his students dare not dispute him either persistently or importantly, he is always right; and as fierce and predatory as the bureaucrat who knows that ten percent of his job is doing his job and ninety percent is neutering, incapacitating, discrediting, demoralising, and enslaving every single living person out to the greatest possible range. The three of them were there that evening for bayonet practice upon the dangling carcass of Dewey Knott, hoping that one of the president's smug, empty-headed snots would note their service to the president's campaign for re-election and reward them suitably in times to come.

"Senator Knott," began a disgusting, scrofulous fiend whose name was actually Glister Heinie, "a statement was issued, in your name, criticising the administration for circumvention of the MTCR in return for alleged campaign contributions from the Chinese People's Liberation Army. Senator," Glister Heinie asked, about to plunge the knife into flesh, "what is the MTCR?" He knew, of course, that Dewey Knott was famous for his inability to understand the basic principle behind acronyms, having publicly asked the CEO of International Business Machines, "Why in God's name do you call it IBM, and what's a CEO?"

"The Missile Technology Control Regime, obviously," said Freddy.

"And how does this figure in?" Glister Heinie asked, waiting for a famous Dewey Knott special, such as when he somehow got it into his head that Greek Orthodox nuns were called nymphomaniacs, or when, confusing the words *tornado* and *volcano,* he told a group of stunned Nebraska farmers, "When I was young, I looked up and there was my father, running as fast as he could from a volcano. No one knows why God chose to put so many volcanoes in Nebraska, but He certainly did, didn't He?"

But, luckily for Dewey, he was unconscious. "It figures in," Freddy answered in his behalf, and as if with cold steel, for the Prince of Wales did not enjoy arrogant impertinence, "in potential contractor-sanctioned and thus government-sanctioned (for it was government that created the exceptions attributed to the contractors) violations in regard to certain category-one items."

"Like what?" Glister Heinie insisted, hoping to chase Dewey out from behind his briefing.

368 FREDDY AND FREDERICKA

"Like guidance sets capable of achieving system accuracy of three-point-three-three percent or less of the range; that is, a circular error probability of ten kilometres or less at three hundred kilometres. Like technical assistance in regard to rocket engines having a total impulse capacity of one-point-one times ten-to-the-sixth-power seconds, or two-point-five times ten-to-the-fifth-power pound-seconds or greater, as specified in paragraph two, section G, subsection one, part five, 'Consulting Services.' To put it bluntly in terms that can be understood other than by mandarins, the president took from the Chinese government laundered campaign contributions not laundered well enough to escape detection, and, in a double scam, from American companies that provided the Chinese missile forces with the guidance capability they require for reducing their CEP, or, rather, for better accuracy, which is essential in the strategic nuclear calculus. It was done ostensibly to help the Chinese launch our communications satellites, but precision in hitting an orbital aim point is all a ballistic missile needs to achieve a trajectory for hitting a terrestrial aim point. That, Mr Heinie, is the substance of my comment."

Freddy continued in this vein for half an hour, humbling his questioners not only with the force and precision of his answers but with stray erudition that softened and adorned his necessarily technical responses. Of Glister Heinie, who tried to stump him on the characteristics of the North Korean Nodong-2 missile—the Prince of Wales knew even that its diameter is .88 m—Freddy asked, "You speak of the Nodong, but do you know what it means?"

"Means?"

"In Korean."

"No."

"It means *labour,* which is what I recommend to you so that you may hone your so-called expertise."

He quoted La Rochefoucauld to vitiate the sweetness of the moderator's astonished praise, saying, in perfect Freddy French, *"Si nous résistons à nos passions, c'est plus par leur faiblesse que par notre force."* He cited, at first in French, Napoleon's comment about a commander's original sin being to form a picture, and held forth about the pitfalls of various approaches to international relations. He was, all in all, scathing, brilliant, funny, noble, and precise, even as he spoke through a wad of absorbent cotton. And when the little fellow on the mushroom in front of the blue curtain closed the interview with an expression of amazement and delight, Freddy said, *"Ac veluti magno in populo cum saepe corta est seditio, saevitque animus ignobile volgus, iamque faces et saxa volant (furor arma ministrat), tum pictate gravem ac meritis si forte virum quem conspexere, silent arrectisque auribus adstant; ille regit dictis animos et pectora mulcet."*

"I beg your pardon, Senator? Most of us have long forgotten our Latin. What does it mean?"

Freddy informed him that it was from Book One of the *Aeneid,* and translated: "And as, when oft-times in a great nation tumult has risen, the base rabble rage angrily, and now brands and stones fly, madness lending arms; then, if haply they set eyes on a man honoured for noble character and service, they are silent and stand by with attentive ears; he with speech sways their passion and soothes their breasts."

"Senator, I'm astounded. And, I have to say, I'm excited. I congratulate you, sir. And, please send my best to Dot."

"To what?" Freddy asked.

"To Dot."

"What is that?"

"Dot, Senator."

"Yes, but what is it?"

"Your wife, Dot. Dot Knott."

"Oh, I'm sorry," Freddy said. "That's a name?"

"It's your wife's name, sir," said the host, even more astounded than he had been.

"Dot," said Freddy, listening to the sound, "Dot." He looked at the absorbent cotton. "Bloody hell."

Usually the host of *Nightline* gave a fairly eloquent summation at the close of the show, but on this night he did not. He just sat there, unmoving, deaf to the shouted importations in his earplug. He didn't even say good-bye to Dewey Knott, and they rolled the credits over him as if he had been paralysed by a Pygmy arrow.

AFTER A SHORT INTERVAL in which Finney walked moon-dazed from the communications van to the house, Freddy and Fredericka heard a quiet, polite knock accompanied by Finney's by-now-familiar voice through wood: "You can let me in now. I know he must be unconscious."

Freddy unlocked and opened the door. Finney's immense anger was held in check by nascent gratitude. Then he looked at Dewey, motionless in the chair. "Is he alive?" he asked.

"Yes, he's alive," Fredericka answered indignantly. She had been making sure that his heart was still beating.

"Is he in a coma?"

"We are a dentist and a dontist," Fredericka said. "We're not brain surgeons. We're not veterinarians. We don't know what a coma is."

"Nonetheless, you can put someone in a coma by starving his brain of oxygen, can't you," Finney asked rhetorically without so much as a question mark.

"Well," said Fredericka, with what Finney took to be astounding gall, "they should have a warning on the machine, don't you think?"

"Do you realise," Finney asked, "that this is the majority leader of the United States Senate, and his party's presumptive presidential nominee, and you may have made him brain-dead?"

"Really, I don't think so," Freddy offered, "and, besides, it's just a colony."

"What's just a colony?" Finney asked. "Is this a dream?"

"I think your leader, or whatever he is, is perfectly all right," Freddy said firmly.

"You do. That's terrific. But he is unconscious. You have no idea what trouble you're in. And I'm not impressed by your fake English accents. Bad job. You're trying for Oxbridge, but it's off somehow, like cheese or fish, or a record that revolves just a bit too slowly. You sound like Terry Thomas on Benadryl. You're not dentists, you're con men." He looked at Fredericka. "Con people. But guess what, con people? This house is surrounded by a protective cordon of the Secret Service, and you will be held responsible for what you've done."

"Come come," Freddy said in the buck-'em-up tone that he had inherited from his father (who used it exclusively for dogs and horses), "it's not all that bad. He may wake up."

Both Freddy and Fredericka had been deeply impressed by Finney's diagnosis of their manner of speech, because they did not speak with Oxbridge accents. Theirs (and particularly Freddy's) was a royal dialect that was unique. Freddy was frequently mistaken for affecting a fraudulent tongue. He wanted to tell Finney that it was probably due not merely to the isolation of the royals and the need to speak with what Freddy called *a certain blasé favösh*, but also to the family's German origin. Thus, no one could tell the difference, when Freddy's father was speaking, between *plea-sure* and *pressure,* both of which were rendered more or less as *pwreh-shah.* Even the queen tended to pronounce *book* as *booook,* after the German *Buch.* But of course he could tell Finney no such thing, even if Finney were indeed the first person they had met in a long time who had some awareness of the wider world. They knew that many Americans were eru-dite and well informed, but they hadn't met any. The oceans seemed to have washed away the immigrants' connexions to their pasts.

As for Finney, he thought they were cheap and peculiar quacks feebly attempting to capitalise upon a vague resemblance to the Prince and Prin-cess of Wales. She was, no matter how attractive, not nearly as stunning as Fredericka, and he was ignoble and his ears were even bigger than Freder-ick's. They were nothing more than flea-bitten white trash affecting fake English accents to run a dental scam in a dying town where they could scratch out a living by pulling and polishing teeth. The contempt he felt for them was limitless. If you were going to impersonate a dentist, or a dontist, you might as well do it in Biarritz or Beverly Hills, where you could make some money, not in Siliphant. But how did they know so much diplomatic history and Latin?

As Finney was about to use his cell phone to call the Secret Service, it rang. This seemed to affect Dewey, who said, "Hello?" and swung his right arm off his chest, where it had been resting. Finney took the call while Fredericka put a dripping cloth on Dewey's forehead and squirted some mouthwash into his mouth. "Hey, whadaya gonna do?" he asked, sitting bolt upright. Freddy used the foot control to bring the back of the chair up to him.

"That's magnificent," Finney said into the phone, but he was not allud-ing to the resurrection of Dewey Knott, not, at least, as it was playing out in Dewey's body. "It's amazing. I don't believe it, but it's true."

"What's true?" Dewey asked, but soon forgot his own question as he realised that he was no longer in pain. "My tooth," he said, feeling gingerly about his face, putting a finger or two in his mouth, "my abscess. It's gone. How'd ya do that?"

"The abscess caused a wrinkling and tangle of the nerves in the inter-lobular spaces of Czermak, or, as some choose to call it, the granular layer of Thappy. We went in through the peristootial odontoblastic tubuli," Fredericka said earnestly, "and spliced the quadrigeminal bigemina with the upper mesial epiplastic pons. *Voilà!*"

"Dewey Knott doesn't have pain," said Dewey. "I owe you."

"Senator?" Finney said.

"Hello, John. These guys are terrific. How much do I owe them? How much do *we* owe them? Can we pay for this with soft money?"

"Senator. . . ."

"When you're in Washington," Dewey said to Freddy and Fredericka, "stop by. See me. I'll give ya a tour. The Capitol. Big building. Beautiful. Great view."

"Senator!"

"John! What?"

"We just got the results of the instapoll."

"What instapoll?"

"After *Nightline,* Senator."

"What for?"

"To see how you did."

"I haven't been on *Nightline* in years. They don't like me. It's that goddamn elf."

"You were just on, Senator, half an hour ago."

"I was?"

"Yes."

"Oh. What did the polls say?"

"Senator, what happened is a miracle. Your performance on *Nightline* has closed the gap. You're now running in a statistical dead heat with the president, and you pass him on charisma, honesty, and expertise. It's predicted that, among likely voters, if you stay on track, by November you'll go to sixty-five percent."

"What's a statistical dead heat?"

"You're even, neck and neck."

Dewey left the chair. He brushed aside Freddy and Fredericka and came fully awake. "It's a landslide!" he said. "How'd I do it? How'd I do it?"

"Your magnificent performance on *Nightline,* sir."

"My magnificent performance on *Nightline!*" Dewey said, beaming, glowing, bouncing on his laurels.

"Yes!"

"But, Finney. . . ."

"Senator?"

"I wasn't on *Nightline.*"

"You were, Senator, this evening."

Dewey dredged his memory. "I was?"

"In a way," Finney said.

"Whadaya mean, 'in a way'?"

"Actually, your answers were relayed, as you were in treatment."

"I didn't answer anything. Who relayed my answers?"

"Dr Moffat."

"Who the hell is Dr Moffat?" Dewey asked, more nervous as each second passed.

"He is."

"Him?"

"Yes."

"You gave answers for me?"

"I had to. Your mouth was in traction," Freddy said.

"About what? What did you say?"

They told him.

"I don't know anything about those things. How could you have. . . . You just did this on your own?"

"You were unconscious," Freddy said. "I had to."

"It was brilliant," Finney declared. "*The Washington Post* is going to lead with it tomorrow and say that not since Theodore Roosevelt and JFK has a public figure been as forceful, erudite, and charismatic. *The New York Times* will also lead, I'm told. They say you've revolutionised American politics merely by not being dumb. Someone from *Time* called in to leak that their cover is going to read 'American statesmanship awakens from its slumber of half a century.' We're back on track. We are, as you like to say, Senator, *smoking!*"

The phone rang. It was Dot. Dewey spent the next ten minutes saying, "Yes, Dot. Yes, Dot. Yes, Dot," and then hung up.

"What did she say?" Finney asked.

"All her friends are calling her. They say it's a miracle and that she should forgive me. What did I do? *What's* a miracle? I was sleeping. What the hell happened?"

For the next forty-five minutes, Dewey and Finney plotted strategy, answered calls, and worked on the terms they would offer Freddy and Fredericka in regard to their employment. During this time, Freddy sat at a little desk the colour of summer sausage and wrote furiously without any sense of what was going on around him. Outside, the press agitated like rabid squirrels. Phone lines in newsrooms were jammed. Planes were chartered.

When Freddy finished, he looked up to see Dewey Knott smiling at him. It was the political equivalent of a come-hither look.

"Is that your real name, Moffat?"

"No," Freddy admitted.

"Whoever you are, I want you to work for me, but we've got to keep it quiet," Dewey said. "What's your real name?"

"My Druidical name," Freddy said, "is Lachpoof Bachquaquinnik Dess Moofoomooach. And this is Mrs Lachpoof Bachquaquinnik Dess Moofoomooach."

"What kind of a name is that?" Dewey asked.

"I don't know exactly," Freddy told him, "but I do know that we can't work for you. You have too much television around you. If we're on television, we'll turn into gourds."

"Hell, you were just on *Nightline,* and you didn't turn into gourds, did you? Biggest political audience in the country."

"Visual blackout," said Freddy.

"Are you fugitives?" Finney asked.

"Are you?" Fredericka returned, stingingly.

"No," Finney retorted, "and I'm not afraid of being turned into a gourd, either."

"We'll come to some kind of understanding," Dewey said. Although he had yet to see a tape of *Nightline,* he realised that his hope of being president would, in Freddy's absence, be dashed in his next appearance before the press. "I need a really capable adviser, and the press seems to like you, even if they don't know you exist. You see," said Dewey, letting everyone in on what he had discovered, *"they think you're me."*

"Look," said Freddy, "we can't work for you, but do this and give this speech"—he handed Dewey the papers he had written—"and you'll soar in the polls."

"Do what?" Dewey asked. Finney seemed to sit back, although he was standing, as if he were watching something not quite subject to the laws of nature.

"Resign from the leadership of the Senate and from the Senate itself. That will be very dramatic. It will show the American people that you aren't interested in position, that you're decisive, that you can concentrate, that you can risk, that you have gravitas, that you put them, and the country, ahead of yourself. Announce this in the speech I have prepared for you. It's about Siliphant, the Plains, and America. These campaigns are concerned too much with the candidates and too little with the country. Change that."

THE LAST THING Dewey Knott ever wanted to do was to leave the Senate, which was his life. He never felt natural there, and had not quite gotten used to it even after decades of service, which was all the better. Unlike the patricians and egomaniacs who had grown up assuming that they deserved election to it and that by their association with it the Senate would vastly improve, Dewey was the son of a small farmer who had been wiped out in the Depression. It hadn't mattered to Dewey's father that one dust storm after another killed his crops, that when he was able to grow something he had so little of it and the market price was so low that it didn't cover the cost of planting, or that half the farmers in Siliphant went under with him. Such facts were, in his eyes, excuses. And he knew that he was not being punished for sinning, for he had not sinned, not enough, anyway, to justify what had happened to him and his family. His view was that he had failed, as his father before him had failed, because he was not as good as other people, not part of a natural aristocracy so broad that it included people like the druggist and the town clerk, the people who had parlours and pianos. There were the lords and there were the peasants, and the peasants had something about them, as did the lords, that kept them in their place. It had been decided over thousands of years, in combat after combat, contest after contest, in which those who were better rose to the top. In America, the impulse was always to start the pieces at the same line, and the rules were not asphyxiating, but, still, blood was blood, and the great ones rose, making a new aristocracy and reconfirming the old. In this aristocracy the Knotts had never had a place and never would.

The Senate was an august and prestigious body like no other, and Dewey Knott had not only won entrance but risen to lead the majority. His suite of offices was the most impressive (even if, compared with Freddy's various studies, libraries, and galleries, it was little more than a broom cupboard); his the longest limousine; and his the biggest staff. It meant nothing. He was his father's son, and that was the place—next to his father—where his heart was and he wanted to be. Whereas most politicians consumed privileges like fish feeding on minnows, Dewey had them mainly for keeping himself from too deep a despair. His feeling that he had no business there, and that he properly belonged as an employee in a grain elevator or in a school as an assistant custodian, was what enabled him to harvest the votes of such people, was what made him, to the extent that he was, a great man, and it was what, as he heard his own polished heels click across marble floors in towering halls, kept him alive.

Never in a million years would he have thought to resign from the Senate had Freddy not suggested it, pulled a spike from his gum, and given him the speech with which he could do it gracefully. "I'm gonna do it," he said, shocking Finney as they rode in the pre-dawn to Dewey's restored boyhood home, where there was now a sauna and a squash court, and, next to the squash court, a garden court in which Dewey's caretaker grew squash, which was Dewey's favourite vegetable. "Dot's gonna have a mammoth, but that's okay. It's understandable. It's her rice bowl, too."

"Forgive me, Senator," Finney said, impressed no end at Dewey's decisiveness, "but you aren't usually as quick in your decisions. Are you sure? It's astoundingly risky."

"Yeah, I know, but this dentist guy's real smart. I didn't know, but he figured it out. It's easy to see once you do."

"What is?"

"If I win, I won't be able to stay in the Senate. If I lose, I'll be thrown from the leadership post like something that went bad in the refrigerator. Having lost twice in a row, like my father, I wouldn't be able to bear staying on. You know, he lost the farm twice, and each time he was offered a job at the Huebner place, which was real big and had irrigation pumps, so they could grow things even in the dust. Didn't take it. That's why I'm so thin. Didn't eat. I might as well go early and make a virtue of going. What's the speech like?"

Finney looked at the speech, which was in Freddy's royal handwriting on the back of four manila X-ray sleeves. It wasn't a long speech. Dewey stared out the window and let his eyes tumble over Siliphant in fraying light. It was going to be a day of rain, he could tell, though none of the press corps had a clue. He could feel the huge black clouds building and the vertical rivers of air as they began to flow. Siliphant was good in the summer rain, when each house seemed like a boat floating down the Missouri with a light burning on the mast.

Finney finished reading, and dropped the X-ray sleeves on his lap. He seemed preoccupied.

"Whadja think?" Dewey asked, turning to his chief of staff. When Finney looked up, the tears that had welled in his eyes streamed down his face.

"Uh-oh," said Dewey.

AT NOON THE NEXT DAY, two hundred people and a thousand reporters assembled in Siliphant's town square to listen to Dewey as he spoke from the courthouse steps. They were there because they knew they had a story. Either Dewey would be his usual self, in which case the story would be the fall of Dewey Knott, or he would continue in the vein of his exceptional performance the night before, in which case the story would be the rise of Dewey Knott. It was a natural drama that five hundred television cameras would document for viewers everywhere, even in Tazerbo at the verge of the Rebiana Sand Sea. If Dewey had suddenly and inexplicably been granted erudition, wit, and charisma as well developed as if he had been the cross between an Oxford don and a British field marshal, it would be a miracle, and rightly the world loves miracles as it loves nothing else.

All bets were intensified by the rain, which provided an adagio as background and focussed attention on Dewey, who was not so good at competing with long views, blue sky, and wind-stroked wheat undulating in the sun. The black-and-whiteness of the clouded scene said to generations that had risen by the hearths of colour television that here would occur something old and authentic, that it would be simple, direct, and sincere. It would be genuine history, as in the low-production-value film clips of the lost early days of the century.

And so, with most of the ponytails tucked under rain hats, and hundreds of black umbrellas shielding hundreds of lenses, Dewey began to read his speech. He knew well that, in his parlance, he had to hit the ball "under the fence" at Yankee Stadium, and was certain that he would not be able to do it. Never in his life had he given a good speech, much less a great one. So wedded was he to Mushrom's pap delivered in a monotone that made a buzz saw sound like Mozart that he had come to see it as a virtue. Anything else, because he could not do it, was fakery and showmanship, somehow effeminate, and inappropriately European. He recoiled from rhetoric that took on a life of its own, and mocked it as "a string of ten-dollar words." His speeches were laden with the words *freedom, liberty, justice, great,* and *Gotham.* Of late he had added *caring, compassionate, diverse, future,* and *change.* Finney told him that he would find none of these in Lachpoof Bachquaquinnik Dess Moofoomooach's speech, and that the best thing he could do would be to read it fresh and awkwardly, hearing it for the first time as he spoke.

"That's crazy," Dewey had protested. "Who is this Lachpoof guy? Isn't he a dentist? What is he? He fixed my tooth. I don't get it."

"What can you lose?" Finney had asked.

"We closed a gap of forty points, that's what we can lose."

"No, Senator, Lachpoof closed a gap of forty points, and if Lachpoof can do that in half an hour, you should read his goddamned speech."

"Why? It made you cry. What if everyone cries?"

"I cried because, in all my career, it was the first political speech that has passed through my hands that is both beautiful and true. Isn't that what Keats said is all you need to know?"

"Keats? The party chairman of Nemaha County? What the hell would he know? I think I'm going nuts. I never want to see that Lachpoof guy again. He really bothers me. He does. A speechwriting dentist who knows all about military technicalities and the history of diplomacy? Why can't I see the speech?"

"Because you'll fuck it up," Finney said, most uncharacteristically. He never spoke like that, because he was raised in a family where no one ever spoke like that except when assembling a gas barbecue.

Dewey looked at him in amazement. "Can't we try a focus group before I deliver? It's important. Lots'a planes have been landing at the airport. I even saw a Japanese one. I even saw one with a picture of an Eskimo. Eskimos are coming to Nebraska to hear me give this speech, and I can't even look at it?"

"No," said Finney, and he meant it.

So when Dewey began to read, he was as grave as the slate-grey clouds that glided above him, and sure that he could never fulfil the heightened expectations. His idea of triumph was to win the South Carolina primary with a surprise buy of airtime. He melded little things like this into a magic political carpet that made him a leader. To be tested in speech, like Lincoln or Churchill, was not done any more by anyone, much less Dewey Knott, the monotone son of Siliphant, "the aluminum-tongued orator of the Platte," and proud of it. His manner, therefore, was curious and delicate, as if he were reading the report of an autopsy. This was notably different from his normal football-rally, tub-thumping style, and even before he had said ten words—and they were all simple words, Anglo-Saxon in origin—the commentators in their studios or on the spot signalled to the audience, in expressive silence, that, yes, indeed, this was a different Dewey Knott.

The speech was a declaration of love for America, with Fredericka present in every word but invisible to anyone but Freddy, who had fallen in love with her and his former colony simultaneously and could not in his heart of hearts completely separate the two. Just as Liberty, a woman in flowing robes, symbolised the country, so that country symbolised the woman with whom he had fallen in love. She had brought to him, in his middle age, the excitement of youth. Everything now seemed new and saturated with energy.

Thus, what Dewey Knott read, with uncharacteristic expression and emotion flowing from him readily and naturally, was a song in which were memorialised the things Freddy had seen—from the preternatural blue of the great inland seas that Americans modestly call lakes, to the sweet smell of evergreens near a rail bed on a mountain curve in the spring sun. Freddy had put into the speech the wake of the barge on which he had ridden down the Mississippi; the bone-white monuments of Washington rising from green water-rich land in spectacular heat and waves of elemental colour; and the greatness even of little Siliphant, that sat on the prairie like a boat sea-anchored on an open undulating ocean. On summer afternoons in Siliphant, the wind came up and rattled the sun-drenched leaves of the oaks and cottonwoods, turning up their white and silvered undersides in hysterical palsy, as if to accompany the grass on the prairie as it moved in sinuous waves. No dancer could dance more beautifully than the grass rising and falling as far as the eye could see.

He spoke of these, and stated for Dewey, more or less, that neither the Senate nor any power of politics could distract him from them; that these elemental things were all he needed to sustain him now and forever; that the ground—the land and the people—from which the structure of governance had risen was of a higher value, interest, and attraction than governance itself; that he asked plainly to lead, because he was in no need of it, being enraptured of the foundations from which the art of governance had been gratuitously separated. Therefore, he would resign from his leadership post in the Senate and from the Senate itself, and go forward toward the presidency having thrown down everything but what was pure and ideal.

Freddy captured the spirit of this in ringing perfection, for he was, after all, a royal prince who sought his kingdom by paradoxically and truthfully abjuring it, and it was only after he had lost his position and fallen low that he had learned to love. He had written this up, translated for Dewey, knowing, from having walked it, the path Dewey would have to tread. Freddy had always had a way with words, but these words were like the narration of a soldier who has just returned from battle, and they held the country for a long and reflective moment. Nonetheless, Freddy would have had no idea what the fuss was about. It was the language he used to direct his valet, or praise a particularly fine example of Begonia, mixed in with a bit of Shakespearean rhythm, some elegiac tone he had picked up at funerals, a ribbon-cutter's forward-lookingness, and his purely factual observations on both policy and the beauty of the country. It was a good speech, but the reaction was due to the fact that politics are madness, and even if one does not know it, a country in electoral season experiences flares of lunacy like the great storms that sometimes march across the golden surface of the sun.

Still, it was indeed a triumph for Dewey, who skyrocketed in the polls. The president had no idea what to do now that Dewey had become an original. The things Dewey was doing and saying came from the man himself, instantaneously, without study, conference, or script.

But Dewey himself didn't know what to do next. These were not his words and this was not he, or as he would have said, *him*. He was, in his view, defrauding the American people. No matter that when he had read a Mushrom speech the Mushrom-like expressions hadn't been his either. If he did things artificially, spoke other people's words, calculated, and it didn't work, it was forgivable. A thief who never takes anything cannot be said to have sinned, and that was what, in his eyes, Dewey Knott had been doing all his life: stealing without taking. And, as he might say, now Dewey Knott was not doing it. His fraudulence was a success, and he felt honourably guilty.

The major journalists were not content to believe in Dewey's sudden transformation, and pressed him in public and private for the name of the ventriloquist. At first, swayed by Finney's logic—"Did you ever, once, credit Mushrom? Why credit Moofoomooach?"—he skilfully abstained from answering. That was easy, his stock-in-trade. If someone asked him a question about, for example, nuclear weapons, he could effortlessly divert the line of questioning to chronic disease in gerbils, interstate piano moving, turtle protection, etc. But it was a torture for him to avoid the question of authorship, because he was fundamentally honest. So, only hours after the speech, when in Siliphant the press swarmed and agitated as if awaiting visitors from another world, and as the instapoll numbers pushed Dewey into the stratosphere, Dewey cleared his conscience. He was sitting with the dean of the print journalists, who, without a single word, had put Dewey on the rack.

He and Dewey were drinking bourbon. Dewey was sweating, and he was not. Dewey was squirming, trembling, suffering. It was like the story of Dr Faustus, and the journalist knew, that, with no action on his part, the truth was pecking more and more rhapsodically against the inside of Dewey's egg and would soon tumble out, as it did.

"I didn't write the speech," Dewey said, immediately feeling a few demons flee his soul. "Nope. Didn't. Didn't do the *Nightline* thing, either. That's the truth."

Finally, the journalist spoke, as delicately as if he were carrying nitroglycerine with his voice. "Who did, Senator?" he asked so quietly that it could hardly be heard.

After a pause in which Dewey decided to take the real plunge, he said, "Idoh know. God, Idoh know. This Lachpoof guy. This Moofoomooach. Says he's a dentist. Got a real beautiful wife. Right here in Siliphant."

The next morning, the vast press contingent that had swelled Siliphant into a kind of First Amendment boil learned from *The New York Times* that the new force behind Dewey Knott was a dentist and his wife with the unfathomable name of Moofoomooach. Now, this was a story, and had Siliphant in fact been a boat it would have capsized as virtually everyone in town raced toward the side of town where the dental office was situated, but the eminent journalist of the *Times* had already been there and gone.

In the house where the miracles had transpired were dental books and equipment. Food was in the refrigerator (what the hell was Bovril?). Everything was sparklingly clean. But no one was there, no Moofoomooach, no tall athletic dentist, no exquisitely beautiful dontist. They had been there, as the locals were glad to attest, but they had gone, and no one, not even Dewey Knott, knew where.

FLASH FIRE

THOUGH THE SUN was not directly visible, Freddy could tell their direction of travel by the light behind the clouds, but he had neither map nor watch, and could only approximate a guess as to how fast they were rolling west-south-west. Then again, neither did they care. They had no place in particular to go and no schedule to keep. The empty boxcar was clean, the doors wide open, the air sweet, and they had escaped from Siliphant before dawn.

Back in Siliphant—crowded with politician and the press—time, deadlines, meaningless manners, tight ties, and invasive cameras were everywhere. Those who had arrived in chartered planes or helicopters, in large rented automobiles, or in buses with dressing rooms, had positions to keep and defend. Every moment of their lives was spent building the bulwarks that kept from them the peaceful anonymity Freddy and Fredericka now enjoyed, knowing that neither a single question would they answer nor into a single lens would they blink.

They sat in the south-facing doorway. In the distance, thunderstorms swept to the east in cliff-like formations, their lightning palsied and golden against black cloud. This was to the saffron yellow of random swales a painterly adornment worthy of Giorgione, but Giorgione had never seen the American Plains with their banks of purple thundercloud in long easily moving fronts of a hundred miles or more. To this royalty of nature was added music from the rolling of the wheels and their perfectly timed syncopation as they crossed small gaps in the rails.

"I have the map only partially by memory," Freddy said. "It's easy to know that Nebraska sits on top of Kansas, and that given our direction we should be heading toward and across the western part of Kansas and into Colorado, but the scale is hard to understand. I wish I had a superimposition of, say, Watford to Luton, so I could have a sense of time and distance."

"What about Malmesbury to Crudwell?" Fredericka asked. "We cycled that once."

"We did?"

"Viscount Ellesmere and I."

"I didn't know you saw him," Freddy said, displeased. "He looks like a pig."

"No he doesn't, he's very handsome. He has quite small ears."

"Did you kiss him?"

"Of course I kissed him. He was my boyfriend."

"Wait," Freddy said, with an abrupt movement of his hands that signalled her to be silent. He listened.

"What?"

He pointed at the ceiling, his eyes following heavy footsteps on the catwalk. He counted: "One, two . . . three," he whispered, even if no one on the roof would have been able to hear him in his normal voice.

"What is it?"

"Three men," he said, "have hesitated here."

"Freddy?" Fredericka was about to ask a question she hadn't yet entirely grasped when they both saw a head appear at the upper edge of the door. Though it was upside down, it was easy to read. The man had long black hair, he was unshaven, his neck was tattooed, and his eyes were like a hunter's. After discovering them, he was pulled back up.

"Oh Freddy," Fredericka said, sick with fear because of the cruelty in the man's eyes.

"I think they're going to attack us," he said.

"How do you know?" she asked, hoping that Freddy would not be able to come up with a logical answer.

"No greeting. He surveyed us. It was as if he were shopping for food."

"What are we going to do?"

Freddy was taking all things into account, too busy for the moment to answer.

"Since we've been here, we've seen no violence," she said. "The country's reputation for violence is much exaggerated, isn't it?"

"We have no weapon other than the folding knife with the wooden handle. Get it out of your pack quickly but calmly. I don't know what they may come up with."

Her hands trembled as she undid the straps.

"Don't worry. They're not down yet, you have plenty of time, and they may be peaceful."

A pair of legs appeared in the upper door, dangling. Then a man slithered down to position himself for a swing and a jump.

"Be calm, Fredericka."

"I've never done this."

"I'll do it."

She came to the clasp knife Freddy had taken from the dental office. Its walnut handle was oiled with time and cracked about the rivets, and the Henckels Solingen steel was as grey as nickel. The handle was five and a half inches long and the blade four inches. Freddy always measured any knife that came into his possession and examined it most carefully. He would then clean it and sharpen it, as he had this one, until it could cut silk in air. She handed it to him.

He opened it, shook it a bit, passed it from hand to hand, all while keeping an eye on the dangling legs, and then folded it and put it in his pocket.

"Oh God, Freddy," Fredericka pleaded, "can't we jump?"

"The train's going too fast," he said. The man swung to and fro, looking down, and when he saw his moment, let go. He hurtled in, crashed to the floor, and rolled. Then he stood, as if to protect himself, and stepped back. Freddy remained seated.

"Aren't you going to get up?" Fredericka asked.

"Better this way."

She was perplexed. It seemed senseless to stay on the floor while one's attackers were on their feet. New legs appeared on either side. In a short time, two more men were in. They stood together, breathing rather hard and joyfully in light of the fact that they had yet to accomplish anything. Their clothes were piratical, they had universal convicts' facial hair, tattoos, and bandannas. All that was missing to complete the picture was a good parrot.

"I can't do anything," Freddy said to Fredericka, as tranquilly as if they were discussing this over tea at the Connaught, "until they make their intentions clear. It wouldn't be right to attack them without knowing what they want. They may be just farmworkers."

"No," Fredericka said.

The one in a blue bandanna looked alternately at Freddy and Fredericka, like a mouse who looks alternately at the trap and the cheese, and was finally overcome. He grabbed his groin and, popping his pelvis in imitation of copulation, began to strut toward Fredericka. This clarification of his intentions brought forth from the rest of them expressions that clarified theirs.

Freddy addressed them as if giving instructions to a driver: "If you intend to kill me, gang-rape my wife, and then kill her, you should jump off the train while you can."

The one in the red bandanna reached into his trouser pocket and withdrew a black switchblade that he held ceremoniously in front of his face before he opened it with a shock to the air.

"That doesn't make the knife any more lethal," Freddy told Fredericka, like an instructor. "It's to help them work themselves up. We, too, can work ourselves up."

She nodded, too afraid to speak.

"First, remember that we are just. Then, that we are conquerors, and not to be conquered. For a thousand years and more we have steadily prevailed. The Vikings who came to our shores were more fearsome and frightening than this, and we dealt with them by raising good yeomen, who were not afraid, and who beat them back. I'm not afraid of a cruel face or Satanic hair, neither of which is a qualification for combat. Nor should you be. If you have to, fight like your ancestors."

"My ancestors who were knights and generals were not women."

"If women defend their children, they can fight magnificently well."

"We have no children, Freddy."

"We shall."

"We shall," Fredericka said, and to the shock of her husband and her would-be oppressors, was the first to charge. Tactically, it was a risk, but it worked, in that the pride of these men obliged them to be amused, and they tried not to handle her too roughly, so as to preserve her for the use they intended. She rammed blue-bandanna against the oaken walls of the freight car and was tiger-scratching him well enough that he was completely distracted.

The other two went for Freddy, who had remained on the floor, one leg almost stretched out and the other partially folded beneath him. Brandishing the knife, red-bandanna came forward expecting Freddy to move, which would have led to a natural placement of the blade. Like cats, knife fighters prefer moving targets. But Freddy stayed still, and red-bandanna, not knowing what to do, looked at no-bandanna and laughed nervously, as if to say, how can I slash him if he's not moving? Then no-bandanna angrily took the knife and threw himself at Freddy, who caught the knife-hand at the wrist and pulled forward. In sitting, Freddy had a much lower centre of gravity than his assailant, who was on his feet and arched over. Staying low, Freddy pushed him rapidly toward the door, lurching this way and that to knock him off balance, and, after a second or two, tossed him out.

For a moment Freddy watched no-bandanna cartwheel into the airstream, the switchblade following its own trajectory after it was released from his hand. Then Freddy stood. He was a head taller than red-bandanna, who, now terrified, began to strike Freddy with karate blows he had copped from the movies. Freddy blocked each one until he had manoeuvred to a clear space. Then he seized red-bandanna's arm and bent it back in contravention of the ordinary movement of the joint. Hoping to be released from this agony by being thrown from the train, red-bandanna moved, screaming, toward the south door. Freddy waited an instant for softer ground, and then ejected him with the same push that he customarily used to throw his royal cousins into swimming pools. Pivoting around, he saw blue-bandanna strike Fredericka on the face. Her hands blocked the next blows, but some were getting through, and she was going under.

Freddy ferociously pulled her tormentor aside and broke his jaw with a stunning blow from the right hand. With fury and clenched teeth, he was about to kill him when he realised that it was unnecessary. Seizing the man's ear, he led him to the door and threw him out onto the prairie. It had all happened in about a minute.

"I'm sorry," Freddy said to Fredericka, touching her face as she cried, rocking her back and forth. He surveyed her bruises and cuts, saying, "All this will heal. Don't worry."

"How do you know they haven't got back on the train?" she asked.

"The train is going sixty miles an hour, and they didn't land softly."

"What if there are others?"

"There probably aren't, but, if there are, you know what to do. You were magnificent."

"Oh," she said modestly, "that just happened."

"So did Trafalgar," Freddy said, "and Waterloo."

IN KNOTT-SPEAK, what Dewey called the "proposition" *this* signified that the word it preceded was desirable, of value, and of use to Dewey. The "proposition" *that,* however, denoted the opposite. Dewey never had to fire anyone. All he had to do was say, "Where is that advance man we hired in Cincinnati?" and Finney passed the word. If on the other hand Dewey were to say, "Who is this blonde in the press office?" Dot would run to her gastroenterologist. It was a primitive system, but it worked so well among those who knew him that he assumed everyone else knew what he was saying when he used differential "propositions," even if not everyone did.

Shortly after his election to the Senate he had discovered that he no longer had to use verbs. He might say, "Cattle. Fat. Lots'a money. Good year. Farmers. Happy." This Amerindian syntax suited him well, and the electorate had a sense of what it meant. But very few people knew the full range of Knottisms, such as that when he said, in answer to a town meeting question, "When I'm president, we'll talk to that country," he meant he would destroy it, or that if he said, "Dewey Knott will examine this bill," the bill was certain to pass, because the industry that would profit had just, out of principle, donated several million dollars to the party in soft money that would nevertheless be channelled to Dewey's campaign. Because someone who seldom uses verbs has even less use for conjunctions, Dewey used *that* mainly as a demonstrative, which made Finney's task in deciphering him easier. But Dewey was unpredictable.

On the campaign plane as they made their way back to Washington, Finney felt that he had reached a tranquil ledge of some sort. Down on earth the lights were coming up as the jet pushed east into rapidly falling darkness. Though he hadn't slept in several days, he felt calm. Dot was in her cabin, with the door shut, in Byzantine conspiracy with nameless aides. Mushrom, rapidly going downhill even as the plane gained altitude, was sitting on a pile of luggage near the galley, a bottle of vodka held by its neck in his left fist as if he were choking a goose. Dewey was in his cabin, listening to be-bop music and reading a cake-decorating catalogue. Finney was wonderfully alone behind his own partition, with a drink on his left, six newspapers on his right, his shoes off, and his bleary eyes watching dim constellations, strings of lighted towns, and silent chains of moonlit mist floating like chimney smoke over the Alleghenies. It was quiet. He had merely three journalists on the line, one to whom he was actually talking and two who were for the moment only blinking red lights.

One was an investigative reporter who, with the tension of an assassin, was tracing rumours that in his youth Dewey had clubbed a seal. Finney said: "I know, I know, I know. That's what they say. But I tell you, Roberto,

I've seen him with seals. He loves seals. No guilt, no apprehension. This was before the rumour. He's definitely pro-seal. . . . I did ask him, and he was vehement, vehement. I give you my word, there are no seals in Nebraska outside of zoos. Yes. Yes. No, I don't expect you to stop seeking the truth. You should always seek the truth, but this is the truth. Senator Knott never clubbed a seal, has always been pro-seal, and as president will continue to be pro-seal. . . . That's Canada, Roberto. We can't promise to invade Canada to stop seal clubbing. What? Yes, I know they're just Canadians, but we still can't invade. Well what *about* the president? He's president already, and we haven't invaded Canada, have we? Can I say this off the record? We're off the record, right? I have no idea if this is true or not, but a source I have who was a classmate of the vice president tells me that, when the vice president was in college, he made disparaging remarks about otters. I'd look into that if I were you. Yes. Yes. Even jokes. That's right."

While Finney was having this conversation, his end of which he could have held up in his sleep, he was reading editorials and analysing poll data. The second light was the *Bhutan Register-Bee,* calling for the fifteenth time about a one-on-one interview Dewey would never grant because no one in Bhutan voted in American presidential elections, and the Bhutanese community in the United States was, in Dewey terminology, not exactly the biggest enchilada on the tray. All Finney had to do was tell them gently that he didn't think it would be possible, and, unlike American journalists, who would at that point inflict upon him a thousand ferret bites and make ten thousand threats, the Bhutanese would apologise profusely and hang up. The third light was a reporter for a woman's magazine who wanted Dewey's—specifically not Dot's—recipe for fried chicken. The angle was that, because of "the new androgyny," Dewey should have the recipes and Dot should do woodworking and subscribe to *Field & Stream.* By the time Finney had picked off the other two lights and taken Naomi Schreckstein's fried-chicken call, he had finished his drink and was dreaming of living in Bhutan, with a deferential Bhutanese wife, on top of a mountain with views of half the world, and lots of heat and hot water.

"Naomi." He hated her. "Yes, I did. I asked him. Do you want the fried chicken he makes at home for a romantic dinner with Dot, or the fried chicken he makes for large groups?" She asked for the romantic dinner. "He changes the recipe sometimes, but, basically, you take two and a half pounds of fryer parts, bind them up with twenty or thirty feet of titanium wire, and attach each end to a one-hundred-and-twenty-five-volt power source. Brush the trussed parts with single malt Scotch, shake a mixture of saffron and tapioca over it, plug in the wires, and, as it cooks, baste with Coca-Cola." She had stopped typing. "Yes," Finney told her, "I'm serious. He got the recipe from Justice Izzblind. Saffron, did I forget the saffron?" She typed the rest and went to file. Finney had a clear conscience, because this was, in fact, the way Dewey cooked fried chicken, and it was delicious, even if, as it was cooking, it tended to explode.

For a moment, all was quiet. No phones, no blinking lights except those of distant cities in the dark and planes speeding silently west; editorials finished; polls analysed; only the steady sound of engines thriving in air. In near silence high over eastern Kentucky—to the north, Cincinnati looked like a blazing star, and beyond it Cleveland was but a glow—Finney was at the same altitude as Bhutan. He was just about to rest when suddenly Dewey burst in.

"Where's this Lachpoof guy?" he asked. "That Lachpoof guy . . . who the hell is he? What are we going to do about that guy? This guy's crucial. He's a pain. What a speech! He fixed my tooth. Is it what the voters want? I don't want defeat to slip through my hands again. Whatever it takes. If it takes that guy. . . . Finney, find this Lachpoof."

"*That* or *this*, Senator?"

"Doesn't matter. Do we not know where he is?"

"You do?"

"What?"

"You know where he is?"

"No, where is he?"

"I don't know," said Finney. "Wait a minute." He picked up the phone and called the intelligence agencies' liaison at campaign headquarters in Washington (the candidates needed frequent briefings). "You know the Lachpoof guy, Dr Moofoomooach?"

Finney nodded to Dewey Knott. They knew. They read the papers. That's how they did their job.

"Do we not know where he is?"

"No I don't," Dewey protested.

Finney put his hand over the mouthpiece. "No," he said to Dewey, "*Do we not* . . . know where he is."

"I toldya, I don't have a clue."

"*Do we! Do we!*"

"You're drunk."

"No, I'm not."

"No, *I'm* Knott," Dewey said, "and I don't like it when you say my name like you're calling a pig."

"No, Senator, I said 'Do we not,' as in 'Are we not?'"

A fierce look came over Dewey. He pointed his right pinkie threateningly at Finney, and said in a low growl so that the press in the back of the plane wouldn't hear it, "It's okay if, sometimes, when you're drunk, you push the limit with me, Finney. But, Finney, don't ever, ever, screw around with my uncle. I get crazy, you know."

"Your uncle, Senator?"

"I loved my uncle. Good man. I don't care if I'm president or not, don't insult my family."

"You never told me about your uncle, sir. Who was he?"

"My uncle Arwe, my father's older brother, an enzyme in the navy. Watch your tongue. I mean it."

"I'm sorry."

Only now did Finney remember a picture in Dewey's office of a man at a Midwestern carnival, cotton candy in hand and a broad smile across his face. Once, Dewey had pointed to it and said, "Arwe Knott having fun." Now Finney understood.

Dewey looked down rather sadly. "Can't bring those days back—the China Station, Babe Ruth, no air-conditioning, Wild Root Creme Oil. Find him."

"Arwe?"

"No, Lachpoof."

"What if we can't?"

"Then I lose the election. What am I supposed to do, go back to Siliphant? I'd rather kill myself."

Dewey left. Never had Finney felt more for him. Dewey was not as insensate as he sometimes appeared: he suffered. Dewey ducked back in. "He's a dentist, for Chrissake. Dentists are not counterfeiters, they leave tracks, big tracks, should be easy to find, get on it."

IN LESS THAN TWO DAYS, Freddy and Fredericka were carried into the landscape of the Mountain West, which was sometimes a desolate moonplace and sometimes overwhelmingly beautiful. Even were you used to it, it kept opening up to you and pulling you in. It was as wide and bright as the sea, but you could walk across it, rise into the meadows of its mountains, and move forever in its sinuous riverbeds and across its high plains. It was so wide that it was virtually untouched, its settlements having little sense of permanence. None of its cities was anchored even half as much as Boston, Bath, or Marseilles. Though the water gushed upwelling or was piped and pumped, by instinct not a single living thing trusted that it would keep running. Thus everything was as ephemeral as the quick and disappointing rains, and except in the mountains that waylaid Pacific clouds, the land was too dry to have a long history or a permanent future. Still, it was beautiful, a transient paradise for transient souls, a place of little record and less contemplation, but of a present that burst forth like a river in sunlit leaps through the gorges its ancestors had prepared for flight.

Freddy had been to all the major places in America that were even vaguely like England. In favour of playing polo in Virginia or making a speech in Cambridge, he had skipped the West except as a place, in the late fifties, to kill large animals, and was unfamiliar with it other than by looking down from the Concorde on his way to Los Angeles or San Francisco. And these, as far as he was concerned, were cities with a tenuous hold not only upon America but upon earth. The first time he had seen San Francisco he had come from the sea on *Britannia* and had assumed he was hallucinating. He loved it, but he never stopped believing it was only a puff of ether. He had gone inland in California, once, to visit a walnut ranch, but apart from that had known nothing other than a strip of Pacific coast ten miles wide. Now they were in the West that neither he nor Fredericka had experienced except as a terra-cotta-coloured carpet so distant that it might have been the textured wall of one of the neopalaeolithic buildings Freddy so disdained.

Awakening in the evening of the second day and having eaten all their rations that required no cooking, they were tired of the noise of the train and they wanted hot food, hot tea, the smell of a fire, and quiet. "Where are we?" Fredericka asked, because Freddy always knew where he was.

"I don't know," he admitted. "I was totally confused when we crossed the mountains, and I have no idea how long we've slept."

A sharp line of blue-black mountains ran close and parallel. The train was slowing on a grade. "Look, Freddy," Fredericka said, pointing out and to the right. "Look at that." Forward of their position the serrated edge of the mountains was diffused with a pink glow, and the stars that rested on the dark ridge looming above them had a different character than those on either side.

"It must be a town or a city," Freddy said.

"Not the setting sun?"

"The setting sun would line the tops of the mountains along their whole length, and dim the stars that ride close over them. And because the air is so clear that most of the light escapes through it, what we see must be the remnant of a powerful emanation. It has to be a large city."

"What city?" she asked.

"Perhaps it's Amarillo," he said, pronouncing it *Amariyyo*. "When the train slows, let's get off and climb to the top of the ridge. There we'll see what kind of town it is, and as it will probably take several hours to get to the top, we can prepare a meal at the summit before deciding where to go."

"What about snakes?" she asked.

"What about them?"

"Won't we step on them?"

"Do you think the land is covered with snakes?"

"Once, in Greece, I saw a hill covered with snakes."

"Someone must have fed them. They'll be scarce here. To survive on land so dry, they need a large territory. And if they hear us they'll run away or rattle." The train shuddered as it took the grade. "Come, it's time to get off."

Freddy went first. Sitting on the floor with legs hanging down, he gripped the handle of the open door and pushed himself out, right hand on the handle, left hand on the steel rim of the floor. Holding on to the train, he had time for his feet to find the ground, come to a properly paced run, and feel what was beneath them. Then he disengaged and, still running, dropped his pack so he could keep up with Fredericka, who threw hers down and did what he had done, though he helped her by clasping her waist so she would not fall when she let go.

They slowed from their run, grateful that the ground was even and not too rocky. As the train passed with great booms of hollow steel, they stepped back to catch their breath, holding one another in what they did not know was an embrace common in square dancing. Within a minute or two, everything was quiet. While they walked along the ties on their way to retrieve the packs, the wind came up, and they buttoned their jackets.

"It smells good," Fredericka said. "They sell that kind of herb in fancy cosmetic shops, in little metal tins, for ten pounds," she marvelled, "and here the air is saturated with it."

"You see," said Freddy, "the sweat and sacrifice, the loss of life, the life-long work and discipline, that it took to make a class of people who could afford to buy that herb in Mayfair for ten pounds an ounce, is here confounded and contradicted as transcontinental winds blow it in a volume a fifth of the American sky over distances that make of Mayfair a stupid little snuffbox of vanity and pomposity that God crushes with the railroad track of His foot."

"Freddy," Fredericka asked, "are you insane?"

"Absolutely not."

"You sound like Cheverly de Montbasse Blasson-Couville when he was on LSD."

"Who was he?"

"He was a boyfriend."

"How many bloody boyfriends have you had? I've never heard of him."

She stopped on the ties. "I've had many," she said. "Some people think that I'm beautiful. That's a power, like the power of royalty. It's why you chose me, is it not? After all, you didn't know me. But I've dismissed all of them and devoted myself to you. I've given myself to you, Freddy. You may have my body, soul, everything. Time passes, and all I want is the intimacy that slows, defeats, and confounds it. Love, Freddy, that's what it is. You've always made the mistake that men often make, and carried forward the great fault that mars civilisation, which is that you believe that your philosophy is deeper than love."

Freddy stopped abruptly. He had fallen in love with her in America as if she had been something as natural and unconscious as a sea fan waving in the ocean above a reef. Now he had discovered that her philosophy was indeed, and had always been, deeper than his—something that now made him desire her without limit.

He guided her off the tracks, his hands on her broad and lovely shoulders.

"Freddy," she asked, although she did not have to, "what are you doing?"

He brought her to rest on an earthen bank of dry dust. "Fredericka. Fredericka Whitaker Nicols Marshall Seaforth Kent . . . Fredericka, Fredericka." Never had he been able to say her entire name: even she had great difficulty remembering it. They had thudded down, and on the rough ground of the high desert, on a dark hillside by an empty track, in escape from the terrible gravity in the lives of commoners and kings alike, a queen of England was conceived.

NAKED, AMAZED, freezing, shocked, and shivering, they awoke at three in the morning, covered themselves, and spent the next two hours climbing to the top of the ridge. The glow from the city on the other side made the edge a salmon-coloured line pulsing like a sunset. Perfumes of the desert rose with them in their ascent, and when they reached the summit thousands of feet from where they had started they saw on the other side a most extraordinary thing, as if they were not on earth but in a kind of heaven where entertainments of light were the chief concern.

Beneath them was a city stretching to a horizon of distant mountains in a meadow of a hundred million lights. Rigid lines of rubies and pearls blinking red and white travelled as smoothly as blood surging through a beast on the Serengeti. Like traversing shotguns, the royal eyes moved to the centre, where the scintillating arteries led to glowing boxes, light-washed pyramids, and jets as white as maggots, sucking passengers from gangways like piglets alongside a sow. Filled and happy with power after feeding, they ran down purple-spotted tarmacs and left the earth behind.

In the midst of all this was, obviously, a giant sphinx; delicate rows of royal palms by the thousand, each illuminated by an individual spotlight; and fountains in fake Egyptian gardens that shone like rayon. Always through everything moved the red bloodstream of cars, twinkling cells streaming along broad boulevards through the black of undeveloped sand waiting for the mitosis of a casino. Its lights were as riotous as bubbles in a mountain flume, and absent astronomical or galactic metaphor this city, which seemed to be on fire, made no sense whatsoever.

"What is that?" Fredericka asked. "Is it a city? Is it a hallucination? Is something wrong with us?"

"It is a city," her husband answered, happy, spent, and delighted, "a very strange city in the desert. They don't have any water: they have to pipe it in, and I think that they may gamble there."

"What's it called?"

"I don't really remember. Ciudad de something or other. Though the lights are fascinating, you can see even from a great distance that it's ugly and dangerous, and we shan't go there. We need wilderness now, and purity, and, God knows, neither wilderness nor purity is down there."

Dewey Knott called Finney into his office three times a day to ask, as if he had never asked before, "Where is this Lachpoof guy? Have you found him?" Finney was beating the bushes all over the United States in an increasingly obsessive search. Teams of investigators—some freshly retired from CIA or the FBI; others hard-bitten, heavily accented, former New York cops who normally could find a drop of water hiding at the bottom of the ocean—made life very difficult for dentists, endodontists, pediatric dentists, orthodontists, cosmetic dentists, periodontists, dental surgeons, hygienists, technicians, enamelists, and receptionists. Unsuspecting presidents of state dental societies were rousted in the middle of the night or easily pulled over in their Cateras, Mercedes, and Excelsiors with license plates like *Bicuspid, Fang,* and *Bite.* The former agents and police would flash their federal gun permits and say, "Just a few questions, Dr Megaloseras. We're looking for two dentists; last names Moofoomooach, man and wife, his name Lachpoof Moofoomooach, her name, we think, Popeel Moofoomooach." The universal response to this was a narrow-eyed gaze, a slight turn of the head, and then the incredulously phrased, "What?"

It was easy to disappear in America. A man had only to grow a blond moustache, lift weights, buy a pickup truck, and wear a tool belt. A woman had only to frost her hair, wear a blue suit, and drive an SUV. By adopting names other than Lachpoof or Popeel, such as Randy, Jason, Jennifer, or Cheryl, you could walk through walls. Though neither Freddy nor Fredericka knew that they were being sought, and had not thought to hide, they could not have been better hidden or lost more than they were in the mountains, weaving unseen to one side or the other of the Continental Divide as they made their way north through evergreen forests, open meadows, and across blindingly bright snowfields in a patchwork that covered the high mountains like the coat of a dappled horse. They went almost five hundred miles this way, skirting settlements except for brief forays to buy food or equipment, until they came to a place where they stopped, and changed direction.

Not quite a town, Pine Ridge floated in clear air and warm intermittent sunshine, the flow of which was controlled by the shutters and apertures of enormous mountain clouds higher and whiter than the snow-covered summits above which they sailed. Like the miscalculations of a pastry chef, they accumulated in rolls and bulges, a kingdom of whipped cream rising into the troposphere on winds aloft. Freddy and Fredericka knew the Alps quite well. These mountains were sharper, younger, lower, and neither half as looming nor half as dark. The greens were lighter, the sun brighter, the air sweeter. And yet they shared with the Alps the high, almost unreachable snow cornices that cut the clouds into clumps of stray sheep, and they shared the great sheer walls. There is no better or purer way to reset the clock of the soul than by reaching the top of one of these massifs, with bloody hands and fingers, ten pounds gone, and the sweet smell of mountain lichen everywhere on your clothes.

They themselves stood in the alternating waves of sunshine and shadow as they watched the light play across high snowfields. Whenever the wind came up, they were surrounded by pacifying scents of pine that perfumed valley after valley and were carried on the air in a world of unnamed rivers. Their feeling of well being, however, was challenged by their sudden immersion in a vibrant youth culture in which they had no place. Nearly everyone in Pine Ridge was a firefighter, a blemishless youth in search of adventure and devoted entirely to fitness, physical tests, and the opposite sex. The young men and women there survived, it seemed, on inedible, foil-wrapped, pseudo–candy bars that went by names such as *Amino-Glycosine Surprise* and *B$_1$ Folic Acid Crunch*. Their skin was smooth, their muscles taut, and their eyes covered in hideous futuristic sunglasses with lizardine lenses and garishly coloured frames. The dress code was as strict and malicious as that which once had governed Restoration dandies, and though neither a frill nor a ruffle was to be seen, the spectrum of colours could easily have outshone a Brazilian Indian in his most extravagant war paint. Freddy was too middle-aged for this, and even Fredericka— young enough to have passed, and who, because of her snow-blinding teeth, could have been taken for a California girl—was too old to feel comfortable. As they walked through the settlement to the Forest Service office, rather than take note of men engaged in pull-up contests or strutting like heroes of battle, or of women so nubile, fresh, and young as to make even Fredericka seem mature, they tended to look into the mountains and up at the sky. Though vitality did not overflow from them as it did from the youths, it filled them nonetheless, quietly, and exactly to the brim.

In the Forest Service office they had only just completed a few forms before they were quickly pulled out of the queue by a grandfatherly uniformed ranger who looked like a badger. Every word he spoke had the grace of age, as if he had come through much that was bitter, only to be kind. "Come in," he said. "You may wonder why I skipped you ahead the way I did. Have a seat."

He gestured to two cane chairs. Then he sat down at his desk, put on his reading glasses, and picked up their applications. "You people have two advantages none of those kids out there has, and I'm hoping that we can put them to good use. One, you're married. And, two, you're old enough not to mind periods of stillness."

"What exactly do you mean?" Freddy asked.

"Long stretches of inactivity. You like to read? You like to watch as the wind pushes the clouds?"

Freddy smiled.

"Yeah," said the ranger. "I'll bet you do. You get a nineteen-year-old kid, and he's gotta move. Doesn't have the attention span of a waterbug. And, here's the thing. The rules may be antiquated, but they do say that if two people man a fire tower and they're of the opposite sex, they've gotta be married. Not one of those kids out there is married, but you are. How'd you like to spend the summer in a fire tower: supplies (or most of them anyway) supplied, money accumulating, and the most beautiful, private place in the world all to yourselves?"

"I would have thought," said Freddy, "that each position would have a hundred applicants."

"You would have been right," said the ranger. "But the couple that manned Centennial Seven is leaving today, because his mother died yesterday. It came through this morning. We're airlifting them to Bozeman, where they'll get a flight to Seattle, and as that's home, that's I guess where they'll stay."

"I see," said Freddy.

"The helicopter will come back here. We can have you up there by tomorrow evening. Lucia, the chief of the Centennial Line, can teach you how to map-read and locate, and you can start forthwith."

"I know how to map-read," Freddy said. "I was trained as a navigator and in route finding."

"Where?"

"The navy and the army. I fly helicopters and fixed-wing, although I don't have my papers with me."

"I understand: this is your vacation. Can I ask you a question or two, just to check, and then we'll leave it at that? Just so I can let Lucia in on it?"

"By all means."

"Good. All right, what's declination?"

"Declination is the angular difference between true north and either magnetic or grid north," Freddy answered.

"What's the back azimuth of one hundred and eighty degrees?"

"Zero, or three hundred and sixty degrees, whichever way you express it."

"Sharp," said the ranger. "One more."

Freddy nodded.

"Last question. How do you plot an azimuth from a known point?"

"If necessary," Freddy told him, "you convert from magnetic to grid. You place the index mark of a protractor at the mass centre of the point in question, with the zero/one-eighty baseline parallel to a north-south grid line. Mark the map at the azimuth desired. Connect the two. That's it."

"What's it called?"

"The grid direction line."

"You are a navigator."

"I said so."

"Take the job. You and your wife will keep a twenty-four-hour watch. It isn't difficult at all. I'll put you in at the highest grade I can, and I promise to do my best when we load up the helicopter with supplies. We want you until the middle of September unless the whole damn forest burns down around you, in which case the job is over. It happens sometimes, and it's been very dry. Probably, though, you'll get through the summer and remember it as one of the best things in your life."

ALTHOUGH THEY HAD not known they needed rest, at Centennial Seven they would get the rest they needed. Rest, Freddy had told Fredericka when he was courting her, was like the willow tree at Moocock. At first its leaves grow almost imperceptibly. In the beginning of the world no bookmaker would have given odds that such a skinny, stringy thing would ever become full. But the willow in spring explodes in green so suddenly and quickly that it can fill out in hours. Rest works ever so slowly, but on every single cell at once, so that when one has been repaired, so have all the others, and strength returns as if in a flood.

They shopped in town for personal items the Forest Service did not provide, and Freddy hired a youth to obtain some necessities for them in

Cheyenne. Just before the helicopter was about to lift off, and after ducking beneath its rotor blades and handing Freddy a book and two slab-like
packages, the youth became five hundred dollars richer. The packages
contained a copy of the Iliad in Greek, each page reproduced on a sixteen
by twenty-four sheet of bright white paper; and a copy of the Liddell and
Scott new abridged *Greek Lexicon,* of 1871, with four pages on each sixteen by twenty-four sheet, the text nicely enlarged and bright, two hundred
sheets in all, quite easily manageable. Freddy was going to have another go
at the Iliad, hoping to make a leap from these light-filled mountains to the
light-filled Aegean.

And he was going to teach it to Fredericka. He knew from the story of
Paolo and Francesca that nothing could match the intimacy between a
man and a woman as both studied the same text over days and weeks.
Then it is that love and desire fuse most powerfully, that one soul becomes
the other and the other becomes it. With the world spread out before
them and the perfume of uncountable pines filling the air, they would
lose themselves entirely in imagination of the Mediterranean and its
ancient wars.

They laid out the texts on a long desk beneath one wall of windows
in the observation room, and worked on them side by side. To fulfil
their obligation to the forest, they merely had to look up every half hour
and scan the distance for smoke. As they did this, slowly over 360 degrees,
they found that the forests and mountains sharply compressed in their
binoculars were as beautiful and fascinating as anything that had ever been
written.

At Centennial Seven they had among other things a Winchester Model
70 in case grizzlies should attack; pure water from an icy torrent two hundred feet down the mountainside; six weeks of supplies neatly stacked in
pine cupboards; a radio that seemed to crack with the static of the galaxies
and nebulae; a terrace on the roof, accessible by hatch and ladder; and a
beautifully drawn, highly detailed map under glass on a huge table in the
centre of the room. With this they could locate any fires they might detect
by plumes of smoke in daylight and orange sparks at night. Their foam
mattress was underneath the table, beneath the map's many shades of green
that spread over them like a baobab tree.

The tower rose sixty feet from the crest of a ridge, and they could look
over the treetops with ease. From windows on all sides the world was visible to the horizon, except that to the north a massive rockface rose

abruptly and blocked the view. On the other side of this wall, seven miles distant by a trail that led through forests and over alpine meadows the home of bear and elk, was Centennial Six, the centre tower, where Lucia lived and from which she managed the line via radio. She was alone there, and awakened only every hour to observe. This was allowed to her because some of her sector was covered by another line of towers to the north, a lot was rock, and even in summer much remained blanketed in snow.

The helicopter pilot had said that the previous occupants of Centennial Seven had dispensed with clothing. Except for Lucia, who announced her visits beforehand, even in midsummer only a few people a month came within ten miles of the tower. You could live there, if you wished, like Adam and Eve.

"Adam and Eve Piesecki?" Fredericka had asked, to put the pilot off the subject, but later, in private, she seemed quite interested.

"You'd like to be a nudist?" Freddy asked. "I bloody well will never be a nudist."

"Of course not, idiot. Nudists live in camps. This would be just the two of us."

"Even when we get water, and work? I would be carrying a rifle in the buff? What if someone came? What if a bear came?"

"Bears are naked, too. That's why they're called bears."

"It's libertine."

"It is permitted," Fredericka stated, slowly and seductively, "by the bonds of holy matrimony, which permit the other things that we do, in their great variety, and that, I should think, would flourish here, where we are entirely alone and no one could possibly hear any sounds." She cleared her throat.

"What about accidents?" asked Freddy. "Things getting caught in things where normally they would not be extended, in hinges and doors and hatch covers."

"I will make sure," Fredericka said, "that whatever is extended is protected. I will keep on top of it meticulously."

"You will?"

"I will."

Thus, the first time they sat down to read the Iliad, they had been naked for days.

"Here is the Greek alphabet," said Freddy. He had written it out in fluid strokes on a lustrous sheet of paper.

"Is that the telephone?" asked Fredericka.

"No, it's the alphabet."

"Not the alphabet—I know that the alphabet doesn't make a noise—the telephone."

"We don't have a telephone."

"Shhh! That."

"That's a woodpecker."

"It sounds like a telephone."

"Nonetheless, it is a woodpecker, and this is the Greek alphabet."

"Look at that," Fredericka said. "You could be Greek. Where did you learn it?"

"I began when I was five years old."

"It's beautiful."

"Yes. This is *alpha.*"

"You mean as in *alphabet?*"

"That's where the word *alphabet* comes from. The second letter is *beta.*"

"Marvellous. What do they mean?"

"*Alpha* is *a,* and *beta* is *b.*"

"Why did they have to do that? Why not just say *a* and *b?*"

"*Alpha* and *beta* came before *a* and *b.* We're the ones who 'did it.'"

"Then why did we do it?"

Freddy pondered. "I don't know. Fredericka, are you anxious?"

"Yes."

"Why?"

"I've always thought Greek was too difficult, and only for boys."

"That was one of the injustices of your education. Now you can learn it in full confidence."

Thus began their study of the classics, as they sat together, unclothed, high above the forest floor, beyond the tops of the trees, as alone in the warm sunlight as if at the very beginning of time.

THE BOOK that the youth had brought to Freddy along with the Iliad and Greek lexicon was a memoir recently released by a cousin fairly far removed, François-Trotsky Snatt-Ball, Viscount Stansfield. Less controversial in England than perhaps it might have been, it was an indictment of Freddy via the questioning of his sanity. Though Snatt-Ball had hardly known Freddy, they had been together in enough group photographs for him to make the case that he had. And he had had one famous encounter with Freddy, the subject of the memoir's central chapter.

François-Trotsky, or, as Freddy called him, with a treacherously steep *a,* Viscount Snatt-Ball, was a huge, fat thing with no self-discipline, and the way Freddy and his father devoted themselves to physical pursuits offended him. He had written a catty article in which he suggested not only that this was a middle-class-German characteristic they could not shake, but that both had undergone electro-shock therapy for the purpose of making them less compulsive, and, for good measure, that Paul liked to wear the queen's dresses.

After the article was published, Freddy appeared with Snatt-Ball in a discussion of Maori immigration rights, and was content to ignore him until Snatt-Ball once again insulted the two princes. Freddy could no longer hold himself back, and joined in battle. "It is one thing that the not-so-right-honourable gentleman insults me, but it is another that he attempts to sully the name of my father, who's sane, who, he says, is not."

This was heard by everyone not as "my father, who's sane," but as "my father, *Hussein.*" The audience was whiplashed.

"Your father, Hussein?" Snatt-Ball asked, delighted.

"Yes," Freddy answered, with finality, "my father, who's sane."

"But he isn't."

"Of course he is," Freddy said. "Everyone knows it. It's been obvious since he was born. It's clear in everything he does. I suspect, furthermore, that, although he is, you are not."

"Of course I'm not. Are you?"

"Yes," said Freddy, laughing at Snatt-Ball's admission (he had him now), "absolutely."

"Both of you?"

"Both of us. The queen can confirm this, as can just about anyone else in the world."

The moderator asked, "When did Your Royal Highness assume this name?"

"Whose name?" Freddy asked. Primed for it, everyone in the hall thought he had said not *whose name* but *Hussein.*

"Yes," the moderator answered.

Because Freddy was puzzled by this answer, he repeated it. "Yes?" he asked.

"When?" the moderator asked.

"When what?"

"When did you assume your name?"

Quite amazed, Freddy looked sceptically at the moderator, and perhaps amusedly, but with an edge. "When I was born," he said, emphasising every word to ridicule such a stupid question. But the moderator and everyone else, knowing Freddy, assumed that he had lapsed, as was his frequent custom, into Pidgin English, and that he had, therefore, just asked a question.

"Don't you know?" the moderator asked.

An exasperated Freddy was beginning to lose patience. "What's going on here?" he asked. "What is it that you want to know?"

This was for Britain a moment of high drama, and the moderator screwed his courage to the sticking place. "I suppose the audience would like to know, Your Royal Highness, if you are the Prince Hussein, and, then, if your father is the Prince Hussein."

Freddy sighed condescendingly. "I can assure you that we both are." He tapped his head as if knocking on oak.

"Hussein?" Snatt-Ball asked loudly and incredulously.

Thinking this a question, Freddy replied very firmly, "*I* am."

No one knew what to say, but thinking to press on and exploit the oddity, Snatt-Ball asked, "Are you, then, an Arab?"

"Am I an Arab?" Freddy repeated, breaking out into laughter. Answering sarcastically, and thinking that Snatt-Ball had really dug his own grave, Freddy said, "Of course I'm an Arab. Every Prince of Wales is an Arab. And," he said, enjoying himself immensely, "a *Jewish* Arab—a Jewish *Eskimo* Arab; a Jewish, Eskimo, *Mongolian* Arab. Aren't we all?" Freddy laughed uproariously at this until he noticed that he was the only one laughing. He stopped suddenly, having not the slightest clue as to what was happening, and looked searchingly at the audience. "Are you mad?" he asked. "Are you all mad?"

The newspapers seized upon this unfortunate misunderstanding, as they did always, like bears grasping salmon. The leader of *The Times,* and every other newspaper in the world, read, more or less, "Last night, with absolute sincerity, the Prince of Wales declared that he is a Jewish Arab by the name of Hussein. In the silence of Wigmore Hall except for the peals of his own laughter, the prince asserted repeatedly to a shocked audience these new facts that he vigorously claims." And then it went on, "In interviews with experts in psychiatry here and abroad. . . ."

Viscount Snatt-Ball was now making immense amounts of money from the sale of *My Cousin Freddy: A Viscount Tells All,* and after reading about this in a newspaper, Freddy had secured his copy. Because Fredericka had to memorise various fundaments of grammar and vocabulary, she and Freddy took a break from the Iliad and he spent the day angrily peering into Snatt-Ball's vicious memoir. He was halfway through when Lucia hiked over from Centennial Six to introduce herself and run through the procedures they had to follow.

"Hello!" she called up from the base of the tower. "Hello? Hello?"

They scrambled to pull on their clothes, from that moment on ceasing to be nudists. It had been interesting, even if unhealthy, to lie in the sun at the top of the world with neither a jot nor a tittle of cloth upon them, but after a short time they hadn't even noticed.

When Lucia entered they greeted her with their customary formality. People in fire towers don't say, "How do you do?" and "Delighted," they say, "Hi," and "Great!" She found them tremendous, curious, and horsey-looking, like the Prince and Princess of Wales. But they could not have been any such thing, even if they did speak like a sleep-deprived Laurence Olivier. "Are you English?" she asked, their resemblance to certain royal personages refusing to exit her awareness.

"Not really," Freddy said.

"We're from *Ahlahbahmah,*" they both said at the same time.

"You don't sound like you're from Alabama."

"Our parents were English," Freddy told her. "War brides and all that. You know."

"And Desi has a speech defect," Fredericka said.

"That's not true, Popeel."

"Just a little. Where are you from, Lucia?"

"Gloucester."

"In England?" Freddy asked, warming tremendously, until Fredericka side-kicked him.

"Massachusetts." Lucia was intensely beautiful, with a delicate, finely drawn, small face surrounded by flowing jet-black hair; eyes so wet, deep, and blue that they could have driven sapphires to suicide; and freckles, thrown across her cheeks and nose, that broke up the perfection of her face and by competing continually with its magnificent features put the beholder entirely off balance. Perhaps in all the world a hundred faces were as beautiful, but not more. It was shocking, stunning. In comeliness she far outdid

Fredericka, and neither Freddy nor Fredericka could take their eyes from her. She wore a set of sapphire earrings and a ring that perfectly matched her eyes. No jewellery had ever been more breathtaking on any queen.

Her great beauty was, however, a fortress that kept her from the world, for virtually no one was capable of taking her for what she was. People would follow, revile, worship, disparage, and envy her. So many men had fallen so hard in love with Lucia at first sight, and so many women, that she considered herself as much a casualty of circumstance as if she had been hideously deformed. Tired of continual overtures not to what she was but merely to the light she reflected, she chose to live in isolation. And having made the choice of how she would live and, presumably, die, she had the grace of the self-disciplined and the serenity of someone who has bowed to the truth. She was as well, and had always been, cheerful by nature.

Better and more experienced than most at taking people for what they were, if only because the people they had had to encounter were so many and various, Freddy and Fredericka would have been perfectly at ease with her. But because they feared discovery, they were slightly nervous, which she mistook for their being overwhelmed, and she therefore attempted to make them more comfortable—just as they did with nervous commoners. In fact, she expected them not even to be able to talk to her, as often happened. Noticing the Iliad on the desk, a work which she herself had read in Greek, she asked modestly, "How's the book?"

Freddy, who had been deeply absorbed in *My Cousin Freddy,* which was out of view under the map table, said, "Quite frankly, I think the little shit who wrote it should be put to death."

"Really?" Lucia asked. "I've read it, and although I'm no classicist, I thought it was rather good."

Freddy took her remark about classicism to be mockery of Snatt-Ball, and he assumed, therefore, that she was witty and sympathetic. He assumed as well that they were in the midst of a kind of literary game, as in the court of Louis XV or, in lowly fashion, George IV.

"Death would be a synonym for justice," Freddy said.

"But he's already dead."

"He is?" Freddy asked. "When?"

"I don't know the exact date. No one does."

"Maybe he was crushed by an escalator," Freddy speculated. "That's an especially painful way to go. Are you sure he's dead?"

"I'm absolutely sure, and I doubt that he was crushed by an escalator."

"Fredericka," Freddy said, forgetting himself. "Did you hear? He's dead. May he rest in peace, but, I must say, it is delicious."

"Delicious?" Lucia asked. "What is it that you object to?"

"The pettiness of it," said Freddy, getting agitated just in thinking about it, "the stupidity, the inaccuracy, the slanderous and dissolute gossip."

"What about the poetry?" Lucia asked.

"Poetry!" Freddy exclaimed. "There's less poetry in that stinking book than on a condom wrapper."

Astonished, Lucia said, "Then why are you reading it?"

Entirely forgetting himself, Freddy said, "Because it's about me."

"It is?"

Before Fredericka could shut him up, Freddy, oblivious of everything, said, "Yes. He's the one who accused me of thinking that both my father and I were Hussein. I said, 'my father, who's sane,' not, 'my father, Hussein.'" (This sounded to Lucia like one and the same thing.) "He made that the theme of the book."

"That would be news to Achilles," Lucia said, charmed by Freddy nonetheless.

"Who's Achilles?" Freddy asked.

"He's in the book, too."

"No he isn't," Freddy declared authoritatively.

Fredericka was behind Lucia, frantically pointing to the Iliad. Now Freddy understood, but, wanting to camouflage his indiscretions, was forced to continue. "Ah," he said, "Achilles. Yes, he is in the book. I had forgotten."

"Of course, who needs Achilles?" Lucia said.

"Actually," Freddy told her, "I was speaking indirectly. That's what literary critics do."

"They do, don't they."

"Yes, it's a way of expressing the essence of a work by venting one's imagined passions. In truth, I don't like that technique. I detest it. I had to do it," he said, pointing to Fredericka, "because she wanted me to demonstrate and practise it."

"I did not," Fredericka protested.

"Yes you did, remember?"

"Oh, yes, I do remember. I did."

"All right," said Lucia, "can we start from the beginning?"

"Of the Iliad?" Freddy asked.

"No, of the fire tower."

Then ensued a long and pleasant conversation, during which they looked out at the great and immobile range of mountains over which masses of white clouds were sailing like ships of the line.

Though impressed by Freddy's and Fredericka's presence, and by Freddy's knowledge of things like map reading and the staging of firefighting crews (which was similar to deploying infantry), Lucia was suspicious. When queried about the operation of the military radio, Freddy had said, "I've been using this for years: I have one in my American helicopter."

"I don't understand that," Lucia said. "I don't understand that construction."

Periodically Freddy was unable to speak, drawn as if by a tide to Lucia's ineluctable beauty. She had mistakenly worn a single gold bracelet—with her sapphires, which stopped the clocks—and Freddy could not take his eyes off of it as it bounced gently near her extraordinarily beautiful hands. With Freddy temporarily speechless, Fredericka jumped in to answer Lucia's question. "You've heard of *Doctors With Wings*?" she asked, thinking of an Australian television programme, aired in Britain during her youth, about medicine in the Outback.

"No," Lucia answered, under the impression that Fredericka was alluding to people with wings.

"Not everyone saw it," Fredericka went on, further puzzling Lucia. "It was on Gorilla," Didgeridoo's independent station broadcast from a gorilla-shaped blimp moored over Pangbourne, "and Didgeridoo is partial, of course."

Lucia was completely lost. "Of course," she said. "Didgeridoo is partial. Why didn't that occur to me?"

"We're dentists," Fredericka continued, "and Ahlahbahmah has so many on the dole that no one in the place can afford a motor. In our entire town we have only a Belisha or two. So, to get to our patients, we have helicopters. Most are Brazilian or Japanese, but one is American. That's what Freddy meant. Isn't it, Desi?"

"Indeed," said Freddy.

"Where did you go to dentistry school?" Lucia asked.

Thinking that she was trying to trap him, Freddy thought of a place that he knew and she probably would not. "The University of New Guinea," he said.

"New Guinea?"

"Yes."

"They have a dental school?"

"Why not? They have teeth. It's absolutely first class, too. You get to practise on macaques, who stay very still after the banana liqueur enemas administered by the Anti-Fox-Hunting League in off-target practice of mouth-to-mouth resuscitation."

"Shut up, Freddy, this is not the place."

"Well they should," Freddy said, forgetting about Lucia, "the bloody self-righteous prigs. They eat beef, chicken, lamb, pork, and fish, and then they throw eggs at Mummy's train. Does that make sense?" he asked, turning to Lucia.

"I really can't tell," Lucia said. "Did you go to dental school in New Guinea as well?" she asked Fredericka.

"Yes," Fredericka answered, somewhat apprehensively.

Realising that Fredericka had not been to New Guinea, Freddy determined instantly the most exotic country she knew passably well, and said, "No, Popeel, you went to dental school in Egypt."

"Egypt?" Fredericka asked, in surprise.

"Yes. You remember. In Cairo, at Forshaatu Asnan University."

"I did?"

Freddy nodded.

Attempting to deal with this, Fredericka said, "I did graduate work there, Freddy. My undergraduate dental degree was somewhere else."

"Where?" Lucia asked.

"Burma," Freddy answered.

"Burma?" Fredericka asked. "Are you mad?"

"That must have been my *first* wife," Freddy said, which precipitated an argument between the two of them, during which they called one another Desi, Freddy, Popeel, and Fredericka, and referred to smouldering resentments and half-forgotten things. "At Moocock," Freddy said, "every time you toasted my bap it came out of the Aga looking like a piece of anthra." At the end of half a dozen completely mysterious impassioned tirades, they remembered that they were not alone, and Fredericka turned to Lucia to ask, "Have we offended you?"

"No," said Lucia. "You haven't offended me."

"Right," said Freddy, continuing a previous comment that, to Lucia, had been incomprehensible. "Why don't they just leave us alone? Even when you go to the beach they use five-thousand-millimetre lenses to get close-ups of you that are so blurry they make you look like a cross between Isadora Duncan and Hosni Mubarak. You try to say the right thing at the right time, and they distort it to make it seem as if you're insane."

"That's right," said Lucia, edgily, "they do." Then she laughed nervously, and asked, "Who are they?"

"To hell with them," Freddy said. "Would you like to stay for dinner? We're going to shish-kebab some smoked mutton. It's been marinating in duck urine." *Duck urine* was what Freddy had always called white wine even if other people didn't. In restaurants, he often stunned sommeliers, who, not wanting to offend or contradict the Prince of Wales, would sidestep the query, "We'll be drinking duck urine tonight, can you suggest a good one?"

Lucia explained that she could not remain away from her tower that evening, but invited them to come to her at the end of the week. They accepted.

Fredericka sensed that this was dangerous. Freddy had been lost in Lucia's eyes and she in his, although both had attempted to avert their gazes (which made them seem particularly awkward even though both had inborn grace). The next step, as sometimes could happen with royalty (at least with Henry VIII), would be a Freddy-Lucia marriage, and Fredericka would be left alone with his child, the advent of which she knew but he did not. Even had he been more observant than he was, it would have made no difference. In school he had been sick during the unit on the female reproductive system (the source of a number of his problems, such as the famous television interview in which he had expressed shock that he did not have a uterus). Perhaps had Fredericka not been with child she would not have had the fortitude to recognise that Freddy was in fact falling in love with Lucia, and to do something about it.

Although Lucia had long before disqualified herself from love, and knew that Freddy was married, she walked back to Centennial Six as if God had forgotten to create gravity, with her heart full and each inhalation of mountain air an intoxication. She knew that nothing would come of it, but she was in love with Freddy, because, among other things, she felt that he could see her for what she was.

And as for Freddy, his thoughts in the days and nights that followed, in clear sunshine and beneath processions of stars, were complicated and painful. What if he took her as a mistress? That was always possible for kings, except that Fredericka had laid down the law about such things and would be a savagely possessive queen. And except that, unlike many kings (for whom women were nothing more than were cars or horses) and like the great-uncle they had always warned him about, Freddy was one to fall in love. He almost enjoyed the war within him between duty and passion, but not quite. And passion and duty notwithstanding, he knew that Fredericka would win, but he didn't know how.

At Lucia's, Freddy and Lucia often found themselves locked in the oblivious-of-the-world-young-courting-couple gaze, the Launcelot-and-Guenevere trance, the Tristan-and-Isolde longing, and whatever else it is. Fredericka appreciated the delicacy of what she was about to shatter, and though she empathised deeply with Lucia, she did not regret that she was going to win the battle.

During a dinner of fresh brook trout that was taken from an olive-oil-and-wild-berry marinade directly into a glowing sear pan, and then served with wild salad and new potatoes, Freddy was his most charming self. His anecdotes about horses alone were captivating enough, but when the subject turned to painting, his passion and erudition were irresistible. All her life, as Fredericka had not, Lucia had read. To her, Freddy—the physical Freddy, the completely unself-conscious Freddy, the unbelievably gauche Freddy, the brilliant and learned Freddy, the inexplicably self-assured Freddy with his striking peculiarities and traits—was the end of loneliness, the salvation of her line, her last chance for love and life, because, somehow, as if he were a king, he could approach her with confidence that she had never seen in any man except in an egomaniac, which Freddy was not.

"Freddy," Fredericka told her husband, "why don't you go up to the roof and look at the sky while Lucia and I clean up, and we'll call you for dessert."

"Oh, I can do it," Lucia said, noting that Fredericka had called him Freddy again.

"I'll help," Freddy volunteered.

"No," Fredericka said. "We'll do it. You go to the roof."

After Freddy had left, Lucia and Fredericka cleared the table in total silence, hardly looking at one another. When the dishes were done, Lucia looked up, and that is when Fredericka said, "Will you sit down for a moment so that we may speak?"

Lucia nodded, half in shame and half in sadness, knowing that what had not even begun was now at an end. She thought that Fredericka would flay her, but Fredericka, whose heart was of great capacity, and who had always in all incarnations known how to love, had no such intention. She grasped both of Lucia's hands. Lucia was moved by that alone. "You are obviously a fine woman," Fredericka said. "I have no animus for you. Everything I believe and feel tells me that you deserve what your heart desires. And if," Fredericka continued, "if I were gone, I would be happy to see you with my husband, bearing his children, sharing his throne."

Lucia looked up sharply. Still holding her hands, Fredericka said, "Yes, we are who you think we are, and I am carrying a child, recently conceived in the dust next to a railway track, a child who, I believe, is a boy, and who will be a king of England in his own time. Of a long and great line that even if imperfect has lasted a thousand years, two kings are here tonight. Assuming that all comes right in the end, you will have received two princes, a princess, a queen, and two kings."

"That sounds like a poker hand," Lucia said, laughing, as a tear dropped onto her cheek.

"It does, doesn't it? The strange forms on playing cards, that people find so familiar and yet so offputting, are our family portraits. Kings. And queens," Fredericka said, most sadly. "It is said that monarchy is no longer of any import, and that when it was, it was an injustice. Perhaps. But I believe in and credit the heart of man, and for a thousand years the heart of man has kept and created kings, who, when they were not selfish oppressors, have borne the burdens of their countries and often sacrificed themselves. My husband, though selfish from the ignorance of having been born to be king, is no oppressor," she said. "There may come a time yet when Britain may need a king once more, as in the war not so long ago when a great king, despite and perhaps because of his modesty and simplicity, helped to focus the soul of the nation upon the essential task of survival." She stopped there.

Lucia was hardly sure that all this was true, but the more it settled in, the more she realised that, as unlikely as it was, it was true, and that her first suspicions had been correct. Heartbroken, she had nonetheless been fulfilled, for the royal work was to direct attention, including the king's, to duty, process, and the slow unfurling of history.

"It is true, isn't it?" Lucia asked, not unmoved.

Fredericka nodded gently and briefly closed her eyes.

. . .

SITTING IN SWEATERS and wind shells, with much appreciated mugs of hot tea cradled in their hands, Freddy and Fredericka listened to the mountain wind rise and pass through the steel girders of Centennial Seven. They were just cold enough to be intently aware of what kept them warm, and to look forward to going to bed. They had dimmed the light, because a sweep was coming up and their eyes had to grow accustomed to darkness.

On the way back from Centennial Six, Freddy had been at his most dog-like and transparent. Fredericka had seen more than her share of men become that way when they were infatuated. She took a sip of tea. "Freddy?" she asked.

"Yes?"

"Something didn't happen that was supposed to happen."

He looked at her blankly.

"Well?" she asked, knowing that he was ordinarily quick of mind.

"Well what?"

"It didn't happen!" she shouted, but, then, remembering her purpose, calmed.

"What didn't happen, Fredericka?"

"Don't you know?"

"Am I supposed to know?"

"You should."

"Was it connected to world events?" he asked as if she had engaged him in yet another game of Twenty Questions.

"Yes, actually," she said, not wanting to play but unable not to.

"Was it a threatened invasion that did not materialise?"

"No," she replied, barely audible.

"Did Russia default on its debt?"

"No, Freddy," Fredericka answered quietly. "It's something that happens every month, and it didn't happen."

He thought. And he thought on. He talked to himself in a kind of buzzing. He counted on his fingers. Then he looked up. "The meeting of the Royal Historical Society?"

"No."

"It's the greyhound races, isn't it?"

"No, Freddy, it has to do with us."

"It's not a banking matter, is it? Anyway, in our situation, how could you know? With us, with us. What?"

"I didn't have my period." She was moved, for she had just told her husband that his line would continue, and hers. Theirs. Heirs.

"Does that happen, sometimes?"

"No, it doesn't happen, sometimes."

"I see. Well, perhaps you'll get two the next time."

"Two the next time?" she repeated in astonishment. "Don't you know what it means?"

"I don't know," he said. "I don't know about those things. Why should I? I trust you to take care of them. I don't burden you about my prostatitis from jumping with a full load, do I?"

"Is that obscene?"

"You see? A full combat load. In a fast descent in hostile conditions, striking the ground with the weight of weapons and stores in addition to one's own weight puts a great deal of sudden pressure on the bladder, which, because you can't use the WC whenever you want while you're waiting to get to the drop zone, is often quite full. The liquid acts as what is called a water hammer, on the same principle as hydraulic power, and the prostate is subjected to severe shock, which can then lead to inflammation and infection. If. . . ."

"*It means I'm having a baby!*" she screamed, having given up entirely on a poetic moment.

Freddy was silent for just a brief instant, and then he said, "It means you're having a what?"

"A baby, Freddy, a baby."

"A human baby?"

"I hope so," she replied, feeling faint. And then, "Are you mad? Are you implying that I've had sex with animals?"

"No, no, no," he said, sweeping the air in front of him with his hands. "I was just confused. In the laboratories that we visit they fertilise eggs in a dish. Sometimes a droplet can fly inadvertently across the room and a gorilla, for example, will be crossed with a yak. Unsuccessfully, of course, I hope. Can you imagine, a gorilla and a . . ."

"Freddy!"

"Fredericka?"

"*Our* baby. *You* fertilized *my* egg with *your* sperm on the embankment near the railway line."

"Ah!" he said. "Oh, I see." Now he was moved. "A king," he went on, staring at Fredericka's aerobic instructor's abdominal region, "or perhaps a queen. It doesn't matter. Even without a title at all, that child, that child is, for me—will be, for me—the centre of the world. I would throw over England for his sake, or hers. I would walk into fire. I've been made second before I've even been first, but never have I felt greater satisfaction." It was true.

"That's the way of the world," said Fredericka. "I feel it, too. I feel content. I feel full of love."

He took her into his arms.

"Be kind to Lucia, Freddy, but nothing more."

"I'm sorry," he said. "I had no intention of behaving badly, but I did. It's all so confusing. Something's in the wind."

SOMETHING WAS INDEED in the wind, although they were unaware of it when they made their initial sweeps to scan the darkness in search of a spark or smouldering glow. Freddy awakened first, sighted nothing, and then, half an hour later, it was Fredericka's turn, and so on, into the night. Though their interrupted sleep was difficult, their awakenings were gentle. They would roll off the foam mattress and out from under the table, stand up, seize the binoculars, and do the well practised scan, a restful traverse across a black void. After putting down the binoculars and sinking to their knees, they would roll quietly back into place, pull up the still-warm sleeping-bag, and fall immediately into an oblivion they had not quite left. And then, in another half an hour, a chime would sound and one of them would rise.

At four-thirty, when on clear days the east had already begun to brighten, Freddy got up to make a sweep. In his half-dream-like state, he thought the light on the horizon was the dawn. But dawn does not flicker, and dawn is confined to the east. The light he saw, though distant, dim, and sporadic, jolted him awake, for lightning lit the horizon in a complete circle as if the world were an artillery battle everywhere but in one dark lake.

"Fredericka, Fredericka," Freddy called.

"What?" She had expected to sleep.

"You'd better get up."

"It's not my turn."

"Something's happening."

She arose and looked out into what should have been black night but was a horizon-line of silent flashes such as she had never seen. Turning slowly, she soon realised that it ran all around in a ring. "What is it?" she asked.

"Lightning."

"I've never seen anything like this. Have you?"

"The closest I've come," Freddy said, "was in a flight over Africa, in a lightning storm half a continent wide. From the air you could see hundreds, perhaps thousands, of lightning flashes all at once. The farther away you got, the more integral it seemed. I imagine that from space a storm like this looks like muffled light."

"Muffled by what?" she asked, her eyes filled with distant flashes.

"Clouds."

"Why can't we hear it?"

"It's too far away. The sound dissipates, but the light doesn't. That's why, even were I allowed, I would not go into politics, where, in contradiction of all nature, the reverse is true."

Fredericka knew that Freddy had thought a great deal about physical science. He frequently spoke to her in terms she didn't understand, like foot-pounds and joules, which as far as she knew were coupons for buying shoes, and what you wore to important ceremonies. He somehow seemed to be able to predict where things would land, what the weather would be, or how long a mechanical part would endure. So, as she usually did, she asked him what would happen. At that moment, the radio woke up.

"Centennial Two to Control." Switch-over was accompanied by loud snaps and clicks as the background static commemorated every distant lightning flash.

"Control by, Centennial Two."

"Report lightning, heat, three hundred and sixty degrees. Three six zero degrees. Range approximately one hundred miles, a hundred and twenty to two hundred flashes per minute. No apparent movement. Over."

"Read you, Two. Further?"

"Negative. Two out."

"Roger, Two. Control out."

And so it went, in desultory fashion, every tower making its report. Freddy, meanwhile, had set up the transit, and by the time he was ready to answer Fredericka's question, had recorded the heights and bearings of the flashes above the horizon. "Either," he said to Fredericka, "it will move over us, retaining its shape, or it will move over us, the shape collapsing, or it will fill in around us, which would be inexplicable."

"Why weren't we given a heads-up when this damned thing was in Oregon?" one of the towers asked.

The answer came immediately. "It was never in Oregon. It was never anywhere. It started here."

"Like this?" was the incredulous reply.

Freddy again consulted the transit, made some calculations, and went on the radio. "Good morning, Control, Centennial Seven here."

"Centennial Seven, Control by."

"I've charted the expansion of the storm, and it appears that the circle in which we find ourselves at the moment is filling in at approximately eight miles per hour. By nightfall or earlier we should be under intense bombardment. Over."

"Thank you, Seven. I'm going to check the Snake and Yellowstone to see if I can find anything about this. Will be back in a short time. Over, out."

"Oh, Freddy," Fredericka said, in the sad and noble tone that women can produce when something terrible is about to happen. "What will we do?"

"We'll take cover on a hillside, in the lee of some rocks. It's just a storm."

"Have you ever seen such a storm?"

"No."

Then came a report on the radio. The lightning was dry. The fantastically thick mass of gunmetal-coloured clouds had held back their emotion in favour of a barrage of light. This changed everything. All the towers were now fully awake and preparing. The Forest Service had announced that it would mobilise everyone and call for as much help as it could get, but throughout the West fire crews were already working at full tilt. What awakened the watchers in the towers to a fervent pitch was that they knew that as the storm moved through it would drop fires like incendiary bombs. Fires would begin everywhere, evenly, almost simultaneously. There would be no front, no directional trend, no untouched areas, no refuge. The only question was how long it would take until the circles of fire joined and everything came alight. For the observers and the young fire crews, most of whom were summer hires, the world was about to change. No one backed off or away, but all understood that, for some, the courage they showed would be their last memorial.

As the storm filled their lake of peaceful air, the show of lightning grew more spectacular. Though the clouds from which it shot maintained altitude, in closing they seemed to rise up. What had first been visible as a kind of volatile grassfire, made low and linear by perspective, was now a cirque of overspilling clouds from which lightning leapt as if in irritation. The wind howled so fiercely that Freddy and Fredericka decided to leave the tower, for fear that it would be lifted like an umbrella or simply blown apart.

They packed furiously, though with less speed than they might have. Freddy knew that in battle, or its equivalent, slowing down one's reactions as much as one could afford made them more reliable and precise, while at the same time depriving panic of its most potent fuel. Although this tactic came naturally to him now, when first he had employed it, in the Falklands, when a group of SAS he was leading came under mortar and heavy machine-gun fire, it had been quite deliberate. Now, in advance of the lightning, the thunder of which they had begun to hear, Fredericka rushed, her hands flailing to get things in her pack, and Freddy seemed maddeningly slow.

"Freddy!" she yelled. "Let's go! Pack!"

"Fredericka?" he asked calmly.

To mock him, she slowed for a moment, and in imitation she said, ever so slowly, "Yes, Freddy?"

"I believe you've packed wrongly."

"Have I!"

"Put in only a third as much food as you have—on the bottom. Then put the first-aid things. Then put in the water, leaving space only for the flame shelter, which should be at the top. Strap the axe and the shovel to the sides, and bring water in as many bottles as you can carry on the belt."

"What about the sleeping bag?" she asked.

He shook his head, rejecting it.

"What about clothes?"

He did the same. "Put electrolytes in the water," he commanded.

"I hate them," she said.

"Just think of all the lovely tastes you will taste for the rest of your life if you live. When you drink it, the water that is now cool will be almost as hot as tea. Everything vital in you will begin to evaporate."

"Come now, Freddy. Do you really think. . . ."

"Fredericka," he said, "the forest has been for years harvesting and storing the energy of the sun. Encased within the pines that make the ocean-like noise when the wind blows through them are trillions and trillions of BTUs, waiting for the liberation of a single spark, much less a thousand lightning bolts. That's why we're here."

"BTUs?" Fredericka asked. "What are BTUs?"

"British thermal units."

"British?" Fredericka asked, forgetting her panic. "Isn't that carrying things a bit too far, Freddy? Yes, you are who you are, and I am who I am, but how do you expect me to believe that this forest in the middle of nowhere is loaded up to the gills with *British* thermal units? Isn't that a trifle self-centred for someone who is always accusing me of narcissism?"

"Not for a long time, now," he said. "It's gone."

She was pleased. "Are you sure they're not French thermal units?"

"They don't have thermal units, they just have cheese."

"Freddy, the way the world seems to belong to you astonishes me every day. Aren't we going to take the Iliad?"

"Of course not," he said as he continued to pack. "It's in libraries. And even were it not in libraries. . . . Do you remember the fire at Windsor? I was the first inside. It was so hot that I had only a few seconds before I left or perished. I was trying to decide which was the greatest painting, so I could save it, and then guess who showed up, twisting about my feet like an ecdysiast?"

"Who?"

"Urqhart."

"Urqhart!" Fredericka exclaimed. "What did you do?"

"You know what I did. He lives. I took him up in my arms, and left the paintings. It was easy. Even in school, when the question was posed, I knew the answer without doubt."

"The cat."

"He was alive. I looked at him, and in that moment, surrounded by fire, I saw a work greater than any work man has ever made. What artist has made an eye so deep and lively? Or a thing that moves with such grace?

The paintings are gone, although we have a record of them, and Urqhart lives even if just for the moment. I was quite comfortable in my choice."

"Freddy, if they knew, they'd crucify you. You, the heir to the royal pictures, a controversialist of aesthetics."

"To hell with them," he said. "My guess is that Lord Clark would have done the same. He knew a masterpiece when he saw it, and so do I."

Then came a concussion of thunder following immediately upon a near and blinding bolt of lightning. Recovering, Freddy said, "An endorsement."

Even at risk of lightning strike, Freddy tried to call the Forest Service and Lucia, but the last bolt had killed the radio. As they opened the door to the stairs, the wind came in as if to levitate the roof, but succeeded only in blasting the pages of the Iliad into weightless commotion, which made those airy quarters look like Freddy's four-foot-wide confetti-filled water globe of Windsor in a snowstorm. Descending, they saw dry lightning out to the horizon, each strike, like a corn driller, planting a seed of fire. When lightning hit areas that already were burning, the trees near the impact exploded. It was an artillery barrage on an unlimited front, with neither lines, corridors, nor areas that remained untouched. By the continually flashing light, which never abdicated to darkness but varied like a rising and falling wave, they saw that the forest was covered in a haze of white smoke.

"Nothing will be left," said Fredericka as they made their way into the choking air.

"Only rock and ash, and perhaps the steel structures if the wind doesn't bellow the fire and melt them down."

"Can this fire melt steel in the open?" she asked.

"People think that a forest fire burns cool, but if the wind is strong it's like a blast furnace."

"If it melts steel," she said, almost indignantly, "what about us?"

"There are a few things we can do—finding the lee of hills, rocky areas, and lakes; short immersions in the lakes; the fire shelters. Perhaps we can be airlifted from H1, if we can find it."

They had a fairly good idea of where they were as they moved at a fast pace through the smoke. "Why not just go to the middle of the lake at H1?" Fredericka asked, referring to their evacuation point, a lake in a deep valley with a little prairie of ten or fifteen acres at its western end.

"If the wind were blowing the heat across the water, because of the flat surface it would leave no pockets of cooler air as it would blowing across obstructions on the ground. When you came up for air, it might kill you. In some conditions, the top layer of water boils."

"Did you know this when you brought us here?"

"Fredericka, almost since the beginning of time, a well ordered line of succession has allowed kings and other royals to gravitate to peril as a bee flies to the rose."

"Yes, but I'm not a bee, and I can hardly breathe," she said, coughing as they went through a ribbon of heavy smoke.

"Think of it as smoking a pipe."

They came to an open ridge where many times they had watched the sky at night. Looking left, south-south-east, they saw a wall of fire climbing up the hill, driven neither by wind nor firestorm but by upwelling heat that led the flames from tree to tree. In the valley it had destroyed, spaces as large as city parks seemed like the interior of a coal stove, with planes of red and black pulsing like an animal breathing in its cave.

They went to the other side of the ridge, farther from H1 but cooler and less smoky. In the valley that fell off to their right, a dozen fires burned, still small. Fredericka had been afraid, but once in motion had lost her fear. "I feel," she said, "as we weave between fires and exploding trees, that I've been here before."

"If there's a conscience of our race," said Freddy, "you have. London was like this, Coventry, and Birmingham, and not for a night or two but for years. You were born to this, as I was. In some ways it's the starting point; it's home."

The forest was completely covered in a pall of white, and walls of flame were everywhere combining and colliding like waves echoing off the sides of an agitated pool. Freddy and Fredericka went where they could. Backtracking sometimes, forced in unwanted directions, they were a false image of randomness, lost now in the darkness from which the lightning had disappeared, navigating by a hellish glow, breathing the rich and offensive smoke, ducking when terrified birds flew past them unknowing that were they to rise for long enough through the smoke they would break out into clear air and blue sky.

Very little daylight filtered through the pall, and by ten they had inhaled enough smoke and worked so hard in the heat that they no longer even thought in terms of night and day. They had finished the water in their belt canteens and now were drinking from the bottles in their packs. In the thick smoke and her fatigue, Fredericka had left her fire shelter behind in some unreachable place soon to be buried in ash. Freddy hadn't noticed, and they walked on, trying to navigate as best they could to H1, which they knew they could reach if they met the river, which they would then try to ride down to the lake. Though at this stage of the fire the river would be cold, later it might steam like a kettle.

By the middle of the afternoon they were as black as coal miners, except for snowy crests of light-coloured ash that clung to them in outlandish designs, making Freddy, especially, look like one of the New Guinea headhunters he had mocked without restraint since the age of five. (Repeatedly criticised for this, he would say, "I'm sorry, but I have always and will always believe that hunting and killing people for food and displaying their shrunken heads as trophies is inferior to, let us say, garden parties or book discussions, or even the savagery of our wars, which we long not to tolerate and perfect but to condemn and escape.") And whereas Freddy looked outlandish, Fredericka's exhaustion and hollowed, soot-ringed eyes made her look like one of the tired and defeated women in a photograph by Dorothea Lange.

They reached the river, which was still cool, and waded in until they were lifted and pulled away by the current. "How do you know there isn't a waterfall?" Fredericka asked. Her hair was washed clean of ash, her eyes cleared, her body cooled, her voice revived.

"If there is, pray that the pool beneath it is deep, and don't let the backwash pull you under."

"How?" she called across the washboard of swiftly flowing water.

"Swim to the side, not against the force holding you back."

"How will I know?"

"You'll know," was all he said before involuntarily taking a mouthful of water. In its centre, the stream flowed rapidly, as if it were panicked by the burning forest.

Swept along, they stubbed their toes and bumped against rounded boulders beneath them. The river sometimes slowed and sometimes sped up, but on average it flowed at about twelve miles per hour. In half an hour, then, they travelled six miles, which seemed a good way to move through a burning forest. In fact, it was so much a triumph over circumstance that they were elated, especially after they passed through lines of fire that would have killed them had they been on foot.

"This is almost," said Freddy, "as if we are being conveyed from hell."

But soon they saw directly downstream a flat line complicated only by a mist of falling water. They tried desperately to cross the flow, but after only a few seconds Freddy understood that they would have to go over. "Save your strength," he said. As they rushed toward the edge that would launch them into the void, they linked arms.

It was too quick even for crying out. As they went over, he looked at her, in those parts of a second just before they knew they would be separated, with the kind of certain love that she might have specified had she had hours to think of the requirements. And then the deepest bond that they had ever had was set permanently as the force of the water pulled them apart.

Anxiety before a fall is a terrifying thing, but in the air, as seconds pass, it vanishes into joy. Everything comes clear, wounds are healed, regrets instantly addressed, complications smoothed, desires satisfied, and gravity seemingly defied even in its triumph. As they fell in the column of water and mist, they neither suffered nor feared, in an instant of perfection such as few will ever know until the end.

And it might have marked a change in the long line of succession had not the falls been only sixty feet high and the pool beneath them very deep. They fell through a froth of water and air into a fast-moving wave that shot them forward as if from a bow. And then they found themselves once more riding the river, feetfirst, alive, packs floating easily because of the empty water bottles inside. They were as alert as hunted deer. On Fredericka's left, Freddy reached out to her with his right arm, and she took his hand.

At this time of summer in England, between the short season of croquet parties and the cruise on *Britannia,* a hundred types of flowers would be blooming in the gardens of Moocock alone, newly mulched with fragrant Scandinavian cedar bark. The new summer-weight blazers and cool shirts would have arrived long before. Freddy would delight in a particular kind of day in London when everyone was on holiday, the parks were empty, the streets quiet, and a stretch of summery blue weeks was surprisingly interrupted by a light-saturated mass of grey cloud that hovered in a flat ceiling over the city, touching it with autumn. In northern latitudes the light had to blaze to keep summer spinning, and the moment it ceased or faltered it made for remembrance of the other seasons. That was when Freddy liked to go alone to his offices and work, knowing that the road outside was nearly deserted.

As they were swept downriver in a world of smoke and heat, and he was thinking of days like that in civilisation, confused and pathetic deer, bear, raccoon, and mountain lion lined the banks in numbers such as he had never seen except on the Serengeti or in the zoo. Pushing in from both sides, the fires had raked the forest of all things living, and they, stopping at the water, probably would die there rather than conceive of the river as a way out.

Unbeknownst to Freddy and Fredericka in their several-hour, exhausting but euphoric swim, the wind had risen. By the time the river widened, slowed, and found its way into the lake, they could hear it roaring along the ridge tops. As they swam slowly to the meadow side, the air that blew over the water was like the air that comes from an oven when the door is opened, and the sky had once again become cloudless, blue, and dry. Theirs was the fatigue of soldiers in battle, who do not have the time to recognise how drained they are. And hours in the water with wet clothes, boots, and packs had made them different sorts of creatures. When they came out on the bank, they crawled at first, comfortable on the sand and undisturbed that they did not rise. When finally they stood, they walked to the centre of the small meadow to join a dozen others who had escaped the fire.

Not having ridden the river, few of the tower lookouts, injured smoke jumpers, and rangers were in as good condition as Freddy and Fredericka. Some were in agony from burns, and had the choice of staying in one-person fire shelters as hot as camp stoves, or suffering in the bright sun and terrible wind. They rocked in pain as if to go somewhere, but there was nowhere to go. Others were so tired and beaten that they lay still, and no one greeted the new arrivals.

"Does anyone have a radio?" Freddy shouted over the wind.

"I have," a young ranger said. He was a college student set loose all summer with a trail hook, radio, and pack. For two months he wandered the wilderness from food cache to food cache, clearing paths and caring for markers. It was a splendid job for a young man of a certain temperament, something that, like military service, would colour the rest of his life.

"Is a helicopter coming?" Freddy asked, knowing better and shouting over the wind.

"Not when the wind's eighty miles an hour."

"Do they have any idea when it will die down?"

"They say this evening."

"Then we just wait?"

"Yes," said the ranger, "and hope that the fire doesn't come down the valley, or up it."

"Where's Lucia?"

"Who's Lucia?"

"The chief of the Centennial Line."

"I don't know her."

She hadn't come in. Freddy looked about. Everywhere his eyes alighted, most of the trees were untouched. Though the valley had been spared, it was pure tinder. "Why are we here?" Freddy asked.

"It's the safest place," the young man answered.

"No, if the fire sweeps over the ridge on these winds the trees will ignite into a firestorm."

"That's why we're in the meadow."

"You don't understand," Freddy told him. "If the wind provides the impetus, the flames could superheat and form into a kind of tornado that as it travels eats up everything it touches. It doesn't have to be fed continuously; it feeds upon itself. Something like that can move right across this open space faster than we can run, and everything standing would go in an instant."

"Are you a forester?"

"I'm not, but the same thing happens in large-scale bombing, even with no wind but the wind created by the firestorm itself. It takes the oxygen from the air. It's bloody hell."

"That's why H1 is the refuge. They must have had experience in other fires. Obviously, it's protected by the topography, which is why it hasn't burned."

"The wind," Freddy said. "We should get the shelters up immediately."

They began with the injured, pegging their sacks to the ground, pulling up the grass around them, and covering them with a spray of earth. It was hard work, and they had to drink from the lake often, because in the high heat water simply flowed out of them. As this was happening, Lucia walked in. She threw down her knapsack, looked over the injured, went to the lake, and immersed herself, staying only as long as she needed to wash off the soot and ash and get cool. When she rose from the water and returned to the group, her black hair was dripping and her eyes were clear.

She knew that no helicopters would be flying: the only things flying were brands, too heavy to travel on ordinary winds, that set clear areas on fire as if a mythological runner had gone from one to the other with a torch. She knew about firestorms, and encouraged everyone to continue with the shelters. Freddy and Fredericka, the least exhausted, were assigned to carry water and pull grass. They doused the ground, the shelters, and the people lying by them. As soon as they wet the earth around the shelters the water disappeared, but it would cool the ground so that if the worst were to occur the ground itself, full of organic matter, might not burn.

When the shelters were up and Lucia and the young ranger took over the bucket transport, Freddy and Fredericka were to set up theirs. Freddy's was out when he looked at Fredericka and saw her clawing through her pack. "I don't have it," she declared.

"Are you sure?" Freddy went through the pack visually and with his hands. She didn't.

Lucia threw a bucket of water at them. "Where's your shelter?" she called to Fredericka over the heightened wind.

"I don't have it. I must have lost it in the river or left it behind when I repacked the pack."

"It's my fault," Freddy told Lucia. "I had her repack it."

"Does anyone have an extra shelter?" Lucia asked. No one did. "Check your packs and your neighbour's packs. It would be a shame for someone not to be in a shelter when one was sitting bunched up right next to him." When this was done, she announced: "We have eleven shelters and twelve people."

Shelters could hardly fit even one: people had died because they were too tall or too heavy to close them properly, allowing the heat to follow them in.

Over the rising wind, Lucia said to Fredericka, "You won't die here."

"That's right," said Freddy, "she won't."

At this, Freddy and Lucia looked at one another, both with love and in a contest of wills that Freddy, who was much older, a royal personage, and a man, was certain he would win.

STANDING IN THE WIND and glare, Freddy was dizzied and almost delirious, but he felt in the diminution of certain of his capacities a transference of strength to his resistance and will. No king of England had ever died in a forest fire, he told Fredericka as they watched a front of flame, like an incoming tide, crest the valley ridge as if climbing a ramp, pause, and flow toward the lake.

"Get in," Freddy told her, with so much love and finality that her heart broke as she knelt, her face now beautifully stained with ash. "I'll submerge myself in the lake."

"You said the surface might boil." Her voice shook.

"I know."

"Freddy," Fredericka said. "Freddy."

"Fredericka, my duty is neither to win nor to survive, but to uphold. If I should fall, blending in with the mass of men, so be it. My only purpose in the world, and the only shining thing, is to have done right."

"But kings take for themselves," Fredericka insisted. "They always have."

"This is a new world, Fredericka. And this is the one glory left to a king. I know that now."

He kissed her, and then he glanced at the firestorm, which was beginning to roar over the lake. "Get in," he commanded, and began to help her in. Looking to his left, he saw Lucia's empty shelter. "Where's Lucia?" he asked.

Lucia, behind him, hit the back of his head with a folding shovel. He fell flat on his face, unconscious.

"Close up!" she ordered Fredericka, as she dragged Freddy toward her shelter. With the last of her strength, she put him in, placing her feet against his shoulders and pushing with her legs. As she sealed the shelter, the wall of flame already reddening her with burn, she saw Fredericka, not yet closed in, tears streaming down her face.

"Why?" Fredericka asked.

"Oh," said Lucia, falling to her knees to lessen the area of pain from the heat that had begun to consume her. "Tell him . . . for mother and child, for father and child." She smiled. "And for king and country."

"My God," said Fredericka, as if to convince her not to do what she had already done irrevocably, "it isn't your country."

And Lucia answered, with her last words, "It was once."

IV.

PARADISE
REGAINED

FREDDY ESCAPES FROM THE MENTAL HOSPITAL AND ENTERS AMERICAN POLITICS. WHAT'S THE DIFFERENCE?

LIKE ALL POLITICIANS, Dewey Knott put out a great deal of information about his work habits and noble qualities. Just as President Self, who since his student days hadn't read anything other than budget documents or captions under photographs of naked women, was said to read four hundred scholarly books each year, so the flacks of Dewey Knott, who knew that Dewey was confused by the Yellow Pages, said he, too, devoured hundreds of tomes, although when asked about this at a press conference he thought that *tomes* was the Spanish word for tomatoes. "Let's see," he said, counting on his fingers. "Every time I have a salad, I finish at least half a tome. Say, about three quarters a day. California tomes, really great. Great state. The Golden State. Florida, too. Yeah, I love tomes. And I think that the people who produce those tomes need all the help they can get because of unfair competition from Mexico."

"How do you find the time, Senator?" asked a sexually magnetic female reporter.

"What time?" Dewey asked, eyes glazing over.

"Ten-thirty, Senator," an aide replied, because Dewey asked the time by saying *What time?*

"What time is she talking about?" Dewey clarified.

The reporter said, "The time to consume all those tomes."

"Are you kidding?" Dewey asked. "It's no problem to consume three quarters a day. If I wanted, I could go through ten a day, really."

In the shocked silence, Sam Donaldson was not about to let this pass. "Ten a day, Senator? Do you stand by that number?"

"Yeah. That would be easy. In the fifties I did that on the advice of Linus Pauling."

"Senator, if you please," said the scourge, "would you name some of those tomes? Right now?"

Dewey laughed at him and said, as if he were talking to an idiot, "I wasn't aware that they had names."

"Titles."

"Titles?"

"Yes."

Thinking that now he really had him, Dewey said, in a mocking tone, "Well, one was called *Lord* Beefsteak, and another *King* California Red."

As this exchange was disseminated around the country and throughout the world, the reporters came alive like sharks on a pod of dying whales. "Who wrote those, Senator?" he was asked from the back of the pack. "Who wrote *King California Red*?"

What cretins, Dewey thought. "My, you people are strange," he said, enjoying what they were doing to themselves. "They aren't something that someone *writes*. They grow in nature, by themselves, on a bush." Dewey looked at the crowd of motionless reporters and laughed out loud. "What's the matter with you people? *Who wrote them?* Are you mad? Do you think that I read them? Maybe you read them. I don't read them, I *eat* them." And then he walked off, laughing and shaking his head.

"Oh," he said to Finney a little later, when informed of the meaning of the word. "Just tell those idiots that it's the Spanish word for tomato."

"But it isn't the Spanish word for tomato."

"It isn't?"

"No."

"What is it?"

"Nothing."

"The Spanish word for tomato," Dewey asked, "is *nothing*? I like *tomes* better. Sounds a lot more Spanish. *Nothing* sounds English, or Ghost."

"Ghost?" asked Finney.

"Well, you know."

"I don't, but *nothing* doesn't mean anything in Spanish. *Tomes* means nothing."

"We've been over that, Finney, and that's wrong."

"Okay," said Finney, "but what am I going to tell them?"

"What *are* you going to tell them?"

"I don't know. Self has just released a list of a thousand books he's supposed to have read since he was sworn in. I doubt that he's read one."

"They'll kill him," said Dewey, "just like they kill me. They'll ask him details from some book about Egyptabology."

"No they won't. They all voted for him. They'll say, 'Mr President, how brilliant do you have to be to read a thousand books while saving the nation?' and he'll say, 'Very brilliant,' and that'll be that."

President Self, who had the lower body of a baby elephant, was reputed to run twelve miles a day and do an hour of weight lifting and gymnastics, so Dewey took up Tai Chi and was seen walking from his house to his limousine in a martial-arts outfit with a black belt (which was actually the tie he used for funerals). President Self was supposedly an expert on pre-Columbian pottery, so Dewey, who had no idea what that was, made a campaign trip to Easter Island and was photographed looking with tremendous suspicion at the statues, perhaps because he had slept on the plane, and believed he was on Martha's Vineyard.

"Boy!" he said to his press entourage. "Look at those crazy things. Who put them there, and why? What happened to the T-shirt shops and frozen yoghurt places? And isn't it impressive," he said, slyly injecting a political point, "that Senator Kennedy swam here all the way from Chappaquiddick?"

So with work habits. According to the serpentine and mendacious White House flacks, President Self worked twenty-hour days and was ever vigilant. Even on the golf course he listened to tapes on monetary theory or studied Tibetan religious documents. Thus, Dewey, who went from couch to couch the way infantrymen in Normandy went from hedge to hedge, and who had seen every episode of *Gilligan's Island* at least twenty times and could and did lip-sync all the parts, had to "put in" twenty-hour days. When the reporters began to stake out the entrances to his campaign headquarters and he no longer could slip away, he began to live in his office, where lights burned in the windows as he counted sheep on an air mattress. He locked the door from the inside and played a tape of him talking on the telephone, typing, dictating letters, and singing along to Patti Page's "How Much Is That Doggie in the Window?" The Secret Service thought he was a man of iron, especially when, at four a.m., rested (as they did not know) from nine hours of sleep, he would emerge in a fresh shirt, newly shaven, cologned, voluble, bright-eyed, and caffeinated, and go downstairs to a press conference at which he would dazzle the half-dead reporters with his energy before roaring off to the airport to fly to a campaign rally in what he once referred to as *West Dakota*.

Finney was delighted with the workings of this scheme, and filled with admiration when sometimes Dewey would emerge dishevelled and as tired as a young lawyer. How clever, Finney thought, for him by imperfection to perfect untruth. But what Finney didn't know was that Dewey had no such stratagem, and that when he appeared fatigued it was because he really was fatigued. Unbeknownst to anyone, including the Secret Service (which Dewey innocently, and perhaps undiplomatically, called "the SS"), Dewey had a secret door in the private study where he played Kate Smith records, drank bourbon, and tried to decipher the racing form. The door had been installed as a defence against terrorists when the building was an annex of the Israeli Embassy. Such security features were ideal for a campaign headquarters, and not even Dewey's closest aides knew of the two-foot-high door that opened out through the wainscotting of a back hall, next to a fire stair. It was under the bar sink, and Dewey had discovered it while looking for a place to hide his malted milk balls from Dot. Every few days, as if he were a grotesque Alice in Wonderland, Dewey used this door to go into the almost empty ten-storey building, as alone and unmonitored as a dandelion seed floating on the wind. He did not simply wander, but went purposefully down to the darkened fifth floor, to a large room that in the daytime was filled with sun-deprived clerks who had not a single window. Here Dewey flipped the switch on a hundred coffered fluorescents that turned the quiet space into the Nevada desert at dawn, and here he stayed until just before he had to shower, as deep in concentration as if he were disarming hydrogen bombs.

This was the mail room, into which flowed the outpourings of an irritable and unsure nation. Letters from bearded automobile mechanics in northern Missouri who wanted to keep their guns, and from silver-haired Philadelphia matrons who wanted to take them away; from people whose entire beings orbited around substances, whether gold, marijuana, pesticides, or potatoes; from those who had recently discovered their strong convictions to those who had recently been convicted; from the pro and the anti to aunties and professionals; from Eskimos who desperately wanted sex change operations (why have two when you can do nothing and get the same result?) to Rockefellers writing about composting toilets; from movie stars, egg handlers, bonefish guides, cashiers, helicopter pilots, sex maniacs, accountants, asparagus farmers, autoworkers, ballet dancers, trick shots, puppet makers, biology professors, and people who lived on the street. Every single one was absolutely convinced that he knew the way and that Dewey should urgently carry out a plan that was invariably presented to him at great length. And every single one expected that Dewey would carefully read his letter and reply in longhand.

As far as anyone knew, no one read these letters other than the high school students who sorted them into 125 different categories for form-letter reply. How amazed they would have been to discover that several times a week Dewey would sit for hours in their chairs, touching the papers they had touched and reading the letters that the letter writers would assume—after receiving a machined reply—he had never seen.

But he did read them, by the thousand, and this fed his uncanny political instincts, without which he might never have entered the District of Columbia other than on a school bus. He read them with Dewey-like randomness, which is to say with no more plan than the wanderings of an unescorted puppy. It frequently amazed people when he would refer to these letters as if they, too, had read them: "What about that girl whose crutches the Social Security Administration wouldn't pay for? Got billed a thousand dollars month after month. Interest. Father's an octopus fisherman in San Francisco. Owes a million dollars. Gotta do something about that. All she eats is octopus. Gotta help her. Gotta do something." This might be on one of the Sunday morning talk shows, in which case Finney in the darkness off-set would mouth the answer to the question that he would surely have to answer in Dewey's behalf: "I don't know. I haven't got a clue. You'll have to ask him." They thought Dewey made these things up.

"What about that nut," Dewey said on *Meet the Press*, "who wants the Indians and everyone else to switch places? We'd go to reservations and they'd get the rest. We can't do that," he said passionately. "For one thing, I have a condo at Chimp Creek, and I'm not going to trade it for a hut in the goddamn Everglades."

Most of the time, Dewey read the mail in the "approve" piles, preferring them, he told himself, because they were near the lavatory and the water cooler, especially the "worshipful" stack. Here were what the teenagers who sorted it called NAROMUCs, for Nauseatingly Ardent Recapitulations of Mushrom's Unbearable Crap. They were all more or less the same: "Senator Knott, you are a man of steel who will fight for the American way and lead us into a brighter tomorrow. I was born in 1897 and I've never voted in an election, but I'll vote for you because you'll bring a new dawn to this great country of ours, from the wheat fields of Iowa to the newsrooms of metropolitan dailies in Gotham City."

After several hours of inflating himself on this, he would read a letter or two from the "disapprove" piles—"Go ahead, schmuck, let's see you leap a tall building at a single bound"—and move on to the pile marked "Various Flavors of Nut." After reading several hundred NAROMUCs he was sufficiently pumped up to wade into the nuts, who, even if they were threatening, were always interesting if only because they never recapitulated Mushrom. Strangely, many of these letters were written in handwriting just like Dot's, and were posted from 20002, the zip code that included the Knotts' own ultra-refrigerated town house, and which Dewey referred to habitually as "Two thousand and two," which shunted his mail to Fort Davis, 20020. The letters in handwriting like Dot's were always the most savage and eerie. Whoever wrote them seemed to be clairvoyant, in that whoever wrote them seemed to know amazing personal details about Dewey that no one was supposed to know, that no one could know, such as the fact that Dewey liked to eat the waxed rind of cheeses and would throw away the cheese itself. How this person, or persons, knew this was an utter mystery. Dewey never showed these letters to Dot, for fear of upsetting her.

One night when Dot was asleep in the town house, curled under six blankets in the twelve-degree air, Washington was in the duck press of August heat. People who slept on the street lay splayed like curing hides. There were no breezes. Had war had to be declared, Congress could not have done it. Every member was on an important fact-finding tour in the Canadian Rockies, the Swiss Alps, the Stockholm Archipelago, or the Maine Coast. That's all right, Dewey thought, I'm the leader. That's why I'm here, and that's why I am the leader. And then he swallowed hard because he remembered that he no longer was the leader. He wasn't even a senator, even if they kept calling him that. Why did he do it? Why did he resign? He had jumped in the polls, but had fallen right back. He hated that Moofoomooach guy, but, on the other hand, look what this Moofoo-mooach guy had done for him. If the son of a bitch had only stuck around, Dewey wouldn't have had to give a thought to Congress except as a place to pass the bills he proposed.

"Damn that Moofoomooach," he growled in the deserted room as he leafed through the nut pile. "Eff ewe see kay him. I don't need him. To hell with him." He glanced at a letter in a hand like Dot's, and saw that it was a protest of the relatively low limits on Dewey's credit cards. Why would anyone care? People were so crazy. He flipped it into the "cold" pile. Another few minutes, and he would have to sneak back upstairs, go through the secret door, deflate his air mattress, shave, and dazzle the hacks with yet another four a.m. press conference. Ten days to the convention. He read one more letter, from a witch in Rhode Island, and flipped it over.

There before him, on the "hot" pile, was a postcard in an uncharacteristically elegant hand. It must have been from a disturbed person, because the return address was N Ward, California State Hospital for the Criminally Insane at Loma Poya.

"Uh-oh," said Dewey. The message was short. He read it out loud, as haltingly as a second grader in a school play: "'If you want to win, I know what to do, and you know it.'"

The signature was bold and almost illegible—did mental patients possess fountain pens? Weren't they too much like knives? It read, "Cordially, L. B. D. Moofoomooach, DDS." Dewey stuffed the postcard in his jacket pocket and bolted from the room.

LOMA POYA was one of those quiet little California towns where the sidewalks are littered with parchment-coloured bamboo and palm detritus that when it rots smells like dead mangoes. The surrounding hills blazed in the sun like Achilles' shield, until the fog came up the valley from the Pacific, almost as chilled, white, and wet as the foam atop a wave. A powerful little river ran through the valley, watering immense stands of fragrant eucalyptus trees with mountain snow melt from the Sierra Nevada. The water was almost as cold as the glass mugs that the high-end Mexican restaurant kept in the freezer, into which chilled beer was poured in anticipation of meals with the red heat of hell. In Loma Poya, little purple Volkswagens with short surfboards on their roof racks were parked along streets of ill-kempt wooden houses with dry frizzy gardens, in which lived razor-clam-thin white boys between the ages of eighteen and twenty-seven, who wore long shorts, Hawaiian shirts, no socks, and went around in a trance on skateboards. In Loma Poya, the sheriff and his three deputies collectively weighed 1,078 pounds. In Loma Poya, the breezes blew, the climate was perfect, the air fragrant, the evenings quiet. And in Loma Poya, there was a huge mental hospital for the criminally insane, that sat upon a rise outside of town, set in a foil of flammable golden grasses and surrounded by a devil's necklace of silvery barbed wire so thick and heavy that it looked like a stormy Pacific with incoming rollers of glittering Slinkys.

At the stroke of eight in the morning of the first Monday in August, Dr C. Cervin Rufus drove his Porsche through the gates of Loma Poya HFCS, sticking his head out the window like a turtle so as to make full eye contact with the guard, who waved him through. Parking in his spot, he left the car and guided a fancy coffee drink through the air like Peter Pan, level and smooth even as he took the steps. Dr C. Cervin Rufus was totally unclassifiable. He was the son of a Finnish-speaking Romanian diplomat and a Bengali Jewish woman who had been raised in New Zealand. After a childhood in Egypt, Holland, and Japan, he matriculated at the Sorbonne and went on to the University of Texas Medical School before taking up a psychiatric residency in a Louisiana hospital that treated mainly Cajuns. His absolutely indecipherable accent was utterly charming—*you* was *yow*, and *business* was *boosy-ness*—he was a wee bit less than five feet tall, with sparkling green eyes and a chocolate complexion that contrasted strikingly with his flaming red hair. He was fluent in many languages but native in none, his hobby was bass fishing, he knew Sanskrit, loved ballroom dancing, was a self-described "night-crawler socialist," carried two dozen tea bags that he sniffed to cure frequent attacks of anxiety and panic, was prone to uncontrollable giggling, preferred German food, took at least six baths a day, and was looking for a wife just like himself.

Trying to saunter into the nurses' station on Ward N with the bored and authoritative air of his peers—something he simply could not do—he cut quite a figure. "Hello, Dr Rufus. How are you this morning?" asked a nurse who seemed twice his height.

"I'm fine, nurse," he told her, beaming at her golden tresses at almost a forty-five-degree angle. "I had some great German food last night, and went to the livestock show."

She eyed him incredulously. "I didn't know there was a German restaurant in Loma Poya."

"I drove down to Palo Cerrito."

"Oh."

"Any new ones?"

"Yeah," the nurse said. "Two. A married couple. I've never heard of that before, but why not?"

"Associative dementia?"

"No, they're young. Here are their records."

Dr Rufus read intently. Then he closed one folder and picked up another, Fredericka's. There was little to go on. The nurse glided back, in her hands a revoltingly pink tray upon which were white cups with individual doses of psychoactive drugs. "Do you want to see them both at once?"

Dr Rufus looked up. "No," he said. "I'm like a squirrel. One nut at a time."

"I'll summon the orderlies."

Dr Rufus shook his head from side to side. "No need. His violence was triggered by a discrete event."

"What was that? I haven't read the chart."

"Evidently," Dr Rufus told her, like the narrator in a Sherlock Holmes movie, "he attacked—they attacked—a souvenir shop in San Francisco, and did a great deal of damage to people and property. The proximate cause is reported to have been his—and then her—reaction to a poster depicting the queen of England in a compromising position with Boutros Boutros-Ghali. The subject claimed to the officers, who just barely subdued him, that she is his mother."

"Probably drugs," said the nurse.

"I don't think so," Dr Rufus opined. "We're not faced with standard hallucinations like bats or gargoyles. I suppose it could be drugs, but I would guess not."

"What about the woman who claimed she was Calvin Coolidge in drag?"

"She looked just like him. I discharged her."

After the nurse left, Dr Rufus finished his coffee and thought about the patient. Then he walked down the hall, unlocked a door, and stepped bravely into Freddy's room.

A FRUIT FLY had landed on Freddy's nose, a baby fruit fly that even he could not see unless he crossed his eyes, which he did. Because he was in a straitjacket, he had no influence upon the fly, and had to content himself with the exaggerated movements of his muscles and joints, and simple verbal abuse. He was so vigorously engaged in this that he had failed to notice the doctor's entrance, and, because the fly was nearly invisible, to Dr Rufus it appeared that Freddy was making faces and talking to himself.

"Hello, I'm Dr Rufus," Dr Rufus said.

Freddy had not heard, and his apparent reply was, "Away, mouse turd!"

Dr Rufus made notes. As he was doing so, the fly flew away and Freddy said, "Thank God you're gone!"

"I'm not gone, and I'm not a mouse turd," Dr Rufus said firmly but without hostility.

Freddy, who in the midst of his passion had not been aware of how he had addressed the fruit fly, replied, "What is that? The bloody Declaration of Independence?"

"I just want to make sure that we start off with mutual respect. I'll respect you, if you'll respect me."

"Fair enough," said Freddy, "assuming that you earn my respect."

"And that you earn mine," Dr Rufus replied. "Do you want to hurt people?"

"No, fruit flies."

"Is that a verb?"

Freddy liked this. "A noun," he answered.

"Do you want to hurt yourself?"

"No."

"Am I a fruit fly?" asked Dr Rufus, cleverly.

"You tell me," Freddy instructed.

"Am I?"

"Obviously not." Freddy looked him over. "What are you?"

"It's too complicated to explain, and I'd prefer to talk about you."

"Unfortunately, most people do."

"If I remove the jacket, will you remain calm and behave in a civilised fashion?"

"Given that I'm in a straitjacket," Freddy asked, "and that I'm three times your size, why would you believe me? Why would you take the risk?"

"I find trust self-encouraging," Freddy was told, "and, that life is full of risks, is to me like mother-of-pearl."

"What's the pearl?" Freddy asked.

"Courage," said the little fellow, undoing the straps.

Freddy was delighted by this, and even more so by his freedom from restraint. He stretched, and breathed in relief.

Dr Rufus relaxed into a chair. This was the moment of truth. What he would say next might reignite the patient into a frenzy. It might even mean the death of C. Cervin Rufus. But he lived for such moments, which were to him like the seconds in which a high diver looks down to where he will strike the water. "So," he said, "what happened up in San Francisco that brought you here?"

To Dr Rufus's relief, Freddy answered with judicious equanimity. "My wife and I were on Market Street, having just arrived in town and walked from the Golden Gate, when we saw in the window of a souvenir shop a faked photograph of my mother in flagrante delicto with Boutros Boutros-Ghali. Outrageous. When I went into the shop and requested politely that the photograph be removed from display, the shopkeeper went mad. He swore at me, foamed, spat, and threatened me with a cudgel that looked like a rounded cricket bat. I refused to back down, and went to the window to remove the libel. Had I a choice? He came after me with his bat, I disarmed him, his cousins appeared with other bats, and a mêlée ensued, during which one of them attacked my wife. I was only breaking their arms, but she grew rather more angry. I'm afraid that, after she began to wield the cudgel, a great deal of damage was done both to the establishment and its proprietors."

"I see," said Dr Rufus. "You know, they would not have sent you down here—it might have been a matter of self-defence, or a tort question solely—but for one thing."

"What is that?"

"In the poster, the woman pictured with Boutros Boutros-Ghali was quite clearly Philippa, the queen of England."

"Yes," said Freddy, "Mummy."

"Then you are the Prince of Wales."

Freddy did not react to this declaration, as it was to him rather obvious.

"Then you are the Prince of Wales."

"That's right," said Freddy.

"You have a slight resemblance. . . ."

"I *bear* a slight resemblance," Freddy corrected.

"But that's all. Obviously, you are not he."

Freddy laughed. It sounded insane.

"This morning," Dr Rufus told him, "I'll call the British Consulate and check on the whereabouts of the prince, who, I suspect, is comfortably ensconced in Buckingham Palace."

"I wouldn't be at Buckingham Palace at this time of year, I'd be at Balmoral. That's what they'll say, that I'm at Balmoral. What does the consulate in San Francisco know? All they know is software."

"I'll call the embassy, then. I'll call Buckingham Palace."

"They'll say," Freddy insisted, "that I'm at Balmoral."

"Why would they say that, when you're here?"

"It's arranged that way. MI5 completely cut me off. I tried calling Mummy's private line, but they changed it. It was part of the plan. I'm stuck here, on my own."

"The intelligence agencies, then, did this," said Dr Rufus, leading the witness.

"And the PM, and the Household, and Psnake, and Didgeridoo."

"Did the CIA do it, too?"

"Probably not. They wouldn't like the underlying premise."

"Which is?"

"Recapturing the colonies for the Empire."

"That was your job?"

"It is my job."

"Alone?"

"Of course not. Fredericka is with me."

"Your wife, the Princess of Wales, Fredericka, the one with the. . . ." Dr Rufus trailed off.

"You needn't be shy," said Freddy. "She's shown it off to three quarters of mankind."

"What?" asked Dr Rufus, not disingenuously but, in fact, shyly.

"Her magnificent bust. Splendid. Young. Overflowing. Firm. Blemishless. Blushing. I took refuge there. I clasped her to me, and it was like being pulled into an airlock on a Russian space ship."

"Have you been on a space ship?" Dr Rufus asked.

"Oh yes," said Freddy, who had toured, as no civilian could, both Baikonur and Cape Canaveral, "although not on it, but, rather, in it. And I have a piece of moon rock on my desk. Nixon gave it to me."

"Nixon."

"Yes. Well, not really. He gave it to the Dalai Lama, who brought it to me."

"You are acquainted with the Dalai Lama?"

"Sure. I taught him how to fly-fish. They have magnificent trout streams in the Himalaya, so I sent him out a full rig of the best equipment. Cost ten thousand pounds, but it was a delight. Capital fellow."

"What about the Pope?"

"Doesn't fly-fish."

"But you know him?"

"Not really, though when I'm in Rome I see him privately. We converse in Latin. Someday I'll be the head of the C of E, which by that time will be a minority sect amid resurgent paganism, but we've been through difficult times before. Because of that, I have to take it more seriously than Mummy, Grandpapa, or any of my predecessors of the last few hundred years."

"Would your wife be able to replicate these details?"

"Most of them."

"If you don't mind, I'll ask her."

"You disbelieve me."

"Yes," Dr Rufus answered, "though I believe that you think, genuinely and sincerely, that everything you've told me is true."

"It is true," Freddy said, and then looked down dejectedly at his hospital-gown-covered thighs. "It is true. I failed in the conquest. All I want is to go home, and, perhaps never to be king, live quietly with the pleasures that once I knew, that seemed then so slight and ephemeral, but that would seem to a man who is dead, or like me, to be inexpressibly good. Oh, if I from this death could touch them, or live once again in their light. Every colour, every sight, was like a mountain river in flood, infilling, flowing in impossibly generous volume, rushing to decorate the world with its rapids and lazy mirrored stretches. How lovely. How lucky I was. And how I long for such things."

Dr Rufus looked intently at his patient. He was much interested in what Freddy had to say. "Tell me what you miss," the doctor said. "Tell me what you love. Tell me what you want to go back to when you leave this place, no matter how long from now that may be."

Freddy looked up, as if he could see through the ceiling and the rooms above straight into the spirit-blue sky. "I miss Fredericka. She's close by. I miss her very much."

"Naturally you do. Our object is to make you and her better, so you can live happily together. But tell me of your past life. Your recollections seem so exact and concrete."

"But you don't believe me," Freddy protested.

"What we try to do in psychiatry," said Dr Rufus, "is to reconcile objective reality—as far as we can know it—with the reality of the heart. Our patients come to us with broken hearts. That's what interests us. Whether it be actually true or not, I will believe what is in your heart, which is often a much finer thing, distilled from the world around it, than what the world around it actually is."

"I would have to agree," Freddy said. "Would you like me to free-associate or something?"

"Yes, please," said Dr Rufus, so graciously that Freddy was put at ease. "I've never done it."

"What about before you fall asleep?"

"But then I sleep."

"Just tell me what comes to mind."

"Melons," said Freddy. "I don't like melons except in France, where they're so magnificently sweet."

"Go on."

"Because they inject them with cane sugar. Damn Frogs, they use too much makeup, too. They're trained in betrayal from an early age, in little things, but little things become big things, don't they, and you go from sugaring melons to Marshal Pétain. What I really can't abide, and have not been able to abide ever since I was a child, are pictures of melons, in all forms."

"What kind of pictures?"

"Every kind. In the fifties I used to see a lot of too brightly coloured representations of bisected watermelons. Then in the sixties it was Kodachromes of cantaloupes. Those I could avoid, but not the old master paintings, still lifes of bloody fucking melons: Juan Sánchez Cotán, a great painter, but why so many melons? Rintel Vorhuis Van Loopen the Elder, melons with flies buzzing about. Giovanni Pizzabianca, melons, melons, melons."

"Melons are a vaginal symbol," Dr Rufus stated.

"Not when they're served as two balls flanking a banana."

"Have melons made up an important part of your life?"

"Of course they haven't. What kind of a question is that?"

"Were you happy?"

Freddy calmed, as if he were seeing invisible beauties. "Sometimes."

"When?"

"I was happy . . ." he said, closing his eyes and infused with memory, "when I would mow hay in a sun-drenched, golden field from which grasshoppers would rise literally by the millions and stream against me like a gravelly wind. Sometimes they would even bite, but their jaws are square and weak, and it was only a nibble.

"When, at Balmoral, I was alone in a cold stream. The sound and smell of mountain water brings you to the innocence of the world's beginnings. Never have I been more content. A long day by a stream—wading to the rocks, feet planted in shallow rapids, rod and line undulating like kelp in a storm (not even the greatest dancer in the world can move as beautifully as a good fly line)—is worth a kingdom. As much as I love Fredericka, and as much as I think she loves me, we know not what we are capable of, not having spent time together in the streams of Scotland. Should we ever get back there, we'll have our chance.

"And whisky and hors d'oeuvres upon returning from a day of cold wind and rain. You sit in a chair with a light plaid blanket drawn up around you, a fire three-quarters front, a tumbler of single malt, and—for example—Plutarch. The thunder cracks outside; the dog is sleeping at the hearth, his golden fur now fluffy and dry; meat and potatoes are roasting in the kitchen; and Fredericka comes in, perfumed and half-naked in an exquisite gown. Was I happy? Yes, often.

"Have you ever heard a girls' choir in a cold but luminous chapel with marble floors as smooth as ice, and jewelled light aflame in the windows like rubies and amber? At university I would go quietly to the most obscure pew and, hiding from all, as I had to, listen to their practice. It didn't hurt to have been in love with this or that girl in the line, but with their voices, their faces, their intensity, and their goodness, you could not help but love them all. They would sing a portion, and the choirmaster would stop them. I loved their expressions as they listened intently to him, taking instruction, embarrassed by what they thought was their lack of skill. And then they would start up again like angels of God. What a deep love I had for them, and for what they did."

Dr Rufus listened intently as well. Whereas most patients remembered fear, humiliation, violence, and abuse, Freddy seemed to run on love and beauty. "Go on."

"Oh, I don't know," Freddy said, closing his eyes again. "I see myself looking out the high windows of Buckingham Palace, at five o'clock, in December. The lights are moving busily in the cold and dark. My heart is pounding, my face burning. Fredericka appears. Her face is hot, the colour of rose petals. You can hear the silence, and the darkness seems to glow.

"Which reminds me of the way the sun lifts me from despair at times, by sending signals about the real nature of things that I have overlooked—by illuminating them truly. It happened with a map once, and it happened with a chop on my desk—a Chinese block of alabaster with an ornamentally sculpted top and a character engraved at the bottom, which I had always thought was dull, until very early one morning, just as the sun rose on a summer day, it was caught in a thin and short-lived ray of sunlight." Freddy stood and went to the window, resting his left hand against the left upright of the window frame, so that his hospital gown, which was of the cheapest blue cloth, extended like a coronation robe. The fall of even this fabric was noble and beautiful, like a curtain draped by an all-pervading and splendid force, and it brightened in the diffusion of sunlight that flooded into the room after having skipped across the golden hills. "Like this," he said. "It almost came alive. The qualities within left on a beam of warm light and filled the room as if with butterscotch and gold. Lovely thing it was. It said to me that even souls of grey are gifted and good, if only they will collide with a glorious and accidental ray. It happens with people, you know. It really does."

FREDERICKA WAS EXQUISITE in her straitjacket. Of white muslin, cut with raglan sleeves, bulky shoulders, and a martial-arts fullness, it was quite chic, and her hair, naturally bleached in the mountain sun and now relaxed in the cicada-dry climate of Loma Poya, was regal. She sat on a clunky enamelled chair in her little cell, eyes fixed on a beam of sunlight that had stolen in through the open window and striped the wall with the pattern of the bars, and she prayed, running through the finer and nobler parts of the services, dwelling on the special prayers for kings lost in foreign lands, and for their chaste and patient queens.

The door opened, and in walked a woman who was Fredericka's opposite. Whereas Fredericka's expression was soft and gracious, hers, despite an obviously fraudulent smile, was hard and tight. Whereas Fredericka's face itself was large, full of planes, sharpness, and firmness, this woman's face was soft, round, and fallow. Whereas Fredericka's mien was graceful and feminine, hers was stiff and defensive. Whereas Fredericka's body was muscular and firm, hers was soft and blowsy.

"Hello," she said. "I'm Tammy Braunschweiger, a doctor on staff. You've been assigned to Dr Rufus, but I thought I'd stop in just to see how you are."

"I don't understand your costume," Fredericka said.

"My costume?" The doctor was offended when she shouldn't have been.

"Your clothing."

"Oh," the doctor said, lifting her serape and tipping her bowler hat. "It's to express my solidarity with the women of Baba Ru. And these beads," she said, lifting a heavy rope of multi-coloured beans, "were strung by the imprisoned rifle-women of Tupac Wenceslas."

"Tupac Wenceslas," Fredericka repeated.

"Dr Rufus is your doctor," Dr Braunschweiger said conspiratorially, "but he's a man."

"Am I going to get a gynaecological exam?"

"No. We're psychiatrists. I thought you might be more comfortable with a woman. If you want a gynaecological exam, it can be arranged."

"I do. I'm pregnant."

"I'll have to put that on your chart. Do you want to carry the pregnancy to term?"

"I beg your pardon?"

"Do you want to carry the pregnancy to term or do you want to abort?"

Fredericka appeared so upset that Dr Braunschweiger suspected the worst. "Did he make you?"

"Did who what?"

"Did your 'husband' make you pregnant?"

"Of course he did."

"With your consent?"

"Yes, with my consent."

"Is he making you carry the foetus to term?"

"Making me?"

"Forcing you."

"Madam, are you mad?"

"No, no, you're the one who's mad, remember? I'm the doctor. You're the one in the straitjacket."

"The world is full of injustices," Fredericka said, "and always has been."

"Absolutely," said the doctor. "You might consider that, in view of your situation, you can't judge whether or not you're being coerced by your husband."

"My husband didn't put me in a straitjacket, you did."

"Yes, and it's within my authority to remove it."

"Then do so, please."

Dr Braunschweiger undid the straps, and Fredericka burst free, throwing off the jacket with great relief. She strode up and down, lifting her arms, taking deep breaths. How noble and statuesque she was, like an exaggerated bronze in the courtyard of a French museum, or a marble in a Florentine piazza, that struggles with a serpent while pouring water from an amphora that never runs dry. For the doctor, it was like being in the same room as a newly awakened tiger.

"I'm going to put you on a thousand milligrams of Proclorox, four times a day," she said, writing out the order on a clipboard.

"No, thank you," Fredericka told her, firmly and royally.

The doctor looked up over her ruler-edged reading glasses. "You have to," she said.

"No, I don't have to. I hate drugs, and won't take them."

"You'll take them if so ordered."

"Sorry."

"Then we'll have to put you back in restraint."

Fredericka knew that the doctor would now summon an orderly, whether by the panic button in her left hand or the one on the wall, and that the orderly—a woman as big as a Melanesian chief—would brutally wrestle her into the jacket. And Fredericka knew that Dr Braunschweiger would watch this with feigned professional detachment and unconcealable personal satisfaction. Why, Fredericka thought, should the doctor get off so lightly? And the doctor didn't.

"YOUR WIFE," said Dr Rufus, opening his second conversation with Freddy, "is a very violent woman."

Freddy jerked his head up. "Is she all right?"

"She's all right, but she's still in the jacket, and sedated."

"That's not all right," Freddy said. "What happened?"

"She attacked a colleague of mine who, because of a mistake in the schedule, went to see her before I did."

"For no reason?"

"Apparently."

"I don't believe it," Freddy said. "She's not like that at all. Let me see her. I must see her."

"She's fine, and she's resting. She's not far from here. We'll bring you together eventually. You may even be allowed conjugal visits. . . ."

"Like rats?"

"In complete privacy."

Freddy said no more, not wanting to prejudice his chances of being with Fredericka. He understood that if they were brought together they would, indeed, make love, even were the whole world watching, because this was the primordial act of survival.

"Soon," said Dr Rufus. "But if one of you is sedated, there can be no visit. The conditions must be parallel."

"Then sedate me."

"We don't do it that way. We move only toward what's better."

Freddy put his head in his hands.

"Have patience. You're making progress. If you and she could control yourselves, your delusions would be harmless and you wouldn't have to be here."

"What delusions?" Freddy asked.

"I spoke to Buckingham Palace itself," Dr Rufus reported. "The Prince and Princess of Wales are on holiday in Scotland, at Balmoral, as you said. He's fly-fishing, and she's making a tour of the crofts."

"It's a lie," Freddy said. "I can prove it." He sat up in his chair with alarming urgency. Dr Rufus was used to such things. "Call the palace, ask for my batman. He'll corroborate details I can tell you that no one else would know."

Freddy had been speaking so fast that Dr Rufus heard not "my batman," but *Batman*.

"Batman?" Dr Rufus asked.

"Yes, Robin," who was the best batman in England and had been at Freddy's side for decades.

"You'd like me to call Buckingham Palace again, to speak to Batman."

"My batman."

"Your Batman."

"Yes."

"You have a special relationship with Batman."

"I do. He's mine."

"He's yours."

"Until his retirement."

"And then, I presume," Dr Rufus said, "Robin will take his place?"

"He is Robin."

"Batman and Robin are one in the same?"

"Yes. *My* batman is Robin."

"But why are there two of them?"

"There aren't two of them. There's only one of them: Robin, my batman."

"But I've seen them," Dr Rufus asserted firmly, "together, talking to one another."

"You've seen *them*?"

"Many a time."

Perhaps, Freddy thought, everyone had always been right, and he was insane.

"You know," said Dr Rufus, "with the big ears."

"No, no," said Freddy, moving his finger to and fro like a metronome, "*I'm* the one with the big ears."

"You're Batman, and he's Robin?"

"Yes, *my* batman. And he is Robin."

"No, I mean, you yourself are Batman."

"No, again," Freddy said with exasperation. "I am not my batman. Robin is my batman. I am I," and then Freddy added, because it was such a famous line, and he couldn't help it, "Don Quixote, the Man of La Mancha."

Dr Rufus was boxed in. He thought and thought, and then he said, hopefully, "Is it a gay thing?"

"It's sometimes gay," Freddy said, used not to the twenty-year appropriation of the word but the meaning of a thousand years, "after rough exercise—you know, all the standard stuff: sliding down buildings on ropes, rescuing people, all that—when Robin draws my bath and pours me a neat Scotch. I often invite him to have one for himself, or two, and then it does get rather gay. I should say, we've been through a lot together."

"So, he's Robin."

"He is."

"Therefore, you are Batman."

"No, Doctor," Freddy said, slowly and with pity. "He is Robin. He is my batman. And I am I"—he just couldn't help it—"Don Quixote, the Man of La Mancha."

"All right," said Dr Rufus. "Batman and Robin are one and the same."

"Yes. You've got it."

"What do you do with them? Who's the dominant one?"

"I'm the dominant one, of course. I'm the bloody Prince of bloody Wales. *He*," said Freddy, "lays out my clothes, helps me dress and undress, polishes my boots and leather, runs dispatches, brings lunch and tea, will go to the shops if I need something, keeps the weapons in order, buffs the saddles, and also serves as a guard and general aide-de-camp."

"Leather," said Dr Rufus.

"Boots, belts, straps, saddles," said Freddy, clarifying, he thought.

"On whom is the saddle placed?"

"Saddles."

"Saddles."

"Mainly on Vercingetorix, but sometimes on Clemençeau, and sometimes on De Gaulle."

"All men," Dr Rufus said.

"Not men," Freddy replied, amused, "*stallions.* But not only stallions. Sometimes, especially if children are present, I mount Christine."

"THESE ARE TWO of the strangest patients I've ever encountered," Dr Rufus said at a staff meeting ten days after his first interviews with Freddy and Fredericka, "and I think we'll probably have to keep them forever."

"I second that," said Dr Braunschweiger, bandaged, black-eyed, and split-lipped. "She almost killed Jolo, and look what she did to me."

"Is she still on Proclorox?" asked the physician-in-charge.

"Yes," said Dr Rufus.

"But they were so resistant."

"Submission is the price they paid for being together. Now they're as placid as two lakes at dawn."

"Good," said the physician-in-charge, "but I see that you have no diagnoses."

"I haven't been able to arrive at any."

Looking over the folder before him, as Dr Braunschweiger tried, painfully and unsuccessfully, to smile, the physician-in-charge said, "A patient believes that he is the Prince of Wales and his mother is the queen of England, that he is also Don Quixote, and the gay companion of Batman and Robin, who are the same person. . . ."

"I know," said Dr Rufus.

"Let me finish. He drops in on the Pope and has ridden on space ships. The Dalai Lama brings him moon rocks from Nixon. What else?" He began to flip pages. "Speaks for the reaccession of the North American Colonies for the British Empire . . . rebuts history (self-supplied) of Tourette's Syndrome by blaming a dog named after a Chinese nutritionist who died of starvation . . . claims to be a dentist by the name of 'Lachpoof Bach-quaquinnik Dess Moofoomooach,' and to have carried his diplomas and professional certifications in his rectum."

"They were parachuted in," Dr Rufus added.

"Dr Rufus," the physician-in-charge said, most seriously and conclusively. "You can't go native in this profession, you simply can't. Do you understand that?"

"Yes, sir."

"This patient is totally insane. He's not ill, he's just crazy. That's the diagnosis. They'll probably have to live in the cottage, milking cows, for the rest of their lives."

"Dr Whippy?"

"Yes, Dr Rufus?"

"They claim that Dewey Knott is going to get them out by insisting that the governor pardon them."

"Naturally. And if not the governor, the Pope; and if not the Pope, Charlemagne. Aren't you on to that one, Dr Rufus? If a patient told you that Napoleon was his wife's divorce lawyer, as a patient recently told me, would you believe it?"

"Not necessarily."

"What do you mean, 'not necessarily'?"

"I think it's strange."

"What's strange?"

"All those limousines and motorcycle police."

"What limousines and motorcycle police?" Dr Whippy asked.

"In the parking lot. I saw them through Miss Durkstein's window as I was coming in."

The silence was broken by the click of the soundproofed door as it noiselessly glided open on its heavy hinges. "Miss Durkstein," said Dr Whippy.

"Dr Whippy," announced a breathless Miss Durkstein, "the governor is here."

"The governor of what?"

"California."

"What's he doing here?"

"It's about two patients," Miss Durkstein said. "He has papers for you to sign."

THREE DAYS BEFORE the convention and sixty points behind Self in most of the polls—eighty in others—Dewey Knott was in despair. Nonetheless, he manfully practised his acceptance speech, a document that had sprung from the head of a manic and resurgent Mushrom, who believed that Dewey Knott was going to be president, and that history would record not only Lincoln and Herndon, Wilson and House, and Roosevelt and Hopkins, but Knott and Mushrom. And if not Knott and Mushrom, then Mushrom at the UN, Mushrom at Defense, Mushrom at State, Mushrom, perhaps, Poet Laureate. The best part of any of these opportunities would be not the job itself but the elegant and beautiful women, who would hang on his every word.

He had pulled out all the stops in the speechwriter's art and thrown in every policy plum that came his way. Dewey Knott had pledged to give each American a dollar, but after deducting postage and taxes it worked out to sixty-nine cents. Hence, Mushrom's line, that Dewey practised at the lectern in his quarters high above San Francisco and the bay: "I pledge, on my sacred honour, for the sake of the dead of Antietam, Iwo Jima, and Bunker Hill, to give every American, woman or man, old or young, living or dead, sixty-nine cents."

"Do you think that will play?" Dewey had asked Mushrom.

And Mushrom had replied, eyes burning with sexual frenzy, "Senator, we're going to win on that. I feel it in my bones."

"What about this line?" Dewey asked Mushrom, as the fog obscured the bay and carpeted the ground below them so that it seemed as if they were two angels in conversation after death.

"What line?"

"'The glory of the flag,'" Dewey read, "'the mackerel seas, the purple plains garlanded with wildflowers, and the forest floors spotted with the noble and brilliant mushroom.' There's something odd about that."

"There is?"

"It . . . it just seems . . . funny. I mean strange, somehow."

"Why?"

"I can't put my finger on it."

"It may not be the most effective line for the convention," Mushrom said, "but it'll be absolutely magnificent on TV."

"Idoh know. Could you change it a little?"

Mushrom bristled, for this was his greatest speech. "How?" he said, which, in the language of the Washington speechwriter, means *no*.

"Maybe," said Dewey, "you could take out the word *plains*. A lotta people won't know what that means."

"What about *prairies*?"

Dewey shook his head. "Too French."

"Fields!" Mushrom said in a burst of inspiration.

"That's good. That'll work. Now, what about this; I don't understand this: 'Tell them on the sea and tell them on the land, tell them in Singapore and tell them in Japan, that America is not in decline, no it's not, it's on the rise, it's going up, like a monkey on the tree, grasping for the nut.'"

"That shows," Mushrom said, "that we're on the upswing."

"Like a monkey reaching for a nut?"

"How about *Ourangatang*?"

"*Orang-utan*," said Dewey. It was, painfully learned, one of the few things that he actually knew.

"*Ourangatang*," Mushrom replied. He was, after all, the wordsmith.

"Orang-u*tan*."

"Tang."

"Tan."

"Tang."

"Tang," Dewey said, wily fox.

"Orang-u*tan*."

"Stop there!" said Dewey. "Put it in." Mushrom did, but spelled it his way, and gave it to Dewey to read.

Dewey's lips moved as he read. Then he said, "*A* ourangatang?"

"Well, you don't want to have two."

"Why don't you just cut out the ourangatangs?"

"I can't."

"I don't want to get up there and talk about ourangatangs."

"We can't use monkeys again."

"Table it," said Dewey.

He grasped the text of the speech, all fifty single-spaced pages of it, which would take three hours to deliver, and walked out onto the terrace. They were thirty storeys above the top of a massive hill. Everything below was a blinding white and everything else a deep bright blue. The sun was strong and the air cool. "I feel like I'm insane," Dewey said to the sky. "I can't take it. We're going down. God help us."

Then Finney tapped him on the shoulder. Finney looked ecstatic. "How many points are we behind?" Dewey asked, hoping that it might be only fifty.

"Still sixty, Senator, but we've found Moofoomooach. You were right. It's a miracle. What a genius you are to have sensed his whereabouts. He *was* in an insane asylum in central California. And he's on his way here, now, with Mrs Moofoomooach."

"Yes, but is he crazy?"

"Who isn't?" Finney asked.

"We've got only three days. How can a crazy person write a three-hour acceptance speech in three days?"

"Senator, only a crazy person could write a three-hour acceptance speech in three days, and it doesn't have to be three hours. It should be forty minutes. Don't worry, we've got seven days to the speech itself."

"What's he gonna want? He has us over a barrel."

"An ambassadorship, probably. He's just a dentist."

"I don't think so. Remember, he's crazy, and he knows about all that foreign stuff."

"Maybe secretary of state," said Finney.

"It doesn't matter. We're going to lose anyway."

"No," said Finney. "Moofoomooach is here. We're going to win."

WHILE FREDDY and Fredericka sped north in the governor's limousine, as silent as two horses staring at the moon, Dewey Knott received Mushrom in the spectacular triplex on Russian Hill. Finney, who, like Dewey, was giddy with the view, called the place "Earthquake Ranch." Mushrom was used to being summoned, but this was different. Now he and the candidate sat on teak garden benches on the terrace in the bright afternoon sunlight, as if they were equals.

"Campbell?"

"Yes, sir?"

"We've been in this together a long time, haven't we?"

"Yes, Senator."

"You know exactly how I think, don't you?"

"I do."

"My words have been your words. My policy has been your policy."

Mushrom nodded.

"Campbell, we have reached the double point."

"The double point, Senator?"

"That's the point, Campbell, where the presidential candidate sheaves off a double, someone who, if the candidate is assassinated or is rendered more incomprehensible, can fill in for him. It's so secret that only presidents know about it, and they tell their opponents only on the eve of the nominating conventions."

"Gosh," said Mushrom.

"Finney has an envelope. He knows that if I'm assassinated or become more incomprehensible, he's to open it. Inside are my greetings to the anchorpeople and a message to the American voter urging him to cast his ballot for my successor. No one has ever asked what happens if the nominee gets assassinated or more incomprehensible before the election. This is what happens."

"Gosh," said Mushrom. "It's Mrs Knott, isn't it?"

"No, Campbell. Dot's a fine woman and I love her, but she's too nervous. She's a . . . what do you call someone who sleeps with clenched fists? It's because, very early on, she took on the business world and conquered it, out of principle, but it wasn't in her nature, and she didn't really want to do it. She had to wear suits and stuff, and work in an office. She told me that every minute of it was torture, and that she just wanted to be outside, taking care of her garden. So did I, Campbell. That's why we're sitting on this bench. It's why I work outside whenever I can, and hold staff meetings in Rock Creek Park. No, it can't be Dot."

"It's Governor Draff."

"Draff is an idiot. I need North Dakota, but the country doesn't need a Draff in the White House, which is why I chose him to be my running mate. Besides, his neck's too long, he'd never fit on a stamp."

"Who is it?"

"Campbell, it has to be someone just like me, someone who almost *is* me, someone who can hit the ground running, fully versed in everything I've done and all that I believe in."

Mushrom began to whiten, but he dared not say a thing. He couldn't believe it.

"Yes, Campbell, you. You are my designated successor."

"Oh God," said Mushrom.

"That means," Dewey told him, "that you must be protected. If I go, you must live. We've got to be in different places."

"Different places. I'll stay in Washington, except when you're there. And when you are, I'll be in San Francisco, Boston, Palm Beach. How about Paris or London?"

"Campbell."

"Senator?"

"No."

"Excuse me?"

"Campbell, Borneo. You've got to make your way into the mountains, find a savage tribe, and become one of them."

"I do?"

"Yes."

"But why?" Mushrom asked, every nerve tingling at what he thought was the prospect of becoming the president of the United States.

"Because it's a place where assassins would not look. No one would know you. You'd be hidden there."

"Aren't there headhunters or something there, cannibals?"

"That's just a myth."

"Borneo," said Mushrom, his eyes swimming.

"Finney will give you the plane tickets. Do you have a valid passport?"

"Yes."

"When you get to the jungle, throw it away."

"How will I get back?"

"Campbell, the greatest power on earth, in need of a leader, will send its armadas to fetch you. And if nothing happens to me, or if I lose, find a consulate and tell them to give me a call."

Mushrom was about to ask if he would have time to buy camping equipment, but he didn't have time even to change his clothes.

"Go, and God bless you. And God bless America," said Dewey.

As Mushrom left, feet hardly touching the ground, he said to himself, "Like a mighty oak risen from the forest floor, from low and dark obscurity, the rounded mushroom rises in rains of adversity and risk, ready to sacrifice for—no, ready to give all for—freedom and the way of—no, the American way . . . no. . . ."

Dewey closed his eyes and breathed deeply. When Finney came in, having given the airline tickets to a now extraordinarily arrogant Mushrom,

Dewey said, "He's gone. For the first time in decades, I'm on my own. I can say what I want in my own words, not someone else's. I feel completely different, like another person. I'm independent, self-sufficient, an entirely new man. Where's Moofoomooach?"

To show that he was presidential, Dewey had to break off from worrying that he didn't have an acceptance speech, and meet the president of Korea as he passed through San Francisco. "There's one issue I want to get clear with you," Dewey told the shocked visitor both impolitely and majestically. "Every time Dot or I go into one of those Korean salad bars and gourmet markets, which we do a lot because Dot never learned to cook, we're treated like dirt, the scum of the earth. The proprietors and employees are offended by our existence, they're rude, they insult us, and they act as if we're bandits and shoplifters."

"Senator, I. . . ."

"I'm not finished yet. What I want you to do is to get the word out. You tell those people to lighten up, to be nice to their customers, to behave like human beings. I don't want to be looked at like Jack the Ripper just because I ask where the tops are for the chocolate pudding containers. And I'll tell you what I'm going to do if you don't. I'm going to withdraw every goddamn last American soldier from Korea, and, believe me, they won't mind. I'll fold up the fucking nuclear umbrella, order the navy to stay east of Japan, and for all I care you can spend the rest of your life scraping Kim Jong Il's garbage cans. Is that clear? I mean, is it clear? It better fucking well be clear. That's it. Meeting's over. Let's go."

Dewey and his entourage stormed out and raced back to Earthquake Ranch in an atmosphere of splendid excitement made more so by the cavalcade of motorcycles and limousines half a mile long, sirens blaring, moving like a black roller coaster up and down San Francisco's hills. Dewey charged into his suite with the same firm velocity that he had had as he stormed out of the meeting. Floods of resolution and authority radiated from him, shutting the mouths and widening the eyes of his staff, Finney included. He was behaving like a determined, resolute, confident, surprising, and energetic leader. It was as if he had had whatever it is that is the opposite of a lobotomy.

Sweeping into the capacious living room high over all the lights of the world arrayed around the night-black bay, he brightened as he saw Freddy and Fredericka sitting on a couch. They were dressed in California casual white muslin, she was as beautiful as ever, more than the match for any model, princess, or movie star, and he looked, in white, reassuringly dental. They also looked quite tranquil.

"Moofoomooach!" Dewey said, voice thundering. "Desi! Popeel! Thank God we found you. Where the hell were you? It doesn't matter: you're here now. It's a new game, a game we can win. And let me get right to the point without being coy. If you stick by me and give me those miraculous speeches. . . ."

"Senator," Finney interrupted, "I think you should. . . ."

"Shut up, Finney. I'm in the middle of this." He turned his attention back to the royal couple. "Stay by my side, be brilliant, hit 'em with all that think-tank stuff and air-you-dition, and—let's not beat about the bush— you do what I think you can do, God, what the whole world knows you can do, and I'll give you the United Nations, with cabinet rank."

Silence captured the room as if with a heavily weighted net. Dewey breathed and waited. His eyes darted. "Okay," he said, "that was my first offer. I'm ready to offer you the post of national security adviser to the president. That's it, you can head up the NSC."

"Senator," Finney said.

"Not now, Finney." Freddy and Fredericka appeared to Dewey to have flawless poker faces. Obviously, he had not gone far enough. They were good, really good. "I surrender," he said, raising his hands. "I'll give you state. You can be my secretary of state." He wiped the sweat from his brow.

"Senator!"

"Finney, do I have to send you out of the room?" And then, turning to Freddy as quickly as someone who has had four expressos, "We've gotta paralyse the intellectuals—you can do that—and the news media. Like we did the last time. And we've gotta get the base roaring. I want you to throw them ten thousand tons of red and bloody meat. You know: battles, George Washington, sacrifice, submarines, distant trumpets. Make 'em feel that if they died during your speech—my speech—it would be worth it. But don't forget women. That means those horrible grocery lists that we're so bad at: education, food purity, safety, day care, all that crap that I can't even bear to think about. Makes my flesh crawl. Puts me to sleep. Body stuff. Sex. Self-concern. Feelings. What does that have to do with statesmanship?

What's going on? If you can't do it," he said, "maybe she can." He pointed to Fredericka, whose eyes were like brilliant and unmoving gems in a case at the Natural History Museum.

"She can do the women stuff. And farmers. You've been out there. I don't know what you've seen, but maybe you know how hard farmers work. It's not much of a vote, though it is where I came from, and the people in cities remember in their blood what it was like to be on the land.

"And talk about the sea. I loved it when you talked about the sea. Even the liberals did. Tell the truth. You can get to people's hearts if you tell the truth. You can get to your own heart if you tell the truth. I've been a politician all my life and I can't do that. I wish I could, but I can't, and you can. Tell the truth, and after it's over, after we win, I won't throw you away like Mushrom. You'll have a shot at the presidency itself. Martin Van Buren was secretary of state. Jefferson was secretary of state."

Dewey smiled. The smile said, Come with me, and victory is ours. "Well? Are you in? Moofoomooach? Desi? Popeel?" He laughed nervously, looked down, and raised his head, smiling his most charming smile. "Okay? Let's do it! How 'bout it, guys? Look, except for vice president, which I've already thrown to Draff, there isn't any higher post. Isn't it enough? You're not Democrats, are you? Finney? Finney?"

THE NIH PHARMACOLOGISTS said it was all a matter of metabolism. Freddy should burn through the residual Proclorox in from twenty-four to forty-eight hours; Fredericka, in the same time, for although she had less muscle mass and weighed less, she was younger. Then again, some subjects had Proclorox "auras" that lasted for weeks or months. The best way to flush the drug would be to walk the subjects all day long and perhaps get them out on the water, where they could breathe massive volumes of fresh air.

Thus it was that before sunrise the next morning, the Prince and Princess of Wales were walked like zombies through San Francisco with a Secret Service agent apiece, another ahead and one more behind. This strange party of six walked from Russian Hill down to the Embarcadero, to the China Basin, through the Mission District, to the summits of Twin Peaks and Mt Davidson, through Stern Grove to Lake Merced, the Zoo, and the Pacific, along the coast all the way to the Golden Gate, and back through the Presidio to Earthquake Ranch. They had two lunches, the first at a goat-meat restaurant in the Mission District, and the second at a stand on the beach, where the party consumed twenty-four skewers of shrimp and twelve bottles of beer. A little later, while Fredericka and a female agent went into the heather to pee, Freddy and the others stood on a cliff and made their contributions to what they thought was the ocean but was actually an adult education class studying the tide pools a hundred feet below.

Not one word did Dr and Dr Moofoomooach speak on this excursion, as the Secret Service reported hourly on its secret frequencies. The agents did notice however that their charges seemed to be awakening. Upon this Senator Knott pinned his hopes as Mushrom winged his way first-class to Borneo, "Hail to the Chief" echoing inescapably within his head.

After a hot shower and a ginseng soft drink, Freddy and Fredericka rode with Finney to the Marina. So as to be inconspicuous, all were clad in yachting clothes. Soon they were out on the bay, their sleek racer ploughing through afternoon sunlight on a steady wind. The sky was the deep San Francisco blue that draws people from across the world, and, as intended, the air forced itself cleanly into the lungs of all on board.

"Would you like another ginseng?" Finney asked Freddy, forgetting that Freddy had not spoken since he had returned to the Knott camp.

Freddy sighed and leaned back, scanning the water. Then he said his first words in almost two weeks. "We milked the cows."

Finney rose from his seat and almost fell overboard.

"Bossy and Bella."

"My cow was Bella," said Fredericka. "I liked her. She gave milk."

"My cow was Bossy," Freddy said. "I liked *him*. *He* gave milk."

"Do you know me?" Finney asked them excitedly. "Do you know where you are?"

"We lived in the cottage," Freddy answered. "We milked the cows."

"They're coming back," Finney said over his cell phone. "They're awakening. Tell Senator Knott." He flipped the phone shut. "Thank God," he said. "Just in time. We'll get them a good dinner—something that sizzles, and strong hot tea." Then he sat back and exhaled in relief.

Freddy trailed his hands in the foam as the water lapped the hull, the wind blew, and he began to awaken. "Milk," he said. And, then, "Not milk." His mind, which had been floating like a blimp, brushed the ground now and then with mooring lines as thin as catfish whiskers. In his days of oblivion he had solved some knotty problems and picked off a riddle or two, and as the world clarified he struggled to bring back with him through the glowing curtain at least some of what he had discovered. Fredericka was following closely behind. Her oblivion had floated her purely on love. Neither riddles nor questions had haunted her, so she came back not wiser but, rather, stronger and lovelier.

But it was hard for Freddy. Never had he been so mentally flaccid. The great store of memories and knowledge within him, intended since his birth and early childhood to personify nothing less than England itself, bubbled disconnectedly like magma that cannot find a vent. He wanted to bring back this stuff of dreams, but it was a battle. And in the battle his allies were dressed in a most distinctive fashion. He saw them in plaids and bearskins, with enamels and royal crests, all the signs and symbols—in his royal wardrobes by the hundreds and thousands—that were earned with the blood of real and courageous men, and that anchored his soul (no matter what anyone thought) in the long history of his islands: too long to know or even fathom, but blessed with a continuity that made it accessible if only the right sign would present itself to pull him from his confusion. He was in danger, as they said at Sandhurst, of failing to pivot upon the point.

In losing the catch of his memory, all would be lost, so he prayed from the midst of his confusion that he would know the things that were calling out to him, and that he would receive a sign.

As the boat cut through frigid blue water, the sign was delivered as if in direct answer to his prayer. As fast as the yacht beat the wind on a north-ward track, or perhaps faster, a ship passed them going south, and when the ship's stern slipped by and skated off to port as it turned—in the most graceful manoeuvre a ship can make—the Union Jack appeared within the ensign of the United Kingdom, furling and unfurling in the strong breeze, blood-red, as blue as the sea off Skye, and whiter than cloud.

Freddy winced under the pressure of many thousands of associations. The red was the colour of poppies that every November his father and mother wore, and the significance of which he had understood even as a very young child. Over hundreds of years, hundreds of thousands of ships had floated under that ensign, harvesting the colours of the world into the story of a magnificent island. On the stern of the passing vessel was its name, *Prince of Mists,* and its port, Glasgow. Suddenly, Freddy was home.

"Fredericka," he said.

"Yes, Freddy?"

"It's all coming clear now."

"Is it?"

"Yes, quite. I saw it in the nether world where we were sent. Mr Neil is an anagram, as is the live ash circle."

"What's an anagram?"

"Fredericka, we found the object of the quest, in the fire, where Lucia died. We have endured what the ancient kings endured, and we have been given, by the grace of God, the most precious gift, as were they. You become a king not by making yourself great, but by recognising the greatness of others and humbly receiving your appointment. Now I know this, like the kings before me, and, as they prevailed, so might I."

Finney had been listening, and was bunched up in a strange position, trying to make sense of it.

"These ramparts," Freddy said to Fredericka, indicating the immense castle that was San Francisco, with its pale towers, hills, and keeps, "in their otherworldly colours, are what Mr Neil called the New Caernarvon—in a land of mists, forgetfulness, and tremblings of the earth. It's a repetition of something that happened a long time ago, in simpler times, to Birchod the Fat. Because I see it clearly now, I know what is to happen. It has occurred before, and will, in forms varying and unfolding, occur again. Past and present are now running together. Can you feel it?"

"Uh-oh," said Finney, having heard all of this.

"You are the equerry of Knott. Are you not?"

"Yes," said Finney. "I am the equerry of Knott."

"He is to battle Self, is that not so?"

Finney nodded.

"He wants me to join the battle, does he not?"

"Yes," said Finney, "he wants you to do some speech work and advise on foreign and military affairs. I wouldn't call it. . . ."

"He wants me to battle for the truth, because he cannot lift his sword for the truth, having kept it too long in the blackness of untruth. That is why he sent you to bring us from the land of forgetfulness."

"That might be one way of putting it," Finney said, remembering that he had, in fact, broken these two out of a mental institution, and that they called themselves Moofoomooach.

"I'll tell you something, Finney," Freddy said, cupping his hands in the bay and drinking salt water as if from a Viking chalice. "You are part of this."

"I know I'm part of this."

"Not the way you think. Hundreds of years ago, your part began when your forbears crossed the great ocean. You are a larva-in-waiting."

"I am?"

"Yes, and you will be rewarded. For rescuing us from the land of forgetfulness, you will be made a knight. But more is to be done, and the way is laid out," Freddy said, smiling like a lunatic. At that moment, *Prince of Mists,* out of Glasgow, gave a blast of its whistle, which swept over the harbour like an invisible tsunami and echoed off the hills and bridges. It thundered in their chests and rattled San Francisco's million windows. Freddy stood to salute as the plume rose from the ship's funnel. His salute was perfectly rendered and distinctly English.

Finney flipped open his phone and pressed a few buttons. "We're coming in. He's awake. She's awake. They can talk."

As the swift little yacht came about and beat on the wind toward a setting sun that boiled as yellow and orange as an egg in a cup, Freddy, and only Freddy, heard the Skye Boat Song repeating again and again, beautifully, delicately, and timed exactly to the waves.

DEWEY'S IMAGE CONSULTANTS had done his hair up in a kind of pompadour, held in place while it set by white netting that made him look like a very homely Amish woman. So as not to disturb the hair, he sat stiffly in an armchair at the centre of his capacious living room. The chances were nil anyway that he would take a seat on the couch, where he might have to sit next to someone who wasn't running for president. A lifetime of politics had taught him to seize any throne-like seat, to move toward the cameras, to get out of the limousine first, to stand on the highest step, and to find the best ray of light in a room, placing his head in it even if he had to walk like Toulouse-Lautrec.

And, of course, Freddy knew what underlings are supposed to do. As he approached he smiled more than Dewey smiled—showing gratitude for having been allowed into Dewey's presence—bent almost as in a bow, and said his own name, to honour the fact that though everyone knew Dewey, Dewey wasn't supposed to recognise anyone but other politicians, movie stars, famous journalists, and people who had given him large amounts of money. "Moofoomooach," Freddy said.

Because Dewey wanted something from Freddy, he responded with contrived modesty. "Knott."

"But I am," said Freddy.

"You are what?"

"Moofoomooach."

"I know," Dewey told him. "You're Moofoomooach, and I'm Knott."

"That's correct."

"I know," said Dewey, who had contended with this sort of exchange all his life and never understood what was happening. "Shall I call you Dr Moofoomooach, or just Moofoomooach? Hello, Popeel."

"Hello, Dewey," Fredericka said, forgetting that it was not her place to be familiar. Dewey's eyebrows arched, but that was all.

"Just call me Moofoomooach," said Freddy, as if launching into a George M. Cohan song.

A steward brought refreshments that Freddy and Fredericka began to devour. The food in California mental institutions can leave much to be desired, and they would eat ravenously for a week. Dewey watched for a while, and then he said, "Moofoomooach, today we're sixty points behind Self. Self has eighty, and we have twenty. That's not so bad. I mean, it could be worse. Two weeks ago, it was worse. But nobody pays attention any more. Self was on the front pages of all the papers this morning, dedicating a feminist horseshoe pitch. I was on page nine, picking fried clams out of my teeth in the blackness of my limousine. They used infrared. You know what the headline was? 'Knott Free-falls in Fetal Position as Election Guillotine Sucks-in His Head: Says a Fried Clam Would Make a Better President Than He Would.' That's what I said. I said, 'A fried clam would make a better president than he would.' I meant Self, but look what they did. We've got no more donors, no more money, no more press. The convention starts tomorrow. My speech is on Thursday and I don't have one. Mushrom wrote all kinds of crap about mushrooms, redwoods, and Superman, and then he took a powder. Draff figures it's all over, so he's blackmailing me to get my former colleagues in the Senate to approve seven billion dollars for rest stops on interstates in North Dakota. Rumours are circulating that I'm a dope addict and Dot is having an affair with Liberace, never mind that he's dead. So, you know, we're going to lose, we're going down the drain, we can't pay you, you'll be mocked . . . but I ask you to write me another speech. The first one did wonders. It put us way ahead. They said I was Lincolnesque, Churchillian, that a new corner had been turned in this country's history. Then you disappeared. Where the hell were you?"

"We were in a mental institution," said Fredericka, perkily.

"What were you doing there?"

"We took drugs," Freddy said matter-of-factly, "we milked cows, and we ate porridge."

"I hear you," said Dewey, which is what he said when Hell's Angels accosted him about helmet laws, "and I'd like to offer you a deal." He looked around. Only he, Finney, and the royals were about. "Now, you know, politicians promise a lot of things, and then you never hear from them. That's how you get people to do things for you: you make 'em think they're going to get something, they put out, and then you walk away. That's how you can give a thousand people one of ten pieces of the same pie. The motto of a good politician is, *Use the pie.* So, if I said to you, or hinted, that if I become president I would appoint you to this or that position, unless you had something on me it would mean nothing. But if I gave you a signed and dated letter, you could count on it.

"Why? Not because it's a pledge. It would be unenforceable as a contract, because there's no legal consideration, since you're not allowed to do something in exchange for an appointment. It's certain because it's illegal. Giving you a written promise is indictable and impeachable. So, if you have the letter, you have the position."

"What position?" Freddy asked.

"Secretary of state."

"That's more like it," said Freddy, "isn't it, Popeel?"

"Finally," Fredericka said, "a leg-up."

"Dewey," Freddy asked, understanding with royal perspicacity that he had the whip hand, "there's one other thing I'd like."

"We haven't got any money," Dewey said. "We're fifty million dollars in the hole."

"I don't want money. I just want complete control of the substance of your campaign."

"What substance?" Finney asked.

"Shut up, Finney. Moofoomooach?"

"I want the last word on policy, rhetoric, strategy, the convention, everything."

Finney was agitated, but Dewey cut him off. "Why not?" he asked. "What have we got to lose?"

.   .   .

To PLAN THE NEW APPROACH, Freddy met that evening with Dewey's inner circle—Dewey; Dot; Finney; Randolph Dacheekan, a prime strategist and money man; two perfect campaign donors, Thaddeus Pappy and Bobby Pinn, who were fabulously wealthy and totally mute; the chief of political advertising, Slogan Beery, who was in the doghouse for having spent several million dollars on a television spot the theme of which was "Dewey Knott is like a friendly scrubbing bubble that gets your porcelain whiter than white"; and Senator Hare of Massachusetts, whose tremendous, blue-grey, cotton-candy-like, African-termite-hill-sized coiffure seemed to grow progressively larger as he aged. At eighty-two, his body was like the stick on a corn dog, and his face peeked out from within the quiffs and curls of his wavy locks like a starving ferret peering from a haystack.

These eight men and Dot gathered in Dewey's panelled library, which, though it seemed to be floating several thousand feet above a maelstrom of seals, fog, and blue water, was appointed like a men's club in the Strand. The rugs were ancient orientals, sharp blues and reds; the woodwork had been removed from a famous English estate; the furniture was noble; and the fire was hot. The table at which they sat was the kind of table, of a vermillion and chestnut colour, that Freddy had not seen since he had last set foot in St James's Palace. A tall-case clock, made in the late eighteenth century by Marmaduke Storr of London, ticked hypnotically and reassuringly in the background.

Dewey opened the meeting. "Moofoomooach here—you all know Moofoomooach—is gonna run the campaign."

"What happened to Plankton Dick?" Dacheekan asked, referring to the former campaign director.

"Isn't that the whale that someone chased in the Longfellow poem about Hawaii?" Senator Hare asked. Just as in the Senate, no one paid any attention to him.

"I fired him."

"What about that tall moose-like fellow you keep around?" Dacheekan inquired.

"Mushrom? He's in Borneo."

"You sent Campbell to Borneo?" Dot asked.

"Yes, Dot, to a place where they do a lot of barbecuing. It's a revolution, Dot. Mushrom's history, Moofoomooach's in." He turned to the others. "Gonna run the campaign. Gonna win. Gonna make history. Gonna get to the White House. Moofoomooach?"

"Dewey?"

"Tell 'em."

"First," said Freddy, "we'll chuck all the polling, focus groups, carnival hats, computers, offices, limousines, and supernumeraries of the entourage. We're going to halve the personnel and pull back eighty percent of the advertising. We will achieve these economies publicly. We'll cut the budget by sixty percent or more, and tell the country that you can run a campaign, and a good one, on virtually nothing, that you don't really need money, that you'd run the government with the same common sense and efficiency, and that you're going fly-fishing in New Hampshire for two weeks after Labor Day."

Dacheekan was so horrified he couldn't speak. Finney smiled. Dot was lost. "We'll fall off the screen for two weeks," Dewey said, "and then what?"

"Even if we did," Freddy told them, "it would give Dewey's every utterance the gravity of a cannonball. But not to worry. The reporters will be there by the thousand. Every night you'll be on the news, fly-fishing and making some pronouncement upon politics and foreign relations. You'll go from being a greedy jerk—that is, in people's minds—to being an oracle. The reporters will love you for bringing them to the White Mountains on days when New York and Washington become giant woks, and their gratitude will effloresce in their dispatches. The people will see that you're above the job, and, when they do, they'll give it to you."

"I can see that," said Dewey. "We'd save millions a week."

"Fine," said Hare, "but what about strategy? What are you going to talk about?"

Dewey looked at Freddy.

Freddy said, "Whatever comes up. You don't have to programme it in advance."

"You don't?" asked Dot.

"No. That would be manipulative."

"Isn't that what we're supposed to be doing?" Dacheekan asked. "Manipulating?"

"Certainly not," said Freddy. "We mustn't try to manipulate anyone, ever. You are bound to respect your subjects. Just tell them the truth at all times, think hard on the nation's problems, and remember your oath."

"What oath?" Dewey asked.

"The one you'll take when sworn in."

"What about issues?" Dot asked. "What about soccer moms?"

"What about them?" Freddy wanted to know.

"What should he say? What would you have him say?"

"Soccer moms," Freddy said, "spend all day driving around in shapeless vehicles that look like Flash Gordon's bread truck, and their children watch television in the back and ape the superficial characters therein. This is the cause of deep unhappiness, because what they want is so different from what they have, even if they don't realise that this is so. They don't want their children to dress like circus clowns, speak like zombie chipmunks, and behave like programmed machines. They want sons and daughters they can talk to; they want a struggle that they can win but that they are not assured of winning; they want to know physical exhaustion; they want to be sunburned; they want to smell eucalyptus; they want to weep; they want to dance naked for their husbands; they want to feel the wind, see the stars, swim in a river, slam the back door, and laugh uncontrollably with their children. That's what they want. They don't want the crap they have, the crap Self promises, or the crap you would promise if you could figure out what to promise. They want to be free, to have dignity, to know honour and sacrifice. What else does anyone want?"

Dot was stunned into silence, because this was what she wanted, too, and had always wanted. Freddy looked at her, understanding that at heart she was a pioneer woman who had been born in the wrong century. By nature she was strong and beautiful, or at least she had been when she was young, and needed neither Washington, nor power, nor prestige, but mountains, rivers, and views so immense that they could fit only in her native West. So Freddy said, "When was the last time you crawled up a mudbank, crashed through the reeds, and tasted the iron in your own blood? When was the last time your heart beat like crazy and you were soaked in sweat? When was the last time you loved, and were loved, so deeply that it possessed your soul? When was the last time you felt the presence of God so strongly you floated upon the rising tide like Moses in his cradle?"

"Whoa!" said Hare. "Young man, are you aware of what happened to William Jennings Bryan? How golden and emotional he was? How many times he ran? How many times he lost?"

"I am aware," Freddy said.

"The American people," Dacheekan said, "are interested only in little things, not big things. They want to be fat. They want to be happy. That's all they care about, all they know. That's the reality."

"I have been with the people of this country from the Hudson to the Pacific," Freddy said, "and I know that you're wrong. It's people like you, who are no better than your contemptuous description of them, who crank the machinery that dulls their lives, who cater to the worst among them. They are a spiritual people. They want love and greatness. I know. I've seen it. I've lived among them as you have not. I was taught to listen to the deeper heart, and from one end of this country to the other, I have."

"That's an illusion, boy," said Senator Hare, bitterly, "that I once shared."

"Whether or not it is, Moofoomooach," said Finney, who by virtue of his position and beliefs was the trustworthy arbiter, "there are political issues that we must contend with, which is hardly a dishonour for us."

"What issues?" asked Freddy, who always preferred the forest to the trees.

"HMOs, for example, which as of today's polling are the top issue, blowing everything else out of the water."

"They are?" asked Freddy, who thought Finney was talking about something else entirely.

"By seventy to thirty over the next strongest category," Finney said, professionally. "You may not care about HMOs, I may not care about HMOs, but the people care about HMOs, and that's a fact. What would you say about them?"

"They have rights just like anyone else," said Freddy.

"You mean cheating people?" Dewey asked. Dewey was mad at his HMO because it had advised him by letter that he was pregnant.

Freddy cocked his head. "Cheating people?"

"Denying them benefits," Finney said.

"I don't think that's the essence of it, do you?" Freddy asked.

"Then what is the essence?" Dacheekan demanded.

"Must we be explicit?"

"Yes."

"I abstain," Freddy said, delicately.

"I don't know what the hell you're talking about," Dewey challenged. "Do you?"

"Yes, Dewey," said Freddy, "I always do."

"Moofoomooach," Dewey said, with some irritation, "HMOs are a burning issue. They can make or break this campaign."

"They shouldn't be a burning issue," Freddy answered. "We've had HMOs since the time of the cavemen."

"Since the time of the cavemen?" asked an astonished Dacheekan, a proud Californian. "What are you talking about? The first HMO was Kaiser Permanente, in World War Two."

"No," said Freddy, with a huge dollop of condescension. "That was World War One, it was Kaiser *Wilhelm,* who happens to be a relative of mine, who was not an HMO, and, believe me, the first HMO much predated World War Two." He was now less frustrated than entertained.

"I beg to differ!" said Dacheekan.

"Take it easy, Randolph," Dewey urged.

"No! The first HMO was Kaiser Permanente, in the California ship-yards, in the Second World War."

"That would be news to Oscar Wilde," Freddy declared, "not to mention Leonardo da Vinci." Everyone looked at him uncomprehendingly.

"Who's Oscar Wilde?" Dewey asked.

"Even he didn't really know," Freddy stated.

Dewey was lost. "All right," he said. "The cavemen had HMOs."

"Of course they did. Even animals—monkeys, lemurs, kangaroos. . . ."

"Fine," said Dewey, "kangaroos have HMOs."

"Yes, Dewey, they do. I've *seen* them."

Dewey looked at Freddy with the air of someone who is being mocked. "Are the doctors kangaroos?"

"The doctors," Freddy repeated. "The doctors. What doctors?"

"HMOs have doctors, Moofoomooach, don't they?"

"Yes, of course they do."

"Well, are they kangaroos?"

"Dewey," Freddy instructed patiently, "kangaroos can't be doctors, they're animals."

"But you said they were."

"I did not, Dewey, you did. You brought it up."

"Drop it," said Finney. "Just drop it. Forget the kangaroos. It's not doing us any good."

There was a long silence in which foghorns were bleating up and down the bay like cows lost in a Cornish miasma. Dacheekan stood up to deliver an ultimatum.

"I know what you're going to say, Randolph."

"Do you, Dewey?"

"I think so."

"What?"

"You're going to say that if I don't throw Moofoomooach overboard, you're leaving with your money and everything else."

"That's what I'm going to say. Consider it said."

"Good-bye, Randolph."

"Dewey!" Dot shouted.

"Shut up, Dot. I don't care what you do, Randolph, Moofoomooach is going to run this campaign. I'm going to introduce him to the press tomorrow."

"You can't do this to the party, Dewey."

"I'm the nominee, Randolph, not you. I've got the delegates, and I've got the votes."

"But you don't have the money, Dewey, not any more."

"I may not have the money, but I've got God, salt water, and Moofoomooach."

"Yeah," said Dacheekan, "and kangaroos."

THE NEXT DAY, Freddy was completely free of Proclorox, and in a symphonic mood. The press conference at which Moofoomooach was to be introduced was in the convention hall of the Archipelago Hotel, a Hong Kong–based chain of which, via complicated and secretive trusts, Freddy was the majority owner. Six thousand reporters were assembled for the announcement. A candidate does not change campaign managers just before the convention unless he is shipping water. On the one hand, this was what the reporters were hoping for, but, on the other, rumour had it that Dewey had found Moofoomooach, and that was a story in itself, especially as the press had collectively decided that the Moofoomooach story was a ruse, and dropped it. After all, no one had actually seen Moofoomooach, and even if someone had, he hadn't been on television, and therefore he was not real. But if he did exist, it would trump even the overwrought portrayal of the Republican nominee gasping for air.

Everyone believed that Moofoomooach was not his true name. No one had a name like that. The prize would be to discover who was behind the pseudonym. Any one of a dozen top Washington political operatives—not one of whom could have written Dewey's "Moofoomooach Speech" if his life had depended on it, and not one of whom could draw upon history or statecraft any more than he could shove his fund-raiser-bloated body into a chocolate mousse cup—was suspected. They all played it up, convincing the press that the genius behind Dewey's brief shining moment had been Phops Brooks (even though he was a Democrat), Louise Trembler, Denis Penis (who for some reason pronounced his name, even if no one else did, in the—sort of—French way, as *Daynee Paynee*), Rickey Champagne, Phil Buckits Whitmony, and others. As the story had built upon itself, excitement had risen, and even before the principals entered a hall buzzing with the murmur of six thousand competitive talkers, strobes popped like a lightning storm that covers ten states. In the gusts of free-floating anticipation, men tightened their belts and women ran their hands through their hair.

When the nominee's entourage arrived, the news spread so fast that it smacked the back wall of the auditorium like a bull whip. The frenzy was sadly reminiscent of the aftermath of an assassination. Once in the hotel, Dewey walked with blistering speed as Freddy shouted out instructions to bellboys and waiters: "Someone dust the chandelier; change the flowers in the centre-court fountain; take that vulgar sign down from the front of the Spreckles Ballroom." Perhaps because of his natural authority and his new-found energy, the people to whom he directed these orders obeyed them, and the people to whom he offered advice took it. In response to Freddy's military-style uniform inspection of a room-service waiter, who actually saluted when called to attention, Dewey said, "Moofoomooach, what the hell do you care what the waiters wear, or how the hotel is run?"

"Perfection is the aim of dentistry, and should be yours if you want to win. You must let everything in the nation flow through you, so you can know it. You must see everything, and forget nothing. The country is a whole, with no part irrelevant. This morning, on the terrace, I spent an hour and a half talking to a single geranium."

"You did?" Dewey asked as they sped along. "How come?"

"It spoke to me, and I answered it."

"You mean you liked it."

"I liked it, but it also spoke to me."

"What did it say?" asked Dewey. "What could it say?"

"Things more wondrous than are dreamt of in your philosophy, Dewey. It told me about the lifeblood of America, and it told me how to run this campaign."

"A geranium?"

"Geraniums are sagacious and beautiful."

"Okay, Moofoomooach. You know that I'm in. You may be trying to test me, I don't know, but I'm in. I made my decision, and I'm sticking to it." They came to the hall, and paused. "All right," Dewey said as applause rose deafeningly, "let's meet the press."

The noise grew so overwhelming that walking against it was hard. Moving alongside Dewey with unconcerned and inexplicable grace was Moofoomooach. Just by looking, the journalists could tell that this was he, a man as mysterious and unknown to them, they thought, as a bog-sleeping Neanderthal in a glass case in the lobby of the National Geographic Society, or, as Freddy called it, "The Putatively Socially Acceptable Excuse to Look at Corpses from the Grave Society, formerly The Putatively Socially Acceptable Excuse to Look at African Women's Bare Breasts Society."

The curiosity of the members of the press was so powerful and acute that they felt it pushing and pulling their bodies. They grunted, groaned, and sighed. "Who is he? Who is he? It's Moofoomooach! He's real. He's here. God! Look! He seems so at ease! He's taller than Knott! He's a natural! What a story! Moofoomooach! Charisma! Charisma! Moofoomooach! Cover of *Time*! This is it! Gotta get this story! What's he gonna say! Moofoomooach! Moofoomooach! Moofoomooach!" It sounded like a New Hampshire pond three weeks before the first frost, when the frogs are overwhelmed by hysteria.

Surrounded by Dewey aides and half hidden by a velvet curtain, Fredericka was worried. This was the first time Freddy had been on a stage in almost two years, the first time he had been before the press, the first time he had been on a "panel" of sorts. She remembered how during an interview with an American television network its correspondent had hesitated in mid-sentence, saying, "I'll uh . . ." causing Freddy to break in and shout vigorously, "is the only God! And Muhammad is his messenger!" The correspondent had had no idea that "I'll uh . . ." sounded like *Allah,* so he said it again, very taken aback, and Freddy screamed, "is the only God! And Muhammad is his messenger!" This played well in certain parts of the world—though not all. She remembered when he had become hopelessly enmeshed in a dispute with Bertrand Russell over the question of whether or not animals have souls. Lord Russell spoke against the proposition. Freddy just that day had suffered the death of Rosebery, his pet tortoise of seventeen years. As a child, Fredericka had witnessed the confrontation on television—the young prince, not yet twenty, raging at the nonagenarian philosopher until the BBC cut him off after he said, somewhat tendentiously, "Fuck you, I loved my tortoise."

But Freddy had learnt a lot, and his confidence did seem to have been justified. He was now the central focus of the vast country in which, a few days before, he had been unknown, incarcerated, and a mental patient. Obviously, he knew what he was doing even if no one else did. She relaxed.

Up stood Elsie Bovine (which she pronounced *Boveen*), a woman of heroic proportions, whose nickname was "The Thunderbird," and whose overwhelming lacquered blond hair looked like a very large piece of furniture in the lobby of a Portuguese hotel. The wife of a billionaire who, in Dewey's parlance, had "pulled Dewey's nuts out of the fire" countless times, she herself had slept with almost every man on the stage except Freddy and Dewey. Having presided at a hundred party functions, she should not have been nervous, but never had she seen anything like this. The stroboscopic attack upon her senses, the hubbub in the hall, and the fact that the mysterious Moofoomooach was just a few feet to her left gave her a stage fright that made her forget the few trite lines that had been supplied to her by one of her husband's many Mushroms.

Hardly able to breathe, she looked at her watch. She thought she was going to faint, for never before had she addressed the whole world. But she couldn't remember what to say. She glanced at her watch once more. Five minutes over, and she hadn't said a thing. She sighed. The way everyone was looking at her, she knew she had to say something, anything. So she looked at her watch yet again, and said, "I'm running behind."

The instant she said it, Fredericka winced. She knew that, having a dozen times on a dozen stages done what he was almost certainly about to do, Freddy would not quit now. No one would think, as Freddy thought, that Elsie Bovine had referred to herself by a parodied Amerindian name. The only person in the world who would have heard it that way was Freddy. "Oh no," Fredericka said, but she could do nothing, for at the instant the woman had said, "I'm running behind," Fredericka had seen an idiotic smile leap to Freddy's lips and disappear. It had to vanish for the next phase, which followed immediately. His expression became strong and grave. He thrust himself from his seat and stood to his full height, raising his left arm and hand as if taking an oath. After silence ensued, Freddy filled the hall in a deep, noble, aboriginal accent he had heard in a hundred movies. "Ugh!" he said, "I am . . . *White Eagle!*" He sat down so hard it almost broke the chair.

At first, no one moved. Then the neurons of the Fourth Estate made their connections, and when it became clear to everyone at the same time what Dewey had done, that this was a year's worth of October surprises, that Self would never be able to get anywhere close, that Dewey had let it ride almost on purpose so he could make a spectacular comeback, that, in the idiom of the press, "This was it" . . . when all this came clear, pandemonium exploded as thousands of journalists began to file stories on cell phones and laptops, and a few thousand others rushed the doors.

And then, spontaneously, everyone stopped again. They stood on their chairs, turned to Freddy, and began to applaud ferociously. It sounded like the ocean upon the rocks of Land's End during a gale. Tears were running down their faces, some wept convulsively, and all were overjoyed. By God, Dewey had done it. The genius behind him was a Native American. Of course Moofoomooach was a name, a name of the great and oppressed tribes of the prairie, the land of Dewey's birth. He had reached back to his origins as if in a magic rite, and found a brilliant Native American to help him repair the broken heart of the country. White Eagle Moofoomooach, or Moofoomooach White Eagle (who knew?), was probably a chief. And he was clearly a genius. He would in one fell swoop transform the Republican Party, restore it to its Lincolnesque origins, rewrite American history, harmonise the disparate forces that had torn the continent in half since the beginning, and save America's soul.

Everyone onstage except Fredericka, Finney, and Dewey joined in the thunderous, unceasing applause. Freddy said to Fredericka, "They got it right off. That's because we're in America. In England, they never get it."

THE NEXT STEP, a day later, was for Dewey to tell Freddy what to put in the acceptance speech. This was a formality. Even Mushrom made the speeches up entirely on his own, but Dewey had to save face. He and Freddy sat on cane chairs in the study at Earthquake Ranch, sherries in hand, leaning forward in conversation.

"I prefer this kind of hard chair when doing something important, don't you?" Dewey asked. "Big overstuffed furniture makes me even more indecisive than I am, I think. People have said that. Do you agree?"

"Yes," said Freddy, "and it's bad for the back."

"So, look," Dewey told him, almost in a whisper, "I'm supposed to tell you what to put in my acceptance speech."

"Yes," said Freddy.

"But, God! I don't know! If I knew what to put in the speech, I wouldn't have a speechwriter, would I? You do it. Just make it . . . you know."

"What?"

"Idoh know."

"Okay."

"You know, the word that sounds like that woman who has a big behind, the singer."

"I'll do my best."

"I don't have time for policy. I don't have time for language. All I do is raise money. Look." Dewey took out of his pocket a piece of paper, unfolded it, and passed it to Freddy. "Those are my fund-raisers just today. I have to go to every one of these places and get money out of nervous people who want to have their picture taken with me in case I become president. Read it."

Freddy read out loud: "'Senator Knott's fund-raisers for today will set up at the following locations: The Legends at Fox Innards; The Whammo Estate at Snake Creek; The Nuns at Aztec Pointe; Chlamydia; The Residences of Potemkin Village; Mer du Cheval; and Eau de Toilette.'"

"Remember when they used to have towns?" Dewey asked. "And at every one of these goddamned things they serve white wine and cheese. Do you know what it's like to stand next to a gorgeous woman with a mouth full of aged Camembert? It's a nightmare. It's worse than having sideburns. How'm I supposed to find time to study economics, strategy, and diplomacy?"

"You don't need much time to study diplomacy," Freddy volunteered. "I learnt it in half an hour, and I'm an expert, really I am."

"You must be. I mean, for an Indian to know all that foreign stuff, that's really compulsive."

"Compelling."

"Whatever."

"Diplomacy is very simple, Dewey. It consists of a body of key phrases with which you can speak portentously and say nothing. I've used them for many years now. You have to if you want to survive among the titled heads of Europe."

"The what?" Dewey asked. "I thought you were an Apache."

"My mother is an Apache."

"We ought to have her for the speech, sitting next to Dot."

"Let's talk about the phrases. What might you say if asked a question about, for example, the budget?"

"I don't know anything about the budget. Remember, Moofoomooach, I don't know anything about anything that I'm supposed to know something about."

"Right. You would say, then, 'The woodpecker of insolvency becomes the dolphin of inexactitude.'"

"I would say that?"

"Yes. What if they ask you about your sexual practices?"

"It's none of their business."

"Yes, but that's not diplomatic. Say, rather, 'The chicken of sexual inefficiency becomes the moose of dismay.'"

"Yeah," said Dewey, "I think that's true."

"There's a phrase for anything: 'The mole of senility becomes the egg of manual dexterity.'"

"I could use that."

Freddy then poured out a dozen diplomatic standards that he had used in England with great effect upon diplomats, journalists, and hysterical pastry chefs: "The bone of precision becomes the duck of anxiety. The worm of sincerity is raped by the snail of deceit. The baboon of ingratitude is rebuffed by the ostrich of self-immolation."

"The baboon . . ." said Dewey. "The baboon of what?"

"Ingratitude. The baboon of ingratitude."

"Oh."

"The fish of insouciance is eaten by the insect of apathy. The outrigger of consideration is smashed by the octopus of petulance. The hippopotamus of generosity dances with the tortoise of disbelief. And the wildebeest of neglect is approached by the goose of democracy."

"But, Moofoomooach," Dewey pleaded, "Dewey Knott can't do that."

"Why not?" Freddy asked. "I know a thousand of them."

"I just can't do it."

"Try."

"Do I have to?"

"You're the one who wanted to learn diplomacy. Let's say one of those pinheads asks you a trap question, on national television, and you don't have the slightest idea what he's talking about."

"I never do."

"All right. Be diplomatic. What would a *diplomat* say?"

Dewey thought, and after some time he groaned and raised his right hand in the air, index finger pointing at an angle toward the ceiling. "I've got one. I've got one."

"Go."

"The cheeseburger of my car runs away in canoes full of nuts!"

"Excellent," said Freddy. "That throws them off balance, makes them look insane. Give me another."

"The chickens of Pearl Harbor scream at Ethel Merman's socks?"

"You've got it!" said Freddy. "Now go with it."

And in the following days, Dewey did. Not knowing what he meant, the press reflexively assumed that he was brilliant. More brilliant even than Self. More brilliant, it was said, than even Albert Einstein. Dewey was on a roll. Freddy was on a roll. It was only a matter of time.

FOR TWO DAYS a storm had beaten against the walls of Balmoral, turning them olive with an almost imperceptible magenta sheen. Storm-filled air flowed down the mountainsides, moving ragged clouds before it; the streams overflowed and their excessive rocking and washing left lines of white froth on the banks; and the sides of trees were lashed black with rain.

On a dark and haystack-levelling afternoon, the queen and Prince Paul had taken refuge by the fire. Their tall windows were so well caulked that the fire brigade could have turned hoses upon them and not a drop would have come through. The queen sat with her back to one of these windows, the fire to her left, Paul in front of her on a chair. Filling the rest of the couch to her right were books and papers. Especially when she could not set foot outside, she loved to read all day. Freddy had inherited from her the maddening concentration he readily directed to works on philology, or naval operations in narrow seas.

Paul tapped his foot and tried to remain absorbed in a polo magazine. They were all so bloody the same. Everyone in them wore polo shirts and helmets. Everyone rode a horse. Everyone had a mallet. The adverts were invariably for the same shops and cars. If you'd read one, you'd read them all. He took some more tea, glanced at the fire, and switched to the newspapers. As he opened *The Times* he said, "I love it when it's like this."

"Like what?"

"Sea state seven. Love it."

"Why?" asked the queen, looking up from (translated) intercepts of Chinese military traffic.

"Because it shows your limitations."

"*My* limitations?"

"Yes. You're treated like a . . . like a god."

"You know that I think it's horrible."

"That's what you say."

"I would trade any day. . . ."

"Yes, yes, I know, to be a country woman who raises dogs and plays the piano. I'd like to see you give all this up, I would."

The queen glanced heavenward. "So would I."

"Then why not give Freddy his chance?"

"It wouldn't change things much for us, and he's still young."

"Have you seen his bald spot of late?"

"Of course I haven't," the queen said wistfully. "How could I have? He's in Pah-kiss-tahn. I hope they have decent food."

"What would it matter?" Paul asked, turning the page. "He's as fat as an Obderoofie."

"He's as thin as a Teensilcat," said the queen, "and I do worry about him."

Paul looked over his reading glasses and beyond the paper. "In that our race was constructed," he told his wife, "to go into strange and inhospitable lands, I would imagine that a two-week holiday in Pah-kiss-tahn is within the limits of his endurance."

"Wasn't he supposed to be going somewhere else?" the queen asked, her brows knitted.

Paul took on the expression of an inmate of Bedlam as confusion and frustration racked his soul. "I have vague memories," he said, "dark memories, at the tip of my tongue, so to speak. But I don't know. He went to Pah-kiss-tahn, didn't he?"

"Pah-kiss-tahn," said the queen. "I, too, have vague memories. I can't summon them. I feel very much as I did when I wanted to remember the sweet I found in the playhouse as a child. I've never been able to recall it. Was it an Exeley Cream? No. A Bittrick's Toffee Melt? No. What was it?"

"Pah-kiss-tahn," said Paul, determinedly. "Pah-kiss-tahn."

"This damnable weather!" the queen said. "I command it to cease!"

"Good try," said Paul, as the rain beat savagely against the glass and even the royal fire hissed as stray droplets rode the air pressure past the baffle in the flue. "Would you like another biscuit?"

"Was it a Derbyshire Chocolate Cherry Cow?" The queen was distracted.

"You know what the Americans are up to now?" Paul asked, referring to a story he was in the midst of reading as he spoke. She saw the animation in his face.

"They're always up to something, aren't they?" she asked in return. "Must we ever go back? Dealing with them is so difficult. The criminals we sent to Australia, the lunatics to America. That's why they have to pretend that something was wrong with George the Third. Remember the crazy fat-woman in Washington whom they chose to have me to tea? She screamed and jumped up and down the whole time. I thought that if she lost her balance she would crush me."

"Yes, but where was I?"

"It was easy for you. You were hunting rogue ostrich. What is it about the Americans? It's as if they are we with a broken nose. They do what we do, but they do it so badly, as if history were not an instructress. Everything immediate, nothing in synchrony, nothing slow, nothing withheld. They are the *Pietà* dropped down a marble staircase and glued back together by a drunk."

"I don't know," said Paul. "They've saved our bacon three times in a century. That's not so gauche, is it?"

"I didn't say that they're not powerful. It's just that they lack every kind of refinement and common sense. And they think they invented the light bulb. Everyone knows it was Geoffrey Deakin."

"Do you know what they've done? Do you remember Dewey Knott?"

"Yes, he's the one who ate the dog biscuits that were in the silver bowl on the coffee table."

"Did he like them?"

"He hated them—I could see it in his face—but he dared not back down. He ate seventeen: liver, liver with chicken, calf's foot, honey glazed tripe. . . ."

"Didn't you stop him?"

"Why should I have? Besides, I was talking to his wife. What was her name? Spot?"

"Dot."

"Dot took one, chewed it a bit, wrinkled her makeup until it looked like a Venezuelan lakebed in a hundred-year drought, and secretly—she thought—deposited it underneath this very sofa. That's why Mitterand always looks there when he comes into the room."

"François?"

"No, the poodle. What about Dewey Knott?"

"He's running for president, you know."

"How pedestrian, to seek office."

"He's come back up miraculously on the eve of his convention, after being behind by sixty points. Now he's ten points ahead of Self."

"Excellent," said the queen. "Self is a psychotic. He pinched my behind. I do hope Dewey wins. Among other things, with Dewey, dinners would be far less complicated—liver, liver with chicken. . . ."

"Do you know how he did it? He brought into his campaign an Indian, 'White Eagle,' who writes all his speeches, dictates strategy, and is, I imagine, a kind of regent. According to the American press, White Eagle can do no wrong. Evidently he was a boyhood chum of Dewey's. They were blood brothers. Strange. White Eagle is said to be twenty-five years or so younger than Dewey. How could they have been childhood friends?"

"Perhaps he's Dewey's son," the queen said. "Things like that do happen." She was referring to Paul's illegitimate daughter, whom he begat with a waitress in a ski restaurant in the Polish Alps.

"I don't see why they should get so worked up over a wog," Paul said. "The whole world's going crazy over wogs."

"Yes," said the queen, mockingly. "Isn't it strange? You'd think there were more wogs in the world than anyone else."

"I grant you that, but, still," said Paul, "everything is wogs. Wogs, wogs, wogs. No one cares about people like us any more. It's not fair."

"Do you suppose, if Dewey becomes president, that we'll meet this wog? What's his name?"

"White Eagle."

"It would be terribly awkward. I'm sure that White Eagle is perfectly intelligent and perhaps civilised. It's just that I've never known a president joined at the hip with an Indian."

"What about Roosevelt and Hopkins?"

"Hopkins was an Indian? I thought he was Jewish. Oh, I so miss Freddy," the queen said. "I hope he comes back from Pah-kiss-tahn soon."

"I just hope," said Paul, returning to *The Times,* "that he's finally lost some weight. God knows, I would if all I had to eat was wog chow."

IT WAS A CLEAR NIGHT in San Francisco, but still the foghorns sounded like the souls of lost seals calling across the bays of the Northern Pacific. The lights of helicopters and boats, like insects engaged on busy errands, made soundless lines as smooth as the tracks of satellites moving among the stars. High above this, Dewey and Finney sat on the teak garden benches of Dewey's terrace, surrounded by potted evergreens. Each morning when Dewey looked out the sliding glass doors of his bedroom he would note that amid the millions of sharp evergreen needles were millions of shining droplets combed from the fog and ready to fall into the planters to water the soil.

"You know," said Dewey, bourbon in hand, "it's really no good going from a hospital, where you hold dying children, to a tortilla bakery with a fucking mariachi band. With all the pressure and attacks, and then things like that, and everyone hanging on your every goddamned word, how are you supposed to stay sane?"

Finney took a long time to answer. He was watching a light on the fan-tail of a freighter make an immensely long blink as it disappeared behind and then emerged to the east of Treasure Island. "What?" he asked.

"How are politicians supposed to be sane?" Dewey said, about to repeat his lament, when Finney interrupted.

"Yes, mariachi bands after hospices for children. The answer is that politicians were never supposed to be sane, and aren't."

"We aren't?"

"Do you think you are?"

Dewey had never been asked that. He screwed up his face and looked at the stars. From Finney's perspective, in the dim light, he looked like Harpo Marx. Dewey's eyes moved about like dogs that dart to and fro behind a fence. "No," he answered.

"That settles it," said Finney, "although I won't quote you."

"It doesn't matter if you do. I'm golden now."

"I know."

"What's the problem then?" Dewey asked. "Why are you so negative?"

"I suppose," said Finney, "that it's just that, the night before your acceptance speech—which will make or break you—you don't have an acceptance speech."

Dewey tapped his foot upon the floor, indicating the rooms below. "He's working on it."

"But have you seen it? Have I seen it? Has anyone seen it?"

"No one saw the other one."

"This is different. Length, policy, importance."

"Don't worry. These days importance is not important. I mean, no one knows anything anyway. I trust Moofoomooach. He gave me seventy points in two days. The whole country's Moofoomooach crazy, and anything he does will work. He could translate *The Hunchback of Notre Dame* into Yiddish, and when I gave it they would say I was George Washington."

"But how are you going to practise?"

"Moofoomooach is going to put it on the prompter himself. Buck showed him how. That way, there'll be absolutely no leaks."

"But how will you have time to practise it on the prompter?"

"I'm not gonna," said Dewey, enjoying Finney's distress. "When I get up there, it'll be the first time I see it. I'm gonna wing it. Moofoomooach said it's the only way for it to seem entirely natural."

"Senator," Finney said, his prudent ancestry arising, "no presidential candidate in modern times has ever 'winged' his acceptance speech."

"What about Prescott Lindy?"

"Who?"

"Prescott Lindy."

"Who was that?"

"Didn't he run against Wickwire?"

"Who?"

"Wickwire? There was a President Wickwire, wasn't there?"

"No."

"Finney, I didn't go to a gold-plated prep school, like you. When I studied the presidents it was in a one-room schoolhouse and there was another class nearby studying accounting. I sometimes get presidents and famous accountants mixed up."

"Everyone does," said Finney.

"Maybe it's true. Maybe no presidential candidate has ever winged his acceptance speech. But no presidential candidate has ever had a Moofoomooach. Seventy points! Seventy points in two days! If he asked me to read the telephone book, Finney, I would."

THE LAST NIGHT of a political convention is always the most spectacular, because, as in war, everyone, even those of the highest rank, has something to do, but no one controls, no one sees all, and no one fails to understand that events take on a life of their own. The great excitement comes of more than noise and the otherworldly wash of white light that, emanating from so many sources and directions, seems brighter than the sun. It comes because the night runs away from its planners, history is made, and the battle begins. The silver-tinted darkness on high near the ceiling, where the balloons ride at anchor, is like something astronomical, a Milky Way with smudges of bioluminescence that suggest life impossibly distant in space and time. The ocean in a high wind on a light-filled June day could not be more exciting.

At the no-frisk door the Secret Service had half a dozen agents and no metal detector. This was the door through which Dewey, Dot, Finney, Moofoomooach, Mrs Moofoomooach, the living Republican presidents, the governor of California, and Charlton Heston would walk. But in addition to these ten were fifteen more whose faces the agents did not necessarily recognise. They were the next highest officials in the campaign, and because the Secret Service agents were rotated among different assignments, they didn't get to know all of them.

The badges, however, were foolproof, with photographs and descriptions of the bearer protected by hair-thin fibre-optic filaments that were connected to a battery and glowed in the colours of the rainbow. Were one fibre cut, all would go dark. "May I see your badge, sir?" or "madam?" the agents would say, and then very carefully compare. Everything went well until, ten minutes before Dewey's speech, the arrival of one of the last outstanding pass holders prompted the entry detail to phone their chief.

"Checking on a late entrant." The agent read the number from the pass. The chief matched it on his computer. The codes were valid.

"Is he the guy?"

"He's the guy, and everything's in order except for one thing."

"What's that?"

"He's got a bone in his hair."

"A bone? What kind of bone?"

"I don't know. It looks like a chicken bone, but it's thin and a foot long. Wait a minute, I'll ask. Sir, is that a chicken bone?"

"No," said the very strange person, who was, nonetheless, totally legitimate. "It's the bone of the yellow flamingo of Sarawak."

"Should I let him in?" the agent asked.

"If he's genuine, let him in."

"What about the bone of the yellow flamingo of Sarawak?"

"Young people do that kind of thing. Remember Lucy-Bird?"

"He's middle-aged."

"Figure it out, Eisen," the chief said. "He's one of Knott's top aides. This is San Francisco. He was probably at a party. Come on."

"Should I frisk him?"

"Let's think. He's been with Knott since before you were born. Should you frisk him?"

THEY KEPT THE convention hall quiet for as long as they could before Dewey took the stage, so that the explosion of music would shock the senses (which Dewey thought was the word for a tally of the population). Finney, Freddy, Fredericka, and Dot stood around Dewey in the green-room. Just before the call, Dot walked up to Dewey and embraced him. They said nothing, having been married for so long that they could speak without words. Then Dewey marched out.

The next thing they heard was a tidal wave of music and voices, and they knew that Dewey was out there, bathed in a million watts of white light, smiling, ramrod straight, and looking the whole world in the eye. Staffers who had come to escort them to their seats onstage held them back until the assigned moment during a lull, before the volume rose again almost intolerably.

Finney turned to Freddy. He had to shout, and was hardly audible even though he did. "I've never been this much out of the loop," he yelled. "Is the speech on the prompter?"

Freddy nodded.

"Is it good? It better be good."

"Don't worry," Freddy shouted over the din. "When I wrote it I drank a whole bottle of Scotch to loosen myself up. After half a litre, the speech came like a flock of wild geese chased by an eagle."

"But, Moofoomooach, when you read it afterward, was it still like a flock of wild geese chased by an eagle? Did it hold together? Was it moving?"

"Read it afterward?" Freddy asked.

DEWEY KEPT RAISING his arms like a Japanese railway crossing guard, first the left, then the right, to request silence, but the sounds had a life of their own and ricocheted around the hall like a plasma in a tokamak. It made Dewey think of the ocean. He had loved the ocean before he was too busy to go there. Dot never had time for the ocean now. She said it was flat and boring and full of "Jellofish," but for Dewey it was the only place in the world where his heart floated. He hoped and expected that Moofoomooach would talk poetically about the sea. What a lovely way to start a speech.

When at last the audience was expectantly quiet, Dewey looked at the invisible glass plates upon which the speech appeared. With his left hand, he would turn the pages of the paper copy on the lectern each time a bright red turnip appeared in the projected text. With his right hand, he kept lively on the forward button to scroll the text, and was always ready for what Mushrom was fond of calling "a little backward action."

Because Dewey had never seen it, the speech would have a quality of absolute freshness. He thought that if he could carry it off he might build his lead and take all fifty states, and thus he began in a noble, confident, ringing tone. His voice reflected that this was perhaps the greatest moment of his life.

"Have you ever had a hair on your tongue?" he asked the entire world. Thousands of people in the hall, and hundreds of millions elsewhere, nodded. An anchorman perked up, and glanced at his guest analyst, who had written Self's inaugural address and was hoping to write another.

Dewey continued. "I have. What a rotter! What a disgusting, uncomfortable feeling! After all, it combines the gag reflex and a natural aversion to serpents. The best thing to do after removing it is to suck on a sweet. I myself prefer Singleton's Lemon Puffs. The American kind—what are they called? Hershorns?—taste like yak pee, and I ought to know: I've drunk yak pee."

Dewey read out loud a notation in the text that said, "Pause and count to twenty." Then he said, "I have?" and, then, thinking he had made a mistake, "Pause and count to twenty. One, two, three, four. . . ."

Before he hit five, the message from a hundred producers to a hundred correspondents on the floor was "What the hell is he saying?" but the correspondents and anchors alike were stunned. The former dropped their pencils, the latter stared at the tiny figure below and at his magnified image on a gigantic screen above and behind him.

"It was in a tent in India near the Tibetan border. I was visiting a team of biologists, who had prepared tea for me, but I drank from the wrong flask. A state in India has a commemorative stamp of it. Funny," Dewey interrupted, commenting on what he had just said, "I've never been to India."

As he pressed on, not a sound could be heard. Had a canary chirped among the armada of balloons, even though invisible and far away, it would have enjoyed the one moment in its life when it seemed to thunder like a train.

"Which," Dewey read, "that is, that I drank yak pee—(here Dewey argued with himself) but I didn't—leads into the body of my speech." He looked up, and read, "Disregard the entire first part and start immediately below." And then he added, "Oh, thanks for telling me."

He paused for a long time as he read ahead. His lips moved as he took in the text. Everyone strained forward to see what he was doing. Then he returned to the text. "I mean, really," he read on, "we are thoroughly disgusting creatures, are we not, who eat dead animal flesh, inhale the smoke of burning leaves, and savour, like vultures or the French, rotted and putrefied foodstuffs such as wine and cheese. We dress in the skins of the dead animals we eat, rub their secretions on our bodies and in our hair, and spend a third of our lives lying unconscious, mute, and vulnerable."

Everyone knew by now that Dewey had dispensed with the conventional opening: "Ladies and gentlemen, citizens of the Golden State, my fellow Americans. . . ."

"Once, when I was playing polo—I've never played polo in my life—a chap was thrown from his pony, and. . . ." Dewey looked up. "But I don't play polo. I've never been on a horse.

"And yet, and yet, we exist in one another's presence as cleanly as gods. It's as if we aren't transient flesh but some impossible royal lobster. How is it that we are able to accomplish this? Is it illusion? Is it accommodation? Is it *force majeure,* or accident? No. What is it? Look up imploringly at audience and say again, what is it? Then say, as if in metred verse, it is, pause, I assure you, pause, nothing more and nothing less than, pause, civilisation.

"That is why I am a Tory. What's a Tory? I believe in civilisation, and what is civilisation if not restraint? What is civilisation if not delicacy of manners; deep concentration; the seeking of truth; the holding in abeyance of actions, which otherwise would result in personal advantage, purely for the sake of justice?

"It is not, pause, the never-ending and always expanding aggrandise-
ment of administration. It is not, pause, the ceaseless and voracious institu-
tionalisation of schemes. It is not, pause, the redistribution of income or the
codification of envy. It is not, pause, a perpetual appeal to grievance. Indeed,
it is more sacrifice than grievance, more forbearance than scheme. It is a
thing almost as silent and pacific as a great and luxuriant tree, pause, that
stands in rain and sun, through nights of wind and stars, in snowstorms
and on perfect days, without a single word, unbent by the wind, for hundreds of years, growing beautiful without presumption, ever suffering, ever
silent, ever noble, ever great.

"Do not trust or follow promises of action unless they are in response
to a threat against that very civilisation to which I ask you to dedicate
yourselves tonight.

"I have been in this country for only a little more than a year. . . ."
Dewey stopped dead, staring at the prompter. "That's not true. I was born
here. If I was here only for a year, how could I have served in the Senate
for so much of the century? I wouldn't even know the language, unless I
came from an English-speaking country. And I couldn't be president.

"I have been in this country for only a little more than a year," he read
again, not arguing with himself any more, "and what I have seen has
taught me many a lesson and inspired me to exceed myself. There is much
that I have permanently taken into my heart, and will keep with me when
I ascend the throne.

"The throne?" asked Dewey. "What is this? I feel like I'm in the fucking Twilight Zone." The only thing he could do was push the forward button, but, going too far and getting ahead of himself resulted in his saying,
"Nor monkeys, nor macaques, nor blasé gelatinous sea creatures, nor the
Red-Tailed Obfusian, nor mice and rats sequestered in their foetid subter-
ranean burrows, nor the fluffy white cousins of Japan, nor cat, nor dog,
nor ibex, skunk, tortoise, bird, or mink. Pause. Look wounded. Look Bib-
lical, a bit like Lear or Father Time.

"No product of nature. No sound. No coalescence of form. No chance
encounter of things molten and hot." This was the end of a section.

In Freddy's view, Dewey was ruining the speech, and Freddy's expression betrayed his annoyance. Fredericka seemed vaguely disturbed as well,
in a patient, detached fashion. The former presidents were, for some reason, filled with glee. Finney was astounded but fearless. And Dot sat with

the same immovable grin that she always had when Dewey was making a speech.

Dewey felt that he hadn't quite connected with his audience. So he raced ahead. "Oh, this debauched and unbearable world," he read. "I would not be bothered were my wife not with child. . . ." At these last words, forgetting that the speech was not his, Dewey turned to look at the sixty-something Dot. The words, "Dot, are you pregnant?" echoed from Spokane to Perth.

Dot tapped her left hand against her chest. "Me?" she asked. "No, Dewey. In case you've forgotten, I'm a sexagenarian."

"You are?" asked Dewey, putting the back of his hand to his forehead. "Oh boy. This isn't my night. In all those years, why didn't you tell me?"

"Finish the bloody speech," Freddy yelled, extremely annoyed at the interruptions.

Dewey nodded and turned back to the lectern. "Debauched and evil and full of suffering as this world is," he read, "and quick as our life may bustle and fade, I have found, and only of late, the consolation I have been seeking all my days, and it is in love. My dear wife, whom I married from royal obligation and pure sexual attraction, has become for me an angel of God." Dewey looked up, extremely puzzled. Then he shook his head and resumed. "Though I may be wrong and suffering illusion, this illusion heals my heart. In her, the open questions have been closed, and in her I am content, and to her, as we grow old, I profess my love and proclaim an island of satisfaction in an imperfect world."

Dewey looked at Dot. A tear was slowly descending her cheek. Though he had always loved her, he felt more tenderness for her, and love, than he had since the Bataan Death March. Strangely enough, Mrs Moofoo-mooach also had tears. Radiant-looking, she gazed at Moofoomooach, who was awkwardly clearing his throat.

Dewey turned solemnly to the lectern once again. "I do love you, Dot. Everyone thinks you're stiff and mean, but I don't. I know you, and I love you. It's true," he said, and now no one knew if he were reading or merely speaking. "Nothing could be truer. All of this," his left arm moved in a simple gesture that took in the great hall and the whole world, "is as nothing to those simple and beautiful things that we ignore in favour of vanity and illusion. I came here for glory, but I find that my heart aches for what is beyond these walls."

Dewey looked out at the crowd. Those in elephant hats had taken them

off. They blinked by the thousand, waiting for the words that would follow. They had no idea what words could follow, which was why they were
transfixed. Their nominee smiled at them, as if for the first time in his life
he were perfectly content, at ease, and in a state of lucid equanimity.

In this graceful elision between one world and another, a figure glided
from the wings quite smoothly. The first person to notice him was a Secret
Service sniper hidden high in the rafters, who put him in the cross-hairs
immediately and called in to request guidance, speaking quietly and calmly
into the microphone of his headset.

"Unscheduled walk-on, stage right. I have him in the cross-hairs.
Guidance."

At control everything jumped up like a cat that touches a live wire.
"Hold," was the command. Then, to the network of agents, "Who the
hell is that?"

Six voices at once said, "Mushrom."

"Is he supposed to be there? He isn't supposed to be there. What's
he doing?"

"I don't see a gun," someone said. No one saw the gun in his hand, in
his jacket pocket, because Mushrom was the kind of person who would
not appear to be carrying a gun even were he bent under the weight of
twenty rifles.

Many voices at once were talking, rapidly losing their professional quality as no one did anything and the tension mounted—all in a few seconds.

"He's got a bone in his hair."

"He's the guy with the bone in his hair."

"It's Mushrom. Hold. Hold."

"Get someone out there. Get him off stage."

Because of the pin-drop silence, the desperate chatter across the Secret
Service net was faintly audible. It sounded otherworldly, and even if no
one could hear the exact words just the tone was enough to tighten every
muscle in the convention hall.

Nothing seemed to move until Dewey noticed Mushrom and turned to
him, smiling, because now he understood that he had to be kind to Mushrom, and that previously he had been very unkind. How best to communicate his deep sorrow? How best to treat Mushrom, finally, like a son?

He was thinking of this, and the solution was clearly on its way, for
little else could explain the aura of benevolence that now surrounded
Dewey like a halo, when Mushrom, full of sorrow himself, elevated the

barrel of the gun in his pocket and pulled the trigger. The noise of the shot was amplified by Dewey's microphone, and everyone in the giant convention hall jumped. Dewey doubled over and stood on his right leg alone, as if he had been shot in the left. "Campbell," he said, before he tumbled forward onto the stage.

As soon as the shot resounded and Dewey went down, the chief of the Secret Service detail screamed, "Rafter one, fire! Fire!" and the sniper amid the balloons carried out the order. Whereas Dewey had taken the bullet straight on, and it had exited from his back and hit a choir girl in the hand, the bullet that hit Mushrom shattered his right arm, passed through his right lung and his liver, shattered his hip, and dug into the floor.

The two men fell into one another. Dewey's hands grabbed Mushrom's arm and shoulder, and then he pulled them back to grip his own wound. By now, thirty people were around them, Dot screaming, Freddy resolute, Fredericka angry, and Finney stunned. Medics crashed through the crowd carrying a worn yellow board with straps the colour of life preservers.

"I went to New Guinea," Mushrom said. "You have no idea what's in the jungle of New Guinea. How could you have hated me and kept me by your side for twenty-five years? I loved you like a son. How could you have hated me?" He died.

Dewey, who didn't know that he himself was dying, said to no avail, "I don't hate you, Campbell. The point is, you aren't my son, so every time you tried to be my son I didn't like it. But now, I think that something has happened to me, and I don't know what it is, but I feel better." By this time, Dot had taken him into her arms. "Hello, Dot," he said, smiling, and then closed his eyes forever.

SELF DECLARED a national emergency (known inevitably as a Self-declared national emergency), mainly out of panic that Draff would be propelled into office as a tribute to the slain Dewey. He prayed vigorously that his running mate, the concussion-voiced, insufferable Vice President Boar, a spritely lummox whose diction was simultaneously so thick and so choked with enthusiasm that he spoke in horrible wads, would die at least a week before the election. The last thing Self's chief of staff heard before the president closeted himself with his vicious, viscous, and vacuous political advisers to work on the strategy of his funeral oration for Dewey, was,

"Get me a list of capital cities with dangerous airports and heads of state who are deathly ill."

The convention had been adjourned until the next night, when, in emergency session, it would choose a new nominee. Having voted for Dewey already, as they were bound, the delegates were now unbound and free to vote as they wished. Draff didn't sleep. He granted twenty interviews and for the rest of the time the phone never left his face. Red and sore of ear, he spoke to every delegation and to the big ones two, three, and four times. All his staff and operatives worked as if shoring up a levy. With television cameras trailing, he paid a saccharine visit to Dot, now a destroyed woman whose hands shook and who was unable to speak.

At four o'clock in the morning, after he had tried to comfort Dot and hundreds of shell-shocked staffers, Finney went to visit Mr and Mrs Moofoomooach. They were in their suite, very subdued, sitting across from one another in a pool of light from a table lamp. Otherwise the room was dark, and the lights of Oakland twinkled like a brazier.

Finney sat down. "Buck tried to retrieve the disk from the prompter, but it was gone," he said.

"I know," said Freddy. "I took it."

"We need it, for history."

"I destroyed it. What Dewey said was transcribed. The rest is immaterial."

"You can't do that."

"I've already done it."

"It's a crime."

"No, it isn't," Freddy asserted.

"It was his speech," Finney said.

"No, it wasn't, it was my speech. I wrote it, and therefore it was mine. It was mine by reason of copyright, and even had it not been copyrighted it was mine by law, and even had it not been mine by law it was mine because I wrote it. And because it was mine, I took it. And after I took it, I destroyed it."

"What for?"

"Why not?"

"What if Draff wants to use it?"

"Well now you know why I destroyed it."

"You were paid to write that speech!"

"Was I?"

Finney remembered that Freddy had not been paid a thing. "Dewey's up in the polls," he said. "He's got almost a hundred percent approval. Can you imagine that? He would have loved it. Dot won't let go of the printout."

"We're going home," Freddy announced, "tomorrow morning."

"You're going to stay," Finney told him authoritatively, "because as someone closely identified with Dewey it would be unconscionable for you simply to disappear."

"The nation grieves," Fredericka said, "or at least it says it does. What does it care about us?"

"Popeel," Finney said to disabuse her, "the nation doesn't grieve. The nation just likes to watch."

"But the people in the long queues, they're so upset, they're so moved, they. . . ."

"Where did you see these people, Popeel?"

"On the telly."

Finney nodded his head. "They come to the television cameras like moths to light. They like to watch, and they like to be watched."

"I find that unjustifiably cynical," Freddy said.

"Oh, really? What about those idiots in England who look like you, my distant relatives?"

"Frederick and Fredericka?"

"Yes."

"What about them?"

"Do you think they could survive a day without publicity? They have actually become publicity and aren't any longer human. People like to watch them, and they like to be watched. That's all there is."

"What if it were not so?" Freddy asked. "What if you were wrong and, in fact, they did not at all like to be watched, and had been alone and anonymous for more than a year whilst, in a charade, the public were made to think they were doing all the expensive things the public so envies, and insists they do for its own gratification and so as to be an anvil to strike in frustration as they object?"

"That's a dream," said Finney. "I know aristo-trash like that well enough, and you, what would you know? You're dentists, you don't know them at all. I assure you that they would rather die than trade places with people like you." Finney was uncomfortable with their reaction. "Why are you laughing? Dewey's dead. Be at the convention tomorrow at six. Out of decency."

"We always have tried," Freddy assured him, "to be decent."

That night, or in what was left of it, Freddy and Fredericka sat in bed looking out at the lights of Oakland. Fredericka was upset because she was not upset. The sheet lay across her breast like a gown. "Why am I so unmoved?" she asked.

"Because we've always run the same risks. In that sense, he was just like us. It may be our turn next. Despite what you may see in the cinema, when their comrades are killed soldiers don't go weeping around on the battlefield. Why should we be grieving when we're lucky enough still to be alive? He would understand perfectly."

"What do you think will happen at the convention tomorrow?" she asked.

"They'll choose a nominee. It won't be dramatic because it's almost certain to be Giraffe. We'll just sit there for eight hours, like mannequins, and then, when it's over, we'll go home. I miss England, and shall never be the king of this country."

Through a bittersweet smile, Fredericka said, "I miss England, too, very much."

AFTER DEWEY'S DEATH the bands were silenced and the only music was the ocean-like sound of thousands of voices, thousands of shuffling papers, thousands of shifting feet, and the rush of air in the massive ventilation system. The press speculated, reported its speculations, and then analysed them as if they were fact. According to them, with Dewey gone, Draff had it sewn up. Correspondents from other countries, who did not even understand the language, repeated as fact the conjectures of their American counterparts in the fantastical glass booths that floated brightly above the mere people on the floor. The whole world was waiting for Draff to seize the nomination, and the whole world was sure that he would.

A chaplain said a prayer, another said another, and another said another. The effect of these on Freddy was walloping, as always. Even prayer in stilted recitation aligned every force within him in what Fredericka thought to have been not a cure for Freddy's madness but its enlargement. When she had seen his expression change as the awkward clerics prayed, she had lifted her head. What would he do? What outrageous thing would he say?

Dacheekan walked across the platform, pausing carefully near the floral arrangement at the spot where Dewey had fallen. But when he stepped up to the lectern he was joyful and fleet of foot. Though Freddy didn't like that, it was inevitable. Draff was Dacheekan's man, and Dacheekan was about to call for his nomination.

"Ladies and gentlemen," he said, his undistinguished, flat voice amplified into nearly booming thunder, "let us bow our heads and pray for the soul of Dewey Knott, and for our country."

"We just did that, three times!" screamed someone about forty rows from the stage. Dacheekan looked out, but only with an instant, cat-like movement of the eyes, head still bowed, hands clasped. There was a murmur, and it unsettled him. Within the murmur, someone shouted, closer now, "Get on with it!" People were upset. But everything was taken care of. Draff had spoken to each of the delegations, and Dacheekan had gone to each one to verify, promise, and threaten. Fifty states would announce for Draff.

"Do it!" came from far back in the hall, where, from the dais, people's faces seemed as small as the erasers on the ends of pencils. One after another of these admonitions, freighted with emotion, floated bodilessly in the open space above everyone's heads, the same open space to which, inexplicably to some, the candidates always addressed their appeals.

"Very well," Dacheekan said. "Tonight, I have the honour to nominate, as the Republican candidate for the presidency of the United States, the former vice-presidential nominee, the governor of the great state of North Dakota, and a man beloved of Dewey Knott—Elwood . . . Lucky . . . Draff!"

A cheer went up, briefly, from the North Dakota delegation. Dacheekan shifted from foot to foot, about to call the roll. He never had the chance. From way in the back, from underneath the balconies, where the least important people were stashed, a strange and insistent chant emerged. At first it was as gentle as ripples in a pond, but by the time it found its way to the open sea at the centre and to the mass of souls who soon came to their feet beneath the empty space the candidates addressed, it was thundering.

Trying to stem it, Dacheekan used his privileged amplification to no avail, for twenty-five thousand voices swept the amplification away like a hurricane bearing down upon a smoke ring. Almost as if by magic, the chant, which now shook the country and the world, divided in two, and, as perfectly timed as a choir of tree frogs, alternated from both sides of the hall. "Moofoomooach!" rose from one side, like cannon fire. It was answered, as if by a tidal wave, with "White! Eagle!"

The air felt like spring. Between the great eruptions of "Moofoomooach!" and "White! Eagle!" it was as if a spark had cleansed and cooled the static atmosphere. The more the delegates shouted "Moofoomooach!, White! Eagle!, Moofoomooach!, White! Eagle!" the more ecstatic they became.

Freddy leaned over to Fredericka, who leaned into him the way only someone who loves someone can, and he said to her, "You know, this may be a little too *moi*, but I feel now, even in August, that wonderful feeling when on the first good night in late spring I open the windows at St James's and the warm night air billows in, carrying the scent of flowers that have just bloomed in the parks. I hope it's not just because they're chanting my name."

"No," she said. "I feel it, too."

"You're Mrs Moofoomooach."

"Everyone in the hall feels it, Freddy. It's not because they want to hear you. They don't know you. You're not important. But, once, they heard you speak the truth. That's all they want."

"The truth?"

"Yes. It makes a lot of trouble, Freddy, but it's worth the trouble. How you know what is in their hearts, I don't know, but you do. Go."

Freddy turned to the vast assemblage and suddenly stood tall in the way he was accustomed to standing on balconies and reviewing platforms and in cathedrals. He felt as straight of back and confident of his position as if he were wearing his naval uniform clustered with the signs and symbols of legendary battles and the work of men who had bravely given their lives. Never had he risen before such a powerful audience, and, knowing restraint, he let the space between it and him fill with the ricochets of invisible urgency that made it go wild. The frenzy was unprecedented, and yet he disciplined it with almost imperceptible changes in expression that swept slowly across his face. By the inlet of his breath and the minute widening of his eyes he told them that no matter how much they cheered, he was firmly rooted where he stood and his feet would never leave the ground. He knew power and never, never would he allow it to run away with him. Always and forever, it would be disciplined, and with this discipline it would become both more concentrated and more precise. They sensed this merely from the way he stood. His dignity, not even the smallest part of which was false, was clear to them, and they gave him their trust.

Slowly and gracefully, he walked to the lectern. Unlike his predecessor there he did not leap up, but, rather, hesitated before he took a firm step, and then he was where destiny had put him. He let the cheering continue, and, as it did, made ready to speak, with no idea whatsoever what he would say.

He lifted his left hand and angled his head down almost microscopically, and the great noise, that had been like the noise of a storm, subsided. Never had anyone seen in recent or long memory such a stupendous racket so quickly stilled. The only thing like it was when in miraculous contrast the eye of a hurricane empties the world of sound and fury in a second or two, and shows heaven to anyone lucky enough to be within its lake of translucent blue air.

He glanced back at Fredericka, whose expression displayed none of the worshipful admiration common to political wives, but only simple pride. This was only an American political convention, after all, and of the party in opposition. She and Freddy had no stake in it whatsoever other than that they had hoped to conquer the country. Not an eye in the house was fixed anywhere but on Freddy or Fredericka. Even the pigeons that had bobbed near the ceiling and fluttered into dark crannies, folding their wings like breaking an umbrella, were totally still.

"How many would-be presidents, and presidents-to-be," Freddy asked in beautiful voice, "have stood on this figurative spot and begun their speeches with meaningless and formulaic salutations? I am not familiar with such salutations, and, even were I, would not start in with anything but something like a love song to this country that you have hinted I might lead.

"I believe, from knowing each one, that your presidents of late"— Finney cocked his head—"have, unbelievably, failed to know and to consider the interests of the country and its people as a whole. Surely this can lead only to disaster. They may know policy and politics, but these, even to someone educated in them, are in the last analysis not much more than a game. Thus the politicians have transformed the life of a nation into a game they play continuously for their own edification. But games are man-made abstractions as weak as water, with none of the fullness, beauty, and consequence of life.

"Life is not a game, nations are not to be gamed, and people are not to be addressed outside their mortal complexities. You may ask what this means. It means that were I to run for the highest office or the lowest, I would not try to determine what you want and then strain to offer it to you. That is what they do, and well.

"If only the satisfaction of want could satisfy, then satisfaction would come upon the first fulfilment of the first request. But it never does. It merely leads to other needs that lead yet again to others, for in the satisfaction of one desire lies the creation of another. Even were the lies you are told by dishonest men actually true, and even if you did truly want what you want, the minute you had it your happiness would depart. This I know because I have had every material thing and privilege in the world.

"The model of a president has been that of a man who comes to you like a salesman, and promises things. I think the model of a president should be a man who comes before you and says, 'This is what I have seen, this is what I believe, this is how I live, and this is what I love.' Surely you would know such a man better for this than you would know a man possessed of a list crowded with numbers and littered with prostituted oaths.

"When confronted with the creatures from whom these words spill like jellyfish vomited from the mouths of whales, my reaction has always been that, though I would like to be prosperous, this is not what I am. What about the little courage that I have, the honour for which I strive, my attempts at faithfulness? These are what you should address. Why do you not see them? Why do you not sense the heart of your own country? Why do you reflexively pull away from deep waters whenever inadvertently you glide over them?

"I will begin not with a salutation but a testament. In the past year or so my wife and I have slowly made our way across the country, step by step, foot by foot. I sank low and felt with my hands, and touched the ground with my fingers. I could smell even the cold streams as they flooded in spring. I listened to the ice on Lake Michigan, grey-black, at three in the morning as Chicago slept. I stood on a mountainside in West Virginia and watched the blue-green horizon as deer rose and dipped in the brush as if on noiseless swells. We passed Baltimore on the interstate highway one night, and saw a city in a fume of gold and luminous smoke from which rose towers encrusted with sparkling lights.

"In all this time we were not attentive to matters of state, we were washing dishes, cleaning bathrooms, serving food, standing night watch in a fire tower and at the bow of a barge, and this was only part of what we did. We came to know the towns and junctions even if often we passed through them unseen. A few months ago, I stood at night on the open prairie under a clear sky of stars as bright as Bellerophon's dripping diamonds, and my wife stood with me. Has any candidate come before you to state how sweet the air is on the open prairie? Probably not. But it is. Perhaps you have forgotten. Perhaps you never knew. But it is, and it is there in infinite quantity, free and unclaimed. And if you watch from on high, from across the Hudson at New York, on a summer night, you will see a construction greater than that of any previous age. You need only look upon it from the proper angle and distance to see that you possess wondrous dimensions that daily you ignore, forgetting where you stand in time.

"I have read your Declaration and Constitution, and though at first I found the former personally injurious, I came to see that these are lucid and perfect documents, and that if you return to them as faithfully as they have served you since the beginning, they will not fail you.

"You have neglected them, and are unclear about the duties of a citizen and what comes by right. You seem to have forgotten the ancient battles in which you prevailed, and, more importantly, those that you merely survived. You seem to have forgotten that your original principles arose in a land that was carpeted with virgin stands of trees, and that the principles by which you lived—immaterial and bright, ever enduring—grew up just as strong and fresh. Return to them. They are waiting for you, as are reserves of honour as vast as the stands of trees that once spread without end.

"In your beginnings you looked down upon spectacle, so why have you such spectacles as this?" he asked, peering out into the gigantic interior in which, it seemed, airships could fly and Roman legions fight unnoticed below. He stared into a network box that floated in the semi-darkness, moored to the rear wall. Bigger than a barn, it was lit like a gem, and as if in another world people moved within it as silently as ants. The celebrated anchor, as lonely as a king, tiny earphones upon his tiny head, stared at Freddy like a rebellious angel who had encamped upon a cloud. "Can you not see that it is of a size unbecoming to a nation whose principles were born in the small farmhouse and on the green of the New England village? Everything I believe about America has its origins in places like that and in the landscape itself."

Here Freddy took flight, his infatuation with the land he had come to conquer driving him on in rapt concentration that pulled the stilled audience after him. He spoke of the most erudite constitutional questions, of the causes of war, of economic theory, of moral philosophy. Freely flowing from him were Latin quotations, statistics, commemoration of battles, Miltonic epithets, and Shakespearean couplets, all as clear as day and illuminated as brightly as he was himself by the column of snow-white light that had been destined to make of Dewey a kind of George Washington, but that now clarified Freddy's words in a blinding ray.

He knew the battles well. His erudition was precise and detailed, and yet he wove his knowledge and his command of things into something like a song, that disarmed the complexities of problems that for decades had hurt like thorns. No one had ever seen anything like it. In his oratory, Freddy made the shape of truth seem beautiful, and not a dishonest or manipulative syllable did he speak as he rolled forward in unsurpassed form. It changed the country. The parties would rearrange themselves, the law would seem just, and even the defeated would feel victorious. The only unconsoled person in the whole nation, including even Self and Boar, would be Dot, whose world had ended when Dewey had left her with the knowledge that she sought the things she sought not because she wanted them but because she, who could not express it in any other way, loved him.

But it was all a dream, a great moment that appeared like a blazing star and then was gone, for Freddy had decided in mid-speech, as he learned the virtues of the country by stating them after he had lifted them from where they had rested unknown in his heart, that there would be no conquest, that, no matter what the price, he would not conquer.

He disappointed his audience bitterly, but was himself quite happy when he said, "I was born to be a king, and you were born not to have one. America does not need and cannot have a king, for it is majestic in itself as perhaps no country has ever been. And its greatest majesty is not the splendid landscape or the long and sunny coasts, not the Mississippi or the snows of the Pacific Crest. Its greatest majesty, its gift to the world, is that it has carried out God's will to make each man a king, subservient only to Him. From the beginning, this has been the underlying force of every footfall, smile, and blink of the eye in this country. It, and not your power, is what has lifted you up, is what distinguishes you from others, and has made you the leader of the world. And may God bless and keep you as you find your way."

He took Fredericka's hand as he walked off the stage and away from the enormous room filled with many thousands of people who stayed silent and motionless for so long afterward that it was almost heartbreaking. As Freddy and Fredericka went into the night no one stopped or followed them, and after a block or two no one even noticed. The fog rolled in, the foghorns sounded mournfully, and they vanished into the city as if they had never existed.

Moocock at Fresh Sight

A ROYAL HELICOPTER flew across London at very low altitude, its rotors clicking like a dragonfly as the city unrolled beneath it at dusk: such a vast and miraculous city, so calm and settled in rows touched with green, and the river snaking, serpentine, in between. And wherever it was choked with steel and glass it soon fled into open squares and broad malls, to colonnaded palaces, and white halls, to carpets of cool grass, and lights on windowsills, like candles by the million, promising and still.

As if awakening from a dream, Freddy and Fredericka looked upon it with new eyes. "It's as if we've been away for centuries," he said, "and now that we're back, I don't know what to think."

"What will happen?"

He glanced her way, still keeping the craft as steady as if it were flying on a track. "They'll tell us, I suppose. We have little say. The queen has some, but only in slow and stately manoeuvre. The quick and animal power is elsewhere. We do what we're told and protest only like obedient horses that sidestep and shake."

"But you've just conquered a country many times the size of Britain, and alone," Fredericka argued. "Surely. . . ."

"In refusing to conquer, therefore I did not, and who knows what price I'll pay for that. Perhaps I'll join my splendid predecessor George the Third, and will be maligned, like him, for having let the great prize slip through my hands. Then again, having failed, I probably will not be king, and may not even be lucky enough in history to be maligned. Perhaps all memory of both you and me will disappear from this earth as it does for ordinary people, whose lives evaporate like mist."

"We knew that coming in, didn't we?" Fredericka asked.

"I didn't," was the answer. "Unlike almost anyone else, I had something of an escape from mortality, even if it were illusory. Now I must look at everything anew, and everything seems lovely at fresh sight."

With the dusk nearly gone and no moon, they dipped down and banked into Moocock, where the lights were on in the pool—a sapphire cabochon surrounded by tungsten-washed emerald lawns—and the lamps were lit in nearly every room. Waiting by the pad were all the servants in their livery. The gardeners held a sign that read: *Welcome Back from Pakistan*.

Alighting from the helicopter, Freddy saw the sign and said, "That's a good trick. I'll bet my father chose Pakistan."

"Your Royal Highness will be disappointed to know," said Lathbury, the kennelman, "that Pha-Kew passed away some time ago, after ingesting too large a piece of wildebeest cutlet. The Heimlich manoeuvre was unavailing."

"What a pity," said Freddy. He turned to Sawyers. "Anything to report?"

"In your absence, Your Royal Highness, we've lost four members of staff to Cunard and Prince Faddle Ibn Rabbiya. They have been replaced."

"Good," said Freddy. "Carry on. Thank you all."

"Are you hungry, sir, ma'am?" Sawyers asked. "The kitchen is up and ready."

Freddy thought for a moment. "Yes," he said, "I'd like some barbecued potato chips and a Dr Pepper."

"I'm afraid that escaped me, sir."

"Barbecued potato chips—mesquite/jalapeño style—and a Dr Pepper."

"A Pakistani treat, sir?"

"No," said Freddy, adjusting. "Bring smoked salmon and Champagne."

"Certainly, sir, and I'll send someone to Brixton to fetch the Pakistani items, if you wish."

"That won't be necessary, Sawyers. We're back now. We're not in 'Pakistan,' and we need not eat 'Pakistani' food."

Having left their American life behind, except in long indelible traces within, Freddy and Fredericka joined hands and walked together toward their house, which glowed from its windows.

SUDDENLY TO HAVE every comfort once again was suddenly to feel very old. All aspects of Moocock were pristine and exquisite. The paintings would have been the pride of a small museum: in the summer-room half a dozen flower paintings by Fantin, Monet, and Renoir (a Van Gogh was in Fredericka's study); in the bedroom, a life-sized Courbet; over Freddy's desk, a Raphael; and so on, all in excellent condition, well placed, and perfectly lit. The library of twenty-five thousand volumes included not one in paperback, for books that came with soft covers were taken to the bindery with the urgency of transporting to hospital a baronet who had tumbled off a polo pony. Cross-indexed on an unobtrusive black laptop, their citations were backed up electronically and in hard copy. The massive ladder that moved silently along its ever-shining brass track had a little platform halfway up, with a comfortable seat and a tiny table. The quality of furniture throughout the house was comparable to that of the solid mahogany dining room table, which was twelve feet in diameter, a foot thick, and polished as carefully as the Mt Palomar mirror. Its surface was an ocean of browns, reds, and buttery colours, with patterns that swirled like a flamenco dancer's shawl. Every thread in Freddy's wardrobe had long been the envy of the world's dandies, and Fredericka's Balenciagas, Wendels, and Ludovicos were hung in her cupboards like carcasses in a freezer. Even in the kitchen, in the caviar refrigerator, the jars and tins were arranged by type, quality, producer, and age. Were Freddy to order any dish, he could specify how many grams of this or that would be in it, its temperature upon arrival and the temperature of the plate, the style of the cooking, the age of the cheese, and whatever else might be required by fancy or need. In the map room were maps of everywhere continuously updated. In winter, fires burned with balanced heat and anarchy in whatever fireplaces Freddy specified, and fresh flowers, placed by a woman with a doctorate in flower arranging from the University of Tokyo, were in almost every room in all seasons. The cars were polished and ready, the guns cleaned, the cream whipped, the metalwork shining, shirts pressed, rubbish baskets empty, gardens fecund, and the light was gorgeous.

This was Moocock, the Garden of Eden, and now they were back, but it seemed too easy. After a few days, not long before they were scheduled to visit the queen and Paul in London, they found themselves, having finished lunch, watching as the dishes were cleared away and the table was quietly refurbished with the most expensive oil from walnut trees grown on the southern shores of Lake Baikal. Then Sawyers backed out, closing the heavy door with a click as only a gentleman's gentleman can.

"It's as if we're dead," said Fredericka. "I didn't really want to come back."

"I didn't want to be the bloody president of the bloody United States, and, besides, the Constitution would have prevented it."

"They would have changed their silly Constitution, and you would have been the first English president. Think of how proud Winston Churchill would have been."

"I was raised to be king. I would have been insufferable."

"And what will happen if you do become king? We have everything we want. We'd just have ten times more."

"If I become king I will do such things as Britain has never seen. I will be the first king of the people rather than over them. I will be the first to speak freely. I will look back to the broad horizons this island once knew, before it became choked with accomplishment, when success was something not to be remembered but to be got."

"And until then?" Fredericka asked. "In America we were always wanting. Here, we want nothing. I wake up in the morning and pray for difficulties—not small ones, not ringing someone up to have him change a light bulb, but the difficulties that, by counterpressure, enliven the soul."

"I've been praying for those all my life, Fredericka, but one needn't even pray, for they come without fail. Tomorrow, you'll see, after Mummy has conferred with her privy councillors. My feeling is that, because I have failed, she'll be in the mood to lay down the law. What could be worse than to be a dumb royal bastard who never moved up, whose cabinets are full, and whose life slips silently away in the smothering silks of privilege? For the rest of my life I'll float like a blowfish in the airless ocean of English aristocracy. I'll give up, get fat, drink, and look fuzzy."

"We'll go back to America. I'll open a restaurant or a hairdressing shop. You'll make millions of dollars tutoring people in classical languages, or writing pamphlets on fox hunting. We can live in Commack. Isn't that a place on Long Island? I've never wanted to live in Commack, but think of how much pleasure we'd get from aching to leave."

"No, Fredericka. We're not going back."

"But, Freddy!" she said, cheerfully.

"What?"

"Whether or not you become king, life will be full, and purpose will be restored." She patted her stomach.

"Ah," said Freddy.

"We'll tell them tomorrow," said Fredericka. "And if you won't, I will."

WHEN THEY WENT to London, they drove, as they often did when they wanted to move about unobserved, in the Aston-Martin bread van, attired in white jumpsuits over their clothes, bakers' hats with red piping, and sunglasses. No one ever would have guessed that it was they in the specially crafted van with *Strathborgie Melba Toasts Ltd* lettered along the sides. Once, they had been stopped for speeding (theirs was the only vehicle of its type in the world that could achieve speeds upward of 180 mph), and the constable had said, "I was going to carry on with this, but it'll be just a warning because you look so much like that bloody idiot the Prince of Wales."

After driving through the gate to the mews, they would shed their uniforms and go to separate appointments. Fredericka was to have tea with the queen and Lady Darlington. Because Lady Darlington was as verbally promiscuous a creature as God had ever created, Fredericka would not be able to mention that of late she had been in America. Perhaps the queen did not want to hear of it. At least not at the moment. That meant talk about racehorses, jewellery, holiday spots in Barbados, dogs, bananas, and other royalty. It was customary for the royal family to turn the conversation to bananas when their guests were insufferable, like a diver releasing a buoy to mark his position in the depths.

Freddy was to meet his father in the private study. "That means we'll talk about dogs and horses," he said. "He doesn't criticise me when we're alone. When we're alone he's too embarrassed and awkward."

"You would think," Fredericka said, "that he wanted to tell you something. Why would they take the trouble to separate us? Perhaps he'll deliver the bad news, if, in fact, by the terms of the test, you have failed irredeemably."

"We did fairly well. We came close enough, but I really think it would have been a step backward to recapture all those Americans. They don't need us any more, and handling them might have been a problem. We'll let my parents know about their first grandchild. We're the ones with the news, after all. What a shame about Lady Darlington. I know someone who had an affair with her. She likes to dress up as a gaucho."

FREDERICKA WAS BROUGHT into the presence of the queen, who, attired in sunny yellow, seemed inexplicably slight and frail. Never before had Fredericka seen the flash of tenderness in the queen's eyes that she registered upon her entrance, and never before had the queen taken Fredericka's hand with such warmth. This was not a stratagem. The queen did not need to please any individual. Previously with Fredericka she had been blunt and cruel. No longer.

"Sit down, dear," she said. "You know Lady Darlington. Dar? Fredericka has been away for quite some time. In Pah-kiss-tahn."

Fredericka could read directly beneath Lady Darlington's enamelled surface that she hated Fredericka, whom she thought only a detriment to her priceless face time with the queen, which she measured as if with a taxi metre and logged cumulatively and life long. "I've heard," Fredericka said, "that you've been in Argentina."

The queen smiled.

"Well, not lately."

"Really? Someone told me just recently that he had seen you with or as a gaucho."

Though the top of Lady Darlington's chest turned crimson, she motorboated about and turned the conversation to dogs and jewellery, which meant that Fredericka would soon have to send up the flag with the banana on it.

It would have been reasonable to assume that the queen and Paul would be eager to know the story of the sojourn in America, or at least to tell Freddy and Fredericka if anything had been decided in their regard. And why Lady Darlington? She was a "royalty expert" who fed shamelessly on the most minor detritus. Like a bird that, chirping atop a rhinoceros, imagines that it weighs ten thousand pounds, she was vapidity in its unburnished essence. What was the queen trying to say? What scarlet thread would she stretch that would require such a monotonous foil?

The queen was inexplicable. The centre of her own universe, she was unique, and communicated in strange ways. And just when Fredericka was about to send up the flag, the queen, with an impish though tired look—as if she was coming down with the flu—beat her to the punch and began a rhapsody about bananas. Fredericka joined in, and Lady Darlington, who couldn't think of anything to say about the subject, looked on in amazement. Soon enough, Fredericka found herself alone with her mother-in-law. For the first time, she felt that the queen was actually going to talk to her as if both Fredericka and the queen herself were human beings. Fredericka was pleased, and looked forward to connecting with the woman who, though more important to her as her husband's mother than as the queen of England, was important as the queen of England nonetheless.

"Fredericka," the queen began, as dignified as ever, and now warm, "forgive my economy of words, that we received the two of you separately, and that I have used that unfortunate woman to dull by custom what is uncustomarily sharp."

The queen spoke with such extraordinary gravity that Fredericka said, "What is it, ma'am?" and moved closer.

"I'm dying," said the queen. "I found out just days ago that I shall probably not live another month. At least that is what they say. It's a secret. Your father knows, two doctors, the PM, and now you. We'll have to plan, for much remains to be done. In the short time I have left, I would devote myself to action rather than reflection. What a pity that in thinking of those I love and in taking leave of them, my heart, which was broken long ago, will break again and again in the weeks to come. Freddy doesn't know. His father will not tell him—cannot tell him. I would like you to do so, and I would like, my dear child, for there to be peace between us."

Fredericka had many faults and many virtues, but the greatest part of her, that overrode her failings where she had them and surpassed her brilliance where she had it, was her heart. And when the queen, who had closed her eyes briefly at the end of her words, opened them, she saw Fredericka, face contorted beautifully, cheeks and forehead scarlet, tears rolling quietly one after another like raindrops steadily falling from the edge of an eave, and landing amid her now glistening pearls and upon her grey suit, its wool soon mottled with dark spots.

"Don't cry," the queen said, as if to a child. "We must prepare Freddy to be king, and, if Craig-Vyvyan will fly, to remain so—with you by his side as his queen."

In her tears Fredericka was unable to speak. The queen was now assured that this lovely girl understood mortality and knew rank for what it was. This made the queen happy, though her happiness was necessarily subdued. She took Fredericka's hand. "You must help Freddy," she said, gently but with unquestionable determination. "Quite soon the world will become very difficult for him. I know, it happened to me. But don't worry, all will come right in the end."

WHEN FREDDY SAT DOWN after greeting his father in the study, he expected the conversation to turn to birds, horses, lubricants for carriage wheels, and perhaps even intra-Tory politics.

"How are you?" he was asked.

"Very well," he answered. He noticed that his father was wearing a rather threadbare suit that he had favoured for decades. It made him look like an academic or a railway worker.

"You're well?"

"Yes," Freddy answered. "And how are you? How are things?"

"Things? What things?" The duke assumed the position of a hunting dog.

"Things in general."

"Oh."

How distracted he seemed. Freddy thought it was because of his advancing age. He wasn't young, even if, as he might have said, once he had been. "Everything's going well, I presume?" Freddy went on.

His father put his hand to his forehead, resting his brow between his right thumb and index finger. "Some dogs ran away," he said with what seemed to be catastrophic sadness.

"From where?" Freddy asked, taking a huge Cuban cigar from a humidor next to his chair. "I like to pick them up, turn them over, and smell them," he said.

"Dogs?"

"Cigars. What about the dogs? Did you find them?"

"Yes, we found them."

"After how long?"

"Five minutes," the duke said. "Some dogs fled an unlatched gate. They were found near a garden shed."

"Are you all right?" Freddy asked.

"I'm fine. And you?"

"Splendid," said Freddy. Neither of them had yet said the word *fish,* even once.

In an awkward silence, Paul began to drum his fingers upon his desktop with increasing violence until Freddy thought that if the rate of increase held steady his father would become a parody of a drummer in a rock band. But suddenly he stopped, and brightened. "Would you like to see my study?" he asked.

"We're in your study," Freddy said, worriedly.

"No no," said the duke, waving his right hand in dismissal. "This one's a decoy."

"A decoy?"

"Yes. You've never seen my real study."

"What about Mummy? Has she seen your real study?"

"No one has, except people who are dead."

Not knowing what to say, Freddy asked, "Then who keeps it clean?"

"I do."

"You do?"

Pantomiming, Paul said, "With a mop and a broom. It's relaxing. I have a stove—it's off the heating systems—and I myself carry the logs and ashes."

"*You* do."

"Yes."

"What if something breaks, a window pane, for example?"

"I fix it. I have books. I have putty and glazier's points. I've done it. So as not to attract attention, I send out for the glass under the name of the Duke of Wellington."

"What do you do there?"

"Nothing much. Come, I'll show you." He stood.

"Why now?" Freddy asked.

The duke said, "There's something I would like to tell you," and motioned Freddy into the hall.

THEY WALKED to one of the rooms Freddy had usually bypassed throughout his life, a guest chamber for elderly female visitors that was decorated in a repulsive French turn-of-the-century motif. It had neither interesting objects, pleasing proportions, nor attractive views. Boxes for false teeth and pin-cushions had been left behind, and next to a doily-covered chair by the window a stack of magazines awaited anyone interested in feminine crafts, cats, and hideous porcelain figurines.

"I haven't been in here since the Duchess of Birdwood read me *Dr Dolittle* stories," Freddy said. "This isn't your study, is it?" Because his father was truly a man's man, stories to the contrary had circulated. Freddy had first been apprised of them by hooligans at his school as they piled on top of him and smashed his face with their fists. Though he had never believed them, he grew nervous when his father put his ear to the door, listened for footsteps in the hall, and turned the lock as quietly as a burglar.

"Of course it isn't," Paul said. "I know where you're going, Frederick, and if I were you I'd put a lid on it."

"Didn't Al Jolson stay in this room?" he asked.

"Yes, and so did Colette, Houdini, and Norman Mailer."

"Not all at the same time, I hope."

"No," his father confirmed. "They came in flights of two. I leave the rest to your imagination."

"But why are we in this room, Pater?" Freddy asked.

"I don't like it when you call me that. Sit down." He took out a pipe, filled it, and lit the tobacco. Freddy had loved the scent of his father's pipe since he could first remember. It calmed him. "What I'm going to tell you, Freddy, is not what I'm going to tell you."

"Then what is it?"

"It's different."

"Different," Freddy asked, "from what?"

"Different from what I'm going to tell you."

"But you are going to tell me."

"Yes, but not what I'm going to tell you."

"I see."

"When George the Third bought this place it was known as the Queen's House."

"Did you say *place,* or *palace?*"

"What's the difference? The point is, it has had a feminine cast since the beginning, probably even when it was a cow pasture. After all, cows are female, are they not?" Freddy looked puzzled, but his father's rhythm did not break. "George the Third was a down-to-earth fellow who hated royal claptrap. He understood perfectly well however that it was required if he were to rule, as Louis the Fourteenth had understood La Rochefoucauld's maxim, *Il faut usurper la déférence des autres,* and built the world's most luxurious birdcage, into which he lured so he could then detain them the nobles who otherwise would have prevented the unification of France. All this nonsense—the gilt, the whorls, the brocade, the huge palaces—as you very well know, serves a powerful political purpose, and always has."

"Yes."

"But we have found ways to get away from it, to pretend that we are normal human beings, to feel the friction and texture of life. We have our fishing places, our secret walks in the Highlands, our high altitude parachute jumps over Africa. George the Third had his ways as well. For him, it was the construction of a royal lair, from which Charlotte was barred. Nor, in fact, was anyone else allowed. Since it was built no one has been in it but the kings of England, Prince Albert, your father, and, to keep the knowledge of it alive, the male heirs to the throne, though it is not theirs to use until they are crowned."

"I've been in every room in this palace," Freddy said.

"No you haven't."

"When I was young, I was like water. I seeped into every cranny."

"Not this one."

"Since George the Third, no one has been in it but kings and consorts?"

"Yes."

"How is it maintained?"

"I told you. We maintain it. Because of that, it's rather rough hewn. We put our initials on everything we build or renovate. Your great-uncle was the best, a natural-born carpenter. I myself installed the stove, to replace a lesser one. I've swept the chimney, changed fittings, painted. All supplies and tools have to be spirited up there in the middle of the night. The rumours about me walking through the palace at four in the morning, covered in soot and hauling bags of rubble, are true."

"Where is it?"

"Above our heads."

"What does Mummy think about all this?" Freddy asked.

On his way to the wall, Paul said, "Given that she hasn't seen it, I think she's a bit jealous, although she puts on that she regards it as an 'I Hate Girls Club,' which, of course, it isn't."

"You don't take women there?"

"I don't take women anywhere, and I don't take anyone there."

Freddy assumed that they would leave the guest room and find their way to the lair by some other route, but Paul stood on his toes and extended his right hand to a rosette about seven and a half feet from the floor. The rosette was indistinguishable from those in its row.

"The shorter kings, I assume, had to stand on something. And God help us if this rather complicated mechanism fails. I'm sure I wouldn't be up to repairing it."

When Paul turned the rosette it released a weight that pulled up the panel beneath. Revealed was a tiny chamber with one narrow window, like a firing slit, that lit the grey stone. When Freddy was in, his father closed the panel. In front of them was a huge steel door. "You know the key on my watch chain?" his father asked.

"Is that . . . ?"

"It is."

"You never would tell me what it was for."

"But I told you that someday I would. You lost interest when you were about five."

After Paul opened the door, they found themselves at the foot of an iron staircase. Closing the door behind him, he said, "It's the best eighteenth-century locking mechanism, but insufficient by today's standards. I haven't got the wherewithal to install a combination lock, which is what should be here. Perhaps you or your successor will be able to. You could always sponsor a locksmithing school and spend a lot of time hanging about. I thought of that, but was too busy saving and killing hippopotamuses. Albert tried to put in a new lock, I believe, but it was beyond him and he must have turned his energies to the museum instead."

They advanced up many turns in spiral stairs within a stone shaft lit occasionally by the narrowest of slits. At the top was another steel door. Paul held the key for Freddy to see, even though it was so dark he could hardly make it out. "Here's the trick," he said. With his thumb he pushed the rear tooth of the key forward and detached it. "It's really two keys. When I die, if you haven't already ascended the throne—in which case I will have given it to you—it will be with me. Ask to be alone with the body. Take it then."

He put the modified key into the lock of the second door, turned the heavy eighteenth-century tumblers, and opened the way ahead.

FREDDY ENTERED FIRST, head tilted slightly upward, walking slowly so as to take it all in. There is a magic to well proportioned rooms. This one, though perhaps a hundred feet long by sixty feet wide and twenty high, seemed spacious rather than enormous. One of the longest spaces within the palace, it was on the highest floor and hidden by the clever device of blocked windows. Although it had four windows looking out upon London, on the outside were eight, four being windows with only black walls behind them. This scheme was carried on in the adjoining rooms in such a way as to confuse anyone on the outside as to which windows gave out from which rooms. And as this side of the palace was the site of the living quarters, no outside work or scaffolds were permitted without notice, allowing Paul to draw the curtains. As the room on one side of the lair had curtains of cream brocade, so did two of the lair's windows, and as the room on the other side had curtains of sage brocade, so did the lair's other two.

"Once," said Paul, "in fifty-six or fifty-seven, a chap who was cleaning windows poked his squeegee through one of the panes and dropped it. Lots of broken glass, terrible noise. Luckily, I was here. His hand followed, looking for the latch. Just as he had got hold, I grasped his wrist and gave him the squeegee. He never saw beyond the curtain. There was a clatter of boards and then the squeak of ropes moving through pulleys. I stood at the window, unseen, and remember it as if it were yesterday. 'Bloody hell, Hayfield! Did you see what I saw?' 'What are you about, Cliff?' 'It's 'im. The monkey! I'm finished with this floor, lower your end.' 'But that's the queen's bloody bath.' 'Better that than the monkey. He tried to pull me in!'"

"Where was Mummy?" Freddy asked.

Suddenly Paul turned away. "You know that Mummy loves you very much. She was at Sandringham. Lucky. She would have been in the bath, and she likes the natural light." He moved toward the far end of the room. "I'll start the fire," he said, his voice cracking slightly. "You take a look around."

"Do you realise," Freddy asked, "that this is the most beautiful room in the palace?"

"That's because it's the simplest," his father called out, "and because it's imperfect, having been awkwardly fashioned not by carpenters but kings. It has the inimitable beauty of the simple, the good, and the true. It is redolent with the fact that here the kings of England, for two centuries, could shed the burdens of royalty. Certainly, in their lives, God touched their souls, and where do you think that happened, on gilt thrones frozen by ceremony, or here, where the smoke doesn't quite draw as well as it should?"

Freddy had always loved the smell of old chimneys—especially in summer when currents of air sometimes sweetened the room unexpectedly. Here, for two hundred years, the smoke had left the life of the forest on every surface. It smelled much like the smoky interior of a stone croft on those islands in the north (where, when Freddy was a child, electricity had not yet come), and the scent carried him back.

The floor was of American heart–pine planks a foot and a half wide, a deep and lustrous auburn, waxed nicely by kings, with ebony-coloured knots, dents, and depressions made by centuries of stray embers that had fallen upon and branded the wood. The most beautiful rugs in the royal family's possession, of the thickest weaves, in pale red and beige with hints of blue culled from distant sky, were scattered over this floor, and the mill-work, decorative moulding, and fluted columns were the colour of parchment. The long interior wall, a hundred feet in extent by twenty high, held a paradise of books—not the brown archaeological relics in the library at Windsor, but books of all stations, in many bright colours, paper-bound as well, each of the highest quality.

Seeing Freddy dazzled by the wall of this gorge, his father said, with delight at divulging the secret, "I read, you know."

"Where are the dog magazines?"

"Don't slight dogs, Freddy."

"I thought that was all you read."

"Really? Are you so dense as not to realise that I cannot outshine your mother in any way, that I must always follow, that I'm mute for life, confined to a particular image of myself? Other than in regard to dogs, horses, lion skins, polo, yachts, and game reserves, the mouth is shut forever."

"You read? You mean, all those Latin and Greek phrases, the Russian and the German, you haven't just memorised them from a book?"

"Of course not. I know and have read extensively in those languages. I know Japanese, you silly twit."

"Japanese."

"I was in one of their prison camps for eighteen months. I would have had to have been a moron not to have learnt the language, wouldn't you agree? I exist," said Paul, splitting a fire log with an ancient hatchet, "in two worlds: one that you have known, and, the other, a prisoner's tight quarters that, nonetheless, open upon the widest spaces of the universe. Though standing still," he said, sweeping his arm to encompass the twenty thousand volumes, "I am able, like John Dee of Mortlake, to tour the universe and circle the stars."

Freddy surveyed the room. On the front and back walls were monumental paintings of such beauty and richness of colour that he was stunned. His expression was like that of a soldier who stands alone and unobserved as long columns of a still-armed enemy walk by in retreat: though he showed the joy of his good fortune, he maintained the stillness of a mouse. Above the fireplace was a Raphael, and on the wall opposite, a Bellini.

In the background of the Raphael, in one small corner, was a patch of silvery blue that took a divine ray of sun shining pale under a distant rim of gold. The painting was of a battle. "That's the biggest Raphael in all the world," Freddy said.

"And the best."

Freddy's eyes swept over the ladders on tracks of dulled brass; the marble busts and friezes as smooth and flawless as cream; the racks of weapons, some ancient and others stacked during the war, for the king's stand had Hitler reached England with more than bombs; the leather-inlaid tables and desks; the saddles and boots; the maps on easels; the seraphim of Grinling Gibbons; the Turner in the corner; the magnificent replica of *Repulse;* Newton's apple itself, withered into mystery; and so on. It was as wonderful a place as Freddy had ever seen.

He joined his father, who sat on a huge hearth of honed slate, staring into the fire he had just lit and watching it take. "The main drawback here," Paul said, "is the lack of heat. In winter it can get extremely cold. That's why the sofas and desks are bunched up somewhat ungracefully at this end of the room. When it's really cold, I nap on the slate, which after three or four hours of a fire has warmed nicely. Get us a drink."

Freddy went to a campaign table upon which half a dozen different single malts stood amid rows of crystal glasses. He chose the Laphroaig because the room with its grandeur was yet like a little house on a Scottish isle. He asked why so many glasses, and the answer was that they looked beautiful when the light played on them—better than diamonds, which reflect too promiscuously and too sharply. The crystal kept as much as it gave, and, in keeping its splendour, took on the quality of warmth.

Paul, it seemed, thought upon the light and followed it for what it did. Freddy had simply not known. Nor did he know at this moment that his father had taken him to this place not only for a practical reason of which Freddy was entirely unaware—which was that he would soon be called to the throne—but to anchor him once again in the world of royalty, lest in the democratic world he become unbalanced in his affections. As darkness fell, they stared into coals that glowed as red as Mars.

FACING THE FIRE, they were, like Englishmen for a thousand years before them, too hot in front and too cold in back. "This is better than central heating," Paul said, "because it's less comfortable."

"I quite agree," Freddy replied. "Central heating has taken the edge off civilisation."

"The question is whether one would want civilisation, as it is now constituted, to have an edge."

"Good point."

They talked in the firelight until they saw and heard things in the darkness that normally they did not perceive. They heard ocean-like murmurs of oblivion, of the abandoned past, of things and people carelessly forgotten, and it kept them still. Within the dimensionless world where they had gone, amidst the sounds of Roman hammers on Roman anvils, of Scottish oats waving in a summer wind of the fifteenth century, of hawsers squealing against the gunwales of the fleet that waited to meet the Spanish Armada, of the click of Arkwright's million gears, of steam whistles, and of the ghostly radar beams bouncing from approaching bombers of the Luftwaffe . . . amidst all this and the void in which it was set, they remembered still that the queen and Fredericka would be waiting for them to go to dinner in half an hour, and that Paul was supposed to tell Freddy something.

"What are you going to tell me?" Freddy asked as Vercingetorix (the man) crossed the space in front of his eyes, with battle-axe and horned helmet, his clothing of skins floating upon his body as weightless as Ophelia's water-borne dress.

"You had to know sometime," said Paul.

"Know what?" asked Freddy.

Thinking he was being asked a rhetorical question, Paul asked, "What?"

Thinking he was being asked to repeat himself, Freddy said, "Know what?"

"What?"

"What do I have to know sometime?"

"You have to know—it's only fair—what happened to you as a child."

"I do know, in general."

"Yes, but you don't know of something quite unusual, that may have made you what you are."

"I'm not adopted, am I?" Freddy asked.

"Of course not. You've got my ears and your mother's nose."

"You dropped me on my head."

"Yes, we dropped you on your head. We dropped all our children on their heads, but that isn't what did it."

"Did what?"

"Made you a little . . . off, Freddy."

"A little off?"

"Most people don't bathe sixteen times a day."

"I rather think it's a virtue," Freddy said, meaning to bathe sixteen times a day, which he did when he could.

"Most people, when interviewed by the BBC, do not howl like a hyena and laugh until they cannot breathe."

"It's just that they're so correct. That's what did it the first time, and ever since then I've tried desperately not to laugh and simply cannot control it. I used to be able to last ten or fifteen minutes. Now, when they say, 'Good evening,' I'm done. The more they look at me in wonder, the more I must laugh. I adopted the trick of howling like a hyena to choke off the laughter, but it works only intermittently. It's really your fault, for not being able to suppress the BBC full hour's special of me laughing. What kind of television is that?"

"Freddy, it's not my fault. And it's not yours, either."

Freddy was now alarmed.

"When you were eighteen months of age, your mother and I took you to Africa. . . ."

Freddy's gaze fixed upon the grizzled duke.

"Your mother had not become queen, and thought that decades might pass before her father's death. We lived then almost like real human beings. The press was not so invasive. We could actually go places without paralysing the life in them. We could actually meet and talk to people and watch as they warmed to us and forgot who we were. We loved this, and, naïvely, we thought it would go on forever. You always think things will go on forever, and they never do.

"In Africa, we stayed so long in a hunting lodge on the plains beneath Kilimanjaro that the locals forgot we were there and England forgot we were gone. We wore nothing but bush clothing, and your mother, who was young and beautiful, was sunburned and rosy-coloured all the time. That was before we knew that the sun isn't good for you. It seemed awfully good for us, I'll tell you that. We had so much life, Freddy, and you were the perfect child. Sometimes we would sit, just the three of us—Sydney was with the queen—and listen to the darkness and feel the heat. Life has never been better, not for me anyway. I knew even at the time; I appreciated it, and I still do.

"One day, having gone out in a jeep to look at one of the great herds of wildebeest, we left you in your carrier on the ground as we observed. We were so excited that we climbed up into the back of the jeep to get a better look. Certainly we checked every now and then, as one does, but then a group of elephants charged through the wildebeest and, I suppose, more time passed than we realised. When next we looked, you were gone."

"I was gone?"

"You can imagine our distress. Without breath, I scanned all around, and to my horror I discovered that, a hundred feet or so distant, you were being carried away by a huge baboon."

"Not!" Freddy exclaimed. "I was raised by baboons!"

"No, Freddy, it was worse than that."

"Worse? What worse? How could it be worse?"

"I picked up my scoped Enfield. Your mother was hysterical and my heart was beating wildly, but I knew that in hand-to-hand combat I was no match for the baboon, and that anyway you could easily have been ripped apart in the struggle. I had to drop the baboon. I had no choice. It was the most difficult shot imaginable, for the baboon carried you in an embrace that gave me no room to miss."

"You shot me?"

"No, Freddy, worse."

"I don't know if you should tell me. Perhaps you really shouldn't tell me."

"I think I should."

"Go ahead."

"I took that shot, and managed it. The baboon fell in its tracks. You rolled away unharmed. Philippa and I jumped down from the jeep and ran toward you. But, before we could get there—and, unfortunately, I was in such a rush that I had left the Enfield in the jeep—before we could get to you. . . ."

"What!"

"You were seized by a Broom-Tailed Ignatz."

"I was seized by a what?"

"A Broom-Tailed Ignatz."

"What is a Broom-Tailed Ignatz? Is this true?"

"If you don't believe me, look in the encyclopaedia: third shelf, behind the bust of Harold the Invincible."

Freddy rose, dashed into the darkness, and rushed back with a volume in hand.

"That's the nineteen seventy-eight edition. Go to the nineteen eleven."

Soon Freddy was back, riffling in the firelight through the pages of the magnificent 1911 *Britannica: "Brooks; Brooks's; Broom; Broome, William; Broome-Rape; Brosch?"*

"Look under *Ignatz*," his father told him.

Then he was back again, with volume 14: *"Iglau; Iglesias; Ignatiev; Ignatius; Ignatz, Broom-Tailed."* He paused, looked up hopelessly, and read: "'Savage animal found in the mountainous regions bordering the Rift Valley, the Serengeti Plain, and the Masai Steppe in East-Central Africa. First mentioned by Pliny as *Insanus vector,* the Broom-Tailed Ignatz is a buff-coloured, chicken-like, semi-canine mammal that, nonetheless, lays eggs and swims like an amphibian. A tubular jaw supporting fine rows of shark-like teeth and joined by the huge tendons of the neck to tiger-sized back muscles enables the Ignatz to seize and rip prey, although it is not an agile fighter. Its prime source of food is the baby ostrich, and it sometimes raids the domesticated livestock of native kraals. Alone among mammals, the Ignatz is equipped with a venom sac and a single hollow fang. Entering the flesh, the gross mandibular fang, because of its large diameter, enables the quick injection of venom. In the Ignatz's customary sources of food, the venom paralyses. In rare cases, when humans have been bitten, the venom induces a'"—Freddy paused, looked at the darkness swirling above him, closed his eyes, and said—"'lifelong insanity.'" He reeled.

"It's worse than that, much worse, I'm afraid."

"What, I was raised by the Ignatz?"

"No. We snatched you away. You were alive. My goodness how you cried."

"You would have, too, had you been bitten by a Broom-Tailed Ignatz."

"No I wouldn't have."

"How do you . . . oh no."

"Yes. He bit me as I snatched you from him."

"Did he bite Mummy, too?"

"He bit her canteen, and then disappeared into the bush."

"But that's it, isn't it? It's no worse than that?"

"Worse."

"Not."

"Worse."

"How could it be?"

"In the camp where we were staying was a doctor—a Pole or a Romanian or something like that: sometimes I don't know the difference. Naturally, when we came roaring in, blowing the horn, everyone ran out, including Dr Lupo—Dr Milhasz Lupo. An English doctor was hours away, so we had to give ourselves over to his care."

"What did he do?"

"He *seemed* well qualified."

"What did he do?"

"He transfused our blood."

"Mine and yours?"

"No. We were both bitten."

"Mummy's?"

"No, she was the heir to the throne. You wouldn't want to have filled her up with Ignatz-treated blood, would you?"

"Whose blood, then?"

"Motta Motta's."

"Who?"

"Motta Motta, the local witch doctor—a quarter of a tonne."

"You mean, we don't have royal blood? We have witch-doctor blood?"

"Yes, but that wouldn't be a problem. He was a kind of royalty, and they're as strong as lions, those Masai. Noble people."

"But there was a problem."

"I'm afraid so."

"What problem?" asked Freddy, drained of reaction.

"Dr Lupo had no way of knowing this, but it seems that Motta Motta had been bitten by Broome-Tailed Ignatzes half a dozen times. That's why he was such a good witch doctor. After the operation, he calmed down considerably. Our blood had been only a hundred proof, but we ended up with his, at six hundred. Of course, there's no way of knowing how the Ignatz venom will affect you. Since then, I myself have been almost totally sane. But, you. . . ."

Freddy finished the last of his Scotch. He laughed a slightly deranged laugh, and asked, "Is this true?"

"I'm afraid, my dear boy, that it is."

"What am I supposed to think?"

"Think nothing of it."

. . .

IMMEDIATELY UPON coming in to dinner, Freddy had noticed that his mother seemed wan and distracted. And when she greeted him, her eyes filled with tears. This he took for her usual disappointment. Knowing that the blood that had run in his veins since his infancy had predisposed him to the controversial incidents in his life that had led others to doubt his stability, he understood her distress. Thus defeated by his very blood, or lack of it, he was uncharacteristically silent. Although he did not know why, so was Fredericka. So was the queen, and so was Paul, who breathed like a fish.

No one touched the hors d'oeuvres. The queen said, "All my life I've loved this salmon that the gamekeepers smoke—all my life. How many times and in how many settings I have eaten it I do not know, but I think that for the moment just the memory of it will be enough. It's very strange, and I don't understand it, but I now find more satisfaction in abstaining than I do in partaking."

As they took their seats, Freddy looked at the menu. "Shish-kebab?" he asked. "Goat curry?" He read the card. "Rawalpindi fruit ice?"

"To celebrate your return," the queen said.

Freddy knew that his mother detested what his father referred to as "wog chow," and he was therefore baffled. "Shish-kebab?" he asked again.

"Yes," the queen said, in a slightly tremulous voice. "Did you enjoy it?"

"I haven't eaten it yet."

"When you were away."

"I don't think we ever did, did we, Fredericka?"

Staring down, Fredericka moved her head back and forth. Her brassy tresses looked like something in a shampoo commercial.

"I suppose their cuisine is quite international now," the queen said.

"It is," said Freddy.

"But when we were there," Philippa continued, "we had it time after time—lamb, goat, mountain burunya."

"You did?" Freddy asked.

"Oh, yes. And cucumbers in sheep's milk yoghurt. Curries even for breakfast. Not my idea of eating."

"Well," said Freddy, "now they have these things called Egg McMuffins, and another oddity, Cheez Doodles. Although I actually like their Cheez

Doodles, frankly, I don't see how they, as a people, have accomplished all they have accomplished on such a diet."

"What have they accomplished?" Paul asked. "They're just a bunch of fly-chewing wogs."

"You may say that, but this year they've won twice as many Nobel Prizes as the nearest competitor."

"They have?" the queen asked. "No one told me."

"They invented the electric light, and the transistor."

"Freddy, that's what they may say, but everyone knows the electric light was invented by Geoffrey Deakin."

"I know you believe that, but, really. They are to this day the only people, among all the peoples of mankind, who have walked on the Moon."

"In their imaginations."

Freddy was astonished. "No, Maman, you know that it's true. Don't tell me that in my absence you've joined the looney left."

"Don't be silly, Freddy," Paul said. "Since they've been on their own they haven't had a pot to piss in. I say to hell with them. They were a drain in the first place. If they want to run around all the time in bedsheets, knifing and stabbing Europeans, that's their problem."

"But Pah-Pah," said Freddy, quite offended, "they came to our rescue in the two world wars."

"Little New Zealand did a hell of a lot more," Paul stated crisply.

"New Zealand?" Freddy asked, stressing each syllable. "That's ridiculous. Without their industrial base, we'd all be Germans now—well, real Germans."

"Oh Freddy, Freddy," the queen said, staring at her plate, pained and disappointed. "They helped us, dear, but it was only a drop in the bucket. That dreadful man who led them—of course, they were all Indians then—had conversations with Hitler."

"Franklin Roosevelt?"

"No," the queen said, rather sternly, "Hitler."

"What do you mean, 'They were all Indians then'? In the Second World War?"

"Ninety percent," Paul said, authoritatively.

"No no no," Freddy said, laughing. "Indians made up only one or two percent."

"And who made up the rest, Freddy?" his father demanded.

"The largest group was of English descent . . ." he began. Paul shook his head in horror, but Freddy continued, "and then, after that, Italians, I believe."

"Italians?" the queen asked. "Italians?"

"Yes, they and masses of Eastern Europeans came in a tremendous wave of immigration"—Freddy could hardly believe that he had to tell them this, and imagined that perhaps they had been drinking—"at the turn of the century. You know."

"No, we don't know."

"Yes. That's why they have so much frozen pizza and everyone knows a few words of Yiddish."

"Freddy," Paul said, "you seem not to be able to tell the difference be-tween the United States and Pah-kiss-tahn."

"I bloody well can, it's you who can't."

The queen was near tears. "We had thought that during your trip you might have straightened things out somewhat, mentally."

Freddy held up his left hand, like a constable stopping a stream of traffic. "Wait a moment," he said. "Our trip where?"

"Pah-kiss-tahn," the queen stated.

"Not Pah-kiss-tahn," Freddy told her. "America."

"Yes, Freddy, we are aware that you stopped in America on your way home. I hadn't wanted to bring this up, but you know it's worse than bad form to use our position to interfere in their politics."

"It wasn't position, it was ability. They thought I was an Indian."

"Let's not get on to that again. Whatever it was, you should have come directly home, over the Pole."

"Mummy, we almost succeeded. It's hard to believe that you won't credit us for that. We almost did it." He looked at Fredericka affectionately.

"Did what?" asked Philippa.

"Reacquired the lost colonies."

"In two weeks?" the queen asked.

"In more than a year, and what a year it was."

Paul leaned forward. He was very serious. "Freddy, you haven't been gone a year, you've been gone two weeks. You went to the hot springs in Bush Nalore. You were to take the cure after you were thrown from your horse at Windsor. Don't you remember?"

"Merlin put you up to this, didn't he."

"Merlin?"

"Yes, *Mr Neil*. It's a simple anagram. What was that all about? The meeting in the chapel at Windsor, the sex toy factory in Naples? Quite frankly, I didn't like him. He was presumptuous."

"Do you mean the gardener, Frederick," the queen inquired, "Mr Beal, who found you after you'd been thrown?"

"Mr Beal? What did he do?" Freddy asked.

"He brought you in, in his hay wagon."

"Was he in the chapel?"

"No, Freddy, and neither were we." When the queen said that, it was clear that she believed she hadn't been.

Freddy didn't know what to do. He looked at Fredericka, who shuddered slightly, in the universal gesture that means "drop it."

"Oh!" said Freddy. "It must have been . . . the wind."

"Yes," Fredericka added, speaking for the first time since dinner began, "it must have been . . . the wind."

"Perhaps it was the wind," said the queen, as resigned as a queen can be. "And it is the wind that must lift the wings of Craig-Vyvyan."

LATE THAT NIGHT at Moocock, Freddy and Fredericka took refuge in themselves. They locked the door of the bedroom, turned off all the lights, closed the curtains, stripped, and lay under the covers pressed one against the other, hearts racing.

The wind whistled outside, their breathing seemed to echo in the room, and in the cool of the pitch black, things that had once been lights seemed to turn like galaxies. He did not tell her about his suspect infancy, having decided to wait until morning, and she did not tell him about Philippa, having decided the same. All they had was their strong embrace. "I don't know which is you and which is me," he stated.

"You never do," she replied. And then, after a pause, she said, "We're insane, aren't we, Freddy?"

"Yes."

"Both of us."

"It appears that way. At least we both think that we've been in America for more than a year, even if the rest of the world thinks we've been in Pah-kiss-tahn for two weeks eating shish-kebab at a hot spring."

"I hate shish-kebab," she said, kissing him.

A minute later, he said, "I don't mind it, but we *were* in America."

A very long time later, in a trance of heat and darkness made all the more lovely by the cool air above the coverlet, she said, "Even if we are insane, we keep on coming closer together."

PHILIPPA

THE QUEEN FAILED to confound her doctors and live on into the spring as she had hoped, and made good on their prediction that she would not see the end of November. To hear a death sentence pronounced with helpless certainty by someone clearly on the side of life was a sad and crippling thing, and when they said that she would not survive, for her husband and children the words were like blows to the face or arrows in the heart.

She was the queen of England, and she had the best possible care in even the tiniest detail. Not only was nothing done that should not have been done, and everything accomplished that was necessary, each action or abstention was decided not instantaneously but in long debates in which the pursuit of exactitude was exhausting and reassuring. Her physicians checked and rechecked. They spent days and nights in medical libraries and at their computers, determining as far as possible the best dosages and most likely outcomes. They spared nothing in their attempts to make the imprecise precise, to attend to the patient, and to defend her from death, their duty not only as her physicians but as her subjects.

As covertly as anything had ever been done in England, a suite in the palace had been converted to a laboratory and treatment facility. The medical personnel were sworn to secrecy, as were the palace staff, and the chemotherapy was administered at night or during household shift changes. Despite all their efforts, not one of the specialists believed that the sum of what they did or any part of it would allow her a single extra day.

She was used to the throne and comfortable as monarch. Even the prospect of death could not pry her from that. As gracefully as a leaf upon surface tension, she floated through diplomatic receptions and tedious ceremonies. Though she had always hated the vapid conversation of royalty-struck interlocutors whose hearts beat as fast as hummingbirds', now she seemed to appreciate every meaningless word, every notification about the beauty of this or that city, every stupid curtsey and bow, every pronouncement that "You wouldn't remember, ma'am, but we've met before," to which she now replied charitably, and as sincerely as if it were true, "I do remember. I remember your face. How kind of you to consider how many people I must greet."

The ambassadors, so often people ill equipped for their role, seemed most interesting to her, and she would ask them all kinds of questions about the sunshine in their countries, the flowers, the birds, and the waters. More often than not, this would put them at ease, and as they spoke she would see every bird, every flower, the mountains, and the surf— especially the surf. A beatific expression would come over her such that for the rest of their lives the ambassadors would remember—and tell their children and grandchildren of—her exceptional tranquillity.

Though the queen's grace in public increased to the point where it seemed unimaginable that she would depart, she knew that she would, and it made her more graceful yet.

IN ONLY WEEKS, she came fully to terms with what awaited her. Very little that people seek and value seemed to please her, but what they pass by and take for granted she fastened upon not to savour but, as a child does, in discovering it. In late October she ordered the gardeners to burn leaves. They protested, warning about the certain fine. "Pay the fine," she said simply, "but burn the leaves."

As the smoke rose she walked about the palace gardens in hope of collisions with its ribbons and clouds that drifted through hedges and trees, and when she did disappear in white smoke she would breathe in, close her eyes, and return to her girlhood, when she was very young and did not expect to become queen. The scent of burning leaves took her back to gardens where she was loved, before she understood the concept of royalty, and when she presumed that what she had and what she knew would go on forever.

The gardeners, who did not know of her illness, were struck by her slow walk, by how often and how long she walked alone, and by the extraordinary sight of the queen of England, on her knees, thrusting her hands into a flower bed, lifting the loam close to her face, and smelling it as appreciatively as if it were tea. They even saw her cup her hand, draw some water from the fishpond, and taste it. To them this seemed insane, but, to her, to taste the brackish, dirty water full of life of all kinds was a better thing than to taste Champagne.

She stared at objects closely; not as if seeking answers but rather as if she were learning the new vocabulary, new shapes, and new colours of a new world. It was apparent that she was beginning to cast off her lines, that this was something that had come to her as a gift of nature, that she was indeed preparing for another world or the lack of it, and had changed. Her family suspected that she was coming to know things they could not even imagine, or at least they hoped so. She seemed pleased and tranquil so often, and would relaxedly stare at clouds and sky, or at a pool of light beneath a lamp, or a vase of moist red roses, not merely to help her by association to plumb the past, but for a reason more wonderful. The things that made her happy when she looked at them, and filled her with a secret joy, she took not merely as signs and symbols everlasting, but as emissaries.

Needless to say, no one could follow her to such places and in such spaces as she went, but she elevated everyone around her, not least Freddy, who despite his fear was forever changed by the fact that she was not afraid.

"You don't fear," he observed, when they were alone together on a surprisingly warm day early in November, and the sun streamed through the high windows.

Slowly, she turned her head, and smiled.

"How can you not?"

"Freddy," she said, "the water has risen and the painter has slipped. All is lost, but everything is buoyant. I feel much as I did as a small child—close to something that gives me absolute comfort."

"God?" asked Freddy.

"Yes," she answered. "Not the God I have come to know, but the God that I knew before I knew what God was, before I knew language, before I knew His name."

HAVING A GREAT DEAL of jewellery, perhaps more than anyone in the world, Philippa was aware that lucidity and transcendence must be set in a foil that is opaque. It was important to her to carry on, to take care of her affairs, and to prepare Freddy for the responsibility to which Craig-Vyvyan's flight might set the seal after Freddy had become king and before his coronation. This involved many hours of practical advice concerning what was in the dispatch boxes, dealing with foreign heads of state, and the extent of and necessity for royal influence on the governance of Britain.

Freddy had his own ideas, and most of what the queen said slid right by. This was the way it had to be and always had been. Were he to be king, he would have to be his own king. His reading of history would bring him—indeed, had brought him—general principles. Her particular experience as a monarch was unprecedented, but being particular, it would not be repeated. Besides, almost since his birth, he had been studying how she got along. Because her life had been exemplary and clear, he saw no need for further instruction.

He was curious, however, about mysteries. What had really happened to the princes in the Tower? Did monarchs hand down the secret from one to another? Yes, they did, and she let him in on it. Other secrets, too, astounded him. Mrs Thatcher had not been the first woman to be prime minister. Amazingly, Harold Wilson was actually a woman from a small village in Romania. And Britain had discovered a scientific principle that enabled it to build weapons of a power many magnitudes greater than that of nuclear weapons, but the secret had been purposefully suppressed. However, a coded key to it was in a bit of microfiche in the setting of a particular jewel in the sceptre. Even then, one had to know an elaborate series of numbers to release the information. This was written on the back of a floor tile in Paul's bathroom. Yet another code was necessary, which could be teased from the arrangement of numbers on the licence plates in the garage of the royal dollhouse at Windsor. And the proper sequence of these numbers was to be found written in invisible ink on page ten of Philippa's first edition of Nina Salaman's *History of the Potato*. Freddy went to page ten with an ultraviolet light and discovered that the motorcycle plate was first, and then he deliberately shut his eyes. A lot of this kind of thing went on in the last few weeks. It was then that Freddy asked her again about Merlin. The way he brought it up was neither original nor diplomatic.

"What about Merlin?"

"What of him?"

"Either he cast a spell to make you forget what happened, or he cast a spell to make me imagine that it did."

"Merlin the magician?"

"He."

"I don't think so, Freddy. He's been dead a rather long while, you know."

"No he hasn't. He's always about. He was John Dee of Mortlake. He was Isaac Newton. He was Professor Lindeman. Churchill, of course, was Arthur. And Merlin has been God-only-knows how many countless others. We met him, you and I. He sent me to America. He has simply made you forget. Or I'm insane."

The queen had the look of distress and anguish that she had whenever Freddy had done what he called "unconventional things." He had known it even as a child, when, for example, he had had unstoppable fits of laughter on serious occasions. One newspaper headline of the nineteen fifties had read: "St. Paul's Filled with High-Pitched Simian Screams for Ninety Minutes as Prince of Wales Laughs Uncontrollably Through Investiture of Archbishop Spatoola."

"Perhaps," he said to his mother, "it's the Ignatz."

"The what?"

"The Ignatz."

"What is the Ignatz?"

All the while as he told her she shook her head in contradiction. "I've never heard of an Ignatz," she said. "You were never bitten by an Ignatz. We never took you to Africa. Who told you all this?"

"Father. He was also bitten. He also has Motta Motta's blood flowing in his veins."

"Freddy, listen to me. Your father was never bitten by an Ignatz. He has had no transfusions."

"Are you sure?" Freddy asked.

"I'm positive."

"Perhaps it was just he who was bitten?"

"No."

"Why did he tell me, then?"

"He probably wanted to make things easier for you, to give your vexations a physical cause so you might better control them."

"But he showed me in the encyclopaedia."

"You do know," Philippa stated, "that he has a special encyclopaedia that he has been altering for decades. Using the printing press and bindery in the basement, he has remade the world according to his likes and dislikes. De Gaulle was never a chorus boy at the Folies-Bergère, and Ted

Heath did not work for a decade as a Maori gigolo on the South Island of New Zealand. Horses do not talk, Eisenhower's real name was not 'Dr Feelgood,' and your father has not won the Nobel Prize, neither the one for physics nor the one for the protection of hunting dogs."

"I don't understand anything any more," Freddy said.

"Freddy, a son never can understand his father. He isn't meant to. You're a man now. Soon you yourself will be a father, and a king, and we hope you will remain so. Don't worry about things that you simply cannot know. Let them fall back and recede like the foam pushed aside by the flanks of a ship. Leave them behind and let your heart power on."

FOR FREDDY, as long as she was alive, anything was possible and everything was bearable. It was as if he were protected from the coldness of an open sky by the great overhead vault of a cathedral. It was she who had been steadily fixed between him and the iciness of the stars, and had sheltered him from the heart's knowledge of what could not be borne. No matter what he knew and what was apparent, he could not imagine that the woman who had brought him to life would actually die. And then, one day, she did.

It seemed inappropriate that it was a soft, spring-like day. Although the flowers were not in bloom, the gardens of Buckingham Palace were a rich green and filled with sweet smells and warm breezes. The sun burned hot and yellow, a disk of brass revolving in the wind. It was the kind of day, few and far between, when the world is given the chance to start over, when the sick are healed, the weak made strong, and the cowardly made unafraid. What sadness, then, that on this day the queen was not allowed to begin anew, and had instead to leave forever the earth, air, and sea.

By her deathbed her elder son sat or knelt, overcome with grief and fear, occasional glances at the mild blue sky filling his heart with the incorrigible and regretted happiness of being alive, unbelieving that his mother, whose hands and arms were already as cold as the chrome rail of the bed, was going to leave him.

She no longer spoke, but when she could she had told him that they had at last come to the garden wall, beyond which only she could glimpse the world in which she would float up to the light, no longer a queen, no longer imprisoned by the fact of being royal, and that on this day they would be just a family, their privacy finally granted. It would be the second time she would surrender her life, the first being when the crown was lowered gently upon her head. "It had the effect," she said, her frailty slowing her speech as it did her breathing, "of freezing me in place. They will never understand, as they will never be us, that we live like soldiers who sacrifice their lives for king and country. They have granted us our privileges so that they need not be troubled by this sacrifice, and these we have accepted purely from distraction. You'll be a better soldier than I've been, Freddy. Men are harder by nature, born for this. When I understood for the first time that someday I would be queen, I cried. When they told me that my father had died, and I would be queen from that moment, I cried as well. And when I was crowned, I cried again. I wanted then to get on a boat and drift away—and now I have my chance. All our lives, we are held apart from others. But there comes a moment when we are not. Royalty is a contrivance of man, and I have lived within that contrivance for most of my life. Though I have always wanted to leave it, I must admit that at times I did love it, such as when the rain washed the stains from the gold on the gates of the palace, and they blazed back at the sun as if to say, *This is the house of a queen.*"

Being inexperienced, Freddy thought that she was about to die. He looked at her for a long, breathless moment until he realised that she was only sleeping, and doing quite well. In dying there are long declensions and there are stretches when one is not dying at all and the body seems to strengthen, until a message from somewhere most compelling bids it look over the crest of a heart-dropping hill and start down once again out of control and despairing of equilibrium.

As Freddy sat by his mother's bedside while she slept, the monarchy seemed stripped away, diminished, and reduced to nothing in light of his love for her. And yet he felt the monarchy also throbbing with life and rising to glorious proportions. The less he knew it to be, the greater it seemed. That it could have survived a thousand clarifying deaths, that it remained, so stubbornly, after those who made it had gone, forced him to see it in a new and admirable light even as it was diminished. Caught in such a cross fire, he was powerless. He had the distinct impression that something was happening, as if a wheel that had turned many times before was turning again, and that he was not actor but object. The primacy of family and the inescapability of death, both of which made monarchy look small, were as well its two great pillars, and as force drained out of it, force was flowing in. It was like the lock of a canal, in which the draining of one chamber lifts the boat in another, and the chamber that has been emptied is refilled by an ever-flowing stream.

With Philippa slipping away, speaking as beautifully and tenderly, perhaps, as George III, who believed that he conversed with angels, Freddy felt the world realign. He had been the end of a miraculous process, the promise of the future, the heir, and now he was moving to the middle rank, where he would be merely a custodian waiting his turn to depart. The miracle and heir was Fredericka's unborn child. Although the power and whatever glory was left in the throne would be his, now he could not help but be as sober as his mother, with a full understanding in his heart of what was to come and what was demanded of him.

"I did not abdicate," Philippa had told him not long before, while she lay in the bed in which she was now dying, "because of your father. It was difficult enough for him to be the husband of the monarch. To have been overshadowed by his son before my death would have been intolerable. And I did not abdicate because, to be a king, you must know . . . this."

"Know what, Mother?" Freddy had asked, too quickly.

"This," she repeated, with angelic calm.

All the while that he had been desperately thinking, comforted and afflicted equally by memory and regret, the sun had run its unvarying course and paused for nothing and no one, and now it was nearly dark. The newly cold air fell to the ground, displacing warm air laden with the perfumes of the grass, and this scented air invisibly unrolling and unfurling in the dusk now came through the windows.

Upon realising that several hours had passed, Freddy went to his mother. She breathed weakly and fast. When he kissed her, she opened her eyes and looked at him with such an otherworldly tranquillity that he knew she had begun to rise from her body. He could sense the slow but unmistakable progress of ascension. The lines had been cast off, as she had said, and he could almost make them out trailing gracefully like the weightless things they were. He told her that he loved her, and that he would get the others.

Then, concentrated and determined, he left to tell them that she needed them right away. The steps from her bedside to the door seemed like the distance between the stars, and by the time he opened the door, he could not speak.

The doctor passed Freddy on the way in, and Freddy, unable to say anything—for now he realised that he had seen her die, and that he had known it, and not known it—simply stood in place, tears falling silently from him, his world in full collapse.

Paul dropped his head to his chest. With his left hand, he hit his right shoulder. Freddy's brother and sister wept. Now they were just a family, whose mother had died. They went in. Freddy would never understand how he had had the strength to turn. He would have no memory of how he had moved himself from facing one way to facing another, but he had, and, somehow, he and they had come into the room where Philippa lay.

The doctor was bent over her, with the understandable curiosity and efficiency of a physician making this, the last of determinations. It was his job, and he did it gently but fast. When he finished, he disengaged his stethoscope, let it clasp around his neck, and straightened.

He was an old-fashioned man, and the long history of Britain ran through his heart and his mind. A loyal subject, he acknowledged the others, and looked directly at Freddy. And then, bravely, but with great emotion, he said, "The queen is dead. Long live the king."

Craig-Vyvyan and Coronation

ANY ESTEEM in which Freddy had been held by the public after Philippa's death quickly vanished during her funeral in Westminster Abbey. Hearts primed for sympathy, all of Britain and a great deal of the world saw an extraordinarily self-contained new king whose expression revealed nothing. This was no longer the way even of the English, who had come to love public display of emotion. Still, the fleet of crows and jackdaws that provided commentary to accompany the televised images drew out their viewers' disillusion and anger—for their stock-in-trade was prolongation—with the observation that perhaps Freddy was so distraught as to be dazed, and that he was undoubtedly overwhelmed by the prospect of being king and the possibility that, due to his chequered past, he might be called upon well before his coronation to give way in favour of his stable and boring younger brother.

For the first hour of the ceremony, the public vacillated between its views of Freddy the daft and Freddy the burdened, withholding judgement until some word, sign, or action would solidify opinion one way or another. This then came as Philippa's coffin was lifted by the prime minister and other unworthies and borne past the new king as he knelt in his pew.

How shocked the world was, from Stockholm to Peru, to see the casket float past a son who did not even look in its direction. This was unforgivable, and when the scene was replayed and analysed, close-ups of his face showed an unmistakable indifference, as if the coffin visible over his left shoulder did not hold the remains of the departed queen, his mother.

In newspapers and over the air, in living rooms and in the pubs, one commentator after another said more or less the same damning thing. *What kind of a king is he? What kind of a man is this former Prince of Wales? When his mother's coffin was borne past him, it was as if she were not in it.*

And, in fact, she was not. In a mystery for archaeologists a thousand years hence, who would wonder what had become of this millennial queen whose recorded burial place was false, the coffin lowered into the floor of the abbey held her weight in sandbags. Her family would go to their graves without mentioning Philippa's last deed, though for years to come they would catch each other's eyes—at stifling dinner parties or in royal ceremonies—and, in the triumphant smile that only the eye can smile, communicate to one another their delight at her escape.

IMMEDIATELY UPON her death, the family had been shepherded by their father into her sitting room. Numbed or weeping, they settled into chairs and sofas. Paul rested his head upon his hands. Everyone thought he would say nothing and that time would continue to pass grievously. But soon he raised himself in his chair and pulled a thick envelope from his jacket pocket.

"She wanted me to read this," he said, fielding his reading glasses, "to all of you. I don't know what it is."

He held one of her envelopes, sealed with her seal, and this he opened like a householder unveiling an electric bill. Inside was a slightly smaller envelope, also sealed, and a sheet of notepaper, from which he read: "'Only the immediate family should hear this. You must, all of you, agree to keep what follows with you forever, and never divulge it—even on your deathbeds, even to your beloved children. The beauty of a secret actually kept is how it purifies the heart that keeps it.

"'Make sure the doors are locked and that no one is listening. At this moment, your privacy will be respected, and no servants should be about. Freddy, now king of England, make a fire in the fireplace. As I write I can picture you, in your special way, cutting the kindling into beautifully hewn sticks, halving them, building a structure like a house, sweeping up the chips and shavings to light first. Never since you were a very young man have I seen you miss with the hatchet, and your force and judgement with it have given me comfort that eventually you would have the force and precision required of a king. I know that Craig-Vyvyan has yet to fly, and that you may not remain a king, but, Freddy, now you are one, so make this fire accordingly.'"

Paul looked up at his son, who moved toward the fireplace. They watched him as he followed his mother's command slowly and with the satisfaction that she was still speaking to him, and that, at a time when it felt as if things had come to an end, the act of building a fire would lead on. With each ring of the hatchet, the practical placement of the newly hewn sticks, and the elevation of split logs upon the structure Freddy had built, the grief of a small family had first begun to subside. When the new king was done with cutting the wood and building the fire, he heard his father say, "Light it." Freddy struck a match, staring for a moment into the flame. Then he touched it to the shavings, which were quickly transformed into light and smoke. The light had come as if from nothing, and the light and heat grew until the fire burned as the queen had commanded.

Freddy stayed at the hearth, his arms around his knees in the manner of a flexible adolescent. Fredericka went to join him. It was an extraordinary picture, the king and queen by the fire, both ordinary and blessed, in the full stream of life, powerless and waiting, as the bereaved husband read.

"'The fire is for burning this and the letter that follows after they are read. Now burn this and the envelopes, so that only the letter remains. And when you see them take flame, remember that life is short, and let nothing keep you from the truth. As I write in anticipation of death, I regret every moment that I could not stay steady in truth.'"

Paul cast the note and envelopes into the fire. The family watched in silence as the heavy paper momentarily resisted the flames, browned, was surrounded by a small storm of combustion, and then lost its substance as it rose up in bright yellow light on its way to somewhere beyond reach. He replaced his glasses and, holding the letter in a way that showed that he knew that it, too, would soon be gone forever, read the familiar and impressive script.

"'All my life, except when I was a very little girl, I have stayed at my station on behalf of Britain, the Empire, and the Commonwealth. Though accustomed to comforts and privileges, I would have preferred to do without them if that had been the price for escaping a life lived entirely according to the expectations of others. I believe that I have been put in this position by God—otherwise, how could I have got here?— and although one cannot say so these days, I believe in the divine right. I do not, however, find the system of aristocracy, with its thousands of prissy, rotted, and rarified layers, either justified or attractive. Fortunately and unfortunately, we are at the head of that system, and as a family we continually sink back into it, for, as there is only one sun, there can be only one monarch.

"'Many times, I have wished to abdicate, but in view of the last crisis of succession I could not, and stayed to make the best of it. Having served during the war and been relatively free before my father's death, I know enough of the world to understand how foolish it is for people to direct their curiosity, envy, and dreams at us. It is they who possess the wide world, not we, they who go freely beyond the garden walls, in a vast, rich, ever-changing hive, and we who are trapped in strange costumes and drafty rooms.

"'I find unbearable the thought of lying forever within a royal tomb and hearing for eternity, were I able, the murmur of tourists piecing out my epitaph. That would be like writing one's name on a blackboard twenty million times in a strange alphabet. I would prefer to avoid the indignity of serving as the bones in an architecture of momentary and superficial curiosity, although that is what the government and people will demand.

"'I would rather that you set me free, and have arranged that you may do so. When we were young, in a different era—unplasticised—your father and I spent several weeks on the island of St Rose in the Leewards. I was the heir to the throne, but as I had not ascended—and mightn't have—far less attention was devoted to me, and we could break from our escort and motor up into the mountains. This we did on more than one occasion, and, once, we found a river with a fall that had a deep pool at its foot, an hour from the road.

"'We forged through the brush, and when we arrived we were scratched and bleeding in hundreds of places, our clothes torn, sweat and dirt on our faces as if we were miners. But we were alone. The water washed us clean and cooled us, and the continuous sound as it thundered down brought us somewhere we had never been before and have not been since. We stayed there the whole day. We ate the fruit that hung on the trees and drank the water in which we swam. No palace and no luxury I have seen in my long life can compare.

"'It is, nonetheless, not where I have chosen to spend eternity. I do not wish to be taken up into the vines and fragrant soil of that place, and spread among the mangrove roots and the mud where the river flows into the sea. I would rather be in the sea itself, in the warm translucent glass of

waters that surround the island with blue and green. I am unusually familiar with sapphires and emeralds, but whereas in their purity these are cold,
the sea is not. They are still, and it moves. They are dead, and it is alive,
flowing without cease, and that is where I want to be, drifting free across
windblown waves, sparkling in the sun, riding the foam in storms, or
sleeping in the silence of the deep. If I may have it.

"'I knew upon my coronation that such rest would not be allowed to
me, so I have taken various steps, though you must take for me the last.
Soon after my coronation, I started the much resented practice of taking
on ancient chamberlains and other staff, and then, after a year or two of
their service, setting up their families upon their deaths. This was inefficient, frowned upon by the monsters of the Civil List, and apparently
without purpose, but it was excellent charity, and these old fellows, the last
of whom passed on fairly recently, connived with me and then took to
their graves the knowledge of what we had arranged.

"'Thus, you will find a simple pine box in the room next to the room
where my elaborate casket lies in wait. No one has been in that room and
no one knows what is there. The keys for each coffin are taped to the
upper left undersurface within the large drawer of the hunt table in my
study, the one where I keep books that are next to be read. In the pine box
you will find, for a Mrs Wicks—a maid long in my service who, needless
to say, never existed—a death certificate, cremation order, transport direc-
tive, etc. You will also find some bags of sand to weight the more elaborate
of the two coffins.

"'I know from experience that it is not too unpleasant to be near the
body of someone familiar even after the soul has departed. There is no
horror, but a comfort that comes of love. Know that even if my hand falls
like a semaphore, I appreciate now that you will carry me. It is my wish. I
trust you to honour it, and hope that swimming in the same sea in which
I will stay for the rest of time will be as satisfying for you as it is for me
to anticipate it here in England—which I love beyond measure—now
that, as I write, the leaves have fallen and are flattening beneath a cold
driving rain.'"

IT SEEMED TO FREDDY that the plane that carried the royal family ascended all the way across the Atlantic. Though they had reached cruising
altitude less than an hour after departure, still it felt as if they rose gradually

and without cease. He listened to the sound of the engine, and thought carefully upon it. It was an all-encompassing, wind-like roar that seemed somehow to be green (Freddy associated all words, sounds, ideas, and sights with other things, and was unable to exist for even a second without a flood of images that multiplied the glories and wonders of the world). He saw in his mind's eye the turbines spinning in a blur of jungle colours. That is what the frequency and pitches, combining, said to him. He knew that to keep the four turbines rotating, a thousand things had to go right, that forces, stresses, and chemical reactions by the trillion had to be disciplined to one purpose, and that as the plane lifted through the clouds its forward momentum contributed to the certainty of such things, overriding what might have been explosive anarchy.

He was the king of England now, and even though it did not know it, all England paused a little in his absence as his procession took him overseas. How many illustrations had he seen of the monarch proceeding with a train of splendid horses and retainers under flags as uncountable as wild flowers in a field? As a child he had watched from the royal train as it steamed through the countryside and people stopped, turned, and put down their tools, shielding their eyes from the sun, to salute the queen even when they could not see her. While the queen was on it, that train, trailing a lariat of white steam as it rushed north to Scotland or out to Bristol, was the centre of Britain, because the people had decided that it would be.

Freddy was born at the tip of an ancient, fast, and steady arrow that nonetheless was falling to earth. To stay steady upon it, he had to master the art of stillness, of doing nothing, of the unquestioning acceptance of the fate that had put him in such a position. It was hardly a coincidence that his life heretofore had been a study in waiting, for the job of the king was to be the unmoving centre of countless orbits. Immense power merely flowed through him, and was not his to exercise. The object of his life was to be the exemplar of restraint. Freddy thought to write a letter to the emperor of Japan, discussing this, but he then realised that neither he nor the emperor would ever write such a letter, that duty and restraint prevented it, but that, still, the emperor knew, and he knew, and that when they met they would not even allude to such a thing.

For hours Freddy stared out the window and down at the sea. Sometimes he saw ships, which from forty thousand feet seemed the size of paperclips, and he believed he could know, and perhaps he could, when they were British. No one interrupted him: not Paul, who might in other days have ordered him to read a particular article or chapter; not his sister, whose company he loved; not his brother, who had now to experience briefly some of the madness of being next in line; not the stewards and retainers, who dared not serve lunch until Freddy gave some sign that he was ready. When he had been the Prince of Wales, people interposed themselves to ask if he wanted a cup of tea, to tell him that such and such a person had arrived, to ask how he wanted his steak cooked. Not now: they did not know him yet, and were far more tentative—except for Fredericka. Only she could come to him without inhibition. Only she had not had to adjust to his elevation.

Paul watched her as she settled into the seat next to Freddy, and was moved, for he remembered how he had been the only person in the world who could sit in comfort and nonchalance next to Philippa. He had been the only one who could sneak up behind her and grab her waist so as to tickle her into an explosive shriek. To see Fredericka, in her extraordinary grace and beauty, next to the king, his son, made him feel that all things were rightly taking their place.

How miraculous, in the modern age, that the eternal beauties were not overwhelmed. The plane roared quietly through ragged skeins of cloud pressed into slipstream and contrail, the pale blue patches of sky pulsing through gates of mist. West of the Gulf Stream the aircraft wheeled south, mitres of sunlight tracking across the cabin floor like a moving compass card. Everything west and to the right was America, a solid line where the sea stopped at the coastal plain in a purplish haze two thousand miles long. Freddy turned to Fredericka and took her right arm. In anticipation of the warm air of St Rose, she was wearing a sun dress, and her arms and shoulders were bare. He kissed her hand, and looked back out the window. Then, turning to her once again, he said, "We made only one thin line perpendicular to that coast, and it went three thousand miles deep. Imagine how many more we could have made along the entire length, and think of the power and rhythm of the ceaseless turning of that country, like a great engine, its cities jewelled bearings, their lights and fires shining like beacons into space."

She nodded, for she had seen it.

"I'm glad we were there," said the king, and for the more than two hours that they flew parallel to the purple coast, he did not take his eyes from it.

FOR BANNERMAN, the king's falconer and an earl, rising up into Scotland, whence he had come, was like ascending to heaven. For he believed that in Scotland each moment was a credit to life. When the cold wind drove the rain into your face, that was. When the clouds skidded by above so fast they were like an army of kilted soldiers, that was. When the sky over the sea moved from grey to gold, that, too. Just standing on a heather-covered plateau with the world dove-coloured for as far as the eye could see, and nothing but the wind for twenty miles or more, was so good a thing and so beautiful that one knew that if one were there to die it would be in fullness. This was how it was for Bannerman, who took the charge of life from wind and smoke.

In the smallest and poorest stone house in the hills above Kilmuir, he found the boy Craig-Vyvyan's father, who would not have been home only a few days before, but who had brought his sheep down just then and was sitting on his step, face burning from weeks in the wind, and a little whisky. As Bannerman approached—an extraordinary figure in his fine Scottish garb—Mr Cockaleekie rose. "May I introduce myself?" Bannerman asked. "I am Joseph Sussingham Bannerman, Earl of Dalnessie, Falconer to the King, looking in behalf of His Majesty for Craig-Vyvyan."

Mr Cockaleekie looked Bannerman over. Had he a pipe he would have taken a puff. "So," he said, "he's not mad after all."

"The king?"

"Craig-Vyvyan. We thought he was daft. It woulda been one thing had he just told that story once and been done with it. No one believed him. Would you? We woulda forgot it in a week: he's just a lad. But he kept at it, he did. Said he had to prepare. Said the Prince of Wales told him to. Taught himself to read thick books." Mr Cockaleekie's eyes rolled heavenward.

"Did he?"

"He did. For two years now we've not been able to shut him up. History of this, history of that; figures of trade; geography of England; geography of the world; started to study Latin; started to study—good God, man—Greek. He has a book," Mr Cockaleekie said, holding his right hand up and sticking out the little finger, "that tells him how to hold a teacup and a fork, and how you go about having dinner with the queen."

"Good lad," Bannerman said.

"Lost a dozen sheep because he was staring at books."

"It may be, sir, that his loss will be made up, and then some."

Mr Cockaleekie bobbed his head in hope. "It was my loss, anyway, but he isn't here. He went to work in the library at Waterstein."

"Waterstein?" Bannerman asked. "Is that in bloody Germany?"

"No, it's not in bloody Germany, it's on Skye, as far west as you can get."

Which library, of whitewashed stone, and one room, at the edge of the Sea of the Hebrides, Craig-Vyvyan was about to close up when Bannerman burst through the door and, after his eye had fastened upon his prey, said, "I've found you."

"I learned to read and write," Craig-Vyvyan told him in near shock, pushing back against his chair as he sat behind the other piece of furniture in the room, a long table. "It took three days," he said, still amazed, "and then I was reading almost as fast as I can run. Before, it was one word at a time."

"Excellent," said Bannerman, stepping into the yellow light that came, somehow, from a student lamp with a green globe. "That's what you were supposed to have done."

"I've read three hundred books," Craig-Vyvyan announced, still amazed. "I know about England, I know about France, I know about the world." He stopped to reflect. "Your lordship," he said, picking his words carefully, *"I know about time."*

"Well then, that's it, Craig-Vyvyan," Bannerman said, "for a man who knows about time will be pressed into being an educated man, or perhaps it's vice versa, I'm not sure myself. Get your things. Tomorrow at noon, in the Forest of Balmoral, we'll stand with the king at the summit of Lochnagar."

"We," repeated Craig-Vyvyan, as a squall peppered the sea.

And Bannerman replied, "He hasn't forgotten, as kings often do. Not this one."

LOCHNAGAR WAS COVERED with snow. Though Bannerman drove as far as he could go on the inner roads, getting to the summit would be an ordeal. They had driven through the night and were tired and unshaven, but they eagerly put on military cold-weather parkas and snowshoes, and shouldered packs. Having retrieved the tiercel falcon Craig-Vyvyan from Balmoral Castle half an hour before, Bannerman removed him from a cage in the back of the Land Rover.

"How can you carry him, with your arm up, all the way to the top?" Craig-Vyvyan asked, looking at the mountain, rose-coloured in the light of dawn and crowned by mists of snow tossing in the wind.

"The frame," Bannerman said, placing a frame between his waist and arm.

"And the king?" Craig-Vyvyan asked, looking at his hooded and restless namesake on the arm of the huge earl.

"The king?" Bannerman asked in return.

"Where is he?"

"The king set out a week ago in heavy snow, and I assume he has been walking ever since. He was to have made a circuit of the mountains and glens, and probably he has walked two hundred miles and not seen a soul or been inside a building in all that time. But he will come to the summit of Lochnagar at noon, because he said he would."

"And what will he be like when he gets there?" Craig-Vyvyan asked somewhat apprehensively.

"What will he be like?" Bannerman echoed. "He won't be like us. He'll arrive clean-shaven, having moved heaven and earth to make a fire in the snow, to heat the water. He will have washed his clothes. He will look, despite seven days in the wilderness, like an officer on parade. He will have strained as we have never strained, carrying the burden of the whole country and its history. And he will have carried, its weight far heavier than any gear a soldier has ever carried, his reputation as a madman and an idiot. For a person of honour, that is a difficult thing indeed. He will not be like us, Craig-Vyvyan, because he is the king of England, and no matter what anyone may say, no matter what you may hear, no matter what the law or what his fate, that still means something."

They began the climb in the dawn-light from the north, on the palace side, as the king, they trusted, climbed toward them from the south. They did not know that throughout the morning Fredericka watched from a south-facing window at Balmoral as they made their way. She did not care that Freddy would come back to her fully confirmed, but only that he would come back. And she did not hope that Craig-Vyvyan would fly, and thereby open a new chapter. She hoped instead for whatever might be. Of late she had discovered that when others prayed to God to save the king, her husband said his own prayer, that God would favour that which was right. So it was, when she stayed in a high room and looked out at Lochnagar as it brightened in the sun, that she prayed for the right.

The higher Bannerman and the boy climbed, the brighter the world became. And the higher they rose, the more the falcon stirred, something within him waking with the altitude. "Look at him," Bannerman said as the boy Craig-Vyvyan bent to retie one of his snowshoes. "He's edgy because he loves the air. All my life I have taken care of falcons, and I will tell you this. The closer to heaven they rise, the happier they get. They understand that when they go very high something changes in the world and in them. I have seen them, a minute speck that you can hardly keep in sight, twirling in the blue, and I am convinced that this is what they live for."

The way they came was such that they could see neither the flat of the summit nor the more luminous and warmer south beyond the rim they were soon to crest. In the last half hour of the climb they moved at a heated pace, all forces in balance, delighting in the effortlessness of their effort, taking cues from the falcon as he thrust his head up or from side to side to smell the wind. The thin crest of the summit, backlit by the sun, was crowned in every blast of wind by glassy sprays of gold and white. Just to reach such a summit in the snow drew them on, but to know that, a little beyond it, the new king would be waiting, propelled them like birds on the wind.

When they crossed the rim, the falcon lifted his wings as if to catch the air, but then settled back, restless still. The boy, who now knew something of the great history of Britain, was moved by what he saw. For standing on a broad patch of snow, looking south over lands as far as he could see, was their king.

Bannerman had been right. Seven days or not, Freddy's uniform and parka were clean and crisp. He himself was clean and clean-shaven, every patch and badge level and shining, a tie knotted perfectly at his neck, showing through to the air where his jacket lay slightly open and luffing in the breeze. Even his pack, at some remove, was filled, balanced, and neatly closed. These were the kind of details to which he had attended all his life. But the best of them was the way he stood, without any self-consciousness but as straight and tall as in an ancient story of a king standing on top of a mountain. The greatness that Craig-Vyvyan and Bannerman felt flooding in came not from Freddy himself, who was, after all, only Freddy, but from what Freddy saw. They could tell from his eyes that he was looking over things, both visible and invisible, that they might not themselves have seen. The sky outstretched before him was only blue, but for him the idea of England was as legible in it as if it had been hanging there like an ornament. When his eyes fixed on what might have seemed to some to be nothing, it was only because the eyes of the king were fixed on constellations in daylight. This was the royal task, which he was discovering in that very moment.

They approached the sovereign of all the isles of Great Britain, which is to say Freddy, and Bannerman made a little bow.

"Bannerman," said Freddy.

"Your Majesty."

"You're late." Bannerman understood the tone in which this was said, although the boy Craig-Vyvyan did not at first.

"Sir," Bannerman said.

"And you, Craig-Vyvyan, you came," Freddy said to Craig-Vyvyan the boy.

"Your Majesty the King asked me to."

"You were a little vague on that before, as I remember."

"I've been reading, sir. I know how to hold a teacup."

"Good," said Freddy. "Otherwise it's hard to get the tea into your mouth. Have you read Gibbon?"

"Aye, sir."

"Carlyle?"

"Aye, sir."

"Yeats?"

"Who?"

"You'll have to get to him. And what do you think of the others?"

"I love them, sir. They have lifted my heart into another world." This was so true in the way the boy said it that it virtually rang through Bannerman and the king, for Craig-Vyvyan's transformation was itself a coronation, and his elevation into that other world was something close to what happens to a king when at last he takes on his responsibilities.

"I promised you Strathcoyne," Freddy told him, "and though in my absence my mother gave it away, the quiver is not empty. It's fuller than I had known, and should your namesake fly we will pull out for you a very good arrow indeed."

"Even if it were nothing, sir, it would be all right," Craig-Vyvyan said.

"It won't be nothing," Freddy assured him.

He turned slowly to Bannerman, as if to say, "Let's begin." Craig-Vyvyan, now a spectator only, became appropriately silent and moved back a few feet.

Freddy met the eyes of the falcon. Four other times he had done so. Once he had been afraid. Next he had been anxious. Then he had been arrogant. And then he had been puzzled. Now, for the first time, he was his own man. He felt that although it was surely true that he was to be judged in this venerable rite, he was in certain respects beyond judgement. He was confident, but not expectant. For whatever the decision, his heart would not change and he would be the same, having learned the same lessons and understood what it is to be a king, even were he not to remain one. If Craig-Vyvyan the falcon would fly, that would be a magnificent thing, but if he did not, it would be magnificent still. Understanding this as he had come to understand it allowed him finally to look upon the falcon with detached affection. The falcon seemed to take notice of this, and to stir with respect, as if he were in the presence of someone he had been born and bred to recognise.

In gusts of wind that flapped his jacket and blew up a furore of glittering snow that then fell like fairy dust, Freddy held out his arm, and Bannerman transferred the falcon. "Let him get accustomed to you, sir," Bannerman said.

Freddy nodded, turned south, and took a few steps into the glare of the sun. Now he was, as it were, alone, and all of England was spread out in blue at his feet. These minutes were to be his own, for he, his parents, and their parents before them, had spent their lives in contemplation of such moments (and on yachts and at race tracks), and perhaps it was this that enabled him to see things in the blue that others could not. It is true however that he did see them, in a vision as real as anything that ever was.

There on the summit appeared before him, not in catalogue but in moving images of all colours, the bravery, the genius, and the heart of England that it was his calling and destiny to serve. He saw before him the outline of a lion rampant, and knew that this was the after-image, projected by reflected sunlight, of the shape of Britain echoing back and impressed upon the sky. And like a lion rampant it was not still, but, to keep balance, made of its paws a whirlwind, as if there were a hurricane buffeting the Irish Sea. The paws being of light, the whirlwind was of light, like a golden engine, like thread whirling on a bobbin, or a wheel driven by steam until its spokes made a maelstrom. From within this generation, things arose that it was Freddy's fate to see for a fleeting instant but to know forever.

He saw the little ships, crescent-shaped, recoiling bow and stern from the sea like a silkworm contracting. He saw them from afar, by the thousands, in a long sunlit line making their ways over the oceans of the world. He saw a patchwork of fields so vast that it looked like the sun reflecting at high speed off an agitated lake. In an agricultural summary that no statistical branch could hope to match, each of these fields, changing its dimensions, went rapidly through every cycle of growth it had seen in two millennia, blinking first as the trees were felled, and then flashing like sparks from an acetylene torch as each harvest was taken. Within each flash of years were the flashes of days, and within each flash of days were the flashes of changing light over minutes and seconds, every turn of every blade or golden stalk, each windswept pattern casting back at heaven the richly complicated shower of light that heaven had sent to it infinitesimally divided and yet flowing as smoothly as a swelling stream.

This was a sight for kings, a gale of sensation sweeping by in black light as if in an unimaginable transit of the universe, and the king in its midst stood fast and stared ahead. Every microscopic field fled past at unfathomable speed, with each flash awakening him from the exhaustion the previous one had occasioned. When these images joined the chain of ships circling in the whirlwind on the sea, Freddy was knocked back a bit by a wave of battles compressed as if all battles had combined into one. He had to put his heels down hard, and yet, on this front that was like a tidal wave, every pewter helmet, every arrow, every banging shield, every shot from every cannon and gun, every bomb falling, every black night made red by artillery, every line of khaki or cavalry, every sword floating timelessly in the air before its strike, was visible individually. Now Jutland, blinding; now Lexington, and Ladysmith, and Passchendaele, Anzio, Trafalgar, and Arnhem. There was no way properly to credit or acknowledge the scores of millions who had fought in the name of the king, and the millions who, in the name of the king, had died. Only God could so acknowledge, and, as for the king, this was the unbearable burden that would press him down for the rest of his days.

Then, to balance the lion rampant, came gentler things, and things more pleasant, by the millions, but these, too, were a burden. To see every bud that had ever bloomed in England, and every bird that had ever sung. To see each parson talking to himself as he made up his sermon walking down the lane. To be present when Newton and Shakespeare by divine grant opened clear prospects in the confused air of blackness and storm, like spinners who make flowing thread from tangled skeins. Dresses were sewn, blue satin smoothed, and garden paths laid out in numbers great and indeterminate. And then the pace picked up and reddened with the rhythm of industry: more wheels, hammers, and levers than the eye could see, turning, striking, and rocking against a background of fire and flame sometimes as yellow as brass.

Not even a minute had passed, and Bannerman and the boy were aware only that the falcon had once arched his wings as if in preparation, that the king stared into the wind, and that the wind itself was of the densest compression, flowing past with messages all its own.

Freddy looked south past Dundee and Edinburgh, and with most of Scotland at his back let himself fly in a leap over the Trent, the Severn, the Wye, and the Thames, all the way to the Channel. And the strange thing was that, with all that he had ever seen and all he was obligated to see, which had many times overcome him, there was one thing that, finally, his vision came to.

Now he slipped back only a little bit in time. After what he had just been privileged to behold, it was easy to get there. It was something so small and quiet that by comparison it was the most stunning thing of all, for he was brought to see, from a little way above her, a girl of sixteen or seventeen, bicycling on an empty macadam road between ranks of tall trees laden with young green leaves. She was wearing the kind of spring coat that girls used to wear, and her hair was tied back with a velvet ribbon. She was coming up a hill, and stood on the pedals, sometimes pivoting the front wheel to keep the slowly moving cycle upright. In her face was all the beauty of the world and no knowledge of what was to come. He was there, but she thought she was alone. It was, of course, Fredericka.

DEEPLY MOVED and grateful that God had set this seal upon his royal vision, Freddy looked kindly at the falcon. Without words, he said, *Lift your wings,* and the falcon did, extending them not to be folded again that day. Bannerman and the boy drew in their breaths and did not exhale. Even before the falcon lifted off, they saw Freddy smile. And then, without words, purely by grace, Freddy said, *Fly.*

The tiercel falcon Craig-Vyvyan, of ancient lineage, took fully of the wind that came soaring up from England, and knowingly changed the camber of his wings until that constant air lifted him from Freddy's arm and, once clear, he beat the air with all his power and was raised thirty feet above the summit of the mountain, where he paused as if for confirmation, which Freddy gave him straight from his heart.

He had a long flight, and he had started on high. Down he glided, into the blue over England.

EPILOGUE

As ANYONE NOW LIVING in England knows, all this took place a long time ago. The reign of His Majesty King Frederick has not been uneventful, and he has risen to the full measure of kingship on many an occasion: in the many Middle Eastern wars; in the great destruction during the twelfth year of his reign; in the revival of culture; and in the formation of the English-Speaking Union.

Most difficult for him, and for the nation, was the death of Fredericka, when the Princess Lucia, heir to the throne, was not even twenty years of age. This tore at the heart of the king and country. But we continue, and expect that Lucia's reign, when it comes, will be as just as that of her grandmother Philippa. For in this she will have not only the blood of her father, but of her mother, too.

When Fredericka died, so much did he long for her that the king asked me to write down the early part of their story together. He wanted, by relating it to me, to stoke the fires of memory. I am astounded still at the detail he has summoned, at his objective recollection, and at the precise descriptions of scenes and sunsets that for many decades have been alive only in memory. Knowing that the truth is greater than any man, he made no attempt to hide his faults or peculiarities, and admitted freely to the desire to justify his acts and views, instructing me to "put a bit on them," as he said, and verify everything as far as possible in the public and private records. This I have done, and although I cannot confirm incidents and events that no one now living or accessible can second, if the record of those that are indeed subject to proof is in any way representative, this is a very accurate account by a very meticulous king.

Going down on the north side of Lochnagar that day, when the light at our backs gave us a view of what seemed a world of myth, Bannerman and I felt change on its way. The king had been confirmed, and although that has happened often, sometimes it is a hinge of history, as it was this time. Although it is hard to be a king, it is harder yet to become one. He had been schooled by his own idiosyncrasy and courage to see and insist where others were blind and shy. He had studied both formally and on his own, working like a scholar or a mystic, always with his eye on the truth. He had embraced a life of action as well, learning and exercising physical courage as part of the tapestry of endurance and discovery that is laid out before any man (if he will only make his way upon it) by a divine hand. And, unlike any other English king, he had been schooled in America. There he had discovered that the aim-point of the impossible is the best aim-point of all. He had made his way with only the princess at his side and no advantage other than that which was within them. In America he had learned to be a king, not least because in America he discovered the sacred principle that every man is a king. If no man there is less than a king, then he became a king by right even before his return home and the death of his mother.

And in America he learned forbearance, humility, and something far greater. As he tells it, he pierced the fog that had bedazzled him, saw Fredericka for what she was, and learned to love her as she deserved. Thus giving themselves the chance, by wit and luck they grew up together and made a bond. And in conceiving a child they retreated from the self-spun illusion of primacy. This, which in its totality is called love, saved them.

I mentioned that I was with the king on Lochnagar. I was, for I am the boy Craig-Vyvyan, hardly a boy now, from whose confusions of childhood the king drew me as he left his own. I had thought for a time that—while keeping my name and thus keeping faith with my forbears—I was to be known as the Lord Strathcoyne. But then in her last months Her Majesty Queen Philippa went on a spree of awarding titles and honours, and Strathcoyne and its emoluments went to an already wealthy West End impresario who looks like a lamb chop, and sings like one, too. In fact, despite Freddy's (I call him Freddy in private, and he has never objected) declaration about the quiver being full, precious little was left by the time it was my turn, and I got Piggleswade.

I use it for formal occasions, and the first name, too. Materially, I am far better off, having received in an instant both Gower Lodge, Mortlake, and a magnificent flat in Belgravia, each free of charges for my lifetime. The problem is buying groceries at a decent price, but I have resigned myself to motoring quite a distance or paying double. As Lord Piggleswade, I was entitled to free tuition and living quarters at Magdalen College, Oxford, and I took it. I wish you could have seen the expression on the face of my late father at the granting of my several degrees, in the presence of the king, who came especially on my behalf. And, lastly, as Piggleswade I am the owner of a flower farm at Hampstead Court, near Syon Lodge. I have five large greenhouses there, and fields for the summer cultivation of peonies, carnations, and roses. Middlemen and taxes take most of what flows through, but in the end I am left with £20,000 to £40,000 a year, depending upon the economy, the weather, fashions, and pests.

That was not enough for Lord Piggleswade, Lady Piggleswade, and their children who have matriculated at various expensive universities here and abroad, so I took to writing books. Books are like flowers. No matter how beautiful or colourful they may be, you cannot tell what they will return to you once you cut the stem and send them into the world. But, though they may return nothing, like flowers, they are a reward unto themselves.

The king now wants me to write of his reign. Because it has been a noble and extraordinary reign, I am sore tempted, but I do not think I will. For this was the book in which he and Fredericka were merely two young people, and in this book their youth and charm were unconstrained by the severity of position. Everyone is interested, it is said, in kings, but I myself am interested in kings before their time. For kings before their time are like us all, and may God bless them for that, and save them, too.

FOR THE BEST IN PAPERBACKS, LOOK FOR THE

In every corner of the world, on every subject under the sun, Penguin represents quality and variety—the very best in publishing today.

For complete information about books available from Penguin—including Penguin Classics, Penguin Compass, and Puffins—and how to order them, write to us at the appropriate address below. Please note that for copyright reasons the selection of books varies from country to country.

In the United States: Please write to *Penguin Group (USA), P.O. Box 12289 Dept. B, Newark, New Jersey 07101-5289* or call 1-800-788-6262.

In the United Kingdom: Please write to *Dept. EP, Penguin Books Ltd, Bath Road, Harmondsworth, West Drayton, Middlesex UB7 0DA.*

In Canada: Please write to *Penguin Books Canada Ltd, 90 Eglinton Avenue East, Suite 700, Toronto, Ontario M4P 2Y3.*

In Australia: Please write to *Penguin Books Australia Ltd, P.O. Box 257, Ringwood, Victoria 3134.*

In New Zealand: Please write to *Penguin Books (NZ) Ltd, Private Bag 102902, North Shore Mail Centre, Auckland 10.*

In India: Please write to *Penguin Books India Pvt Ltd, 11 Panchsheel Shopping Centre, Panchsheel Park, New Delhi 110 017.*

In the Netherlands: Please write to *Penguin Books Netherlands bv, Postbus 3507, NL-1001 AH Amsterdam.*

In Germany: Please write to *Penguin Books Deutschland GmbH, Metzlerstrasse 26, 60594 Frankfurt am Main.*

In Spain: Please write to *Penguin Books S. A., Bravo Murillo 19, 1° B, 28015 Madrid.*

In Italy: Please write to *Penguin Italia s.r.l., Via Benedetto Croce 2, 20094 Corsico, Milano.*

In France: Please write to *Penguin France, Le Carré Wilson, 62 rue Benjamin Baillaud, 31500 Toulouse.*

In Japan: Please write to *Penguin Books Japan Ltd, Kaneko Building, 2-3-25 Koraku, Bunkyo-Ku, Tokyo 112.*

In South Africa: Please write to *Penguin Books South Africa (Pty) Ltd, Private Bag X14, Parkview, 2122 Johannesburg.*